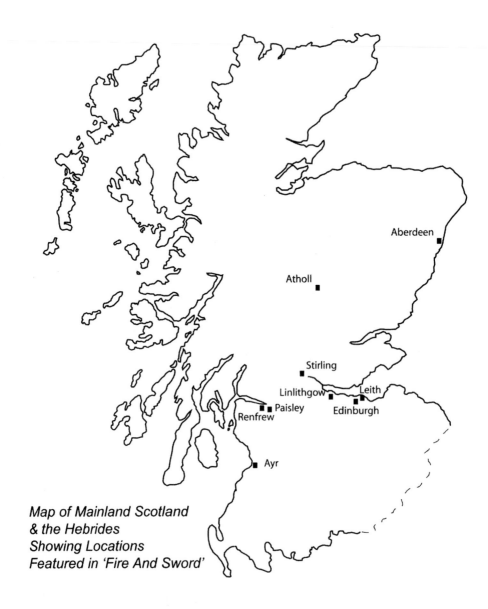

Aberdeen

Atholl

Stirling

Linlithgow   Leith

Paisley

Renfrew   Edinburgh

Ayr

Map of Mainland Scotland
& the Hebrides
Showing Locations
Featured in 'Fire And Sword'

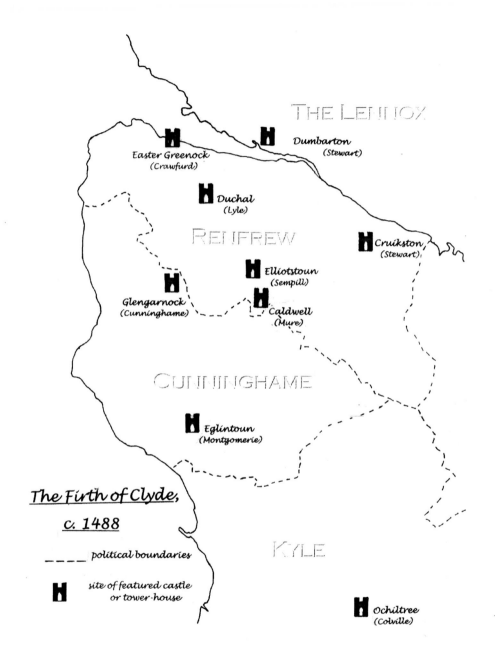

THE LENNOX

Easter Greenock
(Crawfurd)

Dumbarton
(Stewart)

Duchal
(Lyle)

RENFREW

Cruikston
(Stewart)

Elliotstoun
(Sempill)

Glengarnock
(Cunninghame)

Caldwell
(Mure)

CUNNINGHAME

Eglintoun
(Montgomerie)

The Firth of Clyde,
c. 1488

- - - - political boundaries

site of featured castle
or tower-house

KYLE

Ochiltree
(Colville)

Fire and Sword

Louise Turner

HADLEY
RILLE
BOOKS

Published simultaneously in the United Kingdom and the United States of America by:
Hadley Rille Books
Eric T. Reynolds, Publisher
PO Box 25466
Overland Park, KS 66225
USA
www.hadleyrillebooks.com
contact@hadleyrillebooks.com

Publisher's note: This book contains a mix of UK and US typesetting conventions. For the most part, UK spellings are used, and US quotation styles are used.

To Jim, whose enthusiasm for castles, tower-houses and things medieval made me realise that there was still beauty and wonder in this world after AD43.

In September 1489, letters of fire and sword were issued by King James IV to Sir John Sempill, Sheriff of Renfrew.

They referred to "burnings, hardships, and destruction" in Renfrewshire and to an attack made by Sempill on the Place of Duchal in times bygone.

This novel was inspired by these events.

* * *

It can be observed that men use various methods in pursuing their own personal objectives, that is glory and riches. One man proceeds with circumspection, another impetuously; one uses violence, another stratagem; one man goes about things patiently, another does the opposite; and yet everyone, for all this diversity of method, can reach his objective.

From *The Prince*, by Niccolo Machiavelli (1513)

Author's Note

There's a special significance in names. Surnames, forenames, place names, each has their meaning, and their resonance. Because Fire and Sword aims to recreate real characters and real places wherever possible, I've left the names very much unchanged. This may cause some confusion, because it means that every other man is called John, and every other woman, Margaret.

This reflects the fashions of the time. Towards the end of the fifteenth century, Scotland was still a deeply Catholic country. Children may have been named after prominent family members (grandparents, perhaps), but these names were derived in turn from popular saints—such as John, Margaret, Mary and Katherine—or prominent figures from Scotland's past, like David, William, Robert, Malcolm, Constantine. Classical literature was just beginning to make its mark: by 1488, there were a few pretentious folk out there who gave their children Classically-derived names like Helen and Hector.

This plethora of Johns could be confusing, but thankfully I've been able in most cases to make use of another characteristic trait of the Scots nobility: the linking of people and places. For Lords and Earls, the title is enough, as in Hugh, 3rd Lord Montgomerie. For barons, we inevitably link the man with the lands, such as John Sempill of Ellestoun. Younger brothers or cousins, who aren't titled, will also be linked with their lands. So we have John Montgomerie of Hessilhead or John Semple of Fulwood. This proved very helpful, because these supporting characaters can be called 'Hessilhead' or 'Fulwood' in the narrative, though of course, just to further confuse things, their friends will call them 'John ' in the dialogue!

You will also notice that the names of the prominent families may be spelled differently according to the individual being referred to. The senior branch of the family often has a different spelling to the junior or cadet branches. Hence the senior branch of the Montgomeries is spelled with an 'ie', the junior with a 'y'. With the Semples, the senior branch is spelled using 'pill' as opposed to 'ple'. The Cunninghames are a law unto themselves, variously using 'Cunninghame', 'Cuninghame' and 'Cunningham', depending upon which branch they derive from. Cunninghame, as applied to the political and judicial region, is however always spelled 'Cunninghame'.

The official origins of these differing spellings may be quite recent, with their roots lying in the past 400-500 years. Late fifteenth century documents often still vary in their spellings, though it was around about this period that literacy was becoming more prevalent and the written word more accessible to the wider population. But since that time language has continually evolved and those of you familiar with the area will no doubt be aware that some of the names I use are not the same as those in common use today: Ellestoun has become 'Elliston', and Eglintoun has become 'Eglinton'.

The narrative itself is written in English, with some Scots added to give it a local flavour. Though I was born in Scotland and have lived here all my life, I can't speak Scots. Nor can I write it. The language used by John and Hugh and their contemporaries would have been Middle Scots—think a combination of William Shakespeare and Rab C. Nesbitt with a bit of Chaucer thrown in for good measure, and you won't be far wrong. For the modern international reader, this may be virtually unintelligible, so please bear with me, Just imagine that what I've given you instead is a translation from the original.

Cast of Characters

1) <u>Allies of King James III</u>

Courtiers and Counsellors
John Forbes, 6th Lord Forbes,
William Forbes, Master of Forbes, his son
Alexander Gordon, Master of Huntly
William Keith, Lord Keith, Earl Marischal to the Kings of Scotland
Sir John Ross of Montgrennan, Lord Advocate to King James III
William Scheves, Archbishop of Saint Andrews
John Stewart, Earl of Atholl, half-brother to King James III
John Stewart, Master of Atholl, son and heir the Earl of Atholl

The Sempills of Ellestoun
Sir Thomas Sempill of Ellestoun, Sheriff of Renfrew
Lady Elizabeth Ross, his wife, sister to Sir John Ross of Montgrennan
John, Master of Sempill, son and heir to Sir Thomas
Marion Sempill, youngest daughter of Sir Thomas
John Semple of Fulwood, head of a cadet branch of the Semple family

The Crawfurds of Kilbirnie
Sir Malcolm Crawfurd of Kilbirnie
Lady Margery Barclay, his wife
Robert, Master of Kilbirnie, his eldest son and heir

The Rosses of Hawkhead
Sir John Ross of Hawkhead, kinsman to Sir John Ross of Montgrennan, and Lady Elizabeth Ross

The Cunninghames of Glencairn
Sir Alexander Cunninghame, 1st Earl of Glencairn
Sir William Cunninghame of Craigends, younger son to Sir Alexander
Andrew Cunninghame, eldest son and heir to Sir William
Sir Humphry Cuningham of Glengarnock, head of a cadet branch of the Cunninghame family

2) <u>Allies of King James IV</u>

The Privy Council
Colin Campbell, 1st Earl of Argyll, Chancellor
Archibald Campbell, Master of Argyll

13

Robert Colville, Director of Chancery, kinsman to the Colvilles of Ochiltree
Andrew Gray, 2nd Lord Gray
Patrick Hepburn, Lord Hailes (later Earl of Bothwell)
Adam Hepburn, Master of Bothwell, eldest son and heir to Sir Patrick
Alexander Home, 2nd Lord Home

The Church
William Elphinstone, Bishop of Aberdeen
George Schaw, Abbot of Paisley

The Montgomeries of Eglinton
Hugh Montgomerie, 3rd Lord Montgomerie, Bailie of Cunninghame, Justiciar of Arran and the West
Lady Helen Campbell, his wife, daughter of Earl Colin of Argyll and sister to Archibald Campbell, Master of Argyll
John Montgomerie of Hessilhead, cousin to Lord Hugh
James Montgomerie of Bowhouse, younger brother to Lord Hugh
Robert Montgomerie, younger brother to Lord Hugh
John, Master of Montgomerie, eldest son and heir to Lord Hugh
Bessie Montgomerie, half-sister to John, Master of Montgomerie

The Earls of Lennox and their Allies
John Stewart, Earl of Lennox (formerly John Stewart of Darnley)- uncle to Hugh, 3rd Lord Montgomerie
Matthew Stewart, Lord Darnley and Master of Lennox, his son and heir
Robert Lyle, Lord Lyle, ally of John Stewart and future father-in-law of Matthew Stewart
Margaret Houston, wife to Robert Lyle

The Colvilles of Ochiltree
Sir William Colville of Ochiltree
Lady Euphemia Wallace, his wife
Robert Colville , Master of Ochiltree
Margaret Colville, his sister, betrothed to John, Master of Sempill
James Colville, half-brother to Robert and Margaret Colville

The Mures of Caldwell
Sir Adam Mure of Caldwell
Lady Margaret Sempill, his wife, older sister of John, Master of Sempill
Hector, Master of Mure, oldest son and heir to Sir Adam
John Mure, younger son of Sir Adam

Other Ayrshire Lairds
Constantine Dunlop of Hunthall
Sir Patrick Wallace of Auchenbothie

3) <u>Servants & Tenants of the Sempills of Ellestoun, Burgesses of Renfrew</u>

These characters are entirely fictitious, for the common man scarcely ever warrants more than a fleeting mention in the sources at this time. I have, however, done my best to try and recreate authentic names and to link them with appropriate landholdings wherever possible.

William Haislet, manservant to Sir Thomas and later, John, Master of Sempill
Alan Semple, Tacksman to the Sempill family, distant kinsman to Sir Thomas and John Sempill
Hugh Alexson of Barr
Mary White, his wife
John Alexson, his eldest son
Hugh Alexson, his younger son
Janet White, sister to Mary White
Henry Hammill, husband of Janet White
Master John Mossman, Burgess of Renfrew
Master John Montgomery, Burgess of Renfrew
Master John Montgomery, son of the above, also a Burgess of Renfrew

Chapter 1
The Place of Ellestoun, February, 1488

"They say he's in league with the Devil." Marion Sempill paused with her hand on the latch. The candle guttered in the draught, giving her a fey, unearthly look. "From the looks of him, I wouldn't be at all surprised."

John caught his sister's eye, curious, a little concerned. "What's he doing here, anyway?"

"How should I know?" she retorted. "I'm just a woman!" She patted his arm. "Rather you than me." Opening the door, she swept from the chill darkness of the stair-tower to the light and warmth of the hall.

John followed close behind.

Outside the sun was shining; there was a faint warmth in the air that heralded the coming of spring. He should have been out hunting deer in the hills. Instead, he was trapped indoors doing his father's bidding.

Marion halted; lost in thought, he nearly trampled her gown. She glanced back reproachfully, but John couldn't apologise. He'd seen his father's face; it wasn't the time or place for frivolity.

His parents stood with their guest by the fireplace: his father, Sir Thomas Sempill, spared him no more than a brief glance, while his mother Elizabeth Ross was too absorbed even to acknowledge his arrival. Her neglect went unnoticed; of far greater interest to John was the man who stood with them: the Lord Montgomerie.

John had heard of Hugh Montgomerie. There wasn't a soul in the Westland who hadn't. Over the last few years, Lord Hugh had earned quite a reputation as an arsonist, a murderer, and an abuser of the King's laws.

It was impolite to stare, but John stared regardless. He'd expected Hugh Montgomerie to be a big scowling hulk of a man; instead, the much-feared Butcher of Eglintoun was a long lean creature with a pale imperious face and dark hair hanging about his shoulders. Montgomerie could only have been thirty or thereabouts, but already he carried himself with the measured elegance of a seasoned courtier.

Before John knew it, Montgomerie's gaze was on him. It was too late to look away; it was as if in that brief moment, the cold grey eyes had bored right through him.

"It would be splendid to have another son," Montgomerie said. "I'd welcome a Bishop in the family. Perhaps even a Cardinal! But I mustn't be selfish. I already have my heir, and my wife would relish a daughter. Rest assured, Lady Elizabeth, that I'll greet whatever God sends me with a cheerful face and a joyful heart." He smiled and leaned closer to Lady Elizabeth, who clapped her hands and laughed in coy delight.

"Ah, there you are, John," Sir Thomas Sempill said. "I'm glad Marion caught you before you disappeared with the hounds." He grasped John's arm and steered him before Montgomerie. "You've not met my son, my lord?"

"No, I haven't yet had the pleasure," said Montgomerie. "Good day to you, Master Sempill."

"Good day, my lord," John replied. Looking at their guest, he sensed a restless undercurrent beneath the polished facade. Given the right circumstances, he supposed it might erupt into violence.

For once, then, he'd met a man whose reputation was justified. As he watched his father usher Montgomerie to the stair, exchanging token pleasantries all the while, John wasn't sure if he should be impressed, or alarmed.

* * *

It was already late morning, but the day had not yet dawned in the laird's chamber, where the shutters were closed against the cold. Flames roared high in the fireplace, and candles blazed in every corner, a forlorn attempt to hold back the darkness. The black, heavy beams of the ceiling only added to the wintry gloom of the place. But first impressions were deceptive. John looked up and couldn't resist a smile, for lining every joist and timber were painted strings of flowers and leaves. They lifted the heart, glowing like stars in the velvet black of a midwinter sky, a delicate detail lost on those who gave the room no more than a casual inspection.

"Fetch our guest some wine." Sir Thomas sat down in a heavy chair beside the fire. He was fifty years old, strong and proud. The thick mane of tawny gold hair he'd once borne had faded largely to silver, but his face remained smooth, flawless, as if untouched by time.

Wine had been left on the carved wooden kist by the far wall, next to the vast curtained bed that dominated the room. John poured two measures, one for his father, one for their guest.

His father gestured to a nearby chair. "Please be seated, my lord."

"I'd rather stand." Montgomerie halted with his back to the fire, hand resting on his sword hilt.

"As you wish." Sempill's neutral expression did not waver.

"Your wine, Lord Hugh." John delivered the goblet into Montgomerie's ring-encrusted fingers.

"Thank you so very much." Montgomerie's smile didn't quite reach his eyes.

"Sit *down*, John." Sir Thomas snatched the remaining goblet from John's grasp.

Stifling a sigh, John settled in an unobtrusive spot by the window. A sliver of clear bright blue was visible through a gap in the shutters; he stared at it transfixed until the frustration grew too much and he slumped against the panelling, arms folded.

"I can guess what brings you here," Sir Thomas Sempill said. "I hope you've come seeking guidance."

"I don't need guidance."

"Then why are you here?"

"You helped me in the past," Montgomerie said. "I don't forget such favours."

Sempill gave a mirthless snort. "So you're not entirely bereft of honour? That's comforting to know."

Hearing the disdain in his father's voice, John sat up, his resentment forgotten. He swivelled unobtrusively round, planting his feet square before him and clasping his hands loosely in his lap.

"I won't waste your time, Sir Thomas. Argyll's washed his hands of King James now. He's backing the Prince. So am I."

"Do you think that's enough to make the Sempills ride with you?"

"I thought you might consider not riding against me."

"This is treason, Hugh. It'll give Kilmaurs the excuse he needs to hang you."

"I've nothing to fear. There are too many of us."

"What have they offered you?" Sir Thomas Sempill's voice was chill. "A remission for the burning of Kerrielaw? Or Cunninghame of Kilmaurs' head on a platter?"

"You malign me. It's the fate of the kingdom that's at stake here."

"Oh, for God's sake!" Sir Thomas snapped. "This holier-than-thou air doesn't suit you. They must be paying you well, I must say. And don't try and resort to bribery—"

"Nobody mentioned bribery," Montgomerie countered. "I was trying to appeal to your common sense."

"Common sense? Christ, don't patronise me."

"He's betrayed our trust in him. He's incapable of ruling fairly—"

"He's incapable of favouring you, you mean—"

"He should be removed."

"He's the King!"

"Thank you," Montgomerie said. "It's good to know where the Sempills' loyalties will lie in the months ahead."

"We'll be fighting for the King." Sir Thomas pushed himself stiffly to his feet. "Now, I think you should go. Forgive me, if I don't offer you lodgings. I can't give succour to a traitor and a rebel. John, go to the stables. See that His Lordship's horses are made ready."

* * *

John smoothed the horse's rough black coat one last time before he heaved the harness into place.

He leaned against its shoulder with a sigh. His quiet existence here at Ellestoun was in jeopardy, thanks to the scheming of men like Montgomerie. Rage coursed through him; he banged the saddle down so hard the horse flinched and grunted.

The sense of shame was quick to follow and he stroked the creature's neck to reassure it. It wasn't as if the beast was responsible for its master's misdeeds.

His father called him weak, because he had the decency to regret angry words and harsh deeds. Sir Thomas would have far preferred his son and heir to be gifted with a stronger spirit and a weaker conscience. But perhaps Sir Thomas Sempill was right. Perhaps John would change, become harder, more vindictive. More like his father.

"You don't have to do what he says, you know." It came as a shock, to hear Montgomerie's voice so close. John hadn't even heard him approach, but there he was, standing just a few feet away at the horse's tail. "You could ride with me," Montgomerie continued, in that same mild, pleasant voice. "I'd see you were looked after. You wouldn't be the first to change sides. Your kinsman Adam Mure's already pledged his support."

"Adam's always been prone to false counsel."

"Ah, quite a profound statement! From someone who's said to be dull and lacking in spirit."

"Adam said that, I suppose." He boldly met Lord Hugh's gaze.

Montgomerie's steely expression didn't waver. "I think there's more to you than meets the eye."

"Complimenting me won't help you. I might be dull and lacking in spirit. But at least I have my principles. I'll be fighting for the King."

Montgomerie smiled, faintly. "You don't want to offend your father, do you? You're in his thrall. I'd guess he never lets you have your say in anything."

"My time will come."

"He's a stubborn old fool. He'll live to regret this day."

John irritably secured the final strap-end. "If you think that insulting my father and flattering me will change my mind, then you're wrong."

"Actually, Master Sempill, I wanted to make sure that you're doing a reasonable job of tending my horse." Montgomerie smiled again, more obviously this time: it was an unnerving smile, wild, faintly bestial. "You shouldn't leap to conclusions. I'm only trying to save your neck. I've nothing against you, I've nothing against your father."

"Your horse is ready now, my lord." John sidled deep into the stall. Pushing his fist into the horse's chest, he watched in grim satisfaction as it moved back, quickly.

Lord Hugh stepped aside just in time. "Are you always so sanctimonious? You look like you've just come face-to-face with the Devil."

"The similarities aren't lost upon me. Like the Devil, you're tempting me. Your horse." He thrust the reins into Montgomerie's hand.

"Temptation has nothing to do with it. This is a friendly warning, nothing more. You'll face more than forty days and forty nights in the wilderness if the King's defeated."

"We haven't lost the battle yet."

"No, I don't suppose you have." Montgomerie teased some hay from his horse's forelock and flicked it lazily to the ground.

"There you are!" Marion appeared, breathless at the door. "Oh, forgive me. Am I interrupting anything?"

"Lord Hugh's just leaving," John told her.

"Oh!" She feigned ignorance. "So soon? John, Father would like a word. . ."

"Your father calls," Lord Hugh said. "You'd best run along. Like the dutiful son you are."

* * *

"It wasn't an excuse," Marion said. "One of the servants saw Lord Hugh follow you into the stables. He told Father—"

"God, can he not trust me this once?"

"He's in his chamber. You'd best go and explain. . ."

"Alright!" He took her arm and steered her to the door. "Get inside now, Marion. It's cold out here."

No sooner had they started up the stairs than they nearly collided with their mother, who came bustling out all brisk and business-like from the hall. "Where's Lord Hugh?" she demanded.

"He's just left," John said.

"But I was expecting him at the board! The cooks agreed to prepare something special. I believe he's partial to duck—"

John shrugged. "I'm sorry, Mother."

"This is terrible news! What will everyone think of us, sending a guest away like this? Without feeding him? Or offering him a place to rest for the night? Thomas? Thomas!" Her voice, shrill as a banshee, could have wakened the dead.

Sir Thomas Sempill ventured down the stairs. "Yes, my dear?"

"What's the meaning of this? John tells me that—"

"He tells you right," Sir Thomas said, firmly. "He won't be present."

"It'll reflect badly on me!" she snapped. "Can't you understand that?"

"God," said Sir Thomas Sempill, and that was it. He glanced at John, a weary, hunted look in his eyes. Then the impassive façade was back. "Come on," he said. "I want you upstairs. Now."

* * *

"Get in." Sir Thomas hauled John into the laird's chamber. "Sit down."

John sprawled into the nearest chair with a sigh.

"I'm told he spoke with you alone. What did he say?"

"He asked me to ride east with him."

Sir Thomas stood before the fire. He stared into its depths, saying nothing. He rarely lost his temper, but John had weathered his father's rage enough to know the pattern of it.

Sir Thomas whirled around, his face dark, ominous. He marched over and hauled John close, almost dragging him from his seat. "I expect obedience from you!" he snarled, blue-grey eyes bright, unreasoning.

"Father—"

"—I don't care that you're my only son; if you take up with *him*, I swear to God I'll disinherit you!" He pushed John back down, so hard he gasped.

Scowling, John straightened his doublet. "How can you think me capable of such treachery?" he demanded. "Have I ever questioned your judgement? Have I ever disobeyed you in any way?"

"That's enough!"

"I've always been loyal, but all you ever do is dismiss me as irrelevant. I'm nineteen years old. I'm not a boy anymore." John broke off. For nineteen years, he'd bowed his head and agreed to everything. Now, for the first time in his life, he'd spoken back.

"No, John, you don't understand," his father said. "It's not your age." There was a momentary silence, then, "If you want the truth, I'll give you the truth. It's because you're so damned useless!"

"But—"

"What good's the knowledge of a few dead ancients when you're up against an English sword, eh? When I was your age, I'd already slaughtered a score or more English dogs at Roxburgh. You know what your problem is, boy? You're too damned soft!" He smiled with stern satisfaction. "I hope to God this *does* come to war. If you ask me, a good battle's just what you need. Maybe it'll knock some sense into you!"

Chapter 2
Near the Sauchie Burn, Stirling, 11ᵗʰ June, 1488

The horse stamped and snatched at its bit, maddened by flies.

John tightened his reins and muttered a few soothing words. He could forgive the beast for being restive. They'd been waiting here for hours. It was as if, even now, both armies were reluctant to give the order that would finally tear the country apart.

The heat had been building throughout the afternoon and John was sweltering inside his plate armour; sweat drenched his quilted arming doublet and streamed down his forehead into his eyes.

When he'd first lined up here, he'd been terrified, but the fear had faded long ago. He just wanted everything to be over. He stared at the facing hillside, repelled yet fascinated by what he saw. The rebel host was made up of rank upon rank of mounted knights and men-at-arms. Their surcoats formed a swathe of colour against the drab tones of the land, their banners hanging listless in the gnat-clouded stillness of the evening. The tips of countless spears glinted in the sunlight, a bristling thicket that sprang from the ground below.

Things had changed since yesterday, when John had ridden back from his first battle, heady with victory. He remembered how he'd fought and killed his fellow men, how he'd revelled in the carnage, too. A dark excitement gripped him as the enemy lines broke and the frenzy of the rout began. Men fled, he'd hacked them down without mercy.

They were his fellow Scots, but he'd slaughtered them just the same.

Victory seemed just a hair's breadth away then, but late last night the Prince's reinforcements arrived, and suddenly the King's future was precarious. Rumours were running rife through the Royal host: *James has brought four hundred German mercenaries to the field; he's so confident of victory, his army's already flying the Lion Rampant that marks the rightful King of Scots. . .*

John was more concerned by what he saw with his own eyes. There, massed ahead, were the blue-and-red quartered colours of the Montgomeries.

"He's here for Cunninghame, isn't he?" John asked his father.

Sir Thomas smiled. "He'll get more than he bargained for."

"What d'you mean?"

"I've made a wager with the Earl of Glencairn. Twenty pounds for the man who returns with Hugh Montgomerie's head."

"That's absurd!" He'd blurted out the words before he could stop himself.

His father wasn't even listening. "A pity," he said. "He showed great promise once. But when the hound turns and bites his master there's only one way to deal with him—"

"I don't see why we're involved."

"What the Devil do you mean?"

"Why waste our men and risk our own lives in bringing down Montgomerie when Cunninghame can do the deed for us?"

"I thought," Sir Thomas said, coldly, "that we'd put an end to all this nonsense."

"I just wanted to say—"

"It's no shame to fall in battle. Only cowards fear such an end. I sincerely hope, John, that my son's not a coward."

John glowered at his horse's red-brown neck and said nothing.

Further up the line, the trumpet sounded.

Sir Thomas drew his sword. "Prepare yourselves! And remember: you fight for the King, and you fight for what's right! Let that strengthen your arm as you strike down Montgomerie's rabble!"

Carried along on a torrent of dread and relief, John cheered with the rest of them. A flick of his wrist brought his visor down, and his surroundings shrank. The countryside was a distant memory, a sun-drenched strip which beckoned through a grim and claustrophobic world.

The trumpet rang out again.

John drove his heels against his horse's flanks, felt it tense beneath him and spring off at a canter. He leaned back against the high cantle of the saddle, revelling in the comforting presence of the riders pressed close on either side. The canter became a gallop, the snorting horse pounding onwards, the unbroken wall of men coming ever closer.

No way out. Nowhere to go but forwards, through the enemy lines ahead. *Holy Mary, Mother of God, protect me. Holy Mary, Mother of God. . .* The words circled around and around in his head. Terror brought a foul taste to his mouth. Was that really his own voice, yelling out in wordless frantic terror as the collision approached? Just audible over the sound of his own ragged breathing, and the pounding of the blood in his veins.

A Montgomerie man-at-arms approached. The frenzy had gone, John's mind was clear. He made a feint to the left, but when his opponent counteracted the move, he was prepared. He swept his lance to the right, then gritted his teeth as the point caught the Montgomerie soldier's shield full-square. The shield cracked, and the enemy horseman was knocked from his mount.

One down. John dropped the broken remnants of his lance, and drew his sword.

Just in time. His next foe was already upon him, horse jostling shoulder-to-shoulder with his own. The blades of the swords met, clanging loud as one blow blocked another. His attacker made a feint and John parried in response, but the enemy sword came down, a direct hit. Jagged shards of wood jumped from his shield, and John snarled and cursed at the force of it.

The fight ground on and John could gain no advantage. He slammed his blade down upon his opponent's shield, again and again, great bone-jarring thumps that tore chunks from the wood. He had to destroy the shield, but his adversary was defending himself fiercely. The man-at-arms struck out with his sword, hitting John's shoulder, but John escaped unscathed, protected by his armour.

There it was. The opportunity he'd been waiting for. With the enemy's right side exposed, John swung his sword down: it sliced into flesh and bit deep, digging into his opponent's collar bone and lodging there. The wound was mortal, the artery severed. John struggled to free the blade, and succeeded instead in hauling the dying man off-balance. The soldier slumped against him, the two of them were locked together while the blood sprayed everywhere, misting John's armour, staining his ivory jupon.

John grimaced, wrenched the blade loose and pushed the other man roughly away. His foe slumped forward, eyes glazing as the life ebbed from him. It was a welcome sight, and John felt once again that strange flush of elation bloom within him.

Another gone. God only knew how many were left. He struggled to breathe beneath his helmet, heart pounding, blood roaring in his ears. When he looked about him, he found himself alone in a corpse-strewn clearing. To the left and the right tangled knots of men chopped and hacked at one another.

John swallowed, grateful for the respite. It didn't last long; he jerked up his head, startled, as riders approached. In their midst was a knight, horse shrouded in azure blue.

The Lord Montgomerie himself, riding as if the Devil were at his heels. . .

John's heart missed a beat. It was hard enough at the best of times to take on a man of Montgomerie's prowess and win. Today it was unthinkable; Montgomerie looked fresh and untried, while John's strength was almost spent.

But confrontation was not what Lord Hugh had in mind. He swept his arm to the side, indication that he wanted a clear path.

He wants Cunninghame. And I'm in his way. John looked wildly about him. Part of him longed to flee, but at the same time, stubborn pride made sure he held his ground.

He tightened his fingers about his sword hilt, but the horsemen never reached him. As John looked on bewildered, Lord Hugh and his men slid to a halt, hauling their horses back so hard they sat down on their hocks and drove furrows into the mud.

John was no longer alone. Half-a dozen Sempill men-at-arms were gathered about him. There, too, was his father, sitting still upon his horse.

Impasse.

The Montgomeries conferred amongst themselves, while behind them Lord Hugh shook his head and railed at the delay. A momentary lull, that's all it was, before the Montgomerie soldiers surged forward once again and battered into the waiting Sempills.

The two knights, Montgomerie and Sempill, remained quite still, points of calm amidst the storm as their men ebbed and flowed around them. Lord Hugh moved first, lifting sword to visored face in brief salute as his horse skipped and plunged excitedly beneath him. Sempill returned the gesture. They shortened their reins, held their impatient horses back a moment longer, then launched themselves at one another, swords held high.

John watched their battle unfold, gripped by foreboding. He opened his mouth to call out to his father, but the words died on his lips.

It wasn't his place to interfere. But he couldn't let his father fight Montgomerie alone. John wheeled his horse around, let out a blood-curdling yell of mingled fear and ferocity and raced straight for Lord Hugh.

He'd only gone a few yards before more of Montgomerie's men closed in around him. Two were almost as well-armed as Lord Hugh; his brothers, perhaps, or cousins.

I'm as good as dead. It was a strangely liberating thought, and John launched himself on the nearest man with renewed determination. But his blow never hit home. A flail, wielded outwith his vision, caught the blade and hauled the weapon from his grasp. He yelped with dismay, his bravado gone.

The man before him lifted his visor. John Montgomerie of Hessilhead, it was. "That'll teach you, whelp!" Hessilhead called. "Keep your nose out of other men's business."

John cowered beneath his shield. He heard them laughing as they decided how best to bring him down. There was a resounding crack, as the flail battered against his shield. The wood disintegrated; shafts of pain lanced their way up his left arm and squirmed into his shoulder.

Hessilhead grinned. "Not so cocky now, are we? Will you yield, Master Sempill?"

Undeterred, John unsheathed his knife. He'd have died rather than suffer the indignity of being captured by his neighbours.

"It's always the same with the young ones," Hessilhead remarked, sitting relaxed on his horse as if he had all the time in the world. "They never know when to give up."

John had barely registered the jibe when something struck his head from behind. His helmet reverberated with the impact, and a blinding pain seared through him. He cried out and felt himself falling.

He landed flat on his back. He couldn't move; the wind was knocked from his lungs, lights shimmered in his vision.

"He'll fetch a pretty ransom," someone was saying. "How much d'you think he's worth?"

You're not taking me. His lips moved, but he could manage no more than a wheezing cough. He took a great gulping breath, and somehow forced himself to his feet. The world swayed; no sooner had he steadied himself than a horse barged into him and knocked him to his knees.

"Come on now, lad." His tormentor almost sounded sympathetic. "You've had enough punishment. Yield."

He might have done, if he hadn't spotted an abandoned sword, lying there in the mud alongside. He gasped with relief and grasped a hold of it, then pushed himself resolutely upright once more.

One after the other, they brought their horses close and struck out at him. He fought them off as best he could, though his strength was failing and he could hardly see for the blood streaming down his face. Faster and faster they wheeled around and thundered past. He lashed out, but each time he was too slow. Then as he blocked a blow, the blade in his hand snapped—he was holding a shattered stump of metal. He stared at it stupidly, he'd have wept if he wasn't too numb with pain and exhaustion.

"Yield!"

His defiant retort came out as a hoarse gurgle. He was reeling, then falling. . .

When he opened his eyes, he saw blue sky above him. Then it was eclipsed by the vast dark belly of a horse. Its hooves threshed the soft ground all around him, its caprison brushed his armour. He wondered groggily how long it would be before it trampled him.

"Come on, men!" Lord Hugh's voice called out. "Don't loiter here when there's Cunninghames to slay. A silver penny for every Cunninghame you kill tonight, and a gold lyon to the man who brings me Kilmaurs. *Garde bien,* Montgomeries! Follow me!"

The horse leapt away, there was vivid blue sky above him once again. He lay still, dazed with the madness of it all.

He'd survived. He smiled faintly, even as the wave of blackness rolled around and pulled him under at last.

Chapter 3

The grey horse thunders through the spears of growing barley, alone, riderless. Its ears point forward, its tail drifts like a gossamer plume behind. Broken reins trail around its legs, its knees marred by mud and congealing trickles of blood.

It shows no fear, for all its life it has been taught to confront the battlefield with courage and exhilaration, as if war is nothing more than a wild hunt.

The sun is dying in the west. Its rays paint the landscape an eerie red, making the horse appear like some strange bloodied spectre which haunts the land. Its nostrils flare as distant sounds assault it; the neighs of horses, the roars and screams of men.

As the stallion runs on, its rider lies where he fell on a river bank, a crumpled figure who languishes there delirious for a time, undisturbed.

Eventually, some men venturing out from a nearby mill discover him. They note the fine quality of his arms and clothing, but as they carry him back to the comparative comfort of their dwelling, they are unaware of his importance.

They pour a little water on his lips, and he awakes with a start. He is confused at first, but gradually, his senses return. He reaches out, clutches the garments of the nearest man, and whispers, "Pray help me, sir. I'm your King, and I'm dying. Fetch me a priest, so I can make my peace with God."

They find a priest. Or at least a man who claims to be a priest. But this supposed man of the cloth proves less than sympathetic to his king's predicament. No sooner has the stricken monarch confessed his sins, than the assassin's blade gleams as it is plunged down into his body.

James the Third, King of Scots by the Grace of God, is dead.

Chapter 4

His sense of taste returned first. John licked his lips and swallowed, gagging at the salty metallic tang of blood and sweat.

He was lying stretched out in the mud. At first he found his weakness strangely comforting, but gradually his stupor receded. Pain gripped him; his left arm and shoulder throbbed and his head ached, while his ribs felt as if they'd been crushed.

A sound distracted him, a faint skittering scratch close by. The scratching ceased, and his visor quivered.

John opened his eyes. He saw a black shape through the slit of his helmet, silhouetted against a red, lurid sky.

The creature pecked hopefully where his bloodied face was revealed. *Hell*, he thought, numbly, but his body reacted of its own accord, his right hand flicking weakly at the demon perched upon his chest.

It flapped lazily away, heading off into the blazing sky. A raven, here to feast on dead men's flesh.

John stirred. There'd soon be other scavengers prowling the field, a hundred times more dangerous. He forced himself to his feet, though the effort made him retch. He fumbled with his visor, but it didn't move. He tried again, desperate now, and it opened just in time before he heaved up what little remained in his stomach. He spat out what he could; his mouth tasted vile and he needed a drink, but the pools of water at his feet were tainted with blood and dung.

John wiped his lips against the leather palm of his gauntlet. All around him ragged figures scuttled like rats across the battlefield, drawn to the dead and the dying. They clawed at armour and clothing and hacked at men's hands so they could steal the rings on their fingers.

Gradually, it sank in. That even though the world around him was mad, chaotic, he at least was safe. He thanked God for his deliverance, then, ever-cautious, wasted no time in finding himself a sword.

The battle had moved on, the rout was over. A group of men loitered some way away, beneath a blue-and-red quartered banner.

The Prince had won.

He'd been lucky. He should have been dead. Or captive, at least. Instead, he'd been abandoned and apparently forgotten. Others hadn't been so fortunate; amongst the corpses that littered the ground, eight bore his family colours, the red-and-white chequered chevron upon a bright white ground.

One was clad in plate mail like himself.

It was his father.

He squeezed his eyes shut, hoping he'd been mistaken, but when he opened them again, the body was still there. He broke into a stumbling run, remembering the last glimpse of his father, pitched in battle against the Lord Montgomerie.

Now Sir Thomas Sempill was dead. It was hard to say what blow had killed him, for the body appeared perfect, white jupon untainted by gore.

John dropped to his knees alongside. His hand trembled as he pushed back the visor.

Sir Thomas Sempill's eyes, bright grey-blue like his own, stared out from an alabaster face.

It took a while to sink in.

He was alone. The father who'd always seemed as strong and unchanging as the land itself was gone. The realisation hit him so hard that his limbs wobbled anew. He had to sit down, despite the clammy, blood-soaked mire which sucked and squelched around his haunches.

"Oh, Holy Mary. . ." He thumped the unheeding corpse, choking back tears. "Damn you! He only wanted to settle his scores with Cunninghame."

A trumpet sounded, far across the field. John clambered stiffly to his feet, suddenly ashamed. "I'm sorry. I didn't mean that." He crouched down and touched the lifeless arm. "Please understand! I don't want to leave you. But I must get home. For Mother, and for Marion." He gently lowered the eyelids then replaced the visor, so the crows wouldn't gorge themelves on his father's flesh just yet.

Drawing his knife, he cut the purse from his father's belt. There'd be money inside, enough to get him home. There was also a seal marked with the family's arms, and a ring, items of which he was the rightful guardian now.

And that would be all he could salvage, apart from the armour he carried on his back.

John straightened with a sigh. He had little hope of finding a horse, but there was no harm in looking. Some wandered loose nearby, but most were wounded or hobbling. A bedraggled group stood huddled a few yards to his left; amongst them he saw a chestnut gelding with a broad white blaze running the length of its face.

It was the same horse from which he'd fallen earlier that evening. Its saddle was askew, but the beast itself was apparently unharmed.

He was about to approach when a low moan distracted him. Peering through the gloom, he saw the glint of an unsheathed knife. Right before his eyes, one of the foul figures that prowled the battlefield was about to take another life.

The scene revolted him, but he couldn't look away. The murderer straddled its victim, ready to strike; he heard the wounded man pleading incoherently for mercy, which only sickened him more.

He saw a flash of ivory cloth. It was one of his own men.

"Leave him!" He scrambled over, dagger drawn, and plunged the blade deep into the creature's neck. There was a shriek, which faded into a rasping wheeze. A pair of withered hands seized his arms, an old hag's face stared up into his own. Her eyes were bright, her mouth twisted, like the carving of a damned soul from a cathedral frieze. He wanted to move, to cry out, but the horror of it locked his limbs and choked him into silence. Her grip loosened, her hands pawed at his body and his legs as she slid slowly to the ground.

At first he couldn't take his eyes off the ragged heap which lay slumped over his feet. He felt sick, his limbs shaking.

He hauled the corpse roughly aside. "Come on now." He crouched down by his retainer. "We're going home."

The wounded man stared up at him, bewildered. "The Laird."

"Don't say anything."

His retainer's surcoat was stained red down the left side and he'd lost the top of an ear in a glancing blow to the head. *Rescuing him's madness*, a rational part of him protested. *He's as good as dead. He'll just slow you down.*

John hauled the injured man to his feet. "Let's waste no more time!" he urged. "We'll find a horse and go."

* * *

Like a caged beast the Lord Montgomerie strode back and forth before his banner.

He'd led the chase at first, while the lust for killing gripped him. But when he'd hacked down a score or more Cunninghames and he still hadn't found the Lord Kilmaurs, he'd reluctantly turned back, leaving his kinsmen to continue the search.

Now all he could do was wait, and he found that more of a trial than anything else.

Suddenly his pacing ceased. Quite by chance, he'd looked up. The setting sun was burning a fierce red in the west, while the sky above darkened to a deep vibrant blue.

Gules and *azure*. His colours, painted bright across the heavens for all to see. A sign that God Himself was with him on the field this night. Heady with victory, Hugh spread his hands wide, threw his head back and laughed.

But not even the glory of the sky could settle him. Soon the pacing resumed. Restless, unthinking.

A horse whinnied, and Hugh stood taut with expectation. He could hear the thunder of hooves, distant, subdued. It grew ever louder, interspersed now with the jingle of harness and an occasional snort.

They crested a nearby hill, a mass of red-and-blue liveried men. And there, shining pale amongst them, a solitary knight, white jupon shining bright in the dusk.

They'd brought him Kilmaurs.

Hugh closed his eyes in silent prayer as the horsemen came closer. The ground shook beneath the seething mass of horseflesh; undeterred, Hugh strode towards them. At the last moment, he raised his hand, like Canute trying to halt the tide. The gesture was enough; thirty horses came to a stamping halt, just feet away. The smell of them, hot and lathered from the gallop, filled the air.

He waved at Kilmaurs. "It's been a long time, Alex. You're keeping well?"

Kilmaurs said nothing, just sniffed disdainfully. He was hunched on his warhorse, wrists bound before him, a venomous scowl on his face.

"That's a fine horse." Hugh wandered over and clapped its speckled neck.

"No doubt you'll take him for yourself."

Hugh closed his fingers tight about the reins. "Oh, I'm worth more than a knock-kneed English nag." He gestured alongside. "Join me, please. We can't talk when you're perched up there."

Kilmaurs looked unenthusiastically to the ground.

"John." Hugh beckoned to his cousin. "The Lord Kilmaurs needs assistance."

"Happy to oblige." John Montgomerie of Hessilhead slid from his horse and stamped over. He seized Kilmaurs' arm. "Get on with you!" he snarled, pulling so hard that Kilmaurs tumbled to the ground. Agitated horses spilled to either side, and Kilmaurs had the misfortune to roll into Hessilhead's legs as he landed.

"Damned clumsy fool!" Hessilhead hammered into Kilmaurs with his mailed fists.

Hugh smiled sourly. And they said that *he* had a vicious temper. . . He watched a little while, until he grew bored with the delay. "Enough!"

"Get up!" Hessilhead gave his captive one last swipe across his head. "Stand like a man, you dog!"

"That's no way to talk to your betters!" Kilmaurs snapped back.

"I said enough!" Hugh hauled Hessilhead back. "Here, let me help you." He unsheathed his dagger, sliced through the rope that tied the old knight's wrists, then reached out his hand.

"May you roast in Hell." Kilmaurs pushed him away. "Savages, the whole damned lot of you." He clambered to his feet. His jupon was torn and muddied, fresh blood seeped from his nose. "What do you want with me?"

"I'll take the Lord Kilmaurs under my protection, and treat him with all due courtesy—"

"Courtesy!" Kilmaurs spat. "You don't know the meaning of the word. You don't even call me by my proper title. I'm the Earl of Glencairn—"

"A false title, bestowed by a false King. And might I suggest, my lord, that you choose your words more wisely. If you want to live the night, that is. . ."

"You ungrateful wretch!" Kilmaurs clenched his fists. "I provided for you, when no one else cared what became of you. I took you under my roof. Fed you, clothed you—"

"You were well rewarded for your pains." Hugh idly scuffed the grass with his foot. "Let's not waste time arguing. There's a certain matter on which we differ. I want it settled tonight."

"You'll settle it your own sweet way, I'm sure."

"I'm an honourable man, my lord. You have my word that I'll let you live tonight. I'll set you free, with your horse and your arms and anything else you might require. Why, I'll even waive the ransom—"

"It's not like you to be so generous."

"—All I want in return is an assurance from you, in writing, witnessed by a dozen men of my choosing, that you'll withdraw any claim to the Bailie's title."

"It belongs to the Cunninghames."

"It's ours now."

"But you're not even worthy of that office, Hugh."

"And you are?" Hugh said. "It's not your place to make such judgements. You're not my guardian anymore. You can't bully me, or tell me what's right."

Kilmaurs licked his lips. "We can take our grievances to King and Parliament. Let them decide. . ."

"We did that, years ago. They ruled in my favour. But that wasn't enough, was it?"

"The situation was different then."

"It's a pity you're so stubborn. I thought we'd come to some agreement." He glanced around his men. They wanted a spectacle, and he wouldn't disappoint them. He gave a heavy sigh, and shook his head. "What are we to do?"

Kilmaurs shifted uneasily and coughed deep in his throat.

"I know!" Hugh slapped a comradely arm about Kilmaurs' shoulders. "We'll put our differences before the highest authority of all!" He gestured towards the blazing sky. "God Himself will judge us." He paused, to let the words sink in, then, "We'll fight this out together, you and I. The righteous man will prove strongest and he'll keep the Bailie's title. The loser must relinquish all claim to it."

"Don't be so damned ridiculous!"

"I swear, on the graves of my ancestors, that if you defeat me then you can leave this place with your life. You'll be granted safe conduct from the field, and the Montgomeries won't make any further claim. The office can remain with the Cunninghames in perpetuity. Is that agreed, John?"

"Hugh—" Hessilhead was dubious.

"*Is that agreed?*"

"Yes," Hessilhead muttered.

"Well, Sir Alex? What do you say?"

Sweat shone on Kilmaur's face, but his expression revealed nothing. "Very well."

"*Outrance?*"

The old knight's shoulders sagged. "*Outrance.*"

* * *

Outrance. To the death.

Hugh gripped the sword hilt with both hands. He knew he wasn't going to die this day. He'd known from the moment he looked up and saw the sky alight in blue and red that God was with him.

The sea of faces blurred at the limits of his vision. He was aware of them, yet not aware. He could hear the noise, though. Fifty, sixty men, maybe even more now, cheering, shouting his name, *Hugh! Hugh! Hugh!* over and over again.

He was their champion. He would not fail them.

It was like a dream. His fatigue was forgotten, he was in absolute command of every muscle, every sinew. He moved with the grace and precision of a dancer. The great six-foot sword twisted and turned in his grip, he blocked, he thrust, with eerie accuracy.

He did not think about what he was doing. He did not have to, for it felt as if hands more skilled and stronger than his own were guiding him. As the light of the dying sun shivered along the blade, his soul soared. It was a wondrous thing to be alive and in the prime of his strength.

Kilmaurs stumbled.

It was the sign of weakness he'd been waiting for. He struck Kilmaurs in the neck, then turned the weapon deftly around and bludgeoned his opponent's helmeted head with the pommel, again and again. Kilmaurs swayed, then sank to his knees. One last blow and he was prone on the ground.

Hugh tossed aside his sword. He'd called on higher powers to help him, but now God and the saints were forgotten. He was gripped by a raw desire to kill; it took all his strength of will to fight it.

He dropped to a crouch, and ground his armoured knee into Kilmaurs' groin.

Around him, the circle closed in. Men loomed over him, shaking fists and screaming at him to strike the final blow. Amidst all the frenzy, he was suddenly serene. He smiled as he pulled out his dagger.

Carefully, he placed the point at the vulnerable place below Kilmaurs' oxter, then thrust it home. The blade slid deep, but still the old knight struggled. Hugh held him down, relentless, weathering the death throes like a lion savouring its kill.

The twitching ceased.

Cunninghame of Kilmaurs was dead.

Chapter 5
Near the Kippen Muir, Near Stirling

The horse thrust its nose into the pool. It gulped down water, ears flicking back and forth as it drank.

Exhausted, John dropped to his knees alongside, one hand loosely clasping the reins. It was foolish to let the creature take its fill. But John didn't have the heart to haul it back. Or the strength, either.

John sagged forward, leaning on one arm. It was still early morning, but the sun was burning fierce already. The weight of his armour pressed upon him. He wanted rid of it, but was too weary to move.

He closed his eyes. The sound of running water was all around him. It soothed the soul, after the clamour of a battle. . .

His arm gave way; he pitched towards the water. "Christ!" he snapped, hauling himself back just in time.

The horse raised its head and stared, water dripping from its jaws.

"You nearly had to fish me out." He let the reins fall. "Too tired to wander far, aren't you?" He sat down with a sigh, and turned his attention to the armour. He had to remove the gauntlets first, but unaided even that was a struggle. In the end he tugged on the strap with his teeth, and at last the gauntlet slid off.

John raised his hand and gazed in wonder at his own exposed flesh. The fresh air against his skin revived him a little; he freed his right hand next, then off came helmet and mail coif, and the quilted cap beneath. His tangled gold-brown hair fell loose about his shoulders; he shook his head, groaning with pleasure and relief. Plunging his head into the depths of the pool, he gasped as the cold water slammed against him. As he sat up, strands of water ran from his hair, sliding down his neck, seeping cool into his sticky, sweat-soaked clothing.

He remembered then that he wasn't alone. He cast a guilty glance to where his retainer sat shivering in the sunlight, then grasped his helmet. He filled it with water, and carried it carefully to the other man.

"Here. It's water, I'm afraid. It's all we've got."

His companion took a few hesitant sips.

"It's Hugh Alexson, isn't it?" John wasn't granted a reply, but then he hadn't really expected one. "You're safe," he said. "We made good progress. We're up in the hills now, on the Kippen Muir." He talked as much to comfort himself, in an attempt to keep the prowling loneliness at bay. "A leech can see you once we're home. I'll try and staunch the bleeding meantime."

He dressed the wounds as best he could, with strips torn from his jupon. Alexson sat still throughout, then shook his head and sank down without a sound into the heather. Looking at his henchman's pallid face, John couldn't help but wonder if he'd ever wake again.

John yawned. The crushing exhaustion was back, but somehow he found the strength to take a drink and pull the harness from his sweating horse. He hauled the heavy saddle to a grassy bank and set it down, then flopped alongside. Piece by piece, he removed the rest of his armour, then lay down, head propped against his saddle, with his drawn sword close to hand.

He wouldn't sleep. It was too dangerous. He could rest, though. For just a little while...

He closed his eyes. A buzzard keened, high overhead.

It was a sad sound. It stung him, deep inside.

He saw them clear as day. Standing by the gate to wave him goodbye, their hoods flapping in the stiff April breeze. There was his mother, beaming broadly at him. He could hear her voice. *Serve your King and serve your father well. Make us proud of you.*

Marion just stared at the ground. But when he gathered up his reins, ready to depart, she stepped forward. She pressed her fingers to her lips, then took his hand. *Hurry home, John. I'll pray to God every night to keep you safe.* She looked up, and he'd been shocked to see her crying. *I couldn't bear it if anything happened to you...*

We failed them. I failed them. God forgive me... Tears pricked his eyes. *Oh God, how do I tell them?* The breeze flicked pleasantly against his face, he toppled into a dark, untroubled sleep.

* * *

Sunlight beat through the silken walls of the pavilion; it glowed so bright it was hard to look upon the figure enthroned there, James Stewart, Duke of Rothesay.

Their future King.

James was fifteen years old, a slender, fresh-faced boy. But he carried himself with the poise and confidence of a man twice his age. His throne was a chair, his cloth-of-state a banner brought from the battlefield. Despite these shabby, makeshift trappings of authority, James was still a glorious figure in their midst.

Hugh half-closed his eyes and basked in the splendour of the moment. A golden age was dawning, and he was there in the vanguard to welcome it.

"Not feeling the worse for wear after yesterday?"

Hugh's eyes flicked open. The speaker was his cousin, Matthew Stewart, son and heir to the Lord Darnley. "I thought you were in London."

Matthew swilled his wine around in his goblet. "Ah, you know. Changing circumstances." There wasn't much of the Montgomerie about Matthew Stewart. He was his father's son, a Stewart through and through. Stocky and strong, with a cocksure look about him that came from knowing he could count the King of Scots amongst his kin.

"So you fought with us?"

Matthew puffed up proud, like a black grouse in the lek. "We showed our northern kin a thing or two."

Hugh stifled a yawn.

"But that won't impress you, will it?" Matthew gave him a hefty slap on the back. "Congratulations! It's said you were the hero of the day."

35

Bruised and battered as he was, Hugh wasn't going to give Matthew the satisfaction of seeing him wince. He just shrugged and smiled, all false modesty.

Matthew glanced carefully around to see who was in earshot. "Is it true? That you killed Glencairn?"

"It was a fair fight."

"And what did the good Bishop say?"

"I've confessed my sins, and paid my dues."

"Of course," Matthew agreed, cheerfully. "You always do." He raised his goblet and battered it against Hugh's. "Here's to us then, cousin. May we both prosper, in the months ahead."

"Amen to that."

"What of the Sheriff of Renfrew?"

"I can't say, hand on heart, that my blows killed him. He was old, Mattie. No match for a man with youth and vigour on his side."

"Whether it was God's work or your own, it's still a grievous blow for them. And the Master of Sempill?"

Hugh hesitated. With Matthew's bastard brother married to the eldest of Sir Thomas Sempill's daughters, his interest in the Sempills' misfortunes was understandable. "By all accounts the lad did well," Hugh said, eventually. "He fought bravely, even when he was unhorsed. James knocked him down, but tried not to hit him too hard."

"Do you have him?"

Hugh fought the urge to frown. Matthew could at least have been more subtle about his intentions. But Matthew, being a Stewart, had no grasp of subtlety. He had no need for it, when his father was one of the most powerful men in the land. "I'm sorry." There was a certain perverse pleasure to be had, in being the bearer of bad tidings. "We had to leave him. I didn't want to lose Kilmaurs."

"He escaped then?"

"Good luck to him. I've nothing against the Sempills."

"Let's pray they don't hold it against you," Matthew jabbed a conspiratorial elbow into Hugh's side. "Cunninghame might find an eager ally in young Master Sempill."

Hugh took a deep draught of wine.

"We could have dealt with him. Saved you some trouble as well as helping ourselves." Matthew gave a heavy sigh. "Ah, well. Can't be helped." He sipped his wine. "Besides," he added. "It's early days yet, isn't it?"

"Yes." Hugh tugged his gown higher onto his shoulders. "I suppose it is."

Chapter 6

John hugged his knees and squinted through the sunlight at the approaching strip of land. The waters of the Clyde sparkled so bright that it hurt to look on them, but he braved the glare regardless. From his perch in the boat he could just make out Renfrew town, lying upriver from the green fields of Inchinnan. There was the Royal castle on the King's Inch. And, further inland, the belfry of the parish church reared high amongst the houses.

The last two days had been Purgatory. John wasn't accustomed to walking, but Alexson needed the horse. John had been glad to rest during the ferry journey, but now he dreaded the moment when he would have to move again.

Lulled by the slap of the oars, his eyes grew heavy. His stomach grumbled, and he pulled his legs in tighter still. Food had been scarce; on the first day, they'd shared some cold oatmeal gruel before they left the hollow on the hill, and later that afternoon John had negotiated with a farmer's wife for some bannocks and cold mutton and a measure of ale. Those meagre provisions cost a small fortune; she saw his horse and arms and raised the price accordingly. He'd been too weary to argue. He'd paid up, knowing he'd have to set the rest of his funds aside for the river crossing.

At last the boat bumped against the jetty. The horse threw up its head, nostrils flaring, and John held the reins tight and whispered quiet words to settle it.

"Here we are now!" called the ferryman.

"Thank you." John grabbed hold of Alexson with one arm while hanging onto the horse with the other.

"If I were you, lad, I'd find a place to rest in Renfrew. You travelled far?"

"A fair way." John steadied his retainer for the short climb onto the jetty. "You all right there?" he asked. Alexson nodded, faintly, so John turned his attention to the horse.

"Fine-looking beast," said the ferryman, turning covetous eyes upon it. "Yours, I suppose."

"Yes." John gritted his teeth and dragged upon the reins, but the horse wouldn't budge, its legs braced square against the deck.

"Get on with you!" The ferryman slapped the beast hard across its quarters. It sprang awkwardly onto the jetty, hooves battering loud against the timbers. "That shifted him." He scrambled out after it, looking hopeful.

"Here." John pulled the last of the coins from his purse.

"That's most gracious of you, sir. You're a fighting man yourself, are you? The ferryman made no attempt to hide his curiosity. "You from these parts?"

The ferryman was a Lennox man, born and raised in Dumbarton. There was rivalry between the towns of Renfrew and Dumbarton, and it wasn't always good-natured. With John's return, the rumours would soon follow, that something had happened out east, that two of Renfrew's men had come crawling home looking no better than beggars.

"None of your damned business!" John snapped, hurrying Alexson away. He was grateful his coat-of-arms wasn't visible; they'd enjoy his misfortune all the more if they knew he was the Sheriff.

"And a good day to you, sir!" the ferryman called after him.

* * *

John pushed himself on a little faster, dazed but determined, like a pilgrim nearing the journey's end.

At the top of the hill, the cottage of Nether Bar squatted on its stone foundations, smoke drifting out through the thatched roof which hung low over its daub walls.

Chickens clucked and scurried aside as he crossed the sun-baked yard; breathless after the climb, he barely noticed them. He halted, and braced his hands against his knees.

The slopes below were a sprawling patchwork of small fields, the green of the growing crops fading into swathes of sun-ripened gold. Further away, on the valley floor, there grazed a herd of black cattle. A brace of small boys attended them, dogs darting alongside.

He savoured the sight. If anything, the colours seemed more vivid; the green of the crops, the vivid splashes of red, purple and white that marked poppies, thistles and gowans. After the carnage of battle, it was comforting to know there was still beauty in the world. But everything seemed more fragile now. It was as if he looked upon a thin pane of painted glass that might shatter at any moment.

Lights flashed before his eyes, he bowed his head and blinked. He lifted a trembling hand to his forehead, fighting to remember why he'd come here in the first place.

Then he saw Alexson, who sat unheeding on the horse. "Wait here," he said. "I'd best tell them you're home."

He shouldered his way past the ox-hide curtain, cursing under his breath as his sword-hilt caught against the jamb.

Inside, the cottage was dim and filled with peat-smoke. A young child howled, drowning out his entrance. He spotted her first, a girl of three or four years who sat on the packed earth floor. Her golden hair shone against her dull clothing and she clutched a wooden doll in her hand.

Behind the child, two women worked feverishly at their chores. One chopped kale for the pot, while the other sat with a bowl in her lap, preparing dough for tomorrow's bread.

The child saw him. Her crying stopped.

"Good ladies—"

They shrieked. One sprang to her feet, brandishing a knife. "There's no alms here. Be off with you!"

He raised his hands. "I won't hurt you." He could forgive their hostility. He was filthy, stained with mud and blood and dusted with horsehair, with his long hair hanging bedraggled about his shoulders. Dressed like a ruffian, too, with his heavy quilted arming doublet hanging open over what had once been a fine white sark and light blue hose. "I'm looking for Mistress White."

"My goodness!" The woman set her knife down. "There's nothing to fear, Janet. It's the Master." There was a brisk, stern air about her, even though she was tired and red-faced from her chores. She curtsied, briefly. "I'm sorry, Master Sempill. I didn't recognise you. I'm Mary White of Bar, sir."

There was broth stewing in an iron cauldron that hung over the fire. His mouth watered at the smell of it. "I've brought your husband, Hugh Alexson. He's wounded—"

"Dear God!" She pushed straight past him into the sunlight.

He followed, half-expecting an outburst. But she was stronger than that. She just looked silently up at her husband, her face inscrutable.

* * *

He helped them make Alexson comfortable in his bed. After that, there was nothing more for him to do. As they hurried about the place, fetching this and that, he was forgotten.

"Can I help?" he asked.

Mary White looked up from where she'd been crushing dried herbs in a bowl. He might have been speaking Greek, judging by the confounded look on her face. Then she smiled. Her features softened, warmed as if by a sudden shaft of sunlight on a grey winter's day. "If you could mind the water, Master Sempill. Fetch some in a bowl when it's hot."

* * *

Once she'd dressed the wounds, Mary covered her husband with a blanket. "He's in a fever. How long's he been like this?"

"He seemed quite lucid for a while. But this morning he grew worse again. I think the journey was too much."

"It's God's will," she said, distantly. She rinsed the blood from her hands and wiped them dry on her skirts. "I've done what I can."

"She has the hands," Janet explained. "If there's a soul on earth can save him, Mary can."

"He can rest now." Mary straightened. "Thank you, Master Sempill," she said, real warmth in her voice. "For bringing him back."

He shrugged. "I couldn't leave him there." He felt suddenly faint. And so very cold, despite the suffocating warmth of the place. "I'm very hungry," he told her, and then his legs buckled.

"Lord save us!" She caught him just in time. "Janet! Fetch him somewhere to sit." She put her arm around him and steered him towards the stool that Janet set out for him. "There now." She sat him down, gently patting his back as if he were a sick child. "I'm forgetting my manners. The broth'll be ready now. And there's fresh bread baked, too. It won't be what you're used to, mind, but you're welcome to eat with us."

He nodded, too spent even to thank her.

She ladled some broth into a wooden bowl. As she placed it in his hands, her arm brushed against him. Her sleeves were rolled up past her elbows, the muscles of her forearms taut beneath the glowing gold of her skin. Her warm musky scent filled his nostrils, making his flesh tingle with anticipation. Then she'd gone, and all that mattered was the food. He leaned low over the bowl, tearing great lumps from the bread, soaking them in the broth and scarcely chewing each piece before wolfing it down.

When he next looked up, he'd devoured half his meal.

Both women were staring at him, curious, a little disappointed, and he blushed, ashamed because he'd been eating like an animal. His hair had been trailing in the broth and he hadn't even noticed.

Mary smoothed her skirts self-consciously. "How went the battle, Master Sempill?"

"The Laird is dead."

"At least we still have you," Mary said.

"A laird's a laird," he muttered. "One's much the same as another."

"Better the laird who brings his men back home than the one who leaves them to rot."

"I did what I could, Mistress White. I only wish I could've done more." He drained the dregs and pushed himself upright. "Thank you." He placed the bowl in her hands. "I'll be off now. I'll send the tacksman round, to see how your husband's faring."

She followed him to the door, still gripping the bowl. "Thank you again, sir," she said, as he untied his horse. "With all my heart. At least here his passing'll be sweeter—"

He seized her shoulders. "You mustn't talk that way!"

She shook him loose, a warning grimace on her lips.

"Don't lose hope, Mistress White," he said. "I'm going home by Pennald. I'll speak with the priest at St Barchan's. He'll be able to help—" He drifted into silence. There was something unsettling, even intimidating, about her. It was the way she looked straight through him, bleak, distant, as if she saw beyond the realms of the living. "I'll pay the costs myself," he added, cautiously.

"Save yourself the trouble!" Then she added, more gently, "He's dying, Master Sempill. He's in God's hands now." She looked away. "For all the good that'll do him."

* * *

Ellestoun. He saw its tower standing tall and proud across the valley just as soon as he left Pennald, but it was another half-hour before his horse clattered through the gates.

The hounds bayed, but there wasn't a soul in sight. It wasn't the welcome he'd expected. He'd dreamed of far better, of being hailed a hero as he rode back in triumph with his father. . .

"Alright, alright!" A cantankerous voice called to the hounds. "Quiet now!" It was Henry, the family's head groom and huntsman. He stamped out from the stables, clutching a pitchfork, a thunderous scowl on his face. "What the Devil's this?" His failing eyes recognised first the horse, then John, and he broke into a toothless smile. "Master John! You're back, sir." He looked close to tears. "By God we missed you!"

"Yes, I'm back." John slid to the ground. Crouching down, he greeted Henry's entourage of hounds. They swarmed around him, putting huge paws on his shoulders and painting his face with their tongues.

"It went bad for us, didn't it?" Henry asked.

John fought off the seething mass of hounds and stood tall. "Sir Thomas is dead."

"Saints preserve us!" The old groom crossed himself.

"They're dining, aren't they? Don't say anything yet, Henry. I won't spoil their meal."

"But the Lady Elizabeth should be told!"

John rested a reassuring hand on his shoulder. "I'll see to it. Once they're finished, find Marion. Ask her to come to Father's chamber."

* * *

John paid a brief visit to the kitchens, where the cooks took pity on him and sent him on his way with a platter piled high with food.

He limped up the stairs. At the open door to the hall, he paused, drawn by the clatter of utensils and the cheerful murmur of voices beyond. But the burden of his news was too great, he needed some time to compose his thoughts. Like a ghost he moved on, unseen and unheard.

Up another storey, and then he'd reached his father's chamber.

He unlatched the heavy door, and stepped inside. The room had been cleaned and aired, there was an air of tidy expectation about the place. The wooden shutters were open, shafts of gold light gleamed their way across the dark timbers of the floor towards the elaborately carved bed. In the harsh light of day, the rich furnishings showed their age. The dark-red velvet curtains that hung about the bed were faded and slightly worn in places. So too were the hangings and tapestries that adorned the walls.

John sat himself down by the window. Setting his goblet and platter nearby, he pulled off his shoes with a groan. He stared numbly at his feet; his hose were worn through from walking and stained with blood.

He sat back, and closed his eyes. The sun felt warm against his face. He thought of his father, and that cold February day when Montgomerie came calling.

The grief was like a blow in the pit of his stomach. He slumped forward, dropped his head in his hands and wept. He didn't weep for his father, he wept for all of them.

"John?"

It was Marion. She was standing over him, but he could barely make her out through the tears. He tried to speak, but there were no words, just another choking sob.

"Oh, Johnny!" She sat beside him, and put her arms around him, heedless of the state of him. "My poor little brother." She patted his back and stroked his tangled hair while he sobbed all the harder in her arms. "It's alright. You're home now."

He drew a deep shuddering breath and shook himself loose.

She released him and slid away, hand lingering briefly against his shoulder. "Are you better now?"

41

He sniffed one last time. "Yes."

"Here." She handed him a handkerchief. "Wipe your eyes. And blow your nose. It'll upset Mother, to know you've been crying." She was a slender willow of a girl. Tall and dark-haired like their mother, with porcelain pale skin. "Poor John." She ruffled his hair. "You're an awful mess. You look like a wild man from the north."

"I smell foul, too."

Marion smiled, slightly. "I didn't want to say. Did you take Confession?"

"No. . ."

"You should take Confession, soon as you can." She sat back with a sigh. "You blame yourself, don't you?"

"I couldn't reach him."

"It wasn't your fault." She paused. "What happened?"

"He set us against the Montgomeries. He fought Lord Hugh. I tried to help him, but I was knocked senseless. When I woke up, the rout was over, and he was dead."

"You survived. We should be thankful for that."

"Oh, God, I dreaded this moment. I didn't know how to tell you. . ."

"Henry told me you were back. That's when I knew." She sighed. "Poor Father."

"I don't know how you can take it so bravely."

She gave a hollow laugh. "I hardly knew him."

"I suppose." He didn't press her further.

"So what was it like?" she asked. "To fight your fellow man like that?"

"Everything they told me, everything I learned over the years, it all meant nothing. It's every man for himself, and you just have to hack away at anyone coming at you, because if you don't, they'll kill you—"

"Shhh. . ." She brushed the hair back from his face. "Don't get upset. It's over now."

"No, it's not." Panic rose afresh within him. "It's only just begun. They'll have his body. They'll know he fought for the King. Who knows what they'll do to punish us? They could take everything away, they could even hang me as a traitor."

"But it's so unjust! You didn't do anything."

"That won't matter."

She took his hands in hers and squeezed them tight. "Now come on. Put on a brave face, for Mother's sake."

"What will I say?"

"Just tell her the truth. There's no softening the blow, is there?" She broke off as the latch rattled.

They both stood as the door opened, and Elizabeth Ross came hurrying across the room, all smiles. "John! My boy's come home at last!"

"Mother—" His voice faded.

"Holy Mary," she whispered. "Thomas. . ."

"He was defending the King." His voice trembled, he broke off and swallowed. Somehow, when he carried on, the words came out steady. "He led his men with courage, and—" He couldn't look her in the eye. "He was slain."

"And the King?"

"He was defeated."

"No. . ." His mother closed her fist and put it to her lips.

"I'm sorry."

"Is there news of my brother?" Lady Elizabeth asked, warily.

His uncle, the Lord Ross of Montgrennan. Who'd been the Lord Advocate, and one of the most hated men in the King's circle. His uncle's notoriety had been a source of pride once. Now it was a shameful liability. "I don't know."

"He'll know to come here," Lady Elizabeth declared. "We'll give him shelter."

"We can't do that!" It was the hardest thing, to say such cruel words to her. "If we help him, we're as good as dead. If he's got any sense, he'll flee to England."

"Dear God!" Her voice was touched with fear.

"Mother, you mustn't worry," Marion put a comforting arm about her mother's shoulders. "John'll take care of us."

Lady Elizabeth pulled a handkerchief from her sleeve and wiped her eyes. "You're right." She made a brave attempt at a smile. "Oh, John. You're a light in the darkness."

"Mother, there's no need for that—"

"No. Let me finish! Your father. . . He was harsh sometimes, I know, but he only wanted the best for you. He'd be so proud of you, taking up this burden so bravely." She stifled a sob. "I'm sorry. You must be so tired after your journey, and your poor old mother is too wrapped up in her own troubles to look after you. Marion, ask the servants to prepare the room for your brother. He's the laird now."

"Of course."

"Oh, God. . ." She turned away. "Forgive me. I'll miss your father very much." Her voice cracked, she hurried from the room. Her footsteps plotted the course of her retreat, up the spiral stairs to the ladies' chambers above. A door slammed, and through the timber floor they heard her keening wails.

He's the laird now. . .

It was a terrifying thought. The future of the estate lay in his hands. His decisions wouldn't just have consequences for him, they would affect the lives of everyone around him. There was so much he didn't know. And so much at stake. He clenched his fists tight at his sides, trying to shut out the sound of his mother's despair.

"John?"

"What's the matter?"

"I should go to her."

"Of course. Go on now."

"Is there anything else you need?"

"I want to bathe. If you could speak with the servants…"

"I will." Marion inclined her head, an unexpected gesture of subservience. The red-brown folds of her dress rustled as she swept quietly away.

Half-way across the room, she paused. "There's one last matter." She studied the floor, shoulders tense, hands clasped nervously before her. "What'll happen to me?"

She was twenty-one years old, and still unmarried. She'd had two suitors over the years. Good men, rich and well-connected. But she'd refused them both.

"I'll never turn you out of this house," John reminded her. "You know that."

"It's just that Mother—"

"She'll do what I say now."

She nodded, reassured. But at the door, she halted again. "John. . . What of the Crawfurds?"

"I'm sorry. I hadn't even spared a thought for them." A terrible admission, for he considered Robert Crawfurd his closest friend. John scratched distractedly at his forehead, wincing as his nail tore the scab there. He inspected the fresh blood on his fingers, then looked up, puzzled. "Why do you ask?"

"No matter," Marion said, then she, too, was gone.

Chapter 7
Edinburgh Castle

"You've brought food and ale?" Sir John Stewart, the Lord Darnley, called as he crossed the yard.

"Of course." Matthew Stewart sounded bored.

Stewart scowled. "Wake up, lad!"

"He's not said anything yet, has he? What makes you think he'll be any different today?"

"Because we're Stewarts, Mattie. His kin." Stewart was a massive man, strong and broad-shouldered. He was an accomplished knight, nearing fifty now, with a presence that befitted a commander of men. "He's from the north. These things matter to them." He waved to the gaoler. "Open up."

The key grated in the lock, the door creaked inwards.

Stewart took one last breath before he stepped inside. The room was small and dark, lit by a small window set high in the wall. It was furnished only by a privy in the corner, which reeked in the baking heat of the afternoon.

Matthew coughed behind him. For all his swaggering bravado, he had yet to develop a strong stomach.

As for Stewart of Darnley himself, he was well-used to squalor. In his youth, he'd fought in France against the English and he'd endured enough of it then. He saw the stink of sweat and human waste as the stench of defeat. If a man was careless enough to be caught in the rout, then squalor was all he deserved.

The prisoner sat hunched against the wall, arms wrapped around his knees. He was another John Stewart, the Earl of Atholl, who'd been a close ally of King James during the last months of his reign. As they approached, he scowled defiantly and muttered a few uncomplimentary words in Gaelic.

Stewart pretended not to understand. "It's a glorious day out there, cousin John," he said, lightly. "Pity you can't enjoy it with us."

Atholl was a contemporary of his but he looked ten years older: pale and haggard, still clad in the blood-stained arming doublet and clothing he'd worn when he was captured three days before.

Stewart shook his head. It was hard to believe that this pitiful figure had been a powerful courtier in James's court. "Still keeping your lips sealed?" He beckoned to Matthew, who handed him the flagon of ale and the loaf. "Here." Stewart crouched alongside Atholl and held them out towards him.

Atholl snatched both. He lifted the flagon to his lips, drinking so fast that the ale spilled out and trickled down his neck.

"There's really no need for this," Stewart said, as Atholl savaged the bread. "Why must you be so stubborn?"

There was no reply.

"All we want to know is what became of the King's treasure."

"Damn you. . ."

"Listen to me." Stewart pulled the remains of the loaf away. Atholl tried to grab it, but Stewart held it just out of reach. "I said listen, John."

Atholl shrugged, still eyeing the bread.

"The gold won't be any use to him now he's dead, will it?"

"What d'you mean?" Atholl's attention was full on him now.

"I'm sorry. I thought you knew."

That rebellious glint showed in his eyes again. "You're lying."

"Alas, I'm not."

"Murderers!" He moved, quick as a wildcat. Grabbed Stewart's gown and hauled him close. "They killed your King. And you stood by and let them do it!"

Stewart heard Matthew stirring behind him. He didn't shout out. He didn't need to; his son knew better than to intervene. "It was a battle." Stewart gently prised him loose. "People die."

"But he was never supposed to fight," Atholl argued. "We sent him away." The fire went out of him, he slumped forward, head on knees. "Ah, dear God. James. . . You never deserved this. . ."

"Who went with him? Bothwell? Montgrennan?"

"They were to meet him at the ships if the battle turned against him."

"And the treasure?"

"Alright!" Atholl thumped his fist against the flagstones. "He gave me two boxes of coins and jewels. I sent them to Atholl for safekeeping. The Countess has them."

"We want them back."

Atholl stared silent at the wall.

"I'm not lying to you, cousin. By God's truth, it's over. He's gone."

"Send her my seal," said Atholl. "Give it to some men you can trust. She'll hand over the boxes if she's convinced no harm's come to me."

Stewart smiled and patted him on the back. "Thank you. And the rest of it?"

"He didn't tell me."

"Who did he tell?"

"Who d'you think? Ramsay of Bothwell. Ross of Montgrennan. They were the only men he ever trusted." Atholl slumped back against the wall. "He never trusted me, that's for sure."

"He was a fool, John. He could never tell his friends from his enemies." Stewart rose to his feet. "You've done well, cousin. I'll have you moved to more comfortable accommodation this afternoon. And I daresay, once the King's boxes are safely restored, we can release you. I think you've kept your part of the bargain. So it's only fair we keep ours, isn't it?"

The Place of Ellestoun

A cockerel crowed, and John stretched with a luxurious yawn.

It was as if the nightmare had never happened. He was safe, the perils of the world shut out by the curtains round the bed. He almost expected to hear his father's voice, telling him to rise without delay.

"John!" The summons came from his mother. "Get up now. We must go to Mass."

John lifted his head with a sigh.

"Are you listening?" Her footsteps marauded beyond. "Don't forget; you're back amongst civilised folk now."

"Yes."

"I've set your clothes out ready. Make sure you comb your hair. The Good Lord won't be well impressed if you set foot in His House uncombed and unshaven—"

* * *

The gathered clergy at Saint Bryde's poured out a poignant song, and John dug his nails fierce into his palms, fighting back tears. On either side, his mother and Marion clutched him close and wept loud for his father.

He swallowed. He had to be strong. For their sakes.

After Mass, he confessed his sins. Shame-faced, he told the priest about the slaughter, even admitted that he'd found pleasure in the carnage. Told him that he felt it was his fault his father died. *I tried to help him. But I didn't try hard enough. I should've saved him. . .* The words spilled out, and so did the tears, while the priest listened patiently.

It's wrong to kill, the priest said at last. *You know that. It's true that to enjoy the spilling of another's blood makes the sin a thousand times worse. But the workings of this world mean that Man, sometimes against his better nature, is forced to sin. You've had the courage to admit your failings. God will look kindly on that.* He didn't even demand much of a penance, before he laid his hand upon John's head and blessed him. *Don't blame yourself for your father's death,* he added, as they walked from the chapel. *It was God's will. If you were meant to save him, you would have.*

* * *

Afterwards, John returned to Ellestoun for the reading of his father's will. Sir Thomas had made Elizabeth Ross his executor; an astute choice, for it gave his widow a renewed sense of purpose.

Reluctantly, John sat with her while she went through the will in painstaking detail, right down to every feather mattress and brass candlestick. He didn't dispute a thing. There was no need to. It all went to him, except for the necessary payments to Crown and Church and token amounts for his three sisters.

"The estate's in good shape. You'll do alright with it." She rolled up the charters and documents. "I'll send for a notary, to record everything formally. And I'll send word, to Margaret and Elizabeth. They should be told about their father's death." She turned to him, face lit with enthusiasm. "I'll ask Margaret to dine with us. She must be so lonely, up at Caldwell. What with Adam away. . ."

"What makes you think she'll come?"

"She's your sister."

"She's married to a traitor."

"She's a Sempill. She won't betray her kin." She looked close to tears.

"I wouldn't be so sure." He rose to his feet.

"Where are you going?"

"Out into the hills. I've been cooped up all day."

"But there's so much to do," she protested. "Your marriage—"

"It can wait."

"No, it can't!" Her hands fluttered in desperation. "This is too important."

"Mother." He leaned upon the table. Looked her in the eye, a direct challenge. "It can wait."

"But who's going with you?"

"I don't need a wetnurse."

"You shouldn't go out on your own!" she called, as he strode away. "It's too dangerous—"

"God," he muttered, and slammed the door behind him.

* * *

John sought refuge in an old camp, high in the hills. Its earthen rampart had been raised long ago by the King of the Britons; it was said Wallace had rested there during his wars against the English.

Most men shunned the place. They swore that it was haunted. But John had always relished the isolation and tranquility. Now, with summer upon them, the overgrown interior was bright with flowers. A few deer lazed at the far end; they eyed him warily at first, until they realised he wasn't there to hunt them.

He lifted the hawk high. "Go on."

It flapped off into the blue realms above.

Watching it, he felt a pang of envy inside. What a comfort it would be, to have the means to fly away and leave the problems of this world far behind.

Leaving his horse to graze, he scrambled up the grassy rampart. From there he could see the distant spire of Paisley Abbey amongst a cluster of smoke plumes, set within a vast rolling landscape of fields and woodland.

It all seemed so peaceful.

John slid back down to the camp's interior. He'd given the hawk ample time to stretch its wings. He took out the lure and swung it around over his head, whistling.

The hawk didn't appear at first. His heart sank; he wondered if its betrayal was a portent of worse to come.

But at last it returned, falling from the sky like a missile. It dived again and again; eventually, he let it seize the lure and drag it to the ground. He grasped its jesses, then coaxed it onto his gauntlet.

His horse whinnied and jerked up its head. It blew through its nostrils, then strode off, ears pricked, eyes fixed on the gap in the ramparts.

"Whoa!" John set off in pursuit. "Come back here, damn you!"

The walk became a trot, it whinnied loudly once again. This time, its call was answered. By another horse, which threaded its way through the gap.

His heart lurched at first, for the horse was unfamiliar. But he knew its rider well enough. "William!" He quickened his pace, hawk clinging tight to his glove.

William Haislet was a sturdy man of forty years. Waves of frosted dark-brown hair hung down his shoulders, he was still dressed for battle in a bloodstained brigandine. He dismounted and caught the straying horse, then held out the reins as John approached. "You'll be wanting this."

"Thought I'd have to walk home." John grabbed William's shoulder and skidded to a halt. "You're not a ghost?" He prodded the older man's arm, just to make sure.

William chuckled. "Takes more than a few Montgomeries to finish me." He was more than a servant; he was one of the finest minstrels in the Westland. He could have found a patron anywhere, but instead he'd settled at Ellestoun. Serving in such a small retinue had its drawbacks, for William earned his keep by doubling up as manservant, messenger, and armed retainer.

"I don't know the horse." John said.

"Came courtesy of the Lord Montgomerie." William stroked the horse's face. "The lad looking after him had to answer a call of nature. When he turned back the beast had gone." He winced. "Don't know how he explained that one to His Lordship."

"We'd best feed the poor brute to the hounds. Lord Hugh'll burn the place if he finds we've stolen one of his nags."

William blew softly through his teeth. "A hanging offence for sure." There was silence, then he said, gently, "You should come home. Your mother's fretting. She says you parted on bad terms."

John kicked irritably at the ground. "Why must she always worry?"

"Women are like that," William said. "Besides, Lady Margaret's come down from Caldwell. . ."

"Now that's a surprise! I didn't think she'd want anything to do with us."

"She always had a soft spot for you." William hauled himself into the saddle. "Ah, well. Here we go again. No peace for the wicked."

* * *

"I tried to find you," said William, as they rode back together. "I saw you go down, but then the lines broke and we were routed."

"You're lucky you survived."

"Their heart wasn't in the chase. As soon as they sighted Cunninghame's banner they were off."

"How many made it?"

"Five."

Just five, out of eighteen men. John took a deep breath, trying to comprehend the scale of their losses. "You shouldn't have looked for me," he said. "It wasn't worth the risk."

William shrugged. "If they'd caught me, I'd have offered my services to Lord Hugh."

"If his men didn't gut you first," John retorted. "You lost out there. He'd have doubled your income."

"There's more to life than money."

"I'll remember that, next time you ask for more." John stretched in his stirrups with a sigh. "Ah well, Lord Hugh's loss is our gain."

"I've no desire to move on, thank you. Though I was beginning to wonder if my services would still be required. When I couldn't find you, I feared the worst."

"I recovered my senses and fled the field," John said. "I took Hugh Alexson with me. But I had to leave Father. Did you see him?"

"There was no sign of him."

"They seized his corpse then." John frowned. "We'll hear from them soon enough. Lord Hugh'll want to know how much I'm willing to pay to get him back."

"There's more," William added. "Sir Alexander Cunninghame. . . Montgomerie killed him."

"Murder?"

"Not exactly. They fought it out man to man. But Lord Hugh had around two score Montgomeries with him, while Cunninghame was alone. Foregone conclusion, really."

Despite the blazing heat of the afternoon, John felt cold inside. "So Montgomerie's unleashed and unmuzzled? Sir Alex was the only man who could bring him to heel."

"God help the Cunninghames."

"If Montgomerie casts his gaze further afield, then God help us all."

Chapter 8
Edinburgh Castle

"Sit down, Hugh." Patrick Hepburn, Lord Hailes, gestured to a vacant chair. "And thanks, for coming so promptly."

Lord Patrick was not the most approachable of men. He seldom smiled, and there was a slight twist to his narrow lips that gave him a sardonic, even slightly cruel air. But it was important to remain on good terms with him. It was no exaggeration to say he was the power behind the throne. He was like a father to the young King, and had been his close confidante for many years now.

It was a good sign, though—Hugh noted, as he pushed his sword aside and settled into his seat—that for once Hepburn actually *was* smiling.

Hugh made sure he didn't look too curious, though the situation would have roused any man's curiosity. He'd been brought right to the heart of the Royal household, to a small anteroom beyond the King's privy chambers.

He recognised the place; he'd been there before, six years ago, in very different circumstances, when King James had been held captive here by a group of rebellious nobles. It was Ross of Montgrennan who'd come to Hugh and asked him to help secure James' release. He'd promised Hugh that his Bailie's title would be restored, but, as usual, Montgrennan hadn't delivered on his promises...

Strangely enough, the tapestry that faced Hugh now was the same one that had hung there six years earlier; a wistful vision of Eden, where the ground was strewn with flowers and birds and beasts peered sadly from the bushes. Hugh remembered hurling an unfortunate man-at-arms against it, the thud of the body against the wood-panelled wall. *Don't play games with us. We want to see the King. Where's the King. . .*

Hugh shook his head. It was a long time ago. He'd never have dreamed of rebelling back then, but things had changed.

For the better, he hoped. He cocked his head as voices came from the bedchamber beyond; a youth's excited chatter amongst the deeper tones of older men.

"We're very busy at the moment," Hepburn explained. "In between official business we're trying to organise a coronation. The tailors are measuring His Grace for the robes just now, but it's a Devil of a job getting him to stand still." He gestured towards a kist which stood against the wall behind him. "Some wine?"

"If you please."

Another man stepped forward, goblet in hand. Robert Colville was his name. He was the Director of Chancery, and another of young James's favourites. He poured the wine, and handed the goblet to Hugh, a bright, unconvincing smile on his lips.

Hugh grasped it with a nod.

A private meeting with Hepburn and Colville. . . The omens were looking better all the time. But then, wasn't it about time he was rewarded for his loyalty? He'd been praised for his role in the battle, but he hadn't received anything more than kind words. Which was galling, considering that many others had already been granted gifts of land and titles.

He raised his goblet. "His Grace the King."

"The King." Hepburn took a draught from his own goblet, but Colville just flashed Hugh a suspicious look.

Hugh stared back, undaunted. He didn't know what to make of Robert Colville. Colville was a lawyer, kinsman to a lesser baron in Kyle. An elegant man, Colville dressed bright as a papingo in the finest silks and velvets and he always dripped with gold. He had an able intellect, and he was fiercely loyal to young James. Too loyal, perhaps, for he gave the impression that he suspected every man of plotting against the lad.

One last wary glance over his shoulder, then Hepburn leaned closer. "You've heard the rumours?" he asked. "About King James?"

"I don't listen to rumours."

"This time they're worth heeding."

"He's dead then?"

"Oh, yes." Colville barely concealed his glee.

"It's said he was murdered."

"He was," said Colville.

Hugh shook his head, mock-sorrow. "A pity," he said, then added, "What of His Grace? How did he receive the news?"

"He's but a boy," said Hepburn. "Of course he's upset. But he's resilient. He'll know soon enough that it's been for the best."

"What of Ramsay? And Ross of Montgrennan?"

"No sign," Colville said. "Sir Andrew Wood's ships were seen off Leith. They'll be in Berwick by now."

He couldn't resist a dig. "That was careless."

"They won't show their faces past the Tweed in a hurry." Hepburn tapped his fingers idly against his chair. He was smiling again. "The charges of treason are being drafted as we speak."

"So who gets their estates?"

"It was agreed—" said Colville, "—that the Lord Patrick was a worthy successor to the Earldom of Bothwell."

No surprises there. "And Montgrennan?" He didn't want to sound too hopeful, but with Montgrennan's Cunninghame lands bordering his own, he was an obvious choice.

"We don't know. John Stewart of Darnley, perhaps. . ."

"Ah." Somehow, Hugh kept himself from scowling. "Patrick, why have I been summoned here? I'm in no mood to celebrate other men's successes."

Hepburn half-closed his eyes. "Whatever do you mean?"

"My claim to the Bailie's title. . ."

There was an indulgent chuckle from Hepburn. "Of course it's yours. Who else was worthy, or suitable?"

"Then why wasn't I told? You've been pouring accolades on every man but me since the damned battle."

"There have been so many pressing matters. I'm sorry."

Hugh shrugged. "No matter." He looked up. "Is that it, then?"

Hepburn and Colville exchanged glances. "Not exactly," said Hepburn.

"Then what can I do for you?"

"The Treasury's been robbed," Colville said. "Our beloved King ransacked it before he died."

"Oh dear." A lame response, but it was all he could think of. He wanted to laugh, for the irony was magnificent. Throughout his life, King James had been thwarted by his nobles at every turn. Now, in death, he'd outfoxed them all.

"All's not lost, though," Hepburn said. "A Master Simpson delivered into our hands two boxes of coins. And a sword. Bruce's sword, no less. From what we gather, the items were found close to the Sauchie Burn, where His Grace the King fell from his horse."

"So he expected defeat."

"Yes, but I don't think he expected to die."

"You think he shared out his riches amongst his friends."

"We know he did. The Earl of Atholl was captured after the battle. He'd spirited away two chests of treasure."

"Ramsay, and Montgrennan. . ." Hugh tapped his chin, thoughtfully. "They'll have the bulk of it."

"We don't know, though, if they kept it to themselves. They could have passed some on, to others they trusted."

"And that's why we wanted to speak to you," Hepburn said. "You fought the Cunninghames and you fought the Sempills. Montgrennan was always hand-in-glove with Kilmaurs, and the Sempills were his kin."

Hugh shrugged. "We searched the field," he said. "There was nothing worth reporting. Just horses, arms. . . A few trinkets and a handful of coins." He closed his fingers tight about the chair arms. "You don't suspect me?"

"Not at all," Hepburn said. Too smoothly for Hugh's liking. "We've never had any reason to doubt you."

"It's just that certain crucial figures escaped the field," Colville added. "The Master of Kilmaurs. And the Master of Sempill."

"And, since you are an authority on the Westland. . ."

He relaxed at that. "What's my reward?"

Hepburn steepled his hands. His smile grew even broader. "What do you want?"

"I want to be appointed Justiciar."

The bright smile clouded over. "Out of the question."

"Why?"

"There are certain issues in your past."

Hugh ground his teeth with frustration and gripped his chair even tighter.

"You mustn't take this as a slight," Hepburn said. "Your time will come. But for the moment it's best we appoint someone less contentious."

"Who?"

"Lord Lyle."

"Lyle!"

Hepburn cast a warning glance towards the bedchamber. "Keep your voice down! Have some thought for His Grace!"

"You make Lyle the Justiciar, then order me to carry out his duties. Let him find the King's gold!"

"To be blunt," Colville spoke out. "We don't trust Lyle."

"Obviously, you don't trust me, either," Hugh muttered. "I joined you in good faith. I pledged myself to you when it wasn't even certain that we'd win."

"You must be patient." Colville topped up his goblet. "We promised you a remission for the burning of Kerrielaw. You'll be granted that, of course. And you're Bailie of Cunninghame and Chamberlain of Irvine. That's what you wanted all along. There'll be much more to follow, I'm sure."

"Surely you understand our situation," Hepburn added. "We need to win allies, not make enemies. And it's a sad fact, Hugh; winning allies isn't a skill that comes naturally to you, is it?

The Place of Ellestoun

They strolled in the gardens before dinner, enjoying the fresh air and the scent of the roses. Marion went on ahead, walking side by side with their mother along the cinder path which wound between the beds of herbs.

John accompanied Margaret. She'd been like Marion once, lithe and winsome. But years of good eating and an arduous succession of childbirths had taken their toll. Every time John saw her, she reminded him more of his mother. Like Lady Elizabeth, she moved slowly, leaning upon his arm with every stride.

"Have you thought about Marion?" Margaret asked.

"She can stay here as long as she wants," John said. "I'm not putting her in a nunnery."

"What about marriage?"

"She's twenty-one years old. What man would want her?"

"If one did?"

"Who's to say she'd want him? I know how much it frightens her."

"Perhaps she's not so set against it as you might think."

"What d'you mean?"

She looked towards Marion, and pursed her lips. "I don't want to speak out of turn, John. I promised Marion. . ."

"What's this then?" He tugged on her arm, smiling. "Some horrible conspiracy that's been going on for years?"

"Oh, for Heaven's sake!" Her voice dropped to a whisper. "Get your nose out of your books and look around you. Has it never occurred to you that your sister's unhappy?"

"I never thought. . ." He broke off, frowning. "Can anything be done?"

"She'll come to you in her own time. Until then, don't speak a word of this, please. I don't want her to think I was interfering—"

"Come on now!" Elizabeth Ross turned and clapped her hands, a mother hen rounding up her chicks. "We must head back. They'll be expecting us at the board."

* * *

The strains of William's lute drifted through the hall as they dined. Outside, the kingdom was collapsing into chaos, but here life was civilised.

John presided over the top table, sitting in the carved chair that was once his father's. Today, though, no-one mourned Sir Thomas. Instead, they celebrated John's safe return. The cooks had prepared a feast worthy of an earl, and there were flagons of wine on every table.

"—He's a fine-looking lad now." Margaret Sempill picked up a morsel of meat and dipped it delicately in the bowl of black sauce. "He's filled out over the last few months, and he's very shapely. Such strong shoulders on him!"

"Stop talking that way," John muttered. "I'm not a horse."

"He carries himself well, too," Margaret continued. "He's in his prime, Mother. It's high time he was wed."

"You're right, of course," Elizabeth Ross agreed. "I'll see to it."

"I can see to it myself," John told them.

Margaret gave a little snort of laughter. "You!" She took another piece of meat from her platter. "You'd never get around to it."

"Poor John." Marion shook her head. "There's no escape for you." She laid a hand upon his arm. "Chained at last to the yoke of matrimony."

"Oh, rest assured. No woman'll break me."

"Brave words, John! I'll wager she soon has you whipped into submission."

He shrugged her briskly away. "What is it about women?" he demanded, as he refilled her goblet. "They're so very cruel. When there's no bear to hand they'll bait the only man about the place."

"Perhaps she'll enslave your heart. . ."

"Over my dead body." He piled more meat onto their platter. "Try the goose, Marion. It's delicious."

"There's no time to be lost," Margaret persisted, suddenly serious. "What if something should happen to him?"

He laughed. "Come now! Why should anything happen to me?"

No-one spoke. The women lowered their heads, his mother coughed. There was nothing but the sound of the lute and the murmurs of the diners at the lower tables.

He couldn't bear the silence. He slipped a scrap to the hound that slouched at his feet.

"John, stop that! Were you born in a byre?"

"I can do what I like now."

"It's not good manners!" Lady Elizabeth burst into tears.

"Oh, Mother," Margaret took her hand.

"It's so hard for us," their mother sobbed. "Your father's gone, and God knows what fate's befallen your uncle. And there's your brother, without a wife, without an heir—"

"Mother. . ." Margaret soothed.

Lady Elizabeth clutched her daughter's arm. "He's my only son. You know what it's like. To raise them, watch them grow."

Marion fixed disapproving eyes on him. "Now look what you've done."

John glowered down at the platter. "I'm sorry!"

"He's such a bonny lad—"

"When he's not scowling." Margaret handed her mother a handkerchief.

"And the image of his father." Elizabeth Ross dabbed her nose. "I couldn't bear it, if something happened to him."

"Nothing will happen to him," said Margaret. "He's young. And he's very personable. He'll find favour, sooner or later. But you mustn't take unnecessary risks. Send someone out to Ochiltree tomorrow." She patted her mother's shoulder. "Please don't worry. Adam'll look after him. He has powerful friends now."

Chapter 9
The Place of Ochiltree

The Place of Ochiltree didn't have much of a garden. Just some stunted rose bushes and a few clumps of herbs. But when she closed her eyes, Margaret Colville could imagine something far better. A wondrous bower, choked with all manner of herbs and flowers, with her sitting at its heart, a princess, surrounded by adoring ladies-in-waiting.

In reality, the ladies-in-waiting were two lowly cousins and the tacksman's daughter. And she was no princess, just the offspring of a lesser baron from Kyle.

"Have you seen her?" She laid her sewing in her lap. "She's so undignified! Stuck on her back like a flyblown cow. . ." She paused, while the chorus of guilty giggles died down. "What if the child never comes?" She beckoned her maids closer. "She'll be like that forever!"

They shrieked in delight at the thought, and Margaret settled onto the stool with a comfortable waggle of her hips. "You know?" She picked up her sewing once again. "Who's to say she won't die in the labour?"

There was silence. The girls fidgeted and studied the ground.

Margaret smiled, enjoying their reaction. "Sooner I'm wed, the better. Then she can't order me around. I'll have my own household, everyone'll do what I say for a change."

Her maids made impressed noises.

"Do you think he'll be handsome?" Alison asked, wide-eyed. At fourteen years old, she was the youngest amongst them.

"It doesn't matter what he looks like. As long as he's strong."

Katherine cast her a sly look. "You'll look mighty silly at court with a fat, ugly dwarf on your arm."

"Like I said. It doesn't matter what he looks like. He's going to be a Sheriff. Why, he's bound to be a knight already! The most powerful man in Renfrew. No one'll argue with him."

"Or with you," said Katherine.

"Exactly," Margaret smiled.

* * *

The horseman arrived that afternoon. A well-built man, with greying dark-brown hair, on a horse that puffed after the journey.

Messengers were few and far between at Ochiltree, so they followed him inside. At a discreet distance, so no one would know they were eavesdropping.

They crouched together in the darkness of the stair-tower and peered through a crack in the door to the hall. "D'you think that's your husband?" Katherine pressed close, trying to get a better view.

Margaret cuffed her head. "Don't be silly! He's too old."

"—What did you say your name was?" asked her father.

"William Haislet, sir." His voice sounded rich, sonorous. "I've come on behalf of John Sempill of Ellestoun."

"And what can we do for him?"

"He asks that the marriage be progressed with the Maid of Ochiltree."

"John Sempill of Ellestoun?" That was her mother, Euphemia Wallace. "That's the Master of Sempill?"

"No, my lady. He's the laird now."

Silence.

"How very sad," Lady Euphemia said at last. "What happened?"

"It's not my place to discuss such matters, my lady."

"I understand, Master Haislet. You'll pass our condolences on to Master Sempill?"

"Indeed."

"You'll stay with us tonight, of course. We've eaten, I'm afraid, but I'll make sure the cooks bring food to your room."

"That's most gracious of you, my lady." A pause, then, "What word should I give Master John?"

"We'll discuss that in the morning, once you're rested. It's such a long way from Ellestoun. Did you ride down in one day—"

Footsteps approached. Margaret tugged at Katherine's arm, and together they fled up the stair. As the door opened below, they hugged each other. "He's coming for me!" Margaret breathed. "At last he's coming for me!"

"I thought you said he was a knight." Katherine sounded smug.

Margaret didn't reply.

It struck her then, that perhaps her husband wasn't going to be half as worthy as she'd hoped.

But she wasn't going to admit her fears to Katherine. Not yet, anyway.

* * *

Margaret made sure she was passing the door to the guest range when her parents emerged. Like the garden, the range wasn't much to look upon. Its walls were daub-and-wattle, and they bulged slightly, while the roof was shabby thatch. Her father had always intended to rebuild the range in stone, but he'd not yet found the money. There'd been a disaster thirty years ago in her grandfather's time; a dispute with the mighty Douglases which had ended in the burning of the Place of Ochiltree and the slaughter of her grandsire. The tower-house had since been rebuilt, but the family had been left near-destitute.

It was a wonder they'd even found the money for her dower.

Margaret wrinkled her nose in annoyance and wondered what the man from Ellestoun would make of it. She wondered, too, what Ellestoun was like. Whether the tower was old or new, whether its windows were small, or large and airy. She hoped there were gardens. And orchards, too. . . She sighed, closed her eyes, and gave a twirling side-step at the thought.

Strong hands grasped her arms and shook her. "Where have you been?" It was her mother, Lady Euphemia. She stood half-a-hand taller than her husband, a broad-shouldered woman who took no nonsense. *Queen of the Amazons*, Margaret's half-brother Jamie snidely called her, but then she was a Wallace, and Wallaces were supposed to be indomitable. "Your sister was looking for you."

She's not my sister. She's William's wife. But she knew better than to argue. She clasped her hands behind her and looked demurely to the ground. "I was in the garden. I didn't know she wanted me."

"Margaret," her father said. He was a frail man, snowy-haired and gentle. "Elizabeth needs your help. The child's due within a month."

She gave one of her glorious smiles. "It won't happen again. I promise."

"I'm sure," her mother said, dryly.

Margaret gazed coyly at her father. "Who was he?"

"None of your business," came her mother's sharp retort.

"Oh, Effie. Let her be. Of course it's her business."

"Has he come about the wedding?"

"Yes. He has."

"Then when's it to be?" She tried not to sound too excited.

Her mother looked at her father, who grimaced.

Her heart quickened. "What is it?"

"Be quiet, girl!" Lady Euphemia snapped. She grasped her skirts in one hand and stormed across the yard, face like a thundercloud.

"We have to discuss it," her father said, putting his arm about her shoulders. "You'd best come with us. Your mother won't approve, I know. But I think you should be there."

* * *

"What are you doing here?" Lady Euphemia demanded, as Margaret strolled into the laird's chamber, just ahead of her father.

"Effie, please." Sir Robert Colville sank into his chair. "Be reasonable. The girl needs to know."

"Wine, Father?"

"Yes, please." He bowed his head and rubbed his forehead. Margaret handed him his goblet, and he managed a smile. "Thank you, my dear."

His wife strode briskly back and forth. "You indulge her too much," she said. "You always have." She stopped, hands on hips, and scowled at Margaret. "You'd best change that manner when you're wed, girl, or you'll regret it." She waved an irritable hand. "Sit down then. And don't interfere."

Margaret sighed, and perched on the arm of her father's chair.

Lady Euphemia closed the door. "Well? What d'you make of that?"

Sir Robert shrugged. "I don't know. . ."

"It's odd, that he should press to be married. So soon after his poor father's death." She didn't sound remotely sympathetic.

He shook his head. "I don't see what you're getting at."

"I find it strange that he's returned at all, when William and the others aren't home yet. . ."

"These sly insinuations are all very well, Effie. What am I supposed to do?"

"Nothing. Just do nothing. Bide your time, and wait."

"But it's a legally binding contract!"

"Why should that matter? Let him bluster all he likes. If he escapes this crisis unscathed, then we'll rethink matters. If he's put to the horn for treason then it'll be the least of his worries."

"Treason. . ." The world swam around her, her face glowed hot with shame. She knew her mother would be angry, but she couldn't contain herself. "I can't marry a traitor. I *won't* marry a traitor!"

"You'll do what you're told," her mother countered.

Her father looked up, and gripped her hand, tightly. "Don't jump to conclusions, my dear. And don't worry. As if I'd give you away to a man of dubious reputation."

She managed a smile at that. Her father would look after her.

He always did.

* * *

It was the twenty-fourth of June. One hundred and seventy-four years, to the day, since the Bruce defeated an English army at Bannockburn.

An auspicious day for a coronation, Hugh Montgomerie reflected. And an auspicious place, too; Scone Abbey, where James's great-grandfather had been crowned, half a century before.

The nave of the abbey church seethed with courtiers. They formed a sea of silk and velvet; blues and reds and ochres set against more sober blacks and browns. Sunlight drifted through the coloured glass of the windows, flashing from a hundred gold chains and jewelled pins.

It wasn't like the Scots court to dazzle, but today, dazzle it did. What made it all the more incredible was that half its courtiers weren't even there. The half that *had* turned up, though, more than made up for the lack of numbers. Their voices droned so loud that the choir could barely be heard.

Hugh was halfway down the nave, so he wasn't well-placed to see what was happening. Being tall helped, and better still, he was conveniently close to a pillar; if he pushed himself up against the mouldings at the base, he could get a better view.

He found it fascinating. It wasn't the ritual itself that intrigued him, for that was laid out in time-honoured fashion. He was more concerned to see who was present. He was curious, too, to see how James dealt with the circumstances that brought him here. Patrick Hepburn and the others had worked hard to distance the young King from his father's murder, but it was too late.

James was tainted. They were all tainted.

James, however, handled his dubious inheritance well. It was a stroke of genius to have Saint Fillan's Bell carried at the head of the procession; it was probably Patrick's idea, but James himself might have had a hand in it. The bell was a saintly relic known to ease troubled hearts and souls, and it was only right that James showed all the signs of being troubled. As he strode up the nave to the strains of the introit, James was as much remorseful son as magnificent king. Dignified, solemn, he gave the impression that a great burden of guilt and responsibility rested upon his slight shoulders.

Bishop Blacader of Glasgow was the man who set the crown upon James's head. A twisting of the rules if ever there was one, for it should have been the

Archbishop. But Archbishop Scheves of Saint Andrews was still counted amongst the enemy.

Hugh stifled a yawn. He shifted his weight, wincing as a joint creaked in his hip. The ceremony had lasted an hour already, and there were still the oaths of loyalty to come. . .

Trumpets sounded a strident fanfare as the crown was placed on a cushion before the King.

He straightened with a sigh. The time for lurking unnoticed was over; like the rest of them, he had to pledge his allegiance to his new King.

Amongst the nobility, the earls formed the vanguard. There were some new faces there. Such as Patrick Hepburn, who'd recently been granted Ramsay's earldom of Bothwell. John Stewart of Darnley, too; under James the Third's rule, he'd struggled for years to be recognised as Earl of Lennox. Just two weeks into the new king's reign, he'd already been given the title. Most of the Highland earls were conspicuous by their absence, but one at least was present, Hugh's gude-father Colin Campbell, the Earl of Argyll.

After the earls, it was the turn of the Lords of Parliament. Some key supporters of James the Third were there, the ones who'd switched sides just before the last, decisive battle. Perhaps the most prominent amongst them were the Darnley Stewarts. There, too, was Robert, Lord Lyle, who'd been their close ally for several years now.

Lyle knelt and swore his oath before the King.

He was an insubstantial man, with a perennially mournful look about him. Just looking at him made Hugh bristle with indignation. Despite Earl Patrick's attempts at reconciliation, Hugh considered Lyle's appointment as Justiciar an insult. It was blatantly unfair; Hugh had worked hard for James, but his sacrifices meant nothing. Instead Hepburn had given the Justiciar's title to a man whose loyalty changed like the weather.

Lyle disappeared back into the crowd, and the ceremony ground on.

More lords passed before the king, Matthew Stewart amongst them. Matthew climbed onto the dais, knelt before James and laid his hand upon the crown. As he took the oath he smiled at his royal kinsman, and was granted a distant nod in return.

Hugh had to wait a little longer. Then at last the moment came. He took two springing steps towards the throne and dropped to one knee before the king. "So might God help me, as I shall support thee." He looked young James full in the face and wasn't surprised to see the lad staring elsewhere, a weary glazed look in his eyes.

Their king, for all his poise and brilliance, was still only a boy.

* * *

When the ceremony was over, they retired to their lodgings to change their clothes then gathered in the cloisters to await the call for dinner.

"Hugh!" A commanding voice rang out.

Hugh looked up and searched the crowds. He glimpsed his gude-father, the Earl of Argyll, and raised a hand in acknowledgement. A summons from Campbell of Argyll was not to be ignored; the earl had been restored as Chancellor, which made staying on his good side even more important.

Hugh quickened his stride. As he approached Argyll, he caught sight of Lyle, huddled near the cloister arches with Matthew Stewart and his father, John Stewart of Darnley—*that's Lennox now,* he reminded himself.

Almost as if he'd read his thoughts, Stewart caught Hugh's stare. He raised an amicable hand, and as he did so, Lyle turned, too. He looked at Hugh, and smiled, furtively.

Hugh drew a sharp breath. True, the man always looked furtive. Was it his imagination, thinking there was more to it. . .

Nonsense, he told himself. *Patrick wants you to think he mistrusts Lyle. Sweetens the gall of rejection, that's all.*

It didn't bode well, though.

Barely two weeks into the reign, and already the cracks were appearing.

Chapter 10
Renfrew Town

There'd been a mass that morning, celebrating the anniversary of Bruce's victory at Bannockburn. All the local dignitaries attended; once the ceremony was over they'd processed from the church to the tolbooth, for a meeting of the burgh council.

Though John attended Mass, he didn't take his place amongst the office holders. There was no avoiding the meeting, though. He'd been summoned a few days before; the Sheriff was to attend or arrange for a deputy to take his place. No names had been mentioned. The council either knew, or suspected, that Sir Thomas Sempill hadn't returned from the east.

Entering the tolbooth was a relief, for it brought escape from the busy market day crowds. John enjoyed his anonymity while he could, but it didn't last long.

Someone seized his arm. "It's the Master of Sempill, isn't it?" The speaker fell into step alongside, a moon-faced burgess, richly dressed despite the heat of the day. His gown was trimmed with the fur of marten and beaver, and he bore a heavy chain of gold about his neck. He was paying for his vanity; his face shone with sweat and he looked profoundly uncomfortable.

"No longer the Master of Sempill, sir," John said. "The Laird of Ellestoun now."

"Then it's true? Sir Thomas is dead?"

"I'm afraid so, Master, er—"

"Mossman. John Mossman. Please, Master Sempill. Come this way." He steered John to a dais at the far end, where a long table and a row of benches had been set up in readiness. Most of the places were already occupied by venerable figures.

"The Sheriff," Mossman explained.

They were too polite to voice their disapproval. There were coughs and rumbled greetings, as John sat down amongst them.

"Good burgesses of Renfrew!" Mossman called.

The chattering ceased.

"Master Sempill—" Mossman clamped a hand upon John's shoulder, "—has confirmed the rumours. Our Sheriff, Sir Thomas Sempill, is dead."

"How can we be sure?" someone asked.

"I saw his corpse," John said. "He fell in battle."

"This means, of course, that we have a new Sheriff," said Mossman. "He must be approved by the King. But I suggest we let him carry out his duties until his succession's confirmed. Is that acceptable?"

"No it's not!" called another burgess, seated further down the table.

"State your objections, Master Montgomery."

"Look at him!" Montgomery gestured towards John. "He's too young."

"I'm lacking your years, perhaps." His retort raised a chuckle from the crowd, for Montgomery was bent with age. "But I'm as loyal to this burgh as the next man."

"Your commitment's not at issue here," Montgomery sounded vexed.

"Then what is?" called an angry voice from the floor. "Is it because Master Sempill is loyal to King James?"

There was a ripple of disquiet amongst the crowd.

"Who would you have in his place, Master Montgomery?" the same voice demanded. "That appalling kinsman of yours?" The speaker threaded his way to the dais, a grim-faced man approaching his fortieth year, fit and strong. It was the burgh's Coroner, Sir William Cunninghame of Craigends. The younger son of Sir Alexander Cunninghame, Earl of Glencairn.

"Sir William, please!" Mossman called. "I know that the Cunninghames and the Montgomeries have their differences. Surely we can work together for once? For the good of the burgh?"

"By all means." Craigends sprang up onto the dais. "The Cunninghames won't interfere with Renfrew's business, providing the Montgomeries do likewise." Halting before Montgomery, he leaned upon the tabletop. His sword hilt clattered against the board, a few feet from Montgomery, who shook his head and knotted his snowy brows. "Master Montgomery should withdraw his objection. We don't want a lackey of the Montgomeries foisted on us. Most certainly not in Master Sempill's place."

Montgomery's frown deepened. "All I'm saying—"

"It's shameful that you question his right to inherit the title." He hammered his fist upon the board. "Shameful!"

"Thank you, Sir William," Mossman acknowledged, nervously.

"I'm not finished. I won't have Master Sempill's reputation tarnished like this. You dismiss him as a youth, sir, but we say he's fought like a man. He had the courage to stand up for his King. Which is more than the most of you did. Where were you, when the Sheriff summoned you to the wappenschaw?"

"We sent who we could," another burgess replied.

"Aye, and that was half the men required! We lost the battle. We may have lost our King. Hang your heads in shame, every one of you, because you're all responsible!"

* * *

Hours of debate followed. There was anxious talk concerning the long-running disagreement with Paisley; it was rumoured that Abbot Schaw had petitioned the Pope to make Paisley a burgh in its own right. Which was bad news for the Renfrew burgesses, who always taxed the goods sold at the Paisley markets.

Then, inevitably, the talk turned to duties and levies.

John's eyes grew heavy. Thankfully, he didn't nod off. Nor did he yawn. But it was a relief when business came to an end and the meeting was closed.

As John left the dais, Cunninghame of Craigends approached. He greeted John with a gruff nod and a smile.

"Thank you," John said. "Your support was very helpful."

Craigends shrugged. "Old allies should stand together."

"How did you fare? In the east?"

"Lost half our men," Craigends replied. He had a melancholy air about him, even when he smiled, but today it was more marked than usual. "That devil Montgomerie was on us in the rout. He slew my father."

"I'm sorry to hear that. The Earl will be sorely missed."

"We're united in misfortune, Master Sempill. And we share a common enemy." His face hardened. "We'll be avenged. If Lord Hugh lingers too long in the east, he'll have nothing to come home to." He leaned close. "You'll join us, of course?" he asked. And when John didn't reply, "It's what your father would have wanted."

"I'm not my father." Glancing aside, he noticed that Master Montgomery was standing conveniently close.

"Meaning what?"

"It's not my place to take sides," John said, loudly.

"Damn you!"

"I'm the Sheriff now. I can't aid and abet any acts of insurrection within the bounds of Renfrew. And I won't be drawn into your Cunninghame feud."

"If I'd known you'd be so ungrateful, I wouldn't have been so quick to help."

"Someone has to keep their head in all this. You'll thank me in the long run."

"You'll change your tune soon enough." Craigends turned on his heel and stalked off, hand on his sword hilt. He barged into Montgomery as he passed. "Oh, excuse me!"

Montgomery ignored the discourtesy, nodding instead towards John. "Good day, Master Sempill."

"How can I help you, sir?" John's tone was chilly.

"Please don't take it as a slight." Montgomery said. "We were concerned, that's all."

"You think I'm in the pay of the Cunninghames?"

Montgomery spread his hands wide. "I didn't say that."

"You implied it!" John retorted. "Well, you needn't worry. The Cunninghames won't get any favours from me. Nor will the Montgomeries. If the truth's told, I don't have much liking for any of you. Now good day, sir."

He walked away without another word. Fixing his gaze on the open door of the tolbooth he quickened his stride, determined to escape.

A voice hailed him. "Hello, John. Do you have a moment?"

John paused, his scowl melting away, for there amongst the crowd was Sir Malcolm Crawfurd of Kilbirnie, his eldest son Robert alongside.

"Sir Malcolm!" John seized Malcolm's hand and shook it warmly. "And Robert, too." He slapped the young man's shoulder. "It's so very good to see you!"

"And you, John," Malcolm replied. The family resemblance was unmistakable; both men were lightly built and bore raven black hair, though Robert stood a good four inches taller and Malcolm's hair was fading to silver. And, while Robert was clean-shaven, Malcolm sported a neatly trimmed beard.

Malcolm nodded towards Master Montgomery's retreating back. "You handled them well."

John looked heavenwards. "They'll be the death of me."

"They'll be the death of us all." Malcolm glanced towards Robert, who frowned at the floor. "We're sorry," he said. "About your father."

John nodded.

"Least you made it back safely," said Malcolm.

"Dame Fortune smiled on me that day." He tried hard to sound cheerful, though there was something odd about Malcolm's demeanour. The Laird of Kilbirnie seemed awkward, uncomfortable. But Malcolm's reticence was nothing compared to Robert's. Robert didn't even look him in the eye, which hurt, for Robert had spent much of his youth in Sir Thomas Sempill's service, and John still considered him a close friend.

"John, we have a question," said Malcolm. "This isn't really the time or place, but we'd rather not wait."

"Ask away."

Malcolm beckoned to Robert, who cleared his throat and said, "It regards Marion. I'd like her hand in marriage."

* * *

Even late in the afternoon, it was hard to find a clear path through the crowds. People flocked around the booths and stalls that were crammed against every inch of house frontage. The cries of the vendors rang loud; they sold everything from livestock to rolls of Flemish velvet and finely wrought jewellery. Scents assaulted the nostrils; the tang of animal spoor and unwashed bodies mingling with more welcoming wafts of freshly cooked meat and bread.

John split a roast peapod and scraped out the innards with his teeth. He tossed the husk over his shoulder. "Why didn't you tell me?"

"You'd have tried to speak out on our behalf," Robert Crawfurd replied. "You'd have suffered for it, too. And he wouldn't have changed his mind."

"But where was the sense in it? It's not as if you were the kitchen boy!" He waved at a goodwife behind a booth. "Hey, I'll have a wafer. Freshest you've got." He handed her a small coin and was given in return a hot waffle that dripped with cheese.

"You'll get fat," Robert said. "Your teeth'll fall out."

"Sheriffs are supposed to be fat." He held the waffle gingerly and blew on it.

"Try telling your horse that."

John took a tentative mouthful. "Ow, it's too damned hot."

"Serves you right, you greedy hog. God, we only dined two hours ago, and you're stuffing your face already."

"Blame those damned burgesses. I get hungry when I'm nervous."

"That's the worst excuse I ever heard."

John laughed, and gobbled down the rest of the waffle. He licked his fingers, and wiped his hands against his hose. "Delicious," he said, then added, "So what of Marion?"

"She was fifteen and very determined. She told Sir Thomas that if she couldn't have me she'd have no other man."

John winced. "He wouldn't have liked that."

"He didn't."

"Why didn't she say something? I've been home a week."

Robert shrugged. "Perhaps she doesn't want to trouble you."

* * *

"Have you finished yet?" Robert asked, crossly.

"Nearly." John laced up his hose and set his doublet straight. "That's better." He presented a coin to the thin-faced young woman who waited nearby. "That'll be all."

Robert frowned as the girl dropped into a curtsey and scurried away. "Why in God's name don't you get a mistress? It's better than banging a whore against a wall on a stinking street corner."

"You did a grand job, Robert. I'm intact, my purse is intact, and the young lady'll have food in her belly for the next three days. Everyone's happy."

"Except me. Do you think I like watching your back while you're pushing away like a damned buck rabbit?"

"What in God's name's the matter with you?" The wine was taking hold; he swayed and reached for Robert's shoulder.

"Come on." Robert grabbed his arm and hauled him down the narrow wynd towards the main street. "It's well past nine. The bailies'll lock you up for breaking curfew."

"Like Hell they will."

"Still, it'd give them something to talk about. Their beloved Sheriff, fornicating so elegantly. Like a stray dog." Robert's grip tightened.

"Tomorrow I'll admit defeat. And join the ranks of respectable men."

"Not a day too soon. Now stop dawdling. I don't want to be out here when they start throwing shit out the windows."

"Don't be daft! There's plenty of time left." John halted. "Christ, you're in a foul mood. You scarcely touched a drop all night and you're holier-than-thou about the whoring." Understanding dawned in his face. "It's love, isn't it?"

"You've drunk too much."

"You're in love with my sister—"

"John!"

"She's robbed you of your manhood!"

Robert swatted his head, making John laugh and clutch his bonnet. "I'll rob you of yours," Robert said. "If you don't stop baiting me, I'll cut off your parts and throw them to the fishes. And toss the rest of you in afterwards for good measure."

"That's no way to speak to me," John slipped his arm about Robert's shoulders. "When you wed her, we'll be brothers."

"God help me," said Robert. But he was smiling.

Chapter 11

It was a fine day when they laid Hugh Alexson to rest in the kirkyard at St Barchans.

Mary White didn't think it right, that the sun shone and the birds sang so loud on the day her husband was consigned to the ground, but the earth, the skies and the wild things cared nothing for her sorrow.

She hadn't expected much of a funeral, but as soon as Alan Semple the tacksman learned of her loss he called by and told her not to worry. The Laird had said that Master Alexson was to be given a proper burial, should the worst happen. That very day, the tacksman talked to the priest and arranged for a requiem mass to be sung.

Mary felt strangely detached as the priest stood at the grave and talked in the Romish tongue. Mary couldn't understand a word, but she knew what it meant. Promises of everlasting life with the Heavenly Host. What better reward could be granted to a man, after the trials of this earth?

The gravediggers picked up her husband's corpse, limp in its linen shroud, and dropped it heavily into the ground.

She was too numb and exhausted to weep as they shovelled earth back into the hole. She knew she shouldn't take it personally, but she felt that God had failed her husband. And He'd failed her, too.

She would never forget that.

"Say goodbye to your father," she told the children. The boys were old enough to understand, but young Meg knew nothing. She just clung to Mary, staring in wonder at the bees and butterflies that plied the churchyard.

* * *

"Damn the Laird," Mary said to Janet, as they trudged home. "Church has already taken four cows. Daresay he'll want another four." Meg weighed heavy in her arms, she hitched the child into a more comfortable position. "All his fault, anyway."

Janet looked worriedly at her. "You mustn't say that."

"I'll say what I like."

"Promise me you won't curse the lad." Janet's tone was earnest. "His own mother has enough grief, without you giving her more."

Mary would have taken her hand to console her, if she hadn't been gripping Meg so tightly. "Upon my soul, Janet," she said. "I won't curse him. There's enough ills already in the world, without me adding to them."

The Place of Ellestoun

"You wanted to see me?" Marion asked. Her rosary was clasped in her fingers, she toyed nervously with the beads.

John poured himself some wine. "Marriage, Marion."

"You know my thoughts on this," she whispered, head lowered.

"Do I?"

She didn't reply.

He shrugged and ambled over to his chair, then sank into it with a groan. "It's a long journey. And in this damned heat. . ."

Marion looked up. "John. . ." Her voice trembled.

"Enquiries were made. By a noble family, of good reputation and excellent means."

"What did you say?"

"He's a good man, Marion. I can vouch for him."

"I couldn't—"

"Not even Robert Crawfurd of Kilbirnie?"

She said nothing.

He wondered, briefly, if Robert had been mistaken, then realised that he'd misread his sister's silence.

She was weeping.

"Marion?" John scrambled to his feet. "I thought you'd be happy." He hurried to her side and put his arms around her.

"I- I prayed to God for help." She leaned close, sobbing. "I asked Him to grant me Robert's hand. For years I kept asking, and He never heeded me. I thought it wasn't meant to happen. Then you came home, and told me Father was dead, and I was glad, because I knew that with Father gone, all would be well." Marion broke off and swallowed. "It was my fault, wasn't it? He took Father away to punish me, because I asked too much."

"Hush." He patted her shoulder. "It's Fate, that's all."

"Oh, dear God." She sniffed. "A weight's been lifted from my shoulders. It was so hard to keep it secret. But we didn't want you involved. Relations were already sour, between you and Father. It would just have made matters worse."

"I knew you valued Robert as a friend, but. . . I had no idea you felt so strongly. Christ, I'm such a fool!"

"You must hate us for it."

"I'm bewildered, that's all. And perhaps a little hurt. But I'll survive."

"What about Mother?" Marion asked, suddenly stricken. "She'll never agree. She knows Father wouldn't have allowed it."

"I'll deal with her," John said. "She never warned me of this. The Crawfurds approached me and I gave my consent in good faith. I can't renege on the agreement now, can I?"

Marion laughed and wrapped her arms about his neck. "God bless you, John!" she cried, and hugged him closer still.

The Place of Eglintoun

"Quickly now!" Helen Campbell beckoned to the maids. She was a lithe young woman of twenty-five years, bright-eyed and cheerful. "He'll be here any moment."

They lined up behind the crib, hands clasped before them, heads bowed.

Not a moment too soon. The door crashed open, and Hugh Montgomerie thumped across the timber floor, sword belt creaking, spurs singing out with every stride. "Let's have a look at him!"

He was still dressed for travelling, caked in mud and rank from the journey. There was a waft from him as he passed, bitter male sweat mingled with damp horse and leather.

It was all too much for the wetnurse, who hadn't met their lord and master at such close quarters before. She blanched at the sight of him.

Hugh stopped dead and glared. "What the Devil's the matter with you?"

Blushing, the girl mumbled an apologetic reply. The child, woken from his nap, started to wail.

Hugh's bewildered look made Helen smile. It never occurred to him that when he came battering in like this it was enough to make even a strong man cross himself and pray for deliverance.

Hugh peered at the tiny, red-faced mite who lay swaddled inside the crib. "He's an ugly little devil," he said, raising his voice to be heard over the cries. He looked at Helen, suddenly serious. "Are you sure he's mine?"

"You said that last time," Helen said.

"He howls loud enough to wake the dead." He smiled, and for a moment he was like a child himself, full of wonder for something he couldn't quite understand. Then his vacant expression vanished. He seized her shoulders, and planted a kiss upon her forehead. "Well done, Helen! I'm proud of you." Still clutching her shoulders tight, he continued, suddenly sheepish, "I'm so very, very sorry. I tried so hard to get back in time. But Fate conspired against me."

"I know."

"My chamber's yours." He sounded hopeful, apologetic. But there was a lively sparkle in his eye; he knew full well that after six months of abstinence, she hungered for him as much as he did for her.

She patted his arm. "I won't keep you long."

"Good." He turned on his heel, and was gone.

"Give him to me," said Helen, as the wetnurse plucked the child from his crib. She rocked the infant in her arms and gradually the howls subsided. "That was your father," she said. "You'll get used to him soon enough. His bark's worse than his bite."

* * *

Helen lifted the latch and peered inside the laird's chamber.

Servants fluttered about Hugh's shoulders like corbies mobbing a falcon, chattering away while he tolerated their presence in silence. At the same time Ringan, his long-suffering old manservant, tried to disrobe him. An impossible task, with Hugh pacing back and forth like a creature demented.

Helen slipped inside and quietly closed the door.

Hugh looked up as the wood creaked. His eyes met hers, his glance one of desperation.

While Hugh accepted hardship on campaign, he changed as soon he crossed the threshold. He wanted to put the grime of the road behind him, soon as he could.

Woe betide anyone who stood in his way.

He was trying very hard to be polite to his trusted servants, who in turn wanted to impress *him* with their dedication and efficiency.

Their persistence was admirable, but ill-advised. Helen braced herself, wondering how long it would be before Hugh's patience finally gave out.

"They invaded your lands and made off with five cows," said the tacksman.

Hugh's face remained impassive as his sword belt fell to the floor with a clatter. Ringan closed in to unlace his doublet, but Hugh was on the move again. "Where are they now?"

"In the dungeon."

"You remembered to feed them?" Hugh halted so quickly Ringan almost ran into his heels. "They smell bad enough when they're alive." He cast a ferocious scowl over his shoulder. "Hurry up there!"

"You needn't worry," Helen stirred from the bedside and slipped in behind him. Nudging Ringan aside, she took the laces of the doublet in her hands. "I saw to it."

Hugh nodded. Her presence settled him; he managed to keep still for a few seconds before he twitched into life again. Soon as she felt him stir she yanked him firmly back; he snapped his teeth and hissed like an angry gander, but didn't move.

"What are we to do with them?" the tacksman asked.

"Who are they?" Hugh wriggled out of his doublet, and let it drop.

"The boys are Cunninghames, my lord. From Auchenharvie."

Hose came next, joining the untidy constellation of garments on the floor. Hugh trailed wearily over to the bowl of water that had been left ready on a kist near the bed.

"My lord?"

He braced his hands against the wood, breathing deep.

"My lord?" The voice persisted, more querulous this time.

Hugh swept his arm aside, and the bowl crashed to the floor. "Hang them!" he roared. "I won't have Cunninghames thieving on my lands." He turned around, glowering. "Now get out! All of you."

* * *

"Heaven help me!" Hugh splashed water over his face. "I'm surrounded by fools."

"They only want to help." Helen picked up the fragments of the broken bowl. *Plenty more where that came from,* she reminded herself, setting the pieces down upon the kist, alongside the replacement which had been hurriedly sent up from the kitchens.

Six months it had been, since she'd last set eyes on Hugh. Since then, she'd spent many sleepless nights fretting over him. When he'd last left Eglintoun to ride against the King, he'd risked everything. His lands. His reputation. Even his life.

Helen had been married to him ten years and she'd endured four births already, but she still burned with lust for him. She felt it most at times like this, when he hurled himself back into her life, furious, vital. Perhaps it was because he never changed. Most men grew fat at court, but Hugh always came home without an ounce of spare flesh on him.

Helen hummed a little tune as she picked up his discarded clothes and laid them out over the nearest chair.

"I'm the Bailie of Cunninghame," Hugh said, all matter-of-fact.

"At last." She took a cloth and rubbed his back dry. "And Kerrielaw?"

He gave a wolfish smile. "I'm forgiven."

"What of the Cunninghames?"

"Kilmaurs is dead." He turned to face her. His nostrils flared, there was an angry light in his eyes. And he was roused, too. "I killed him."

"That's all very well, my love. You've proved your worth amongst men. Now prove yourself to me." She ducked away, giggling, as he reached out with a roar to seize her arm.

* * *

They lay together afterwards, stretched out on the bed. She clasped Hugh tight; his body felt firm and warm, the flesh of his calf pressed against her own. He was still for once, at peace with himself and the world.

Helen buried her face in his shoulder and breathed deep. A faint smell of leather and damp horse still clung to him, and behind that, there was the comforting scent of *him*. She closed her eyes, treasuring the moment.

"The King was murdered," he said.

She wasn't sure what shocked her most; the knowledge that someone been bold enough to kill King James in the first place, or the thought that Hugh might in some way be involved.

"I don't know the details," he added. "There's rumours, of course. Some say Sir William Stirling did it, because the King sanctioned the burning of his place. Others say it was Lord Gray. Because he wanted to."

"Just as long as it wasn't you."

"I don't kill kings."

"I'm right glad of that." She hugged him tighter. "I couldn't bear it, my love. If they strung you up for all to see and carved the guts out of you." She traced a finger lightly up his belly from his loins.

A tremor coursed through him and he laughed, uncomfortably. He was a fearless creature, but the thought of being hung, drawn and quartered was too much even for him to stomach. He patted her hand. "No chance of that. No one'd think to pin such a crime on a lowly soul like me."

"Except the Cunninghames."

"They're more likely to ambush me on the Irvine road and slit my throat."

"Heaven forbid." She stretched slightly, and sighed. "At least you were granted the Bailiery. And the remission for Kerrielaw, besides."

"Patrick Hepburn honours his promises. Unlike that vile creature Montgrennan. . ."

"Did they give you anything else?"

He was silent.

"They should have. You deserved far more."

72

"They rewarded men who did much less." He brightened. "But they did say that more would follow."

"And you believed them?" She stroked his hair. "You're too loyal for your own good sometimes. If they thought you might turn against them, they'd have been more gracious."

"They gave me what I wanted, and that's a start. Six months from now I might think differently." He rolled over and wrapped his arms about her. "Rebellion?" He kissed her neck. "Perhaps. I did it once and lived to tell the tale. Who's to say I can't do it again?"

* * *

Hugh disliked early mornings.

He never had much of an appetite on awaking. Now, though, he was getting hungry. He stretched his fingers out before him and studied them intently, anything to keep his mind off his empty belly. A speck of dirt under a nail annoyed him, he picked restlessly at it then gave up and clenched his fist with a sigh.

The boys snuffled and whimpered as they were hustled up the hill towards the gallows.

He found it all rather embarrassing. But he said nothing as they stumbled past. He supposed he should be charitable at a time like this.

"Damned Cunninghames," he muttered to his tacksman. "Can't even die with dignity." He didn't look up, just waved his hand. "Let's get on with it."

As the two captives were strung up, he glanced out to the west, where Arran's hills rose stark and glorious from a restless sea. It was a much more appetising view. Behind him, the ropes creaked, the cries were replaced by gurgling gasps, and even those could scarcely be heard over the cheers of the crowd.

Hugh frowned. God alone knew how so many had come to hear of the execution, but hear of it they had, and they'd come flocking. He wasn't sure what the fascination was; he found hangings rather tedious.

But then, he'd seen it all before.

"Let's hope that'll be a lesson to the rest of them," said the tacksman.

"I doubt it." Hugh cast a disinterested look at the scrawny bodies twitching on the gallows. They were pinch-faced, underfed wretches. If anything, he'd done them a favour by ending their miserable lives.

"Place the corpses at the bounds with Auchenharvie's lands," he said. "They'll serve as a reminder that I'm not to be trifled with. I'm going to Mass."

He hurried towards his waiting horse, past the men-at-arms who held back the crowd.

Voices hailed him. "God bless you, Lord Hugh!" someone called.

"God bless *you*, good lady." Hugh headed towards them. A flock of women crowded close as he approached. Some reached out to touch him, while others held babes in outstretched arms.

He gripped each hand in turn, admired every infant that was presented, and listened attentively as the grievances poured out.

"It's been so hard since the menfolk went away—"

"For six months they've raided us. It was a hen or a few cabbages at first. Then they started lifting the kye and burning the byres—"

73

"It got so bad I couldn't even sleep at night—"

"You've all endured much in my absence." His voice was firm, brisk. "But I'm back now. And everything's going to be all right. I promise."

Chapter 12

"More wine, Sir Patrick?" Halting by the sun-drenched window of the hall, Marion lifted the flagon high.

"Yes please, my dear." Sir Patrick Wallace of Auchenbothie had sixty summers under his belt, but he was a sprightly little man nonetheless, with silver hair and quick bright eyes. His lands bordered those of Ellestoun, and he'd always been an impeccable neighbour. He waited while Marion filled his goblet, then raised the vessel with a flourish. "Congratulations, Master Crawfurd. She's a fine girl."

Robert shifted, suddenly awkward. "Thank you."

"We're delighted to welcome her into our family," said Sir Malcolm. "We're also delighted that you accepted our invitation to celebrate with us today."

"I'm honoured to act as a witness," Wallace told him. "And it's a pleasure to dine here at Ellestoun. Sir Thomas always kept a good wine in his cellar. And I'm told young John here's in possession of an equally discerning palette." He nudged John in the ribs.

"Why, thank you." John allowed himself a modest smile. "I'd just like to add my thanks to Malcolm's. We both thought you might not want to attend. Considering the circumstances. . ."

"We're neighbours," Sir Patrick replied. "Can't let politics get in the way of friendship, can we? Life's too short for that."

"Master John," William whispered in John's ear.

"Excuse me." John stepped back from the circle. "What's the matter?"

"It's Adam Mure. He's on his way."

John turned to his guests. "Forgive me, gentlemen," he said. "The Laird of Caldwell's arrived. I'd best go and welcome him."

* * *

Ten horsemen thundered into Ellestoun; Adam Mure was at the front of the pack, mounted on a stocky brown horse. The beast snorted loud as it trotted across the cobbled yard, its mealy nose thrust high in the air.

Red-faced, Adam hauled upon the reins. "Whoa!"

John winced. "That's a new one," he said to William. "It's not much better than the last."

"He isn't the best judge of horseflesh."

"Hush! He might hear you!"

The horse stepped forward unbidden, and was rewarded for its insolence by another jolt in the mouth and a string of curses.

"Damned beast!" Adam snarled. He looked anxiously about him. "Where the Devil's Constantine?"

"Trailing in your wake, Adam. As always," Constantine Dunlop of Hunthall called from amongst the men-at-arms. He was the antithesis of Adam, long and lean and quietly patient.

Adam shrugged and dismounted. He scarcely reached John's shoulders, but he'd earned a fearsome reputation as a fighter nonetheless.

"Thank you for coming," said John. "I feared you might still be away."

"We came back a week ago." Adam sounded uncomfortable. "His Grace was out this way. On a Justice Ayre. The court was in Paisley, you know."

"I hadn't heard."

There was silence.

"So Marion's to be wed then?" Constantine said, climbing down from his horse. "Not before time, I say."

"We're all delighted, of course. Come inside, gentlemen. You'll dine with us, I hope?"

Adam seemed reticent. "I don't think so," he said. "There's too much to do, back at Caldwell."

"Constantine?" John asked.

Constantine clapped John firmly on the back. "Set me a place at the board, John. I'd be delighted to join you."

"Come on, Adam," John encouraged.

Adam's plump face coloured. "It's *Sir* Adam now."

"Sir Adam, eh?" John tried to look impressed. "So congratulations are in order. The campaign went well, then?"

"Well enough," said Constantine. "Though some of us weren't granted our knighthood."

"Don't be so coy," snapped Adam. "Your wine cellars have never been so full. Nor your coffers so swollen with gold."

"Not that I was moved by wealth alone," Constantine told John. "We have a new Bailie in Cunninghame. It's wise to keep on his good side."

"The Lord Montgomerie, I suppose?" said John. "That explains the fiery glow over Kilmaurs last night."

"John—" Adam warned.

"You're right," John agreed. "It's none of my business." He gestured to the door. "Come inside, gentlemen. A goblet of fine claret awaits you."

Constantine bounded over the threshold without another word, but Adam lingered.

"John. . ." he began. He glowered at the cobbles. "I hope you don't think me rude. Riding off like this. I don't mean it that way."

"You don't want to be seen at Ellestoun."

"No. It's not that at all." Adam had never been a good liar. "Look," he said, and for the first time he met John's gaze. "I'll do what I can. But don't expect miracles." He forced a smile. "Now come on. Let's get this over with, shall we?"

The Place of Ochiltree

Jamie agreed to walk with her after dinner. *Heaven help me, Margaret,* he said. *I rode halfway across Scotland last week, and I'm fit to drop. But if a lovely maid like you asks me to spend some time in her company, then I'd be a fool to refuse.*

Jamie was a hefty creature. Wild and boorish in his manners, and reckless, too. Scarcely a week went by when he didn't come back from Ayr or Kilmarnock bruised from fighting. He scarcely shaved, wore the same clothes three days running and stank to high heaven. His lack of cleanliness annoyed Lady Euphemia no end, but when she voiced her disapproval it only made him worse.

Lady Euphemia always said that Jamie was vulgar because he was a bastard. She may have been right, but Margaret couldn't help thinking that Lady Euphemia's attitude hadn't improved matters.

Margaret felt sorry for Jamie. He'd been taken from his mother as a child and brought to live with the rest of them. Lady Euphemia despised him, and never ceased to tell him so. It wasn't fair on Jamie; he wasn't to blame for his own illegitimacy, but Margaret understood why her mother felt so strongly about the cuckoo in their nest. She thought it would be horrible, to have to confront the consequences of a husband's indiscretions, day in and day out, for twenty years or more.

"Tell me about him," Margaret begged, as they strode arm-in-arm through the apple trees.

"Oh, for God's sake." Jamie reached up and plucked an apple off the bough. It was too small to eat; he regarded it disappointedly then hurled it at one of the dogs that loitered nearby. He caught the beast square on the rump; it fled, yowling.

"Jamie. . ."

"I've told you twice already!"

"Please. . ."

"If you insist. . ." Irritation gave way to sullen admiration. "Well, a fairer youth you'd never hope to see. He's slim and tall, with such a noble look about him. He's every inch a King."

She clutched his arm. "I'm in love with him already."

"He's skilled in the arts of war, as every monarch should be. He wields the lance as well as any man, and he's a master with the bastard sword. And he's so finely educated. He speaks the Romish tongue. And the Greek, too."

"Is he married?"

"No."

"So he's seeking a wife?"

"My Lord, Margaret. You've quite an imagination."

She cast him a sly glance. "Am I not worthy of a King?"

James laughed. "Course you are, sweet princess. But a King can't marry whom he chooses."

"His mistress, then."

He nearly choked. "Lord save us! What the Devil are you thinking?"

"Wouldn't Father be pleased?"

"Of course not! He wouldn't want his only daughter to be a whore. Even a King's whore. You're worth more than that."

Margaret pulled back slightly. "So what am I worth?"

He stepped closer and laid clumsy hands upon her shoulders. "I know just the man for you. He's your second cousin. His name's Robert, he's thirty years old and he's a handsome devil. Not an ugly soul like me."

Margaret smiled up at him. "Oh, you're not ugly. Just a little battered around the edges."

He patted her cheek. "You can be so very charming when the mood takes you, dear sister."

"Tell me more. About my kinsman. . ."

"He's one of the mightiest men in the Kingdom. He's the Director of Chancery."

"He's not a knight?" Margaret pouted, just a little.

"He's a notary."

"I don't want to wed a notary," she sniffed. "I want to wed a knight. Who'll ride to my door all handsome and dashing in full array, on a great big horse."

"Don't forget the long spear to prick you with."

Margaret thumped his chest, laughing. "Don't be so vulgar."

"Master Colville doesn't need to be a knight. He's one of the king's right-hand men. Why, I daresay his arms are richer than most knights' round here. And his horse a thousand times better."

"Perhaps Father should approach him. . ."

"Aren't you forgetting something?" He rested his forehead lightly against her own. "You're as good as wed already."

She clicked her tongue in annoyance. "Unfortunately. Have you met him?"

There was an unruly guffaw from Jamie. "Wouldn't want to!"

"Why?"

"Because — how can I put it kindly — he's not in favour right now."

"Meaning what?"

"Don't be so damned silly, Margaret. What d'you think?"

She shrugged.

"His father died fighting for the wrong side at Stirling. His uncle's been charged with treason. Master Sempill might think he's safe just now, but there's bound to be someone who wants his lands. It's only a matter of time before the wolves come howling at his door. And he'll deserve everything he gets. Because, dear sister, your betrothed is a traitor."

* * *

"I won't do it," Margaret said in a low voice, as she lay awake in bed that night, squeezed close between Katherine and Alison. "I won't marry a traitor."

"Who told you that?" Katherine asked.

"Jamie has heard rumours. At court." Tears stung her eyes. "I'm telling you, Katherine. I won't do it. I'd rather go to a nunnery. I'd- I'd rather die."

"If he's a traitor, then they'll hang him. And you'll be rid of him. If you do things right, you'll be carrying his son when he dies and you'll be mistress of your house for twenty years before the boy comes of age. You'll be free to live alone or marry again as you see fit. Why, you might even find a man worthy of your love. . ."

"Ah. . ." Then she stirred, suddenly vexed. "What if they don't hang him?"

"There's always poison," came Katherine's bright response.

"Poison!" A forbidden thrill coursed through her. Then, once she'd thought it over, "Ugh, no. They might hold me responsible."

Katherine clutched her hand. "Perhaps together we could pleasure him so much that his strength fails him and his heart gives out."

Alison giggled at that, and Margaret, too, had to smile. "You say such wicked things."

"I know. But you're laughing, aren't you? And that's all that matters." She squeezed Margaret's hand tighter. "You mustn't despair. Your father won't let anything horrible happen to you, will he? So there's nothing to be afraid of, is there?"

"I suppose not."

"And besides. . . Whatever happens, you'll still have us. We can look after each other."

"Yes."

"And when the time comes to bury him, we'll celebrate together. We'll look back on this day and wonder what all the fuss was about."

Chapter 13
Saint Bryde's Chapel, Near Ellestoun

Late September brought summer's last flush. Though the sun still shone the morning air was chill, a sure sign that winter was coming. The leaves of the trees turned russet and gold and the hips burned red on the rose trees, while the cows called sadly in the morning mists.

John always regretted the passing of summer, but this year it was to be especially poignant, for Marion was leaving them at last.

"He's a good man. He'll take care of you," John said, as they stood together at the kirk door.

"I know." Marion shivered, and smoothed out her skirts yet again. She'd chosen a sober hue for her wedding gown; a deep wine red. *I can't dress gaily,* she'd said, *not so soon after Father's death. . .*

"It's what you wanted, isn't it?"

"Yes, of course." She twisted the posy of flowers around in her hand. "But Ellestoun was my home. I'll miss you. And I'll miss William, and dear old Henry." She cast a sideways glance towards where Elizabeth Ross talked with the priest. "I suppose I'll miss Mother, too."

John smiled. "And she'll miss you. Though she'd deny it, of course."

The wedding party approached.

At the fore rode Robert Crawfurd. He looked impassive, but as he halted his bay horse at the gate of the kirkyard it stamped and side-stepped, betraying its rider's agitation.

Robert dismounted and strode towards them, ahead of his father and brothers. He had dressed formally for once; over a doublet of dark blue velvet, light blue hose and a white sark he wore a long black gown trimmed with martens' fur. Doublet and sark were densely embroidered about collar and sleeves, and he bore a chain of gem-studded gold about his neck. On his head he sported a neat bonnet of black velvet, which was adorned with a jewelled pin.

As he approached, Marion drew herself taller. She pressed close to John, who took her hand and squeezed it tight.

Robert halted before them. He pushed his hair back from his face and fidgeted with his bonnet. He glanced anxiously towards Malcolm, who smiled and nodded.

"If that's how a man looks when he wants to be married," John whispered in Marion's ear. "Then Heaven help those of us who don't. . ."

Marion giggled, even as the priest spoke out, "We may proceed, then. Master Crawfurd?"

"Er, yes," Robert replied, brow faintly furrowed. He cleared his throat, then announced, in a firm clear voice, "To my future wife, Marion Sempill, daughter of Sir Thomas Sempill of Ellestoun, now deceased, and sister to John Sempill, Laird of Ellestoun, I give a dower of three hundred merks, as agreed in the contract signed upon the fifteenth of August, in the year of our Lord fourteen hundred and eighty-eight, between my father, Sir Malcolm Crawfurd of Kilbirnie and John Sempill of Ellestoun."

One of his younger brothers stepped forward. The lad bore a silver tray, which held a pile of coins and a delicately wrought ring of gold.

"As a token of your dower, I offer you this silver. And as a symbol of our union as man and wife in the eyes of God I give to you this ring." Robert fumbled for the ring and held it aloft, while the priest blessed it and sprinkled it with holy water.

Marion offered her hand. As Robert gently placed the ring upon her finger, a smile crossed her lips.

"Now you must make your vows to one another," the priest said, "so you can be properly joined in the holy state of matrimony. Robert Crawfurd, do you solemnly swear in the presence of God the Father that you will take the hand of Marion Sempill in marriage, and love her and cherish her until you are parted in death?"

"Yes," came Robert's reply. "As God is my witness, I do."

"And do you, Marion Sempill, swear in the presence of God the Father that you will take the hand of Robert Crawfurd of Kilbirnie in marriage, and love him and honour him until you are parted by death."

"Yes," Marion whispered, hoarsely. "I do."

"Then we shall celebrate the union of these two young people by taking Mass together. Let us go inside."

* * *

The priest led the procession into the kirk, his vestments glowing in the dim interior of the nave. Ahead, two boys held a canopy of velvet over the steps before the altar, while the voices of the choir soared loud around them.

Together, Robert and Marion knelt beneath the canopy. John had never considered his sister beautiful. But as Marion accepted the blessing of the priest and took the Eucharist, there was a radiance about her that he'd never seen before. She reminded of him of the Blessed Virgin, her face was patient, lovely. He didn't care if his thoughts were blasphemous; at that moment he loved her so deeply he'd have risked his very soul for her.

He bowed his head in prayer. *Oh, Holy Mary, look after them both. They've waited so long. Surely they should be rewarded for their fidelity. . .*

His mother sniffed back tears, all objections conveniently forgotten.

John patted her hand. Then he snapped back to full awareness. Above the singing of the choir and his mother's quiet sobs, he'd heard hoof beats. It wasn't just one or two beasts, either.

It was a whole pack that approached.

His mother was oblivious. So were Marion and Robert. John glanced over his shoulder, wondering what calamity would follow.

The hoofbeats died, a horse snorted from beyond.

The door opened, and in sidled Adam Mure of Caldwell, Margaret Sempill at his heels. Half their brood was with them; Hector, their eldest son, their two

81

daughters, Lizzie and Janet. And following them, Constantine Dunlop and Patrick Wallace of Auchenbothie.

Adam caught John's eye, and raised his hand. Margaret stood alongside her husband, eyes bright with tears. She clasped her hands in excitement, a broad smile upon her face.

John breathed a quiet sigh of relief, and turned back to the altar.

There, beneath the canopy, Robert and Marion were sharing their first kiss as man and wife.

* * *

"Marion!" Margaret hurried forward just as soon as the recessional music faded. She seized her sister and kissed her on both cheeks. "Oh, my dear, dear sister. I'm so happy for you."

"I never thought you'd come!"

Adam looked skywards. "I'd have never heard the end of it if she hadn't." He shook Robert's hand. "Well done, sir! If she's as fecund as her sister, you won't want for an heir."

Margaret gave a girlish laugh. "Oh, Adam! Enough!"

"Thank you all for coming," said John. "You can join us for the wedding feast, if you like. There's more than enough to go round."

"It'd be a pleasure." Adam gave an embarrassed smile. "I'd best warn you, though. I didn't travel here alone."

"What d'you mean?"

"These are dangerous times. Why, just three days ago a party of Cunninghames rode out from Glengarnock and raided the Montgomerie lands of Hessilhead and Giffen. I couldn't risk my good lady by riding through these parts unarmed. I brought my retainers."

"They can ride with us!" John laughed. "They won't make trouble if they're well-fed." He turned to the priest. "Now, Father. You'll return to Ellestoun with us, of course. To bless the bedchamber, and eat at my table?"

* * *

The subtleties were presented towards the end of the wedding feast, to loud applause from the guests. There was a battlemented castle, baked in pastry, each of its turrets stuffed with delicacies. And, befitting the occasion, there was a bed wrought from sugar paste. Marchpane figures completed the scene; a woman, her belly swollen with child, strained to give birth as the midwife urged her on.

Marion turned bright red at the sight of it. She dropped her face in her hands and laughed till the tears rolled down her face, while Robert smiled patiently as he endured a tirade of bawdy quips from friends and family.

Then, once the feast was over, Robert and Marion disappeared to the wedding chamber. The priest went with them to bless the bed. So too did their parents; Elizabeth Ross, and Sir Malcolm Crawfurd and his wife, Marjorie Barclay. Priest and parents returned soon enough, leaving Robert and Marion alone together.

John had insisted that the bride and groom use his own room as the wedding chamber. Where he'd be sleeping that night, he had no idea. He guessed he'd be settling down in the hall with the servants or scrounging some space in the guest range with Adam and his retinue.

But that wouldn't be for a long while. The night was still young, and there was music and dancing to be enjoyed. And vast quantities of wine to be drunk, too.

"Just one more dance," Janet Mure tugged on John's arm as he tried to head back to the benches.

"I told you. That's enough for the moment. Why don't you dance with Hector?"

"Because he's a clumsy oaf."

"He's your brother."

"He's a clumsy oaf."

"If you say so," John said, wearily. "I'll dance with you later, my lady. Once I've rested my aching feet." He put his arm around her waist and steered her across the hall.

Janet muttered her dissent, but went with him. Like her sister Lizzie, Janet was a strong, broad girl, with Adam's ruddy look about her. She'd just turned fourteen and she'd changed markedly since John had last seen her in the spring. She filled her gown nicely now, and, like Lizzie, was learning to flaunt her charms to best advantage.

John happily took Adam's girls under his wing for the evening. Far better they dogged their uncle than another man who might take advantage of them. Besides, it was a welcome change to endure shameless flirting instead of constant teasing.

Lizzie stood up in readiness.

"No!" John said, with a stern wave of his hand. "I'm exhausted. I'm thirsty. I need to sit down."

"He thinks we should dance with Hector," said Janet.

Lizzie pulled a face. "Not likely."

"Your father, then?"

"Oh, no!" Lizzie looked with horror towards Adam. "A woman wants to look her best, Uncle John."

"Well you won't look your best if I collapse from exhaustion." He sank down onto the bench, and retrieved his goblet from beneath it.

He sipped his wine, feeling pleasantly light-headed and well-disposed towards the world. William had rounded up the best musicians in the Westland, and the guests were enjoying themselves. Malcolm was dancing with Elizabeth Ross and Constantine Dunlop with Marjorie Barclay. Even Adam was joining in, though he wasn't the most nimble of men. But his wife, who had coaxed him out onto the floor, didn't mind that.

"Marion's lucky." Janet sat down on one side, while Lizzie settled on the other. "Robert Crawfurd's a fine catch."

"Janet's like a bitch on heat at the moment." Lizzie pushed her shoulder close. "She'd marry you if it was allowed. She thinks you're very handsome."

Janet went scarlet. "No I don't!"

"Don't be cruel to your sister, Lizzie."

"Any word of your wedding?" Lizzie asked.

"I'm afraid not. I remain a free man."

"Don't you think it's unjust? That they're treating you this way?" Her wide, pleasant face stared into his own.

"I think I've been granted a stay of execution."

"Why?"

He set his wine down. "Because I might be wed to a sly young vixen like you." He tapped her nose, gently.

"John Sempill of Ellestoun!" Robert Crawfurd's voice bellowed loud across the hall.

The dancers faltered. So too did the musicians. They talked amongst themselves, curious, more than a little concerned. But William's lute kept going, strong and undaunted, and gradually the other players joined in.

John crouched low in his seat.

"He's over here!" Janet called.

"Whatever's happened?" Lizzie asked. "He looks angry."

"I left them an extra wedding gift," said John. "Obviously, they found it."

Robert approached, scowling. His hair was dishevelled, he was missing his doublet and his shoes and his sark hung loose over his hose. And there was a large rabbit tucked under his arm.

John ducked behind Lizzie with a laugh.

Robert hauled him out and thrust the rabbit into his lap. "A full hour we've wasted!"

The rabbit looked equally perturbed. It sat quite still, eyes bulging, body trembling. John picked it up and stroked it, gently. "You didn't like my gift?"

"Eight of the damned things, hopping about the wedding chamber. Just what a man needs, when he's eager to bed his wife."

"Why waste more time remonstrating with me? Go off and bed her, for God's sake."

"If you're not careful, I'll dream up something worse for your wedding day," Robert grumbled.

"You'll appreciate her all the more after the delay!" John called after him.

"What did you do?" Janet asked.

John smirked. "I left a sack of coneys on the bed. What's more, they were daft enough to open it."

* * *

"There were rabbits everywhere." Marion's lips twitched. "Robert spent ages trying to catch them."

"I can't believe you opened the bag." John checked the straps of the harness one last time. "Weren't they moving?"

"It was Marion's doing," said Robert. He nudged John aside. "No need to do that now. It's my task."

John shrugged, and stepped back.

"Robert didn't think to warn me," said Marion, as Robert helped her up onto the horse. "His thoughts were elsewhere."

"I'm sure they were." John stifled a laugh. "God, I wish I'd seen it."

"He was calling you everything."

"Thankfully, I have great capacity for forgiveness." Robert patted her thigh. "All set there?"

"Yes." She looked wistfully down at John. "Goodbye," she said, reaching out her hand. "You'll visit us, won't you?"

John raised her hand to his lips. "Whenever time permits, sweet sister."

"And you'll tread carefully?"

"Don't worry about me," John said. "Adam wants me to dine with him in a few weeks' time. That's a good sign, I think. It probably means the worst is over."

Chapter 14

"Hup, Zephyr. Come on now." Hugh sat firm as the grey stallion heaved itself up the steep slopes of Lochlands Hill.

It was a crisp October day, and Hugh was making the most of the good weather. He'd left Hessilhead early, and had taken a roundabout route that passed east of Beith.

Zephyr's legs threshed a swathe through the deep drifts of dead leaves and decaying vegetation. Its hoof struck a hidden stone, and the horse stumbled. The sudden movement threw Hugh forward in the saddle. He tightened the reins, but his relaxed expression didn't waver. Venturing so close to hostile territory, he had to appear confident before his men.

From here he could see right across the vale of the Cart. Mist still hung heavy in the valley, but here and there large plumes of smoke rose above it. They marked the tower-houses of the local lairds; in the east, Ellestoun, to the west, Ladyland and Kilbirnie.

And, tucked away in a valley to the north-west, Humphry Cuningham's place of Glengarnock.

He hissed with frustration. So close, but still out of reach. . .

"Lost another five byres last week," John Montgomerie of Hessilhead growled. "It's Craigends, I'm sure of it."

"There's a surprise."

"What're we to do?"

"Raze more farms round Kilmaurs and Auchenharvie. Take enough stock to cover our losses. Oh, and impound a few more cartloads of stone bound for Kerrielaw. Might as well put the fear of God into the masons, too."

"It's not enough."

"To reach Craigends I'd have to cross another man's estate."

"Yes, but—"

"Under what pretence? It doesn't lie within my jurisdiction."

"Glengarnock, then."

"Too dangerous."

"Not like you to be so cautious."

"I'm not cautious. I'm practical," Hugh replied. "When we strike, I want no half-measures." He swivelled his horse around. "Let's go. It's not as if we'll pass unnoticed."

"Whose fault's that?"

Hugh laughed, and clapped Zephyr's neck. The big grey had been a gift from the King. "Why keep a fine horse if you're not prepared to flaunt him?"

"It's criminal, to use him as a common courser."

"It's criminal to make him fret in a stable all day." Hugh stretched with a sigh. "We'll deal with Glengarnock soon enough. And Craigends, too. But we can't afford to tread on too many toes round here. I daresay Craigends is already trying hard to discredit me to his neighbours."

"God rot the man."

"Be patient. There's ways round it." He cast a last wistful look towards Glengarnock. "Well, I'll be on my way. Before I'm late for dinner."

* * *

"Good of you to come, John!" Adam Mure waved from the doorway. "And you brought William, too. . ."

"William's quite used to singing for his supper," said John.

Adam laughed, but he sounded strained. "Well, let's waste no more time. It's no day to be lingering outside."

* * *

"Uncle John!" The small boy raced across the hall and wrapped his arms tight about John's legs.

"Hello, Johnny!" John ruffled the child's tawny hair. "You've grown."

"He'll be eight next spring," said Margaret.

"Eats more than ever," Adam added.

"Wait till Constantine gets a few more years under his belt," John replied. "Then you'll have real cause for complaint."

"The girls'll be wed by then, I hope," said Adam. "Two less mouths to feed. . ."

"I have a new pony." Young Johnny Mure seized John's hand. "Come and see him."

"Oh, not now!" Adam cast a despairing look at the joists.

"Where's the harm in it?" John laughed. "Come on, Johnny. Show me your mighty destrier."

* * *

"Where have you been?" the boy asked.

John glanced uneasily about the courtyard. Caldwell was normally a relaxed place, but today it seemed unsettled. Servants bustled here and there, unloading supplies, tending horses and delivering barrowloads of fresh rushes to the range. "I was in the east."

"With Father?"

John's breath caught in his throat. "Not exactly."

"Father was knighted. By the King."

"I know."

"Were you knighted, Uncle John?"

"No. I wasn't."

"Why not?"

"Well. . ." Thankfully, they'd reached the stable, and he was spared any further interrogation. "Ah!" he said, halting beside a tiny bay pony. "Is that your steed?"

"Do you like him?"

John tried not to smile. The creature looked faintly absurd alongside the riding and sumpter horses. Its short legs, rotund belly and bellicose look were oddly reminiscent of Adam. "He'll teach you well, I'm sure," he said. "This time next year you'll be tilting before the King."

"Father's teaching me to use a sword, too. But it's just made of wood." The child looked close to tears.

"All in good time."

"I'm supposed to practice with Hector. But he just scoffs and knocks me over."

"Well, if Hector won't help, then you'll have to make do with me. Fetch your sword. Show me what you're made of."

* * *

John lingered in the stables for a while. Satisfied that his horses were settled, he wandered back outside.

More horsemen were arriving; Constantine Dunlop of Hunthall, and his entourage.

"Good to see you, John!" Constantine dismounted. "I'd best go inside and ask after my godson. Are you coming?"

"I'm afraid not," John replied. "I've a tryst to keep. With a master swordsman."

"Eh?" Constantine turned pale.

"Young Master Mure," explained John, as Johnny came galloping out with two wooden swords gripped tight in his hands.

There was an uneasy laugh from Constantine. "I'll leave you to it then."

* * *

The encircling wall at Caldwell was freshly harled, but as Hugh drew closer, he saw that its masonry had crumbled in places, with saplings rooted in the exposed rubble core.

Caldwell's shabby defences came as no surprise. Though Adam Mure tried hard to appear educated, and civilised, he was just another provincial laird; raw, uncompromising and vicious.

For all Adam's faults, he made a useful ally. Men of his ilk were honest and straightforward, and a little generosity went a long way with them.

Hugh halted at the gates. The tower-house reared tall ahead, an enticing sight.

"Good day," he said to the steward. "Tell Sir Adam that the Lord Montgomerie's here."

The path ahead was cluttered with servants, grooms and carters.

Hugh forged his way through. As usual, his reputation went before him. All stepped aside; nervous faces looked up, then turned away.

He tightened his reins and touched his spurs against Zephyr's flanks; the stallion arched its neck and sprang forward at a slow, high-stepping trot.

People stopped and stared. Hugh sat tall, revelling in their admiration. Even here, men appreciated a thing of quality when they saw it.

Somewhere nearby, a child's laughter rang out. The mood was spoiled, his audience shrugged and returned to their duties. Intrigued and irritated, Hugh halted his horse and twisted around in the saddle.

He glimpsed a boy, darting through the carts with a wooden sword in his hand. The child was fighting someone, a brother perhaps. He disappeared, there was a rattle of blows as the blades met.

His curiosity roused, Hugh steered his horse closer.

The child was a Mure. No surprises there. But his opponent was a different matter. A slender young man, with bright gold-brown hair.

John Sempill of Ellestoun. Scrapping with his nephew as if he hadn't a care in the world.

Hugh almost felt sorry for him. In the same dispassionate way he felt sorry for the stag when the hounds closed in. The young man's future was bleak; why, just next month Parliament was meeting to decide the fate of men like Sempill.

The boy tapped his kinsman smartly in the chest; Master Sempill doubled over with a groan, clutching the blade.

Sempill straightened, looked around and saw Hugh. For a moment, he looked mortified. Small wonder, after being caught engaged in tomfoolery with a child.

"It's Lord Hugh!" The child seized his uncle's hand and dragged him forward.

"Good day, Master Mure," Hugh said, cheerfully. "And good day to *you*, Master Sempill. I hope you didn't draw your sword on my account."

John Sempill's surprise briefly gave way to raw distaste. Then he nodded and smiled, pleasant, unassuming.

Hugh remembered Adam Mure's exact words: *Young John? Oh, he's a lad of little consequence. He's a dull soul, a little naïve and lacking in spirit.*

Looking at John Sempill now, it was easy to be think he had neither the wits nor the inclination to harm anyone.

Dangerous, Hugh told himself, as he dismounted. *Damned dangerous. Just like his uncle.*

"He's a wonderful horse," the boy told him. "Can I pat him?"

"Better still. You can take him to the stables." Hugh hoisted the child onto the horse's back.

"Thank you!" Young Master Mure nestled comfortably in the saddle. Clutching the reins with one hand, he waved wildly with the other. "Look at me, Uncle John!"

Master Sempill muttered a few half-hearted words of admiration, then looked relieved as Adam's voice boomed out, "Welcome to Caldwell, my lord!" Adam shouldered his way past Master Sempill, clapping the young man on the back as he passed. "I'm sorry about the boy," Adam said. "It was gracious of you to humour him."

"It'll do him good to sit him on a real horse once in a while," Hugh replied.

"He's a fine horse," said Master Sempill. "He's of Spanish stock, isn't he?"

"On both sides." Hugh wasn't quite convinced by Master Sempill's amicable tone.

Adam leaned a hand on the young man's shoulder. "You know my gude-brother, John Sempill of Ellestoun?"

"Our paths have crossed." Hugh shivered. "It's a chilly morning," he said. "Forgive my presumption, but some refreshment would be appreciated. I've been in the saddle some hours; I can scarcely feel my feet."

"I thought it was just an hour's ride from Hessilhead," Sempill said, all-innocence. "Less, on a princely steed like that. Did you get lost, sir? Or was there urgent business to attend to?"

Adam flashed his kinsman a disgruntled look, then smiled at Hugh. "Step this way, my lord. Margaret's in the hall. She'll look after you."

* * *

"Alright!" Adam closed the door behind him. "You wanted a word? Well, now's your chance. And don't say I'm not good to you, John. My guests are waiting—"

"It's a trap, isn't it?" He should have been frightened. Instead, all he felt was cold hard anger at Montgomerie's contaminating presence in the hall below.

"What in God's name are you talking about?"

Rage coursed through him, his eyes blurred. "He's a butcher! He killed my father."

Adam swallowed. "I didn't know that."

"You should've warned me."

"You wouldn't have come."

"You're right. I wouldn't have."

"John. . ." Adam hesitated, searching for the right words. "Lord Hugh's called many things. . . But he's not a coward. Your father was a bold man, too. Sometimes, when two such men meet in battle, only one lives to tell the tale."

"Ask him how Glencairn met his fate. He murdered the Earl, Adam. Just like he murdered Lord Boyd—"

"That's enough!" Adam clenched his fists, face dark with fury. "Young fool!" he snapped. "I've done my best to help you. And all you do is throw it back in my face—"

There was a knock on the door.

"Yes?" Adam barked.

Lizzie opened the door and peered round. "Mother wondered when you and Uncle John will join her in the hall. She says it looks rude."

Adam pulled off his bonnet with one hand and smoothed back his thinning hair. "We'll be down shortly." He looked, and sounded, exhausted. "Well?" he added, replacing his bonnet. "Will you humour your sister?"

John said nothing.

"He knows the King. . . And it'd ease Margaret's worries, if she thought you were trying to get back into favour."

Fear gave way to numb resignation. If they planned to trap him, he was doomed, whatever he did. He shrugged. "Alright."

"Good lad!" Adam gripped his shoulder. "I thought you'd see sense. Now be wary. He has sharper wits than most men. And a quick temper. Treat him with respect, John, however much you dislike him."

* * *

John took a deep breath, and stepped into the hall.

90

He found Lord Hugh the centre of attention. His presence filled the room; he carried himself with grace and careful elegance, like a hawk perched on a falconer's wrist.

Snatching a goblet of wine from a passing servant, John loitered near the door. From there he watched Montgomerie's audience carefully. What he saw sickened him; men puffed themselves up tall because Lord Hugh chose to speak with them, while the women looked flattered when he merely glanced in their direction.

He glowered at the floor. He wouldn't succumb to the lure of Montgomerie's presence just yet. He ambled round the panelled walls, and halted by the aumbry. He made a show of admiring the contents, then chanced a quick glance towards the crowd.

Montgomerie's bright gaze flicked briefly in his direction. John stared back, unbowed. Lord Hugh's jovial expression didn't waver, then his attention was elsewhere.

John gave a relieved sigh. He continued his prowl around the hall, halting by a tapestry. It was a hunting scene; the stags almost seemed to smile as they hurled themselves into the waiting nets. . .

"Master John?" William whispered alongside. "Thank God you're safe."

John glanced towards Montgomerie. "Look at him. He swaggers as if he owns the place."

"He has more reason to swagger than most."

"Be careful tonight," John said. "Sing some songs of unrequited love and give them some of the Wallace tales. You can't go wrong with Wallace in these parts."

"A wise choice. And watch yourself." He gripped John's arm. "I've no wish to serve a new master."

With that, he'd gone. John shivered, and turned back to the tapestry. In the foreground a knight and his lady held hands; theirs a chase of a very different kind. . .

"John!" Margaret spoke sternly in his ear. "Come on now. Lord Hugh's eager to speak with you."

"I'm sure."

"Stop it." She tugged him towards the fire. "I won't have you cluttering up my hall."

* * *

"Ah! The Laird of Ellestoun!" Montgomerie raised his goblet. "I see you've set the sword aside now. That's comforting, I must say." He laughed, and everyone else laughed with him.

John kept a straight face. "Good day, Lord Hugh. It's been a while since we last met."

"It has," Montgomerie agreed. "And I'm pleased to see you made it back safe and sound after our disagreement in the east."

John smiled, tightly.

"You seem preoccupied." Lord Hugh made a show of looking concerned. "You've suffered no troubles since your return?"

"Actually, no."

"You see?" Lord Hugh proclaimed. "The world's been put to rights! Justice has prevailed, we have a wise and noble King upon the throne." He flourished his goblet once again, looking straight at John. "The King."

"The King." John readily joined the chorus.

"We've talked enough of politics," Lord Hugh said. "We're boring these lovely ladies, and that's unforgivable." He leaned close to young Janet Mure, and smiled his charming smile; she blushed and sighed, but he didn't even notice. His gaze was back on John once more. "Tell me, Master Sempill, do you hunt with us tomorrow?"

"I'll be there, my lord. Though whether my poor nag'll keep up with your fine steed remains to be seen."

"There's few men alive who can keep up with me, Master Sempill. In fact, there's few men bold enough to even try."

"Can I take that as a challenge, Lord Hugh?"

Montgomerie smiled. "If you like."

Chapter 15

Hugh should have been bored. He hated dining with country lairds; they never cared for much beyond their estates and were seldom capable of witty conversation.

But the baleful presence of Master Sempill at the table meant Hugh couldn't afford to drop his guard. The young man had been itching for an argument all afternoon. So far, though, Sempill hadn't said a word, except on one occasion when he'd asked Sir Patrick Wallace to pass the salt.

"It must be so exciting," said Margaret Sempill. "To be part of such a lively court."

"Oh, it is, Lady Margaret," Hugh said. "The King's such a vibrant young man. His wits are second to none, and he makes entertaining company."

"If life at court's so magnificent—" John Sempill said, deceptively mild, "—then why did you come home at all?"

An embarrassed silence fell across the board.

Hugh caught the young man's gaze. Sempill, unlike most men, had the gall to stare right back.

He was an angelic-looking lad. He appeared younger than his twenty years. That would have fooled some men, but Hugh wasn't going to let it fool him.

Hugh dabbed his cloth against his lips and took another sip of wine. "My lands don't manage themselves," he said. "Besides, I'm Bailie of Cunninghame now. The King was kind enough to grant me the title; I must make sure its duties are performed to his satisfaction."

Adam and the others nodded politely, but John Sempill just gave him an icy glower.

"Well, I'm pleased to see you back," said Adam. "It's well known that you keep a tight rein on rebels and reivers."

Master Sempill frowned and fiddled with his goblet. "Since you've come from the east, my Lord, perhaps you could give us word of the King?"

Hugh feigned misunderstanding. "Whatever do you mean?"

"The King I served. King James the Third. If I remember right, Lord Hugh, you were once his loyal servant too. . ."

"John!" Adam gasped.

"He hasn't been forgotten already? Why, his crown is scarcely cold."

"You're right to express concern," Hugh countered, smoothly. "He died, I'm afraid. He fell from his horse as he fled the field."

"That's unfortunate," Master Sempill said, in that same innocent voice. "There'll be an explanation, of course. I suppose his steed tripped in a rabbit hole. Did they hang the guilty rabbit? Or weigh him down with gold for his pains?"

"That's enough!" Adam cast a pleading look at Hugh. "Forgive him, my lord. He's young."

Not that young. . . Hugh shook his head, feigning irritation. A warning sign: Don't press me further. He didn't really mean it. He just wanted to see whether that would be enough.

"It might be useful to take that rabbit and make him a peer of the realm. Who else'll sit in Parliament? Half its Lords are dead. Or skulking in their towers, too frightened to come out."

Adam turned a deep shade of purple. He gazed helplessly at Hugh. "My lord. . ."

Hugh gave Adam his best benign look. "Master Sempill is nursing a grievance," he said. "I hope he'll share it with us sooner rather than later. We mustn't let it fester on all afternoon." He slapped his palms against the table. "Well out with it, man!"

"Since you ask, Lord Hugh, then yes, I am aggrieved. I lost a father, just a few months ago."

"If you hold me responsible for your father's death, then I'm sorry," Hugh said. "What did you expect me to do? Bow my head and let him strike me down, like a sheep before the butcher's knife?"

"What's done is done, Lord Hugh." Sempill's tone was infuriatingly self-righteous. "It's God's place to pronounce judgement, not mine."

"How very magnanimous of you."

"I'm concerned that my father's lying amongst strangers," Sempill gripped the board before him, staring at his platter. "My mother's pain is much worse, because she can't visit his grave." He turned accusing eyes on Hugh. "What did he do to deserve this? What did *she* do?"

Adam dropped his head into his hands and moaned.

"Your kinsman's like a mastiff," Hugh said. "Once he gets his teeth in there's no shaking him." He took a leisurely mouthful of his wine, and smiled. "You're right to speak out, Master Sempill." He paused to take another sip. "I shall make enquiries, and do what I can to have him restored. For the sake of his widow, as well as for yourself."

The young man unclenched his fingers, and somehow managed a smile. "Thank you, my lord," he said. "Your generosity is appreciated."

"It's the least I can do." Hugh felt pleasantly satisfied. He'd come through with his reputation not just untarnished but actually enhanced. All credit to his opponent; unlike many men, Master Sempill had the good sense and the grace to back down and let him emerge victorious.

* * *

From the way Adam stabbed his spoon into the plum pudding, it was as if the plums were to blame for everything. John noticed how his gude-brother didn't so much as look at him; he'd have turned his back, John reckoned, if that had been physically possible.

At least John could console himself with the knowledge that William's playing was impeccable, and his recital of Wallace's escapades was very well received. Whatever else Adam found to complain about, he couldn't complain about *that*.

As for Montgomerie. . . Though men spoke in hushed voices about Lord Hugh's quick temper, evidently the famed Montgomerie fury didn't flare quite as readily as popular opinion had it. If anything, John thought, the atmosphere had lifted.

He sighed, and chased a plum about the platter. He felt a little guilty about ruining Adam's festivities, but couldn't help thinking that his gude-brother's fury was misplaced. "The minstrel." Lord Hugh leaned back in his chair.

"He's not ours," Adam said. "Music's a luxury we can't afford."

"A sorry admission, Sir Adam. A gentleman's house isn't complete without music." Lord Hugh looked towards John. "Master Haislet's in your service, isn't he?"

"Yes, he is."

"Will you be keeping him?"

"William's in command of his own destiny," said John. "He's been in our retinue for a good many years; I hope he'll stay with us."

"Ah." A look of undisguised avarice crossed Montgomerie's face.

"No harm in asking," John said. "But he'll say no."

"That's a confident assertion." Montgomerie sat up, and beckoned to Adam. "Your hospitality's been peerless," he said. "But now it's time for business."

"Excuse me." Adam rose from his chair.

John's misgivings returned. "What in God's name—"

Constantine Dunlop lifted his head, mildly interested. "Who knows?" He chuckled. "That was quite an afternoon, John. I never thought you'd take on Hugh Montgomerie and live to tell the tale."

"The day's still young," said John. "Who says I'll survive it?"

* * *

Margaret at least had forgiven him. Within minutes she was badgering him about marriage. "There are good notaries in Paisley," she said. "You should find one. It's the height of discourtesy, to treat you like this."

"I've better things to do." He almost wished Lord Hugh was still there, for then he'd escape Margaret's nagging.

"You'll be saying that on your deathbed."

"Oh, let the boy be!" Constantine laughed. "When the sap rises in spring, he'll think differently."

"The frosts are getting heavier now," Sir Patrick Wallace said. "The kye'll be coming in soon."

"It's been quite dry so far," Constantine replied. "The roads are still passable."

John picked up a slice of gingerbread, grateful for the respite.

A hand closed about his shoulder.

It was Adam. He'd returned alone. "Come with me," he said. "Lord Hugh wishes to speak with you."

* * *

Night had fallen, but in the laird's chamber only one or two candles were lit. Darkness prowled the corners of the room, held at bay by the fire that burned in the hearth.

Hugh Montgomerie sat at the cusp of its glow, midway between the shadow and the light. He slouched back in his chair, legs crossed before him. He was staring into the fire, seemingly preoccupied.

John swallowed. He glanced cautiously about him, searching the gloom for hidden attackers.

There were none. Montgomerie was alone.

Montgomerie kept looking at the fire. An attempt to unsettle him, John supposed, so he just stood there, humouring the man.

"Sit, please." Montgomerie gestured to a vacant chair.

He sat down.

Lord Hugh stared at him now. The dancing flames of the fire cast an unearthly light upon his face; he looked pale as a corpse, his cheekbones stark, gleaming, his eyes sunk deep in their sockets.

"Wine?" Montgomerie pushed himself to his feet. He headed for a kist by the far wall, where John heard liquid being decanted from a flagon.

"Adam thinks he's done you a favour," Lord Hugh said as he wandered back, goblet in hand. "But I'd have sought you out, sooner or later. I remember our meeting at Ellestoun. You impressed me then." Handing John the goblet, he sat down. "You impressed me today, too."

"Flattery didn't help you then, my lord. What makes you think it'll work now?"

"You need my help."

John stared at the goblet. In the near-darkness the wine looked black, putrid.

He couldn't bring himself to touch it.

"Oh, for Heaven's sake. . ." Montgomerie seized John's goblet and swallowed a hefty draft. "There. Perfectly safe." He handed it back.

John sighed, and took a sip.

"Kilmaurs," said Montgomerie. He picked up the goblet which rested beneath his own chair. "You fought alongside him at Stirling."

"It was my father's choice to face you. Not my own."

"I know that. I bear no ill-will towards the Sempills. But anyone who assists the Cunninghames will feel the full force of my wrath."

"Craigends approached me in September. I told him I'm not prepared to take sides. If you ask me to join you, my lord, I'll give you exactly the same reply."

"Thank you," said Montgomerie.

"You don't think I'm lying?"

"I know you're not." Montgomerie sipped his wine. "Now," he added, setting his goblet back down, "I think it's my turn to be helpful. As you know, I've not long returned from the east. I'll tell you what I heard there, if you like."

"Is it over?"

Montgomerie leaned forward, frowning. "It's hardly begun."

"Do you know what will happen?"

"The Lords meet in October. They'll decide then what's to be done with men like you."

"But I've done nothing!" He winced; he'd sounded petulant.

"You were defeated," Lord Hugh said. "And you hold some desirable lands and titles. It doesn't help that your father died a traitor and your uncle's been charged with treason."

"Dear God. . ." His head swam, he gripped the arm of his chair.

"Brace yourself, for it gets worse. The King's Treasury was almost empty when we found it. We think His Grace put much of his gold into the care of those he trusted most. Men like your uncle, Ross of Montgrennan."

"And you think I've spirited some away?" His voice shook.

"The facts could be twisted, could they not? A short sail up the Forth, a quick transfer of baggage and another short sail to Renfrew. Why, the missing treasure would be safe in Ellestoun's walls within a week!"

"But Lord Ross would never have given it to me!" John protested. "He might have entrusted some to my father, or to Cunninghame of Kilmaurs. But they both fell in battle. Perhaps questions should be asked of those who searched their bodies—"

Montgomerie leaned close, his eyes bright, agitated. "Do you think I don't know that?" he snapped. "My honour's at stake here, too." He slumped back, and stared at the fire. "There was no treasure. If it's anywhere, it's with your uncle, in England. But that's not going to help you, is it?"

"What do you mean?"

"You're unmarried, with no heir."

John swallowed, sickened by the implications. If he died, his lands would go to the first-born son of his sister Elizabeth. . . "It's the Stewarts, isn't it?"

"And Lord Lyle. He had reason to hate your father."

He didn't know what to say. He hoped Montgomerie was lying. But there was something horribly plausible about Lord Hugh's words. He'd been a small boy when Elizabeth married William Stewart of Glanderston, bastard son of John Stewart of Darnley. He barely even remembered her.

"Lyle's the Justiciar now," said Montgomerie.

John wondered numbly if Montgomerie derived pleasure from tormenting him this way, feeding him one morsel of bad news after another. "I had no idea," he said. "To have Lord Lyle as a Justiciar! And to have Darnley working with him!"

"Darnley's an Earl now. Earl of Lennox."

John shook his head. "What hope do I have?"

"Forewarned is forearmed," Lord Hugh told him. "Besides," he added, "It's not in my interests to see you turned out of Ellestoun. You'd run straight to Kilmaurs for protection. What good would that do me?"

John was silent.

"It's not an ideal situation. But you're bold. And determined."

"You're flattering me again."

Montgomerie gave a thin smile. "Yes, I suppose I am." He sighed, stretching clasped hands before him. "You don't trust me."

"Why should I?"

"Your father helped me once." He stared into the fire. "What happened between us was unfortunate. I didn't want things to end that way."

Liar. Somehow John kept the scowl from his face.

"Perhaps it's my duty, to keep a watchful eye on you. But I must be careful. I can't be seen to give you assistance—"

"I don't expect any."

"—But I'll bend the King's ear to your situation. When the time's right. . ."

John looked Montgomerie in the eye, searching for deceit, but found none. Which reassured him a little. He nodded, too overwhelmed to speak.

"There's one more thing. Your marriage to the Maid of Ochiltree. They've failed to honour the contract, haven't they?"

His surprise must have shown. "Yes."

"There could have been better matches. But they're respectable enough."

"I don't think they'll honour their obligations."

"I know a Colville. I'll speak to him, and put in a good word." He sat back. "And that, I think is that. It's been a pleasure, Master Sempill. And I'm sure we'll find plenty to discuss in future."

* * *

The grey stallion was skittish in the chill of the morning. It gave an ear-splitting whinny then sat back on its haunches and thrashed the air with its forelegs.

John thought Lord Hugh would take a whip to the beast; instead he reacted with surprising good humour. "Patience, Zephyr," he soothed, running his hand down the horse's dappled neck. "Just a little longer."

"Needs less oats," Adam suggested.

"Nonsense!" Montgomerie sat deep as his horse reared up again. "He's eager to be off, that's all."

"He's not the only one," said Adam. "Margaret, would you hurry along!"

Margaret arranged her gown carefully over the hooked pommel of her saddle. "I'm ready now, dear."

"Sound the horn!" Adam called. "Let's be off!"

John tightened his reins as the horn rang out. He should have been enjoying himself; it was a rare treat, to take the horses out on an exhilarating chase across the parkland.

Today, though, his thoughts were elsewhere. He'd lain awake most of the night, trying to convince himself that Montgomerie was lying, that Lord Hugh had spun this tale about the Stewarts to win his confidence and wean him away from the Cunninghames.

But Montgomerie's words had an uncomfortable ring of truth about them. Try as he might, John couldn't shake them from his mind.

The huntsmen led the way to the hunter's mark, while they all trotted along behind. The legs on young Johnny Mure's pony moved twice as fast as those of the horses, while Montgomerie fought his mount all the way; it bounced along at a sprightly canter, tail switching in annoyance.

John winced as the big grey barged close. "Is he trained for war?"

"He's exemplary," Montgomerie replied, as he wrestled with the reins. "That's why I indulge him once in a while."

"It seems risky, to run him on ground like this."

"A horse that's used to the rigours of the chase serves you better in war than one that's never ventured beyond the tiltyard."

John could see the sense in that. Even if he didn't want to admit it.

* * *

They sighted the stag at last. It grazed halfway up the hillside amidst a group of hinds. Heavy antlers crowned its head, it gazed imperiously over at them, then moved off at an elegant trot. The cry of the hounds went up; the hinds scattered, and the stag pushed itself into a cumbersome canter.

They were off at a gallop.

The ground passed by at giddying speed. The wind whistled in John's ears, tugging at his hair, driving the breath from his lungs.

His troubles were forgotten. He was lost in the thundering beat of the hooves, the rhythmic snorts of the horse. It pulled at the bit, until his arms ached with the strain of holding it back.

Ahead, Montgomerie's grey was a teasing apparition. The Spanish horse looked slow, but try as he might John couldn't catch up.

He spurred his horse on faster.

* * *

The stag bounded down into a stream then vanished into a copse of trees. The hounds faltered at the water; heads lowered, they searched for the scent.

Montgomerie reined in beside the stream. His horse was blowing from the gallop, neck lathered with sweat.

Adam and the others were still specks in the distance.

"Adam's loitering," Montgomerie remarked. "No surprises there."

The huntsman sounded his horn to reform the pack, but the hounds ignored him. They'd already picked up the scent. They bayed loud and set off once more.

Montgomerie wheeled his horse around, and urged it across the slippery rocks of the stream. "Well?" he asked. "Are you coming?"

John cast a guilty look back towards his gude-brother. Adam was hailing them, but his words were lost in the tumbling water.

With a sigh, John hauled upon the reins and splashed after Montgomerie.

* * *

They followed the hounds to a stand of trees. The growth was too dense for the horses, so they halted beyond while the hounds flushed out their quarry.

They didn't speak. Montgomerie held his head on one side, listening.

The hounds called, unseen. Twigs cracked; the stag crashed from the undergrowth, just feet away. Its head drooped low, its breath came in wheezing rasps.

"Almost over," Montgomerie said, with airy confidence. "He's spent."

As if determined to prove him wrong, the stag groaned and forced itself back into a gallop.

"He's a real fighter," said Montgomerie. "I almost hope he gets away."

"He won't. Adam wants a kill."

"He thinks I'm easily impressed by carnage?"

"He judges men by his own standards."

"Do I detect an air of disdain, Master Sempill?"

"If you did, it wasn't intended." To his relief, he saw Adam and the others approaching.

* * *

There was their quarry, scrambling up a rocky hillside ahead. It stumbled, slowed to a faltering trot then heaved itself back into a canter. Its tongue lolled, streams of saliva trailing from its open jaws.

The hounds were almost on it.

The stag slithered back down the slope, a last desperate effort to escape. As it swerved and jumped to avoid a boulder, its knees buckled. Already, the lead hound snapped at its haunches.

It staggered to its feet and turned to face its tormentors. With legs splayed wide, it lowered its head and swept its antlers from side to side to keep the hounds at bay. Its nostrils were bloody pits, it shuddered as the hounds closed in and tore into its flanks and hindquarters.

"Mort!" Adam shook his fist in triumph as the huntsman waded through the hounds with his knife drawn.

Margaret crossed herself. "He showed such courage, to turn on the hounds like that."

"A good chase," Montgomerie said. "He was a brave and worthy foe."

John didn't speak. He'd witnessed the kill a thousand times before, but it had never touched him like this. The stag's body twitched as the blood poured from its throat; as he watched it, he sensed his own doom.

It was a sign. His ancestors had chosen a stag's head as the crest that adorned their arms. They'd valued its steadfastness, its loyalty. Until this morning, this particular stag had gone about its business without a care in the world, fearless, lordly. But the hounds had marked it, just as Fate had marked him. He wondered if he'd suffer the same fate, brought to bay then slaughtered by those so much mightier than himself.

His head reeled, he clenched his hands tight in his horse's mane and looked away.

"He's *so* handsome," Janet said.

"Are you talking about me?" He wasn't sure how he managed to sound light-hearted.

"No, silly," said Lizzie. The two girls had reined in their horses alongside. "She means Lord Hugh. She's in love with him."

"He's married already. So you'd best forget him. Unless you'd care to poison his wife?"

The girls giggled.

"Hark at him," said Lizzie. "Sounds like he's jealous."

"Poor old Uncle John," Janet added. "No one wants to marry him. He's hopeless."

"Excuse me, ladies." He steered his horse away.

"Idiot!" Lizzie's voice hissed behind him. "You shouldn't have said that."

He didn't know where to go. The last thing he wanted was for Montgomerie to see his agitation. And he couldn't bear the thought of Margaret fussing. He needed sympathy even less than ridicule. He steered a course for Sir Patrick

Wallace and Constantine Dunlop. But to reach them, he had to march straight past Montgomerie. He didn't want to acknowledge Lord Hugh, but good manners prevailed. He looked up, hoping Montgomerie's eyes were elsewhere.

Montgomerie leaned upon his pommel, watching him.

He muttered a barely audible nicety in Lord Hugh's direction and hurried onwards. He chanced a backward glance. To his horror, he found that Montgomerie's relentless gaze was still upon him.

As if Lord Hugh knew what he was thinking. . .

He shuddered, like someone had walked over his grave. He missed Ellestoun, so much he ached inside.

Tomorrow, he reminded himself. *Tomorrow. You'll be safe behind your own walls. It'll all seem better there.*

He laughed inwardly. *It's just delaying the evil hour. When the time comes, not even Ellestoun's walls'll protect you.*

You're finished, John Sempill. He knows it just as well as you do.

Chapter 16

"Montgomeries," William called from the wallwalk. "A whole pack of them. And armed, too."

Scarcely a fortnight had passed since John's return from Caldwell, and now a band of armed Montgomerie retainers were heading for Ellestoun. John scrambled up the steps, joining William at the parapet. "Prepare my horse," he called. "And ready five men-at-arms. I won't have them trespassing on my lands."

There were ten of them in all, their red-and-blue liveries bright against the clammy grey-green fields. All were mounted, but their pace was slow.

John squinted into the distance. "They're escorting a wagon."

"Twenty barrels of pickled herrings for the Abbot of Paisley?" William suggested.

"Let's find out, shall we?" John was already heading for the yard.

* * *

One man broke formation and approached at a canter. He was bearded, thickset, and arrayed in plate armour.

"The Laird of Hessilhead," John told William. "Last time we met he gave me the hiding of my life." He raised his hand. "Halt! You're on Sempill lands."

Hessilhead reined in his steed. "I'm here on behalf of the Lord Montgomerie. He entrusted this cargo to my care, and asked me to ensure it reached you safely."

It was only now, that John could see what they'd brought. A dull grey casket, about six feet long and wrought of lead.

"What—" His voice shook so much he had to start again. "What does Lord Hugh want in return for this gift?"

"He asks only for your goodwill. And hopes that you will find it in your heart to forgive him for any part he played in your father's death." Hessilhead urged his horse closer. "He also wanted to give you this." He handed John a soft bundle wrapped in wine-red velvet. "We found it on the field. We couldn't leave it there."

Balancing it against the pommel, John untied the ribbon that secured it. Ivory silk was revealed, and a flash of crimson.

It was the banner they'd abandoned in the rout.

"Thank Lord Hugh on my behalf." Somehow John held the grief at bay. "Now bring him home, if you will." He turned to William. "Ride back to Ellestoun. Tell them to open the gates and offer these men our hospitality. And find my mother. Tell her that Father's come back to us."

* * *

The casket was laid on a table in the nave of Saint Bryde's.

"Open it." Lady Elizabeth jostled close.

John held her back. "Let me do this."

One of the chaplains took her arm and tried to lead her away, but she pulled free. "Thomas!" Her cry rang out as the seals were chiselled open.

The stench of decay rolled out from within, and John's stomach heaved. He steeled himself, concentrated instead on pulling the lid away. The lead sheet clattered against the bright tiled floor, but he was scarcely aware of it.

The corpse lay neatly wrapped in its linen shroud. The priest pulled at the cloth concealing the dead man's face, then fixed John in a long, sober stare. "It's Sir Thomas."

"Let me see!" Lady Elizabeth Ross called.

John delicately loosened the bindings a little more. He shivered at the sight of his dead father. The corpse had been sealed in its coffin for three months, but it was as if it had been placed there yesterday. The proud profile was as John remembered it, the hair that same fading mane of golden-brown. With his eyelids closed over the voided sockets beneath, it was as if Sir Thomas Sempill were caught in a deep sleep.

"Thomas. . ." His mother clutched John's arm. "It's a miracle!"

But the false bloom of life was fading fast, the dead man shrinking and dwindling before their eyes.

"Come on now," John said. He wanted her to be gone before the reunion was spoiled by harsh, inevitable decay.

She shrugged him aside. "No, John. I'll sit with him a while. Leave me, please. I want to be alone."

* * *

It was a dank, cold night. The sky was black with cloud, but occasionally John glimpsed the star-flecked heavens.

Lights still burned within the distant chapel.

His horse faltered at the ford. He spurred it gently forwards and it ventured cautiously out into the water. His mother's palfrey balked alongside, but when he clicked his tongue the beast reluctantly followed.

Leaving the horses at the gate of the kirkyard, John hurried inside.

His mother knelt by the open coffin, hands locked about her rosary, head bowed. He'd never seen her look so tired, her shoulders sagging, her face etched deep with despair.

John crouched alongside. "It's late."

She looked up, face streaked with tears. "I don't want him to be alone."

"He's not alone. He's with God. And his ancestors." He straightened. "Come on," he said, tugging her arm, gently. "You'll catch your death. Would you have me bury both my parents within a week?"

She seized his arms and hauled herself up. "Goodbye." Her face crumpled. "Oh, Thomas. How could you leave me?"

"Hush now." John held her close while her sobs subsided. "He wouldn't want this."

She took his hands and gazed into his face, desperate, hopeful. "Twenty-six years we were married." She sounded lost. "I loved him, John. I loved him."

* * *

"They were Montgomerie's men," Elizabeth Ross said, as they rode back through the darkness to Ellestoun.

"Lord Hugh was at Caldwell. I told him I wanted my father back."

"Hugh Montgomerie won't grant favours for nothing," she retorted. "What did he demand in return?"

"My forgiveness."

She drew a sharp breath. "Don't be lured by his promises. He's a serpent."

"I know that."

"Don't be so complacent!" Her tone was agitated. "I know what he's capable of. Do *you*?"

"He'll do what he can to make sure I stay impartial."

"He'll trap you, John! And you won't know it till it's too late." She sighed loud in the night. "I just hope to God it's not too late already."

* * *

October, and Parliament had gathered in the tolbooth at Edinburgh. It was a respectable turnout, given the circumstances; the benches were crowded with the red-robed figures of the assembled Lords of Parliament.

Hugh slid forward on the bench and tapped Matthew Stewart's shoulder. Matthew took the hint and leaned back. "Interesting," Hugh whispered. "Bishop Elphinstone's here."

Matthew squinted round to face him. "Archbishop Scheves, too."

"And did I see Lord Carlyle?"

"You did. Keith's come along for good measure."

"Give them credit, Mattie. They're bold."

Matthew arched his brows. "Won't do them any good though."

Hugh smiled at that.

"Do you think they'll keep their mouths shut?" Matthew asked.

"Scheves and Keith?" Hugh stifled a laugh. "I don't think so. I've seen more sense in drunken nuns."

"Has Earl Patrick sought you out?"

"I only reached my lodgings last night."

"He'll send for you."

"Good news, I hope."

"Oh, yes." Matthew faced the front once more, as the call went out for the day's proceedings to begin.

Hugh concealed a yawn. He was bored already.

But no sooner had he resigned himself to a long debate about nothing, than an unexpected voice called out across the chamber, "Your Grace, might we open the proceedings with a discussion about what happened at Stirling last June?"

It was Archbishop Scheves of Saint Andrews. He stood tall, proud, amongst the seated clergy, a vibrant figure in his episcopal robes.

"All in good time." Patrick Hepburn stared back across the tolbooth.

"There's no time like the present," Keith added from the peers' benches. "We have concerns. We want them addressed as soon as possible."

James stirred. "My lords," he said, before Hepburn could speak out. "We've had our differences, but we must work together now. For the benefit of this realm. If you have concerns, then you must air them." He cast a warning glance at Hepburn, who stood stiff with disapproval alongside.

104

Keith stood up and bowed his head, briefly. "I'm speaking for those who aren't here today, the heirs of those lords and barons who died defending your father. I want an assurance that these men won't be punished for their fathers' loyalty. I want an assurance that these men will be granted their inheritance."

"These men are the offspring of traitors!" someone called.

Ahead, Matthew folded his arms and sat back with a comfortable sigh. Hugh clasped his hands before him and studied the floor, trying not to smile. The hairs on the back of his neck were prickling already.

It was going to be a long week.

* * *

"A fair decision," John Stewart leaned across the table and poured more wine into Hugh's goblet.

"And a lucrative one," Hugh agreed. "Why, once each dissenter's paid his brieve of service, His Grace'll hardly notice the dint in his Treasury."

"Good time to be a Sheriff." Matthew said.

"Or a Bailie." Stewart was smiling slightly. "How many of Cunninghame's people fought for King James, Hugh?"

"Each and every one of them." Hugh tried not to sound too gleeful.

"So you'll collect twenty pounds from all of them? Wouldn't hurt to ask for another thirty on top of that. Just to cover the costs."

"Kilmaurs can afford more."

"Much more," said Matthew.

"I'll have the new guest range built at Eglintoun yet," Hugh said, then added, "It's a pity you can't enjoy these rewards yourself."

"All in good time." Stewart sat back in his chair as the servants set a roast fowl upon the table. "Matthew, the meat if you please."

"Certainly." Matthew rose to carve.

"We thank God for his generosity." John Stewart bowed his head and clasped his hands upon the table. "And hope He will continue to provide."

"Amen," said Hugh and Matthew together.

"To us." Stewart raised his goblet. "The Lords of the Westland."

* * *

Another long day of debate drew to an end, and they filed out from the crowded tolbooth.

"About our last meeting." Earl Patrick fell into step alongside Hugh. "You were right to be aggrieved."

"And?"

Hepburn glanced cautiously about him, but the peers and barons were more interested in retiring to their lodgings than eavesdropping on affairs of state. "Master Colville and myself discussed the matter, then raised it with the King. Obviously, we can't make you Justiciar now Lyle's in office-"

"This is old ground. Let's not churn it up again."

"We have something better in mind."

"What, exactly?"

"We anticipate trouble in the Westland. We want it nipped in the bud."

"There are procedures."

"Not anymore." A smile slid across Hepburn's lips. "We're granting you special powers. No need to wait for the assizes. Just mete out justice as you see fit. Use fire and sword, if necessary."

"In Cunninghame?"

"No. Throughout the Westland. Cunninghame, Kyle and Carrick. Renfrew. And the Lennox, too."

The scale of it all was breathtaking. For once, Hugh was lost for words.

"You were an obvious choice, Hugh. We need a man who's strong, forthright."

Hugh chuckled, deep in his throat. "No need to flatter me."

"The fines can be set at your discretion. And, as a token of our goodwill, we'll grant you the Royal lands of Arran. They're yours, for life-rent."

"I'm overwhelmed."

"I said you'd be rewarded in due course. You're not disappointed?"

"Oh no," said Hugh. "Most certainly not."

* * *

"—We can't rely on men who took up arms against the King to defend his interests in the assizes," Hepburn said. "We propose that all hereditary Sheriffs who fought for King James the Third should be removed from office, and not re-instated until His Grace the King agrees to it—"

Matthew turned around and beckoned to Hugh. "An excellent suggestion," he whispered. "Scheves looks sick at the thought, but he's hardly in a position to argue."

"Furthermore—" Hepburn continued, "—those who inherit their Sheriffs' titles from men who died at the field of the Sauchie Burn will be removed from office for three years, or until His Grace the King decides that they are to be restored—"

Scheves leapt to his feet. "Outrage!"

"Ah," Matthew sighed. "They'll be looking for a man to replace Sempill of Ellestoun."

"Your father, perhaps?"

Matthew's smile grew more entrenched. "Looks like you won't be alone in reaping rich rewards."

Chapter 17
The Place of Ellestoun, November 1488

It had rained almost solidly for three days, but that morning the sweeping sheets of water dwindled to a drizzle. The kye stood shin-deep in mud; soon they'd be brought inside for the winter. The geese and the swans were returning, another sign that the cold weather was on its way.

Despite the foul weather, life had to go on. John hunted when he could, bringing home deer and hares and wildfowl for the pot.

But the winter was already taking its toll.

The hound lay upon a mound of straw, eyes half-closed, ribcage heaving. John crouched beside it, stroking its head, gently. The beast tried to lick his hand, but barely had enough strength to move.

Two nights they'd nursed it, dropping warm milk into its mouth and wrapping it in blankets. To no avail; the weight had dropped off it and now the waste ran like stinking water from its rear.

"She's dying," Henry looked close to tears.

"Are the others alright?"

"So far."

"Master John?" It was William.

"Make her comfortable," John instructed Henry. "And stay with her until it's over." He rose to his feet. "What's the matter?"

"It's the King's men."

* * *

"John Sempill of Ellestoun?" The name was barked out like a challenge as the horseman charged through the gate. His armour was covered with a fine mist of water, his bright yellow jupon rain-damp and mud-stained.

"Aye, that's right." John recognised his visitor. It was Matthew Stewart, son and heir of Sir John Stewart of Darnley. "How can I help you?"

Stewart gave him a look of undisguised contempt. It wasn't entirely his fault; the lift of his eyebrows and the line of his mouth made him seem insolent. "I'm here with Bute Pursuivant," he said. "We've come to defend the King's interests in Renfrew."

"You think we're incapable of doing that ourselves?"

Stewart didn't deign to reply.

"Please," John gestured half-heartedly to the door. "Come inside. You can rest a while before you continue on your way."

The herald looked visibly encouraged. He was about to reply when Matthew Stewart spoke out. "That won't be necessary. We'll return to Paisley, soon as we can, where we'll find more comfortable lodgings."

"If you're so anxious to be on your way," John retorted, "then deliver your message from here and be done with it."

"This isn't good weather for travelling," Bute Pursuivant interjected. "It's not my place to speak for the Master of Lennox, but. . . I'd be grateful for some warmth in my bones."

Scowling, Stewart shrugged.

"I'll show you to the hall." John beckoned to William. "Warm some wine. I should be courteous, even if Master Stewart doesn't know the meaning of the word. Oh—" He broke off, then added, quietly, "The sword. . . The Sheriff's sword. It's hanging in the hall. It must come down. See to it please."

*　*　*

John stalled for time as best he could. He paused on the threshold to ask how His Grace the King was keeping, then loitered on the stair to enquire about their journey.

Until he could delay their entrance no longer. He opened the door to the hall and showed them inside.

The wall of warmth hit them right away. Bute Pursuivant planted himself before the fire with a martyred sigh, holding his hands towards the flames.

Matthew Stewart, meanwhile, wandered around the room. Studying the tapestries and examining the best plates in the aumbry as if he already had a God-given right to treat the place as his own.

John glanced towards the wall where the Sheriff's sword of office should have had pride of place. A tell-tale ghost of its presence could be seen, a clean dark patch on the wooden panelling beneath.

As for William. . . He stood next to the curtain that closed off the privy, hands clasped behind him, a guarded look on his face.

"So," John said, warmly, as one of the servants entered, bearing a flagon of steaming wine and some goblets. "The King's at last sent word?"

Stewart said nothing. He'd spotted the trace of the sword in the panelling. He examined it intently, frowning.

The herald offered John an apologetic smile. "Indeed he has, Master Sempill. I've brought news for yourself in particular." He pulled a roll of parchment from the pouch at his belt. "Shall I read it to you, sir?"

John snatched it. "No, thank you. We're not entirely uncivilised here in the Westland." As he broke open the seal he noticed that Stewart was smirking to himself.

John's fingers shook as he unrolled the parchment. The words were scrawled in Latin, he stared at them, concentrating. . .

Matthew Stewart sighed.

The sound distracted him; John looked up, glowering.

Stewart stared back. "We'll announce it if you like. Saves us being here all day."

John shrugged aside the jibe and kept on reading. What he saw was reassuring. He was to keep his father's lands, providing he paid the King twenty pounds. It was a significant sum, but it wasn't an impossible one.

He'd escaped quite lightly.

"You have seven days." Stewart said. "I'll return then for the required payment of two hundred pounds. If it's not paid in full, then the Sheriff will seize whatever goods or livestock's needed to make up the difference."

"What?" John frowned, wondering for a moment if he'd misheard.

"Must I repeat myself?"

"No, of course not." He wanted to argue, but knew already there was no point in trying. "You mentioned the Sheriff."

"Parliament has decreed that the traitors who fought the King aren't capable of upholding his laws. You're no longer the Sheriff, Master Sempill. You won't be for at least three years." He wandered round the hall again. "After that, who knows? It depends how you conduct yourself."

"Who'll replace me?"

"My father, the Earl of Lennox." Stewart halted before him. "You'll answer either to him, or to myself, for I'm the Sheriff-depute."

John blinked, fighting back the panic.

"Seven days." Stewart jabbed a finger into John's chest.

At that indignity, fear gave way to anger. "I heard you the first time," John snapped. "Get out of my house!"

* * *

"Don't look so hard done by," said Stewart, as he settled into the saddle. "Your kinship with Montgrennan is enough to have you hanged." He tightened his reins. "It might still be, if you don't co-operate." His horse sprang off down the hill at a canter with the herald and the escorting men-at-arms close behind.

John watched them go.

It was only then he realised his hand was gripping his dagger-hilt, so tight his fingers ached. He opened his fist and turned around, to see the entire household watching. Men-at-arms loitered on the wall-walk, cooks peered out from the kitchens. And in the midst of them all was his mother.

His head throbbed. He wanted to tear the King's letter into tiny pieces and stamp it into the slippery mud.

"What did he say?" Lady Elizabeth demanded.

"Two hundred pounds!" He crushed the offending parchment in his fist. "Where in the name of God will I find two hundred pounds?"

He broke off. He'd never lost his temper like that before. The servants glanced nervously at him and at each other. He wondered what had upset them most, the bad news or the way he'd reacted to it.

His mother dropped her face into her hands. "By the saints, John. We're ruined."

Chapter 18

A dozen men in plate mail were lined up beyond the gates. Most bore the Darnley livery: a chequered blue-and-white bar on a gold ground. But some wore the diagonal gold-and-red stripes of Lord Lyle.

Matthew Stewart sat at the head of the party, face hardened by a scowl.

"So Matthew's in charge," John said to William.

"A young hound being trained for his first kill," William replied.

An appropriate comparison, for Matthew wasn't alone. Behind him sat Robert, Lord Lyle. He was familiar enough, even without the livery; a thin-faced, sullen-looking man. And next to him was the Earl of Lennox himself, a battered old knight, stern and solid on his horse.

"God," John whispered to William. "Look at them. Am I really worth that?"

"I should take it as a compliment."

Matthew Stewart advanced. "John Sempill of Ellestoun? We've come on behalf of His Grace the King to receive your payment. Open the gates."

"I have the money," John replied. It was easy to sound bold, though his guts churned with terror. "I have the twenty pounds that His Grace requested."

"That's not enough."

"It's all you're getting!"

"You're defying us?" Matthew Stewart couldn't hide his incredulity.

"Yes, I am." He felt oddly calm inside.

"You're a fool!" Stewart raged. "We want our payment. We won't leave until we get it!"

"Then you'll be waiting a long time." John gripped the edge of the parapet wall. He had to appear unbreakable. If the Stewarts saw a hint of weakness, then all was lost. "Pitch your tents and get on with it. You'll break first, I assure you."

His men cheered at that. They thumped their spear butts down upon the wall-walk so hard the timbers shook.

"Master Sempill." It was the Earl himself. "I admire a man of courage when I see one. But only a fool would take on a fight he can't win."

"I'd be more of a fool to pay you. Who's to say you won't be back next week asking for more?"

"Two hundred pounds. That's all we ask." The Earl's voice was soft.

"You don't want two hundred pounds. You want to bleed me dry."

"That's ridiculous!" Then Lennox added, more gently, "Come now, Master Sempill. We're not vindictive. As a token of my good intent, I'll give you two more days. You can deliver yourself up to Lord Lyle's place at Duchal or my own place at Cruikston with your payment."

"I won't do it."

"You're an insolent whelp. You deserve all that's coming to you," Lennox steered his horse around. "Come on, we've wasted enough time here."

Matthew loitered, red-faced with fury. "We'll soon crush your arrogance," he called. "You'll be on your knees begging for mercy by the time we've finished with you." He kicked his horse in the ribs; it leapt away.

Ellestoun's garrison jeered as he departed.

"Least we gave as good as we got," said William.

"They'll probably be back on the morrow. Along with a small army."

"Not the best time of year to beseige a castle. Lennox knows that. He's no fool."

"But he'll think I just took him for one." John leaned against the rough stone of the parapet and closed his eyes. The wind whipped cold in his hair, he found himself wondering if he'd even live to see the spring. "Ah, William," he said. "What in God's name have I done?"

* * *

There was no besieging army camped outside Ellestoun's walls the following day. Nor the day after that, so when the burgesses of Renfrew summoned John for a meeting in the town, he rode out that same afternoon.

The following morning, he made his way into the tolbooth.

"Have you heard the news?" Master Mossman's broad face shone moist with concern.

"About our new Sheriff? Oh yes, his son rubbed as much salt into my wounds as he possibly could."

"It's intolerable! Paisley's request to become a burgh has been approved by the Pope. Now His Grace makes things by worse by demanding a tax. A token of our loyalty, they said, but we paid our taxes in July."

"It's small consolation, I know, but he's demanded similar payments from his lairds."

"As for his emissaries!" Mossman choked. "We explained our grievances to the Master of Lennox. He was most dismissive. He cares nothing for Renfrew."

"He cares nothing for any of us. His prime concern is filling his coffers." John stepped up onto the dais, and filed his way past the burgesses to the chair that had been set aside for him. Sir William Cunninghame of Craigends sat nearby; John nodded to him in passing.

Mossman hammered on the table. "Quiet, please. The Sheriff's here now."

The Sheriff. Even now, they insisted on giving John his rightful title. It was so typical of Renfrew. Their traditions had been upended, and yet they still insisted on carrying on as if nothing had changed.

At once, the floor erupted. "I had goods impounded by the Bailies last week!" one merchant complained. "They said I hadn't paid duty on it. But the duty was paid up six weeks ago—"

"Some Stewart men-at-arms stopped me and demanded a groat to let me take my beasts to market," another called. "They said that if I didn't give them the money, they'd take the pick of the herd instead."

"Enough!" Mossman called. "We'll deal with your grievances, one at a time. To be blunt, Master Sempill. We fear for the future. They want to punish us for our loyalty. They've given us a Sheriff who's more sympathetic to Dumbarton and they want Paisley to prosper at our expense."

John looked round the faces, marvelling at the transformation; the normally mild-mannered burgesses were restless with rage and injustice.

All except Master Montgomery, who sat there stone-faced.

"I know what you intend," said John. "As your Sheriff I support you wholeheartedly. Withhold the taxes! And suspend the wappenschaws. Don't co-operate with His Grace the King until he sends an intermediary you approve of." He had to shout to be heard. "Rest assured that throughout the land barons and burgesses will be doing likewise. Myself included; His Grace won't be getting a penny from me until he treats me like a loyal liege, not a traitor!"

Craigends slouched in his chair. He beckoned to John, a faint smile on his face. "Well done, Master Sempill," he said. "You've put the iron to the touch-hole now. Cunninghame's in chaos, and Renfrew won't be far behind. They've lost the Westland for sure."

John glanced towards Master Montgomery. The old man looked regretful.

The flush of excitement faded.

Treason. There was no other word for it. Before, they'd have been hard-pushed to find a reason to hang him.

Now he'd given them just the excuse they needed.

* * *

"A warband!" the sentry called. "I saw light catch a spear."

"Lock the gates!" John crossed the yard at a run. He sprang up to the wall-walk, William close behind him. "And bring crossbows!"

It was six days since he'd turned the Stewarts away from Ellestoun. John leaned against the parapet; the stone felt reassuringly solid beneath his hands. Men shouted to one another, making final preparations for the onslaught. The gates creaked closed; there was a comforting thud as a solid length of timber was drawn across to bar them.

Soon men-at-arms lined the wall-walk, crossbows ready.

"What do you reckon?" John asked William. "A score?"

"More, by the looks of it."

"Can't see any livery." He wondered if he should tell the cooks to boil up some fat. But something didn't ring true. He drummed his fingers against the stonework, thinking. . . "They've come from the west. From Beith. Or Kilwinning. . ." He paused. "Why would Lennox do that?"

His eyes settled on the horse that cantered smoothly in the vanguard. It was a great big grey. . . "They're not Stewarts. They're Montgomeries."

His men exchanged uneasy glances.

William voiced their concerns first. "Then what're they doing here?"

John shrugged.

The horsemen climbed up the hill towards Ellestoun. He counted them; *thirty-five, thirty-six, thirty-seven. Christ Almighty, he's brought a small army. . .*

"He's Lennox's kinsman," William muttered.

The warband halted; the grey stallion approached alone.

"Hello!" Lord Hugh waved as he rode brazenly up to Ellestoun's walls. If it hadn't been for the horse, it would have been hard to recognise him; he was arrayed in lightweight field armour, shabby and battered from hard use. "I've caught you unawares, Master Sempill."

"I'm surprised, certainly." John beckoned to his men. "Lower your arms!"

They reluctantly obeyed.

"So. . ." John called to Montgomerie. "What does the Lord of Montgomerie want with the Sempills?"

Lord Hugh leaned on his pommel, considering his reply. "I ask a favour, Master Sempill."

"Ask away." It was hard to muster much enthusiasm; Montgomerie's manner was too cheerful for his liking. "But don't wait outside like a stranger." He signalled to the men in the yard. "Open the gates!"

"They outnumber us threefold," William said, as the armoured horsemen poured in.

"He sent Father home," John replied. "What else can I do?"

* * *

The yard bristled with Montgomeries; John picked a careful course through their midst, searching for Lord Hugh's dappled grey steed. The scent of lathered horses and sweating men was heavy in the air.

He spotted the Spanish horse at last. "This is an unexpected pleasure," he told Lord Hugh.

Montgomerie was about to reply when a shutter clattered open above. They looked up, to see Elizabeth Ross peering down.

"Lady Elizabeth!" Lord Hugh bowed his head. "You're keeping well?"

The shutter slammed closed once more.

"The wounds are still raw." John grasped the grey horse's reins. It blew through its nostrils wearily and rested its velvet muzzle in his hand. "Thank you. For what you did."

"I was glad to assist," said Montgomerie. "One good turn deserves another. I thought you might help me in return."

"What do you want?"

"Hospitality, for two nights." Lord Hugh spoke lightly, but his eyes were cold as a snake's.

John scratched the horse's forehead with a sigh. *What can I do? To turn away a traveller who comes seeking shelter for the night is unforgivable.*

Even if he's come to wage war on a neighbouring estate. . .

"Tell your men to dismount," John said. "They're welcome at Ellestoun. They may stay as long as they wish."

* * *

That afternoon, an extra table had to be brought into the hall. Throughout the meal, William played his lute, but for once the music could scarcely be heard over the laughter and talking.

John shared his platter with Lord Hugh, while Lord Hugh's brother James and his cousin, John Montgomerie of Hessilhead, sat close by. Lady Elizabeth was conspicuous by her absence.

Today Montgomerie didn't entertain them with cheerful anecdotes about court life. Instead, he sat sullen and silent at John's side.

But Lord Hugh's kinsmen were better company. They discussed the weather, the recent harvest, and the breeding of hounds; mutual interests guaranteed not to offend.

They'd scarcely started the last few dishes when Lord Hugh took up his cloth and dabbed it against his lips. "A fine meal," he said. "I'd remain a little longer, but I'm tired."

"The range should be warm now," John told him. "I'll send a man there with you, if you like."

"That won't be necessary," Lord Hugh replied. "Tomorrow, I'll break fast with my men. There's a chapel nearby, isn't there?"

"Saint Bryde's. It's just across the river. I'll be taking mass there in the morning."

"I'll come with you. I want to pay my respects to your father. And I need to make my peace with God, just in case. . ." He drew his gown close with a sigh.

John shrugged.

"Of course, you're welcome to join me," Montgomerie added, and no trace of fragility remained. "There's few pleasures on earth that can match the thrill of the chase."

"I've had a bellyful of war just recently."

"You weren't with me then." Montgomerie slid from the bench and beckoned to his kinsmen; while they extricated themselves, he gripped John's shoulder. "My thanks," he said, "for being such a gracious host."

Chapter 19

Lord Hugh was an incongruous sight when he strode into the chapel the following morning. He was already arrayed for battle, though he at least had the decency to come before God unarmed. He stared single-mindedly at the shining glory of the altar and murmured the words of the liturgy with careful precision, then, when the time came, he knelt before the altar and took the Eucharist.

Watching Montgomerie, John's thoughts wandered. He wondered how a man could be so determined to follow his own path that he became impervious to others' distress. And how he could then remain so dedicated to his faith.

It was a contradiction which Montgomerie thrived on.

Ah, Holy Mary, grant me skills and prowess like his own. His enemies call him a tyrant, but he's good to his kin and his tenants. He must be, for them to follow him so blindly.

He looked up to see Lord Hugh fold his hands in prayer as he accepted the blessing of the priest.

As the priest lifted his hand, Lord Hugh glanced to the door. His eyes shone bright, his nostrils flared. A strange feral smile tugged at his lips.

The singing faded. Outside, the rattle of hooves grew louder.

* * *

Montgomerie straightened his helmet as his sword-belt was buckled into place. "We'll return by evening," he said. "Keep some food, if you can."

"I'll do that," said John. He stepped aside, as Hessilhead brought the grey horse close.

"Are you content?" Hessilhead asked.

"Yes. All's well." Lord Hugh clambered onto the horse and took the reins. "Let's be off then!" he called. "Sooner we go, sooner we return." Drawing his sword, he waved it high. "*Garde bien*, men! For honour and justice!"

He cantered off up the road, forty men in close pursuit.

John frowned. Only six were liveried; the Laird of Hessilhead, and five of his men. The rest, including Lord Hugh, were not.

"It's been a very bad year." The priest spoke softly at his side. "And I think the worst is yet to come."

"Pray for us, Father," said John. "Pray for all of us. We'll need God's help and strength if we're to survive the months ahead."

* * *

A mile from Glengarnock, they paused.

"You're happy to do this?" Hugh asked.

"As long as that rogue Craigends gets a hiding," Hessilhead replied.

"We'll be there."

"I know." Hessilhead grinned. "The look on his face will be priceless."

"I can't wait to see it," Hugh reached for his cousin's hand. "God be with you."

115

"And you." Hessilhead briefly gripped Hugh's fingers.

* * *

Hugh halted close to the fringes of the woodland with twenty of his men. Horses stamped and snorted, twigs snapped as heavy hooves crunched through the leaf litter. They were safe from casual observation; with no livery to mark them, the dull grey of plate armour and the muted browns of studded leather brigandines just merged into the leafless trees.

From here they had a good view of Glengarnock Castle. It was an old stronghold, built on a rocky promontory high above the River Garnock. Too well-placed for all but the most determined attacker.

Hugh watched the small band of Montgomeries approach the castle. He knew how the scene would play itself. Hessilhead, on Hugh's behalf, would announce the warrant for Craigends' arrest.

The pronouncement was made; the gates remained stubbornly closed. The Montgomeries went back the way they'd come.

Hugh's grey stallion stirred impatiently.

At the ramshackle settlement that sprawled across the hillside Hessilhead's men faltered. Three headed straight for an animal pen, cutting open the gates and freeing the beasts within.

Hugh heard his cousin's shouts and smiled.

As the hue-and-cry went up, some farmers came running, pitchforks held ready. Hessilhead still roared out orders, a man at his wit's end.

Hugh stretched in his stirrups. *Not yet. Not yet. . .*

Glengarnock's gates creaked open, chains rattled loud as the drawbridge dropped. Hooves thundered against the timbers as the Cunninghames sent men out to finish the work their tenants had started.

Ten of them, no more than that.

Hugh pulled his sword from its scabbard and held it high. His men's eyes were on him. He could almost taste their anticipation. His heart beat loud. He knew this feeling well; the heady rush that always fuelled him through the fray. He closed his eyes, briefly savoured it.

His eyes flicked open.

The Montgomeries in the fermtoun below turned tail and fled. They headed up the hill, pursued by the Cunninghames.

A smile crept across Hugh's lips, he breathed deep. "*Garde bien*, Montgomeries!" He sliced the air with his sword.

His horse surged downhill at a canter. Men shouted, joining the charge. The pace picked up, Hugh threw back his head and laughed; he rode the crest of an armed wave that swept aside all in its path.

The beleaguered Montgomeries raised their weapons and cheered, while the Cunninghames faltered.

Craigends was amongst them: Hugh homed in on him like a hawk after the lure.

He'd been spotted; Craigends drew his sword and urged his horse towards him. But wisdom got the better of valour. Craigends hesitated, then rode straight for one of Hessilhead's lightly-armoured men-at-arms.

Hugh set off in pursuit. But two Cunninghame men-at-arms were moving in to block him, swords drawn.

Hugh cursed and hauled upon the reins. He roared loud and rode straight at one. At the very last moment, he attacked the other. He swept his sword around in a smooth arc, taking the sword arm clean off and biting deep into the torso beneath.

A man screamed, but Hugh scarcely heard it. He wrenched the blade free and turned his horse.

The other man-at-arms was already fleeing.

Hugh scanned the melee, looking for Craigends. There he was, fighting alongside one of his retainers.

"Craigends!" Hugh bellowed. "I'm here for *you*. Face me, you coward!"

Craigends glanced towards him, face ashen white. He wheeled his horse around and galloped towards Glengarnock's walls.

Hugh followed, his grey stallion moving so fast its hooves hardly touched the ground. Its snorts blasted loud in his ears; he sat light in the saddle, at one with the horse, mesmerised by the sound of its breathing.

Almost there. He leaned forward, lifted his sword. He could almost hack off the fleeing horse's tail. . .

Glengarnock's curtain wall loomed closer.

Craigends' mount put in one last burst of speed. It reached the drawbridge, hooves thudding loud across the timbers.

Hugh shouted out, frustrated. Then realised that he'd ventured too close.

He peeled away just in time. A shower of arrows pierced the spot where he'd been a moment or so before.

He trotted up and down the length of the wall, a tantalising target. The arrows rained down, feet away. "When I catch you," he called after Craigends. "I'll slit your belly and hang your guts like ropes around your neck!" He halted. One touch from his spurs and the grey stallion reared high, lashing out with its hooves. "Sir Humphry Cuninghame?"

"Damn your black soul, Hugh Montgomerie!" The Laird of Glengarnock watched from the wall-walk. He was a bent old man. Married to a Montgomerie, too, but Hugh wasn't going to let that little detail deter him. "May God preserve my kinsmen from your so-called justice."

"Stop playing the innocent, Sir Humphry. You're harbouring a felon."

"That's nonsense!"

"Tell your Godless kinsman Craigends that this is just a taste of what's to come. If I ever catch him thieving on my lands I'll have him quartered and his four pieces hung from the ports at Irvine!"

* * *

With the fight in progress, James Montgomerie arrived with the last of his men.

Now every rick, byre and house was alight.

The livestock had been loosed before the burning; cattle and sheep, many heavy with next year's calves and lambs, and a few thickset ponies, too. Anxious farmers tried in vain to round them up. But the mounted soldiers cut past them, shouting, whistling, waving their spears. Some beasts lost their reason entirely, galloping straight for the ravine that ran beyond the castle.

Hugh picked a careful course through the fermtoun. The air around him shimmered with heat, the sound of women wailing bombarded him from all sides. They screamed and wept, they called him a devil and cursed the ground he walked on.

In the heart of the fermtoun he stopped. He breathed deep, savouring the scent of burning thatch and timber. Orange light danced across his armour; fire lit the dark depths of his horse's eyes.

His spirit soared with the flames. Here, amidst the destruction, he felt at one with the world.

Chapter 20

A pall of smoke hung over the hills to the west. Glengarnock was burning.

John took mass for the second time that day. But for once, the chanting, the music and the incense brought scant solace.

He gazed upon the altar. *You knew what he intended. If Cunninghame retaliates, you'll deserve whatever punishment he metes out.*

I had no choice. . .

There's always a choice. Women and children will starve and die because of what he did today. And it's all your fault. You gave him succour. . .

He bowed his head. Tears stung his eyes, he choked back a sob.

God forgive me. Have mercy on my soul.

* * *

It was a cold night.

John retired to his room after dinner. His favourite hounds, Caesar and Pompey, were sprawled next to the fire. He pushed them aside with his foot and pulled his chair closer. But not even that kept the chill at bay; he wrapped a thick fur-lined cloak about him and pulled his legs in close beneath its folds. He balanced a book in his lap; a well-leafed copy of Homer's account of the Siege of Troy. He'd arranged the candles so they cast light over his shoulders, but it was still almost too dark to read.

John persevered. Anything, to keep his mind off the Cunninghames' plight.

He found comfort in these tales of a more heroic age. Though on reflection, he wondered if it was right to relish the triumph of the Acheaens. It didn't seem very heroic to win Troy by treachery, breaching the walls inside a wooden horse.

The hounds sat up. Pompey barked, sharply.

There were voices outside and the gates creaked open. Hooves clattered loud, men's laughter rang out.

He closed the book and slipped out of his chair. Near to the window, the air grew markedly colder; he shivered and drew the cloak tighter.

John pulled back the shutter. He saw horses lit pale by the moonlight. The mist from their nostrils shone like dragons' breath.

With a sigh, he closed the shutter, holding back the night, and the nameless dangers it contained.

* * *

"Lord Hugh returned a good half-hour after the others," said William. "He took Confession down in the chapel."

"Has he eaten?"

"Yes. He's in the hall now. He wants to speak with you."

"Show him upstairs. And bring some wine."

William's footsteps dwindled down the stair.

119

John sank back in his chair with a sigh. It was a month since he'd climbed up to Adam's room at Caldwell, trying to look bold as he was summoned into Montgomerie's presence.

More footsteps on the stair, and William's voice. "Step inside, my lord."

The door opened and Lord Hugh entered. He looked tired, a little preoccupied. If John had been a small-minded man, he'd have made him wait a while, just to return the courtesy that had been granted to him on their last meeting.

Instead, he gestured to an empty chair alongside. "Good hunting?"

A smile sprang out of nowhere on Lord Hugh's face. "Oh, yes." He stepped carefully over the dogs. The scent of musk and rose water drifted out from him as he passed; he'd washed after the raid, but even now the stink of woodsmoke clung to him.

It befits a man of his hot temperament, John thought. *He'll belong to a sign of fire. The Lion, I'd guess. If his roar's anything to go by. Not to mention his vanity. . .*

"William's bringing wine."

"That would be most welcome." Lord Hugh hitched the sleeves of his gown carefully over the arms of his chair. Caesar and Pompey came to greet him; he rubbed their heads and pulled their ears while they laid their chins in his lap and wagged ecstatic tails in response.

"I must thank you, John," said Lord Hugh. "You granted me a rare luxury during my stay here."

"I wasn't aware that I granted you any luxuries at all."

"You allowed me to be myself." He paused. "You'll hear rumours," he said, "about what happened today."

John couldn't bring himself to look at him. "You asked for hospitality, nothing more."

"Your conscience is tormenting you, isn't it?"

John closed his teeth about his nail again.

"If it's any consolation, my soul is troubled, too," Montgomerie said. "I don't justify my actions to any man, but sometimes I must justify them to myself. And to God. . ."

"I don't know what you mean. . ."

"Oh yes, you do." He leaned close. "What's happened? Between you and the Stewarts?"

There was a knock at the door. Lord Hugh sat back, his eyes fixed upon the door, hands gripping his chair.

"It's only William," said John. "He can be trusted." He passed a goblet to Montgomerie, then took another for himself. "That's all. Thank you." He sipped his wine as William retreated. "I'll put it plain," he said. "They called here a week ago. They asked me to pay a brieve of service. His Grace wanted twenty pounds."

"But the Stewarts wanted more."

"Two hundred pounds."

"It's as I thought," said Lord Hugh. "They think you have Montgrennan's money."

"Hasn't it occurred to them that I might not?"

"Doesn't matter. Either way, they win. Either they return a portion of the King's missing treasure and earn his gratitude, or they ruin you and take your lands. What can possibly go wrong?"

"I turned them away. I told them they weren't getting a penny."

"My God!" Montgomerie surged forward in his chair, eyes bright. "Do you have any idea what you've done—"

"Yes, I do. . ."

"This is incredible!"

"I had no choice."

"How do you hope to defeat him?" Montgomerie asked.

"I have justice on my side."

"Justice has never won a conflict yet," Montgomerie reminded him. "Not without a mighty army to assist, at any rate."

"Is there any other answer? If I pay him, I'm finished. If I fight him, I'm finished. All I can do is stand firm. Some day the King'll see that I am loyal, that I'm the victim of an impartial judge."

Lord Hugh locked his hands before him and frowned at the floor. "It's easy to be self-righteous. But it's the innocents who'll suffer."

"I know."

"God help you. He's the only one who can."

"Can I ask you one thing, my lord?"

He shrugged slightly. "Ask away."

"You're his kinsman. If I make a stand against the Stewarts, will I also offend the Montgomeries?"

"The Montgomeries don't meddle in other mens' affairs."

"But the Earl may ask you to assist."

"If you're put to the horn, then the situation may change. And if there's armed rebellion, I'll be forced to quell it. But if order's maintained, I'll remain impartial. You should bear that in mind, if you commit yourself to other parties. . ."

Meaning Renfrew. He knows then, or he's guessed, at least, that they'll turn to me.

"You'll recognise, too, that I most certainly can't intervene," Montgomerie added. "But if you continue to assist me as I go about the King's business in the Westland, then you can be sure you'll win my tacit support."

"I did you a favour today, Lord Hugh. I wondered if you might return it."

"Ask away."

"The Crawfurds of Kilbirnie. They're my kin by marriage. I wondered if you'd collected the brieve of service. . ."

Montgomerie smiled. "There'll be no burdens placed upon the Crawfurds. You have my word on that." He glanced at the dogs. "They're splendid fellows."

"Caesar's five now. And Pompey's coming up for two. I reared them myself."

"I daresay the hunting's good."

"We're never short of quarry."

"We have a well-stocked deer park at Eglintoun. You should hunt there some time."

121

"That's a gracious offer, my lord." John rose from his chair. "The night's still young. William could entertain us. Or perhaps you'd prefer chess?"

Montgomerie slouched back and stretched out his legs; it was the first time John had seen him look so relaxed and comfortable. "I can't promise to do the game justice," he said. "But I'll try."

* * *

"I'm in your debt," said Lord Hugh, once he'd mounted his horse the following morning. "I don't forget those who help me."

"Your kind words are appreciated, my lord."

"It's scant comfort, I know, but it may ease your burden a little. You'll understand, though, that I can't intervene in your dispute with the Stewarts."

"Yes, of course."

"But I'll keep an eye on your situation, and do what I can to assist. It'll be a grim day for the Westland, if a Stewart makes gains at a lesser line's expense."

"God will settle the dispute as He sees fit."

"A noble sentiment. You can be sure I'll pray for you." Montgomerie stared out to the rolling hills beyond. "Back at Caldwell, you asked after the King."

"I didn't mean to cause offence."

"I've given the matter much thought. And I think it better you hear this from me. King James was murdered. Stabbed through the heart by a man disguised as a priest."

"I suspected as much," John said.

"The matter weighs greatly on His Grace's conscience." Lord Hugh took up the reins. "It's difficult to lose a father, whatever the circumstances. At least you know that Sir Thomas died with dignity and honour."

John didn't reply.

"When you mourn him, remind yourself that you're blessed compared with your King. He lives out his days knowing his father was murdered in his name. It's a heavy burden for any man, let alone one so young."

"I bear no malice towards him."

"I know that," Lord Hugh said. "Well," he added. "We'd best be on our way, if we're to reach Hessilhead before dinner." His horse stirred. "Move on, men!" As he passed through the gates, he raised his hand in farewell.

John returned the gesture, but Montgomerie didn't look back.

Chapter 21

The following day, another visitor appeared at John's door; Robert Crawfurd of Kilbirnie.

John hurried out to meet him. "Hello, Robert! How goes matrimony?"

Robert slid from his horse, grinning. He embraced John, warmly. "Life's never been so rich, John."

"It was worth the wait?"

"Oh yes."

"So what brings you to Ellestoun?"

"Father's sending us down to Easter Greenock. He thinks it's high time we learned the skills of running an estate."

"We won't be seeing much of each other then. It's a long hard road to Easter Greenock."

"You'll survive without me."

"What d'you mean?"

Robert shrugged. "It's said you're making new friends now." He glanced away. "Best not talk about it. Not when there's better news to share."

"Such as?"

The grin crept back. "We think she's with child."

"That's excellent news!" John seized Robert's hand. "Oh well done, Robert! Well done!" He steered Robert to the door. "You'll come upstairs, I hope? We can toast the health of mother and child?"

"I can't stay long. You wouldn't understand, but. . ." He blushed. "It's hard to be parted from her. She wanted to come here today. But Father wouldn't hear of it."

"She'll hate that. God knows how she'll take it when the lying-in's upon her."

* * *

They sat in the laird's chamber and talked a while. About Marion, and the times they'd shared together.

But there was something different about Robert Crawfurd. He seemed guarded, distant.

"John," he said at last, leaning forward with his goblet cupped in his hands. "We've known each other for years, and all that time we've called each other friends."

"Of course."

"You won't put that friendship aside lightly?"

"Why should I?"

"I've heard rumours. I wanted to hear your side of the story, before I made judgement. . ."

John was silent.

"You'll have heard the news?"

123

"No," John said. "I haven't."

"The Montgomeries attacked the Place of Glengarnock two days ago. They drew the Cunninghames out and set on them with a force much greater than their own. Eight Cunninghames were wounded, three died. The fermtoun was laid waste, the livestock slaughtered."

John couldn't bring himself to speak.

"It's said you welcomed Lord Hugh into your place while he planned the raid and carried it out." He looked John in the eye. "Is it true?"

"He stayed here, yes. But I didn't ask his business."

"Men are dead. And many more will starve. And yet you played a willing part in all of this!"

"I'm sorry about the Cunninghames." John gazed into the fire. "But he'd have attacked them anyway."

"God help you, John. Before your soul ends up as tainted as his." Robert grasped his shoulder. "You're treading a dangerous path. For all his charming words, he's no better than a wild beast." He squeezed his fingers tight. "Be careful. He'd stab you in the back without a second thought."

* * *

The Cottage of Nether Bar, November, 1488
* * *

The last of the spring calves were going to market. One final chance to earn some pennies before the lambs were born next spring.

Not that she'd see much of it.

"Mind you don't spend everything, Henry Hamill!" Mary called, as Henry clambered into the ox-cart.

"I'll spend *my* money how I like." Henry had been a handsome man, before the drinking made him red-faced and bloated. "And I won't have you telling me what to do. You're a scold, Mary White."

"This time, Johnny, leave him in the whorehouse!"

Her son smiled, feebly, from where he sat hunched alongside his uncle. He was a slight lad of twelve, still too young to speak out on her behalf.

"If you ask me," Henry said. "That damned husband of yours was lucky. Least in his grave he's granted peace." He goaded the oxen forward.

"God rot you, Henry!"

The cart creaked down the track.

Mary shivered. "You shouldn't take such nonsense from him," she told her sister. "He'll ruin us."

"Stood up to him once," Janet said. "I won't try again."

* * *

The kye were tied in their stalls; eight stocky black cows and a stately bull. They lifted curious eyes as Mary trudged through the byre.

"Patience," she told them, as they stamped and called for food. "You're not forgotten."

Mary sighed as she forked stained straw and dung from the byre. It was hard, to do a man's job about the place. Last year, they'd hired cottars, but since Hugh had died, money was tight.

She was coping, but only just. Janet was a great help; she kept the children fed and watered, while Mary did everything else.

As for Henry. . .

He'd always been a drunken layabout. But recently he'd grown worse; she reckoned it was because Hugh wasn't here to bully him into doing his fair share of the work. But when the time came to take the beasts to market, he changed. He'd swagger in and say, *It's a man's job to trade, Mary White. You just stay home and mind the wee ones.*

Each time he'd come home with scarcely a groat to his name. *Times are hard,* he always said. *Couldn't get any money for the kye. Was damned lucky to sell them at all. . .*

Mary stabbed the pitchfork into the dirty straw with renewed vigour.

If there'd been any justice in the world, God would have taken Henry and left her Hugh behind.

*　*　*

When the soiled bedding was piled high on the midden, Mary laid down fresh straw, then filled the mangers with hay. The kye had only been indoors a fortnight and were still fat with grass. All the cows were plump with calf; God willing, she'd have enough put by to buy more milk cows in the spring.

She filled the troughs with water. The sheep were next, and then it was back to the household chores.

She sank down onto the packed earth floor; she'd been on her feet since dawn and it was already well past noon.

Mary wiped a grimy sleeve across her eyes as tears gathered. Three months it had been since her husband had died. Sometimes, it still felt like she'd lost him yesterday.

Just one or two sobs at first, then they came thick and fast. She hugged her knees and moaned, rocking back and forth like a child roused from a nightmare.

*　*　*

That evening, Mary scarcely started her pottage when the dog barked in the yard. One thing was certain; it wasn't Henry returning.

Mary set the bowl down. "I'd best see what's amiss."

"Be careful!" Janet called.

Mary ventured out into the night, shivering as the cold hit her. The sky above was velvet-black, a full moon hung high overhead.

She tilted her head. More barking. And voices. Men called out, a woman screamed.

She whistled to her dog. It came skulking round the wall of the cottage, tail clamped low against its legs. Then it froze, hackles raised.

A rumbling growl awoke in its throat. It was staring down the track towards the village.

Mary pulled her cloak tighter. "Go on." She sounded much bolder than she felt. "See them off."

It bolted away.

A few moments' silence, then more frenzied barking. A man shouted. The barking stopped, there was a yelp, then nothing.

125

Suddenly anxious, Mary whistled to the dog. "Come back now!" she called. "Come home—"

She broke off.

She heard hooves, thudding in rhythmic unison. Harness jingled, a horse snorted.

They crested the hill. Firebrands bobbed in their hands. There were seven or eight of them; she could see their plate armour and the swords at their sides in the glow of the fire.

I have to fetch Janet. But her legs wouldn't move. She couldn't even find the strength to call out.

They rode into her yard and one of them trotted straight towards her. It wasn't courage that made her hold her ground; it was fear. She fixed her gaze on the big black horse, and swallowed.

He pulled the horse to a savage halt.

"What do you want with us, sir?" she whispered.

His visor was pushed up; she could see his face in the orange light of the torches. He was a tall, solid man, with heavy dark brows and a haughty, determined face.

"Mary?" Janet hailed her from the door.

"Wake your children," said the knight. "Get them outside."

You must be strong. For Janet. For the children. Mary took a deep breath. "Do as he says," she said, firmly. "Be quick about it."

The knight dismounted. He waited impatiently at the door. "Get out!" he said, and as Janet shepherded the young ones outside, he pushed her so hard she stumbled.

"No need for that!" Mary hurried to her sister's side and helped her stand.

"What's happening?" Janet asked.

"He's going to burn the house."

"But he can't!" Janet wailed. "What'll we do?"

"Get on with it." The knight sounded bored.

As the men-at-arms moved in and set the thatched roof alight, Janet screamed. The children started to howl.

Despite the noise and the smoke and the knowledge that their home was burning, Mary felt as if she were watching the scene unfold from afar. It wasn't *her* knees that trembled uncontrollably, it wasn't *her* throat that felt so tight she could scarcely breathe...

The young knight seized a torch and headed off towards the byre.

Somehow, she shook free of her stupor. She trotted after him. "For pity's sake, sir!" She seized his arm, clung to it. "Our beasts are in there!"

He turned on her, lip lifted in a warning snarl. "Don't you dare touch me!" He hurled her roughly aside.

She lay where she fell, fingers curled in the chilly mud. She watched in horror as he pushed back the door and hurled the torch inside. The cows called out, terrified, as the fire took hold.

"Come on, Mary." Janet crouched at her side. "On your feet."

"They're killing them." Her strength had gone, all she could think of was the suffering of the beasts. Tears ran hot down her face. She pulled herself to her feet, suddenly resolute. "I won't let them burn."

"Mary, no!" Janet held her firm. "Don't interfere."

Mary shrugged her aside. Picking up her skirts, she strode over to the knight. "Have you no shame?" she called. "Burning a poor widow from her home on a night like this?"

His horse loomed black and tall beside her, she could feel its breath hot against her face. "Save the complaints for your laird," the knight said. "He's defied the King; now you'll reap the consequences."

He rode off.

There was a soft sound of stone hitting flesh. The knight's horse squealed loud, and kicked out.

Mary turned to see her boy, Hughie, standing unrepentant alongside. There wasn't a flicker of fear on his face; he was only eight years old, too young to understand.

The knight saw him, too. "How dare you!" He spun his horse around and spurred it forward, mailed fist raised high.

"Leave him be!" She threw her arms around the child just in time.

The knight lashed out as he thundered past. His gauntlet struck the side of her head; lights flashed in brief brilliance before her eyes as she fell. Hooves pounded the ground close by; she tightened her grip about her son and curled up tight, praying for deliverance.

The hoofbeats receded. Mary lifted her face from the dirt, to see the young knight cantering after his companions.

She shook her head. Blood ran warm down her cheek, she could hear the cows groaning, bellowing, as the fire took them.

She scrambled to her feet. "I'm coming. . ."

Janet pulled her arm. "You mustn't!"

"I can't bear to hear them!"

"They're dying," Janet told her. "There's nothing you can do."

Mary closed her eyes, suddenly exhausted. Her limbs wobbled, she wept, as Janet held her and her children gripped her skirts.

With a groan the roof of the house collapsed, sending sparks shivering high into the night. The timbers of the byre were quick to follow.

At last the stricken cattle were silent.

* * *

"There was a whole army of them," the old man told John. "On great big horses. I thought they'd kill us all."

"Around eight, actually," the miller whispered in John's ear.

"Eight was enough," John replied.

"There was no stopping them," a woman added. "One of them was a knight. A young man, with a sneering look about him. *Tell your laird*', he says to my Davey, *This is nothing to what he'll get if he doesn't give what's owed.*'"

John sighed, and leaned against the old carved stone cross that stood at the heart of Pennald. William had woken him that morning to tell him the bad news.

He'd ridden out as soon as he could, with Alan and William and six of his men-at-arms.

As soon as word spread that the laird had come to see the damage for himself, they'd come flocking; men, women and children. They were bewildered and frightened, but hopeful.

In spite of everything, they still believed in him. He was humbled by it, and a little despondent, too. He wondered how long it would be before their feelings changed.

"What'll we do, Master Sempill?" the woman asked. "I've six bairns to feed."

"I won't let you starve," John told them. "As long as there's food in my stores, you're welcome to share it. Those who can should lodge with your kinfolk; Master Semple will provide you with flour and ale to feed the extra mouths. As for the rest of you. . . Make your way to Kenmure. We'll find lodgings for you there."

"What about our homes?" someone asked.

"No sense in rebuilding your cottages yet. Not until we settle our dispute with Master Stewart. We'd best wait and see how this plays itself."

* * *

"How many altogether?" John asked.

"Six cottages razed," said Alan. "Eight byres gone. And three-dozen ricks burned. Even where the kye survived there's no fodder to keep them."

"Pennald bore the brunt of it?"

"Pennald, and Bar."

"Bar. . ." John frowned. "Nether Bar is where Hugh Alexson lives."

"Lived, sir."

"Lived?"

"He died, Master John. Back in August."

* * *

A dead dog lay by the track that led to Nether Bar.

John dismounted. He crouched alongside the corpse and lifted its head. It was a rangy, ill-bred creature; it had been felled with a sword blow that hacked deep into its backbone.

"Poor beast," John said. "He tried his best to defend them." He retrieved his horse. "I hope you're proud of yourself, Alan. Hugh Alexson's widow is wandering out there in the cold. There's no roof over her head, and no husband to support her."

"My lord—"

"I was to be informed if Master Alexson died."

"I'm sorry, my lord." Alan bowed his head. "I thought there were more important things to concern you. Besides," he added, cautiously, "we paid for his funeral, and waived our claims to his property."

"I'm the one who'll judge what is and what isn't important. I promised that woman she'd be provided for. And now I've failed her."

"We'll find her, my lord."

"Make sure you do. And when she's found, you'll bring her before me. I'll decide then what's to be done with her. I don't want you making any more decisions on my behalf."

* * *

John cursed under his breath as he rode into Nether Bar. He remembered coming here on a sunny summer's day. There'd been a prosperous cottage with smoke seeping from its roof, and chickens scratching in the dusty yard.

Now all that remained of the cottage were its roof-couples, which stood proud like the ribcage of a rotting beast. The stench of burned wood and flesh was rank in the air. He had to take a handful of his cloak and raise it to his face to keep himself from retching.

Least the chickens are still here, John thought, as a sorry-looking hen picked its way over the smouldering remains of the house.

* * *

The more distance he put between himself and the ruin of Nether Bar, the more the despair and self-pity diminished.

In its place was cold, hard rage. The words circled in his head like a demented rosary: *He must not win. He will not win.*

"What are we to do, my lord?" asked Alan.

"This is arson," John said, tightly. "It's been committed in the King's name, but it's still a crime. We can't pay Lennox what he wants. And we can't fight him with arms. Our only recourse is the law."

"My lord. . . Given everything that's happened since King James died. To the Cunninghames, and now to yourself. . . Do you really think the law can help us?"

"We'll just have to hope and pray it will. It's our only hope of salvation."

Chapter 22
The Place of Eglintoun

"I don't know you keep your fingers nimble," said Hugh. "The air's perishing!"

"If it wasn't light, we couldn't see to sew," Helen retorted. "There'd be holes in your sarks and we'd never hear the end of it."

He was barely listening. Hugh was in one of his restless moods; as he knelt along the cushion beside her, he leaned his elbows on the ledge and took great interest in the mouldings round the window.

Helen left him to it. She was too busy making sure that Bessie's sewing was acceptable. Bessie perched at the other side of her: twelve years old, with a thick rope of black hair and Hugh's fine-boned look about her.

When Helen had first come here to Eglintoun, Hugh had thrust Bessie into her arms and earnestly explained that the child was his daughter by a mistress he'd once kept. Perhaps he'd expected a tantrum or a chilly silence; instead, Helen had just shrugged and smiled. She came from the north, and had no trouble treating Hugh's flesh and blood as her own.

Besides, it wasn't difficult to like Bessie. She wasn't particularly clever, but she was a pleasant soul; always cheerful and obedient, and a good sister to the boys.

"Is that alright?" Bessie asked.

Helen put down the garment she'd been stitching and examined Bessie's handiwork carefully. "It's splendid. Show your father."

Hugh was still in a world of his own. He frowned as he drew the shutter closed and opened it again. "Glass," he said.

Helen picked up her sewing once more. "Whatever are you talking about?"

"If they can have a glazed window in a humble parish church, then why shouldn't we have that luxury?"

"Because there's better things a man can spend his money on." Bessie still loitered by her side; Helen sent the girl on her way with a quick push on the rump.

"If you insist. . ." He had the grace to look impressed as Bessie presented her work. "How elegant!"

"Can I be excused now?" Bessie asked, plaintively.

"Don't ask me. Ask your mother."

Helen smiled at that. "Of course," she said. "You've worked very hard."

"Can I go out to see the deer?"

Hugh sprang to his feet and seized Bessie's shoulders. "We'll see the deer together. Just run along to the stables and have the horses saddled." He kissed her forehead. "Be off now. I'll be with you shortly."

Bessie skipped away with a delighted squeal. At the doorway, she paused. "What about John?"

"I think the poor lad's suffered the trials of Latin grammar for long enough," Hugh agreed. "I'll fetch him. We can take the ponies for a gallop."

* * *

Young John was just eight and his pony was half the size of Bessie's palfrey. But she held her horse firm as they galloped, and let the pony edge ahead as they thundered down towards the tree that marked the end of the race.

Their laughter rang loud through the parkland. "I won!" The Master of Montgomerie raised his fist high as they circled back to where Hugh and Helen awaited them.

"You earned your dinner then," said Hugh.

"Come along now!" Helen called. "You must wash and change your clothes before we dine."

"Why?"

"Because your mother says so," said Hugh.

They rode side by side behind the children.

"So what did the herald want with you?" Helen asked.

"I've been asked to spend Yuletide at Linlithgow, with His Grace the King."

"I thought that's what it would be," Helen said, wistfully.

"I'd rather stay here. With you." He looked sincere at least.

"No, you wouldn't."

He grinned at that. "You'll ride with me some day. We'll go to court together."

"I'd like that." She sighed. "I can't complain, though. I've had you to myself for the best part of a month."

"And you'll have me back again once the New Year's on us."

"You'll hurry home?"

It was that grin again. "Dragons and gryphons won't stop me." He steered the grey horse close and stretched his hand towards her.

She gripped his fingers, tightly.

As they rode though the gates, the steward came to meet them. "Forgive me for intruding, my lord," he said. "But a visitor arrived, just ten minutes ago."

Hugh groaned. "Ah, can't a man get any peace?"

"It's your cousin, the Master of Lennox," the steward explained.

"Matthew?" Hugh cast an anxious glance towards Helen. "What the Devil's he doing down here?"

* * *

"A penny for your thoughts," said Helen.

Hugh settled on the cushion beside her. "I was thinking of Renfrew."

"Mattie seemed very coy through dinner. What did he have to say for himself?"

"He stayed at Skelmorlie last night. He wanted to thank me for the hospitality. He said his business took him to the Sempill lands at Largs and Southannan."

"I would guess then," Helen said, quietly, "that he's not left much standing at Largs and Southannan."

"He's heard. About my little sojourn to Ellestoun. He was asking questions."

"I hope you were opaque in your answers?"

"Of course." Hugh pulled his knees close with a shiver. "But there's something else. He said the most curious thing. *Doesn't it concern you,* he said, *that there's none but Homes and Hepburns at the heart of our government?*"

"It's quite natural for him to feel left out in the cold. He's a Stewart. He'll think it only right that a Stewart's role is to be close to his kinsman the King."

"That's what worries me." Hugh laid himself down along the cushioned seat beside her. Resting his head in her lap, he closed his eyes. "He wants too much, too soon. He thinks the sun and stars should revolve around him."

"When we all know full well that the sun and the stars revolve around *you.*" She played with a lock of his hair, turning it over in her fingers.

He smiled.

"Mattie can look after himself," she said.

"Yes, I know."

"So what's worrying you, then?"

Hugh opened his eyes. "Oh, nothing much. . ."

"Are you concerned for young Master Sempill?"

"Strange as it may seem, I quite like the man."

"That's not like you." She patted his chest. "Most of the time you don't have a good word to say about anyone."

He smiled, faintly. "You'd find him delightful, I'm sure. He's young, and vigorous, and very pleasing to the eye."

"Dark and dangerous, like you?" She gently teased out his hair.

"Oh no. Fair, like his father. He has a thick mane of hair, dark gold like a lion's."

"Magnificent."

"He'd have gone far in King James's court. He has all the qualities that James favoured. Charm, and wit, and a very pretty face." He looked up at her with a mischievous grin. "Oh, and did I mention his arse? Tight and well-muscled, just the way His Grace liked it."

"Don't be so horrible!" She cuffed his shoulder.

"No smoke without fire, they say. . ."

"Yes, but it's cruel to mock a dead man."

He sat up with a laugh, then slumped forward, locking his hands before him. "He's a bold lad. And he's determined. But I don't think he quite understands what he's let himself in for."

"You should help him. If you can."

"Whatever for?"

"Because it's the charitable thing to do." She put her arms around him and pulled him close.

Hugh made a half-hearted attempt to wriggle loose. "I'm charitable enough. The church bleeds me all the damned time."

"That's just because you let them." She felt herself slip forward on the cushion, but didn't ease her grip; together, they slid to the floor. "Because you swear," she said, pressing her lips against his own. "—and lie—" Another kiss. "—

and eat meat on a Friday—" And another. "—and you take great pleasure in fornication."

"It's a wonder I have any money left at all."

"I daresay young Master Sempill hasn't yet learned these vices." She snuggled closer.

"He is the embodiment of virtue," he said, with mock-bitterness. "His soul is purer than the driven snow."

"What a wondrous man!"

"Either that, or he's the worst kind of hypocrite. . ."

"Well, I'm touched by his tale of woe. It seems terribly cruel, that he should pay such a heavy price for something which wasn't of his doing."

"The sins of the fathers. . ." His fingers gently traced the embroidered pattern on her arm.

"You were that age once," she reminded him. "And the world was very cruel to you. I'd have thought that since you'd endured all that already, you wouldn't want to inflict it on another."

"Perhaps. . ." He sighed. "Ah, Helen, I can remember a time when the motives that moved me were purer, more noble. . ." He turned to her, puzzled. "Whatever happened?" he asked. "Is it the world that changed? Or was it me?"

The Place of Ellestoun

"John Sempill of Fulwood," William announced.

John rose to greet his kinsman.

Fulwood nodded to him as he entered. He was in his forties; from the dour look of him he wasn't relishing the prospect of sharing his bad tidings with a man half his age.

They clasped each other close, then John gestured to a vacant chair. "So what's your news, cousin?"

Fulwood studied the floorboards, bleakly. "I've been attacked."

"The Stewarts?"

"Them, or Lord Lyle."

"Lyle? What makes you think he was involved?"

"A week ago, he sought an audience with me. He told me he was 'concerned', because you hadn't paid a sum requested of you by the King. He wanted me to try and make you see the error of your ways."

"What did you say?"

"I told him it wasn't my place to lecture you."

"Good."

"So then he said that if I paid him twenty pounds, he would take it as a token of goodwill. *That way,* he said, *you can distance yourself from Ellestoun's rebellion.*"

"So how did you reply to that?"

"I told him it wasn't a decision I could rush into lightly. I said I needed time to raise the necessary funds." The old laird bowed his head. "When they came, my tenants tried to fight them. . ." He swallowed. "Two men died. Their son escaped and brought me the news."

"I'm sorry," John said. "But we can't hit back."

"I know that."

"I can only do what I'm entitled to do, in the eyes of the law."

"Oh, for God's sake, John! Pay him what's due."

"He wants two hundred pounds."

The older man's face blanched. "God Almighty!"

"He doesn't want the money. He wants rebellion."

"So what are we to do?"

"We must sit tight and hold our ground. That's all we can do."

"Master John?" William poked his head around the door.

It wasn't like William to barge in like that. And there was something about his face. He looked grey, exhausted. . .

"What's happened?" John asked, quietly.

"We've just received word from Southannan. It was attacked two days ago. They destroyed almost every cottage and byre on the estate."

* * *

"There's thirty-five, altogether," Alan Semple said, as they hurried down the stair. "And there'll be more to follow, I don't doubt."

"Poor souls," John muttered.

"I don't see how we can provide for them," Alan added. "It'll soon be midwinter. We can't afford to keep them till spring."

"Do you expect me to turn them away and let them starve?"

"But it's not our place to be charitable. That's what the Church is for."

"They'd beg to differ, I'm sure."

"They can't stay here, at any rate."

"Then we'll find them places to stay in Kenmure."

Alan pursed his lips and shook his head. "The good folks of Kenmure won't like it."

John paused at the door. "They'll damn well put up with it."

* * *

They raised grubby, hopeless faces as he approached. Their clothes were sodden and caked with mud; children clung to them, too cold and tired even to cry. They hadn't brought much with them; some had rescued a cow or a couple of chickens, while others carried light bundles on their backs.

"Come into the hall," John told them. "You can dry off by the fire and have some food while we find you lodgings." He gave a weary sigh as his bedraggled tenants filed their way past. "Damn him," he muttered to William. "Master Stewart might be of Royal blood, but he's no better than a brigand."

"Blessed are those who ride roughshod over others," William said. "For they'll be richly rewarded here on this earth."

Chapter 23

Henry had been confident he'd find work in Paisley or Renfrew. But he didn't have any skills, and there wasn't much demand for a labourer at this time of year.

They weren't alone in seeking help, either; the churches and hospitals had been full of needy souls begging for alms. *Go back to your parish,* a lay-brother at the Abbey told them, when Mary explained their situation. *If your priest won't help you then go to your laird.*

Should've gone to the laird first, Henry had said, as the Abbey doors closed against them.

He'd sounded almost smug.

Mary knew better than to argue. But inside, she was glad they'd at least tried to make their own way in life.

Unlike Henry, she had her pride.

* * *

It was getting dark by the time they reached Kenmure. Mary could scarcely feel her feet, and she was glad of it, too, for until now they'd ached incessantly. They'd walked all the way from Renfrew; they'd been forced to sell the cart there to pay for food and lodgings. She supposed they were lucky they still had the oxen.

For an hour the children had been silent. Not a whimper, not a grumble.

The silence worried her.

"Nearly there," she told little Hughie, who stumbled along at her side.

"Where?" he asked.

"The church. They'll help us."

"Last one didn't," he replied.

And she didn't know what to say.

* * *

The priest came to the door. "Best see the laird," he told her. "Last thing I knew Master Semple was trying to put folk up with the tenants of Kenmure. You from Southannan?"

"No, we're from the parish of Kilbarchan. We tried to find work so we wouldn't impose."

"Bad time of year for it," he agreed. "Where are your lands?"

"Nether Bar, Father."

"Well bless my soul!" He opened the door wide. "Come inside, all of you. We were wondering where you'd gone. You were widowed in the summer, weren't you? Your husband fought for Sir Thomas."

"That's right."

"The Laird was looking for you. Master John doesn't forget his obligations, see. I'll send word to Master Semple right now."

* * *

135

It wasn't the tacksman who came to fetch her. It was Master Haislet, a quiet, well-spoken man, who was, he explained, a manservant to Master Sempill.

At this moment in time, she didn't really care who he was, though she supposed it was a refreshing change to hear a friendly voice.

"I knew your husband," said Master Haislet, as they made their way through the gates into the busy yard at Ellestoun. "He was a good man."

"He's sorely missed." She wanted to trust him. He had a kindly face, and a pleasant manner.

"I'd like to help, if I can," he said. "I have a cottage in the village. My daughter lives there, with her husband. Your family can lodge there, if you like."

"We don't have any money."

"There's none wanted."

"Thank you." She saw the tower-house rearing high ahead, and her steps faltered. She'd never been so close before; it looked such a cold, stark place.

"It's warm enough inside," Master Haislet said by way of encouragement as he opened the door for her. "Now just go on up the stairs. He's waiting for you in his chamber."

Mary frowned. It worried her, that a man she scarcely knew was showing such an interest in her business. "Master Haislet." She paused on the stair. "Is your master an honourable man?"

"The most honourable man I know, Mistress White. You mustn't be afraid."

* * *

The chamber was full of light and colour. Candles burned bright in the corners, and two sleek hunting dogs lay slumped before a pile of blazing logs in the fireplace. Embroidered hangings adorned the panelled walls; at one side, Adam and Eve stood side by side in the Garden of Eden, on the other a knight galloped through a forest in pursuit of a distant stag, his lady perched behind him.

Even the timbers above her head were painted with flowers.

She wanted to run. It all seemed so far removed from the earthy reality of land and byre and growing crops.

"Mistress White?" The laird stood to greet her.

He looked nothing like the bedraggled creature who'd stumbled into her cottage on his way back from the war. He was in his natural element here, brilliant and opulent as the room itself. His dark red velvet doublet was embellished with pearls and gold thread, his boyish face smoothly shaven and his gold-brown hair combed neatly about his shoulders.

She felt suddenly ashamed. She didn't want to be scrutinised so closely by a man who seemed so perfect. Not when her clothes were stained and torn, her cheek still swollen from the knight's blow.

"I'm sorry about your husband." He sounded painfully earnest. "I asked Master Semple to keep me informed, but he failed me this time. You must think me very cruel."

She was still too embarrassed to speak. She wondered why she'd ever thought his motives less than pure; he almost looked young enough to be her son.

"Would you care to sit down? You must be very tired." He took her hand, as if she'd been an elegant lady, and led her to the fireside. His fingers were soft and smooth against her own. He didn't even smell the way other men did; raw, bestial. Instead he carried with him a scent of lavender and musk and rose water.

Mary looked at the chair, with its pretty embroidered cloth cover and snatched her hand from his. "No, thank you."

"What happened to your face?" he asked.

"My son threw a stone at the knight who burned my place," she told him. "The knight was going to strike him. I took the blow."

"Then you're very brave. You both are." For all his grace and polish, he was only a young lad, whose curiosity had got the better of him.

"Thank you." For the first time, she met his gaze. Though his face appeared youthful, unblemished, his eyes seemed much older. They looked dark, haunted.

"I can offer you work," he said. "Here at Ellestoun, amongst my household. You can lodge in the tower, if you like."

"What about the children?"

"How many are there?"

"I have four. Two boys, of eight and twelve. A girl of three, and another a year old."

"The eldest could help in the stables. But the others would be a problem. This is no place for young children to roam unchecked. Have you no kin who could help you?"

"I can't betray my children," she said, firmly. "They're all I have left of him."

"I understand," he said. "Though you might serve them better if you accepted my offer. If you reconsider, then you know where you can find me."

* * *

Master Haislet showed her downstairs to the hall.

"He doesn't sleep well, does he?" she asked.

"What makes you say that?"

She shrugged.

He took a deep, troubled breath.

"It's a sin," she said, "that someone so young and so fine is weighed down by such troubles."

"There's no justice in the world," Master Haislet replied. "If there was, then our laird would prosper. And poor widows like yourself wouldn't be forced out of their homes in the depths of winter."

* * *

With every passing day, there were more of them.

As well as those who'd been burned from their homes, there came others; families for whom even the rumour of attack was enough to drive them away. They came with their possessions piled high on carts, herding cattle and sheep before them. They tethered their beasts on the common, and set up bothies nearby.

Those who'd suffered the wrath of the Stewarts brought with them the news that the Master of Lennox had changed his methods. Instead of burning everything to the ground, his men were emptying the byres of every beast and fowl before they set the fires.

They were thieves now, as well as arsonists.

Each afternoon, the queue of people at the gate asking for alms grew longer. The servants would go out bearing loaves and flagons of ale and pottage. There were scuffles and arguments when the alms were given out, but the men-at-arms would always intervene.

After that, there'd be no more fighting.

But beyond the castle walls, the situation was more precarious. A steady stream of tenants came to John's door, mostly residents of Kenmure. They complained bitterly about trampled gardens, straying cows and stolen chickens. The atmosphere in the village had changed; where once there had been friendly smiles and idle chatter, now there were only sullen faces and voices raised in argument.

* * *

They couldn't fit everyone inside the great hall at Ellestoun, so they held the court outdoors, near the kirkyard.

Kenmure Hill formed a grim backdrop to the proceedings, a massive rocky knoll that rose tall from the plain of the Cart. As the crowd gathered, the wind whipped across the land, swooping and diving around their ears.

John glanced up at the leaden sky. At least the rain was holding off.

He didn't like to flaunt his authority so boldly, but these were unusual circumstances. Today, he had William at his right shoulder and Alan on his left, and another ten men-at-arms lined up for good measure. They were all mounted, and the men-at-arms carried spears.

"So much discontent," John muttered to William. "It's drifting from the village like a vapour."

The faces of his tenants stared up at him. Most were pale and gaunt and hopeless, but one or two looked resentful, even rebellious.

It was for the benefit of those few that John had summoned them all into his presence. He had to maintain order; if his tenants turned on Lyle and Lennox, or if they turned on *him*, then all would be lost.

He tugged upon the reins and pressed his spurs against his horse's sides; the chestnut gelding skipped up and down and shook its head. Its hooves battered loud against the ground and ropes of froth dropped from its jaws.

The crowd shrank back.

"You know why you've been summoned here," John told them. "Many of you are relying on goodwill and charity to survive this winter. Compared to these poor souls, those of you with a roof and a barn and the means to keep your kye can consider yourself blessed.

"Life will be hard this year. But this cruelty is being carried out in the name of our King, and we daren't oppose his will. All we can do is pray that some day soon God will deliver us from our misfortune.

"Until that day dawns, we must be patient. We must help those less fortunate than ourselves, and be tolerant towards our fellow men." His voice hardened. "Remember that God is watching you. He'll see your actions here on this earth, and He will judge you accordingly. And never forget that I, too, am watching you. If there's disorder, I'll curb it." He nodded to Alan.

"Alright!" Alan said. "Get back to your homes. And pray to God you're not brought before the Laird for judgement."

They wandered away in knots and huddles.

"Master Sempill!" A woman's voice hailed him.

It was Mary White of Bar. John spotted her trying to forge a path through the crowd towards him. "There she is!" he called to William. "Help her."

William dismounted, and disappeared into the throng. He soon returned, with Mary White at his side. She was shivering, her shawl drawn close.

John nodded. "Good day, Mistress White. How can I help you?"

"You said I might reconsider your offer. Well, I spoke to my kin, and they said they'd keep the wee ones." She looked up at him with a hesitant smile. "If it please you, sir, I'd be glad of work for me and my eldest."

* * *

A week passed before John next set eyes on her. The sun was shining; it was the first time it had shown its face for the best part of a fortnight. The sight of it lifted his spirits a little; he whistled a merry tune as he bounded down the stairs to the yard. He skidded to a halt at the door and was about to lift the latch when it opened from the outside.

And there she was.

Uncertainty flickered in her face. She blinked and, smiling half-heartedly, reached up to straighten her hood. She didn't curtsey; his mother would have been outraged at her arrogance, but he found it quite refreshing.

Her short spell at Ellestoun had transformed her. Her drawn face had filled out, and a rosy bloom touched her cheeks once more. The swelling on her cheek had gone down, though the deep cuts left by the knight's gauntlet could still be seen. And the shabby clothes she'd worn on her arrival had been replaced by an elegant gown of brown wool.

He nodded, and touched his bonnet. "Good day, Mistress White."

She curtsied then. "Master Sempill." She looked him in the eye and smiled.

It was, he thought, rather a glorious smile. She always seemed so staid, so solemn; to see a smile grace her face warmed the soul.

"You're looking well, Mistress White. Is everything to your liking here?"

"Oh yes. I'm very comfortable." She glanced furtively about her, then leaned closer, hands clasped before her. "There's just one thing. . ." she confided. "I miss my little ones."

"It's not right, that a mother should be kept apart from her children. . ." He paused, then added, "You'll be attending mass on the Sabbath. Perhaps you should spend the rest of the Lord's day with your family."

"I wouldn't be missed?"

"William can fetch you in the evening."

She smiled again and clapped her hands. "Oh, God bless you, sir!"

"Not at all." He stepped aside to let her pass.

It was only when she vanished round the curve in the stair that he realised he'd been staring after her.

His reactions surprised him. Before this day, he'd never looked twice at any of the servants. But then, most of the women who served at Ellestoun were twice his age or more. The rest were skinny little maids.

Mistress White was altogether different. Her hips were broad, inviting.

As for her breasts. . .

Ample, he supposed the word was.

He shook his head, and continued on his way.

Chapter 24
The Place of Ochiltree

It was her mother's duty to wash the corpse. *A wife cares for her husband in life,* Lady Euphemia said. *It's only right she prepares him for the grave.*

Margaret couldn't understand how her mother had taken it so calmly. But that was her mother all over; cold, indifferent.

Once it was done, Margaret crept into her father's room and sat there at his bedside. He looked so serene, with the coverlet drawn up over his shoulders and his eyes closed, his snowy hair combed neatly out upon his pillow. He looked as if he were fast asleep, but she knew from the grey-white pallor of his skin and the bluish tinge to his lips that he was dead.

Her eyes filled with tears. Ten days ago, he'd been his usual self. A little frail perhaps, and plagued by his regular winter pains. Then the aches had started in his limbs, followed by a harsh cough and streaming nose and eyes.

As he'd lain in his sickbed, racked with fever, she'd prayed and prayed for a miracle. She'd called on the Holy Virgin and Saint Margaret to intercede on her father's behalf, but her pleas had gone unheard.

It was only now, as she sat at her dead father's side listening to the priest chant psalms for his soul, that it finally hit her. He was gone. She'd never again hear his voice or have the reassuring grip of his hand about her own.

She bowed her head and wept, stricken with grief for her loss, and terrified at the prospect of the future.

* * *

"Well, I'm sick and tired of her," Elizabeth Kennedy said. "I have to put up with that sullen face staring at me all day long."

Margaret gripped her knees close against her chest with a sigh. She was tucked out of sight by the window, too tired and miserable to argue with them now. The shutters clattered at her back as the wind caught them, and she shivered. It was a miserable night out there, but for once she felt no safer indoors. She was fighting a losing battle; ever since Elizabeth had borne him a son, William always did what she wanted.

"Just marry her and be done with it," Elizabeth continued. "She's a burden on the household."

"You mustn't do that!" Jamie argued. "We can't let her wed until we know what the future holds for her."

"What right do you have to tell my husband what to do?" Elizabeth countered. "You're only his bastard."

Margaret squeezed her eyes tight. She heard his angry hiss of breath from where she sat. But other than that, Jamie took the insult remarkably well.

"It's almost Yuletide," he said. "The court will be gathering at Linlithgow. Our cousin will be there; we should tell him of his kinsman's passing. At the same time, we can find out what's happening in Renfrew and then decide what's to be done with our sister."

"James is right," Lady Euphemia said. It was the first time Margaret had ever heard her mother speak out in Jamie's defence. "We've held back this far. Why rush into things now?"

"Alright," William said, in a defeated tone of voice that suddenly reminded Margaret of their father. "James and I will ride to Linlithgow. I'll speak with our kinsman, and find out what the situation is."

Margaret breathed a sigh of relief.

She was reprieved, for a little while at least.

The Place of Ellestoun

They didn't take kindly to strangers, the folk who lived and worked at the castle.

During the first week, Mary sat by her son's side through dinner. She listened patiently while he told her how he'd been taught to groom the horses or exercise the hounds. Then he made friends amongst the stable hands and the huntsmen, and soon he spent most of his time with them.

Without her boy's company, she felt out of place. But she wasn't quite alone there; Master Haislet often went out of his way to speak with her. He talked of things she could understand, like the land and the crops and the kye. He spoke about her husband and asked after her family. He'd lost his own wife just two years earlier and knew how difficult it was to put the grief aside.

As for the laird. . . He dined with them each day in the hall, and he would nod politely and pass the time of day when their paths crossed.

But those moments apart, he might as well have been living in a different world.

* * *

It was Christmas Eve.

"Yuletide tomorrow," said Mistress Semple. "And once that's behind us, it'll be Saint Stephen's Day. I daresay Master John'll be following old traditions and working in the kitchens for the day."

"Whatever for?" young Mariota asked.

"Things are turned upside-down on Saint Stephen's Day. The Boy Bishop sits in pride of place in the Abbeys, and the Lord of Misrule reigns in the castles." Mistress Semple was a bent old woman, who'd weathered sixty summers. She thought herself superior because she carried the same name as the laird, which meant she was distantly related. "I doubt Master John will give the kitchen boy free rein for the day, because of his troubles. . . But he'll still be helping the cooks and letting the lad sit in his chair through dinner." She grasped her mug and gulped down some ale. "That'll be a sight to see. Hot place, the kitchens. He'll be stripped down to his shirt and hose in no time."

"D'you think the cooks'll need our help?" asked Christian.

Mistress Semple crowed with mirth at that. "That's the first time I've ever known you to volunteer your services!" Then she added, suddenly serious, "We shouldn't speak of him like that. He's a fine, upstanding man, our laird."

Mary kept her head down, and concentrated on her darning. Sometimes, it felt as if there was no end to the washing and the mending. She didn't mind the work so much as the company she had to keep. For all her mighty words, Mistress Semple had as much in common with the laird as a corbie did with a peacock.

And then there were the two girls, Christian and Mariota. . .

"It was so kind of him to take Lady Elizabeth to Caldwell for Yuletide," Christian said.

"But he *is* a kind man," Mariota agreed. "So good to his mother."

"He looked at me this morning and he smiled," Christian added. "He has such a lovely smile."

"It's such a cruel thing, that he can't find a wife. And he's been cooped up here the past month. It's not good for a man of his age to live this way."

"I'd have him," Christian sighed.

Saints preserve me... Mary frowned as she stabbed the needle into the fabric. *I'll have lost my mind before this year's through.*

* * *

Christian shot a frosty glance in Mary's direction. "But it's not right!" she complained, in that whining way of hers. "She's not even been here three weeks, and she's being given privileged duties."

"Master Haislet put it plain enough," Mistress Semple said. "It's indecent for a young maid to enter a man's chambers when he's still in his bed. Mistress White's a married woman."

All this fuss, Mary thought, and just because she'd been asked to take a pot of hot water up the stairs so the laird could wash each morning. It had been Mistress Semple's task until now, but she was finding the climb too much.

"Mistress White doesn't have to do this, you know," Mistress Semple retorted. "She's doing it to be charitable."

"I'm sure," Christian muttered. "She wants into his bed, that's what she wants—"

"What a wicked thing to say!"

"It's true." Christian's tone was sullen, rebellious. "He looks at her. And she smiles and leads him on. It's disgraceful."

"That's enough!" Mistress Semple gave the girl a sharp cuff across the ear.

"I'm sorry." Christian lowered her head, but didn't sound at all repentant.

* * *

That night, Mary lay awake a long while, thinking about Christian's words.

Yes, she'd been guilty of nodding to the laird and exchanging greetings with him. But that wasn't a sin, was it? It was just common courtesy, towards a man who'd gone out of his way to help her.

From then on, she kept a careful eye on him.

It was true. His eyes would linger on her. She thought she was imagining it at first, but the more she watched him, the more she knew she wasn't mistaken.

She was more intrigued than frightened. She knew full well that a man in his position didn't have to ask for anything; if he'd wanted his way with her, he'd have taken her.

He was more like a bashful young lad who couldn't pluck up the courage to approach. If their eyes met, he'd look away and blush.

For all his courtly manners, he was just a man like any other. And a young one at that, who still lacked experience and understanding in the ways of the world. When he looked at her, he always seemed wistful, a little sad.

Poor soul's lonely, that's all. Needs a woman in his bed at night, to hold him close and tell him everything'll be alright.

He was the laird. He was richer and more powerful than most men. But he had his troubles, same as the rest of them.

It was the strangest thing, but she felt sorry for him.

Chapter 25
Cruikston Castle, December, 1488

Matthew stalked back and forth before the fire. "He asked us to join him at Linlithgow, and we turned him down. He'll take it as a slight!"

John Stewart clasped his hands with a sigh. "He won't be well impressed if Sempill's not brought to heel by New Year."

"Well, I don't see any sign of him capitulating."

"Why's that, I wonder?"

"I've done what was expected of me," Matthew countered. "There's scarcely a cottage left standing between here and Largs. And he still won't give in. What's the matter with him?" He shook his head. "Sempill by name, simple by nature. . ."

"He's been protesting his innocence too long. He genuinely doesn't have Montgrennan's money."

"Then we've been using fire and sword against an innocent man." Matthew sank into a vacant chair with a groan. "James'll never stand for that."

"We need rebellion."

"There's not a hint of it yet, is there."

"Every man has his breaking point. We just have to press him until we find it." Stewart briskly cracked his knuckles. "Easter Greenock's just an hour's ride from Duchal."

Matthew sat up tall. He was actually smiling. "Of course!"

"Ride out to Duchal tomorrow. Robert'll grant you some men. As for myself. . ." Stewart added. "I'll go to Linlithgow for New Year and speak to James. I'm sure I'll convince him that we have matters well in hand."

"And what about cousin Hugh?"

"What about him?"

"He stayed at Ellestoun. Last month."

"He'll have his reasons," Stewart said. "If Master Sempill hopes to enlist Hugh's help in all this, then he's more foolish than I thought. Hugh knows who his friends are. And John Sempill isn't one of them."

The Palace of Linlithgow, December, 1488

The bear was a mangy creature. It swatted at the dogs and managed a roar or two, but gave the impression it was too tired to care if it lived out the day.

Small wonder, for it was the third bout of baiting it had suffered that evening.

Young James had grown bored of the entertainment and had left the hall an hour ago, but some of the barons along the lower tables were still roaring loud at the contest.

Hugh supposed he ought to take an interest. He had five unicorns staked on a particularly grim-looking mastiff that the Laird of Sauchie had produced for the occasion, but after a week of endless blood-letting he was almost as weary of it all as the bear was.

A hand pressed his shoulder. "Lord Hugh?" It was Robert Colville. "I'd like a word, if it's not inconvenient. Come to my chambers, if you will. Later this evening. And make it discreet."

Hugh sighed, inwardly. All week long, the rumours had been rife, and the Darnley Stewarts' absence from court over Yuletide had only served to fuel the gossip. It was common knowledge that the situation in Renfrew had grown dire in the last month. Men thought it amusing, that the Earl of Lennox hadn't managed to beat a lowly laird into submission after weeks of trying.

Secretly, Hugh was relieved that John Stewart's troubles had festered; unrest was just as rife in Cunninghame as it had ever been.

But nobody was interested in Cunninghame. The court had scented John Stewart's blood, and now they cared for nothing else.

* * *

Hugh wasn't the first to arrive at Colville's apartments. Two men were there already. He didn't recognise them; their gowns and doublets were worn and faded and they looked more like provincial lairds than courtiers.

"My kinsmen," Robert Colville said, with an embarrassed little smile. "They're just leaving."

"Aren't you going to introduce us?"

"Sir William Colville, the Laird of Ochiltree, and his half-brother James. They fought for us last year." He took Hugh by the arm and presented him before them. "Gentlemen, this is His Grace Lord Hugh, the Lord Montgomerie."

"Delighted," said Hugh.

Ochiltree doffed his bonnet and bowed. "You've earned a fearsome reputation, Lord Hugh."

Hugh gave a little smile. "Ah, yes."

"Lord Hugh's been given special responsibilities in the Westland," Colville explained. "Your co-operation with His Grace would be appreciated. And in return, I'm sure he'll deal directly with any specific grievances you may have. . ."

"Perhaps Lord Hugh would like to visit us at our place in Kyle," said Ochiltree. "We could discuss matters further, and establish how we might best assist him in his duties."

Hugh inclined his head. "That would be most welcome, Sir William. I'll call by your place, when the new year's upon us."

"Good night then, cousins," said Colville, hurriedly. "We'll speak further about these matters." He shepherded them away without another word.

* * *

When Colville returned, Hugh was already seated by the fire. "I thought the Laird of Ochiltree was an elderly gentleman."

"Sir Robert died three weeks past."

"I'm sorry to hear that. They came to tell you?"

"Yes." Colville handed him some wine, then sat down nearby. "But they also came to ask my advice." He smiled, thinly. "We have a mutual problem; John Sempill of Ellestoun."

"The marriage, I suppose."

"They want to break the contract. They want me to wed the wretched girl myself."

"What age?"

"Fifteen. A very pretty creature. Allegedly. . ."

"You're not tempted?"

"It'd cost just as much to pay off the damned Sempills as I'd make from the dower."

"I can see their problem though. Master Sempill's reputation isn't exactly wholesome."

"Earl Patrick and myself wondered if you'd pursued the matter we discussed back in August."

"I did. I've spoken to the lad on more than one occasion, and I've been his guest at Ellestoun. He's not seen a penny of the King's treasure."

"Then why's he not co-operating with the Stewarts?"

"Perhaps you'd best ask the Stewarts that. Or Master Sempill himself."

"You don't consider him a threat?"

"Not while he remains in possession of his lands and his titles. If he's forfeited, then that might prove a very different matter."

"So what's your advice?"

"Send in a third party to negotiate between the Stewarts and the Sempills. Someone who can remain impartial to both households."

Colville nodded. "That sounds reasonable."

"I could do it, if you like."

Colville said nothing.

"You'll act accordingly?" Hugh asked. "It'll save us trouble in the long run."

Colville shrugged, and gave one of his non-committal smiles.

* * *

"How about a wager, Lord Hugh," said Lord Gray, as they filed into chapel the following day.

"That all depends on the nature of the wager. And the stake."

"This dispute in the Westland. Between His Grace the Earl of Lennox and Sempill of Ellestoun. I say it'll be over by Twelfth Night, and Sauchie says it's settled already. The Master of Bothwell has opted for New Year. We're each offering a stake of twenty unicorns."

"Twenty unicorns. . ." Hugh pursed his lips and frowned.

"Come on, Hugh. It's not like you to be timid."

"Twenty unicorns isn't even worth my while! If you want to name a stake, then make it a respectable one."

"Such as?" Gray looked wary.

"Forty unicorns!" Hugh replied. "I wager forty unicorns that John Sempill of Ellestoun won't have paid so much as a penny into John Stewart's hands by the Feast of Saint Valentine. And I wager twenty more that he'll remain defiant until Lent's upon us."

Gray drew a sharp breath. "Thus speaks a man whose courage and conviction can't be rivalled." He slapped Hugh on the back and offered his hand.

"Done, sir. I'll be the first to congratulate you when you come to collect your winnings."

But from the neat little smile on Gray's face, Hugh could tell he thought exactly the opposite.

Chapter 26
The Place of Ellestoun

Scarcely a day passed without the death knell sounding at Saint Bryde's, and the gravediggers were always busy. Fresh mounds of earth sprouted in the burial ground, visible testament to their labour.

It wasn't famine that claimed so many lives. There must have been a hundred people or more queuing for food each day, but supplies still held out. Though John didn't ask for aid, it came nonetheless. The Crawfurds and the Mures rallied to their kinsman's side, and the Dunlops and the Wallaces gave what they could. So too did the monks of Lochwinnoch.

But despite everyone's efforts, people died. Sickness was rife amongst those who camped in squalor on the common grazing, and the good folk of Kenmure lost loved ones, too.

Each day, John trudged his way to mass past lines of hopeless faces.

He tried to keep cheerful for the sake of everyone around him. Inside, though, his spirits ebbed ever lower. It was hard to stay strong, when his tenants were suffering so much hardship.

He found it hard to grasp how much his life had changed. A month ago, he'd been free to roam the hills alone, and travel to Renfrew as the fancy took him. Now he never went anywhere without a dozen men for protection; even then he flinched at every unexpected sound.

He might as well have been captive behind Ellestoun's walls.

During the day, he'd bury himself in routine; he'd attend mass, first thing in the morning, then he'd either practice his swordplay or hunt fowl in the marshes until dinner. Then, with dinner behind him, he'd help distribute alms to the begging hordes at his gate.

It was the nights he dreaded.

He'd lie awake in his bed for hours. His heart would race with fear, or he'd feel so profoundly alone that he wanted to weep; even the heavy warmth of a hound pressing down upon his legs and the familiar sound of William snoring quietly from beyond the bed brought little consolation.

When he did sleep, the terrors only grew worse. He was chased through endless stone corridors by something dark and nameless. Tendrils snaked across his path and twined around his limbs, while the whispering forms of his pursuers grew closer.

He'd wake up gasping for breath, too rigid with fear even to cry out.

But as time passed, his dreams were tainted by something even more insidious. He'd be lying bound and naked in that same cold place, with the rough stone beneath him and darkness clouding his eyes. He'd hear women talking and laughing, he'd feel their hands as they roused and teased him.

And then he'd come to his senses, hot and wet with desire.

149

He prayed endlessly to God for deliverance, but the more he tried to shut lust from his mind, the more his nights were fouled by it, until he dreaded sleep more than ever.

What made matters worse was that in his waking hours his desires had a name, a face; Mary White of Bar.

He hated himself for harbouring such thoughts about her. She was no whore. She was just an unfortunate mother trying hard to help her children. All along, she'd borne her troubles with the saintly courage of the Madonna, and he respected that.

But every day her presence preyed more upon his mind, until he could think of little else. He took every opportunity to visit the kitchens or the stables in the hope he'd glimpse her. And when she talked to William as she brought water to his room each morning, he'd grow stiff with longing.

He was ashamed of his ardour and he spoke of it to no one. He hoped to God that no one would notice. Least of all her.

She'd suffered enough trials over the past six months, without him adding to them.

* * *

Head in hands, John stared at the parchment spread out before him. Each tack was noted there, along with the tenants' names, and the rents that they paid.

So many farms burned, in the space of one short month. . . His head swam at the scale of it, the silence of the deserted hall seemed to press upon him.

He started as the door crashed open and Alan stormed in. "Master John!" In one hand he clutched a dead pigeon. With the other, he dragged a young boy by the ear. "Look at this!"

He slammed the bird's corpse down before John. The powder from its plumage settled to form a pale halo about its head, and its neck was broken.

From the look on Alan's face, it was as if murder had been committed. "He was in the doocote. Henry found him there. With *this* in his hands." He grasped the bird and shook it again.

"It was dead anyway!" howled the boy. He was no more than eight years old. Flaxen-haired and blue-eyed, like an angel.

"Master John, this can't go unpunished. You feed them every night, and they repay you by plundering your stores."

"He's just a child."

"Aye, maybe, but this is how it starts. Once they get the taste for thieving and poaching, there's no stopping them."

John leaned his brow against clasped hands and closed his eyes. His head throbbed. "Lock him in the pit. We'll discuss this further."

Alan bowed and hauled the boy away.

The child clung to the door-jamb. "Ma!" he wailed. "Where's Ma?"

"Get on with you!" Alan slapped the boy across the ear. It only made things worse; the boy started to scream and bawl.

Alan swore, then picked him up and carried him, the child squirming and kicking in his relentless grip. They disappeared down the stair together, the boy's cries ringing shrill in the stair-tower.

The clamour receded.

John sat back with a sigh. He knew full well what Alan would recommend. But to mete out such a harsh punishment on a young child seemed inhuman.

Picking up the dead bird, he wandered over to the fire. He tossed its remains into the flames, watching dispiritedly as the feathers charred and burned.

* * *

As he made his way back to his chamber, he found it a struggle even to move. And the aching in his temples was growing worse.

He'd nearly reached his door when he heard a scuffle of feet behind him.

"Keep back!" William's voice was sharp with authority.

"No! I must see him!" It was Mary White. "For pity's sake, Master Haislet. Let me through!"

John turned to see them grappling together on the stair. "What the Devil's going on?"

She reached out towards him. "Master Sempill!" She tried to dive forward, but William blocked her. She hissed an oath, then sank her teeth into his arm. William bellowed, with surprise more than pain, and she darted past. "Master John, I must speak with you!"

William reached out to grab her skirts and hold her back, but he was too late; she fell to her knees before John and grasped his hand. "Please, sir. Grant me a few moments of your time."

She'd never grovelled to him before; it seemed so out of keeping with her nature that he didn't know what to say. He cast an uncomfortable glance towards William, who was rubbing his arm and scowling at her back.

"I'll fetch Alan," William offered.

"No," John replied. "I'll deal with this."

For once, the look William gave him was unconvinced.

"Now come along." John took her arm and helped her stand. "Of course I'll speak with you. William, bring some wine."

"As you wish, my lord," William replied. He still looked sceptical.

* * *

"Sit down."

She didn't move.

He shrugged, and sank down in his chair. "What's the matter?"

"He's my son." Her shoulders shook as she fought back tears. "My sister tries hard, but she's got wee ones of her own. And Master Semple. . . He says his ear is to be cut off." Her voice cracked, she stifled a sob. "I know he's done wrong, sir, but to have him marked for life as a thief. . ." She looked him in the eye, almost a challenge. "It's my fault. I shouldn't have abandoned him. I'd do anything to have him pardoned."

It was the first time he'd studied her so closely. Her eyes were soft hazel, faintly touched with green. The creases at their corners only made her more intriguing. There was wisdom in her face, earned through years of hardship and misfortune.

Was she a saint or a witch? He didn't rightly know. But he could read her thoughts, clear as day. *I know you want me. Take me then. Just spare my child. . .*

He looked away. He felt his cheeks burn hot and he hated himself for it.

"Please spare him!" She rushed across and dropped to the floor at his feet. She seized his hands, her head sank against his knees.

Her hands were heavy in his lap, her face warm against his legs.

The lust awoke within him. He shuddered, all too aware of the possibilities. It was all up to him. Whether the boy was maimed or left unharmed. Whether she retained her honour or yielded her body to him. And he could scarcely think, for he wanted her so much he ached inside. "I'll speak with Alan. He can't go unpunished, but. . . I'll be merciful."

She looked up, face streaked with tears. "You're a kind man," she whispered. Her fingers caressed his palms, while he sat there, too unnerved to react.

The door opened. It was William.

John jerked his hands away.

William's expression didn't waver. "Wine, Master John."

"For the lady," said John. "Find Alan. Tell him not to be hasty."

William bowed, and retreated.

As she lowered her head to drink, John stared at her, entranced. She was like a hind sipping from a woodland stream, tense and wary. Fronds of copper-gold hair drifted out beneath her hood, her neck stretched pale and enticing to the line of her gown.

He closed his eyes, but the image was still there, a ghost in his thoughts. He could feel the stirring in his loins once more, stronger this time. "Leave me," he said. "I have to be alone."

Chapter 27

John sighed and pulled his hood lower to conceal his face. Never before had the narrow wynds of Renfrew town felt so threatening. Houses loomed tall and black on either side, they seemed to be crowding closer. Some light shone from cracks in the shuttered windows above, but it only served to make the shadows look darker, more ominous.

"I don't like this." William glanced nervously around him.

John irritably hitched up his hose. He'd worn coarse garments of wool and linen so he wouldn't draw attention to himself. He hadn't realised just how uncomfortable he'd be; they didn't fit properly, and they itched. And he felt naked without his sword.

Footsteps shuffled towards them.

"Who's there?"

"I've got what you're looking for," a man's voice replied. He drew closer; he was shepherding a reluctant girl before him. "Is she suitable?"

"As long as she hasn't got the pox..."

"She's only been doing this a week. She's as pure as they come." The girl was pushed roughly towards him.

She sighed, and lifted her skirts resignedly.

He swore as he fumbled with his hose. The urge in him was so strong he wasn't sure he could contain it much longer.

She gasped as he pushed her against the wall, again and again.

One brief surge of pleasure, enough to make him groan aloud, and it was over.

He let his head sink against the cold stone building. He was weary to the core. But despite his fatigue, a nagging doubt still gnawed away inside him.

He could've sworn he'd heard William call out to him. . .

"Hurry up," the girl said, crossly. "I've better things to do than spend my time mothering you."

John laced up his hose. "Do you want paid or not?"

He heard a rustle behind him, and reached instinctively for his dagger.

Too late. There was a thump; something struck him across the shoulders. He gasped and groaned and fell to his knees, winded. Then, as he fought for breath he was struck again.

He was lying face down in the dirt. His attacker's knee pressed hard into his back; he wanted to whimper but somehow he gritted his teeth and endured it without a sound. His arms were hauled behind him; every instinct told him to fight but instead he went limp.

"Oh, watch yourself!" the girl's voice said.

"Must've got his head. He's not moving."

Hands grasped his body and turned him over, they let him sprawl on his back while they groped at his belt for his purse.

"There won't be much on him." The girl again.

"Just as well. It doesn't pay to rob the gentry. They'd gut you soon as look at you."

He lay still as the thief cut his purse loose; thankfully, the man didn't think to look for a knife on him.

"There's a chain round his neck," said the girl. "Let me see. . ." Fingers tugged at his clothes. His doublet was torn open, then she hissed, "What's this?" She'd found the silk sark beneath. Her small hand caressed his chest. "Oh," she whispered. "I must have that. . ."

John moved then. Grasped his knife and heaved it upward with all his might, roaring aloud as he did. He struck flesh, there was a gurgling groan and a body sagged down onto him.

He wriggled free and hauled his knife loose. Then he struggled to his feet. He was breathing fast, his instincts roused.

The girl was there; she stared at him, open-mouthed. "You killed him!" Her accusation rang shrill in his ears.

He retrieved his purse and shook it in her face. "No one steals from me." Then he strode down the lane. "William?" His pace quickened. "William!"

He heard a moan nearby. John peered into the shadows, saw something stir there. Dropping to a crouch alongside, John reached out his hand. "William?"

"God forgive me. I tried to warn you. He knocked me over. I think I cracked my head. . ."

"We'd best go," John said. "Can you move?"

"What's happened?"

"Murder!" The girl's scream pierced the night.

* * *

John didn't notice the pain at first; he was too heady with rage and nervous excitement.

But by the time they reached the inn, it was a different matter; he was nursing a sore back, and he was limping.

He hated to flee, but running away seemed infinitely preferable to being brought before the Stewarts for judgement. Most of the time no-one cared if a cut-purse met his end in a back street; in these circumstances, John feared that the recently-appointed Sheriff of Renfrew might not be so lenient.

"We'll get the horses, and we'll leave," John told William, as he pushed open the door of the inn. "Soon as we can. Any stragglers'll just have to—" He broke off. "Oh, Holy Mary. . ."

It was chaos. A fight had erupted; tables and benches were strewn over the floor. His own men-at-arms were involved, along with a few others that he recognised; Stewarts, mostly, with one or two Lyles for good measure. One man was sitting on the floor with his head split open; he wasn't a Sempill, John noted with satisfaction.

John spotted the innkeeper, cowering by the stair along with a few well-to-do merchants.

154

"Master Sempill!" The innkeeper scuttled nervously across the battleground to join him.

"Christ Almighty. . ." John began. Then he groaned as he saw firelight chase along the blade of an unsheathed dagger.

It belonged to one of his own men.

"Oh no!" The innkeeper clutched his arm. "Do something, please. I won't have this in my place."

"I'll see to it." And before William could stop him, he was wading into the fray himself.

He ducked to avoid a blow from a Stewart man-at-arms. Side-stepped, as a battling knot of men thudded to the floor alongside him.

"Put that down!" He seized the offender and pushed him back against the nearest table.

Blinded with wine and rage, his retainer didn't even recognise him. He spluttered an oath and stabbed wildly at John's chest.

His aim was dire; the blade passed harmlessly past John's shoulder. "Hey!" John struck the man across the head. "It's me! See sense, damn you!"

Recognition glinted in the other man's eyes and John clapped his shoulders. "That's better. Now let's—"

An arm was clamped around his neck. He was hauled backwards.

He couldn't breathe. Lights flashed before his eyes, his chest heaved, again and again. He clawed wildly at the arm that crushed his windpipe, and kicked out.

They just tightened their grip.

The pressure eased. He gulped down air and blinked back tears. The world swam back into focus; he found himself wondering why they'd released him. Then he saw a knife flash in the corner of his eye.

The hold on his throat resumed. There was no strength in his limbs, he felt light-headed, detached, as if in caught a dream. *They'll butcher me*, he thought. *Like a hog in the shambles. And I'll go to Hell. I've enjoyed carnal pleasures and I haven't confessed my sins*. . .

A great weight struck him, and he fell, still locked in his attacker's embrace.

He was pressed against the floor beneath another man. He was suffocating now rather than choking, the arm no longer wrapped round his neck.

John squirmed loose. Waves of blackness still lapped at his vision; he crawled away on hands and knees, retched a few times, then sat back on his haunches and looked around.

He saw William straddling a fallen Stewart man-at arms nearby.

"Master John?" William looked up, anxious.

The Stewart retainer stirred. William hadn't knocked him senseless after all. And he had a dagger.

"William, look out!" John threw himself at William, knocking him aside. The dagger shredded the air, dangerously close. John wrenched his opponent's wrist back and twisted it, then slammed the hand against the cobbled floor, again and again. There was a yowl of pain, and the fingers went limp.

John tossed the discarded dagger aside. He sat back and grinned at William. "That was a close call!"

"You're bleeding!" William's eyes were wide with horror.

John looked down. Blood already spattered his doublet, but there was another vivid crimson stain spreading out across his left sleeve.

He hadn't even known he was hurt. He clenched and unclenched his fingers, realising with relief that everything still worked as it should. "I'll live."

William's face hardened. "How dare you!" He grasped the fallen man-at-arms by the tunic and smashed his fist into his face. Blood exploded from the man's nose, but as William pulled back for a second strike, John caught his hand.

"That's enough."

The anger melted from William. "I'm sorry," he said. "He shouldn't have done that." He looked reproachfully at John. "And you shouldn't have taken such risks for me."

"Strong arms are ten-a-penny round here," John said. He grasped hold of William's shoulder and hauled himself up. "Minstrels are less easy to replace. Come on." He held out a hand. "Let's go home. Before our crimes catch up with us."

Chapter 28

"Don't fuss," John muttered. "It's just a scratch."

"Any deeper, and it would've cut the sinew," William said. "It's not your sword arm, I suppose."

"Does he need a leech?" Elizabeth Ross prowled anxiously at his shoulder.

"No," William said. "It'll mend itself. Just slap a poultice on it."

"Whatever possessed you?" his mother lamented. "To go to Renfrew? Surely you knew how dangerous it would be."

"Leave him be, Elizabeth." It was Sir Malcolm Crawfurd. "He's made a mistake and learned a valuable lesson."

"Malcolm?" John hadn't even noticed the old laird's presence. "I didn't realise- Ow!" He snarled as one of the cooks slapped a steaming poultice down onto his arm.

"You've had other things on your mind," Malcolm said.

"I suppose so." John gritted his teeth as William bandaged the poultice deftly into place. A servant pressed a mug of mulled wine into his hands; he wrapped his fingers gratefully around the green vessel. He started to shiver, despite the warmth of the fire that blazed nearby.

"This is intolerable," said Malcolm. "What's the world coming to, when a laird of your standing is hunted down like a dog. . ."

"I'm sorry. You're our guest, and you've been caught up in all this. What brings you to Ellestoun?"

"I was looking for you. Your mother told me you'd gone to Renfrew. I thought you'd be back sooner rather than later." He shook his head, a faint smile on his face. "Things could've been worse."

John shrugged. "It was my own fault."

"It's not a good time, I know, but I just received word from Robert. Our lands have been attacked. A dozen kye were stolen, and five cottages razed."

"It's those accursed Stewarts, isn't it?"

"I fear for Robert. And for Marion, too. I want them back in Kilbirnie, until all this is behind us."

"Then tell him to return. He'll obey you, surely."

"Marion's with child. He won't want to move her. I thought perhaps you could persuade him. He'd listen to you."

"It means riding right past Duchal."

"I know."

"I'll do it." John leaned forward with a sigh. "I'm sorry it's come to this."

"Not as sorry as he'll be. . ."

John looked warily at the old laird. "What do you mean?"

Malcolm's gaze was fixed on the fire. "I'm not a patient man."

"You're not thinking right," John said. "You can't make things worse at Easter Greenock. Do you want to drag Marion into a war?"

"I don't want Marion involved. Or Robert, either. I want them away from there. Once they're safe, it won't matter anymore. The Stewarts can burn the damned place down for all I care. What's stones and mortar, compared to two precious souls. . ."

"They won't burn Easter Greenock," John said. "They'll burn Ellestoun. And hang me for good measure. You must hold back. The longer we stand firm, the stronger our case will be when we plead it before the King."

"The moon's full in three days," Malcolm whispered. "It'll be a perfect night for raiding."

* * *

Henry's sick, Janet said, when she came to the gates for food that evening. *I've done what I can, but . . . I think he's dying. . .* She'd looked into Mary's face, stricken. *What are we to do? They'll take away our tack, for sure. . .*

Leave it with me, Mary had said, taking Janet in her arms and holding her close. *I think I can solve all our troubles.*

She hadn't said how.

* * *

Mary kept her head down during the chaos of the master's return. She'd heard the rumours. That he'd disappeared to Renfrew that very morning, disregarding everyone's advice. *He'll be whoring, I expect,* the cook said. *Can't stomach the loneliness any longer.*

William Haislet climbed the steps ahead, a mug in his hands.

Mary fell into step behind him. She wasn't frightened of William. She wasn't frightened of the young master, either. The only worry she had was that in some way she'd offend her husband. *I'm sorry*, she whispered under her breath. *But it's for the best. For me. And for the children, too.*

"Master Haislet!" she called.

William stopped. He'd been in the wars himself. His face was grazed, and there was a bruise above his eye.

"Is he alright?" she asked.

"He'll get over it."

"It's because of me, isn't it?"

He didn't reply.

"Here." She reached out to take the mug. "Let me take it to him."

"I don't think that's wise. He's not in the best of moods."

"You're worried, aren't you?"

"Of course I am. And I don't think it's kind of you to torment him."

She patted his shoulder, gently. "I'll take good care of him. And that's what he needs, isn't it?"

* * *

Mary paused at the door.

It was almost a year since she'd lain with a man. Her heart was beating fast with excitement already. She hadn't thought she'd feel this way; perhaps it was against nature to abstain so long.

She'd heard William's knock many times before, she mimicked it now, then entered the room.

A candle still burned on the kist beside the bed, the curtains closed against the cold. Setting down the mug, she tugged back the curtain. At first she thought he was asleep. He was buried beneath the embroidered coverlet; all that could be seen of him was a tangled mass of dark gold hair against the pillow.

The hound that lay upon the bed looked up, then yawned and slid lazily to the floor. Its claws rattled across the floorboards, there was a soft thud as it settled beside the dying embers of the fire.

"William?" He sat up, dazed and half-asleep. The covers fell into his lap, he shivered as the night-time cold hit his flesh. "Mistress White." He looked shame-faced as he pulled the coverlet up around his waist. "I'm sorry. I didn't expect—"

"It's alright," she said, briskly. "I've seen a man before." She handed him the mug. "Some *uisque beatha?*"

He pushed her hand away. "No, thank you."

"It'll help you sleep."

"I don't want it, thanks."

Mary shrugged, and set the mug back down again.

She tried to act as if nothing was amiss. Some clothes had been placed ready for him on the chair by the fire. She rummaged through them, aware all the time of him watching her.

She didn't think he was angry. Wary and a little hostile, perhaps, but she could hardly blame him for that. She straightened, and met his gaze. "You need your sleep."

He looked away. The mask cracked briefly, his young face was bleak, frightened. "I—I don't like to sleep."

Mary took the gown back to the bed and draped it tenderly about his shoulders. "You dream, don't you?" She made the bold step of sitting down beside him. He was bruised about his back, and around his neck, too; she reached out and touched the discoloured flesh lightly with her fingertips. He was tense beneath her touch, like a wild creature poised for flight. "Is it the dreams you were running from today?" she asked.

He swallowed, but his face was inscrutable. "Did William ask this of you?"

"No." She lightly brushed his hair back from his face. "It's my fault, isn't it?" she said. "It's no shame, to feel that way towards a woman."

"It's a sin."

She smiled. "Then take Confession tomorrow."

Chapter 29

Mary stirred alongside. "I should go."

"There's no need." John supposed it was the right thing to say; it seemed unfair to make her run the gauntlet of gossiping servants in the hall.

Mary settled back down, and wrapped her arms about him. The coarse cloth of her gown felt rough against his skin, but he thought it rude to insist she took it off.

Instead, he suffered her presence in silence. She took great delight in touching him; he could tolerate it at first, when she didn't stray beyond his shoulders. But when he didn't protest, she grew bolder. Her fingers brushed his belly and his loins; he tensed with a warning growl, but all she did was laugh softly and hug him tight.

"It's new to you, isn't it? You've never allowed a woman to get so close. . ."

It wasn't something he cared to admit. Part of him yearned for her touch, but at the same time, she frightened him. She knew too much about the desires of men, she could rouse or soothe him at her pleasure.

She buried her face against his neck. "There's no joy to be had in rutting with a whore." When she spoke, her breath blew soft against him, making him shudder with apprehensive delight. "You'll learn that soon enough. Now just lie still. I won't harm you." Her fingers kneaded his muscles as she whispered loving words into his ear. And gradually, he let himself relax, until he lay loose and sleepy in her arms.

Her lips brushed his forehead, and she clasped him close against her breast. "You're a sweet young thing," she said. She was solid and enduring, like the land; she even smelled of the land, earthy, wholesome. "And you'll sleep now. Close your eyes, my love. There'll be no bad dreams tonight. I promise."

* * *

He awoke to the sound of William's voice beyond his bed. Mary was there, too; he heard her laughing aloud as they talked together.

William always brought his clothes so he could dress without having to venture out into the cold. But he didn't want to look feeble in front of *her*, so he took a deep breath, pulled back the covers and the curtains and stepped out of bed before he could think better of it.

They were sitting by the fire. They didn't hear him at first as he hobbled unsteadily towards them. He ached from the pounding he'd taken in Renfrew; he hadn't even noticed it when he'd been lying in her arms.

"Am I late for Mass?"

"By the Saints, lad!" Mary sprang to her feet. "You'll perish out here!" She grabbed the embroidered cover from the chair beneath and wrapped it round his shoulders. She didn't seem like a woman who'd just shared his bed. She was more like his mother or his wetnurse.

The thought brought a wry smile to his lips.

William tossed him his sark. "Here."

John struggled into it, then sank down with a shiver into the chair that William had just vacated. "It's late, isn't it?"

"At this rate," William said, "you'll just make it downstairs in time for dinner."

"Why didn't you wake me?"

"You were sleeping like a babe." Mary rearranged the chair cover, then settled down again.

"But I was meant to ride to Easter Greenock!"

"Sir Malcolm agreed that you shouldn't be disturbed," William told him.

John gave an irritable sigh.

"So how are you?" Mary leaned forward and rested a hand upon his knee.

"Refreshed."

"See?" she said to William. "I told you he'd feel better." She took John's hand, and tapped the bandage on his arm. "And the wounds?"

He pulled an unenthusiastic face.

"You took a right good battering yesterday." She patted her lap. "Will you let me see?"

John shrugged, and ambled over to join her. He sprawled like a hound at her feet, sinking back into the comfortable folds of her skirts.

"There now." She teased his hair out in her lap. "Just rest awhile. . ."

He felt his eyes closing. He basked in the warmth of the fire, stretching his legs towards the heat. Pompey was lazing there; the hound's coat was sleek beneath his toes, its flesh moving loose over the thin ribs beneath.

As Mary stroked his face, his neck, the troubled world outside his walls no longer seemed important. All that mattered was that which was here, and now; the crackle of the logs, the comfort of the cushions beneath his haunches and the solid weight of the hound at his feet.

And all the time her fingers moved soft against his skin. He was so overwhelmed by sensual pleasures that he felt he might suffocate. He knew it was wrong to savour the fruits of adultery but all of a sudden he didn't care.

There'd be time for atonement another day. . .

"You're in no state to be tearing across the countryside," she whispered. "Leave it until tomorrow. Then everything'll be fine."

"Until the next time," William muttered, darkly.

"There won't be a next time," she said. "He'll stay safe now. He won't go risking his neck in Renfrew hunting for whores."

"I'm off to fetch some water," said William. He hadn't sounded that cheerful in weeks. "I won't hurry back."

* * *

They watched the laird's party depart from the window of his chamber.

After two days in his company, they were on first name terms now. But there were still times when he seemed remote and unfamiliar. When he was dressed in his rich clothes, telling everyone what should be done and how to do it, and walking with that proud swagger in his stride, she'd shake her head and marvel at the change in him. It might have been a different man who smiled and laughed and whispered poetry in her ear when they nestled warm together in his bed.

Mary folded her arms and stifled a shiver. Her heart was heavy with misgivings. Johnny was on his bright red-brown horse, riding stirrup-to-stirrup with the Laird of Kilbirnie. He'd done his best to look inconspicuous, wearing a battered old cloak and hood that he'd gleaned from one of the huntsmen.

It was no good.

There's no mistaking him, Mary thought. *He sits so fine and proud in the saddle. Oh, Dear God. They'll know it's him.*

William watched alongside, leaning against the wall with one arm crooked up to cushion his head. His gaze didn't waver until the horsemen disappeared behind the shoulder of Kenmure Hill.

"He's like a son to you, isn't he?"

William smiled slightly. "I've known him since he was a babe."

"I'm sorry," Mary said. "You should be with him."

William shrugged, all false confidence. "He'll survive." He straightened with a sigh, then wandered through the chamber, folding clothes and rearranging the chairs.

"I didn't need this," she said. "I can look after myself."

"He's right to worry. Once word gets out, they'll call you a whore. Or a witch."

"The women will. The men have more sense."

William said nothing.

She sank onto the cushioned seat by the window. "So what am I to do now? I can't sit here all day."

"He doesn't think you should go back to the other women. Perhaps I should speak to Lady Elizabeth."

"I'm no seamstress. I'd wreck his silk sarks. Besides—" she added, "—she'll hate me for this."

"Not unless he asks you to marry him."

That made her smile. "Nothing to fear there. He's a good lad. He knows his duty." She looked wistfully at him. "Would he mind very much if I went to the village? To visit my family?"

"Not at all. I'll come with you, if you like. We could visit the kitchens first. You should take something special, for the little ones."

* * *

There were seven of them crushed into one end of the Haislets' barn in Kenmure. It was cramped and airless and smelled of the kye that lodged with them, but at least it was warm and dry.

"Here." Mary squatted on the floor and emptied out the contents of the bag before them. "A flagon of wine. Some slices of goose, cooked fresh today. Some rabbit pie. And some sugared plums, too. We can all feast like kings tonight!"

The children laughed and clapped with delight, but Janet wasn't convinced. "Did you steal it?"

"Of course not." She squeezed her sister's arm tight. "I'll tell you all about it later. How's Henry?"

Janet shrugged. "Come and see him. Perhaps you'll be able to do something."

* * *

Henry lay on a thick nest of straw by the wall, wrapped in blankets to keep out the draughts. He was mumbling to himself. His face was white and rimed with sweat, his breath weak, rasping.

Mary laid a hand across his brow. "Did you give him draughts?"

"Couldn't find the right herbs," Janet said. "Needed you to tell me what was what. Besides, everything's withered and dead."

"I'll see what can be done," Mary said. "I've brought some dried herbs down from the castle. But don't hold out much hope. He's on his way to God."

* * *

Once they'd eaten their dinner and settled Henry for the night, they sat together by the fire. It was good to be with the children again; Mary had little Meg curled up like a cat in her lap, and wee Hughie was snuggled up at her feet.

Hughie had been clinging to her skirts all night. He was a bold child, but his adventure in the doocote had left him shaken. He'd had been locked in the prison pit at Ellestoun for two days with just a chunk of bread and a small pot of ale each morning. *That'll teach you,* she'd told him, when he complained about the darkness and the cold and the horrible smell. *I know you meant well but you mustn't go stealing the Master's birds again, or he'll put you back in there. And he says that next time he might just forget all about you and leave you there forever. . .*

She ran her fingers gently through the boy's hair, and smiled to herself. Hughie had escaped lightly; Johnny had said he'd be merciful and he'd kept his word.

"I don't know what'll happen when Henry goes," Janet was saying, as she pulled her shawl closer about her. "We'll lose the tack for sure."

"No, we won't." Mary settled Meg more comfortably in her lap and held her hands out towards the fire. "Things are different now."

"What do you mean?"

"You'll hear the gossip soon enough. I thought I should tell you first. I—" She didn't quite know how to begin. "I've taken a lover."

"It's been almost six months. I think you've mourned long enough."

"It's the laird."

Janet blinked a few times while the news sank in. "But. . ." She frowned, searching for the right words. "It's not right! He's just a lad!"

"He knows what he's doing."

"He's not like us. He's different."

"When he's naked in his bed at night, he's just like any other man." She sighed and hugged her knees close. "He's a kind soul; I know he'll let us keep the tack."

"Thank God. . ." Janet cast a sideways glance towards her sister. "So what's it like then? Lying with him?"

Mary closed her eyes and shivered. "He's firm and lean and smooth, the way a young man should be. And he smells different. Like the Orient; all exotic spices and perfumes."

"Do you love him?"

"No. And he doesn't love me. But he thinks he does." She stretched her hands before her and yawned. "He'll be wed soon. To some poor unsuspecting maid who won't know what to do when she sees the beast in him."

Janet giggled. "You're doing her a favour. When she gets a hold of him, he'll be a well-mannered beast at least." She shook her head. "Christ. . . You and the laird. . . Who'd have thought it?"

Chapter 30

As they rode through the fermtoun of The Green, John sat tense on his horse, hood pulled low.

Lord Lyle's tenants didn't give him a second glance. He didn't really look out of place; every traveller on the road that day was wrapped up warm against the biting wind.

Men forked soiled straw from the byres; children laughed as they chased each other round hayricks piled high with winter fodder. And it seemed so unjust. That his tenants were suffering so much hardship while Lord Lyle's prospered.

Gradually John's resentment cooled. He looked about him with chill detachment, briskly noting the location of every house and barn. Dogs snarled around his horse's legs; he made a quick tally of their numbers.

When the time for reprisal came, he'd take no half-measures.

* * *

They'd left the fermtoun far behind them when the landscape changed. All around them, the blackened ruins of cottages were stark against the winter landscape, smouldering hayricks clustered about them.

They'd reached the lands of Easter Greenock.

Halting his horse, John pulled back his hood for a better view. He crossed himself. "This can't go on."

"How can we stop it?" Malcolm asked. "They're doing this in the King's name." Then he added, quietly, "Robert tells me that you've grown reliant on Montgomerie's goodwill. You've misjudged him, John. There's not an ounce of generous flesh in his body."

John didn't reply.

"If you think the King'll see sense and take the side of righteousness, then you're mistaken. He won't even hear of our plight. We're condemned. We might as well be rotting in a stinking prison pit somewhere."

"I hope you're wrong."

"You're still young. And ignorant of the world. Men do unspeakable things in the name of justice. You'll understand that soon enough."

* * *

"Robert?" Malcolm climbed the spiral stair towards the ladies' chamber. "It's not like him to neglect a visitor," he remarked to John. "We'd best see what's amiss."

They halted outside Marion's door, and Malcolm rapped smartly upon it. "Robert?" He stepped inside, John close behind.

The room was unbearably hot. A fire burned heartily in the grate and the shutters were closed. As for Robert. . . He sat by the bed where Marion lay. He didn't even hear them enter, too absorbed by his worries, hands wrapped loosely about Marion's.

John swallowed. He found it hard to believe that this whey-faced young woman was Marion. Her half-closed eyes were set deep in their sockets, her cheeks hollow.

He didn't wait for his arrival to be announced. Instead, he just pushed past Malcolm to Marion's bedside.

Robert looked up. He brightened briefly when he saw John, then the worry returned. "John's here," he said.

Her eyes flickered open. She smiled, and struggled to sit.

John seized her hands, and lightly kissed her forehead. "How are you?"

"I've been sick a few weeks now. They say it's only to be expected, but I've had such pains in my belly! Everyone's says that all's well, but— Ah!" She snatched her hand away and clasped her abdomen tight. "It hurts. I wonder sometimes if the child's already on his way."

"That's ridiculous!" Robert spoke with unintended sharpness.

Malcolm gave a weary sigh. He was standing by the window; he'd pushed the shutter open and was gazing out at the grey waters of the Clyde and the snow-capped hills beyond. "Have you eaten today?"

"I took a few mouthfuls," Marion told him.

"You must eat, Marion."

Robert turned on his father. "She ate what she could!"

Malcolm threw his hands up. "Alright!" He looked at John, then said, "We must talk, Robert. Downstairs, in the hall."

* * *

"—I never thought they'd come so close." Robert pushed his hand nervously back through his black hair. "We could see the glow of the fires from the parapet."

Malcolm nodded. "He's getting bolder then."

"But why's he doing this?"

"Because you're married to a Sempill," said John.

"So I'm guilty by association. What am I accused of?"

"I think John's the best man to answer that," Malcolm said, softly.

"They wanted money."

"So that's it," Malcolm muttered. "Twenty pounds. That's all it was. Damn you, John! Couldn't you even spare that?"

"They asked *you* for twenty pounds. They asked me for ten times that." John sank down upon the window seat. "They want my lands. Perhaps they even want me dead, I—I don't know. . ." He couldn't bring himself to look at them; he could sense their fear, their incredulity. "I never thought they'd involve you."

"But if the Stewarts are attacking Easter Greenock, then why isn't Montgomerie joining them and attacking Kilbirnie?"

"He has no interest in you."

"He said this, I suppose?"

"He gave me his word that he wouldn't trouble you."

"And you believed him?" Robert slammed his fist against the stones of the fireplace. "Damn you, John! Taking up with him was bad enough. Discussing our business with him's unforgivable."

166

"He'll be lurking in the background like a hoodie craw," Malcolm said. "Waiting to pick your carcass clean."

"He's not our enemy. The Stewarts are."

"Where's this going?" Robert looked suspiciously from John to his father and back again. "You've been conspiring behind my back, haven't you?"

Malcolm looked expectantly at John.

"Marion can't stay here," said John. "She must travel to Kilbirnie. Her safety's guaranteed in lands under Montgomerie's jurisdiction. It's not guaranteed here. Matthew Stewart will keep pushing and pushing until we break."

"But I don't see—" Robert argued.

"When that happens, we'll be at war."

There was silence.

"A pregnant woman can't live in such conditions." Then John added, more gently. "Would you risk her life? The life of your child?"

Robert looked away. "This quarrel's of your making," he said. "I won't be party to it."

"But you *are* party to it! Do you think Master Stewart cares—"

"Marion's not leaving. I'd sooner trust the Stewarts than Hugh Montgomerie."

"Oh, for Heaven's sake! Stop being so stubborn!"

Robert shrugged and headed for the door. His face was grim, unyielding. "Marion remains here," he said.

* * *

"Where's Robert?" Marion asked.

"They're discussing what's to be done." John sagged forward in his seat.

Marion stretched her hand towards him. "You look worn out."

He grasped her fingers. "I am worn out."

"Robert told me. About your woes." She closed her eyes. "How can the Stewarts be so cruel? You're their kinsman."

"If I die, Elizabeth's son will inherit my lands."

"She wouldn't want that, surely?"

"I don't know."

"Poor John," Marion whispered. "You're still not wed?"

"The Colvilles don't want me."

"It's not right, that you should be living like this. You have so much love to give." She squeezed his hand. "You're blushing. There's a woman now, isn't there?"

He smiled. "Some people would say it's not appropriate, but. . . She has a kind heart. . . She's good to me."

"So long as it brings you happiness, then what does it matter? Just make sure you treat her kindly."

"You must rest now, Marion," John said, softly. "I'll sit with you, if you want."

A smile touched her lips. "I'd like that very much."

* * *

167

That evening, John sat alone in the guest chambers. Malcolm and Robert had both retired early; *It's a long journey tomorrow,* Malcolm had said. *An old man like me needs his rest. You young bucks'd be wise to follow my example.*

John didn't argue. He was exhausted, and still a little stiff and sore after his trials in Renfrew.

But after just a few minutes of sitting alone in a silent room the old fears were back. He dreaded the prospect of sleep; he knew he'd miss having Mary's comforting warmth in the darkness. He took another sip of wine, hoping that if he drank enough he'd be so numb he wouldn't dream. . .

"John Sempill of Ellestoun!"

He sat up with a start, heart scudding in terror. His name, called out from far away. . . The goblet slipped from his hands and fell to the floor.

"Show yourself, Sempill! Are you too craven to face us, you gutless coward?"

He moaned and sank his head in his hands. Matthew Stewart had braved the cold and the hostile terrain and followed him here.

Or was there more to it? Had Malcolm arranged this, in one last-ditch attempt to make peace with the Stewarts and the Lyles?

John sprang to his feet. His vision was blurred with drink, but he could still make out his sword-belt, lying on the kist that stood at the foot of the bed. He grasped it, and buckled it clumsily into place.

He'd moved too fast. He swayed and leaned against the bedpost, eyes closed.

"What's the meaning of this?" Malcolm's voice bellowed out.

"Sir Malcolm Crawfurd of Kilbirnie?"

"Are you lost, Master Stewart? It's late to be wandering abroad."

"I'm here on behalf of the Sheriff. You're harbouring a fugitive. A man wanted for treason by the King. Deliver him into my hands with all due speed."

"A fugitive, you say. Who might that be?"

"I want John Sempill!"

"What would he be doing here? We're miles from Ellestoun."

"You were seen this afternoon, riding out with a man who matches his description. A man with hair like last year's mouldy straw, riding a horse that's red as a mangy fox."

"What if I did? What do you want with him?"

"He was responsible for the malicious wounding of five of my men in Renfrew town three nights ago. Bring him out, so he can answer for his crimes in person."

Malcolm laughed. But there was fear beneath his bravado. "You think I'd throw my gude-son out to endure your so-called justice? Be off with you! You're not welcome here."

The shutter slammed below.

"Can you hear me, Master Sempill?" Stewart called. "Come out! Let's settle our differences once and for all at the point of a sword." Silence. Then, "You're afraid to face me, aren't you? You're not man enough to try!"

John sank down upon the edge of the bed. He threw his arms over his ears to drown out the taunts.

Footsteps rattled up the steps beyond. There was a knock upon the door, the latch lifted.

He leapt to his feet with a roar. He strode forward, pulling his sword from its scabbard.

The door opened and he was face-to-face with Robert. "Out of my way!"

"What in God's name—" Robert's face went white. "Put the sword down, John." He glanced behind him. "Father! Come quickly."

"Let me pass." He pushed Robert roughly in the chest.

Robert stepped back. His foot slipped, he nearly fell back down the stair. But his hands were gripping the door-jamb; he was able to recover himself. "I won't let you kill yourself."

"I told you." John raised his sword. "Get out of my way!"

"Strike me if you must. I'm not budging." Robert pushed the blade aside.

"What's happening?" Malcolm came running from below.

"It's John!"

Malcolm paused at the curve in the stair. "Rest easy, John. We're not the enemy."

"No. He's right. This is between us. By God, I'll kill him. Or he can kill me. It makes no difference." Matthew's taunts still rang in his ears; he feared that if he didn't strike out at something he'd crack completely. "Just let me pass!"

"Give me the sword, John." Malcolm advanced, cautiously. He stopped alongside Robert and held out his hand.

John took a deep shuddering breath. He couldn't think properly. He could hardly even see straight. "No, I can't—" He gasped; the headache that had plagued him so frequently over the last few weeks was back, worse than before, throbbing so hard he thought his head would burst. His hand dropped, the tip of his sword bounced against the floor.

"Now!" They set upon him, one to each arm. They half-dragged him across the room; he fought them every inch of the way. The bedpost struck him in the back; he yelped and doubled over.

"That's enough." Malcolm wrenched his sword from him. "You'll get it back when you're in a better mood to handle it. Now sit down." He pushed him down upon the bed. "Take his dagger, Robert. And keep the door locked. In case he tries any more heroics."

He'd have given Malcolm an assurance of his good behaviour, if he'd been able to speak. But it hurt even to breathe. He lay stretched out along the bed, unable to move.

Robert sat alongside, saying nothing.

Gradually, the crushing in his chest eased. The blinding headache faded, he pushed himself up onto his elbows, wincing. "I'm sorry."

"We'll forgive you." Robert shivered. "Listen to them! They're like cats, serenading the Devil by the moonlight."

"Montgomerie warned me of this. He said it would take a mightier man than me to take on the Stewarts."

"I wouldn't be so sure. This reeks of desperation. There'll be men watching and waiting with bated breath across the land to see how this turns out. They'll have expected you to break before a month was out. And yet you've confounded everyone by holding your ground." He patted John's shoulder. "Are you alright? We didn't mean to be so harsh. But you can be quite a handful sometimes."

John sat up, grimacing. "I deserved it." He folded his arms across his knees and laid his head upon them.

"Marion's leaving here tomorrow," Robert said. "She says she'll walk to Kilbirnie if she has to."

"Thank God. . ."

"Now get some sleep, damn you. Your sister needs you."

* * *

He lay there for hours, unsure whether he wanted sleep or not. The room was dark, cold, unfamiliar. He wanted to know that William was there beyond the bed, he wanted his dogs, and above all he wanted *her*.

John curled up in his bed with a whimper and gripped his knees tight against his belly. The fear still gnawed away inside him, he felt too weak to fight it.

He dozed off, at last.

He was in that same barren grey place, shivering and frightened. A great weight pressed down upon him, he could scarcely breathe. He groped his way along the floor, knees and hands scraping along rough stone.

The shadow was coming, but he couldn't move any faster. He swivelled around to face it; a grey mist rolled through the passageway towards him.

Hooves. They battered against the flags at a canter. A horse screamed out from afar.

He saw it then. A mighty warhorse, charging out of the mist towards him. Black and solid, its nostrils flared wide and its yellow teeth were bared. And on its back, a knight. Armoured in black plate mail, with his spear couched and ready.

He was unarmed. He didn't even have the strength to pick himself up off the ground. He raised his hands to shield his face as the horse reared high above him. The spear flashed bright as it came down, it pierced him right through the belly and pinned him to the ground. He felt nothing, but the blood was flowing fast from the wound.

He screamed. . .

"—John! For God's sake!" Someone was shaking him.

It was Robert. He was standing over him, wearing just his sark, and holding a candle in his hand. "You let out the most terrible howl. Christ, we thought you were possessed."

"No," he whispered. He sat up. He was still trembling, the sheets soaked with sweat. "I'm fine now."

"I'm sure you are. How long's this been happening?"

"This was the worst yet."

"You should see a leech. Perhaps it's your humours."

"It's not me that's out of sorts. It's the world." John leaned his head upon his knees. "Oh, God. . . You don't know how hard it is. To take all this punishment, and not fight back. . ."

"If this is what it takes to stand up to him, then it's not worth it. Sooner or later, it'll break you." Robert sighed and sat down beside him. "When will it end?"

"When the King puts a stop to it." He gave a hollow laugh. "I just pray to God it won't be too late for me."

Chapter 31

They gathered in the yard once they'd broken their fast the following morning.

"Will we head straight over the hills to Kilbirnie?" Malcolm suggested. "We could travel by Glengarnock and shelter there tonight."

"No thanks," John said.

"The Cunninghames have no love for you just now. But they'd do what they can to help the Crawfurds."

"It's not that." John cast an anxious glance over his shoulder, towards the band of dark cloud hanging low in the west. "If the weather turns when we're in the hills, we'll perish. If we take the coast road, we can seek shelter in Renfrew if needs be. Or visit my kinsman at Fulwood."

Malcolm nodded. Worry showed in his face a moment, for he, too, had spotted the clouds. But his voice remained cheerful. "The coast road it is," he said, briskly. "Come on, everyone. Let's not loiter."

* * *

There were precious few out on the road that morning. Those they did encounter hurried on their way without so much as pausing to pass the time of day.

By the afternoon, the black clouds covered half the sky and the wind was rising.

They made good progress until the rain started, near the Cunninghame lands of Craigends. Just a few drops fell at first. But by the time they reached Pennald it was a curtain of biting cold that soaked their clothes in minutes.

"Oh, God!" Marion clasped a hand to her belly.

"What's the matter?" Robert halted his horse alongside.

She stared at her husband, her face pale. "It's started. I know it has. Help me!"

"It's just a little further," Malcolm said, gently.

"But it's happening! It shouldn't be, but- Ah, God!" She doubled up in the saddle. "Holy Saint Margaret!"

"Even if this is the birth approaching, then the pains'll start long before the child drops," Malcolm's voice was steady. "Come on, Marion. You're from hardy stock. Robert, take the reins. And John, ride to Ellestoun. Tell the ladies to prepare for the delivery."

"She's my sister. I can't leave her. . ."

"You must!" For the first time, Macolm's voice cracked. "Go, damn you!"

* * *

The horse ran faster and faster, hooves thundering in desperate rhythm beneath him.

The lashing rain blinded him, but John didn't care. All that mattered was reaching Ellestoun.

They were still opening the gates as he arrived. He charged into the yard, travelling too fast to pull up in time. He wrenched the reins to circle the horse around, its hooves slid on the slippery cobbles and its legs nearly went out from under it.

William was there. He grasped the reins and whispered soothing words to the frightened horse, guiding it round in an ever-tighter circle until at last it halted.

John slid from its back. He clutched William's shoulders, unable to speak. "Go . . . inside," he said, eventually. "Tell Mother that Marion's pains are starting. . ." He took another gulping breath. "Tell her to prepare the chamber."

* * *

His horse was lame. John could feel the jarring break in its stride. But Marion was still out there, and the rain was turning to snow.

John pushed the horse back into a lurching canter, and headed out into the gloom.

They'd scarcely travelled half a mile since he'd left them.

"They're expecting us!" he called.

"Thank God." Malcolm's voice was tight with relief. "Hear that, Marion? It's just a little further."

They forged forwards through the tempest. Soggy flakes of snow fell so thick they could scarcely see the road ahead; it formed a heavy crust along the horses' necks and made them sidle sideways into the darkness.

John dismounted, and pulled his sodden cloak closer. He edged forward, the cobbles hard beneath his feet; without them, he'd have lost his way.

By the time they reached Kenmure, the snow was easing. They could see the faint glow of lights ahead.

It was Ellestoun. The shutters had been opened in the leeward walls of the tower-house, and candles placed there to guide the travellers to their destination.

They were almost home.

* * *

"A midwife!" Lady Elizabeth seized Marion in her arms and held her as she hobbled into the tower. "John! Go to Kenmure and fetch a midwife."

John shook his head. Trails of ice-cold water streamed down his neck from his lank hair. His heart sank at the thought of going back into the night, but it was for Marion. He took a deep breath, bracing himself.

"Master John?" Mary hailed him.

He was too exhausted to show any enthusiasm. "What?"

"I'm a midwife. I could help the lady."

"God bless you, Mary!" He seized her shoulders. "Why didn't you say this before?"

"She wouldn't have listened."

"No matter." He pushed her gently up the stair. "Go on. There's no time to be lost."

"I must be with her," Robert whispered.

"Leave them be, lad," Malcolm said, sharply. "If you want to be useful, then go to the kitchens and fetch some water. And don't fall over your feet when you're bringing it." Then, when Robert had gone, he added, "John?"

John halted. "Yes?"

"We need a priest. I'll go to St Bryde's and fetch one. You stay with Robert. He'll need you there. If things go wrong. . ."

* * *

"Mother?" John opened the door and stepped inside, Mary at his heels.

The women shrieked. "Get out!" his mother snapped. "Have you no shame?"

"I'm sorry." He couldn't see why they were upset; they'd done no more than remove Marion's cloak and unlace her dress. "It's just that Mary here's a midwife."

She curtsied briskly as he spoke her name.

"Come quickly, woman!" Lady Elizabeth snapped. "Leave us, John."

He cast an anxious glance towards Marion. His sister was groaning, like a wounded creature close to death.

"John?" Robert called, panic-stricken, from below. "Where is she?"

"Keep him out of here!" barked his mother. She turned away, but Mary hesitated, giving him a little private smile. *It's alright,* she mouthed.

Reassured, John ventured out onto the stair.

Robert came scrambling towards him. He carried a flagon of steaming water in his hands. "Is everything—" He broke off as a loud cry came from within the room. "Marion!"

"Give me that." John snatched the flagon. "You can't do anything more. Let the ladies do it their way." He leaned close to the door. "Mother? There's more water here."

One of the maids opened the door just wide enough to take the flagon.

Robert sank upon the stair with a groan. He let his head fall against his knees.

John sat alongside. He gripped Robert's shoulder, offering silent support as best he could.

Outside, the wind howled like a damned soul. The water dripped from his clothes and pooled around him, but John couldn't bring himself to move.

Robert's face crumpled. Tears ran down his cheeks. "It's all my fault. I've damned her. I've damned myself, too. If anything happens to her, then I don't want to live."

* * *

The priest came later. He stayed a while then left, his face grim.

At last Marion's cries stopped. There were no wails from an infant, no sounds of any kind at all. *She's dead,* John thought, numbly, and Robert must have thought the same. He seized a tight hold of John's arm.

The door opened, and Lady Elizabeth looked out. "It's done."

"Marion?" Robert scrambled over John's shoulders and bolted into the chamber.

John followed, more cautiously.

"Shame on you!" His mother didn't have the gall to turn on Robert; she made up for it by grabbing him. "Show more respect to your sister."

John shrugged her loose and pushed her gently away.

Marion was sitting up in bed. She wore a long white kirtle, and all around her, there was blood. It stained the bed linen, it soaked the cloths that were being gathered up by the maidservants.

It wasn't so much the blood that disturbed him. It was the look on his sister's face. Haggard from weeping, she sobbed uncontrollably, holding in her arms a tiny, cloth-wrapped bundle.

She looked up at Robert, shame-faced. "I'm sorry."

"It doesn't matter!" Robert sat at her side and put an arm about her shoulders. "I still have you."

"The poor thing was dead in the womb," Lady Elizabeth said. "The saints have smiled on you, Marion. I've heard tales of women wasting away because their child rotted inside them and poisoned their blood. Now, I'd best speak with Malcolm. Mary—" she called from the door, "—remove that thing at once."

"As you wish, my lady." Mary looked up from where she'd been wiping her arms clean by the fire. Once she'd dried them off, she went over to the bed. "Mistress Marion," she said, softly. "You must give him to me now."

Marion clutched the bundle close, sobbing with renewed vigour.

"He was never intended for this place," Mary said, in that same reassuring voice. "God took him so he'd never know the trials of this earth."

"But he'll never know God. He'll just be buried in some cold hole somewhere." Marion drew a sharp breath. "Oh, what did I do to merit this?"

"Don't fret," said Mary. "I know that's what the priests say in church, but. . ." She glanced towards the door. "They don't know everything."

"We won't let any harm come to him," John said. "Now give him to Robert. We'll take care of him tomorrow."

Chapter 32

The world glowed in a ghostly half-light, the ground was cloaked in a pristine layer of white. It was doubtful the snow would lie long; the air felt warm and the sound of water dripping from the drains and the roofline of the tower-house was indication enough that the thaw had already set in.

Within the chapel, lights were shining. Prime was in progress, first mass of the day.

"Come on!" John scrambled over the wall.

Robert passed him first the spade, then the infant's remains, and once that was done clambered quickly after him.

Taking the spade, Robert pried away a lump of turf close to the wall.

It started to rain.

Robert crouched down by the hole and placed the bundle tenderly within. "I know what they'll say," he whispered, as John filled the grave and stamped the soggy soil back down. "They'll say she was too old."

"It happens to the youngest of brides, too." John pressed the peeled-back turf into place.

"It wasn't her fault," Robert said. "Fate's been against us from the start. Your father stood in our way so long, and now. . . She's been worried sick about you and the way you've been treated by the King's men. How's a woman meant to keep her health in these circumstances?" He sniffed and wiped his nose against the back of his hand. "I blame *them*, Lennox and Lyle and that damned Matthew Stewart. Let them burn. I'll rejoice at their misery. I'll be proud to throw the first torch. They deserve to suffer, after all the suffering they've inflicted on us."

"We can lace some meat with poison," John said. "With the dogs dead, they won't even hear us coming."

The Palace of Linlithgow

Dawn revealed a light dusting of frost over the hills. The loch shone like a looking glass, reflecting a weak blue sky. A flurry of ducks quacked furiously as they rose from the ice-bound reeds that skirted the shore.

James was in a lively mood this morning. The hawks had been brought out for inspection before the hunt; he paused to admire their fluffed-up plumage and commend their keepers on their condition.

Once he'd spoken with his falconers, James turned his attention to his courtiers. He was liberal with his presence; he'd talk to each man in turn, and listen to their views, nodding sagely as they spoke.

Then he'd move on.

The spell he wove was slow to fade. Men's faces would lift at the sight of him, and the brightness would linger, long after he'd gone.

Hugh watched patiently as lesser men grovelled or jostled for James' company. He almost pitied them, for they'd mostly be forgotten in a week.

A lesser laird veered close; Hugh briefly half-closed his eyes, feigning inattention, a way of warning men that he didn't want the burden of their company.

But there were some he was prepared to make an exception for. He stood tall, for there was James, striding towards him.

"Lord Hugh!" James called.

Hugh bowed his head, carefully courteous. "Your Grace."

"We haven't seen much of each other just recently," James said. "I'm pleased you could take your leave of Cunninghame and spend some time with me."

"It was gracious of you to invite me."

"You're always welcome in my house. You know that." James laid a hand upon Hugh's arm. "Walk with me," he said. "I must speak with you alone."

"Of course."

"I have such plans for this place," James said. "My father wanted to build a new range here, in the west." He gestured towards the sheds and stables that flanked the western wall. "I'll make that dream real. Linlithgow will be transformed into a palace so splendid that men will talk of it from here to Rome."

"A worthy fate, for a place close to your heart."

"My mother was happy here. I want these works to be completed in her memory." James stared beyond the walls, his radiant face suddenly clouded with gloom. "Doesn't it tire you? That the world thinks nothing of the Scots. . ."

Hugh was silent.

"I want this land to be great, like Florence, or Rome. I see it as a rose in bud, tightly furled. If I could coax that bud to open. . ." He spread his hands.

"A noble sentiment, Your Grace. And I don't see why your dreams shouldn't be realised. We're all part of God's great design, as capable as beauty and brilliance as anyone else on this earth."

"But I fear my plans will come to naught," James said. "So many can't comprehend this vision of mine. Sometimes, I wonder if my people find pleasure in tearing the land apart. If my father had lived, there would never have been peace. I thought things would change when I took the throne."

"They *are* changing."

"Not soon enough." The young king spoke softly. "I want to be remembered as the man who took this fractured land and forged it into unity." He looked at Hugh; his gaze was sharp as an eagle's that had sighted its prey. "How would you have history remember you, my lord?"

Hugh felt his heart beat quicker. For once, he'd missed the warning signs.

"I stand here in the courtyard and when I look to the west, I see that something's lacking," James continued, his voice misleadingly gentle. "And what's true for this place of mine is also true for this land of ours. I've told you of my hopes and dreams, Lord Hugh. If they are to be realised, then I must have peace in the Westland. Grant me that peace, my lord. Or is that asking too much of you?"

* * *

"He arrived yesterday," said Patrick Hepburn. "He asked to see the King. They spoke together for over an hour."

"What did he say?" Hugh's voice was chill.

"He says you're spreading dissent in the Westland."

"Why?"

"Because making mischief's in your nature."

Hugh rattled his fingers against the arms of his chair.

"It's known that you've been associating with Master Sempill," Hepburn said, in that honey-smooth tone of his. The one he used when he bore bad news. "It doesn't look good," he added. "To be seen conspiring with a traitor."

"I approached him at your behest. I reported back to Master Colville, and told him everything I knew."

Hepburn gave a little smile. "I know."

"And neither of you said a word to His Grace?"

"The arrival of His Grace the Earl of Lennox has pre-empted things somewhat."

"Speak to him now!"

"All in good time. . ." Hepburn said. "Hugh, you must have faith in me. I doubted John Stewart from the very beginning. And I doubted Robert Lyle—"

"That's reassuring."

"I was right to be wary. They'll make their move, sooner rather than later."

"Until they do, I'm left on this spit to roast, am I?"

"John Stewart has failed to administer the King's Justice in Renfrew. He's blaming you because he won't take responsibility himself. James'll soon work that out."

"I hope so."

"How well do you know Master Sempill?"

He didn't quite know how to respond at first. Most of the time, Hepburn wasn't quite so obscure in his intentions. "What do you mean?" Hugh asked, cautiously.

"We need peace in Renfrew. On our terms, and not on John Stewart's. Will Master Sempill do what you say?"

Hugh scratched his chin. "Yes. I think he will."

"You're our eyes and ears there. Keep the peace as best you can. And don't forget how John Stewart betrayed you. He's your kinsman, but that doesn't mean you can trust him." Earl Patrick rose to his feet. "I'll talk to the King."

"I'll return to the Westland tomorrow. To see what mischief's been done in my absence." Hugh scowled. "With luck, I won't meet *him* in the meantime. If I do, I'll probably kill him."

"There's to be a Justice Ayre this spring. We'll be heading south. Perhaps we'll summon you to Paisley or Ayr." Hepburn smiled. "Don't forget," he said, "when Lennox falls from grace, there'll be openings at court."

"Such as?"

"Master Colville and I have already decided. You're to be appointed to the Privy Council. A gesture of thanks, from us both. . ."

Chapter 33

They took mass at St Bryde's before their departure.

John knelt before the altar to take the Eucharist. He clasped his gauntleted hands before him and closed his eyes as he accepted the blessing of the priest.

It struck him then. That he'd seen all this before.

Only this time, it wasn't Hugh Montgomerie who asked for God's help as he rode out against his enemies.

* * *

No snarling dogs came to meet them as they rode into the fermtown of The Green.

The place was silent. Like the grave.

John halted his horse. All around him, the shapes of cottages were black against a silvery landscape.

So still. . . So peaceful. . .

Robert drew up alongside, a lighted firebrand in his hand. "This is folly."

"I'm not wasting the kye."

* * *

Inside the barn, the air was sharp with the smell of livestock. Hooves rustled amongst straw, there were anxious snorts as the beasts caught scent of him. He could see their eyes, reflecting the glow from Robert's torch.

One by one, John loosed the ropes that tethered the cattle. He half-expected to hear voices from the adjoining house; every noise seemed loud in the still night air, the creak of the hurdles, the clatter of his plate armour.

He hauled the nearest animal over to the door; it balked and blew through its nostrils, so he slapped its rump and jabbed it in the side with his dagger for good measure. It gave a little kick, and trotted out.

The rest were quick to follow. He counted six altogether as he strode out after them.

"Satisfied?" Robert asked.

"No. It's not nearly enough. The next one. And quickly."

* * *

Two dozen kye ran loose, hooves drumming across the frozen ground. William and the others had arrived; slowly but surely they were herding the beasts away from the village.

"One more," John said.

"John—" Robert began.

John didn't wait to hear him out.

"Thieves! They've taken every beast in the place."

John flinched as the cry went up outside.

He cast a reluctant glance at the frayed rope in his hands.

"Leave it!" Robert hissed. "Get out now, you idiot!"

John grinned, and sawed at the rope with his dagger.

It gave way at last. He pulled the gate open, then thumped the nearest cow on the quarters.

"That's our kye." A small boy stood at the hide curtain that led to the adjoining house. He yawned and rubbed sleep from his eyes as the cows barged out into the night. "Da! He's taking our kye."

* * *

Robert was waiting with the horses. His face was anxious beneath the up-tilted visor. "Come on!"

John broke into a run.

"Damned thief!" A man called out behind him.

"Watch yourself!" That was Robert.

John chanced a glance over his shoulder. The farmer was pounding towards him, shouting obscenities as he closed in.

John cursed and pushed himself onwards. Fast as he could go, with the weight of his armour pressing down upon him.

He only hoped it was fast enough.

The solid flank of his horse loomed ahead; John gasped in relief as he grabbed his reins and set his foot in the stirrup.

He'd almost hauled himself up when he started sliding back.

Someone had a hold of his leg. "I'll gut you for this. I'll skin you!"

John lashed out with his foot. The jagged rowel of his spur dug into something firm. He hauled it free and wriggled into the saddle, as Robert snarled threats alongside.

The shouts ceased.

John looked down. The pursuing farmer was on his knees, hands at his throat. Blood poured through his fingers, staining his pale sark.

"Da!" It was the boy who'd confronted him in the barn. He threw his arms about the stricken man.

A woman was there, too. "Beast!" she wailed. "Animal!"

He spun his horse around on its hocks and trotted away. She ran after him. Her pace quickened, she kept up as long as she could, battering her fists against his thigh. "I hope you rot!" she yelled. She hit armour most of the time, but even when she did strike flesh, he hardly noticed it. He was too intent on what was to follow. He felt strangely serene as he took the torch that hung from his saddle, and lowered it towards the lighted firebrand in Robert's hand. As he paused for the flames to take hold a stone was hurled at him; it bounced off his cuirass with a clang.

He took a deep breath, and tossed the torch over the woman's head. It tumbled through the air, and landed on the thatched roof of the cottage.

The flames caught. They spread like orange serpents through the straw. The woman dropped to her knees, hands clenched in her hair. She gave a low moan as the blaze took hold, then she turned on him. "How could you?" she howled. "I've bairns to feed."

* * *

William and the others had discarded their torches before they departed with the stolen cattle. By the time John and Robert rode back through the fermtoun, it felt as if the whole world were ablaze.

Women shrieked and prayed to God Almighty for deliverance. Men blundered back and forth, dazed and half-naked; those who'd tried to fight had long since thrown aside their weapons.

Or they'd been slain in the fighting. . .

John checked his horse. It was like a dream; he knew he should have felt compassion for the innocents who'd lost everything this night, but compassion was dead in him.

Someone stumbled towards him; John raised his sword with a bellow then laughed in heady delight as the unfortunate man dropped to the ground with a howl and wrapped his arms about his head.

Then, in the midst of all the chaos, a deep rumbling boom rent the air, as if the King's bombards had been fired close by.

Malcolm's party had struck the mill.

* * *

Mary buried her face in his hair and breathed in deep. "You smell of justice," she said.

John laughed and rolled onto his back. He stank of woodsmoke and sweat, but it hadn't deterred her. If anything, it had roused her more. "You should have seen it. . ."

"I wish I had. . ." Her fingers lightly caressed his chest. "They got what they deserved. My poor beasts had never harmed a soul. But they burned them so cruelly. . ." She squirmed closer. "If I could," she whispered, "I'd take that young knight who killed my kye and I'd do the same to him."

"He's a Stewart. A kinsman of the King."

"Then he should know better than to abuse a poor defenceless woman."

John propped himself up beside her. "There's some fine cattle in the yard," he said. "Take a look at them in the morning. You can take some if you like. To help you start afresh."

He lay back down with a sigh. The memories were flooding back. But this time there was no joy in knowing he'd put the fear of God into everyone who'd encountered him that night. He kept seeing the stricken faces, hearing the desperate cries. "Oh, God, Mary. They were just poor folk. Like you. Their lives are ruined." He swallowed. "What have I done?

She squeezed him tight. "You did what you had to," she said, firmly. "And your people will love you for it."

Chapter 34

"I hope you're pleased with yourselves." Grimacing slightly, Marion pushed herself up onto her elbows. "Why didn't you warn me?"

"You'd have tried to talk us out of it," John said.

"What did you hope to achieve?" Marion raised a hand. "No, don't tell me. You did it for me, didn't you?"

John glanced towards Robert, who sat nearby. He was staring at the floor, chin in hand, trying not to get involved.

I'll have no help there, John thought, sourly. "Malcolm suggested it."

"That's right. Blame Malcolm." She lay back against her pillows, eyes closed. "Blame anyone but yourselves." She sighed. "He'll come for you, John."

"We're ready. The women and children are sheltering in the hall and every beast in Kenmure's locked in the yard. If he hopes to pillage my lands, he won't find much to take."

"It's not the cattle I fear for. It's you. They'll drag you in chains to Blackness and then they'll hang you. Or worse. . ." She started to weep. "Oh, Holy Mary. . ."

"Marion, please." John reached out and took her hand.

"You're my little brother."

"It'll be alright—" He broke off as William's knock sounded on the door.

"He's here," William said.

"Oh God. . ." Marion gripped him tighter. "John, be careful!"

He squeezed her fingers one last time and smiled. "Don't fret."

Robert rose in readiness.

John pushed him back down as he passed. "You're staying here," he said. "Best I suffer the consequences alone."

* * *

The yard at Ellestoun resembled market day in Renfrew. Cattle milled everywhere, grumbling as they searched in vain for fodder.

John navigated a route through the sea of shaggy black hides, side-stepping as a horned head swung round to inspect him.

"That's an Easter Greenock mark," John remarked to William. "I daresay some'll carry my mark, too. We've got real proof of his thieving now. It's just too bad we had to find it this way."

He scrambled up onto the wall-walk.

Across the valley, smoke hung in the sky to the north-west. The sight brought a smile to his lips. But the euphoria faded when he saw his men-at-arms' anxious faces.

He nodded to them, and edged his way past.

"There he is," said one of the men-at-arms, pointing to the village. "Just behind that cottage."

John saw Stewart then, seated on his solid black destrier. A group of armoured men followed; they numbered twelve in total. All bore lighted firebrands. They didn't loiter in the village. Instead, they rode on.

Towards Ellestoun.

"We'll defend ourselves if we must," said John, "but don't do anything until I say."

His men muttered their assent. They wound their crossbows and held them ready while the horsemen splashed their way through the ford and climbed the hill at a trot.

The Stewart men-at-arms halted, just a dozen yards away. But Matthew Stewart rode right up to the wall.

John waved. "Good afternoon, my lord! To what do we owe this pleasure?"

Stewart's face was dark as a stormcloud. "You know why I'm here."

"I'm no warlock. I can't read thoughts."

"Enough!" The façade cracked. "John Sempill, you've already been implicated in the assaults on my men in Renfrew town a week ago. Now you also stand accused of the crimes of arson and theft. Twenty-six cattle belonging to Lord Lyle were taken from their byres last night. And twenty houses and a dozen ricks were set ablaze in the fermtoun of the Green. At the same time, the Mill of Duchal was razed. You, sir, are being held responsible for these crimes."

"Then I'm a remarkable man," John retorted. "The Mill of Duchal and the fermtoun of the Green are a good half-mile apart. How could I commit these crimes? I can't be in two places at once."

"Don't mock me!"

"But your accusations are ridiculous!" He was settling into the role of injured party as skilfully as a player in a masque. The apprehension had gone; he was almost beginning to enjoy himself. "If Lord Lyle's cattle stray, then I don't see why the blame should naturally fall upon me. As for the mill . . . I can swear to God that I did not burn it." His tone hardened. "Make your charges. But do so in the proper fashion. I'll fight you all the way, and make accusations of my own besides—"

"Of all the damned arrogant—"

"I want a Justice Ayre. I want to plead my case before the King."

"You're occupying his lands without consent!" Stewart retorted. "Spring's almost on us. When it comes, my father and Lord Lyle will lay siege to this place. We'll roast those walls until they crack. And then there'll be nowhere for you to hide." He turned his horse and walked away.

"He'll burn Kenmure," John muttered, as the horsemen headed back across the river.

"No, look!" William pointed to St Bryde's.

The priests were hurrying out from the chapel. One hailed Stewart, who at least had the courtesy to wait while the churchmen joined him.

Soon knight and priest were deep in conversation.

John clenched his fists tight. "Oh, what I'd give to know what they were saying. . ."

"One thing's for sure; he won't be appealing to young Master Stewart's finer feelings."

"The Holy Father's no fool. He'll be voicing his objections in monetary terms. God, I never thought the day would dawn when I'd be grateful for Bishop Blacader's greed!"

The priest raised his hand in farewell, then walked away. Stewart spoke to his men, then wheeled his horse around.

They were coming back to Ellestoun.

"Give me that!" John snatched a crossbow from the nearest man-at-arms.

Stewart came close to the wall, holding a firebrand high.

"If you toss that here," John said, "then you're a dead man."

Stewart raised his brows. "Really?" He sent his horse ambling along the length of the wall.

John matched him stride for stride, crossbow in hand.

"If you so much as scratch me," Stewart remarked, "then by God you'll hang."

"If you get your way, I'll hang whatever I do."

Stewart halted his horse. He raised his head, and looked John in the eye.

John stared back, undaunted.

The seconds stretched out.

It was Stewart who stirred first. He looked away with a shake of his head and a laugh. "Come on, men," he said. "We'll burn this fox out of his hole soon enough."

John sighed with relief.

But he'd relaxed too soon. The horsemen threshed their way across the gardens towards the doocote.

Stewart squinted back towards Ellestoun. There was something in the way he slouched on his horse, a mocking defiance that set John's teeth on edge. He gestured at the doocote and two of his men-at-arms dismounted. They heaved their shoulders at the door. After one or two attempts it gave way, and then they tossed their torches inside. The fire caught immediately; birds poured from the door and flight holes amidst clouds of black smoke.

Part of him wanted to cry out and beg Matthew Stewart to leave his lands in peace. Instead, he steeled himself to say nothing as Stewart came cantering back.

"The next time you raid the lands of Lord Lyle or the Earl of Lennox," Stewart called, "then, by God, Ellestoun will burn. And I'll make sure you burn with it."

* * *

"My lord?" Alan called desperately from the yard. "What'll we do? We can't lose the birds. . ."

The departing warband had already crossed the Cart. They were heading through Kenmure at a trot, torches spent.

It was risky, for Stewart might have planned this from the outset, but Alan was right. It was still deep in the winter, and they needed all the meat they could get.

* * *

John took his place in the line with the rest of the household, passing bucketful after bucketful of water to the burning doocote. His shoulders ached, sweat dripped into his eyes, but he kept on going. They all did. Until eventually, the remains of the doocote flared briefly in the fading light. The timbers collapsed; the building was lost. Along with half the birds or more.

John folded his arms tight across his chest as he watched its demise.

Malcolm came up alongside and laid a commiserating hand upon his shoulder.

"He's right," John said, softly. "Soon as the weather lifts, it'll all be over." He shivered. "Ah, this is folly. No-one prospers in a world where men negotiate by fire and sword. Is that what Fate's decreed? That Renfrew must follow Cunninghame into the abyss?"

"We must have a choice," Malcolm said. "Why would God grant us wisdom, if we weren't meant to make use of His gifts?"

John turned his back on the burning doocote. "Montgomerie has failed me," he said. "I must rely on my own wits, my own instincts. I don't need his patronage."

"What will you do?"

"I'll seek an audience with Abbot Schaw. He's a powerful man. And he's close to the King. Perhaps he'll intercede on my behalf."

Chapter 35
The Place of Eglintoun

Something had happened at Linlithgow.

Hugh returned earlier than expected; he clattered into the yard at a canter and snarled at the children when they came running out to greet him. Then he stalked off to his chamber and shut himself away, with just his dogs and a flagon of wine for company.

Helen ventured downstairs later on that night and knocked on his door, but all she was granted in return was frosty silence.

Of course she'd been anxious. But there was only so much a woman could do.

Today, thankfully, he'd settled. He knocked on her door bright and early to escort her to Mass; now it was over, their time was their own.

They walked together in the chilly wastes of the garden. The hounds were sniffing amongst the herbs; two hoary old staghounds that Hugh always kept by his side when he ventured alone beyond Eglintoun's walls.

"So when was it confirmed?" He stared absently at the dogs as he spoke, a weary, defeated air about him.

"I've spoken to no-one," she said. "I wanted to tell you first."

"What if you're mistaken?"

"I'm not. A woman knows these things."

"I'm banished from your bed then."

"Why? I've never birthed a monster yet."

"I don't know," said Hugh. "My heir has his moments."

"He follows his father."

That made him smile, at least. He slipped his arm in hers.

"You came home smartly," she said, cautiously. "Was the company of men so tedious?"

He gave a troubled sigh. "There's times when the plotting and ill-will at court sickens me."

"What happened?"

"I'm told that John Stewart holds me accountable for his failure in Renfrew."

"Who said that?"

"Earl Patrick."

"Did you speak with Mattie?"

"Mattie was conspicuous by his absence."

"What about John Stewart?"

"Our paths crossed the following morn." Hugh winced. "He looked me in the eye and smiled. Asked after you, and the children, as if there was no reason for bad blood between us. . ." He trailed off. "It caught me offguard. I've never known any man show such deceit to a kinsman."

"Perhaps Earl Patrick was lying. . ."

Hugh's frown deepened. "That had occurred to me."

"It's a difficult choice. Stand by your kinsman, or place your trust in Patrick Hepburn."

He seized her gloved hands and faced her. "What would you do? If you were a man? And you were faced with such a decision."

"You know what I'd do."

He let her fingers slip from his, and turned away. "You're from the north. Things are different there."

Helen shivered and pulled her cloak tighter. "What have they offered you?"

"A place on the Privy Council."

"Be wary," she said. "It's too good to be true."

* * *

"I don't like Latin!" The Master of Montgomerie pouted at the board. "I want to ride my pony. If I'm to be a knight, then I should practise all the time."

Hugh rested his forehead against clasped hands. At seven years old, the boy was already willing, if not quite able, to confront the world head on.

"It's different these days," Hugh said at last. "Sometimes a knight uses his sword in battle. Sometimes, the theatre of war takes a different form entirely. Then he relies on wit and wisdom."

"I wish it was like the old times," the boy muttered.

"Don't we all?" Hugh cast a sideways glance towards Helen.

"But even then a knight had to be accomplished at many things," Helen added. "To catch a lady's eye he had to sing and dance and make witty conversation."

"I didn't win your mother's heart by piling corpses at her door, that's for sure."

"You learned Latin?" His son sounded incredulous.

"And Greek," Hugh said, wearily. "French, too. Not to mention a little of the *Gaelic.*"

The child gave an impressed murmur, then went back to his dinner.

"So there'll be no more tantrums?" Hugh asked.

"No—"

The door to the hall crashed open.

"Christ!" Hugh put his hand to his dagger.

It wasn't Cunninghame assassins; it was his cousin from Hessilhead, who had, as usual, dispensed with pleasantries. "You didn't tell me you'd come home!" Hessilhead called. "I thought at least you'd pass by my place."

"Move aside," Hugh said, and the boy sidled close to his mother. "I thought it prudent to visit Adam Mure at Caldwell," he added, a little defensively, as Hessilhead squeezed his hefty frame onto the bench. He didn't know why he'd bothered to make excuses, for his cousin didn't seem particularly upset. Instead, John Montgomerie was grinning away like a thing demented, as if party to some great secret.

"Adam said nothing about what's been happening in Renfrew?" Hessilhead asked.

Hugh tore a piece of bread and handed it to his cousin. "Renfrew. It's always bloody Renfrew."

"That young whelp you've been coddling. Master Sempill, at Ellestoun." Hessilhead snatched a choice scrap from Hugh's trencher and wolfed it down. "He's cracked at last."

"Oh." Hugh feigned boredom. "Where is he? Adorning a gibbet in Renfrew? Or has he been hauled to Blackness?"

"Hugh!" Helen chided.

Hugh gave a wicked grin. "She has a soft spot for him."

"She's never even met him." Hessilhead wrested Hugh's goblet from his hand and gulped down some wine. "Well, Lady Helen, you'll be curious to hear that young Master Sempill's making quite a name for himself."

Hugh nudged him, roughly. "Stop tormenting me. Do you want to share your news? Or are you here just to pillage my table?"

"The fermtoun of The Green's in ruins. Sempill razed it."

"Good God."

"Well, word's out that it's Sempill. Some say it might have been the Laird of Easter Greenock. But I have it on good authority that Sempill rode out on Twelfth Night, with eighteen armed men at his back."

"What I'd have given, to see Mattie's face. . ."

"That's not all. The Master of Lennox rode out to Ellestoun the following day.

"Ah."

"He burned the doocote, nothing more." Hessilhead said. "Not like Matthew to be so cautious."

"No. It's not."

"If this escalates. . ."

"We'll make sure it doesn't." Hugh reclaimed his goblet. "Master Sempill's made his point now. Time he started behaving more responsibly."

"And how, exactly, will you get him to co-operate?"

"I'll invite him to Eglintoun. For the festivities here."

"Are you mad? The Stewarts are coming."

"All the better. I'll lock them all in a room and broker a peace between them. The King will be delighted."

"Won't work."

"Then I'll knock their heads together until they're too dazed to argue." He smiled, and picked up some meat. "Mattie will see sense in time. And there are ways of dealing with Master Sempill. . ."

"From what I've heard, he's a law unto himself."

"I'll ride south next week. I'll visit the Sheriff of Ayr. And then I'll travel on to Ochiltree. The distractions of marriage can work wonders on a hot-tempered youth."

Chapter 36
The Abbey of Paisley

"Master John Sempill, Laird of Ellestoun."

John took a deep breath as the door to the audience chamber opened. He'd arrayed himself in his finest silks and velvets, and bore a heavy gold chain about his neck.

Everything hinged on his performance here today; he had to convince Schaw that he was loyal, that he'd been driven from the King's side through the cruel workings of Fate.

John strode down the hall, halted before the dais and dropped to one knee. He grasped the hand that was offered, and touched his lips against the heavy ring that adorned it.

"Rise, my son." Schaw looked kind and inoffensive, but John knew full well that looks could be deceptive.

John straightened. "My thanks, Your Grace, for seeing me so promptly."

Schaw smiled, faintly. "I'm surprised you didn't seek me out before."

"I didn't think my presence would be welcome. . ."

"Your household has served the Abbey well over the years. You and your kin are always welcome." The smile teased Schaw's lips once more. "No matter. You're here now."

"You've heard of my troubles?"

"Of course. You've had to carry a heavy burden since your father died. It's cruel, that a son should have to suffer for his father's loyalty." Leaning his head upon one hand, the old abbot tapped a finger lightly against his cheek. "I did what I could to make Sir Thomas see sense. So indeed did Lord Hugh. But alas, we failed."

"That's all in the past, Your Grace. What concerns me is the future. My future, and the future of those without a voice whom I represent. We need your help. My tenants' homes have been razed; their livestock slaughtered or stolen. I'm doing what I can to aid them, but the deprivations are taking their toll. The poor souls are dying."

A frown touched Schaw's brow. "You're eager to portray yourself as the injured party. But I'm loath to pronounce judgement without hearing both sides of the argument. What of his Grace the Earl of Lennox?"

"He says I'm a traitor." He watched Schaw's expression carefully; it didn't waver. "It's true that I took up arms against the then Duke of Rothesay," he continued. "But I was moved by the purest of intentions. I wished only to serve my King, and obey the will of my father." He paused. "Why must I be punished so harshly?"

"And the brieve of service?"

"His Grace wants twenty pounds. I'd pay that sum tomorrow, if I could be sure it would reach his coffers safely."

"You don't think it will?"

"I can't pay it through the agency of Lord Lyle or the Stewarts," John said. "I fear for my safety. But I would be willing to pass it on to His Grace through another's hands. Perhaps you could assist. . . Or failing that, Lord Hugh. . ."

"I'm sure Lord Hugh, like myself, would be delighted to act as an intermediary," Schaw said. "There remains, though, the certain matter of a burned fermtoun and a razed mill."

John shifted, uncomfortably. "It was wrong to burn Lord Lyle's village. I'm a man. I make mistakes."

Schaw studied him in silence. The moments stretched out; the old abbot was deep in thought. "He harried you a long while before you succumbed to violence," he conceded at last.

"Speak to the King, Your Grace. Tell him that I seek forgiveness." John drew his sword and presented the hilt to the Abbot, then dropped to one knee once more. "I pledge my sword to him. I will fight in his name, whenever he summons me."

"I'll tell him that," said Schaw.

"I need his help. Who else can preserve me from the cruel justice of the Stewarts?"

"Perhaps I can," said Schaw. "I'll go to John Stewart myself, and see what can be done to heal the rift between you." He leaned forward and placed his hand gently upon John's head. *"Gloria patri et filio; et spiritui sancto. Benedictus qui venit in nominee Domini."*

* * *

A dozen men lingered in the road as John approached Kenmure. They looked like brigands, dirty and dishevelled. But as he approached, they touched their tattered hoods respectfully.

He recognised them at last. They were his tenants. They held lands at Bar and Pennald.

"Hope we're not troubling you, Master Sempill," one said. "We asked to see you up at the place and they said you'd gone to Paisley. We thought we might meet you on the road."

"How can I help you?"

"It's nearly spring. The ground'll be warming up soon and the fields need ploughing."

Their faces were gaunt, but there was still hope in their eyes. Still, there was no telling what Matthew Stewart would do, once he heard that work had begun in rebuilding the cottages he'd razed a month before. "All your hard work'll come to naught if there's more raids," John reminded them.

"We'd be better off dead than wasting the land," the farmer said, grimly. "We'll be dead anyway, if we don't find some way of supporting ourselves."

"How soon will you return?"

"Soon as we can."

"You can cut what timbers you need for the roof. And take what stone's necessary for the footings. When you leave, I'll ride with you. I'll make sure you're protected until the building's finished. And I'll give you whatever provisions you need to get yourselves back up on your feet again."

A smile cracked the dirt on the farmer's face. "Thank you, Master Sempill!"

* * *

His meeting with his tenants lifted John's spirits; despite the dankness of the day he was humming a jaunty French air as he tramped into the hall. He shed his dripping cloak into a servant's hands and gratefully accepted the mug of mulled wine that was offered.

"Not a good day for travelling." Robert Crawfurd greeted him. "How was it?"

"He seemed sympathetic enough." John wandered close to the fire and basked in its heat. "How's my sister?"

"She's left her bed, and is walking a short distance. She says she'll be able to travel before the week is out. But your mother thinks she should wait the full month."

"And so she will. I'd rather starve myself than have my sister thrown out into the cold."

"Besides, I might have to fulfil the duties of laird-depute once again in the coming weeks. In your absence, two liveried messengers came to your door. One was from Sir Adam Mure at Caldwell. The other was from Eglintoun. . ."

"From Montgomerie? What the Devil does he want?"

"He asks that you attend him at Eglintoun next month. To celebrate the Feast of Saint Valentine in his company. Sir Adam hopes you will break your journey with a few days spent with himself and Lady Margaret at Caldwell."

John shrugged. "I can't go."

"—I thanked both men and told them that the Laird of Ellestoun was honoured to accept their invitations. They're expecting you, John. You can't wriggle out of your obligations that easily."

"But how can I leave Ellestoun?" He tried to sound calm, reasonable; he grimaced inwardly, for despite his efforts there was desperation in his voice. "The men of Pennald and Bar will be going back to their lands. I told them I'd protect them."

"If you ask me there's no better way of protecting them than to curry favour with Montgomerie. If that's the only way forward, then you must do it. For all our sakes. I'll look after your tenants."

"It's too much to ask," John muttered. "The Stewarts may level the cottages as soon as they're built."

"There's at least ten days before you leave for Caldwell. That gives Master Stewart plenty of time to take up arms against you."

The Place of Ochiltree

Their visitor entered Ochiltree astride a splendid dappled grey charger, which curved its neck and tossed its silken mane as it trotted into the yard. He brought with him a cavalcade of attendants; a dozen men-at-arms liveried in red-and-blue and a line of laden sumpter horses.

There was a presence about him. Margaret found it instantly compelling; she thought he was like an eagle, full of grace and majesty. With his lean haughty face and his bright eyes, he reminded her of Caesar, or one of the Greek heroes.

She watched from the wall-walk as William and Elizabeth greeted him, feeling slighted, because she hadn't even been told he was coming.

Goose-bumps touched her skin. What she'd have given, to be swept up in his embrace, to hear him say that he'd do anything to win her heart. . .

She bounced down into the yard and loitered in the background, hoping that someone would introduce her.

No-one did. She was just William's unmarried sister. Like Jamie, the bastard, she was an embarrassment to the family.

* * *

She cornered Jamie later. "Who is he?"

"Lord Hugh, the Lord Montgomerie. He's Bailie of Cunninghame and a loyal friend of His Grace the King. Descended from French Kings, they say."

She shivered. "He's magnificent."

Jamie smiled, half-heartedly. "Maybe."

"What's the matter?"

"He's not a man to be trifled with."

"Why?"

He grasped her wrists and pulled her close. "When he was twenty-five years old he murdered the Lord Boyd in cold blood."

"Oh." Somehow, that revelation only made him more attractive.

"And just last year, he burned the Cunninghame place of Kerrielaw to the ground."

"I'm sure they deserved it."

"He's earned a fearsome reputation in battle. He slew the Earl of Glencairn at Stirling."

"It's a knight's duty to slay the enemy—"

"Aye, maybe. But Glencairn was his kinsman. The Earl took Lord Hugh into his household when his great-grandfather died and he had nowhere else to go. Treated him like his own son, he did. . ."

Margaret shrugged.

"And if slaughtering Glencairn wasn't enough. . . It's also said that he killed the Sheriff of Renfrew. You know, the father of your intended. . ."

"That's something in his favour, then. You must introduce me."

"Why?"

"Because—"

Jamie threw back his head and laughed. "Because you want him in your bed."

Her face coloured. "No!"

"Margaret." He gripped her shoulders. She'd never seen him look like that, agitated, serious. "You mustn't go near him. He'd ruin you, and he'd break your heart."

* * *

It was the most Margaret could do to sit still through dinner. She sat a few seats away from their guest, who dazzled them all with his wit and his brilliance.

She picked idly at her venison. She didn't want the evening to end; she just wanted to bask in his presence. She glanced at him from time to time and blushed as unfamiliar thoughts coursed through her. She'd never given much thought to men before. But then, there weren't many worth speaking of at Ochiltree.

But though she tried her best to catch Lord Hugh's eye, by smiling and looking demurely down towards the board whenever he glanced in her direction, it did no good.

Instead, he seemed to look straight through her.

She settled next to Katherine that night. "I shall probably dream of him."

"Mmm."

"He's so graceful. And handsome, too. I wonder what he's like, beneath all those fine clothes. . ." She stretched slightly, and yawned. "I think he'd be lean and sleek, like the carving of Our Lord above the altar."

"My aunt says that some men who are hung like goats are hairy from their loins right down to their toes. Just like those creatures that haunted the forests of the ancients."

"Your aunt's silly."

"No she's not."

"Oh, it's not fair!" Margaret rolled on her back with a sigh. "Why couldn't they find me a man like him?"

"Maybe Lord Hugh's heard of your beauty. Maybe he wants your hand."

"Do you think?"

"Who knows?"

Please God let it be so, she prayed. And she could scarcely sleep a wink that night for the thought of it.

* * *

The men talked together the following day. In the laird's chamber, where their conversation couldn't be overheard. Margaret sat in the ladies' rooms above, spinning yarn while her mother and gude-sister discussed what provisions were needed for the kitchens.

There was a knock on the door, and in came Jamie. "Margaret's to join us."

She didn't know whether to be delighted or dismayed. She set down her distaff and looked to her mother, who waved her impatiently away.

Once they'd left the chamber, Jamie put a hand on her shoulder, and steered her down the stairs. He had a sour look on his face.

"What's happened?"

His grip tightened. "Quiet."

"But—"

"Just be quiet!" He rapped on the door to William's chamber.

"Enter!" called William.

She marched bravely inside.

It wasn't William in the laird's chair. It was Lord Hugh. He was sprawled comfortably there, with his elbows resting on the arms of the chair and his legs parted slightly before him.

Those qualities she'd found attractive terrified her now. His thoughts, his motives, were unfathomable. She saw the bulge at his loins and she swallowed; she couldn't look away, she was fascinated and unnerved all at once.

She almost forgot to curtsey. Jamie nudged her, and she sank low.

"My sister," said William.

Lord Hugh looked her up and down. His face was dispassionate, he might as well have been sizing up a brood mare. He gave a nod and a wave. "She'll do."

Rage flared briefly inside her, but she said nothing.

"Your marriage to Sempill of Ellestoun—" William began.

Lord Hugh stirred. "It's to be progressed, without delay."

The news took a while to sink in. She wanted to cry out; tears stung her eyes, she had to gulp them back. But she didn't want them to know how upset she was. She nodded. "I understand."

She looked at Lord Hugh sitting there, with his cold expressionless face, his sumptuous clothes and his careless pose, and the love and desire she'd felt when she first set eyes on him was gone.

She hated him more than anything else on this earth.

But she was born of a Wallace, and Wallaces always bore misfortune bravely.

The Lands of Pennald

Some bothies had been set up at Laigh Pennald; small mound-like structures built from turf. They wouldn't be needed much longer, for the crucks of the house already stood pale and tall against the sky. Now the gable walls were being built, while the women and children gathered fresh turf for the roof.

"Rest a while!" John called. "There's ale here."

They trooped over to join him.

John's heart warmed at the sight of them; they were smiling again, comforted by the hope that soon their troubles would be over.

John lifted his mug. "To the spring. Let's pray that the harvest will be fruitful, and your labours here rewarded."

"Amen to that," someone muttered.

Bread and meat was handed out. They all ate greedily.

"How much longer?" John asked.

One of the farmers shrugged. "We'll have finished the roof before the week's out. Providing the weather holds, that is. . . If the winds pick up, we'll be right back where we started."

"Master John!" One of the men-at-arms hailed him from the crest of the hill. "There's horsemen approaching."

The mood changed; the farmers grabbed what implements they could, while the men-at-arms put their hands to their sword hilts.

"How many?" John demanded.

"There's just the three of them." The soldier squinted down the hill, one hand shielding his eyes. Then he waved. "It's only Master Robert!"

Robert soon appeared at the brow of the hill. He came trotting towards them, face bright with excitement. "Excellent news, John!" he called. "Abbot

Schaw has sent two cartloads of flour and another of seed grain. He asks that you distribute these alms amongst the poor and the dispossessed."

John bowed his head. "God bless the man." He looked up, to where a pale sun glowed behind a veil of cloud. Was it really too much, he wondered, to hope that winter was over, and spring at last was on its way?

* * *

Mary sat slumped against the bedpost. She hadn't moved for ten minutes now, maybe more. The laces of her gown were loose, her tawny hair hung thick over her exposed back.

John sat up. "Mary. . ."

There was no indication she'd even heard him. She'd been taking these fickle moods over the last week or so, ever since she'd heard that her neighbours were returning home.

Throwing back the covers with a sigh, he slid down the bed to join her. He snaked his arms around her waist. "What's the matter?"

She didn't look at him. "You'll catch cold."

"What's wrong?"

"You know what's wrong."

"It's better this way."

"The fields need tended."

"It's too dangerous," he said. "I can't be there to protect you. You should wait here until we know it's safe for you to go back." Snuggling close, he squeezed her tight.

"I'm not a child." Her body was rigid, her voice cold. "I don't need you to protect me."

"If something happened, I'd never forgive myself. Can't you understand—"

"You want to hold me captive here, don't you?"

"No, I don't. Of course I don't."

"Then let me go home!" She raised her fists to her eyes and moaned. "Ah, God. I want to go home. . ."

"Mary, please." He rubbed her back. "You're comfortable here, surely."

"I hate Ellestoun. I hate being your whore—"

John drew back and hugged his knees. "I never thought. . ."

"Oh, Johnny. . ." She turned to him, cheeks streaked with tears. Raising her hands, she cupped them about his face. "Don't take it that way. Of course I care for you. But I can't live this way. If you loved me, you'd understand that. You'd let me go."

He pushed her gently away. "I have to go to Eglintoun," he said. "When I come back, I'll arrange for a new cottage to be built. And I'll send a plough team out to your fields. Will you wait till then?"

She said nothing.

He hugged her. "I'd worry, if I thought you were living out there with just your sister and your children, and the threat of another raid looming over you."

"You worry too much." A smile spread wide across her lips, the light danced in her hazel eyes once more. She pushed him down along the bed and snatched his wrists, thrusting his arms high over his head. Then she straddled him. The folds of her gown enveloped him, her hips pressed against his loins.

He was roused already, but he knew full well she'd make him wait. She always did, these days.

She studied him a while, idly traced the line of his ribs with the fingers of the one hand.

He flinched and swore.

Her smile sprang back. She leaned close, and breathed warm against his chest. "I'll stay here a little longer," she whispered. "If that's what you want."

Chapter 37
The Place of Eglintoun

"This isn't Caldwell," Adam said. "He's in his lair now, and twenty times more dangerous."

"I'm not a fool," John retorted.

"Just keep a civil tongue in your head! And the same goes for you, Hector. Speak only when you're spoken to. And don't drink too much."

"Yes, Father." Young Hector cast a weary glance towards John.

"Best listen to your father," said John. "That way we're all granted a quiet life." He felt sorry for Hector; the lad was fifteen now, big and broad like Adam. Eager to please, but slightly slow-witted. Adam had high hopes for the youth, but John knew that while Hector's qualities would serve him well in battle, they'd do nothing to help him succeed at court.

And success at court meant everything, these days. . .

"This isn't some small intimate affair," said Adam. "The King's come south on a Justice Ayre, and half the court's come with him. I daresay half of them will come to Eglintoun if they can. Lord Hugh's very generous in his hospitality."

* * *

The curtain wall that surrounded Eglintoun was well-maintained and freshly-harled. Montgomerie men-at-arms patrolled the wall-walk above, keeping careful watch as they approached.

At the sight of them, John's misgivings were rekindled; he wondered again if it was all a trap. He'd brought no armed retainers, for they'd all been needed to keep watch over Ellestoun and the newly restored farms of Pennald.

It was just William, and himself.

They reached the gatehouse. Above the entrance was a brightly-painted carving of the Montgomerie coat-of-arms; the quartered *gules*-and-*azure* shield, supported on either side by winged gryphons. It was crested by a shapely maid; she smiled modestly down on them as she held aloft a severed head.

That's appropriate, John thought, as his horse clopped across the drawbridge. He looked up warily at the looming shadows above and the menacing black void of the murder hole.

It was too late to turn back.

* * *

"I've had my eye on this a while." Hugh lazed back in his chair, goblet in hand. "Earl Patrick thought early on that Montgrennan might have entrusted some of the King's treasure to the Sempills."

"A reasonable assumption," Abbot Schaw agreed.

"I found an excuse to speak with Master Sempill in October. The matter was raised, of course."

"What was his response?"

"He seemed genuinely horrified by the suggestion." Hugh picked up the flagon on the adjacent table. "More wine, Your Grace?"

"If you please." Schaw held out his goblet.

"Make no mistake; the lad's matured since then."

"I daresay he's had to."

"He can mask his motives as well as the next man now, but only when he's given time to prepare himself. If you catch him off-guard, he'll either speak the truth, or he'll say nothing at all."

Schaw frowned as he sipped his wine. "I'm relieved to hear this," he said. "I knew Master Sempill was putting on a show for my sake, but I was inclined to believe him." He laughed, quietly. "So that's what John Stewart intended. He wanted Montgrennan's money. For himself, d'you suppose?"

"He's more eager for John Sempill's lands. He thinks that if he conjures up the missing gold and has Sempill denounced as a traitor, then he'll be granted the forfeited estates and titles. Not only that, he'll find the favour at court he's been seeking all along—" He broke off as a knock sounded on his door. "It's only Helen," he said. "Come in!"

Helen peered around the door and nodded towards the abbot. "Forgive me for intruding. But more of your guests have arrived."

"Is it Mattie?"

"I don't recognise any of them. The steward's talking to them now."

"So?"

"Do you want to speak with them?"

Hugh slouched back with a sigh. "I'm not here. Tell them—" He waved her irritably away. "Just tell them anything!"

"I understand."

Hugh rolled his eyes in mock-weariness as the door closed once more. "Where was I? Ah, yes . . . Sempill of Ellestoun. When I visited his place, all was as it should be. He didn't act like a man who had vast quantities of gold stored within his walls."

"I think," Schaw said, carefully, "that if he'd been entrusted with the King's treasure, this whole affair would have played out differently."

"Exactly!" Hugh agreed. "At the first sign of trouble, young Master Sempill would have run straight to you or me so he could be rid of the damned gold as soon as possible. That way he'd have earned the King's gratitude, and I daresay some financial recompense."

"The Stewarts already realise the mistake they've made."

"And that's why they're pressing him so hard. If this becomes common knowledge, they'll lose face at court. The only way they can entice men's attention away from their poor judgement is by making Master Sempill a traitor one way or another."

"They almost had their way, too."

"Burning down Lord Lyle's fermtoun, eh?" Hugh shook his head. "I'll have words with him about that. He *must* come across as the injured party."

"I'd like to have seen you acting with such restraint at that age."

"I suppose," Hugh conceded. "I've invited him to Eglintoun," he added. "But whether he shows his face is a different matter."

"He's a canny fellow," Schaw said. "He'll fear the worst, I'm sure."

* * *

She awaited them in the hall; an elegant lady, slim yet solid in build. She wore a fine gown of dark green velvet, with her hair confined within a gabled hood. A cross of gem-studded gold hung about her neck.

John blinked, entranced by the sight of her. She was Venus and Diana combined; grace and beauty balanced against the fierce strength of the huntress.

She turned dark eyes upon them as they were ushered before her. "Welcome to the Lord Montgomerie's place," she said, a radiant smile lighting her face. Her voice was soft, she spoke with a pleasing northern lilt. "I'm Helen Campbell, the Lady of Eglintoun. I've been entrusted with your care until His Lordship's return. He's hunting at present, and begs that you forgive him his absence."

"My lady," said the steward. "May I present to you Sir Adam Mure of Caldwell and his son, the Master of Mure."

Adam ushered Hector forward. Adam was all blustering pomp and self-importance, while Hector was a tongue-tied wreck.

You shouldn't be here, John told himself, as he watched Hector blush and mumble replies to the questions put before him. *The whole land will have heard of your misfortune by now. They'll be mocking you for it, too. . .*

The steward was beckoning him closer. He didn't know where to look, he wished the ground would open up and swallow him.

"Master John Sempill, the Laird of Ellestoun."

"Oh!" Recognition dawned in her face. "So this is the young lion of Ellestoun? I've heard so much about you."

"Thank you, my lady." He tried to sound grateful.

"You mustn't look so bemused. My lord speaks highly of you. You're the thorn that festers endlessly in John Stewart's side. That's no mean achievement for a man of your years."

"You're very kind." Somehow he found the courage to look her in the eye. "In truth, I don't know why you asked me here."

"My lord says your star will soon be in the ascendant. He's seldom wrong about such matters."

"I'm flattered to hear he has such faith in me."

"I'm sure you won't disappoint him. You carry yourself with such humility and courtesy. They're rare qualities in a man." She seized his hands. "It's a pleasure to welcome you here to Eglintoun."

"No, my lady. The pleasure's mine." He bowed extravagantly before her, then lifted a slender hand to his lips and kissed it lightly.

She tossed her head and gave a little peal of laughter. "You are a flower of chivalry, Master Sempill. And, I daresay, a breaker of young maids' hearts." She gestured to the servants who lurked discreetly nearby. "Wine for our guests, if you please. They must have refreshments, before they're shown to their lodgings."

* * *

They tarried a little longer with Lady Helen in the hall, sipping spiced wine while she asked of their families and told them a little of the Montgomeries' exploits and traditions.

As she spoke in that captivating voice, John looked about him in a daze. Wherever his eyes came to rest, the wealth of the family was evident. Gold and silver plate was piled high in the aumbries, while fine Flemish tapestries hung from the walls.

But amongst the riches there was an incongruous sight. A battered old pennant, hanging in pride of place amongst the rich furnishings. It was emblazoned with a lion, a curious creature whose tail stuck out, straight as a poker, behind it.

Hector voiced the question that John himself was dying to ask. "Forgive me, Lady Helen," he said, "But what's *that*?"

She followed his gaze. "That's the banner of the Percies. It was captured at Otterburn a hundred years ago. Sir Hugh Montgomerie fought the Earl of Northumberland in single combat and defeated him. It was with the ransom for the earl's release that the Montgomeries built the castle of Polnoon. Their seat has moved to Eglintoun now, and it was Lord Hugh's wish that the Percies' banner should be placed here.

"My lord has always tried to live up his ancestor's reputation. He's succeeding, too; there's many men who swear that the spirit of Sir Hugh has been reborn in him. Why, Lord Hugh has already established himself as a leader of his household and a man of great influence in the Westland. God willing, the day will soon come when he can prove himself in battle against our old enemies the English. Just as Sir Hugh Montgomerie did before him."

* * *

"I wish I'd never come here," John said, stretching out along his bed. "I'd give anything to be back at Ellestoun, with the starving hordes clamouring at my door. At least Matthew Stewart doesn't pretend to be my friend."

William looked up from where he was unpacking. "There's worse men to be doing business with, I suppose."

"But I don't belong here!" John thumped his fist against the mattress. "I daresay everyone attending Lord Hugh fought for the Prince. Except me. Yet here I am, like a wolf amongst sheep."

"A sheep amongst wolves, more like."

"They'll hate me. Because my damned uncle's a traitor, growing fat on a pension from King Henry."

"It's no consolation," said William, "but rumour has it that Harry's here."

John sat up. "Blind Harry?"

"Who else?"

John lay back down with a groan. "He'll stir the Wallaces into a frenzy. For want of an Englishman to rend, they'll probably turn on me." He gave a humourless smile. "I shouldn't jest about such things. A pack of drunken Wallaces is one thing. They may be the least of my worries."

"I know."

"Lennox is Montgomerie's uncle. Would Lord Hugh dishonour his kinsman by failing to invite him?"

"I'll sleep by the door," said William. "Just in case."

Chapter 38

When the time came for dinner, John found himself crushed between Adam and Hector at the far end of one of the lower tables. It was an inconspicuous position, and it displeased Adam no end.

They weren't short of company; their table was crammed full of Wallaces. Patrick Wallace of Auchenbothie was a welcome face nearby, amongst a gaggle of Craigie and Ellerslie Wallaces. They were enjoying a raucous family reunion, tossing back vast amounts of wine as they toasted each and every Wallace who'd ever lived, and The Patriot in particular.

The head of the Craigie Wallaces was, however, conspicuous by his absence. As Bailie of Kyle, he was worthy of a seat in Lord Hugh's company. John recognised some more of the men sitting with Lord Hugh and his family at the top table; the Abbots of Paisley and Kilwinning, and Sir Hugh Campbell, Sheriff of Ayr.

There were others, however, whose faces were unfamiliar.

"Archibald Campbell, Master of Argyll," Adam explained. "And Robert Colville."

John nearly choked on his ale. "Colville?"

"He's related to the Ochiltree Colvilles, I'm sure. But I don't actually know where he was born and raised. Stirling, I think. He's a great favourite of the King. I can't for the life of me think why he's come here, because he and the King are thick as thieves. Perhaps His Grace sent him out to Eglintoun to act as his eyes and ears." Adam sat tall as music sounded from the minstrels' gallery above. "No more talking, John. Dinner's served!"

A cheer went up as the serving staff emerged. A sumptuous array of dishes was paraded before them, all beautifully presented on vast gold and silver platters. There were roast swans and ducks glazed with honey, suckling pigs squatting on their haunches, great cuts of venison, stews and pies and a vast quantity of bread. One by one, each dish was carried to the top table and presented to the host and his lady.

The Abbot of Kilwinning rose to bless the assembled company, then John Montgomerie of Hessilhead stood to slice the meat.

Little by little, the dainties that graced Lord Hugh's table trickled their way down. The food was cold by the time it reached the lesser lairds, but it was appreciated just the same. Every dish was flavoured with a host of herbs and spices, each concoction more exotic than the last.

John chewed his meat half-heartedly. He'd never felt so discontented with his lot. He wanted so much to be a part of the privileged group who presided over the top table. He longed for the challenge of their conversation, to prove his worth in a battle of wits that was as keenly fought as any tournament.

He watched Lord Hugh throw back his head and laugh at some jest uttered there. Helen Campbell smiled, her brilliant beauty shining out like a beacon. She turned to her husband and he turned to her, and they looked into each other's eyes, so magnificent, so perfect. . .

"What ails you, John?" Adam wrapped a hefty arm around his neck, nearly choking him. "Your face is as straight as the poker-tail on that damned Percy lion."

"Leave him alone!" Constantine laughed. "Can't you see that young John's tired of our company? He wants a place at the top table."

Adam gave a scornful snort. "He's lucky to be here at all!"

"Pass the bread, please," John spoke briskly to Hector.

"You're fine company tonight, John!" Constantine taunted. "Get some more wine down you." He leaned over Adam, flagon in hand, and made a careless attempt to re-fill John's goblet. Wine spilled everywhere; all over John, all over the table, and over John's dinner, too.

"By the Saints! Don't be so careless." John sighed as he brushed wine from his lap. At least he'd had the foresight to wear a doublet the same colour as the wine. He cast another glance towards the top table, and wished the night could soon be over.

Instead, it had scarcely begun.

They forged their way through six courses, then, when the subtleties were being served, Montgomerie of Hessilhead rose to his feet. He battered the hilt of his dagger against the board. "Silence!" he called. "For our noble laird, Sir Hugh, the Lord of Montgomerie."

The chatter ceased.

Lord Hugh stood tall, leaning his knuckles on the board. He looked about him with one of those charming smiles of his. "Kinsmen, friends, gentlemen. We've almost reached the end of our meal now. God willing, your bellies will be full and your appetites sated. But our festivities are far from over. It gives me great pleasure to present a man whose name is known by all. He's a patriot amongst patriots, a storyteller whose vision can be matched by none. Gentlemen, I give to you; Blind Harry!"

There he was; a shrunken figure entering the hall with his harp slung over his back. Two Montgomerie men-at-arms escorted him, then Lord Hugh himself left his meal to take the poet's arm and guide him to the stool that had been set ready.

John felt the hairs on his neck prickle with excitement. Harry was a legend; some said he was a hundred years old, others swore that he was older than that. That he'd fought at Otterburn, that he'd even met the Wallace himself.

Harry sat himself down, luxuriously slow. He unslung his harp, sat it on his knee and tuned it fastidiously, saying not a word.

The silence was unbroken.

He looked up. His unseeing gaze seared the crowd, twin points of penetrating blue.

The Wallaces erupted into life. "Harry!" They roared as one, lifting their goblets high. "Har-ry! Har-ry!"

One imperious glance from Harry and even the Wallaces were silent. A cough rumbled faintly in his throat, and then his voice boomed out:-

"Noble lords, gathered in this gracious place,
Right worthy sons of Scotia's blessed race.
A shining star amongst you is Lord Hugh
Chieftain of this House; noble, fair and true.
From fine and gracious stock His Lordship comes,
Such wight and worthy blood through his veins runs.
Born of Cath'rine Kennedy, blythe and fair—"

John stifled a sigh. It was understandable, that Blind Harry should curry favour with the man who was giving him board and lodgings for the night. But he was disappointed, for he'd hoped for some of the Wallace tales. . .

"Lord of Montgomerie, a mighty house,
Whose sons have fought right hard for Scotia's cause:
Good Sir Neil, martyred in the Barns of Ayr,
And brave Sir Hugh, a knight beyond compare.
Who vanquished Hotspur, in combat gory—"

The Wallaces were restive. But they needn't have worried; a few more token words of deference to Lord Hugh, and Harry's introduction was at an end:-

"Speak of none," he said to me. *"But Wallace."*
"For do the least of his brave deeds not far
Surpass our own—"

John could barely contain his smile. *You can relax now,* he told himself. *There's no sign of Lennox or Lyle amongst the company. No one knows who you are. No one cares, either. . .*

He held out his goblet as a servant came past bearing more wine. *Best make the most of it,* he thought. *Who knows what tomorrow will bring?*

Chapter 39

A hand shook him. "Master John?" William's voice hissed loud in his ear.

The world was swaying. If he moved, he thought he might be sick. "Go away!"

"It's important."

John groaned and rolled over. He didn't know where he was at first, but little details nagged at him. The bed was too small, he could hear the grunts and snores of sleeping men from beyond the curtains.

His eyes opened.

He remembered then. He was in Eglintoun, with a brace of Adam's men-at-arms camped in his room.

He sat up. "What's-" He broke off as he registered the pained expression on William's face. "-the matter?"

William cast an anxious glance towards the men who lay strewn about the floor. "You're wanted. One of Montgomerie's men, I think. Here." He thrust some fresh clothes at John.

John still felt ill, but his mind was lucid. He wriggled into his hose, and pulled on his shirt, then shivered as he scrambled from his bed. "Dear Lord! It's damned cold!" He pulled on his doublet then slipped into his shoes, somehow avoiding stepping on one of Adam's men as he did so. "Did he say what he wanted?"

"No." William held out John's sword. "Do you want this?"

John pushed it aside. "If this is foul play, then it won't do me much good." He pulled his gown around his shoulders. "But I'll take my dagger. Just in case."

* * *

A shrunken old man awaited John in the corridor beyond. He looked John up and down with a dour frown on his face, then shrugged and shuffled off.

John followed, fully alert now, his heart thumping fearfully.

They reached a door. The old man lifted the latch and gestured for John to step out into the frost-rimed yard.

Lord Hugh was there. Alone, but for two rough-haired old staghounds that lounged at his feet. He stared into the pale blue sky, oblivious to the world, his breath misting in the frigid air. His fur-trimmed collar was pulled high around his neck, his velvet bonnet jammed over his ears. There was a drawn, hollow-eyed look about him; indication that he, too, was paying for his over-indulgences the night before.

The staghounds looked wistfully towards John, and Montgomerie snapped into life. "Good morning! I'm sorry I disturbed you. But it was vital that we talked. And in private, too." He nodded towards the old man. "We'll inspect the gardens. An early morning walk's just what a man needs after a rowdy night." He flicked his hand.

The gesture might have been intended for the dogs. Or the servant. Or indeed for John.

As it was, they all followed.

"You will be careful, Master Hugh." The servant had to hurry to keep up with Montgomerie's long strides.

"Yes, yes. . ."

"You take too many risks. We worry so."

"I can look after myself." He was heading towards the sally port, with a swing to his step that showed he had a sword concealed beneath his gown.

The servant gave John one last mistrustful look, then unlocked the iron yett that pierced the curtain wall.

"Thank you." Lord Hugh patted the old man's shoulder. "Don't forget; you never saw me. Now come this way, Master Sempill. Time is short."

John ventured beyond the gate without a word, and waited for Montgomerie to join him.

The dogs trotted on ahead, crossing the narrow walkway that spanned the ditch. They paused on the other side, looking back towards their master as if they, too, had their doubts.

"Go on!" Lord Hugh urged them. "After you," he said to John, gesturing towards the walkway.

As he crossed the narrow timber bridge, John glanced down. Stinking piles of rubbish filled the ditch; discarded straw from the stables, soiled rushes from the floor, the shrivelled remains of a long-dead cat. *He means to murder me*, he thought. *There's no better place than this to hide a corpse.* He was suddenly grateful for his dagger, though it would be poor defence against two huge hounds and a man armed with a sword.

"You look as if you'd rather be going to your own hanging," Lord Hugh remarked.

"I'm sorry, my lord."

"The Stewarts aren't waiting here to hack you limb from limb, if that's what's worrying you."

They reached the gardens beyond, and paused amongst the ranks of herbs and flowers that waited, frost-shrouded and shrivelled, for the spring sun to coax them back into life.

Montgomerie didn't speak at first. His gaze was fixed on the tall trees in the deer park beyond. Rooks circled the skies, their raucous voices loud in the still morning. "We can talk now," he said. "I like to think my people are loyal, but Cunninghame spies are everywhere. Why, those wretched birds are probably Cunninghames, damn their black hides!"

"You didn't say a word to me yesterday," John said. "Why the sudden change of heart?"

Montgomerie regarded him a moment, face impassive. "What news do you bring me from Renfrew, Master Sempill?"

"Nothing that you haven't heard already. My household's on its knees."

"And still you won't give in?"

"He's wronged me. If I admit defeat, then I might as well admit my own guilt."

"Wouldn't that be easier?"

John shrugged.

"Even Hercules would be daunted by the task you've set yourself. And yet you struggle on regardless. . ." Montgomerie turned with a sigh and studied the trees again. His gown was pushed back to reveal his gloved hand resting lightly on his sword hilt; a far from reassuring sight, John thought, but he was suddenly too tired to care. "You're like your father. Stubborn and determined to hold your ground, and the Devil take the consequences."

"Why did you bring me here?"

"I said I'd give what help I could, when the time was right. I'm not a man to renege on his promises. When you arrived yesterday, I was in counsel with Abbot Schaw of Paisley. He'll speak to the King on your behalf."

"Oh, thank God. . ."

"He's been seeking an audience with the Earl of Lennox."

"I thought they'd already spoken." There was no disguising his surprise. "There's been no attacks on my tenants for at least a fortnight. I thought he'd pricked John Stewart's conscience enough to hold him back."

"Lennox refused an audience with him." Montgomerie paused. "Strange isn't it?" he said at last. "That the attacks on your people have stopped anyway?"

"I don't understand. . ."

"And if that wasn't odd enough. . . The man I sent to Dumbarton requesting the presence of my kinsmen returned with his message undelivered." Lord Hugh glowered at the distant birds, as if they were to blame for everything. "To be treated that way cuts me to the quick."

"But why should he turn his back on you? And the Abbot?"

"Perhaps he has greater quarry in his sights. . ."

John swallowed, throat dry with foreboding. The thought of intrigue suddenly repelled him. It interfered too much with normal life. It was unsettling and dangerous. Yet here he was, being drawn into intrigue of the highest order.

"There's rumours of discontent in the north," Lord Hugh said, in a matter-of-fact voice. "In those places where support for the late King was strongest."

"You think the Earl would strike out at the King himself?" He grimaced at the hypocrisy of it all. "But he justifies the persecution of my tenants by saying that I'm a traitor!"

"He changed sides last year because he knew King James would fall. But he didn't prosper. Men had him marked, from the very beginning. *Why should he succeed*, they said, *when we risked so much more, right from the outset?* He resents their success, because he's a Stewart, and he thinks the Stewarts have a God-given right to be there, at the very heart of government."

"You're his kinsman. Shouldn't you ride with him?"

Lord Hugh sighed, wearily. "The men he'd remove have been good to me. They've promised me a seat on the Privy Council. If the court was clogged up with Stewarts, I'd never be granted such an opportunity."

"So you'd side with me. Against the Stewarts."

"It's not as simple as that. I'd side with the King. Against the Stewarts. And if that means defending you, then yes. I'd side with you."

John breathed out, quiet relief.

"There's just one thing. We must be assured of your loyalty. Some think you shouldn't be trusted. Because of your past, and your family connections."

"When I spoke with Abbot Schaw, I pledged my sword to the King. When my services are required, then I swear by Almighty God I'll be there."

Montgomerie relaxed, visibly; there was a warmth in his smile that John had never seen before. "Good," he said. "Serve us well, and we'll make sure you're rewarded." He stretched out his hand. "We can call ourselves allies? And friends?"

John didn't stir. "I appreciate this, my lord. But I won't be beholden to you."

"I expect nothing in return. Except loyalty to the King."

Reassured, John reached out his hand to grasp Montgomerie's own. For a fleeting moment, his fingers were locked in Lord Hugh's precise, unyielding grip.

"Don't speak of this to anyone," Lord Hugh warned. "Lennox mustn't know that we suspect him of treason. Now, there's just one last favour I must ask of you. . . No more burnings, if you please! Once can be forgiven as youthful exuberance. Any more, and I'll be hard pressed to come up with an excuse for you."

John smiled. "I'll leave the arson to Master Stewart from now on."

"Excellent! Now I'll send word to Ellestoun in due course, and instruct you on what's required."

"I'll await you there, my lord."

"I have a name, John. You can use it, if you like." Lord Hugh cast a gloomy look towards the sky. "Well, we'd best head back. Before we're missed." He whistled to the dogs; they came leaping up alongside. "Sir William Colville's here," he mentioned. "I'll introduce you to him later. You can discuss the wedding. If all goes well, you'll be a married man by Lent. If not, then I'm sure something else can be arranged."

Marriage. He supposed it was a good thing; it would put his mother's mind at rest, at any rate. "Thank you," he said.

Montgomerie shrugged. "Not at all," he said. "What're friends for?"

Chapter 40
The Place of Ellestoun

"He thinks the world of you," Mistress Marion said. "He'll be deeply hurt when he hears you left like this."

"It'll hurt him anyway." Mary stared unseeing at the floor. Mistress Marion was going out of her way to be kind, but it wasn't much help. She still felt like a prisoner.

She'd felt changes in her body the last few days. Her breasts were tender; she knew the warning signs by now. She was determined not to bear his bastard. But there was little she could do to be rid of it here.

"If it's what you want, then I can't stop you," Marion told her. "But I wish you'd reconsider."

"He doesn't need me anymore. He'll be wed soon. I can feel it in my bones."

* * *

That afternoon, she found herself perched in an ox-cart, seated next to Janet and the children. They hadn't left Ellestoun empty-handed: Master Robert had pillaged the stores, filling the cart with all sorts of things. A cage of chickens, sacks of flour and seed grain, an assortment of cooking pots and flagons and a bundle of blankets.

He rode alongside on his bright bay horse, accompanied by a brace of men-at-arms. *Nothing but the best for you, Mary,* he'd said with a smile and a touch of his bonnet. And it wasn't just because she'd been sharing John's bed for the past month. It was because of Mistress Marion; *it's thanks to you she's on the mend,* he'd told her. *I won't forget how you helped her.*

Her heart felt lighter as the cart trundled past Pennald and on towards Bar. She could see pristine thatch on some of the newly-built cottages dotted about the countryside. *Soon*—she thought—*I'll be in my own house, with no-one telling me to fetch and carry for them.*

* * *

Davey Semple nodded to her. "The wife didn't think I should come here," he said. "But neighbours are neighbours, and I didn't want your children to be stranded out in the cold."

"It's none of her business," Mary said. "Besides. . . What's she to be jealous of? Did he shower me with gold and fine gowns?"

Davey shrugged. "Nothing to do with me. She'll change her tune when the next child's due and her pains start."

"We'll help you with the sowing and the harvest. Same as we always have."

"And we'll start on the building tomorrow. This time next week, Mary, we'll have you a cottage to be proud of."

* * *

The Place of Eglintoun

Adam was well pleased that night. "Did you see how he sought me out?" he said, as they headed back to the hall after dinner. "He hasn't forgotten me."

"You said he forgets nothing."

"Is that jealousy I hear?" Adam laughed. "Because he spoke to me and didn't even glance at you? Don't you worry, John—" He wrapped an arm about John's shoulders and hauled him close. "—your kinsman'll look after you."

When they entered the hall, they found that the tables had been cleared and benches set out along the walls so the guests could enjoy an evening of music and dancing.

John sank down between Adam and Hector and stared gloomily into his goblet. He was bored already. He listened for a while as Adam and Constantine discussed the merits of Lord Hugh's claret, but soon his mind wandered.

You're a fool. He's spun this tale of treason so you won't strike out at his kinsmen. You'll hold back as he asked but he'll never come. . . He frowned. *So why aren't Lennox and Lyle here? He must be telling the truth. Unless this has all been a ruse to remove me from Ellestoun. .*

.

The musicians struck up a stately *rondeau*.

Lord Hugh and Lady Helen took the floor; they were performing the dance with as much grace and elegance as they displayed in every other aspect of their lives.

John watched, distantly. At the sight of them, his discontent grew worse. "Ow!" he gasped, as Hector elbowed him. "What in God's name was that for?"

"You weren't listening, were you?" Hector said.

"I'm sorry. What is it?"

"I think I'm in love." Hector's face was bright scarlet. "With the Lady Helen."

"Holy Mary! Don't say that too loud. Lord Hugh'll fillet you like a herring."

"I can't help it."

"No," John agreed. "I don't suppose you can."

The dance was over; Lord Hugh turned to his wife and bowed. She responded with a curtsey and a lively smile.

They walked back, arm in arm, to their circle of kinsfolk and friends. Children came running out to meet them; Lord Hugh ruffled the hair of one small boy and hugged an older girl close.

The ache inside John intensified. *Look at him. He has everything; a glorious wife, a family that adores him. And wealth and influence that matches any man's round here. His reputation's not exactly wholesome, but I suppose even that has its advantages. . .*

Amongst the flock of cousins, a girl caught his eye. She was a shapely maid, fresh-faced and pleasant, with her long brown hair flowing free and unbound down her back. Not as sophisticated as the Lady Helen, but attractive all the same.

And unmarried, too.

John sighed. Now he'd spotted her, he couldn't look away.

He thought of Mary, and he felt a little guilty. He missed her warmth, her kindness, but distance brought an unbiased eye. She always listened, but she scarcely talked, for there wasn't much in his life she could relate to. Her eloquence was in her hands; he could see now that the comforts she brought weren't enough.

You don't love me, she'd said, more than once. Not being reproachful, just matter-of-fact. *You'll understand that some day.*

"Uncle John!" Hector's fingers drove deep into his arm.

Somehow, he kept from wincing. "What the Devil's—"

"Look! She's coming this way."

John reluctantly dragged his eyes off the girl. Hector was not mistaken; Lady Helen was indeed approaching. He thought she'd walk on past, but instead she halted before them. "Master Sempill," she said, clasping pale hands before the red-brown folds of her gown. "My lord remarked that you seemed melancholy. That won't do, sir. You're insulting your host. And his lady. . ."

"I'm sorry." He was all too aware that Adam and Constantine were staring.

"Perhaps our company would cheer you." She reached out her hand.

"It would be my pleasure." He rose and grasped her fingers.

She rested her hand on his arm, and they walked sedately across the hall together.

"My brother wants to meet you." Her eyes flitted up to meet his.

He'd thought a look like that would rob him of his wits. Instead it put him on his guard. He didn't think he'd ever met a woman so magnificent, but at the same time. . .

"—and here he is," Montgomerie announced, as they approached. He was slouched on the bench, elbows resting on the board behind him. "Helen's used her wiles to good effect."

"So this is your squire?" The Master of Argyll said. He was a similar age to Lord Hugh; his brown hair was tinged with auburn, and he had a lively manner about him. He shook his head. "You've chosen a dangerous master, Master Sempill. Learn well; he won't tolerate mistakes."

Lord Hugh waved a hand towards Argyll. "John, may I introduce my gude-brother, Archibald Campbell, Master of Argyll."

Campbell gave a little bow. "At your service, Master Sempill."

"And this," Lord Hugh continued, "is Robert Colville."

"Delighted," said Colville, distantly. He was a perfect courtier; impeccably turned out, with his light brown hair combed sleek about his shoulders, and the velvet of his doublet densely embroidered with gold.

"My sister is concerned for you," Campbell said. "She has decreed, that since we're gathered here to celebrate the feast of Saint Valentine, you won't leave this place without a wife—"

"Or at least the promise of a wife," Lady Helen added.

"You deserve a fine woman, sir," Campbell continued. "A woman of virtue. A woman of courage. A woman worthy of the man who bloodied John Stewart's nose."

"And she must, of course, be a beauty," Lady Helen said.

Lord Hugh stood with a sigh. "Helen's most insistent. I'll do anything to stop her nagging. Janet, my dear. Come here."

The young maid John had noticed earlier stepped forward. "My lord?"

Montgomerie seized her shoulders and manoeuvred her before him. "I have my doubts about the Colvilles," he said. "If they won't deliver on their promises, then I won't have you leave here empty-handed. I have a daughter, but it's Helen's opinion that she's not quite ready for marriage—"

"And she's a bastard," Archie Campbell cut in. "Sired by a peacock, born of a chicken. So don't expect much of a dower from that old miser—"

"Archie!" That was his sister.

Campbell was undaunted. "Be wary, Master Sempill. This man would sell you a two-legged horse and tell you it was bred for going round corners."

Casting Campbell a baleful glance, Montgomerie gripped the maid tighter and shook her gently. "Janet Montgomerie of Giffen. She seeks a husband. A man of sound character and good prospect."

Janet Montgomerie curtsied, and gave a hesitant smile. "Master Sempill."

Lord Hugh prodded her in John's direction. "Go on now."

"Lord Hugh's talked much about you, Master Sempill," she said.

John took her hand and steered her deftly away. "Good things, I hope."

"He says you're an educated man. I myself speak Latin and a little Greek. I sing, too." She cast a shy glance towards him.

She might have been of an age to marry, but there was still something child-like about her; she was trusting and willing and desperate for approval. "You're very accomplished," he told her. "And you'll make a worthy wife, I'm—"

"Come along," said Lord Hugh, seizing the collar of his gown and hauling him away like an unruly youth. "We need you for this dance."

* * *

Eight of them were marshalled in readiness for a round dance. It started sedately enough, but soon became a gallop as Hugh Montgomerie and Archie Campbell vied to drive the pace along.

The ladies were caught between exhilaration and terror; at John's left, Lady Helen laughed in delight, while young Janet clung to his right hand as if he were the only thing keeping her upright.

One dance followed another, with no one wanting to admit they were tired. Montgomerie and Archie Campbell treated the whole episode like a tourney, and the ladies didn't want to let them down.

Eventually, Lady Helen raised her hand. "I'm vanquished!"

Lord Hugh steered her carefully back to the bench. "I think we proved our worth." He snapped his fingers at a passing servant. "Ale, please. Enough for everyone!"

Lady Helen nodded to John. "You're good on your feet," she said. "If your prowess is matched in other ways. . ."

"Alright," Montgomerie muttered. "I'll see to it now. Excuse me." He sauntered off.

John ushered Janet to the bench. "Some ale?" he asked, retrieving mugs for them both.

She arranged her skirts carefully as she sat down. "Thank you, Master Sempill."

"Please." He grimaced. "Call me John." He settled beside her. "Are you enjoying the evening?"

"I'm a little overwhelmed. This is the first time I've set foot beyond Giffen. There's so many people. They're all rich, and grand, and wonderful."

John smiled at that. "Well, I don't know if I'm any of those. But if Lord Hugh thinks I'm worthy of your company, then I won't complain."

"Master Sempill, a word please."

John looked up to see Robert Colville standing over him. He squeezed Janet's hand, gently. "Forgive me. We'll speak later?"

Colville clutched his arm and shepherded him a short distance from Argyll and Lady Helen. "Hugh's moving quickly, I see."

"If the Colvilles won't honour their promises, then I'm sure the Montgomeries will."

"Is it really what you want? She's a very pretty girl, but marrying her would be just one short step from marrying Hugh himself." Colville pursed his lips disapprovingly. "He'd be a very demanding kinsman. . ."

"If you're so eager to wean me away from Lord Hugh's influence, then perhaps you should talk to your kinfolk."

Colville gave a thin smile. "I'm only a humble notary. They'd never heed me," he said. "Besides, why should I get involved? I'm sure Hugh will settle things his way." He turned cold grey eyes on young Janet. "A pity," he said. "The poor maid seems quite fond of you."

* * *

Lord Hugh came back accompanied by two other men. Both were in their early thirties; one was thin-faced and furtive-looking, the other broad and strong and grim.

"Sir William Colville of Ochiltree," Lord Hugh explained, patting the shoulder of the thin-faced man. "And his half-brother James." He gestured towards John, "Gentlemen, can I introduce you to a good friend of mine; John Sempill of Ellestoun."

Ochiltree gave a brief nod, while James Colville just scowled at the ground.

"We discussed the match at Ochiltree," Lord Hugh said, taking a neat side-step and placing himself alongside John. He leaned a conspiratorial hand on John's shoulder. "Sir William assured me that he would progress the marriage." He cocked his head, there was a bright, expectant look about him. "So when may Master Sempill collect his bride, Sir William?"

"My lord, we've had much to concern us," Ochiltree replied. "We haven't yet—"

"But I was so looking forward to the wedding," Lord Hugh protested.

"If Master Sempill wants to be released from the contract," James Colville spoke out, "then my brother would be agreeable."

"There's the question of the dower," said Ochiltree.

"It won't be repaid," John retorted. "I didn't break the contract."

"We'll waive—" James Colville began.

He was silenced by an angry look from his half-brother. "We have to discuss this," Ochiltree said.

213

"No need to worry about finding a new bride." Montgomerie spoke loudly in John's ear. "I'll speak to the Laird of Giffen, and make arrangements for you to wed his eldest daughter." He turned to the Colvilles. "Trying to broker a deal between you has taken great effort on my part," he told them. "Some expenses might be in order. Shall we say, fifty pounds? I'll add half to the dower; the maid's father wasn't expecting to find a husband of Master Sempill's calibre. I hope that's acceptable."

"The bans will be read," Ochiltree said, face pale. "At the parish church in Ochiltree. Commencing this Sunday."

"Most excellent!" Lord Hugh punched John lightly in the back. "You'll be wed before Lent, John." Without another word, he headed back to where Lady Helen and Archie Campbell awaited him.

Ochiltree shrugged and walked away; James Colville cast John one last seething scowl before following after him.

"John! Come here please!" Montgomerie called.

John hurried after him with a sigh.

A goblet of wine was thrust into his hand.

"A toast!" Lord Hugh announced. "To the health of the young couple." He tossed back some wine. "There," he said to Lady Helen. "I've done what you wished, my love. Master Sempill has won his bride." He drew himself tall, a benevolent smile upon his face. "I think I handled that rather well."

"I'm indebted to you, sir," John said, softly.

"Yes," Lord Hugh agreed. "I rather think you are."

Chapter 41

Mary lay awake in the cramped space of the bothy. Outside it was a chill night, but she felt snug enough. She had Janet curled close on one side, while her children slept on the other.

She knew it would be a while before she grew used to life away from Ellestoun. Rich, highly spiced food had been replaced by bread and ale; in a way it felt good to be feasting on plain fare again.

In another week, she'd have a home to call her own, and then. . . She patted her belly and smiled in the darkness. *I'll be rid of you. And it'll all be behind me.* Her eyes filled with tears. *I'm sorry, Johnny. I didn't want to hurt you this way. But you're young. Your heart'll mend soon enough.*

"You're awake, aren't you?" Janet asked.

"Yes."

"Do you miss him?"

She didn't reply.

"It wasn't right, Mary. He's so different. How could a woman like you. . ."

"I know," she said, softly.

"Perhaps he'll visit?"

"The way I left will cut him deep. I don't think I'll see him again."

"I'm sorry," Janet reached for her hand.

Mary squeezed her fingers tight. "It's the way of the world, that's all."

* * *

The following day, the building began. The neighbours came; the men brought axes to cut trees for the crucks, while the women brought bread and ale to keep the labourers fed throughout the long day.

Mary helped the women as best she could, fetching wood for the fire and doing her fair share of the cooking. They were cold towards her at first, until they realised that she hadn't changed. They asked her advice on sick children and barren cows; she gave it freely, as she always had.

It was as if the trying times of winter had never happened. She was home again, and she was happy.

* * *

For once, his return to Ellestoun brought John no consolation. In the cold grey of the morning, his old tower looked tired and worn; its harling was grubby and stained and the pennant hung limp from its flagstaff, while around its walls lay the ramshackle shelters of his tenants.

He was weary already. He'd have given anything to be back in Eglintoun, where life had been vibrant and colourful. Suddenly, the prospect of spending the rest of his days confined within these walls made him want to weep.

Once he'd halted in the yard, he sat still upon his horse a moment, too tired even to dismount.

"John!" Marion leaned from the window of the ladies' chambers. The past week had transformed her; her face looked bright and healthy once more.

That at least made him smile. "Shouldn't you be resting?" he called.

She hesitated. "We must talk," she said at last. "I'll come to your room."

* * *

"Where's Robert?" John trudged to the window and sat down there.

"He left with Alan yesterday. I think they were heading west to Southannan." There was a dejected air about her. She hadn't looked him in the eye since they'd started talking.

He knew full well what was coming, but didn't feel inclined to discuss it yet. "The rebuilding?"

"It's going well. The farms at Pennald are all restored." She paused, then added, "John. . ."

"I know."

"She said she needed to go back. She said the fields had to be prepared. She was determined. It seemed wrong, to keep her here against her will."

The news came as no surprise, but it hurt nonetheless. *Oh, Mary, you could at least have said goodbye. . .*

"John?" Marion placed a hand upon his shoulder.

He shook her away. "I'm alright." He stretched his legs out before him. "Was she provided for?" His voice sounded too loud, too cheerful.

"Robert made sure she had everything she needed. He was very generous; he said that's what you'd have done in the circumstances. He gave her livestock, too; some handsome cows, a brace of sheep and some chickens."

"I'll send Alan to her cottage in a few days. To make sure that all's well." John slumped back with a sigh. "It's for the best, I suppose. I'm to fetch my bride at the end of the month."

"But that's wonderful news!"

"I've decided, Marion. Once I make my vows before God, there'll be no infidelity. No matter what, I'll be a loyal and devoted husband."

Marion sat down alongside. "That's all any wife could ask for." She slipped her arm in his. "You should visit the tailor."

"I can't afford it."

"Of course you can!"

He didn't answer. He stared through the open window, towards the grim grey skies beyond. "I was right. The Colvilles loathe me."

She patted his hand. "You're marrying the maid," she said. "Not her kinsmen. How could she not be charmed by you?"

Chapter 42
The Place of Ochiltree

"I'm sorry," William said. "I tried, Margaret. I really thought the marriage would slip his mind."

Her chest felt tight. She couldn't breathe. She swayed on her feet, and was caught by Jamie's steady hand.

Then the tears started. She shuddered as she fought to contain them, but it was impossible. She cried so hard her whole body shook, the sobs coming so fast she couldn't even see.

"We couldn't afford to break the contract," William whispered. "I'm sorry."

"Leave her be," Jamie snapped. "Come on, girl. Let's sit you down."

He ushered her over to the window.

William muttered his apologies and left. But Jamie stayed with her, patting her back and murmuring encouragement as she wept.

"I won't marry him."

"Margaret. . ."

"I'll kill myself. I'll throw myself off the tower."

"Don't talk that way," he said, gently. He rubbed her shoulders with one of his great big hands; she couldn't ever remember him being so considerate. "Besides, maybe it's not so bad."

"It is."

"He's very personable. I don't think he'll disappoint you."

"I don't care."

"So he's suffering misfortunes just now? Who's to say he won't prosper tomorrow? With Montgomerie's patronage, he'll go far. . ."

"—I shall shut myself away, and I won't eat. When he comes to Ochiltree, he'll find me on my deathbed."

"Now that's plain silly. And you'd best not talk this way in front of your mother. She'll beat you."

Margaret giggled, despite herself. "I'll miss you," she said. "I don't know what I'll do, alone in a strange place."

"You'll have the girls."

"You think he'll let me keep them?"

"He'd be a monster not to. And he didn't really seem like a monster. One head, two legs, two arms, and no forked tail. Least not one I was aware of."

She hugged him tight. "Thanks, Jamie. You're very dear to me. I'll miss you more than anyone." She sniffed back more tears. "When he takes me away, I'll never see you again."

217

He rocked her in his arms. "Course you will, my little princess. I'll come and visit, whenever I can."

"Promise?"

He smiled. "I promise."

The Lands of Bar

I'm going out to gather herbs, Mary told her sister. *I might have to wander quite far. If I'm not back tonight, don't worry.*

Janet shrugged, and didn't question her.

Mary took everything she needed. A knife, some tinder and a small pot to crush and boil the brew.

All that day she searched through thickets and copses, selecting fresh shoots of spurge, henbane, hemlock, and hellebore. It was still early in the year, and there weren't many plants to be found.

But she only needed a little.

Darkness was falling when she settled down by the Lochar Water and set up a fire there. She pounded the herbs together and added a little water, then boiled the mixture up.

Just a few bitter mouthfuls, but she knew it would be enough.

She lay back in the darkness, feeling the wet and cold seep through her clothing, and there she waited, her hands caressing her belly.

She closed her eyes and prayed to God. *I'm so sorry. You've blessed me with the Miracle of Creation, but You know I mustn't bear this child. Please forgive me. . .*

Pain tore through her innards, and she gasped.

She crouched on all fours, steeling herself to the horrors that lay ahead. Despite the cramping in her belly, she felt strangely at peace. *I've sinned, and must bear the consequences. God give me strength. God help me.*

The Place of Eglintoun

"Mattie!" Hugh was still pulling his gown into place as he hurried out into the yard.

Matthew Stewart waved, and slid from his horse. Barely recognisable in thick winter clothing, he strode towards Hugh, laughing.

Hugh quickened his pace. It wasn't like Matthew to make such efforts to conceal himself. But he didn't voice his misgivings. He just opened his arms wide and warmly embraced his cousin. "It's good to see you. Where the Devil have you been hiding?"

Matthew sighed and shrugged. He seemed pale, weary; it suddenly struck Hugh that his younger kinsman had aged five years in just a few short months. "I'm sorry we missed the feast. But Father was away when the message reached Dumbarton. And I was at Duchal. I was told too late; I thought I should ride down and make my apologies in person."

"There's no need to apologise." Hugh shivered and stamped his feet. "Let's go inside," he said, placing an arm about his kinsman's shoulders and steering him towards the tower-house. "Will you stay here tonight, or will you be pressing south?"

"I'll stay here, if that's alright with you. You'll make a welcome change from Lord Robert."

"What's that supposed to mean?" Matthew glowered at the cobbles. "We have little in common."

"I spoke briefly to your father over Yuletide. But we didn't have much time to talk. How's he keeping?"

"He's well enough."

"He's away, you said? What business has taken him from Dumbarton at this time of year?"

"Ah." Matthew winced slightly. "He's speaking with his Stewart kinfolk. You know Father; he never talks much about his affairs. But I'm not here to talk politics. I'm here to see you."

Hugh halted. "He doesn't know you're here."

Matthew took a deep breath. Looked him in the eye, and he was his usual self, bold, defiant. "No," he said. "He doesn't."

* * *

"I haven't seen these before." Matthew held the glass goblet up before the window. He swilled the wine gently around, studying it closely as the light pierced its ruby depths.

"I met a merchant over Yuletide. He brought them all the way from Venice." Hugh pulled a chair up before the fire. "Could've bought a new warhorse with the money, but I thought Helen would appreciate them. Please, sit down."

"I'm surprised they survived the journey intact." Matthew settled into his chair, stretching out his feet with a sigh. "I've been absent from court too long. I've missed all the comings and goings. And all the news, too. How has Fate been treating you, cousin?"

Hugh pulled another chair alongside. "I'm doing very well. I'm told a seat on the Privy Council's beckoning."

"That's good news." Matthew tried to smile, but didn't quite succeed. "Here's to your success," he said, lifting the glass high. "It's richly deserved." He took a sip, then added, "What of the King?"

Hugh shrugged, trying to look as if nothing were amiss. "He's flourishing. Bursting with enthusiasm for hunting and hawking and cracking English skulls. And eyeing up every comely maid who crosses his path."

"I'm glad he's well." Matthew fixed his eyes upon the fire. There was a crack as a log settled there and sparks flew high; he started slightly, like a stag scenting the air for danger. "Has James talked of Renfrew?"

"He hasn't asked anything of me. He still has limited knowledge of the situation, and that's how it will remain. Unless someone decides to tell him."

Matthew frowned, and tapped his forefinger gently against the glass. "You won't be that someone. . ."

"It's Renfrew," Hugh said, quickly. "Beyond my jurisdiction."

"What if you're asked?"

"I'll state the facts as I know them. Nothing more."

"I understand."

He'd never seen Matthew look so glum, so hopeless. "What's the matter?" he asked.

Matthew said nothing. He just sat hunched over his chair, goblet clasped in both hands.

"If you want advice, I'll give it. What's worrying you? Is it the unpaid taxes? Or the fact that Master Sempill won't co-operate?"

Matthew shook his head, a regretful smile on his lips. "You should've finished off that runt on the battlefield."

"Come now, Mattie! Don't be so uncharitable. He's taught you a valuable lesson. You underestimated him from the very beginning."

Matthew didn't reply.

"What of the taxes? Are the men of Renfrew willing to pay? Or are they clutching their purses close and procrastinating?" Hugh paused. "The two problems are one and the same," he added. "Solve one, and you solve the other."

"And how—" Matthew said, "—would you solve them?"

Hugh gave a little smile. "You wouldn't like my suggestion."

"Don't be so damned mysterious."

"Anyway, why should I try and tell you anything? You'll just snort and tell me that it's not what you wanted to hear."

"That's not very fair."

"But it's true," Hugh countered. "You're treading on thin ice. The King wants peace, but in Renfrew he sees only unrest and defiance. He'll want to know why."

Matthew gave a cold laugh. "What about Cunninghame? Why should he question my conduct, and overlook yours?"

"Because the Sempills aren't the Cunninghames. Master Sempill knows he can't defeat you with the sword. So he'll use a weapon he's more adept with: the law. It's something Sir Thomas wanted his son to be familiar with. Thought it might serve the lad well when he came to be Sheriff. So he packed the boy off to the university at Glasgow for a year or two." Hugh snorted with mirth. "Fancy that! A Sheriff who knows the laws of the land. The world's changing, without a doubt."

The moments crawled past and Matthew maintained his sullen silence. Every sound was intrusive; the crackle of the fire, men shouting in the yard, the neigh of a horse.

Hugh could bear it no longer. "Have you heard from Abbot Schaw?"

The scowl he was granted was answer enough.

"You see," Hugh continued, "Your runt knows how to bleat in the right ears. He plays the role of injured innocent to perfection, too."

Matthew still stared at the fire, thick brows drawn tight into a frown.

"Swallow your pride. Declare a truce with Master Sempill, and make no more demands on him financially."

"You want us to give in!" Matthew jerked round to face him, cheeks bright with rage. "What kind of talk is that?"

"That way, you'll get your taxes and your father'll keep the Sheriff's title a little longer."

"We're Stewarts, for God's sake. We won't bow down to a laird like *him*!"

"Don't dismiss him. He's moving in wider circles now. He's a charming fellow. The King will take to him straight away. When he's introduced. And it's just a question of when. . ."

Matthew gnawed at a finger-nail. "This isn't what I hoped to hear."

"He's asked Schaw for protection. Now the good Abbot's determined to champion his cause before James."

"Why should James take his side? And turn his back on my father?"

"James won't want to take sides. But Patrick Hepburn will." Hugh broke off, then added, quietly, "I think I know what your father intends. He mustn't expect James to choose between you and Earl Patrick. Patrick's like a father to him." He leaned close, and gripped Matthew's arm. "You must talk him out of it."

Matthew didn't look at him. He gave a sardonic smile. "I might as well try and stop the tides."

"I know."

"Thank you." Matthew said, distantly. "I appreciate your counsel. Whether I'll be free to act upon it is a different matter. I hope you'll understand, in the months ahead, that whatever happens between us, no malice is intended towards you."

"Will you still be saying that when Kilmaurs is slipping the noose around my neck?"

"It won't come to that."

"Such assurances aren't yours to give." He broke off, searching Matthew's face for indecision. He could see none, but that didn't count for much with Matthew. "Don't do this," he said. "Turn back now, while you still can."

Matthew drifted into an unheeding silence.

And that, Hugh guessed, would be the end of it. He'd done what he could. "Let's head to the hall, shall we?" he said, false brightness in his voice. "Helen'll wonder what's keeping us."

Chapter 43

The fire was dying, and just one solitary candle flickered at the bedside. The floorboards creaked as Hugh prowled like a wolf beyond the bed, moving from the darkness to the light and back, over and over again. He said nothing, but every so often he'd give a fitful sigh.

Helen set the comb in her lap, watching him. She knew him well enough; he'd seethe away for hours, unless something happened to make the anger erupt in earnest. It worried her, to see him wander restlessly like that, wearing no more than his sark, with the night growing colder by the minute.

"Hugh." She patted the bed beside her. "Come to bed. It's very cold."

Not a word.

"Hugo. . . Come here, my love. . ."

Still no response.

"Hugh!" she snapped. "Do you want me to go back to my own bed? Because that's what I'll do. Least I'll be granted peace and quiet, even if there's no man there with me to warm my flesh."

The pacing stopped; she drew a deep breath in readiness.

"Damn him!" he roared. "Why must he do this to me?"

Then, even as the echoes of his rage faded, his mood changed. He looked at her, face ghost-pale. "What am I to do?" Sinking down on the edge of the bed beside her, he dropped his head in his hands. "Ah, God help me. . ."

"Shh. . ." She rubbed his shoulders gently. "You must do what your conscience tells you."

"I can't help him. There's too much at stake now."

Helen said nothing, just wrapped an arm around him and hugged him tight.

"Their plot. . . It's doomed to failure. I can feel it in my bones. And when it fails, someone'll hang. I just hope to God it's not him."

She brushed some stray hairs back from his face. "Mattie's like a cat. Drop him from a parapet, he'll land upon his feet. Even if Earl Patrick wanted him dead, James'd never allow it."

Hugh nodded. He turned to her, weary, but with the brightness burning undaunted in his eyes. "I suppose."

"You can do no more tonight, my love." She ran an idle finger down his back, tracing the hard ridge of his spine. "Come to bed, please."

He shed his sark with a sigh, and shivered, gaunt and pale in the flickering candlelight.

"Are you going to sit there all night?" She flung back the covers and stretched out along the bed.

He settled alongside her without another word. She wriggled out of her kirtle, and pulled the covers over them both.

"So," she said, rubbing her fingers briskly against his chest, "are you going to tell Mattie that you've been asked to Master Sempill's wedding?"

He caught his breath at the absurdity of it, and silent laughter shook him. His mirth was infectious; soon they clung to one another, giggling, like young lovers hiding in the cornfields.

"It was most gracious of them to invite me," he said, pressing his nose close against hers. "I think I'll attend."

"They might not want you there."

"Shouldn't have invited me then."

"You'll have to bring a gift."

"I've already decided. A pair of fine gilt candlesticks. They can throw them at each other."

"Oh, Heavens! I'm sure things won't be that bad."

"If the maid's anything like her mother, then God help him. One look from Euphemia Wallace would freeze a man's blood at fifty paces."

"Young Janet would have made a much better wife."

"He's too expensive for the likes of her."

"It was unfair, to make her think—"

"But to hide herself away and weep for three whole days was ridiculous."

"You don't understand how a maid's heart moves, Hugh."

He snuggled close. His breath was warm against her ear. "I understand yours."

She pushed him half-heartedly aside. "Sometimes. . ."

Hugh laughed and rolled away. Licking forefinger and thumb, he pinched out the candle, and the night swallowed them.

* * *

"Remember what I told you," Hugh called, as Matthew sprang up onto his horse. "Don't dismiss my advice."

There was a careless wave from Matthew. "You're getting soft, Hugo. You should spend more time razing farms and less bouncing babes on your knee."

"Mattie—"

Matthew smiled. "We'll meet soon enough, once all this has been resolved. Until then, take care of yourself."

"God be with you." Hugh closed his fingers tight about his kinsman's hand.

Matthew gave a sober nod. "And you, cousin." He spurred his horse forwards.

Hugh strode alongside, saying nothing.

As Matthew battered his way over the drawbridge with his retainers close behind him, Hugh scrambled up the steps that led to the curtain wall. He leaned on the parapet, watching in silence as the horsemen headed back up the Kilwinning road.

Matthew looked back one last time, and raised his hand in farewell.

Hugh returned the gesture. His hand dropped as the horsemen pushed forward into a trot, but he kept watch there until they'd dwindled from sight.

He straightened with a sigh.

Over the trees in the east the black birds were flying, restless spirits in a heavy sky.

Hugh crossed himself. Pulling his gown tight about him, he trudged back to the yard, wondering if he'd just turned his back on Matthew for the last time.

Chapter 44
Near Atholl, Perthshire

John Stewart cursed as his horse floundered in the soft mud. Holding the reins tight to steady the beast, he urged it onto safer ground. But the earth beneath its quarters was crumbling; the horse lurched to the left, nearly throwing him.

A close one, Stewart thought with a scowl. He sat deeper and ran a reassuring hand down his mount's neck.

The plaid-swathed Northern men who escorted him were grinning at his mishap. One muttered a snide aside in *Gaelic,* but a curt word from the Master of Atholl silenced him.

Savages. . . Stewart wrinkled his nose in distaste.

"Thought we'd lost you there," the Master of Atholl said. "I'd have had some explaining to do, if you'd drowned." Young Atholl was a wiry man in his thirties. At court, he was as finely dressed as the next man. But travelling through his home country, he looked little better than his servants, his rich clothes hidden beneath a plaid that covered him from his hood to his boots. "It's not as if I didn't offer you a more suitable mount," he added.

"That damned nag wasn't fit to feed my hounds."

"No need to get angry. We're nearly there."

"Thank God." John Stewart looked about him with a shiver. The whole world looked grey. Grey clouds hung low over the mountains, while a ghostly vapour drifted up from the stunted pines and birches that clung precariously to the nearby slopes. All around them the ground was alive with water, the path riven by countless burns that surged down from the hills.

Then, just when he thought there'd never be an end to it, the dank trees petered out, and a vast grey-green valley opened out ahead. Clusters of tiny cottages were dotted here and there.

And in the distance he glimpsed a castle. Against the dank misery of the day, the glow of its bright harled walls seemed ethereal, like a vision of Paradise.

The Master of Atholl whooped loud and cantered off, his escort following close behind.

Not to be outdone, Stewart pushed his horse into a trot.

No one wanted to be stranded out in the cold any longer; even the baggage ponies were pressing on towards home, kists and boxes banging loudly on their backs.

* * *

"Welcome to Atholl, cousin John!" The Earl of Atholl smiled broadly as he strode across the yard. "I trust the journey wasn't too unpleasant?"

Stewart shook his head, a flurry of droplets spraying from his hood and beard. "A man could rot here."

"There's worse places to find oneself," Atholl responded, sharply. He gave a quiet little laugh. "You're the last man I expected to see."

Stewart raised his brows. "Stranger things have happened, I'm sure."

"Indeed." Atholl's smile didn't waver. But his eyes were guarded. "Forgive me, but I find it hard to believe you've decided to embrace our cause."

There was a weary sigh from Stewart. "I've had time to reflect, since we spoke together in Edinburgh. You were right about James. His murderers should be found, and brought to justice."

"So you're here to champion Justice!" Atholl laughed. "That's a first, John!"

Stewart scowled. "Don't press me too hard, cousin. Remember what I'm offering here."

All trace of mirth vanished from Atholl. "It's a generous offer," he said. "It's much appreciated."

* * *

"A man in my situation's wise to be wary," Atholl said, as he escorted Stewart across the gloomy yard towards the guest range. "It's been a difficult six months."

"I can imagine."

"Everyone's wondering who'll be next. We've watched our allies in the south suffering such persecution! And we haven't even been able to voice our concerns, for fear of being branded traitors along with the rest." Atholl cast a furtive glance towards his kinsman. "Though rumour has it you've been scheming just as hard to make gains at a defeated man's expense."

Stewart snorted. "In just one day you can hear a thousand rumours. Best not listen to any of them."

"You'll understand why we're concerned, though." Atholl halted at the entrance to the range. "Do you genuinely want to help us? Or will you denounce us all to Patrick Hepburn?"

"I've no loyalty to Hepburn. I'd string him up tomorrow."

"That's reassuring." Atholl opened the door. "Almost there."

They threaded their way through candlelit corridors, until they reached another sturdy wooden door.

"Here's your chamber," Atholl said. "Once you've changed your clothes, you must come to the hall. There's a great fire roaring there, and a stag roasting in the kitchens. And a draught of the *uisge beatha* is waiting to warm your bones. But before I leave you in peace, I'd be grateful if you'd answer just one question. . ."

Stewart shrugged.

"Why have you done this? You've already snatched the Sheriff's title from Ellestoun. We thought it was just a matter of time before you sent him south to join his uncle Montgrennan in exile."

Stewart was silent.

A little smile appeared on Atholl's lips. "So your plans came to naught? Well, that'll save me some trouble. I was going to summon Sempill of Ellestoun to Atholl before the month was out. Along with Ross of Hawkhead, and Cunninghame of Kilmaurs."

"You'll get more men from myself and Lord Lyle than you would from the Sempills and the Rosses combined." Stewart paused. "As for Kilmaurs?" he added. "He has enough problems just now."

Atholl's smile grew broader. "Still trying to protect that wayward nephew of yours?"

"I've been travelling all day," Stewart muttered. "I'm in no mood for chatter."

* * *

"Can we trust Lennox?" asked the Master of Forbes. He was a sullen-looking man, a born conspirator if ever there was one.

Stewart allowed himself a little smile, and tapped his fingertips lightly together before him. "Can you afford not to?"

"My kinsman Lennox has pledged his support," said Atholl. "I trust him implicitly. Alex?"

"We're delighted to have you join us." Alexander Huntly, Master of Gordon, spoke out.

Stewart laughed, inwardly. He would never have guessed that the master plotter was Huntly, a lean, fragile-looking man. Who always seemed mild-mannered and docile. . .

"When Parliament met in January," said Huntly. "I wrote a letter to King Henry. I reminded him of the circumstances surrounding King James' death and asked him to give what support he could. He didn't reply. But John Ross of Montgrennan did. It's as we'd hoped. He's alive and well, living in exile at the English court."

"Well that's no surprise," said Stewart. "What did he suggest?"

"He's urged us to gather what forces we can, to raise arms against James and his counsellors. He says we must strike soon, while the memory of our King's death remains fresh in mens's minds."

Stewart snorted loud. "Oh, that's damned typical! Montgrennan wants us to wage war, while he stays safe in London. Even together, our men might not be enough. Remember what happened last year."

"Yes, yes!" Huntly perched on his chair, face lit with excitement. "There's one thing James lacked when he took to the field last year: mercenaries. This year it'll be different. Together, Lord Ross and myself have sufficient funds to hire four hundred mercenaries if needs be. Men of the finest calibre, from Germany. Or Switzerland."

"But that'd cost a small fortune!" Stewart retorted.

"Before he died, James entrusted a substantial sum of money into my care," Huntly said. "He granted a similar amount to Lord Ross. We'd hoped to use the money to help James regain the throne if the battle turned against him. What better fate for it than to use it against the men who murdered him?"

Stewart slouched back in his seat. "I'm concerned."

Huntly's face twitched with annoyance. "What?"

"You haven't thought this through. All this talk of justice, of retribution. . . What happens if you win? Do you murder young James? And make his brother King in his stead?"

"Absolutely not!" Huntly retorted. "A grievous sin was committed when James was slain in the first place. We don't want to compound it by murdering his son."

"Besides," Atholl added, "how we will we enlist Henry's support if we tell him we want another rightful King removed from his throne?"

"So we keep the King, and replace his counsellors. . ." Stewart gave a satisfied nod. "Who's on the list then?"

"Patrick Hepburn. All the damned Hepburns. And the Homes."

"I agree with that," Stewart said.

"Schaw of Sauchie, too," added Forbes. "And Lord Gray. Bishop Blacader. . . All those men who sanctioned the King's death and let it go unpunished."

"And Montgomerie," Atholl said.

Stewart frowned. "Let's not be hasty."

"He was there from the beginning," Forbes said. "If we're to obtain Cunninghame's support, he must be removed."

Stewart raised his hand. "I absolutely forbid it." He looked around the sullen faces. "I'm being practical. We don't need Cunninghame. The Montgomeries'll ride to my banner if they're asked to."

"More the merrier," said Huntly. "But please tread carefully! Make sure you keep Hugh on a tight rein. He mustn't use this as yet another excuse to attack the Cunninghames."

Chapter 45
The Place of Ochiltree

It was the most beautiful gown she'd ever set eyes on. Pale blue satin, which gleamed when the light caught it. The girls had worked hard to embellish it, embroidering swirling flourishes over the bodice and stitching tiny seed pearls onto the sleeves.

Margaret swallowed as Katherine and Alison pulled the laces tight at her back.

It was the eve of her wedding day. In just a few short days she'd leave Ochiltree forever. She'd start a new life away from bossy Elizabeth, and her overbearing, inflexible mother.

She should have been the happiest maid alive. . .

She wasn't; she kept hoping she'd hear the news that her betrothed's sins had caught up with him at last, that he'd been imprisoned as a traitor and she wouldn't have to be concerned with him anymore.

It hadn't happened.

I might still be granted good news, she told herself. *He hasn't arrived yet. Perhaps brigands will put an end to him on the road south. Or he'll be slain in a brawl at a wayside tavern. . .*

Lady Euphemia stalked about her. "You'd be a perfect bride, if you just took that scowl off your face." She leaned over, and checked the stitching carefully. "It fits you well. Don't be a glutton at dinner."

I won't be attending dinner, Margaret thought. *I shall be here. Wishing I was dead...*

* * *

The groom's party came too late to dine with the household, but their arrival didn't go unnoticed.

Katherine was keeping vigil by the window. She leaned out, peeking through a gap in the shutters, then scurried back to where Margaret lay upon the bed. "They're here!" she gasped. "Shall we seek him out?"

Margaret didn't move. She just stared at the ceiling. "Do what you want. My life is over."

She was beyond weeping. Her heart felt sore, her whole body numb. She thought she'd have been frightened, because tomorrow night she'd have to surrender her virginity to a man she despised. But she wasn't frightened, just bone weary with despair.

She closed her eyes. *Oh Saint Margaret, Oh Holy Mary, Mother of God. Hear my prayer, please. Save me from this. Take me away. Or better still, take him. I don't want to be sullied by him. Grant me a miracle, please. . .*

* * *

Katherine gripped Margaret's arm tight. "Oh, Heavens!" she gasped. "I've seen him."

Margaret shrugged her loose. "Go away."

"No, no! I have to tell you. He's lovely. Tall, and quite slender. But not too skinny, mind. With a thick mane of hair that's a deep, dark gold. And he has a marvellous smile."

"He shows his teeth, just a little," Alison chirped, "—and they're all still in place, without a blemish."

"That wasn't all that caught my eye. You should see his legs! They're long and fine. And his haunches-" Katherine broke off with a gurgling laugh. "You could break your teeth on them, they're so firm and tight!"

"He's such a gentleman," said Alison. "He asked who we were, and when we told him, he gave a little bow and doffed his bonnet, and asked after you."

"If you love him so much, then perhaps one of you should marry him."

"You won't be saying that tomorrow. You'll be spreading your legs wide and begging him to take you—"

"Enough!" Margaret sat up, scowling. She felt ill already. "I hope he drops dead."

"He wanted you to have this." Alison handed her a folded parchment, and a tiny wooden casket.

She opened the casket. There was a pretty brooch inside. A venerable piece, wrought of silver, in the shape of a stag's head. Set with diamonds, with the collar round its neck studded with rubies. "Very nice," she said. "But it'll take more than this to win me."

"And the letter?"

"Burn it."

* * *

That night, she bathed.

Afterwards, she sat wrapped in a sheet, while her mother combed out her long brown hair.

"When the consummation comes," Lady Euphemia said, tugging on the comb with brutal strength, "you must be meek, and yielding. He's old enough to know what he's doing. He'll be gentle." She found a knot and yanked upon it.

Margaret gritted her teeth and clenched her fingers tight around the sheet. "Will it hurt?"

"Of course it hurts. When Eve tempted Adam and caused the fall of Man, she condemned the rest of womankind to pain and suffering."

"But I thought a woman couldn't conceive. . ."

"Nonsense. I bore eight children into the world. I never liked it once."

"You never know," Elizabeth said. "You might be pleasantly surprised." She had such a snide way of talking, even at the best of times. "He's a very pretty gentleman."

"That he is," Lady Euphemia agreed.

"Shame he's such a fool."

"Elizabeth!"

"Well, it's true. Only a fool would have followed King James last year. And only a fool would let the Stewarts trample all over him without so much as trying to fight back. Which makes him craven, as well as foolish." Elizabeth smiled, serenely. "Good luck, Margaret. You'll need it, trying to build a successful marriage with a man like *him*."

* * *

John sighed and flicked an imaginary speck of dust from his sleeve. He had the same empty feeling inside that he felt before a battle, a numb desire for everything to be over.

For good or ill. . .

Robert punched him lightly in the arm. "She took the gift," he said. "And the letter."

"Did she read it?"

"Can she read at all?"

It was a reasonable point, John supposed. He straightened his doublet one last time, then clasped his hands behind him and rocked gently on his heels.

"No sign of Montgomerie," said Robert.

"Are you surprised?"

"I'm relieved."

John had to smile at that.

It was a chill morning. He shivered, and stamped his feet. The chain of gold about his neck snagged upon his hair, and he winced.

When he reached up to free it, Robert elbowed him. "Keep still, for God's sake. She'll think you've got fleas."

John took one measured breath after another. Somehow, he managed to look composed as an ox-cart approached. It was flanked by horsemen; he recognised Sir William Colville, and James Colville, too, with another half-dozen men following on behind.

"She's a very lovely maid," the priest said, by way of consolation. "You won't be disappointed."

The cart halted, and Sir William dismounted to assist the women. The bride's mother emerged first; a fearsome, broad-shouldered woman with the glance of a basilisk.

John nodded to her, and was granted a glower in return.

It was enough to make John wilt inside. He studied the ground with a cough, then braved a glance back towards the bride's party.

The girl's mother was instantly forgotten. Sir William had returned to the cart and was grasping the hand of another.

John's breath caught in his throat as a dainty figure stepped out. Margaret Colville was slight and delicate as a bird, her face as exquisitely pale as her hands. Her body was lithe, swelling with the first bloom of womanhood, while her long hair shone a lustrous dark brown.

He couldn't take his eyes from her as she walked sedately over to the church. When she halted at his side and smiled, it was as if nothing else in the world mattered.

He smiled foolishly back, trying not to blush.

"Master Sempill?" the priest prompted.

"Oh, yes, of course." The tray was offered; he fumbled for the ring. His fingers were trembling, his palm moist with sweat. No sooner had he grasped the fragile piece of metal than he'd dropped it. It fell onto the tray, then, to his horror, rolled down to the ground below.

Robert retrieved it, and pressed it firmly into his hand.

John swallowed. His face burned with embarrassment as he placed the ring on Margaret's finger. And all the while the maid stared back, her face impassive.

* * *

He fared little better through the rest of the ceremony. He'd never before suffered from such crippling shyness; he stammered through the vows, then, thankfully, it was over and he could escape into the consoling depths of the chapel.

Throughout Mass, he knelt beneath the canopy with his young wife beside him. The words and the music rose in ecstatic glory all around him; he thanked God, again and again, for his good fortune.

* * *

Once the ceremony was behind them, he stood with Margaret in the nave to greet the guests.

"Congratulations!" Robert Crawfurd stepped close and shook his hand.

At the same time, Marion clutched his other arm and kissed his cheek. "I'm so pleased for you, John!"

"My sister, Marion," John explained to Margaret. "And her husband, Robert Crawfurd, Master of Kilbirnie."

"I'm honoured." Margaret dipped her skirts politely.

"Well done, John." Adam Mure called.

"Thanks-" John broke off. He'd spotted Hugh Montgomerie, bludgeoning his way through the crowd.

"Are you not the proudest man alive, sir?" Montgomerie called, swatting Robert aside without so much as a glance. He grasped John's hand and shook it, then turned to Margaret. "Why, the Maid of Ochiltree is such a splendid prize! You look magnificent, my dear." He bowed low before her, seized her hand and kissed it.

Margaret curtsied. "Thank you, my lord."

Robert was scowling.

John flashed him an apologetic glance. "I'm flattered you came, my lord," he told Montgomerie. "I thought you'd be too busy."

"It's poor form to turn down such an invitation!" Montgomerie looked genuinely hurt. "I'd hoped to arrive yesterday, but circumstances conspired against me."

"Better late than never," Sir William Colville said. "You'll be most welcome at the board, Lord Hugh."

* * *

"Do you think they're genuinely poor?" Hugh Montgomerie whispered in John's ear. He'd downed an impressive amount of wine and there was a wild, glazed look about his eyes.

John wished that he, too, could have drunk enough to think he was enjoying himself. "I don't think they expected a guest of your calibre."

"I've eaten better on campaign," Hugh grumbled. "Don't they know what salt is?" He took another gulp of wine. "Never mind. In two days' time, we'll be sitting down to a real dinner."

John picked up a slice of venison and chewed it half-heartedly. He didn't think he'd have noticed the poor fare if Hugh hadn't mentioned it. He wasn't really that hungry.

"Christ," Hugh muttered. "I've seen happier faces at a soul mass." He lurched upright. "Gentlemen. Ladies!" Swaying on his feet, he had to lean a hand on John's shoulder.

John grasped a discreet hold of his belt to steady him, and Hugh tossed him a nod by way of a 'thank you'. "And now," Hugh said, pressing his fists firm against the board. "I'd like to say a few words about the groom—" He might have been drunk, but it was still the kind of tone that commanded silence.

Oh, God. No. . . John leaned his head on his hands and studied the table.

"I've known John a year now, and I'd say that no maid could ask for a better husband." Loud cheers came from Adam and the others at the groom's end of the table, but the Colvilles were stone-faced.

Hugh held his hand aloft for silence. He looked imperiously around the gathered guests. "We're all very proud of young John, but even this paragon of manhood has his faults. There's times when he drives us mad with his inattention. You know, I've heard it said that when Johnny was a little lad, Sir Thomas — God rest his soul — took him out into the hills to learn his swordplay. And, thinking it was high time the boy learned about other matters—"

John glanced towards Margaret. The poor girl was picking dispiritedly at the morsels on their trencher. She hadn't looked at him once throughout dinner. *Am I that hideous to behold?* he wondered.

"—Misunderstanding him, young John piped up, 'But how should you thrust it in? With one hand, or with two? And what if it should get stuck there?

"That threw Sir Thomas for a moment, but then he realised, and said, *For God's sake, boy. What did you think I was talking about?*" Hugh grasped his goblet and swallowed back some wine. "There's a sword at Ellestoun," he said. "It hangs upon the wall there. And by God, is it a sword! Nine foot long, if it's an inch. All I can say, Mistress Colville, that if the sword reflects the man, you're in for a treat tonight. Your husband must have the parts of a horse!"

* * *

The girls adored him. When the meal was done and the dancing started, they flocked about him. *He's like the divine Apollo,* Katherine sighed. *His eyes are lovely. And that hair. . .*

Katherine was right, she supposed. He *was* handsome. When Margaret had first seen him standing there at the church door, her heart sank, because he was everything she'd ever wished for and more besides. *More to a man than a pretty face,* she'd told herself. *He won't look anything as handsome when he's choking at the end of a rope.*

You'll forgive him his sins soon enough, Katherine said.

But she wouldn't. She'd show Katherine and the others just how strong she was by hating him. Till the end of time itself, if necessary.

Or at least until he turned his life around and made himself successful.

She stared out into the hall.

He was dancing with Katherine. He'd seemed such an oaf that morning, when he dropped the ring in front of everyone. Now, though, he moved those long limbs with casual elegance. . .

No. Don't look at him. You mustn't give way. Ever. . .

The music faded. He bowed to Katherine, who curtsied, blushing.

She came rushing back, face still glowing.

"That's enough now," Margaret told her.

"It's not as if you want him to yourself," Katherine protested. "Where's the harm in it?"

"There's no harm in it," she said, with a sweet smile. "I don't want you doing it, that's all."

Katherine sank alongside with an angry sigh.

"Don't forget," said Margaret. "We all hate him. We must work together to make his life a misery."

Chapter 46

John danced once with his new wife, at the very beginning of the evening. After that, she sat down. *I'm tired,* she said. *Why don't you find yourself some company elsewhere?*

Undaunted, he sat beside her and tried to strike up a conversation. But she made it quite obvious she wasn't interested, so he soon gave up.

He didn't want to have sit and brood all night. So he threw himself into the festivities. He danced with his sisters, he danced with his mother. He even danced with his wife's maids, until she called them back to her side and put an end to it.

Everyone seemed to be enjoying themselves. Except Margaret. And himself.

How could he, with the consummation looming? At least he was making an effort to look cheerful, which was more than could be said for her.

Eventually the priest beckoned them away to their chamber on the upper storey. Elizabeth Ross and Euphemia Wallace came, too; to her credit, the bride's mother tried to keep a civilised façade in place for the proceedings.

The priest sprinkled holy water over the bed and over them both, then blessed them.

Then everyone left.

They were alone.

Margaret stood rigid, her eyes fixed on the floor and her hands balled into fists before her. She looked as if she were about to weep.

"My lady," he ventured. "You've scarcely glanced at me all day. God made me what I am; I'm sorry if I don't live up to expectations."

"You're pleasing to look at, I suppose." Her tone was grudging.

"Then how else have you judged me? Why won't you talk to me? At least tell me what's wrong."

She glared at him, her pale face fierce. "You're a traitor. People mock you, because you're a fool and a coward. And now I'm your wife. It's my duty to stand by you, no matter what. And I don't want to. I don't want anything to do with you."

He couldn't believe the transformation. Until this moment, she'd seemed so meek, so quiet. He stood there dazed, struggling to find the right words. "I have lands aplenty," came his defensive reply at last.

"How long will it be before they're torn from you?" She took a deep shuddering breath then burst into tears. "Oh, why was I given to you? There's a hundred worthy men in Kyle, and another hundred in Cunninghame besides. . ."

"It's been a bad year. The situation's better now. I know I can improve my family's fortunes. But I need your help, your goodwill—"

She stamped her foot. "I don't care about you!" Her face was contorted with fury. "And I don't care about your family. They're worth nothing. *You're* worth nothing."

235

Be patient, he told himself. *Let her have her say. . .* But it was hard, to take the endless criticism. His temple throbbed, that old familiar pain.

"—I don't want you. My family don't want you. We all pray for the day when you're strung up on a rope, because that's all you're good for. You're a treacherous, useless idiot, and I should never, ever have been contracted to you. I'm worth far more—"

As the endless stream of vitriol poured from her lips, he felt the rage build and build within him. Because she wouldn't listen, she wouldn't pause to let him plead his case. Then all of a sudden, the blinding anger was gone. He breathed deep and calm once more. He'd transcended fury; it was as if ice ran through his veins. When he looked at her crumpled, tear-streaked face he felt nothing.

Had she noticed the change in him? He didn't know. He didn't really care. . .

"—I hope they take you, and slit your belly like they do with traitors—"

He wanted to grasp her neck and squeeze the life from her. She'd be silent then.

He took a step closer.

"I hope you-" Her voice wavered into silence. She glanced behind her and gulped, face ash-white with fear. But she held her ground. Her fists were still clenched, her mouth tight with defiance.

He closed his hands about her arms and gripped so hard she gasped. "I'm not dead yet," he said. He scarcely knew his own voice; it rang out so hard, so clear. "So you'll have to live with me. Now let's get this over with, shall we? And let's hope you conceive, because that way I won't have to blight your bed again until the child's delivered."

She was too proud to apologise. She closed her eyes and swallowed, as he pushed her down upon the bed, and straddled her. The confrontation had roused him, he unlaced his hose and pushed back her skirts and then he entered her.

Once it was done, he sat back on his heels. When he saw her lying there, curled tight and weeping, he hated himself.

I'm sorry. I'm so sorry. It wasn't meant to be this way. . .

But stubborn pride choked his tongue. He swallowed, close to tears himself, and then he left her.

He lay back along the window seat and stared up into the darkness. The night air was chill, so he wrapped himself in his gown for warmth.

Margaret sobbed upon the bed, as if her heart were broken. Perhaps it was. From the ache he felt inside, he thought his might be, too.

The desolation was suddenly overpowering. He wept silently, and wished that he were dead.

* * *

It was hard to keep a brave face when it hurt to pass water and it hurt even to sit down, but Margaret was a Wallace, and she had her pride. At least now she could console herself with the knowledge that she'd been right to hate her husband.

She'd waited a long while until she was sure he was asleep, then she'd crept upstairs to find her mother, who'd been typically unsympathetic. *Least it's done,*

Lady Euphemia had said. *And you've proved yourself a virgin. Now pull yourself together. You're too old for snivelling.*

To Margaret's relief, she didn't insist that her daughter go back to spend the rest of the night in her husband's company.

Margaret lay down beside her mother for the last time, and there she'd prayed. *Oh, Holy Mary, let me conceive. If that's what it's like to lie with a man, then I don't think I can bear it.*

* * *

"We shall miss you," Lady Euphemia said, briskly. She almost sounded as if she meant it. "But it's time for you to move on."

"Give my love to Father," Margaret said. "When you visit his grave."

"I'll do that. Now you'd best go. Everything's packed." She patted Margaret gently on the shoulder.

Katherine and the girls awaited her inside the wagon.

"Come on!" Katherine beckoned.

Margaret hesitated.

The step inside seemed insurmountable. She breathed deep, steeling herself. She didn't want to cry out, but didn't know how she'd manage it without a sound.

But before she could ask Katherine to assist, hands closed about her waist and hoisted her up.

It was her husband who'd helped her.

She didn't know what to say. She didn't want to thank him; if anything, she was annoyed. She didn't see how he could have the gall to treat her with such courtesy after what had happened the previous night.

"We'll be travelling to Ayr today." He didn't quite look at her when he spoke. "The Lord Montgomerie tells me that we're lodging with the Sheriff tonight. After that, it's onwards to Eglintoun, and then to Dunlop. We'll be at Ellestoun by the Sabbath."

"Oh," she said.

"James says he'll ride with you as far as Eglintoun." He touched his bonnet, and then he was gone.

Katherine leaned forward and tugged at Margaret's skirt. "Here!" she said, patting the wooden bench beside her. She'd made space amongst the pillows and coverlets and candlesticks that had been presented as wedding gifts.

Margaret sat gingerly down.

"Well?" Katherine asked.

"I don't want to talk about it."

"Oh, please. . ."

"Mother was right. It's hateful and it's sore. He's not a man, he's a monster."

* * *

Throughout the morning, Margaret dozed despite the discomfort, starting from sleep occasionally as the cart lurched into a deep rut in the road. As the day stretched on, she ate a little bread and cold meat, and drank some ale.

After that, she found her spirits reviving. She pushed back the canvas slightly at the side of the wagon and stared out ahead. Her husband rode at the head of the party, between Lord Hugh and her half-brother. Sir Adam Mure rode with them. So did Master Crawfurd, with Marion Sempill sitting pillion behind him.

Margaret settled back down, and drew a coverlet around her shoulders with a shiver. She was cold and uncomfortable, she wanted so desperately for the journey to be over. . .

* * *

That evening, they dined at the Sheriff's table in his townhouse at Ayr. The Sheriff was a Campbell, which apparently made him a kinsman of Lord Hugh.

The Sheriff wasn't there. But his lady was. She asked Margaret to sit beside her at dinner, then cooed and fussed over her all afternoon.

Margaret had never been granted such attention before. She quite enjoyed the novelty of it. She even found herself thinking, once or twice, that it made it worthwhile being married to *him*.

But when she retired to her bed that night, the fear came back.

She drew the sheets tight up to her chin, and stared out into the darkness, dreading the knock that would herald his arrival.

But it never came.

Chapter 47

"Sir Hugh Campbell's back tomorrow," Hugh said. "I'd like to meet with him. If you want to press on, then by all means do so. Helen's expecting you."

"Would he object if we stayed another night?" Despite Hugh's assurances, John wasn't convinced that he wanted to attend Lady Helen in her husband's absence.

Hugh refilled his goblet. "Of course not. You're with me."

There was silence.

John studied his wine, wondering what to say. Robert and Marion had retired not long before, and Adam was still out in the town with Hector.

Which left the two of them.

He found Hugh's company more awkward than ever. He wasn't talking to a courtier, he was talking to a man, and he still couldn't adjust to the change. Even now he wasn't entirely comfortable being on first name terms. Better he called Hugh nothing at all, than cause offence.

"It's getting late," Hugh said, pointedly.

John shrugged. "She'll be tired."

Hugh laughed. "That's very noble of you."

If Hugh was prepared to believe that, then John wasn't going to contradict him. He didn't want the truth to be out, that he didn't think he'd ever find the courage even to look the poor girl in the eye, let alone invite himself into her bed.

For once, he'd lost his temper. Now, with hindsight, he could see what it had cost him. The more he thought about it, the more he wondered if her fury had been a front. She hadn't wanted to marry him; she'd been disappointed when she met him. Small wonder the girl had reacted that way, faced with the terror of leaving everything she'd known to start a new life with him.

He didn't even know where to begin making amends.

* * *

They attended Mass at St John's Church the following morning. John lit a candle to the saint who was his namesake, asking for guidance and wisdom.

Marion drew him aside afterwards. "Something's wrong," she whispered. "The two of you haven't spoken all morning."

He cringed inside. He knew what she'd think, that by treating Margaret so cruelly, he'd betrayed *her*. "I can't say. . ."

"Then I'll ask her myself," Marion declared.

* * *

"Whatever possessed you? To treat that poor maid so harshly?"

He'd never seen Marion so angry. He squirmed under her sharp gaze, and looked away. He closed his teeth about his little finger, concentrated on the pain; it was the only way he could keep himself from weeping.

"Well?"

"She said the most terrible things." Outside, the gulls cried as they soared over a sparkling sea; the beauty of it all just made the ache inside worse.

"They're just words, John."

"No. . ." His voice trailed off. He leaned forward and glowered at the floor, so she wouldn't know he was crying. He forgot his bonnet. It slid into his lap and made him start; he caught it and wrung it tight in his hands. "What should I do?"

"Hush now." Her anger vanished; she was suddenly concerned. She sat beside him, and slipped her arm about his shoulders. "Oh, Dear God. . ."

"I wronged her." He looked her in the eye, desperate. "How am I to make things better?"

"Don't make any demands on her. Maybe she'll forgive you, when she learns what manner of a man you really are." She cocked her head. "The town's getting busy now. Perhaps we could venture out this afternoon. It's market day; she's probably never experienced such a thing before."

* * *

Someone knocked on her door later on.

When Margaret opened it, her heart sank, for it was *him*.

But he hadn't come to visit her bed. With his bonnet gripped tight before him, he asked her rather sheepishly if she wanted to take a walk and enjoy the town.

"No, thank you," Margaret replied, and shut the door in his face.

Another knock sounded a while later, and in barged Jamie.

He flopped into a chair by the fire. "Still sulking?"

Margaret perched carefully on a neighbouring stool. "That's not fair."

A smile spread across his face. "He wasn't to your liking?"

"He's a beast. I never want him near me again."

"He's alright. I like him."

"He's a beast."

"Oh, Margaret," Jamie said. "What did you do?"

"I told him what I thought of him, that's what."

He sprawled back with a sigh. "Christ. Couldn't you hold your tongue for once in your life?"

"It doesn't matter. I knew I'd hate him."

"No. You wanted to hate him. You pressed him till he turned on you." He stared into the fire. "Did he strike you?"

She didn't answer.

"I would have," he said. "But you wouldn't have dared pick a fight with me."

"You're different. He likes the world to think he's a gentleman. But he's not. He's a monster."

"Are you going to be a martyr forever?" Jamie asked. "You should come and see the town. There's ships out there, and an ocean that stretches to the ends of the earth."

"Do I have to go with *him*?"

"He's your husband." He batted her arm. "Might be worth your while. A man with a guilty conscience is profligate with his money."

* * *

In the end, she relented, and went out with Jamie and her husband. Mistress Sempill and Master Crawfurd came with them. But Lord Hugh did not. She asked her husband why. *He's in council with the Sheriff,* he said, in that pompous way of his, as if the explanation wearied him.

She didn't hurt so much today. And she *was* excited by it all. There were people everywhere, and all manner of things to see. There were acrobats and a dancing bear and countless booths and stalls which dripped with goods and produce. She didn't much like the smell of the place, though; it stank of stale flesh and rotting rubbish. She wondered how anyone could keep their health in such conditions.

He kept close, but never actually touched her. He never spoke, but she could sense his looming presence at her shoulder all the time. She wasn't sure if he was being possessive or protective towards her.

Perhaps Jamie was right. Perhaps he did have a conscience. Remembering her half-brother's words, she wondered if she might work the situation to her advantage. She saw a litter of tiny puppies and gasped in delight.

"Look at him!" She clutched her husband's sleeve. "He's the sweetest thing I ever saw!"

And before she knew it, her husband was delving in his purse. Some money changed hands and the warm, whining pup was pressed into her arms.

A selection of fine fabrics soon caught her eye; before long he'd bought her six ells of green velvet and another six of rich blue satin.

Next time, she was a little more ambitious. She spotted a long string of fat pearls and commented on how magnificent they'd look on her.

He hung his head. "I'm sorry," he said. "But it's more than I can afford just now."

Ah well, Margaret thought, as they all ambled back to the Sheriff's place. *Least I'm not going back empty-handed.*

Chapter 48

It was raining when the wedding party reached Eglintoun, but Helen Campbell braved the elements regardless.

The men were all hooded and cloaked against the weather. Even so, when Helen looked at Zephyr, she knew it wasn't Hugh seated on the grey stallion's back.

She spotted Hugh at last, mounted on a red-brown charger. She caught his arm as he climbed off his horse. "Poor Zephyr," she said. "I hope you won't be so inclined to share your wife."

Hugh grasped her shoulders and kissed her forehead. "He's younger than me. I'd find it hard to match his prowess."

She wriggled free with a laugh. "Be off with you. You're soaking wet. And you smell of that wretched horse."

"Greet our guests, please. I'd best take care of Zephyr."

Once Hugh had joined Master Sempill, the two men stood for a while, heedless of the rain. They were talking about Zephyr; Hugh nodded vigorously as Master Sempill gestured to the horse.

It warmed her heart, to see her husband speak so freely with another man. Hugh didn't believe in friendship; many of his so-called friends had failed him through the years. Helen hoped that Master Sempill would prove an exception to the rule. The lad seemed genuine, and pleasant, with a wise head on his young shoulders. It would, she decided, do Hugh the world of good to have someone sensible on hand to advise him for a change.

At last Hugh and Master Sempill parted company; Hugh delivered the horses to the grooms, while Master Sempill went to marshal his entourage.

It took a while for the ladies to disembark from the wagons, but Helen was patient. Eventually, she approached.

"It's lovely to see you again," she told Master Sempill, taking his hands and kissing him lightly on both cheeks.

Master Sempill looked away, and muttered a few barely audible niceties. He was shy as well as modest, which only added to his charms.

The absolute antithesis of Hugh, she thought. *Strange the two of them should get on so well. . .* She turned to the girl who stood at Master Sempill's side. "You must be Margaret."

Margaret gave a little smile and curtsied, but said nothing. Helen hugged her tight. "Welcome to Eglintoun!"

* * *

"They make a perfect couple," she told Hugh later, as she sat on the edge of the bed and combed her long hair before dinner.

Hugh grunted from where he lay flat on his back alongside.

"But something struck me," she added.

"What?" He sounded bored.

"You'd have thought that being newlyweds, they wouldn't take their eyes off one another."

He was silent for a while. "Ah," he said at last. "You noticed it too?"

"You'd be blind not to."

"Thought it was just me."

"No, it's not." She set the comb down. "We weren't that way together."

Hugh reached for her hand. "Absolutely not."

"Poor Master Sempill. Such a sweet lad, too."

Hugh chuckled. "A sweet lad," he said. "He's caused more trouble than anyone thought possible."

"Fate has been cruel to him."

"I should be jealous," Hugh said, rolling onto his side. "But if you must bestow your favours on a dashing young buck, it might as well be him. At least he's honourable."

She giggled. "You think so?"

"Perhaps I'd best post a guard outside the range tonight."

"As if I'd have the strength to take a lover. Being married to you is exhausting enough."

He didn't answer. His thoughts had moved on, he was frowning slightly. "I'll ride north with them tomorrow."

"Must you?" Helen rubbed his arm, a half-hearted attempt to change his mind.

He settled on his back. Putting his hands behind his head, he gazed at the ceiling. "Patrick should be informed about how things are progressing."

Helen stared towards the window. The skies were grey as slate, the rain lashing down in sheets across the yard. She shivered, despite herself. "It's starting all over again, isn't it?"

"Yes," he said, softly. "I think it is."

* * *

It's a great honour, Sir Adam Mure had said to her husband, as they headed down to dinner. *To be gracing the top table at Eglintoun.*

He'd sounded jealous.

Sir Adam was gracing Lord Hugh's table, too. But he wasn't sitting with Lord Hugh and his lady, the way they were.

Margaret liked Lady Helen very much. She wasn't like the Sheriff's wife, who'd been broad and worn and old. She was like her namesake, the lady of Troy; beautiful and glorious and radiant.

"You must be very happy," Lady Helen told Margaret, as they dined that night. "He's such a lovely man."

Margaret gave a modest shrug. Everyone kept remarking on how pleasant and even-tempered her husband was. She wondered sometimes if they were actually talking about the same person.

She took a mouthful of pie and nearly choked as it seared her tongue. She'd tasted spiced food before, but only on feast days, and even then it had never been so overwhelming. Here, the sauces were so heavy with spices and herbs that she couldn't bring herself to eat much.

She still wasn't sure what to make of it all. But everyone acted as if it were perfectly normal; Lord Hugh, Lady Helen, even her husband.

Margaret plucked up her courage, and dipped her slice of poultry into another of the sauces. Perhaps marrying *him* hadn't been so bad after all. Her life had never been so exciting, and now that the pain was gone she was beginning to enjoy herself.

* * *

When she lay down in her bed that night the terror was back. *Please God don't come.* Then, once she realised that he wasn't going to visit her, the fear gave way to excitement.

She still couldn't sleep. Her mind raced, as she thought back through the events of the day.

How the Lady Helen had praised her husband. She'd called him a man of courage and purpose, and she'd made it quite obvious that she considered him attractive. And from the way her husband had looked at the Lady Helen, it was clear he was rather taken with her, too.

Lord Hugh didn't seem to mind. If anything, he seemed to revel in the knowledge that his wife was desired by other men. But Margaret found it a little discomforting. She knew it was the fashion, for ladies like Helen Campbell to act that way. But she didn't see why it should be her husband who caught her eye.

Margaret didn't want him, but she didn't want anyone else to want him either.

Chapter 49
The Place of Ellestoun

The whole household had lined up ready to greet them. They were immaculate; even the kitchen boy was wearing his best clothes for the occasion.

John pushed back the canvas flap at the rear of the wagon. "Welcome to Ellestoun," he said, giving Margaret his hand and steadying her as she climbed to the ground. "I hope you'll be happy here."

She snatched her fingers from his and looked about her, unmoved.

"It's best that Mother shows you round. Running the household has always been her responsibility. She'll show you how things should be done. But she'll need to rest this afternoon. The journey's been hard for her."

"Where will we be staying?" Margaret's voice was distant.

"In the ladies' chambers. Within the tower. My mother's agreed to move her household to the guest range for the time being. We have a dowager house a mile from here at Perkhead. But I'd prefer it if she remained here just now."

"Show me my room."

He helped the maids from the wagon, then led the way into the tower-house. The girls were all very gracious and thanked him profusely.

But Margaret stayed silent.

He thought she could at least have put their differences aside and shown a little gratitude. Instead she trudged up to her room with as much enthusiasm as she'd show towards a prison.

"If there's anything you want—"

"Thank you," she said, and closed the door on him.

* * *

"Well, here we are." Margaret walked around her room, peering into every corner.

She wanted desperately to find something she could criticise, but found it hard. The room was a good size, its windows satisfyingly large. It had been cleaned thoroughly, so she couldn't even complain about that. She *was* disappointed to see that the panelled walls were unadorned; patches of dark wood showed where tapestries had recently been removed. The bed, hung with gold-brown curtains, was ample.

Margaret frowned. "I suppose his mother took the hangings."

"There'll be others," Mariota said.

"They'll be chewed by the moths, I expect."

Mariota shrugged. "Then we'll make new ones."

"Mattress is very comfortable," said Katherine, bouncing upon the edge of the bed.

"It's probably full of fleas." Margaret took the puppy from Alison's arms and set it gently down upon the floor. She crouched alongside. "Go to the kitchens," she told Alison. "Fetch him some milk."

Katherine left the bed and looked out from the window. "There's gardens," she said. "They go on forever. Lots of vegetables, I think. But more, besides. Flowers and herbs. And an orchard."

Margaret smiled, and stroked the puppy's back. "We'll explore tomorrow."

* * *

But the following day she wasn't granted any time to herself. They went to mass in the morning, then after that she was given a tour of her new home.

He came down with his mother and his sister, but didn't stay long. "Lord Hugh's leaving," he explained. "I have to say goodbye."

"Do what you like," came her stiff reply.

Once he'd gone they visited the kitchens and the stores. There were bread ovens, stills for ale and pots full of spices and salt, and an army of busy sweating cooks who stopped what they were doing and bowed or curtsied to her.

She liked that. But she didn't think much of her gude-mother. Lady Elizabeth fussed and fretted, using ten times as many words as needed. And she worshipped her son. Kept telling Margaret how lucky she was to have such a fine husband.

Margaret bit her tongue and said nothing.

Then at last they were finished with her. "I'd like to see the gardens now," she said. "If that's acceptable."

* * *

Thin paths wound through neat ranks of plants. Dead foliage lay in shrivelled heaps everywhere, but when she looked closely, Margaret could see the sharp green shoots of the new growth.

Margaret had hoped to wander beyond the walls with just her maids for company. But that hadn't been allowed; someone had to go with her.

It was Marion Sempill who escorted her. She'd guessed Margaret's displeasure straight away. *I know how disappointed you are,* she said, taking Margaret's hands in hers. *But it's best you have someone with you at first, at least until people get to know you.*

Margaret didn't argue. She grudgingly supposed her gude-sister was right.

"I spoke to him," Marion Sempill said.

"Oh."

"If he treated you harshly then I can't defend him, but. . . I just can't understand it. It's not in his nature. He's one of the kindest, sweetest men I know—"

"He's your brother. You would say that. I found him neither kind nor sweet."

"Times were very hard last winter. He's not been himself since then. He's prone to melancholy, which worries me." She looked Margaret in the eye. "He's very sorry. But he's a proud man. Please be patient; he'll do what he can to make amends."

When Hell's fires grow chill. That's when I'll spare him a kind word. . . But Margaret just smiled, and nodded, and that was the end of it.

* * *

"Thank you very much." Hugh strode from the stables, grey horse ambling alongside. "It was most kind to invite me."

"We were glad you could attend. And your gift was very generous." John glanced over his shoulder; Robert lounged in the doorway, face disapproving. "Please don't think we're chasing you away. There's good hunting in the hills."

"There's been new developments; the King's councillors should be informed as soon as possible. I'll speak with Abbot Schaw tomorrow, then press east." Hugh sighed, and patted the grey stallion's neck. "There's no peace for the wicked, they say. If that's the case, then I must've sinned most gravely."

John smiled. "What price success?"

"You should make the most of this," Hugh said. "The storm's coming. I don't where it'll break first; here, or the north. I just hope that the men who matter will heed the portents before it's too late." He clapped John's shoulder. "Now remember," he said, emphasising his words with a rough shake, "don't do anything, until I send word. No matter what you hear, from what source, just hold your ground until the time is right. That way, we'll both profit from this."

"I hope Fortune smiles on you—" John said. He broke off, just in time, before the name slipped unguarded from his lips.

Hugh shook his head. "John. . ."

"I'm sorry, Hugh."

"That's better." Hugh swung himself onto his horse's back. "It won't be long now. But miracles can't be wrought overnight." He beckoned to his men, "Come on now!"

Absently straightening his belt, John returned to the tower, and nearly collided with Robert. "Sorry," he said. "Forgot you were there."

"Had more important matters on your mind, I suppose." Robert straightened. "You're on very familiar terms with Lord Hugh."

"What does it matter?"

"So you'd call that man your friend?"

"I'm sorry about the wedding. But he's been quite helpful recently."

"Because it suits him." Robert's eyes narrowed. "What on earth are you plotting?"

"I can't say."

"I hope you know what you're doing," Robert remarked, wearily.

The Abbey of Paisley

With the monks at prayer, they walked the cloisters alone. It was raining; fat drips of water slid down the pointed arches of the arcade that surrounded the courtyard garden.

"Thank you for warning me," Abbot Schaw said. Then he added, "You're subdued, Hugh. Is there something on your mind?"

Hugh didn't speak.

"It's alright," Schaw said. "I won't ask your source." He turned to Hugh with a smile. "You mustn't worry. James will give these erring sheep ample time to return to the fold."

That's what I'm afraid of, Hugh thought.

"You spoke to Master Sempill?" Schaw asked.

"He's pledged his men to the King."

"Good."

"I thought I'd ride east on the morrow."

Schaw tilted his head, considering. "No," he said. "I don't think that's appropriate. Earl Patrick must be handled carefully. Let me talk to James directly."

"It's of the utmost urgency—"

"I know." The old abbot sounded faintly irritated. "Which is why *I'll* set out tomorrow. I agree with you, Hugh. I think we must expect the worst."

"Thank you."

"Go back to your lands. Let everyone think that nothing's amiss, but make sure that you and your allies are ready. I'll prepare the ground for you to argue your case before the King."

Chapter 50
The Place of Ellestoun

Margaret studied the gilded cage that sat upon the kist by the wall. There were two finches inside; red heads flashing bright and wings gleaming gold as they fluttered round their prison.

A gift from *him*.

He'd been embarrassingly generous just recently. He'd ridden away for a few days, and when he returned he brought all manner of presents; the finches in their cage, and more fine cloth to make new gowns with. Best of all, he brought an even thicker rope of pearls than the one she'd admired in Ayr.

He must love you, Katherine teased.

Margaret rolled her eyes. *He's a pathetic soul*, she'd said. And they spoke no more of it.

Beyond the walls, the apple trees were coming into bloom. Margaret desperately wanted to wander amongst them, but it had rained almost solidly for five days now.

The incarceration did little to improve her temper.

"We should go down for dinner," Katherine reminded her.

"I suppose." Margaret tapped the cage one last time but the restless finches were oblivious.

Shrugging, she left them and wandered to her chair. She sat down, and Katherine pinned her gabled hood deftly into place. "I hate the thing," Margaret sighed. "It makes my head hot. And I feel so old and matronly when I wear it."

* * *

She stood along with the rest of the household until *he* took his place amongst them.

He thanked God for their food then sat down.

They all followed.

"Good day." He stared into the distance, as he always did. "You're keeping well?"

"Tolerably so," she replied. *You're the dullest soul I've ever met. You never smile, you never laugh, you just have that same expression, day in, day out.*

A bowl of scented water was brought round and they washed their hands. Then the food was presented. A roast pike formed the main dish, along with some platters of vegetables. There was plenty of bread, too.

Her husband rose to carve. Once he'd piled some of its flesh onto their trencher, he placed more on the platters that would be passed to the lower tables.

Margaret took a cautious mouthful. The pike was mildly flavoured, and delicious.

The exotic spices used so freely here weren't quite to her taste, but she was still determined to learn more about them. She'd visited the kitchens several times to talk with the head cook, who told her all the names; mace and saffron, nutmeg, cloves and galangal. He showed her what they looked and smelled like, too. But when he told her how much they cost the household, she nearly died of fright.

A pie was placed before them. Fish again, because it was Lent.

Her husband sliced it and lifted some carefully onto on their trencher. Then he helped himself to a sprinkling of salt. To his right, Lady Elizabeth complained about a leaking roof in the guest range.

Margaret stifled a sigh.

"Wine?" he asked.

"Please," she replied.

When she bit into the pie, its rich, spicy flavour nearly took the tongue off her.

"Perhaps the cooks could make their dishes a little less *fort* and a little more *douce,*" she said, in the sourest voice she could muster.

His brow creased faintly. He stopped chewing and swallowed. Other than that, there was no sign he'd even heard her.

"It's not as if there's guests at the board," she continued. "Why must the food be so strongly flavoured?"

He fiddled with his goblet, tracing a tight circle on the table with its base. "It's always been this way."

"You eat above your station. You could afford this, if you had your Sheriff's income. But of course you lost that, didn't you?"

He didn't reply, and his blank expression resumed. But after that he just picked at his food. He didn't eat much more before giving up completely.

She congratulated herself, and felt much better. He might have been a man, and so much stronger than her, but now she knew he wasn't invulnerable.

* * *

John lay on his bed, staring at the ceiling. A candle still burned on the kist nearby; he hadn't bothered to snuff it out, and was no longer in any state to try. He'd drunk too much; the trailing patterns on the beams above were blurred.

Three weeks he'd been married. In all that time he'd taken her just once, that first fateful night. Now it was Lent, and he was supposed to avoid sins of the flesh.

But abstinence only seemed to stoke his desire. She haunted his thoughts, all the time. John couldn't understand why he felt drawn to her. She was the cruellest soul he'd ever met. Things hadn't gone well at first, but since then he'd tried hard to be friendly and generous, but all she ever gave in return were stinging criticisms or hostile silences.

He'd thought she would soften. But there was no sign of that happening. He should have shrugged her aside and got on with his life, but he'd taken a vow before God; he felt duty-bound to keep it.

Every night, he'd lie awake wondering whether he should knock upon her door. And every night, he'd lose heart and decide against it. Sometimes he drank to deaden the pain inside. At other times, he'd lie awake all night.

John sat up, and swallowed the rest of his wine.

He could bear it no longer. He'd perform his duties as a husband, whether or not his young wife welcomed him.

* * *

Once supper was over, they shed their stiff, bulky dresses and stifling hoods. It was cold, so they pulled cloaks over their kirtles and huddled on the bed, piling the pillows high around them.

"Just one last game." Margaret gathered together the cards.

Katherine shrugged, and stifled a yawn.

The puppy whimpered by the bed.

"He wants some milk," Margaret instructed. "Don't forget to warm it, or he'll get—"

The door banged open; they all shrieked, and the girls clung close.

It was *him*. He lurched unsteadily towards them, his eyes, bright, desperate, were fixed on her. He wore just his sark and hose; his sark gaped at the neck, revealing the flesh beneath. And he was roused.

Margaret stared back, unbowed. She didn't feel frightened this time. Just irritated.

"You could at least knock," she told him.

His footsteps faltered. "I want to lie with my wife." His breathing was fast, his face gleamed with sweat.

"So you'd damn my soul as well as your own."

Katherine and Mariota clutched her shoulders, unwilling to leave her. Alison started to cry.

"It's alright," Margaret said.

They scurried away.

Margaret lay back with a sigh. She hitched up her kirtle, parted her legs and steeled herself. "Get on with it."

He clambered onto the bed without a word.

Margaret closed her eyes and drove her fingers deep into the coverlet.

He gripped her shoulders, crouching close. His thigh felt hot against her own, his manhood pressed against her. The smell of him was all around her; rich, exotic spices and perfumes, mingling with a hot musky scent that was entirely his own. His breath, warm against her cheek, reeked of wine.

Come on. Get this over with, damn you. . .

"Must I lie here all night?" she asked.

She felt the change, the moment when his lust abandoned him. He moaned, then his stifling closeness was gone. His thighs still rested lightly against her flesh.

She opened her eyes to see him kneeling there, staring at her. He looked lost, on the verge of weeping.

"Aren't you capable?" She hadn't meant to sound so gleeful.

"I—" he began.

"Oh, go away!" She pushed roughly at his shoulder. "I'll lie with you willingly enough, once you're a Sheriff and a knight. Now take me, if you must. Or else get out!"

He didn't speak. There was an air of injured dignity about him as he retreated from the bed.

Once he'd gone, the girls came flocking back. "You were so bold!" Katherine sighed.

"He's a feeble creature," she retorted. She beckoned them close. "If I could, I'd summon a wise woman who'd change him into one of those scrawny hounds that he loves so much. Then I'd show him what it was to cross me. I'd whip those fine tight haunches till they bled, and chain him outside." She stretched her hands before her. "I could lie warm in my bed and listen as he howled himself hoarse in the wind and the rain."

The girls giggled nervously.

She wasn't finished. "What I'd give to have him bound and naked before me. I'd tease him and rouse him, then when he was mad with desire, I'd punish him for his lustful thoughts. I'd pinch his flesh, every inch of it, from the soles of his feet to the nape of his pretty neck. And then—" She clenched her fist tight. "I'd crush his manhood in my hand."

Katherine shivered. "You're so hard-hearted."

She closed her eyes, basking in their adoration. "He's met his match in me."

* * *

When she lay tucked up tight under the coverlet that night, she reflected on what she'd said. Harbouring such dark thoughts frightened her, but they thrilled her a little, too. She wondered if it was a sin, to think that way about a man. *I don't see how it can be,* she thought. *I want to punish his lust, that's all. What's wrong with that?*

He was her husband. He controlled almost every aspect of her life.

She'd savour her cruel thoughts without remorse, for they were the only way she had of resisting him.

Chapter 51

Margaret stood alongside at mass, her triumph palpable.

John couldn't even look at her. He didn't know what embarrassed him most; that he'd barged into her room without asking, or that he'd been incapable of performing as a husband should.

No wonder she looked so pleased.

Last night had proved what he'd suspected all along. He couldn't bear to lie with a woman who so obviously disliked him. Not that there was any point in forcing himself upon her. If she didn't love him, if she didn't gain pleasure from their union, she'd never conceive. All his efforts would come to naught.

After mass, he retreated to his chamber. But sitting there in isolation only served to fuel his unhappiness.

He couldn't shake Margaret from his thoughts. She was like a siren; he wanted to be near her, even though her indifference hurt. He didn't know how he'd win her heart, but he was a patient man. He'd persevere.

"Master John?" William's voice broke his thoughts. "The Laird of Hessilhead's downstairs. He wants to see you."

* * *

John Montgomerie of Hessilhead paced across the hall, scowling. He halted, grunted a barely audible greeting. "Brought you two dozen spears," he said. "Hugh says to make ready for war."

"Has he sent word from the east?" John asked.

"Never went," Hessilhead replied. "Abbot Schaw went instead. Hugh seemed happy with that, so. . ." He gave a non-committal shrug.

"That's it then?"

"For the present. He's been summoned to Linlithgow. To be with the King over Easter. He'll make his move, then, I suppose."

* * *

The Laird of Hessilhead joined them for dinner.

He was a coarse brute of a man, who dropped crumbs in his beard and licked his fingers and chewed with his mouth open.

Margaret didn't think much of him.

At first, she tried her best to be polite and friendly and join in the conversation. But it was hard, when the men at her side talked only about hunting or war.

So she remained silent.

Her gaze kept straying to her husband. She watched the way he held his food so elegantly in those long fingers, then let her eyes wander, along his arm, down past his shoulders and his back to the firm flesh of his leg.

She remembered the fierce heat of him, his musky, spiced scent as he leaned over her. If she flared her nose and breathed in deep, she could just catch a waft of him.

A shudder coursed through her. It wasn't fear, or loathing. She didn't quite know how she felt about him now. She kept picturing those terrible desires she'd harboured the previous night, and that quivering warmth would burn deep inside her again.

It was the first time she'd seen him as a man wrought from flesh and blood, and the realisation disturbed her. Looking at him now, she kept trying to picture him without all the trappings and rich clothes.

She wanted more than anything to stroke and squeeze his thigh, to see what it would feel like and how he'd react. She wouldn't have done it, not in a hundred years, but the desire was there, all the same.

So I want to touch him. On my terms, not his. I want him to lie quiet and obedient in my arms. I most certainly don't love him. I don't even like him. But if I must think sinful thoughts, it's better they're about him, and not some other man. . .

She spared him a smile as he poured some more wine.

Dinner wouldn't ever be dull for her again.

The Palace of Linlithgow

"Congratulations." Patrick Hepburn shook Hugh's hand. "It's good to have you amongst us."

"I'm delighted to be given this chance to prove my mettle," Hugh replied. He'd been expecting this news since his arrival, but still found it hard to contain his jubilation.

* * *

Strange how Fortune's wheel can turn. . . Hugh thought later, as he made his way to the great hall for dinner.

Just one year ago, he thought he'd be put to the horn for the burning of Kerrielaw. Now he was a Privy Councillor.

Many of the court's more moderate men were dismayed by his appointment. But their complaints had been muted. Earl Patrick had been careful to appease them, by appointing one of their number to the Privy Council: William Elphinstone, Bishop of Aberdeen.

Elphinstone had been a senior adviser to James the Third; now he was back, serving James the Fourth. Even Robert Colville had conceded ground to him, giving up his position as Keeper of the Great Seal.

All in all, Hugh reflected, as he sat between Hepburn and Argyll at the King's table, the Privy Council had been transformed. There were the hawks—like himself and Hepburn and Lord Home—and balanced against them, there was Elphinstone. Colville was still there. So too was Hugh's gude-father, Colin Campbell, the Earl of Argyll.

Argyll had never actually said where his loyalties had lain last June. He'd been, conveniently, in London when the battle took place. But Hugh knew the truth. He knew how angry Argyll had been, when King James removed him from the Chancellor's office he'd held for many years. Argyll had never been coy with Hugh; he summoned his gude-son to *Caisteal Glowm* months before the uprising began, asking him to deliver a payment to Patrick Hepburn. *It's best you do it, Hugh,* Argyll had said. *Archie's not well-suited to such subterfuge.*

Argyll's flattery didn't fool Hugh. He knew the truth. That Argyll didn't want his precious son's reputation tarnished if the plot was uncovered. That if someone was to hang for it, better it was the good-for-nothing gude-son. . .

All that was in the past, and best forgotten. Argyll had repaid Hugh in full for services rendered; along with Patrick Hepburn he'd been instrumental in arranging Hugh's appointment to the Privy Council.

A Privy Council place made life much easier, for it gave Hugh an ideal platform from which to plead his case for an intervention in the Westland.

Though whether Hepburn and Argyll would thank him for causing such an upset so soon was debatable. . .

* * *

"I spoke to James." Abbot Schaw took Hugh aside as they left chapel the following morning.

"How did he respond?"

"His curiosity is roused. *How can it be,* he said to me, *that the man whom John Stewart called 'base and treacherous' gets down on bended knee and asks his king for help?* Be warned. He'll soon start asking questions."

"Time to mention it to Earl Patrick, then."

"It'd do no harm," Schaw agreed. "But be discreet. And tread carefully!"

The Place of Ellestoun

"—And another thing. . ." Elizabeth Ross paused for breath at last. "She mocks you behind your back. All the servants talk about it." She cast John a pleading look. "How can you let her away with it?"

John sat slumped in his chair, head propped on one hand. He'd weathered his mother's tirade without a word; he'd known what he was in for when she requested 'a few words in private' after mass.

"What's the matter with you?" Her tone changed. She stalked back and forth, lips pursed tight with rage. "If I'd spoken to your father that way, he'd have beaten me."

He'd listened long enough. "I'm not my father."

"More's the pity."

"Anyway, I don't see how striking her will help."

His mother jerked to a standstill, skirts swinging to a belated halt. "You're half the man you were a month ago. She's robbed you of your strength, your wits."

John shrugged.

"If you want her to humiliate you like this, then that's all well and good. But it does you no favours."

He scowled. "Thank you for that."

"Not only that. . . She has the gall to talk back to me." She wagged a warning finger in his face. "I won't have that. I'm an old lady now. I don't deserve this treatment."

He was in half-a-mind to tell her that playing the injured party would never work, but thought against it. He wasn't in any mood for confrontation.

"I've done what I can," she continued. "I've struggled to help you through one of the worst winters I've known. What thanks do I get? None. Just endless criticism from that little shrew—"

"Alright!"

"—She says you're weak. She's right, you know."

He pushed a hand through his hair, trembling from rage or frustration, maybe both. "Why must you blame me? You made me marry her. If I'd found myself a wife I might've got a woman who wanted me."

"Your father and I worked hard to find a maid with a handsome dower and the right connections at court. Stop trying to shirk your responsibilities. You're the one at fault. Beat some respect into her!"

"I won't do it."

"Then I'll do it for you."

"No!" He met her angry gaze. "I won't have that. I remember how cruel you were to Marion, when she wouldn't marry the man you wanted—"

"What does this have to do with anything?"

"—You battered her, you starved her; she never yielded. I stood back and did nothing, because I was too young, and too frightened. And because the priest told me that whatever happened, I should honour my parents. . ." He drew a sharp breath. "She should've hated you. I know I did."

"John!" There was real hurt in her face.

The blazing anger vanished, as quickly as it came. "I'm sorry. I didn't mean that."

"You did." His proud, indomitable mother looked close to tears.

"She's my wife," he protested. "I'm the one who decides how she should be treated."

"I'll pray to God that you finally see sense," Elizabeth Ross said. "And I'll ask Him to give me patience. But be warned, John. My patience is already wearing thin."

Chapter 52

For five days now, Margaret and her girls had watched her husband unseen from their window.

He'd rise early and descend to the yard, and for an hour or two he'd hone his skills with sword or axe. A stout wooden stake had been set up for him there, the same height as a man. Sometimes he'd batter the stake. Sometimes he'd spar with William.

"Do you think he's practising for war?" Alison grasped Mariota's shoulder and rose up on tiptoe for a better view.

"Undoubtedly." Margaret leaned back against the wall with arms folded tight, a picture of indifference.

"He wasn't doing this before. What's changed?" Alison asked.

"It's something to do with the Laird of Hessilhead," Margaret said. "This all started after he came calling."

They fell quiet, savouring the ring of metal-on-metal, the shouts of two men roaring loud.

"Do you think he knows we're watching?" Alison again.

Margaret smiled, thinly. "I doubt he cares."

Katherine sighed, eyes half-closed. "Such a beast."

Margaret made a show of admiring her nails. "If you say so."

She would never have admitted it, but she was mesmerised herself. When William fought, he always wore his brigandine. But her husband never wore any armour at all. He just went out in his sark and hose, and made sure he moved so fast he never got struck.

He was magnificent to behold; he seemed so lithe and quick when he lifted the blade high or swung it around. She felt proud of him, and proud of herself too. She was proud of him because he could make her girls wilt and groan at the sight of him. And she was proud of herself because she could see how glorious he was, and feel her heart beat fast at the thought of him, but still stay strong enough to keep him at arm's length.

The girls loved her all the more for that.

The clamour ceased. She peered down, saw her husband resting on his sword, talking to William. She'd noticed how, when he grew tired, his silk sark clung to him, and his gold-brown hair trailed damp over his shoulders.

Katherine leaned against the wall, a finger hooked lightly in her mouth, her lean face flushed with excitement.

Like a mare in season, Margaret thought.

In the yard far below, William slapped her husband on the back and ambled off towards the armoury, sword balanced across his shoulders.

He remained there.

A mischievous thought gripped her. She clutched Katherine's hand tight. "Let's tease him. Throw him your handkerchief. Then pretend you want to be his mistress. Tell him you have my permission. Tell him I'll let you lie with him."

Katherine's eyes widened. She gulped, fearfully. "But what if—"

"Tell him you'll have to ask me first." She giggled. "Of course I'll say no."

"That's too cruel!"

"You're frightened of him, aren't you?"

Katherine looked nervously from Margaret, to her husband standing there oblivious in the yard. "No," she said, drawing herself tall. "I'm not."

"Well, go on then." Grasping a handkerchief from Mariota's sleeve, Margaret tossed it through the window. "Fetch it."

* * *

A pale square of silk fluttered down before John's eyes and settled upon the cobbles.

There was girlish laughter, hushed voices whispering.

John stared at the fragile piece of cloth, all too aware that somewhere high above Margaret and the girls were watching. And no doubt plotting some way to make him look foolish.

Katherine soon trotted out from the tower-house. She was the oldest amongst Margaret's entourage, and her closest companion. She waved to him. "Master John!"

He watched her carefully, saying nothing.

Katherine wasn't beautiful the way Margaret was; she had a flat chest, long limbs and a long face, too. She was handsome, he supposed, in her own way. But he didn't much care for her. William had heard it said that, much like Margaret, she'd say the cruellest things without considering the consequences. She'd never been rude to him, but he suspected that all her flattery and pleasantness was just for show.

"I'm sorry if I disturbed you. It slipped from my hand. . ." She blushed brightly, a foolish smile on her lips.

John kicked the ground with his toe.

"I didn't mean to—" She stumbled on the cobbles and came to rest on her rear, skirts forming an untidy heap around her. "Ow!"

Against his better judgement, he set aside his sword and hurried over. He took her arm and helped her up. "Are you all right?"

Katherine held his shoulder, grimacing slightly. "I've hurt my foot. I don't know if I can walk."

"Sit down and rest. Mounting block's just over there." He hadn't meant to sound so terse. She was just a young girl, unfortunate enough to be at the mercy of Margaret's whims.

Katherine muttered an apology, and slipped an arm around his neck. Clutching a handful of his shirt, she leaned against him.

John looked up warily, but there was no one at the window. Together they made their way to the mounting block.

Katherine sank down, wincing. "Do you think the bone's broken?" she asked.

"Of course not."

"But it hurts so." She looked close to tears.

"You probably just wrenched it." He crouched before her. "Lift your gown a little. Let me see."

Without another word she placed her slippered foot in his lap. She pulled her skirt back, revealing a pale ankle beneath.

Her foot looked absurdly slight and small as it rested there upon his thigh. There was no sign of swelling. Not even a bruise. He pressed his fingers gently against her flesh, and she gave a choked squeak.

"Right as rain," he told her.

He was about to stand when her foot slipped back, and prodded him firmly in the loins. Not enough to hurt, but quite enough to be noticed.

She put a hand to her mouth, face scarlet. "Oh, goodness! I'm so sorry!"

He straightened, quickly. "Get inside. Before you're missed."

"Can you help me? Please? It's still sore. . ."

He didn't believe her for an instant. But he offered his hand regardless, and the girl hauled herself up. She held on tight about his waist, and they wandered slowly across the yard.

"Master John." She paused by the door. "Please halt a moment. We must talk."

His stomach churned, and his heart beat faster. "What is it?"

"Please don't be angry. . ."

"Why should I be?"

"I've seen the cruel way Mistress Margaret treats you. I know how much it must hurt you." She gripped him tighter still.

"I don't know what you mean."

"She says—" Her voice dropped to a whisper. "She says the thought of lying with you makes her skin crawl. But. . . She knows you have needs."

It's Margaret's doing, he told himself. *Don't trust her. . .*

"She says she'll let me lie with you. All you have to do is ask. . ." Her hand moved light against his belly.

For a moment, he couldn't think. His heart thudded loud, it was the most he could do to subdue the lust.

He swallowed. She didn't speak, just kept clinging to him, caressing him so gently. . .

Then he thought of Margaret, of how she'd laugh when Katherine told her how she'd had reduced him to a hopeless wreck. Scowling, he shrugged her loose. "Keep your hands to yourself," he told her. "And don't ever speak that way to me again."

* * *

When he took his place at dinner, Margaret and her maids were nice as anything. Which made him wonder what they'd said once Katherine rejoined them.

They frightened him because he couldn't understand them. He felt like a baited bull, chained by the snout to a rock while dogs snapped at his flanks and quarters. He'd speak when he was spoken to, and that wasn't very often, but otherwise said nothing. He always felt anxious in their presence; his belly was unsettled, his appetite almost non-existent.

Margaret noticed something was amiss. She patted his arm and asked him, all concerned, whether he was eating enough.

He was glad when the meal was behind him, so he could escape to the silence of his room.

Were women always this cruel, he wondered. He'd weathered the company of three sisters through the years, and though they'd teased there'd always been good humour.

And Mary. . . He'd tried so hard to forget her. But suddenly he missed her, with a stabbing ache inside that made it hard to breathe. He wanted to hear her voice, feel the deft touch of her hand. . .

But she had no reason to welcome him. She had her farm, she had her children, and she had her memories of a husband she'd once loved.

She had no need for anything more.

Chapter 53
The Palace of Linlithgow

It was nearing the end of a long evening, and Hugh was flagging. He'd drunk more than was sensible; it was time to disappear before his relaxed mood got the better of him. There was no sign of young James, so he wouldn't cause offence by leaving early.

Saying goodnight to Archie Campbell and Robert Colville, he threaded his way through the crowded hall. He'd almost made it to the door when one of Patrick Hepburn's nephews intercepted him.

The child stood square before him and bowed. At just eight years old, the boy already possessed the quiet arrogance of Earl Patrick's kin. "If it please you, Lord Hugh. His Grace the King requests your company."

* * *

"Enter!" James invited.

Hugh stepped from the dark passageway into a room ablaze with candles.

James sat within this realm, a figure of light himself. His doublet glinted as seed pearls and gold thread reflected the flames. "I'm pleased you could join me, Lord Hugh." He waved to the nearby harpist. "That'll be all, thank you."

Hugh unsheathed his dagger and handed it to the page, who bowed then followed the musician from the room.

James watched carefully.

Once the door closed and they were alone, the young King nodded. "My apologies for the inconvenience." He arranged the counters on the backgammon board. "It's late, I know, but I didn't want this meeting to be common knowledge."

"Your Grace." Hugh sat opposite.

James grasped a flagon and poured wine for them both. He pushed a goblet towards Hugh. "Name your stake, sir."

"You caught me unawares, sire. I'm travelling somewhat light." He fumbled in his purse. "Shall we say three unicorns?" He placed the coins in a tidy pile upon the table.

"Three unicorns it is." The young King scooped up the dice and tossed them down. One brief glance to register his score, then his eyes locked on Hugh. "The Westland," he said. "I need your advice."

"Ah." Hugh's response was non-committal.

"I want that advice from the heart, Lord Hugh. I know you're not inclined to speak your thoughts, but I hope this once you'll make an exception."

Hugh looked the young King straight in the eye. No insights there; James was adept at concealing his motives. "Your Grace," he said, "I don't know who's fed you these tales. I swear to God that my loyalty is absolute."

James slouched back and pushed the gaming board aside. "The Westland has vexed us both from the beginning," he said. "I'm content you're doing all you can in Cunninghame. And in trying circumstances, too. . ."

"The situation's precarious, but I can enforce your laws there without a doubt. If Renfrew collapses into disorder then. . . My authority will be compromised."

"Would you blame Lennox for Renfrew's ills?" asked James, all-innocence.

Hugh grimaced, faintly.

A mistake, for James was staring at him with renewed intensity. The old James was back, sharp and devilishly cunning.

Hugh silently berated himself; he'd given James just what he wanted, evidence of a rift between the Montgomeries and the Darnley Stewarts. He gave a taut smile. "Let's just say, Your Grace, that I would have handled Renfrew's affairs differently."

A reflection of his smile shone in James's face. "Then the situation grows ever more complicated. The last time I spoke to John Stewart, he laid the blame for his ills squarely on your shoulders."

The news didn't surprise him. But hearing it from James himself made the outrage flow white-hot within him once again. A muscle twitched in his cheek, he made no attempt to fight it.

"Earl Patrick says you've been pressing for action in the Westland. You're championing the cause of John Sempill of Ellestoun, a man whom John Stewart has declared a traitor and a rebel. Whom should I trust, Lord Hugh. The Earl of Lennox, or yourself?"

"I wouldn't trust Lennox. Not at this moment in time." He felt profoundly uncomfortable.

"Why not?" James asked.

If it hadn't been for Matthew, he'd have heard nothing of the plot. *May you rot in hell, John Stewart. You'd hang me with the rest of them, if it came to it. . .* "I have reason to believe that the Earl of Lennox is plotting against Your Grace and those who counsel you."

There, it was done.

"Good God Almighty," said James. "What makes you think this?"

"Matthew came to me, and hinted of their intent."

"Did he ask you to join him?"

"He did."

"Yet you would not?"

Hugh shifted in his chair. "There were issues in my past you agreed to resolve."

James studied him. "There's one name at the root of all this," he said. "I've heard it countless times over the past few days. John Sempill of Ellestoun. . ."

"I guessed as much."

"John Stewart wants him put to the horn."

Hugh didn't reply.

"Stewart and Lyle were granted powers of fire and sword to bring Ellestoun to heel. But fire and sword hasn't crushed him. Now Ellestoun has appealed to me for help. He says he's a victim of impartial justice." James slumped in his chair. "I'm torn two ways," he said. "My head says I shouldn't trust Ellestoun, but my heart tells me to heed his grievances. The man has appealed to me for aid." Staring vaguely at the gaming board, James grasped the dice, then set them quickly down again. "Tell me truly," he said. "Do you know Sempill of Ellestoun?"

"Yes," Hugh said.

Relief flared in the young King's face. "That's excellent news." He sat tall in his chair. "Tell me what you know."

"I've had dealings with the Sempills for a number of years, but I had little reason to be acquainted with Master Sempill until recently." Hugh paused. His throat felt dry; he sipped some wine to moisten it. "Until his father's death, he had little involvement in his family's affairs."

"He's a young man, is he?"

"In his twenty-first year. He succeeded his father last summer."

"And how did you meet with him?"

"Master Sempill's gude-brother introduced us formally; Sir Adam Mure of Caldwell. But Earl Patrick had already asked me to seek him out. He's the nephew of Ross of Montgrennan; it was thought he was given some of your father's missing gold for safekeeping."

"Is this so?" James lazed back in his chair, suddenly informal.

Hugh stretched out his legs, visibly at ease. "With hand on heart, sire, I'd say he knows nothing of the King's gold. He's not an accomplished liar. If he was harbouring the missing gold, he wouldn't have had the gall to approach you in this way."

"What manner of a man is he?"

"He's an honest man, which is rare in these treacherous times. And he's reliable, too. He's no provincial laird; he's had an education befitting an earl and he's very civilised in his pursuits."

"You'd vouch for him then?"

"I would, sire."

James chuckled, softly. "It's a strange day when a man of your steely reputation is moved by a noble motive like friendship."

Hugh shrugged. "He has rare qualities. They should be nurtured. His situation has been difficult since his father was slain last year. His mother is there to conduct his legal affairs until he finally comes of age, but he needs guidance."

"And you think you're the man to provide such guidance?"

"I think it should be my responsibility." He bowed his head. "I slew his father."

James sat forward. "Does he know this?"

"I suspect he knows far more than he'd ever admit to."

"And he's forgiven you! That's a rare man indeed."

"I think so. I've never had reason to believe otherwise."

A smile spread across James's face. "Perhaps he bides his time. . ."

Hugh said nothing.

"I look forward to meeting this man," James said. "He and I have much in common. We lost our fathers before we were good and ready, and now we must rely on the goodwill of those who stole them away. One last thing concerns me; what of the twenty pounds he owes?"

"He'll want rid of it, I'm sure. He'd have paid it long ago, if he could."

"If he won't trust my emissaries, he can give it to me in person." James slid the board back into place and retrieved the dice. "We can relax now, my friend. Rest assured that your labours haven't been in vain. I'll speak with Earl Patrick and ensure that this matter is attended to at once." He raised his goblet. "To our business in the Westland. May it be resolved with all due speed, and to our mutual satisfaction."

Chapter 54
The Place of Ellestoun

Every day the finches flew to her window-ledge. They'd be there first thing in the morning, and in late afternoon they'd return, waiting hopefully for crumbs.

Margaret had felt sorry for them, trapped in their cage. So one day she opened the door and urged them out. She'd gasped with delight when she saw their bright gold wings glitter against the blue of the heavens. And it was an even greater pleasure to have them sitting at her window the following morning, waiting to be fed.

"I wonder what he does all evening, sitting alone in his chamber," Margaret said, scattering morsels of cake for the eager birds.

"Probably commits unnatural acts with William," Katherine said.

"Perhaps I should find out."

"You wouldn't dare."

"Oh yes I would." She stood. "Besides, I have a score to settle. With William. He talked back to me today. I won't take that from a servant."

So she was exaggerating. But she'd seen the look on William's face when she'd accused his master of being weak and a coward and a fool. His reply had been tight with resentment. *It's unjust to criticise a man who's suffered his misfortunes.*

On reflection, his words were verging on the rebellious.

He'd dared to stand up to her. Now she was determined to have her revenge.

* * *

Once her door disappeared from view, Margaret faltered. She'd never confronted her husband on his own ground before, and the prospect frightened her. She took a deep, fortifying breath, then continued onwards.

Outside his chamber, she halted.

Music. The strains of a lute, sweetly played. She paused, entranced, then shook herself to her senses. *Don't soften. With luck, his mother'll be gone before the month's out. Perhaps she'll take William. Then he'll really be alone. . .*

She rapped upon the door.

"Yes?" That was her husband's voice.

It was the first time she'd entered his room. She'd thought his lair would be austere. Instead, it was finely furnished with tapestries and wall-hangings. The dark red curtains around the bed were embroidered with gold thread, while the ceiling was exquisitely painted. The air was heavy with the scent of herbs, woodsmoke and perfume. And behind that, she caught the scent of *him*.

Thoughts of his flesh rose unbidden in her mind, and she blushed.

She looked instinctively to the big chair by the fire, but he wasn't there. Instead, she saw William. He had a lute balanced in his lap; he'd stopped playing and was staring at her, face impassive.

Please, she almost said. *Don't stop. . .*

But she couldn't retreat now. Not with the girls waiting to hear how she'd fared.

I'm sorry, William. I didn't know there's more to you than meets the eye. . .

"What do you want?" Her husband reclined by the window, legs stretched out along the cushioned seat. He had a cloak pulled up round his shoulders to keep the chill at bay and a thin cap jammed over his head. His hair spilled out beneath, glowing fiery gold where the setting sun touched it. One hound lay draped over his knees and another was sprawled on the floor beside him.

An open book lay in his lap.

"You'll strain your eyes," she told him, helpfully.

He sighed, and snapped the book shut.

"What are you reading?"

"It's Homer," he said. "Tales of Troy."

"Heroes battling over the fair lady Helen," she said. "So, how do you see yourself? As brave Achilles, perhaps. Or the spurned Menelaus."

He shifted slightly. The hound opened its eyes, yawned, then slid to the floor.

"What do you want with me?" He sounded weary beyond belief.

The seam had worn through in his hose, a little above the knee. She glimpsed a pale sliver of skin there.

Gripping her fists tight by her side, she stood tall. "It concerns Master Haislet."

He looked across at his servant, expression unchanged. "William," he said. "Could you leave us a moment?"

The silence stretched tight, unbroken, as William set down his lute and strode off. The door creaked closed behind him, the latch rattled shut.

"Now," he said. "What has Master Haislet done to offend you?"

"He was rude. He questioned my judgement and called me a liar."

He stared at her, frowning faintly. He didn't speak.

A new flush of courage filled her. "He should be punished."

"Do you want him dismissed? Or merely whipped?"

"I—" Now the question was put to her, she didn't know how to respond.

"He was defending me, wasn't he?" His tone was cold.

She didn't reply.

"You want me to punish a man who had the courage to speak out in my defence."

"Yes, but—"

"That's unreasonable."

Her euphoria faded. He always seemed so compliant, but once she'd cornered him, he changed.

Just like that first day. . .

"I'll speak with him," he said. "An apology will be forthcoming." He opened his book again.

She didn't feel inclined to leave just yet. Not while he had the upper hand. "You should say when things need mending."

He looked up. "What?"

"Your hose. They're torn. Here." Before she thought better of it, she crouched down and stroked the offending spot. His skin was cool, smooth. Just as she'd imagined it.

He was such a fierce creature, when he roared and wielded his sword. Yet here he was, trembling at her touch. She felt giddy with wonder and triumph. And, perhaps, a little desire. . . "There now," she whispered. "That's nice, isn't it?"

His manhood twitched, he looked away and swallowed. "Could I visit you tonight?"

"You can visit whenever you like. But I won't welcome you."

"Then what should I do. . ."

Leaning closer, she gripped his shoulders. "Find favour with the King, and I'll love you," she said, whispering soft in his ear. "Until then, you can spend your nights alone." She kissed him lightly on the cheek.

* * *

He didn't visit.

Margaret didn't really think he would.

She lay awake that night, thinking pleasing thoughts. He'd be lying there in the room below, tossing and turning in his bed. Burning with torment because he lusted after a woman who spurned him. She hoped he couldn't sleep. She hoped he was weeping with frustration.

He was a poor helpless fool; he'd do anything to make her want him. Why, he'd even let her tease him. He was weak as water in her hands; she'd despised that weakness once but now she found it somehow endearing.

Margaret stretched, yawning.

A few months of this and you'll crawl to my door, begging me to take you. She smiled at the thought. *When that day comes, then. . . Maybe I will, maybe I won't. It all depends on how you conduct yourself, my glorious husband. . .*

* * *

It was well past noon, and John had been in the saddle five hours or more.

In all that time he'd brought down just one roebuck. The rest of the morning he'd wandered aimlessly, not caring where he headed, just making sure he didn't go home.

He was tired and hungry, his thoughts confused. He kept thinking about *her*, and he'd feel such a painful jolt inside that he'd choke back a sob. He tried to turn his mind to other matters, but she still haunted him, her taunts echoing loud in his head.

He sat up with a start, realising where his path had taken him.

He was half a mile from Pennald, and the lands of Bar. . .

I won't call on her, he told himself. *I'll just make sure that all's well. . .*

* * *

His horse ambled along the trackway which led to Mary's farm. Oats and bere barley grew green and vigorous to either side of him.

His life was barren, but at least the land was fertile and prosperous.

At the halfway point, his courage failed him. John halted his horse, and stretched in his stirrups with a sigh.

You're the laird. She used you.

267

The thought stung him. He swallowed, tears briefly misting his eyes. Gathering up his reins, he was about to turn back when he heard a child's gurgling laughter ahead.

Tottering towards him was a girl aged three, maybe four, years. Her bare legs gleamed pale beneath a gown she'd outgrown long ago, her hair shone bright gold where the sunlight caught it.

Mary's child, wandering alone in the road.

His self-pity was forgotten. "Hello there," he said.

The child halted and stared fearlessly up at him.

"Meg!" A woman's voice called. "Meg? Where are you hiding?"

Dismounting, he dropped to one knee before her. "You're a long way from home."

She chewed on a grubby finger, bright blue gaze fixed upon him.

"Hasn't your mother got enough to worry about?" he asked. "Without you adding to her woes?"

He picked her up and settled her in the crook of his arm. She nestled close without a sound.

"I don't know what your mother will say when she sees me." He winced as the child crooned and grasped the gold cross round his neck. "Oy! Don't tug. You'll break it."

"Meggy!"

Mary's child, but not Mary's voice. Mildly concerned, he tucked the child more securely into place and strode down the track, horse trailing behind him.

* * *

It was as if he'd stepped back through time, to that afternoon long ago when he'd brought Hugh Alexson home from the war.

Things had scarcely changed. The new cottage had been built on the foundations of the old; now, as then, it looked deserted. Someone was there, though. He could hear the rhythmic sound of an axe chopping wood.

He started as a woman appeared from around the side of the cottage.

It wasn't Mary. It was her sister. Janet was her name, as far as he could recall.

"Hello." He blushed as he spoke.

"Oh, thank God!" Janet seized the child and hugged her close. "There you are!" Quick, darting eyes looked out from her careworn face and briefly met his own. She bobbed into a curtsey. "Thank you, Master Sempill. I turned my back a moment and she'd gone."

"She takes after her mother."

Janet sighed and pushed some unruly curls from the child's face. "She's round the back. If you want to see her. . ."

"I don't know—" His cheeks burned a deeper crimson.

She slid a sideways glance towards him. "Well, you certainly didn't come here to see me." She strode away, heading back round the cottage. "Mary! It's alright. Meggy's safe. And there's someone here for you."

John trudged after her.

There behind the cottage was Mary. She was doing a man's job, wielding a heavy axe as she split logs for the fire. She still wore the gown she'd been given at

Ellestoun, but it was patched and stained now. Her hood hung shapeless on her head, her face was scarlet with exertion.

She didn't look up. "If it's the tacksman, tell him—"

"Oh, it's not the tacksman," said Janet.

Mary winced and straightened, a hand on her back. Then her strained expression vanished, and she smiled, faintly. "Why, hello!" She pushed some stray hairs back under her hood.

"I'll leave you," Janet said. "There's work to be done."

Mary sighed and set down the axe.

"You shouldn't be doing that," John told her.

She rubbed her hands awkwardly against her apron. "I'll not shiver and starve for want of a man." She picked up the axe again.

"Get back now." He strode over and grasped the haft, but she tightened her grip. "Oh no! You mustn't!"

"I've a strong pair of arms. Stronger than yours, for sure."

Mary relinquished the axe with a sigh.

John paused to unpin his cloak. "If you want to be useful, look after that." He placed it about her shoulders. "Now stand back." Grasping a log, he balanced it on the cutting block. "So you're not wed yet?"

"No," she replied. "Don't intend to, either." She retreated to the pile of peats by the wall and sat down there.

"How will you manage?" He swung the axe high, let it fall. The wood split and he rearranged it.

"This year'll be hard for everyone. But so far things are going well. The kye have dropped three calves for a start."

"Let's hope we have a good summer."

"We're all praying for that. If the crops fail. . ." Her voice trembled.

"I know." He set down the axe and cleared the wood from the block. "This is hot work," he complained. He unbuckled his sword belt and threw it aside.

"No one asked you to do it!" She rocked anxiously on her perch, arms wrapped about her knees. "I can chop my own wood."

"What manner of a man would that make me, leaving a poor widow to cut her own kindling? Now help me, please. Before I roast alive."

She came over and helped him unlace his doublet. She put out her hand to take it but he'd already hurled it away.

Mary scrambled after it. "Oh, for shame, John!"

"To Hell with it."

Mary settled back down on the peats, doublet folded neatly in her lap. She leaned her chin on her hands, smiling. "It's a sight to see, the laird doing a cottar's tasks."

John wiped his sleeve across his brow. "Each time that blade falls, I fancy it's hewing Matthew Stewart's neck. That pretty thought'll keep me going all afternoon."

* * *

Mary sat there awhile, then left, muttering apologies.

He barely noticed her absence. With every blow, the burden lightened. He no longer cared. About Margaret. About Ellestoun. About his poor impoverished estate and how he'd fare if Hugh Montgomerie's political manoeuvrings came to naught.

Sunlight gave way to cloud, and a light drizzling rain started. But he kept going, the pile of wood beside the peats growing ever larger.

"Johnny," Mary whispered in his ear. Her hands rested light upon his back, then slid about his waist in a caress that made him shudder. "Come on now. That'll last all summer." She kissed his cheek.

"If there's anything else I can do, then I'll try my best. But I'm not much good at being useful." He glanced ruefully down at his hands. They were blistered, bloody.

"You've been a great help already." Taking his hand, she rubbed the palm. "You'll stay and eat, won't you?"

"If it's not too much of a burden on you. I brought some ale. And you can take the deer. But you'll need to hang it. . ."

Mary tugged him close. "Oh, you're coy today. I know what really brought you here. And I'm flattered."

"I didn't mean it that way. I didn't expect you to take me to your bed. I just. . ."

"You just hoped I would." She slipped her arm in his, smiling. "I don't want a husband, but that doesn't mean I don't miss a man's company."

"What about your sister?"

"We share our secrets, always have." She took his hand. "Come inside," she said. "You're wet through."

* * *

As they walked together, she chattered away about how the kye were faring, and how she'd worked from dawn till dusk for a whole week to have the fields manured in time for ploughing. He didn't say a word; he just listened, enjoying the novelty of hearing her talk so much. She'd changed in other ways, too, walking with a confident swing to her hips he'd never seen before.

When they paused at the door, her sprightly mood was gone. "I'm sorry," she said. "It was cruel to leave that way. But I knew you'd soon be wed." She paused. "It's not going well, is it?"

"How did-"

She laid a finger on his lips. "You'd be loyal if you could, just as you're being loyal to me now." She glanced away. "You don't belong here."

"I don't want to offend. . ."

"It's not like that." When she looked up, her eyes were bright with tears. "I'm pleased to see you. But this can't last. You'll be gone soon enough, and I- I *understand* that." She frowned, searching for the right words. "You're like the sun. You'd burn me if I strayed too close."

She rested a hand lightly against his chest. She didn't move at first, just stood there looking at him, austere features softened by a smile. "It's a beautiful thing," she said. "To be touched by the sun. Even in the coldest winter, the memory's still there."

She traced a delicate line down the damp cloth of his sark, to the taut muscles of his abdomen and lower still. Her fingers deftly worked behind his hose, making him shiver and gasp in delight.

He seized her close and pressed his lips against hers.

One long, lingering kiss, then she drew back. She grasped his hands, squeezed them tight. "I missed you, Johnny."

Chapter 55

In the great hall at Ellestoun, the household gathered for dinner. Margaret peered through the crowd, trying to catch a glimpse of her husband.

Katherine nudged her. "Perhaps your harsh words were too much. Perhaps he drowned himself. Or plunged his dagger in his breast because of love."

Margaret fiddled with her goblet. For once, Katherine's words didn't amuse her.

She glanced past her husband's place to the long bench beyond. Lady Elizabeth had noticed her son's absence; she'd summoned William and they were talking together in hushed voices.

Margaret had been there a month, and scarcely knew the man she'd married. But even she understood that he never went off without telling someone where he was heading. She glowered at William, who'd sat down next to Lady Elizabeth.

They waited a long while in the hope that the master would appear. But he didn't. By now, everyone was restive. Even the laundry-women and huntsmen at the lower tables.

"Well," Lady Elizabeth sighed. "I suppose we'd better start without him." She didn't seem too upset. "If you please, Mistress Colville."

Margaret stood. She opened her mouth to speak, but the talking didn't cease.

Together, William and Lady Elizabeth battered their hands against the table. Silence.

"Thanks be to God for the gracious gifts He's bestowed upon us. May He Bless this house, and all who've gathered here to eat with us today."

The food was brought out. Fish again, because it was Lent, but at least the cooks knew how to keep the flavours varied. William sliced and served it, since the master wasn't there.

Margaret wasn't hungry. She kept seeing the empty space in the corner of her eye.

Perhaps he'd fallen from his horse and was lying injured somewhere. The thought unsettled her. She didn't care for him much, and she found great pleasure in thinking hateful thoughts and saying spiteful things about him.

But deep inside, she didn't like the thought of him suffering.

* * *

She tried to catch William after dinner. But he'd already gone out to walk the master's hounds.

So Margaret waited in her husband's chamber. She sat in his chair, and drew her legs up close. *I shouldn't be in here*, she thought. *If he catches me, God knows what he'll do.*

An hour passed. There was still no sign of either William or her husband. Bored of waiting, she wandered round the room. She admired the tapestries, then examined a pile of books lying on the kist next to the bed. There was a venerable

Bible, a Book of Hours, Homer's Trojan tales, and some indecipherable work in Greek.

Picking up the Homer, she sat back down again.

It was dense text, with no pictures. Written in Latin, too. She started to read it aloud, but soon lost interest; she wondered how he found pleasure in reading it.

Eventually, she heard footsteps. The latch lifted, and the two hounds came trotting in, followed by William.

"Mistress Margaret," he acknowledged.

The hounds pressed closed, tails wagging. She pushed them away. "Where is he?"

He swallowed. "I don't rightly know."

"He's sworn you to secrecy, hasn't he?"

"By God's Truth, he hasn't. I don't know where he is."

"This isn't like him, is it?"

William hesitated. For a moment, he too looked anxious. "No."

"Aren't you concerned?"

"Yes, but. . ."

"But what?"

William said nothing.

She wanted to shout with frustration. "I want you to find him." Her voice shook. "He might need help."

"Any message?"

Tell him to come home. Tell him I'm sorry. "No," she said quietly. "No message."

* * *

Mary shook out the thin silk sark and hung it on a peg to dry. She wasn't used to handling fabric of that quality; she kept thinking her clumsy hands would tear it.

She glanced towards John. He'd settled himself down on the packed earth floor next to the fire and was gazing thoughtfully into the flames. She'd wrapped him in a tattered old blanket to keep him warm: he was like a wild Barbarian prince, the blanket was draped over his shoulder, concealing the parts that mattered, if little else. His long pale legs were folded close to his hips, his arms and half his back exposed.

He looked profoundly uncomfortable. Mary guessed it was Janet's presence that unsettled him; he was awkward with women at the best of times.

Janet tried to act as if he wasn't there. But it was hard to ignore their visitor. Even now, bereft of his rich clothes, he possessed a grace and presence that caught the eye. He seemed out-of-place, a unicorn stabled amongst the kye.

Janet bustled past and pushed her hip gently against Mary's. She cast her a secretive smile and a wink. "Get on with it," she whispered. "It's not fair, to put temptation in a woman's way."

Mary laughed and pushed her aside.

* * *

Once she'd laid John's clothes out near the fire, she drew a stool alongside him.

273

He threw an arm across her lap and leaned his head against her thigh. She hadn't ever seen him so subdued. She caressed his arm, offering silent consolation. *What manner of a wife is she*, she wondered, *if she weighs up all your qualities and still finds you wanting?*

She knew better than to pry. He'd tell her his troubles in his own time, if at all. She brushed his damp hair aside and touched his shoulder. The muscles were taut; she pressed gently, trying to loosen them. "Do you want to talk?" When he didn't reply, she ruffled his hair. "Let me try and make it better."

* * *

She didn't have a proper bed. Just a mattress stuffed with straw and a few blankets which had to make do for everyone. But when she explained the situation, he just shrugged and said he quite understood.

He didn't want to make love at first. He was tense and upset and reluctant to let her touch him. But she persevered, stroking and kneading his flesh until he lay soft and supple in her arms.

He was ready then. They lay together, and afterwards she held him close and breathed in his strange exotic scent. "Just rest now," she whispered. "No one knows you're here. You can stay as long as you want."

* * *

The boys hadn't long come home from the fields when she heard hoofbeats outside. A horse snorted, a man called, "Hello?"

"Come inside!" She knew William's voice well enough. "Good evening, Master Haislet!" she greeted him as he dived beneath the ox-hide curtain that served as a door. Grasping his hands, she kissed him on both cheeks.

He gave an embarrassed smile and doffed his bonnet. "Good day to you, Mistress White." He nodded towards Janet, then spotted the clothes that hung by the fire. "He's here, isn't he?"

Mary glanced towards the mound of blankets by the wall. "He's been asleep all afternoon."

William was visibly relieved. "Thought so."

"It'll be dark soon."

"I'd best get back. The mistress'll be worried."

"Then let her worry."

William grinned. "Seems reasonable to me."

"It's better than going outside at this hour."

"A space by the fire'll do me just fine. And I brought some victuals. In case you had an extra mouth to feed."

"God bless you, William!"

He twisted his bonnet awkwardly. "I'd best see to the horse."

"I'll do it." Mary's eldest sprang to his feet. "I saw to the master's, too. Brushed the beast's coat till it shone like copper."

William laughed. "You're a good lad. Henry says he's missing you." He looked at Mary. "You glad to be home?"

"Oh, aye. It's good to have an honest living again."

"We miss you back at the place." He sounded wistful.

"It's no life for me," she told him.

274

He nodded, saying nothing. He was a kind-hearted man. In other circumstances, she'd have considered marriage. She supposed it was too late now. She'd lain with his master too long.

* * *

William sat by the fire and entertained the children before dinner. They hung upon his every word, while he told of fearless knights battling a cruel dragon that despoiled a distant land.

Then at last the bread trenchers were laid out and they were ready to dine.

John still slept. No one wanted to wake him. The rest of them sat down around the table, William jammed tight between Mary's two boys, Janet sharing the other bench with her three children.

They kept the stool free for John. He wasn't exactly presiding over the hall at Ellestoun, but he was still the laird and it wasn't right to lay out the board any other way.

The smell of food woke him at last. He joined them, still yawning, with his blanket pinned at the shoulder.

"Christ, there's a sight for sore eyes!" William laughed, while wee Hughie gaped in amazement.

"It's John the Baptist!" he cried.

"No," said William. "It's your Uncle John from Kenmure. And he'll smash your teeth down the back of your throat if you tell a soul he's here."

"He would, too," said her eldest, helpfully. "I seen him with a sword. He'd slit you open and chop your innards into tiny pieces."

Hughie's horror turned to awe.

"Don't talk that way at the board." Mary patted the stool. "Here you go, Johnny."

He sat down. "What're you doing here?" he asked William.

"Mistress Margaret made me scour the county for you."

John glanced disparagingly up towards the rafters.

There was a bowl of plain vegetable pottage, laid out beside the treats that William had brought; pasties, a whole roast trout (*freshly caught from the loch*, William said, proudly. *Stole it from the kitchens myself*) and some little cakes.

John slid aside, and Mary sat down, crushed against him.

Meg tugged Mary's skirt. Mary plucked her daughter up and sat her in her lap, but before long Meg crawled off and settled on John's knee. The child sat there, straight and self-important, watching everyone with her bright blue eyes.

Mary started as Hughie reached out to snatch a cake. "Don't do that!" she scolded. "We're eating in company. Close your eyes and clasp your hands and wait while Master John blesses the table."

* * *

There was still no sign of her husband. And no sign of William, either.

"His horse has fallen and its back's broken," Katherine suggested. "One of his shapely legs lies trapped beneath its cold body. He's lying alone in the dark, calling for help. . ."

"Maybe he's been set upon by thieves." That was Mariota. "He's been stripped and beaten and he's bleeding to death at the side of the road."

Margaret shivered. She'd said endless cruel things over the past few weeks. She'd even gone down on her knees in chapel, and prayed to God he'd die so she'd be rid of him.

She hadn't really thought God would take heed. Now it seemed the unthinkable had happened, and she felt a little responsible. She felt sick in the pit of her stomach, she didn't think she'd sleep until she knew all was well.

"Margaret?" Katherine sounded worried.

"I'm fine."

"You should get to your bed."

She went to the window one last time. Pushing back the shutter, she peered outside.

The yard was still. A dog barked from the kennels, but otherwise there was silence. Out on the loch, moonlight formed a fractured path across the water.

Margaret gave a heartfelt sigh. *I know he's tedious, but if he dies after what happened between us last night, I won't forgive myself.* She gently closed the shutter. *Look after him, Holy Mary. Keep him safe from harm.*

* * *

The girls were whispering together when Margaret rose from her bed the following morning. They still seemed subdued as they dressed her. Alison's eyes were red; she'd been crying.

Margaret's heart tripped faster. "What's wrong?"

They looked at one another. Katherine swallowed, nervously.

"Is he home yet?" She knew he wasn't. She was sure she'd lain awake all night. Worrying, blaming herself for his death, while she waited in vain for the clatter of hooves in the yard. . .

"Margaret, there's something you should know," Katherine began. A moment's silence, then, "He has a mistress."

She felt as if she'd been struck. She couldn't even speak.

"The servants all think he's gone to see her," added Mariota.

She gulped for breath. "But why should he want a mistress?" Her voice was thin, forced. "He has a wife."

"It's worse." Katherine laid a gentle hand upon her arm. "She's a widow, she's thirty years old, and she's a commoner." She rubbed Margaret's sleeve. "I'm sorry. I didn't want to break the news. But I thought it best you hear it this way."

Margaret still felt numb inside. But slowly the anger was building inside her. She'd worried about him, when all the time he'd been lying in another woman's arms, being pleasured by her.

* * *

William returned later, and at least had the grace to call by her door.

"Where were you?" she demanded.

"It was late."

"You were told to return."

"He told me to stay."

"Where is he?"

"I can't say."

"He's with a woman, isn't he?"

He didn't reply.

Tears pricked her eyes. *Does she love you? Do you love her? Oh God, I can't stand the thought of another woman looking at you. Touching you.* "Please, William." She clutched his arm. "Tell me one thing; is she beautiful?"

Gripping his bonnet tight, William studied the floor. "She's handsome, I suppose."

"Am I prettier than she is?"

"Well, yes, but. . . That doesn't really matter to him. It's—" He broke off.

"Tell me, William. Please."

"It's just that she cares for him. And a man. . . Sometimes he needs that from a woman."

She sat down, breathless with horror. *It's not even lust. He loves her. He's capable of love. . . Oh, God. . .*

"Mistress Margaret?" William sounded concerned.

"Thank you, William," she said. "You've served us both well."

* * *

The following day, Margaret was about to change for dinner when she heard hoofbeats. She rushed to the window and there he was. Sitting relaxed upon his horse as he talked with the grooms, behaving as if nothing were amiss.

"Everything's ready," said Katherine, from where she'd been laying a fresh gown out upon the bed.

"It'll wait," Margaret retorted, face hot with indignation.

* * *

Margaret hurried down the stairs, and halted at his door. She seethed silently, fists clenched.

Footsteps approached. Spurs clinked, the tread sounded weary.

He came round the turn in the stair and saw her waiting there.

He paused.

He seemed bigger and taller somehow, his presence filling the tiny space of the stair-tower. She'd never seen him so dishevelled, hair bedraggled, two days' growth of beard on his face. His clothes were stained and filthy and he reeked, of peat smoke, earth and bitter male sweat.

He seemed alien, bestial.

She was terrified and aroused all at once. "Where were you?"

He looked her carelessly up and down. "That's not your concern."

"I was worried about you. I thought you were dead."

"No need to worry." His voice was brisk, unsympathetic.

She wanted to berate him some more, but when he acted so disinterested, he frightened her more than ever. "Please tell someone next time," she whispered.

He didn't reply, just opened the door and disappeared into his room.

The door slammed behind him.

Margaret couldn't move, stunned because he'd refused to talk to her. Then gradually it sank in. The realisation that, when they'd spoken together, she hadn't any inkling what he'd been thinking.

You misread him all along. You thought him dull, and tedious. He's not. He just keeps his true self buried deep, somewhere you can't find it. . .

She hated herself for not realising it sooner. She'd been merciless in her criticism; she'd thought it would sting him into trying hard to win her love.

Instead, she'd driven him away.

* * *

His mother raged at him. Told him he was a fool, told him he was letting his ancestors down, bedding *that base-born whore* instead of doing his duty and producing an heir.

John let her have her say. He was only half-listening. He couldn't even feel upset. Those precious hours spent with Mary had worked wonders; if he closed his eyes, he could still hear her voice. . .

"—I warned you. But you did nothing. You just let things slip further. What's the matter with you? Don't you care anymore?"

He shifted with a sigh.

"Well, you can rot in this midden. The dowager house is ready and I'm leaving on the morrow."

She wanted him to beg her to stay. But he was sick and tired of trying to appease everyone. He just shrugged. "If that's what you think best."

"John, what are you saying? That little shrew couldn't possibly—"

"You've made your mind up, Mother. I'm not going to change it."

He walked out then.

* * *

John went into the gardens and stayed there a while, picking pests off the new shoots on the roses.

He should have been worried. His mother was right -- Margaret couldn't cope with running the household alone.

He smiled. It didn't matter any more. Nothing mattered.

To Hell with his family. To Hell with the rest of the world.

Chapter 56

Good Friday, and the city of Aberdeen was jammed with crowds. Hundreds had flocked from miles around to witness the Easter celebrations at the cathedral.

Another stranger in their midst wouldn't be noticed by anyone.

Forbes had promised great things for this day, and John Stewart, Earl of Lennox, was intrigued enough to want to see what he had in mind.

Forbes timed their arrival well; they entered the city to be told that Unicorn Puirsuivant had arrived two days previously. The herald had summoned the burgesses, and informed them that an additional tax was being levied that year. *For the sending of ambassadors to foreign courts.*

Everyone knew why *that* was necessary. Murdering a legitimate monarch never went down well with either enemies or allies.

Why should we be punished for their sins? the burgesses asked. *We never sanctioned his murder...*

But they had to pay up all the same.

In the streets beyond the Lord Forbes' townhouse, the atmosphere was tense, angry. Men's thoughts were first and foremost with the martyred Christ, but it was an ideal time to remind them of their martyred King. The good citizens of Aberdeen couldn't take their vengeance on Pilate, but they could vent their anger against those who'd murdered their rightful monarch.

Stewart slouched back with a sigh. Excitement burned deep within him. But he was too old, too experienced, to let anything show upon his face.

There was a knock on the door, and a Forbes retainer came before them. He bowed his head. "My lords, the Passion's just ending in the market square."

Forbes looked at Stewart and smiled. "I think it's time, then."

* * *

They rode out from the townhouse; twenty Forbes men-at-arms and another twenty Stewarts. They battered through the main street at a trot with Lord Forbes at the fore.

Forbes held a spear. Lodged upon its tip was a white silk sark, torn and daubed with blood.

"What's happening?" a woman cried.

"It's the sark of good King James!" Stewart retorted, from where he sat aboard his horse.

* * *

News of their coming spread like plague. By the time they'd reached the market square a great surging mass followed on behind, drawn to Forbes' banner as if it were the relic of a saint.

Forbes pulled his horse to a halt at the mercat cross. He dismounted, sprang up the steps with the spear in his hand and waved it in broad sweeping strokes before him. He battered the butt against the plinth, making the bloody banner shiver in the breeze.

"Good people of the north!" Forbes roared. "I call for vengeance! Vengeance on those who slaughtered our King! Have they paid for their crimes? Have they, by God! They steal our lands, they grow fat on our gold and grant us nothing but contempt in return. They've corrupted Prince James, and now he's King he's entirely in their thrall. Listen, men of Aberdeen and Moray! Should we wring our hands and lament as all our wealth is stolen from us? Of course not! We must fight back. And make them rue the day they martyred our King!"

The crowd swept forward, baying loud support. Distressed faces gazed upon the bloodied garment; eager hands stretched out to touch it. Then a sturdy farmer leapt alongside. He seized the spear from Forbes and waved it. "Death!" he called. "Death to them all!"

The reverence was gone. Hot on its heels came rage. Men and women screamed and howled with fury. Holding the banner high in their midst, the crowd swept up the street like an angry wave. Stalls were overturned; goods and produce trampled underfoot and smashed.

Forbes and Stewart watched from the safety of the mercat cross, savouring the chaos. Their men-at-arms mingled with the crowd, goading the rioters onwards, aiding the destruction.

"Impressive," said Stewart.

Forbes leaned back against the market cross, arms folded. He was smiling. "This is just the start of it," he said. "Mark my words, John. In a few months, the whole land'll be ablaze."

The Place of Ellestoun

Margaret hadn't even finished dressing when the knock sounded on her door. Mariota answered it. "It's the tacksman."

"What does he want?" Margaret didn't much like Alan Semple. He was a huge bear of a man, cold and uncouth, who shouted at everyone. She didn't like to admit it, but he frightened her a little.

"He says he has to see you."

"I'm dressing. He'll have to wait." She waved impatiently at Katherine. "Hurry up!"

Katherine fetched her hood and fixed it in place.

Margaret picked up the mirror and studied herself, carefully. Satisfied, she swept to the door. "Yes?"

Alan Semple doffed his bonnet and bowed. "Mistress Colville."

"How can I help you?"

"The Lady Elizabeth's gone now, if it please you. Could you attend the servants, to discuss business for the coming week?"

Margaret suddenly felt very old, and very important. "I'll be there right away," she replied.

* * *

She knew most of the servants to look at, even if she didn't know their names. They addressed her in turn, bowing or curtseying before they told her their tasks. They explained their needs, and asked about expenditure.

Margaret nodded sagely, and made approving noises. But her heart was pounding. *What am I to do? He keeps the gold in his room, and the accounts, too.*

What if I make a mistake?

She swallowed, realising for the first time what a vast place it was. *I can't do this. . .* she told herself.

You must.

But I can't. Not on my own, without instruction. She told me things, I know. But I didn't really listen the way I should have. Besides, I don't think she wanted me to know everything.

Margaret gulped, suddenly frightened. *I so want to be a good wife, so he can't find fault with me.*

"—is that acceptable?" Alan Semple asked.

"Er, yes, I think so. . ."

* * *

She sat in her room for at least an hour, fretting silently.

Katherine and the others fussed around her. They asked her what was wrong and offered what soothing words they could, but it didn't help. Deep inside, Margaret knew what to do. She was proud, but she wasn't stupid.

Hooves battered outside, hounds sang loud.

Margaret sprang to her feet, shrugging the girls aside. Scurrying down the stairs towards the yard, she hoped it wasn't already too late.

When she burst into the yard, she found the horses ready, the hounds just being mustered. A half-dozen men had gathered, her husband and William amongst them. Her husband stood before his horse, reins clasped loose in his hand. The horse dozed, head drooping; its muzzle rested light against his hip as he caressed its bony face and smoothed its forelock.

Jealousy surged through her. *You care more for that ugly old horse than you do for your wife.*

Taking a deep breath, she headed towards him.

His smile vanished. He nodded briefly. "Good day."

"I don't mean to intrude, but. . . I'd be grateful if you'd spare me an hour or two."

"I have to leave now."

"It's very important." She hoped he wasn't immune to wheedling. "I need to discuss the accounts."

He shrugged, faintly. "As you wish." He glanced at William and the others. "I'm sorry," he said. "But I'm needed here."

* * *

Margaret had to trot to keep up with him. "I don't like to inconvenience you," she said, breathlessly. "It's just that managing your affairs is down to me, and I'm not yet familiar with what's required."

He stopped. "You want advice?"

She wished he hadn't made his incredulity that obvious. "Actually, yes." She felt herself blush. "I need to know what money's available." She loitered at his side, waiting anxiously for a reply. She thought she'd made a reasonable attempt at being nice to him.

He smiled, faintly. "Alright," he said. "We'll go upstairs and fetch the accounts. We can run through everything together."

* * *

It was hard to keep a cheerful face as she sat beside him, elbow just touching his. John kept noticing little things about her; the delicate curl of her lashes, the pale curve of her neck. A tiny blemish on her chin marred an otherwise flawless complexion. Somehow, it only made her more endearing.

The crippling self-consciousness was back; he blushed with every misplaced word and hesitation. He thought she'd mock him but she didn't say a word. She just waited patiently while he explained all the incomes and outgoings.

She grasped the rolls, and scanned the entries, keenly. "The rents are paid at midwinter and midsummer?" she said. "If that's so, then what happened last winter? And midsummer, last year? The incomes were well down, both times."

"We lost thirteen men in battle, and waived the rents for the widows. We didn't press for rents at all over the winter, because of the troubles."

"But. . ." She tugged her little finger with her teeth. "Without the rents, the household won't prosper."

"You can't take rents from starving people," he said. "We'll waive the rents this summer, too."

"Why?"

"A man'll toil far harder if he thinks his labour will benefit his family. We'll be granted the tithes from the mills at least, and a portion of the profits from any kye sold at market. We won't get much income, but at least we can fill up the granaries again."

"But that means there's been no income for a year!"

"It was an exceptional year."

"You're very generous." Margaret looked him in the eye. "I understand what you intend, but. . . What if they realise this? They'll claim hardship even when they prosper."

"Alan and I keep good relations with my tenants. Much can be learned under the guise of casual interest. It makes them feel appreciated, too, if the laird speaks with them personally from time to time."

"So that's why you spend the occasional night away. And return reeking of peat smoke. . ."

He didn't quite know what to say. He stared intently at the rolls, feigning concentration.

"All in all," Margaret said, "we're facing a difficult year."

"I'm afraid so. We lost the income that the Sheriff's office brought, and most of the rents won't be delivered. I won't lie to you; this winter will be hard."

She tapped her fingers lightly against her lips. "What about yourself?" she asked. "How much money do you require?"

"I need twenty pounds to pay the King. I must put aside some spear silver, too, in case we're asked to fund a campaign this summer. There's a suit of armour that awaits shipping in Leith; I should reclaim it soon, before it's pawned to cover storage costs. And His Grace may demand a rental payment on the feast of Saint John. It's symbolic, really; I'm to deliver a red rose to the King if asked."

"There's roses in the garden."

"The finest in the Sheriffdom. But it should be presented properly, and sandalwood boxes don't come cheap. . ." He rubbed his forehead, trying to ignore the ache. "I may have to borrow some money. Or pawn some jewels. I spent too much on my sister's wedding."

"You spent too much on me, too. Whatever possessed you?"

"It seemed right at the time." He stared down at the documents and swallowed. It was worse than he'd thought.

Margaret patted his arm. "We'll manage." She glanced furtively towards him. "The birds you gave me. . ."

From her manner, he half-expected her to tell him that she'd crushed the life from the poor creatures. "What of them?"

"I couldn't bear to see them trapped. I let them go."

It wasn't the news he'd feared, but it still hurt, to think she'd taken exception to his gifts.

"They fly to my window, every day," she said, quickly. "I feed them. . ." Her eyes briefly met his. "I could sell the cage. And use the proceeds to provision the kitchens."

"It's yours now; do whatever you please."

"Don't worry," she said. "We'll manage somehow. But. . . How did this happen? It wasn't a harsh winter."

"Around fifty farms were ravaged last winter. Most of the livestock was burned or stolen."

"Whatever happened?"

"It's a long story. I don't want to bore you."

"I'm here now. So are you." She laid her hand on his, fingers light against his skin.

A shiver coursed through him. He couldn't speak.

"It's alright," she said, softly. "I won't judge you."

Was it an end to hostilities, he wondered, or just a temporary truce? "It began last summer. With the war—" He broke off, hearing the scuffle of hooves in the yard.

"Master John?" William's head appeared round the door. "Master Mossman and Master Montgomery are here to see you. It's very important."

"Just a moment!" John gathered together the jettons and the counting board and the sheaf of rolls and accounts. He thrust the untidy pile into Margaret's arms. "Put these away, please. Can you prepare the range?"

She gripped the parchments tightly, using her chin to steady them. "Of course." she said. "What do they want?"

"They're burgesses. From Renfrew." He walked with her to the door and opened it. "God knows what they want, but it must be urgent. Hurry now. Come back when you're finished. And bring some wine."

* * *

283

Master Mossman looked like he'd been riding for a week. His red face was running with sweat, and he was plastered with mud. "Ah, thank you!" he gasped, taking a goblet from Margaret with one hand and mopping his brow with the other. "It's a hard road at this time of year."

"Please, be seated." Gesturing to a nearby bench, John sat down in his chair. He kept half-an-eye on Margaret, who set the flagon down and swept silently over to join him. She stood at his shoulder, hands clasped loosely before her, looking every inch an elegant, supportive wife.

Mossman plopped down with a groan. While Montgomery loitered by the window, hands behind his back.

Keeping his own counsel, thought John. "How can I help you?" he asked.

"There's been strange goings-on in Renfrew. We hoped you might advise us." Mossman paused, briefly. "Just two days ago," he said. "Bute Puirsuivant read out a proclamation at the mercat cross. Seems the Earl of Lennox and Lord Lyle have been accused of abusing their judicial powers in Renfrew. They must ride to Edinburgh within forty days, to report to the King. If they don't, they'll be charged with treason."

"Did you hear this for yourself?"

"Well, no," Mossman said. "But I heard it from a reliable witness and saw the herald when he left the following day."

"Ah." If he'd learned anything over the last few months, it was the value of being cautious.

"That's not all, Master Sempill," Mossman continued. "They've called a wappenschaw, for the end of the month. We're loath to let them down, sir, but there's no one to summon the households. It's the Sheriff's task. . ."

"I'm not the Sheriff."

"But you know the procedures."

"I don't have the authority. God knows what lies the Stewarts have spread. How will it look if I raise an army without the King's permission?"

"If you won't do it, who will?"

"I'd like to help, but unless I'm given precise instructions by the King's representative, then I won't do so." Behind him, Margaret stifled a gasp. He couldn't even flash her a warning glance; he just had to hope she'd stay silent. "If I hear anything that makes me change my mind then I'll let you know. But for the moment, my hands are tied." He stared past Mossman towards Montgomery, wondering if the burgess might be biding his time to deliver a message of his own. "You'll stay here tonight, I hope? We've plenty of room at the board."

Mossman looked visibly relieved. "Oh, that'd be most gracious, Master Sempill. I don't want to return to the saddle again so soon."

* * *

John hoped Margaret wasn't too offended when he stepped in to show their guests to their lodgings. He knew from her tight-lipped look that she wasn't pleased, but explanations would have to wait.

He had to speak with Montgomery alone.

It was easy to be rid of Mossman. The old burgess was clearly flagging, and eager to escape to his room. Being by far the younger of the two, Montgomery was quite content to be kept waiting.

"Was it your father who sat on the town council last year?" he asked Montgomery eventually.

"He sent me along in his stead. He's reluctant to journey too far these days. And he's awaiting a shipment."

"Trade's going well?"

"Paisley's causing trouble for us now. There's plenty of ill-feeling, I can tell you."

"Have you heard word from your kinsman?"

"Who?" Montgomery looked blank. "Oh, you mean Lord Hugh!" He stifled a laugh. "Beg pardon, Master Sempill, but His Grace won't take much to do with us. Unless he wants money. Then he's sweet as anything." He stared at John, bewildered. "Why?"

John shrugged. "It's not important. I just wondered if he's in the Westland."

"He's still in the east, as far as I know. He'll be back for the wappenschaw, though. That's guaranteed."

"Commend me to him, if you see him."

"I will." Montgomery replied. "If I see him. But I doubt very much that I will."

Don't do anything, until I send word. That way, we'll both profit from this.

Hugh's exact words. . .

What was he to do? He wanted to send a token force to the wappenschaw, just to show his loyalty. But he was more inclined to trust Hugh. Mossman and Montgomery were armed with hearsay, while Hugh was fast becoming one of the King's right-hand men. Hugh was fickle, and treacherous, but John couldn't see what advantage the Lord Montgomerie would find in double-crossing him.

The situation was progressing, out in the east. Whether it was going as Hugh planned was debatable, but John felt it was his duty to hope it was and act accordingly.

John opened the door to the hall. "Sorry about that—"

Margaret whirled to confront him. She was close to tears and scowling. "How could you?"

"Let me explain—"

"This could have been your chance to succeed!"

"Would you listen, for God's sake—"

"You've thrown everything away. How could you do this? To us? To me?" She erupted into angry sobs.

John stepped up close and tried to console her. "Margaret, please. . ."

"Don't touch me!" She jerked away. Her elbow caught his ribs, hard enough to make him gasp.

Her fury vanished. "Why can't you understand?" she asked, laying a gentle hand against his cheek. "I'm doing this for you. You'd sit back and do nothing, if I didn't goad you."

He drew back. "It's not like that."

"I don't want to hear your excuses!" Pushing past, she hurried out into the stair-tower.

John followed. "There's more to this than meets the eye. All I ask is that you trust me, this once."

But she'd already disappeared up the stairs.

Chapter 57
The Palace of Linlithgow

Easter Sunday came and went. Lent was over, there was meat upon the table once more. One hunt followed another, interspersed with eating and drinking and occasional Privy Council meetings, where they discussed trade levies and plagues of corn marigolds.

Then, after two days of normality, everything changed.

Patrick Hepburn tugged Hugh aside during mass. "The King's chamber," he said. "Soon as the last note fades. And no dallying. This is important!"

Hugh shrugged. Despite his Devil-may-care attitude, Hugh *was* curious. Earl Patrick never took things that seriously. Something had happened. Something important. And Earl Patrick wasn't going to say a word until the time was exactly right for *him*.

* * *

"The Lord Montgomerie!" The page announced.

Hugh glanced imperiously around the room as he stepped inside. Most of the Privy Council had already gathered, the Great Seal lying out in full view. He spotted a vacant chair next to Campbell of Argyll; he headed towards it, a deliberate swagger in his stride. He was in buoyant mood, fired by the prospect of pitting his wits against his colleagues'.

That initial display of his prowess was enough. Once he'd sat down, he nodded, all meek deference.

It fooled no-one. Least of all Argyll, who raised his brow and cast him a sideways look.

"Pray rise for His Grace King James of Scotland!"

They stood as one.

James emerged from his bedchamber, with Earl Patrick in tow. The young King sprawled in his chair, looking faintly bored. For a moment, he was just another gangling youth forced to perform unwelcome duties. Then he sat up, the façade of statesmanship in place.

"Please, be seated," James invited. "My apologies for the unexpected summons. We'll have food and drink bought here shortly." He paused. "We've received dire news," he said. "From Unicorn Pursuivant."

Hugh stifled a smile. *That's what you get, Patrick. For mocking me and saying that I'm jumping at shadows. For once in your life, you've been proved wrong.*

James looked at Hepburn. "Earl Patrick?"

Hepburn nodded. "Certainly, Your Grace." He cast his chill gaze about them all, eyes lingering on Hugh.

Hugh stared back, unbowed.

"We sent the herald out to Aberdeen to announce the call for taxes," Hepburn said. "The following day, there was a riot. The town was burned, there were assaults on some Flemish merchants trading there."

Bishop Elphinstone stirred. "And the herald?"

"He was safe in the cathedral precincts. He fled the town that night."

Elphinstone sighed, and shifted, uncomfortably. As well he should, Hugh thought, for the old Bishop's own territory was where the rot was setting in. The rest looked suitably cowed.

"This wasn't a simple riot," Hepburn continued. "Lord Forbes started it. He rode through the streets holding up a torn and bloodied sark. He called for all men to rise up and ride against their King."

James locked his fingers and stretched. "Your thoughts, gentlemen." He would already have decided how best to proceed. But before he announced his intentions, he'd let his nobles voice their own opinions. He had such high hopes for them all. He wanted his counsellors to combine the military prowess of Achilles with the debating skills of Cicero.

"Ah, well," Home said. "At least now we know where our priorities lie. Sorry, Lord Hugh. Your problems in the Westland are trivial compared to this."

"I disagree," Hugh retorted. He disliked Home, always had. Home was typical of the Border lords; arrogant in the extreme, and treacherous, too. He'd do deals with the English while pretending that his loyalties lay with the Scots. "Doesn't this make winning the Westland all the more vital?" Hugh added. "How long will it be before the dissent in the north spreads to the west? And how will we keep a grip on this kingdom if we're fighting on two fronts?"

They were unmoved. Home spread his fingers before him with a sigh and studied his nails, while Robert Colville coughed, awkwardly.

As for Elphinstone. . . He sat upright in his chair, hands folded before him, looking intently at Hugh.

Hugh didn't catch his eye. There was no point in trying to convert Elphinstone to his cause. The old Bishop would never justify a case for war.

Impatience coursed through Hugh. *Are you all fools?* he longed to roar, but somehow he kept his composure. "We'll gain much if we act quickly in the Westland," he told them. "By making an example of the Stewarts, we can show that His Grace the King won't tolerate rebellion. They'll expect us to strike in the north; if we hit them in the west we'll consolidate our own position and weaken them at the same time."

"My dear Lord Hugh," Home said slowly, as if addressing a child. "The evidence against Lennox is tenuous. Waging war on the basis of hearsay may be acceptable to you; it's not acceptable to us."

"It's not hearsay! We have the perfect excuse to intervene. One of James the Third's allies has asked us to intercede in a dispute on his behalf."

He scanned the faces. Home was frowning, openly sceptical, while Patrick Hepburn's face revealed nothing. Argyll sighed and traced patterns on his chair arm with one finger. Colville, meanwhile, stared at his king, waiting for a lead.

James was nodding vigorously. So, to Hugh's surprise, was Elphinstone.

Hepburn and Argyll remained unconvinced.

Undaunted, Hugh pressed his case. "We won last year because for every household that fought against us, another stayed at home. Fortune helped us then, but this time we mightn't be so lucky. If we champion Ellestoun's cause, then no man can say we're blind to the abuses of the law carried out in our name. We'll win over the Doubting Thomases, and guarantee the support of others who fought for His Grace's father last year."

"Oh, bravo, Lord Hugh," Home's tone was bitter. "Why is it I'm not convinced by your plea for justice? Is it because your own abuses of the judicial system are legendary? Why, it's said you're never satisfied with an assize unless it ends with a Cunninghame's corpse swinging from a tree."

"This has nothing to do with the Cunninghames!" Hugh disputed. "The Cunninghames have never accepted our King's authority."

"Neither, it can be said, has John Sempill of Ellestoun."

"Damn you!" Hugh closed his fingers tight about the chair arms. More than ever, he wanted to take Home by the throat and throttle him.

Argyll laid a steadying hand on his shoulder.

Hugh took a deep calming breath, and nodded to his gude-father. Smiling slightly, Argyll relinquished his grip.

Bishop Elphinstone cleared his throat. He was plump-cheeked and portly, with a soft voice that did nothing to reveal the brilliance of the mind within. "From what I understand," he said, "it's not the King's authority that John Sempill of Ellestoun takes issue with. It's John Stewart's."

"It's precisely the same situation," Home retorted. "The Cunninghames would say, I'm sure, that it's Lord Hugh's authority that they object to."

"Then perhaps they should voice their objections differently." Elphinstone's tone hardened. "Gentlemen, we mustn't let personal issues cloud our judgement. I agree wholeheartedly with the Lord Montgomerie. I think we should make this gesture. It would win us more allies, and it would make many men think twice before they offer support to Lennox and the others."

"Thank you, my Lord Bishop." Hugh settled back in his chair, savouring the warm glow of victory.

Home was smarting. As for Patrick Hepburn. . . He still said nothing.

"Thank you, Lord Hugh," James said, warmly. "Earl Patrick?"

"Of course, Your Grace." Hepburn smiled. "Rest assured, noble cousins, that the situation is the Westland will soon be resolved. Bute Pursuivant has already been dispatched to Renfrew town. He's summoned John Stewart, Earl of Lennox, Matthew Stewart, Master of Lennox and Robert, Lord Lyle to Edinburgh. There they'll answer accusations regarding their conduct in the Westland—"

"What?" Hugh gasped.

"We've also summoned the men of Renfrew to a wappenschaw."

"This is too little, too late! We must act now."

"Lord Hugh," James said. "I appreciate your concern. But you're speaking of my kin. And your own kin, too."

"Yes, I know, but-"

James raised his hand. "I won't have it."

"Besides," Hepburn added, "before anyone's charged with treason, we must obtain the approval of Parliament."

"Summon the three estates. Call a Parliament." Hugh nodded to the King. "I know Your Grace is loath to move too quickly. But there are other issues here. A wappenschaw's been called, but there's no one to organise a response to the summons."

"Meaning what?" Home asked, suspiciously.

"The Sheriff of Renfrew's suspected of treason. The Justiciar of Arran and the West likewise."

"Oh, well done, Lord Hugh!" Home said. "You betrayed yourself at last. Pay attention, gentlemen; the Lord Montgomerie fancies himself as the Justiciar!"

Steady. . . Hugh closed his eyes briefly. Angry outbursts were expected of him; he'd obliged them once, he was damned if he'd do so again. He waved his hand. "I've said my piece," he said. "Just don't blame me when your wappenschaw's a travesty."

Chapter 58
The Place of Ellestoun

It was Sunday afternoon, and Margaret had been in charge of the household for the best part of a week when William came to see her.

"Master John wants to speak with you," he said.

"Thank you, William. Tell him I'll be there shortly."

She put on her pearls and made sure her hood was set straight, then dabbed some rosewater about her face and hands. Once she was confident that she looked her best, she headed downstairs.

Taking a deep breath, she knocked upon her husband's door.

William opened it, an unexpected formality which shook her all the more. She nodded to him and smiled, but as usual he didn't respond.

Her husband slouched sideways in his chair, legs draped over the carved wooden arm, feet loosely crossed. The soles of his hose were worn and grey with dust. There was a book in his lap; he was engrossed in it, oblivious to the world.

Margaret wasn't used to seeing him like that, looking so relaxed and unburdened by worries. Her heart scudded faster. *He has an angel's face,* she thought. She curtsied, the way everyone was meant to when they greeted the laird. "You wanted to see me."

"I thought we might walk together."

Margaret waited patiently while he slid out of his chair, set down his book and pulled on his shoes. He grabbed his gown and bonnet from a nearby kist, then gestured to the door.

He didn't say a word as they descended into the yard and headed for the gardens. It wasn't a comfortable silence. But it wasn't hostile, either.

Every so often, she had to trot a few steps to keep up. She was going to ask him to walk more slowly, but he curbed his pace unbidden.

He strode at her side, gaze fixed ahead. Her eyes were just level with the cross that adorned his chest. She marvelled at how imposing he looked, with that stately stride of his.

Remembering the cruel thoughts she'd once harboured, she felt herself glow hot with embarrassment. She'd thought that way because she'd hated him, but she couldn't bring herself to hate him anymore. She could never have hated something that intrigued her so much. He had a name, *John,* but she couldn't really think of him as a John. He shielded his character so well that she couldn't think of him as anything at all.

"I wondered how you'd fared this last week," he said, once they reached the isolation of the gardens.

"There's a lot to master," she confessed. "But I'm quick to learn."

She wished he'd offer her his arm, but he didn't. Instead, he folded his arms before him and surveyed the waters of the loch. "Your mother never told you what was required?"

"Of course she did!"

"But you never listened." A smile touched his lips.

So close, but so distant. Her heart felt sore at the thought. She'd hoped to conquer him and make him surrender to her will. Instead, all she'd won was indifference. She wanted to think he loved and desired her, but every time they spoke, it felt instead as if he were drifting further away.

"We should meet together each week," he said. "At least until you're confident to handle the servants alone. If there's anything you need guidance on, then please ask—"

"Alan says you take nothing to do with the running of the household."

"That doesn't mean I don't know what's required."

* * *

He questioned her closely for an hour or more. Margaret was uneasy at first, in case he tried to catch her off-guard and criticise her. But he never did. Instead, he just asked her views, then he'd reflect on them in silence. Sometimes he'd query her replies. *Have you ever considered doing it this way,* he'd ask, before giving his own thoughts and letting her ponder them a while.

"Well," he said at last. "I think that's enough. We don't want to be late for dinner."

"Will Alan be there tomorrow?" she asked.

He kicked a stray pebble along the path. "He has better things to do."

She nodded and smiled, putting on a brave face.

"I'm sure you'll be alright," he said.

She blushed. "I'd rather not face them alone. I don't suppose you. . ."

"Of course," he agreed. "If that would be of help."

She didn't like to admit it, but she felt a little better then.

* * *

Her throat was dry with fear as she confronted the household the following morning. There were two dozen servants or more; she had the distinct impression that they were waiting for her to put a foot wrong.

He wasn't there.

Margaret swallowed, feeling a fresh wave of panic. *So this is your way of getting revenge. You've thrown me into the lion's den so you can say 'I told you so'.*

Just when she was going to start without him, he came in, dressed ready for hunting, with his long boots, his horn and his stained leather jerkin. He slipped to the back of the hall and sat down on the bench there. His dogs were with him; one sat by his side and laid its head on his knee while the other slumped at his feet. He gently kneaded the dog's ears, saying nothing.

As soon as he appeared, the atmosphere changed. Everyone fell silent.

He nodded, inviting her to begin.

Filled with a new sense of courage, of purpose, Margaret stood tall.

She was mistress of her house at last.

* * *

The Burgh of Renfrew, May, 1489

The rain rattled loud upon Hugh's helmet and battered against his face. The blue and red plumes of his *panache* trailed limply down his shoulders, his hose were soaked through. He'd been shivering for the past hour or more, and could hardly feel his feet.

Three hours they'd been sitting there, with the rain pouring down. Hugh had suggested long before that they seek shelter in the nearby Royal castle, but Patrick Hepburn would have none of it.

They might still turn up, he'd said.

Hugh's grey stallion shook its head, sending drops of water spraying from its blue-caprisoned ears. Raising a foreleg, it stamped the ground.

Hugh read the signs and stood in his stirrups. His horse groaned, and out came a vast ocean of piss that steamed and stank as it hit the grass below.

Hugh settled back into the saddle. He winced; the padding was cold and soggy, and to make matters worse, his own bladder was growing full. He considered voicing his complaints to Earl Patrick, then thought twice of it. He could almost hear the reply; *if you're that desperate, Lord Hugh, then piss in your armour and be grateful of the warmth.*

Earl Patrick sat still as a statue on his horse, face smeared with rain, water dripping incessantly from the end of his hawk-like nose.

A wave of loathing coursed through Hugh. He knew that despite his oblivious façade, Hepburn was feeling the misery just as keenly. But now and then he'd glance at Hugh, then he'd take a deep breath and that look of serene contentment would shine through once again.

The grey horse turned its head and pushed Hugh's toe with its muzzle.

Hugh clapped the velvet-shrouded neck. "Patience, Zephyr. I'm sure His Grace will take pity on us soon."

But he didn't. For another hour they stood there, until even the horses quaked with the cold.

The church bells tolled noon.

Hepburn stirred at last. Gathering up his reins, he turned his bleak, rain-ravaged face towards Hugh. "Let's begin," he said. "But don't think I'm doing this for you. I just feel sorry for the damned horses."

* * *

There were a handful of burgesses present. Apart from them, only the Montgomeries of Polnoon had bothered to send a contingent. Twenty-five of them stood by the butts, casting sullen faces towards their lord as he approached.

Hugh nodded to his bedraggled men as he rode past. It was hardly shrewd thinking, he thought, to mete out such harsh treatment on those who'd at least had the decency to turn up.

"Dismount, everyone." Hepburn's voice was tight with disapproval.

They squelched their way through the soggy grass. A herd of cattle grazed nearby, thick black coats heavy with water. Several boys had been sent out to mind the beasts; they trailed behind the visiting dignitaries, mouths agape.

Hepburn scowled. "Damned idiots."

Hugh fought the urge to smirk.

"Let's begin." Hepburn waved at the herald.

"The burgesses of Renfrew!" Bute Puirsuivant announced.

"Three men," Hugh said.

The clerk cursed. "Damned ink's running!"

"Shut up!" Hepburn spat.

"Sempill of Ellestoun."

"Absent."

"Sempill of Fulwood."

"Absent."

"Mure of Caldwell."

"Absent."

"Montgomerie of Polnoon."

"Twenty-five men," Hugh replied. "Twenty spearmen, five men-at-arms."

"Thank you, Lord Hugh," came Hepburn's graceless response.

* * *

"—Cunninghame of Craigends."

"Absent." Hugh rubbed his gauntleted hands together, in a vain attempt to warm them.

"Cunninghame of Finlaystone."

"Absent."

"Well, here we are then." Hepburn stepped back, hand on his sword hilt. "You have twenty-eight men. You're welcome to take on the Stewarts with this rabble. Perhaps at a push John Stewart will die laughing."

"It's not as if I didn't warn you," Hugh retorted. "We need a Justiciar—"

Hepburn's face darkened. "Don't sound so damned self-righteous!" he snapped. "You've made His Grace look a fool, you've made me look a fool. God, I'm sick and tired of you. And I'm sick and tired of the fucking Westland. Where it's always fucking raining."

Hugh looked him coldly in the eye. "You've a strange way of winning allies," he said. "I should take my twenty-five Montgomeries and make straight for Dumbarton. You mightn't want us, but I'm sure John Stewart will."

Hepburn's eyes narrowed. "Let's not be hasty—"

"I won't be blamed. We need a Sheriff. We need a Justiciar."

"And just who would you recommend?"

"It's not my place to recommend anyone." Hugh said, innocently. "But it'll have to be a man who has influence in the Westland. A man who'll choose a Sheriff acceptable to everyone."

"A man like yourself." Hepburn's tone was ice-cold. "Why do you think you haven't been made Justiciar already?" he demanded. "You're a fucking liability! We'd lose as many allies as we'd gain." He shook his head. "You and your damned foul temper."

"I'm not the man who's ranting and cursing like a peasant."

Hepburn sighed. The fury faded; he looked tired and unexpectedly old. "We'll make haste to Linlithgow," he said. "And you'll explain to His Grace what happened. If he's in good spirits, you'll probably be made Justiciar. If not. . ." He seized his horse and climbed into the saddle. "I daresay you'll be strung from the nearest tree."

Chapter 59
The Palace of Linlithgow

"I thought this would happen," James said. He'd taken the news remarkably calmly. "We couldn't be seen to pander to you," he added. "Not without justification."

Hugh inclined his head, all measured deference.

"I value your counsel," James continued. "I always have."

"Thank you, Your Grace."

"But you're not well-liked at court." James poured some more wine for himself, then slouched back. "Now, you see, we've proved that we can't win the Westland without you." He studied Hugh, frowning. "You're confident that this debacle won't be repeated?"

"With the proper authorities in place, it wouldn't have happened at all. That's what I said."

"I know," James agreed. "I've summoned the three estates," he added. "But it'll be a month. And we don't really have a month, do we?"

"No."

"Then I'll put this to you. Let's assume the charges of treason will be approved. Earl Patrick and myself will work to convince Parliament in your absence. Meanwhile, I'll make you acting Justiciar in Lyle's place. Once I'm convinced you're an appropriate choice, I'll make the appointment official."

Hugh half-closed his eyes. "It's a great honour. But, without wishing to sound ungrateful, it's a heavy burden of responsibility. . ."

"You'll be well-rewarded."

He tried not to look too jubilant. "You're very generous, Your Grace."

"The charges will be read," James said. "But you must win me the Westland. Summon men to fight in my name, for once I'm committed to this, there'll be no turning back."

The Place of Ellestoun

Hooves sounded in the yard below, but Margaret didn't bother to look out. It was Thursday morning. Her husband was riding off alone, as he'd done the previous Thursday, and the Thursday before that.

The servants never dared say anything to her face. But she knew they talked about it behind her back.

Meanwhile the girls tried hard to keep her spirits up. *You don't like him anyway,* they reminded her. *Let him enjoy his whore.*

But it niggled at her more and more. She'd failed as a wife. She'd failed herself, she'd failed her family.

These days, Margaret liked to have him close, sitting by her side at dinner, or walking with her in the gardens. He always looked so fine; he dressed well, and kept himself impeccably groomed. But it wasn't just those qualities that fascinated her. More and more, her thoughts would turn to the unseen promise of his flesh.

Thinking of him now made her face burn hot with desire. She wriggled on her perch, twisting the spindle with renewed vigour.

The girls giggled together as they spun yarn nearby. They seemed so young, so inconsequential. All they had to worry about was looking after her, while she had to worry about everything else. About keeping the household running smoothly. And making sure that all was well with *him*. . .

She wasn't doing a very good job of the latter, and it irked her. It touched her even more keenly at present; her bleeding was due, she'd felt the ache that morning.

Margaret glowered at Katherine. *I'm bored with them. They're just girls. They don't understand what it's like to be a woman.*

And yet she wasn't quite a woman, either. She was doing everything expected of her, but there was no child swelling her belly.

Anger flared within her at the thought. She slammed the spindle down without a word, and stamped off.

* * *

Margaret pushed open the door to the laird's chamber. She wasn't afraid of being discovered; she had the keys to the kists and the strongbox, and he'd told her she could come in whenever she wanted.

But she remained apprehensive. He wasn't here, but it was still *his* room, and she felt she was intruding. The floorboards creaked, she drew a sharp breath and continued on tiptoe to avoid making too much noise.

Everything looked so bright and cheerful; the tapestries, the brocaded curtains round the bed and the painted ceiling. On closer inspection, she saw that the paint was flaking in places and the curtains were worn; there was, she thought, a weary and rather subdued grandeur about it.

It reminded her of *him*.

She saw his books lying on the kist by the bed. She sat down there and picked up the tales of Troy, opened it but couldn't be bothered reading.

Placing the volume back down again, she settled herself more comfortably on the edge of the mattress. Looking around, she spotted some stray dark gold hairs on his pillow. She cast a guilty glance about her, but there was no one there. She snatched the hairs up, twisting them into a taut strand which she coiled around her fingers. Pulling a handkerchief out from her sleeve, she placed the hairs in the centre and folded it up.

Margaret kissed the tiny square of silk, and pressed it down between her breasts.

Her secret. She wouldn't even tell the girls.

When she lay back along the bed and turned her head to the coverlet, she could catch the scent of him. She closed her eyes, and breathed in deep, rubbing her cheek against the cool linen sheets. His perfume was all around her, rich and warm and vital.

She stretched with a sigh, beguiled by his ghostly presence. She smoothed the heavy folds of her skirts down over her thighs, relishing the soft comfort of the mattress beneath.

She could imagine what it would be like to have his arms wrapped tight around her, to have him whisper loving words in her ear. . .

She didn't suppose it would ever happen now.

In the beginning, she'd viewed her marriage as a battle. Every cold glance and cruel word had been carefully crafted so that in the end she'd subdue him.

She'd thought she'd won, too. But now she wasn't so sure. She'd built up bastions that he'd given up besieging long ago; she realised now that he'd done exactly the same to her.

She clenched her fingers in the coverlet, her aching loneliness suddenly unbearable. Burying her face in the pillow, she cried. She cried until her tears failed her, and she was too weary with despair to even pick herself up from the bed.

Shutting her eyes, she drifted off to sleep.

* * *

Foul breath blew in her face, something wet brushed her cheek. She opened her eyes and found a hound's long pale face staring into hers, tongue lolling loose from its jaws.

"Get down, Pompey!" William bellowed, and the hound went scuttling back to his side.

Margaret sat up. "Master Haislet."

William nodded, curtly. "Mistress Margaret."

"I came down to see if anything wants mending." She felt herself blush. "I felt a little tired, so I lay down. Must've nodded off. . ."

William shrugged, and sank down in the chair by the fireplace.

"Please don't tell him I was here."

He smiled. "Your secret's safe with me." He crossed his legs and hauled off one of his long boots, then repeated the exercise with the other. Though William was her husband's most trusted servant, Margaret had never studied him so closely. He'd been quite handsome in his time; he was sturdy and strong with a thick head of frosted dark hair that drifted round his shoulders.

She hugged her knees close. "William?"

He stood briefly, setting both boots out to air by the fireplace. "Yes?"

"About what happened. A few weeks back." She swallowed. "I'm sorry. I didn't think about the consequences."

William sat back down and stretched his feet comfortably before him, the two hounds settling by his chair. "No harm done, Mistress Margaret."

"It was after that he went to her, wasn't it?"

He didn't answer.

"Can I ask you something?" she asked. "Does he hate me?"

That faint smile appeared once more. "Hate's a very strong word." He leaned forward and scratched the upturned belly of the hound that lazed at his feet.

"I'd like to know."

"We don't really discuss such matters, but no. I don't suppose he hates you."

"He treats me like a child."

"He's growing old before his time. You should make allowances for that."

She couldn't quite think how to respond. "William," she said at last.

"Yes?"

"Why won't he speak about what happened last winter? Every time I broach the subject, he talks of something else."

"Perhaps he doesn't want to burden you with his troubles."

"We heard rumours when I was in Ochiltree. We heard he was a coward, and a fool."

He laughed, softly. "Master John was damned whatever he did."

"You don't think so, do you?"

"See the day the Stewarts came here last year?" William gestured towards the window and the yard beyond. "Master John was out there on the wall-walk with the rest of us. He had the Earl of Lennox and the Master of Lennox and Lord Lyle and a dozen men-at-arms confronting him. He knew he had one of the strongest families in the land pitched against him and still he didn't flinch. He just told them to be off, in no uncertain terms." He slapped his hands on his knees and looked straight at her. "Tell me, Mistress Margaret; is that how a coward conducts himself?"

She didn't know what to say.

"Master John's like David. He'll defy a giant, if he thinks his cause is just. And like David, he fights with his head, not his heart."

"He doesn't have a heart."

"Now what makes you say that?"

"He wouldn't leave me alone here if he did." She rose to her feet, and wandered over to the fireplace. Folding her arms with a shiver, she leaned back against the cold stone. "Does he love her?"

"That's another strong word."

"Well, does he?"

"She's a friend to him. She welcomes him into her home. He's happy there; he wrestles with her children and helps her out about the place."

"He's my husband. He should be playing with his own children and helping me."

William reached down and rubbed the hound's ears. "Men are simple creatures. Easily pleased, like old Caesar here. All you need do is feed them and keep them warm and rub their bellies once in a while." He slapped the beast so hard its quarters slid out from under it; it scrabbled to its feet, tail wagging furiously.

"My husband's not a dog, Master Haislet."

William grinned. "No, I don't suppose he is."

"I've some money left over from provisioning the kitchens," she said. "Does he require anything that could be fashioned here?"

"A nice smart jupon wouldn't go amiss, Mistress Margaret. And a caprison for his poor horse. The ones he uses at the moment aren't worth speaking of."

"But a man should always look his best when he's arrayed for battle!"

"There's been more important things to worry about."

Margaret dragged the other chair close. "We'll visit the armoury, and see how much cloth is required." She clutched his sleeve. "I'll give you some money. You could purchase some velvet in Paisley or Renfrew."

"Next week, perhaps. When he's away."

"We'd best see to it soon," Margaret decided. "I won't have my husband riding to war looking like a beggar."

Chapter 60

"You're thinking of her, aren't you?" Mary said. She was lying on her side, propped up on an elbow so she could look at him. She'd set her hood aside, her tawny hair was draped over the grass at her shoulders.

John hesitated. He didn't want to admit the truth, but there was no point in lying. Mary would sense it. She always could. "I think about her all the time," he confessed at last. "It's as if she's bewitched me."

"It's only natural. I mean, a few more years between us, and I'd be old enough to be your mother." There wasn't any judgement in her voice. No jealousy, either.

"I'm sorry," he said.

The laverocks sang loud in the cloudless sky above, and the heady scent of meadow flowers was all about him. The summer sun beat hot through his sark. So much beauty everywhere, but it no longer brought any comfort. His world was grey, and full of sorrow.

"You can't live this way."

He turned his head towards her, shielding his brow with one hand to escape the sun's glare. He could've spent hours just looking at her, trying to comprehend her. She wasn't fresh and young like Margaret, she didn't make his heart beat quicker at the thought of her. But her face fascinated him, the lines of pain and laughter about her eyes that gave her a look of infinite compassion and wisdom.

"You're not eating enough."

"I ate last night, didn't I?"

"Enough for two." Mary settled down upon her back. "But you don't eat well at home." She paused. "I'd have you as my lover if I knew I made you happy. But you're not happy. You want to be with her."

John sat up with a sigh. He didn't know how to tell her. That she was right. That he wanted Margaret to love him more than anything else in the world. That at the same time, he needed *her*, because she was everything Margaret was not; kind, caring, compassionate. "You've made it clear," he said. "I won't visit you again."

"Oh, Johnny. Don't take it that way." Sitting up alongside, she laid a hand upon his knee. "I shouldn't have let this linger so long."

He shrugged her gently loose, and stretched out his legs, all casual indifference. He plucked a gowan from the grass, delicately pulling away each long white petal, one by one. *She loves me, she loves me not. . .* "I don't know where I'd turn, if I didn't have you."

"You can't run away forever," she said. "You must accept that what we have together isn't love."

"Then what is?"

She stared ahead, unseeing. "You know full well," she said. "You're just too proud to admit it."

The Place of Ellestoun

Hugh batted past yet another servant. "It's urgent."

"But it's most improper!"

"It's alright," Hugh called. "I'm a friend of the family."

He leapt up the stairs two at a time, a protesting servant still in pursuit. The sound of a lute drifted down from the hall; *a strange hour for entertainment,* he thought, but it wasn't his place to reason why.

He barged into the hall, then stopped. Like Actaeon, he'd ventured into a forbidden place.

The four girls danced together, heavy gowns doing little to disguise the careless sensuality in every step. They'd set their hoods aside, their long hair hanging loose about their shoulders; they giggled and clapped as Master Haislet made an admirable effort at concentrating on the music.

Hugh felt a brief stirring in his loins. A few deep breaths and the madness was gone, leaving behind it an aching desire to be back at Eglintoun, with Helen cradled warm in his arms.

"Mistress Colville—" A servant called over Hugh's shoulder.

They'd already spotted him. The maids shrieked, and scurried back to their distaffs, while Margaret Colville flung her head high and glared. "It's rude to barge in like that."

"What are you going to do?" Hugh retorted. "Turn me into a stag and set the hounds on me?"

"Why, it's you, Lord Hugh!" She laughed, lightly. "I was about to offer you alms."

He scowled. It must have been eight weeks or more since the wedding, and Margaret Colville certainly wasn't a meek young maid anymore. He could see that she'd learned how to provoke a man's lust. Right now, she was doing her best to provoke *him,* putting that little swing in her stride and casting sidelong glances in his direction.

Hugh pretended not to notice. "Where is he?"

She came right alongside. Looking him up and down, she gave an irritated sniff. Then she whisked herself away, skirts brushing light against his legs. "I'm just his wife. He doesn't tell me anything."

"When's he due back?"

"He left Ellestoun yesterday. I can't say when he'll return if I don't know where he is or what he's doing." Her veiled antagonism vanished; she was suddenly subservient. "I'm sorry, my lord. Would you care to wait?"

"I suppose I'll have to," Hugh muttered. "Can he be summoned?"

"Speak to William. He knows my husband's business better than any of us." Then she added, "You'll eat with us this afternoon, of course."

"As you're well aware, I'm in no fit state to grace your table. I'd hoped to dine in Paisley."

"We'll forgive you this once, Lord Hugh."

Hugh smiled, thinly. "Thank you. Now, if I could speak with Master Haislet alone. . ."

Margaret Colville shrugged. "Of course." She bustled away, maids in close attendance.

* * *

William set down his lute. "I'm sorry," he said. "But I gave him my word."

"Would some gold loosen your tongue?"

William said nothing. His face was inscrutable.

"If you were any other man serving any other lord, I'd break your neck. Do you know when he'll return? It's very important."

"If it's that urgent, I could go out and find him. But we'd probably meet on the road."

"I suppose I can wait a little longer. I've half-killed my horse and eaten nothing but bread and water for three days, but what's a few more hours. . ." Hugh's lips twitched. "It's a woman, isn't it?"

"I can't say."

"So he's straying already?" Hugh laughed. "What a damned hypocrite!"

William's gaze was reproachful.

"Ah well." Hugh slumped down on the nearest bench. "Least he's human, like the rest of us."

Chapter 61

Two strange horses stood in the yard at Ellestoun. Their sides heaved from hard riding, their sleek coats were spiked with sweat. The grooms poured water over their backs to cool them in the heat of the day; as one man tried to wash his charge's spur-raked side, it stamped and tried to avoid him.

John inspected the horse's ravaged flank from the back of his horse. "Ouch," he commented.

"The Lord Montgomerie's here," Henry said, then added, "He was in quite a temper," as if that explained everything.

"Remind me never to lend him a horse." John dismounted, briskly. "Well, if he's desperate enough to wreck a horse in his haste, then I'd best go and find him."

* * *

He paused at the door to the hall. He could hear voices; Margaret, and Hugh. They were laughing together, but the humour was forced. From both of them.

He stepped inside.

"And here he is." Margaret was all feigned lightness. "I knew he wouldn't be long."

"Better late than never," came Hugh's benign reply.

John looked at Hugh, and had to look again. Hugh's sumptuous clothes had been replaced by the plainest of garments, and those were stained with several days' dirt and sweat. His hair was tangled, his face unshaven. He looked exhausted, but behind the weariness, there was something else. An exuberant glow that couldn't be extinguished even now.

John wasn't surprised that the servants had read their guest wrongly. The line between anger and excitement was so thin in Hugh that most men would be hard-pressed to spot the difference.

John nodded. "I didn't recognise you," he said. "Without the horse."

Hugh grinned unexpectedly, teeth gleaming bright as a wolf's in his dust-rimmed face. "Zephyr's travelling back to the Westland in a more dignified manner," he said. "I wasn't granted that luxury."

"Important news?"

Hugh rocked back and forth on his heels. "Very."

"Then we'd best share it. Margaret, bring some wine upstairs for my guest."

* * *

Margaret trudged up the spiral stair, flagon in hand. She knew it was foolish to bait a man with Lord Hugh's reputation, but somehow she didn't care about the consequences. She wouldn't forget how he'd interfered in her brother's affairs, forcing her into marriage with a husband she'd despised. And she wouldn't forget how for one brief night he'd made her sigh and lie awake in her bed, desperate for his love.

She knew better now. She loathed him more than any man alive. Even so, he was everything her husband was not; bold, vicious, full of vitality.

Margaret halted at the door. She'd walk straight in, just as *he'd* done earlier, to see how he would like it.

But wisdom, or caution, got the better of her. She pressed her ear against the timbers instead.

"Left Edinburgh three days ago," Lord Hugh was saying. "Changed horses at Stirling then rode on to Ru'glen. There's been no time to sleep or eat. It's urgent business. We have to be in Paisley tonight."

"We'll leave directly after dinner," her husband said. "The journey shouldn't take more than an hour." There was a brief silence. "I hope I did the right thing by not attending the wappenschaw."

"You did exactly the right thing," Lord Hugh replied. "Things have worked out beautifully for both of us."

It was as she'd suspected. They were plotting something, her husband and Lord Hugh.

"Ah!" Lord Hugh groaned. "That's good!"

Margaret jerked back. She'd joked so many times with Katherine and the others about her husband's inclinations. She'd never for one moment thought they might be right.

And with Lord Hugh. . . She shivered at the thought. *Best you learn the truth now,* she told herself. Taking a deep breath, she opened the door.

Lord Hugh was merely washing away the dirt of the road, and getting as much water on the floor as he was on himself.

And he was naked.

Margaret blushed and tried to retreat, but it was too late.

Scowling, Lord Hugh snatched a cloth to his loins. "It's rude to barge in like that!"

"I—I'm sorry—" She couldn't look away; Lord Hugh was slim and frail as a sapling, but it was all raw muscle and sinew. He was like a fleabitten old tomcat, shoulders and upper arms scattered with healed scars.

Lord Hugh glowered back. "Get a grip on yourself, woman!" he snapped. "Have you never seen a man before?"

"No harm done," her husband said. He'd been rummaging through a kist in the corner, looking out some clothes for his guest. He straightened, carefully closed the lid then joined her, thrusting the clothes into Lord Hugh's arms as he passed.

"I'll take that." He wrested the flagon from her grasp. "Before you drop it." He was trying not to laugh.

"I wasn't to know, was I?" She looked beseechingly up at him. "I was carrying things. I couldn't knock."

"Next time, try warning us." He gripped her arm and steered her back to the door.

Margaret didn't protest.

* * *

"I said I was sorry!" she told her husband, when the door closed behind them and they were safe on the stair. "I *am* sorry. But he shouldn't speak to me like that!"

"He's a Lord of Parliament. He can speak to either of us however he likes." He studied her, frowning. "What did you do?"

"I didn't do anything!"

"Poke a stick into a bee's nest and you'll get stung. It's a fact of life."

"But he's been rude to me since he arrived!" She bit her lip, so he'd think she was on the verge of tears.

"Just be grateful you're not married to him."

"I heard that!" Lord Hugh snapped from within.

"Now, thank you for the wine. That'll be all." He opened the door.

She scarcely dared look. Until she realised that their guest had at least pulled on a pair of hose. Her relief was short-lived; Lord Hugh was staring right at her. "The hounds never tasted stag today," he said. "But there's still time to throw them a small and rather succulent hind." He smiled.

Margaret shivered, and scurried off up the stairs.

"Mistress Colville!" Lord Hugh called after her. "Ask your husband to tell you about Actaeon. You'd enjoy the tale, I'm sure. . ."

She'd never felt so relieved to reach her own door.

* * *

"If she was my wife, I'd strangle her." Hugh buckled his belt deftly into place. The doublet and sark he'd borrowed were too short, but the gown would hide the worst. At least he looked, and smelled, civilised.

John shrugged. "She's only young. She has a lot to learn."

"You have the patience of a saint."

John smiled as he poured out two measures of wine. He handed a goblet to Hugh.

"You look exhausted," Hugh commented.

"If it's not one thing, it's another." John wandered to the window and sat down. "It's been a long year."

Hugh settled opposite. "If it's a question of money. . ."

"I'll manage, if circumstances stay the way they are." He broke off. He didn't want to say any more. *If the Stewarts turn on me again, then I'm finished. It's all finished. . .*

"There's no need to worry any more," Hugh said. "It's over."

"I heard rumours. I didn't like to think—"

"You heard right. Abbot Schaw and myself spoke to the King, and tomorrow the proclamation will be read in Renfrew. John Stewart, Matthew Stewart and Robert Lyle will be charged with treason. Their lands and titles will be forfeit, their strongholds handed over to the King's men."

For so long, he'd prayed for deliverance. Against all hope, it had come at last. John sank his head in his hands. "Thank you."

Hugh snorted. "Wasn't my doing. You asked Schaw for help. He proved a very powerful ally."

"Perhaps. . ."

Hugh gripped his shoulder. "The whole world said you'd fail, but you proved them wrong."

"It's a miracle—"

"You could call it that, I suppose. But don't forget. You've got a new Justiciar now. One who doesn't forget his friends."

It explained so much. Why Hugh had battered his way through the Sheriffdom, why he'd been seething away in excitement ever since he'd set foot in Ellestoun. He'd wanted to find someone, anyone, with whom he could share his good news.

"Congratulations," John said, even as he felt dread tighten inside him. As he thought of the Cunninghames, and what would happen to them now Hugh Montgomerie was appointed Justiciar of Arran and the West.

Hugh laughed, feigning modesty. "It's not confirmed yet. I must prove myself first, by restoring the peace in Renfrew. But I can't do that alone. I need a Sheriff."

"They made a ruling last parliament. Three years, they said. . ."

"At the King's discretion. His Grace has agreed to reinstate you, on my recommendation." He grinned. "Well? What do you say?"

John looked him in the eye. "What of the Sheriff's officers? Who chooses them?"

"I trust your judgement and stand by your decision."

"Very well," John said, firmly. "I'll resume the Sheriff's duties. I'll do what's required. On one condition—" He paused.

Hugh was looking at him, eyes narrowed.

"—Sir William Cunninghame of Craigends resumes his office as Coroner."

Hugh's breath hissed sharp as a snake's. "Judas!"

"You want peace in Renfrew?" John retorted. "Then restore the balance. Give the Cunninghames the respect they deserve and they won't trouble you." He broke off. He hadn't expected to see such hurt on Hugh's face. "It has to be this way."

Hugh sighed, deeply. But his frown had softened. He rested his chin on one hand, thinking. . .

John hardly dared breathe. *Come on. For once in your life, consider the consequences. . .* He grasped Hugh's shoulder. "It's for the best," he said. "If Craigends is kept busy here, he won't stir up trouble in Cunninghame."

Hugh recoiled with a snarl. "You drive a hard bargain!" He slumped against the panelled wall, scowling.

John didn't speak.

Little by little, the scowl faded. Hugh shrugged, carelessly. "Win me a good turnout in the wappenschaw. Maybe then I'll forgive you." He made a brave attempt at a smile.

John raised his goblet high. "Here's to your success as Justiciar," he said. "And to a successful wappenschaw."

"Yes." Hugh's shoulders sagged. "A successful wappenschaw."

* * *

Katherine came bouncing in. "I think he saw me!" she gasped. "I left as quick as I could, but—"

"Never mind!" Margaret gripped Katherine's hands tight. "What were they saying?"

"You'll never believe what's happened—" Katherine broke off, as a knock sounded sharp on the door.

Margaret held her hand aloft for silence. "Yes?"

"Might I speak with you?" It was her husband.

"Oh!" She hadn't thought he'd seek her out: she wasn't even properly dressed. Alison was still fastening her gown, while Mariota combed her hair. "Katherine, fetch my jewels. That way, he won't suspect you were eavesdropping. . ." She fluffed out her skirts. "Come in!"

He paused by the door. "You're busy," he said. "Sorry. I didn't realise." He was staring at Katherine, hands clasped behind him, shoulders hunched slightly.

It unsettled her, to see him look so timid, but Margaret supposed it was understandable. The last time he'd set foot in her room, she'd chased him away like a whipped cur.

She smiled. "How can I help you?"

"I need a sumpter horse sent out to Paisley. Without delay. Pack enough clothes for tomorrow. And the town house at Renfrew must be provisioned. I'll need baggage sent out there, too. Enough to last a week." He was still frowning at Katherine, who sifted through the piles of clothes by the bed, trying to look as if nothing was amiss.

"I'll see to that," Margaret said.

"Good," he said. "William can go to Paisley," he added. "But he's to see me before he leaves. Lord Hugh will want to shave before he dines. He'll trust William to do the job, but I doubt he'll trust anyone else." He paused. "That's all, I think. For the moment, anyway. Thank you."

"Wait a moment."

He paused with his hand on the latch. "Yes?"

"Won't you tell me what's happened?"

He glanced at the girls. "It's not the right time."

Margaret waved her attendants aside. "Leave us, please."

"You're not ready!" Mariota complained.

"My husband can help me."

He moved away to let them pass, but didn't come closer until they'd filed from the room. Even then he halted at arm's length, saying nothing.

She presented her back to him. "Alison was girding me up. Perhaps you'd finish the task."

He didn't stir at first. Eventually he sighed, and stepped up alongside. He grasped the laces and carefully threaded them through the holes at the base of her stomacher.

"You don't like them, do you?" Margaret asked.

There was no reply.

"Why don't you send them away?"

"I'm not an ogre. I know how hard it is for you, cooped up here like this. Is that alright?"

"Tighter, please."

"It can't be comfortable, surely."

"Tighter." She felt the satisfying pull about her ribs and nodded. "Thank you. Now tie it, please." Once she was secure, she turned to face him. "What did Lord Hugh want?"

"I've been restored as Sheriff." His eyes flitted across her face, but didn't quite meet hers. "I'm to ride to Renfrew tomorrow with the herald. The Stewarts and Lord Lyle will be put to the horn."

She seized his hands. "But that's wonderful news!"

He snatched them uncomfortably away. "The baggage for Paisley must be dispatched as soon as possible. Before dinner. If you could attend to it now."

It hurt, to know he wouldn't accept her offer of friendship. But as his words sank in, misery soon gave way to panic. "But *he's* there!"

"He won't eat you." He held out his hand. "I'll protect you."

"I'm not dressed. My hair..."

She thought he might be smiling slightly. "That doesn't matter. Not after what happened earlier. . ."

"Alright." She took his hand and strode forward, head high.

At the door, she hesitated. "John?"

It was the first time she'd ever called him by name. It caught him unawares; his gaze met hers. "Yes?"

She was unprepared for the thought that jolted through her. *You have such lovely eyes. So clear, like the sky on a winter's day. . . I never noticed them before. . .* She gulped, fighting to compose herself. "Who's Actaeon?"

"He's a huntsman, in the old tales. He was so absorbed by the chase that he blundered into the bower of Diana. She was bathing with her nymphs; she was incensed at being glimpsed by a mortal man so she turned him into a stag. He was torn apart by his own hounds." He squeezed her fingers. "Shall we go?"

She gripped him tighter. "Yes."

Chapter 62

John rapped upon the door. "Can we come in, my lord?"

"Of course."

John opened the door and ushered Margaret inside. "We need to arrange baggage for tomorrow."

"By all means," Hugh said. He'd unearthed John's lute and was sitting by the window, frowning intently as he tuned it. The tension he'd shown earlier had gone; he seemed at ease with himself and the world. Margaret's earlier breach of etiquette had evidently been forgotten. She realised it, too; her face flushed with relief and she dipped a hesitant curtsey in his direction.

But Hugh was absorbed in his task, and oblivious.

They hurried across to the kists that lined the far wall.

"What do you need?" She glanced warily over her shoulder.

"Clothes for tonight," John said. "And for tomorrow, too."

"William'd make a better job of this."

"It's best you're seen to do it."

She shrugged, and burrowed deep into the kist. A waft of lavender drifted out, strong enough to make her sneeze.

The idle plucking of the lute-strings ceased. After a brief silence, music drifted through the chamber. Hugh's playing was a little hesitant at first. But soon he began to sing, in a clear tenor voice. It was one of the old troubadour's songs, a lamentation on the woes of unrequited love.

Margaret gritted her teeth, and rummaged single-mindedly through the clothes. She looked some out as quickly as she could, and together they carried the garments over to the bed as Hugh sang of broken-hearted knights and the cruelty of love.

She pressed close as they laid the clothes out. "Will that be enough?" she asked, tersely.

"I think so."

"Then we can leave everything here for William to pack. Can we go please? I must bind my hair before dinner." She looked up at him, pleading.

He offered her his arm as they retreated to the stair. She held on tight.

"Thank you!" John called to Hugh.

Hugh's voice didn't falter. He merely raised a brow in John's direction, then cast a sly glance towards Margaret and smiled at her, a faintly sinister smile.

She clutched John closer, and moved a little faster.

* * *

"Doesn't it worry you?" Margaret asked. "That he was trying to seduce me right before your eyes?"

"I'd be more worried if I thought he was trying to seduce you behind my back."

Her pace faltered and she blinked a few times, the way she always did when he tried to be witty.

"Singing doleful songs hardly counts as seduction," he pointed out. "If ever you give birth to a lean dark child who froths at the mouth whenever the name 'Cunninghame' is mentioned, then I'll be concerned."

"Don't be so coarse! I'd as soon as lie with a snake!"

"I thought you'd do it just to spite me."

"Don't say such things!" She squared up to him, hands on hips. "On the matter of infidelity. . . Where were you last night?"

"Attending my own business."

"Your gown was covered with bits of grass and flowers."

"It's my concern. Not yours."

"Of course it's my concern!" Margaret retorted. "We've only been married two months, and already you're finding pleasure in another woman's bed."

He scowled. "Is it any wonder? You made it clear from the beginning that you didn't want me in yours."

"That was before."

"So you're quite happy to bed a Sheriff? I seem to recall that last time I had to be a Sheriff and a knight. . ."

She studied her skirts. "I didn't mean it that way."

"I know exactly what you meant."

"People are talking. It reflects badly on you, as well as me." She drew a sharp breath, then added, "I want you to stop seeing her."

"God, you're unreasonable. You don't want me in your bed, but you don't want me in anyone else's bed, either—"

"Hear me out, please—"

"Would you rather it was a man?"

"That's disgusting! Of course not."

There was silence. He knew she was distressed. He was upset himself, and angry, too. He certainly wasn't in any mood to placate her.

"I want you to stop seeing her," Margaret repeated, faintly.

"I'm damned if I'll let you order me around like this!" he snapped. "Perhaps I'd spend more time here if I had something worth coming home to."

"John, I beg you." Margaret looked him in the eye. "If you care for me at all. . ." She choked back a sob. "I can't bear the shame."

* * *

Margaret waited by his horse to see him off. She'd tried so hard to keep a cheerful face through dinner. But with reality sinking in, she couldn't conceal the fear any longer.

He was going away. For the first time, Margaret would be completely on her own. It didn't matter that just hours before they'd been arguing. Somehow it felt better to argue, than to have to endure his silent indifference.

Over the last few days, though, she'd noticed he wasn't nearly as silent or indifferent as he had been. When his mood was right, he could be quite forthcoming, in his own peculiar way. His observations were caustic at times, even a little cruel. She found his comments quite amusing, though she was always afraid that some day he'd turn that sharp-tongued wit on her.

As she watched him check his horse one last time, Margaret suddenly realised that she'd miss him. She'd miss having him sit alongside, pouring the wine, serving the meat. She'd miss stealing those secretive looks as they dined.

She supposed, in a way, she'd even miss his company.

"When will you be back?" she asked.

"I don't honestly know." He glanced about him, restless, inattentive. "I'll be in Renfrew tomorrow," he explained. "After that, I'll be mustering the host." He hesitated. "It may be weeks."

"What am I to do?"

"I'm sorry." He took her hands. For once, he looked genuinely concerned. "But the King needs me. And so does Lord Hugh. . ."

"I heard once about a knight who left his place for a week and didn't return for thirty years," Lord Hugh said, cheerfully. "It was something about the Crusades, they said. *I* think he found the charms of a dusky maid from Palestine far more to his liking than the frigid embrace of his dear wife. . ."

Her husband scowled. "That's not very helpful!"

Lord Hugh just smiled.

"Nothing can go wrong," her husband assured her. "If there's anything you need, or can't understand, then ask Alan—"

"Enough!" Lord Hugh circled his horse restlessly around. "I'm sure the world won't collapse around your ears, Mistress Colville."

From the doubtful look on her husband's face, he didn't share Lord Hugh's confidence. But he gave her a smile and a pat on the arm regardless. "Everything will be fine, Margaret—" He broke off as Lord Hugh urged his steed away with a roar and a slap of the reins. "Damn him!" He scrambled up onto his horse's back, even as Lord Hugh disappeared through the gateway.

The chestnut horse sprang away, hooves kicking up a cloud of dust as it thundered after Lord Hugh.

Chapter 63

Sheep milled everywhere, dogs barked as they fought to contain the flock.

"Damned ruffians!" the shepherd bellowed, waving his crook.

John sighed, and tossed some pennies in the shepherd's direction. Glancing up the road, he could just see the dust which marked Hugh's passing.

"Is he always like this?" he asked his companion.

"A man learns to live with it," the Montgomerie man-at-arms replied.

"We're only a mile from Craigends. . ." John pressed his horse back into a canter. "Come on! Before he gets himself killed."

* * *

They still hadn't caught Hugh by the time they reached Paisley. He was waiting at the port, his horse heaving and puffing beneath him. "Thought I'd be in my grave by the time you arrived."

"We kept tripping over the casualties left in your wake."

"They shouldn't have got in my way." Hugh steered his horse alongside John's. "Your horse. How is he with artillery?"

His heart lurched. "Why? What are you unleashing?"

"We can't storm Duchal with strong words and good intentions," Hugh said. "There's unrest in the north. His Grace will use the bombards."

"Bombards!" John's spine tingled at the thought.

"That's why I asked about the horse. . ."

"He's never seen a gun being fired. The shock'll kill him."

"I'll see what I can do." Hugh halted his horse. "I've hired a townhouse for the night," he said. "The food won't be much to speak of, but it'll fulfil our needs."

"We could find a tavern."

Hugh sniffed. "I don't visit taverns."

"But—"

"Oh, talk sense, John! There's three hundred men or more in the Westland who'd like nothing better than to slit my throat or plunge a knife into my ribs. If they found me drunk in an alehouse, I'd never survive the night. God, there's so much you have to learn—"

* * *

Hugh had set his mind on lying low in the townhouse, but John would have none of it. *I'm going to the Abbey for vespers*, he said. *Whether you like it or not. . .*

His announcement didn't go down too well. Hugh flew into a seething sulk, then, just as promptly, flew out of it again and declared that if John was Hell-bent on going to mass, then he would come too.

In truth, John was glad of Hugh's company. The thieves and cutpurses of Paisley town had no respect for the devout; they made most of their money by preying on unwary pilgrims.

313

"I don't know why you bothered with Confession." Hugh prised himself away from a pillar. He had to speak loudly to make himself heard; the nave was filled with the chatter of townsfolk and pilgrims, and the din of a dozen prayers being chanted in the side-chapels. "So you rolled in the grass with your mistress?"

"Would you keep your voice down?"

"For the price of *my* sins, they've raised a new bell-tower at Kilwinning."

"Obviously, since you're so profligate with your money, you'd not risk offending the Almighty."

"No more than you would." Hugh glanced furtively towards the chancel, where the golden crosses and vessels and the rich silks of the altar cloths gleamed in the candlelight. "They sing a mass for me every day. He'll be content with that, surely."

* * *

John soon found a priest and paid for four masses to be sung; one for himself, one for Margaret, another for his mother and a final one for the soul of his father. He lit a candle to the Virgin, too, and another to Saint Mirin.

After that, he felt in better spirits.

The singing began. Strands of music, diving and twisting all around them, a cascade of sound that rained down from the vaulted heights above.

John gasped in wonder, but Hugh shook his head. "It's all the same," he scoffed. "Whether it's Kilwinning or Paisley or the Chapel Royal in Stirling."

John didn't care to reply. He gazed at the brightly painted statues that adorned the rood screen. A whole plethora of saints were gathered there; wrathful, cheerful, pious or forgiving. And, seated in pride of place above, the Blessed Virgin, who smiled softly down at the infant Christ perched on her knee.

John felt a flood of warmth, of hope. *Oh, Holy Mary, life has been hard, but I know now that my trials were for a purpose. I hope I endured them with dignity, and I hope I didn't disappoint You. I know, too, that this couldn't have happened without Hugh's help; I'm probably a fool for saying this, but I think I could call him 'friend.'*

He swallowed, suddenly overwhelmed. *Father would find it hard, to know his son has grown close to the man who struck him down. I wouldn't want to cause him grief, but. . . There was no other way.*

Breathing deep, John filled his lungs with the sweet scent of incense. *There's one last favour I'd beg of You. It concerns her. I think I love her. Please help her to love me in return. For what good is success, without someone to share it with?*

"Can we go now?" Hugh muttered alongside. "It's getting late. And I'm hungry."

* * *

"Just one more." Hugh lifted the flagon.

"You said that last time."

"I paid good money for this. I want it finished before the night's out." He poured the wine into John's goblet.

John reached for his drink. His thoughts were growing vague, the melancholy returning. He'd kept a brave face throughout the evening, when they'd been closer to sobriety. They'd talked of many things; the training of horses, the arts of war and the true meaning of chivalry.

Hugh took a deep draught of wine. He set his goblet down amongst the flotsam on the table; their discarded daggers, a demolished roast fowl, a half-eaten loaf and some empty platters. "A man like me has precious few friends." He slumped his head against his hand, disconsolate. "Most men'd stab me in the back as soon as look at me. But you, John. . . You can be trusted. And I value that. I really do."

John reached for his goblet. His eyes blurred, he shook his head to clear them. "Men say harsh things about you. But you've been a true friend." He stared into the blood-red depths of his wine. "There's something I must say, though. I hope it won't come between us."

Hugh just cocked his head and looked at him.

"I think I love the Lady Helen," John said. "I loved her the moment I first set eyes on her."

"What about your wife?" Hugh asked. Mildly curious, nothing more.

"Of course I love Margaret. She's my wife. And she's very beautiful. But her heart's made of stone."

"A woman's cruelty knows no bounds," Hugh agreed.

"Helen's magnificent. I've never known a woman so accomplished. And her eyes. There's a fire in them that sets my heart alight."

Hugh smiled. "Of course you love her. What man doesn't?" He wrapped his arm about John's shoulder with the tenderness of a brother. "She's a veritable Guinivere. And if any man must play Lancelot to my Arthur, I'd rather it was you, John. More wine?"

* * *

"Wake up now." Hugh spoke loud nearby. "There's work to be done."

John groaned and buried his head deeper into his pillow. He was curled up on his bed, still wearing yesterday's clothes. He couldn't bring himself to move at first. He had a grinding headache and he felt sick.

"Come on!" Hugh shook him, roughly. "I've already let you lie too long."

John reluctantly sat up. He rubbed his eyes, struggling to recover his senses.

It came back to him then. He remembered that he'd burst into tears, and Hugh had burst into tears, and then they clutched each other close and declared themselves devoted brothers. They'd sworn on the graves of their ancestors that they'd stick by one another, no matter what.

He hoped to God that Hugh had been as drunk as he'd appeared, that he'd have forgotten everything by now.

Hugh laughed as he pushed back the shutters. "You just can't take your wine, can you?" He'd recovered remarkably quickly; there was a faint pallor to his face and a hollow-eyed look about him but nothing more.

"I don't remember—"

"You collapsed over the table, so William and I carried you upstairs to your bed. You're not much of a burden. One slap from a mace would knock you into the next county." He gazed out into the street below, where the town was already stirring. "It's a beautiful morning. It's a sin to waste it. There's bread and ale waiting downstairs."

* * *

315

Bute Pursuivant sat slumped on his horse by the mercat cross. He had the air of a man who expected a debacle to unfold.

Hugh reined in his mount. "Good day!" he called. "Don't look so gloomy, sir! I've brought you a Sheriff." He gestured to John. "This is John Sempill of Ellestoun. Have you met?"

The herald smiled. "In different circumstances, yes."

"Then I'll waste no more of your time. Master Sempill knows what's required." Hugh turned to John. "I can't promise to attend the wappenschaw," he said. "But I'm sure you'll cope without me."

"I think it would be helpful if you stayed away."

"I'll bear that in mind," Hugh said. "William has all the documents you need. They're signed by myself and the King. They'll be enough to satisfy most men. Good luck."

And that was it.

Hugh was gone, leaving John with William and Bute Pursuivant and another half-dozen of the King's men in attendance.

Casting his eyes around the assembled company, John wished he could have better appreciated his circumstances. Instead, he was weathering a terrible headache and struggling to keep down his breakfast.

He nodded vaguely towards his men. "We'd best go then," he said, somehow managing to speak with authority, "if we're to make Renfrew by noon."

* * *

It was just striking noon as they rode into Renfrew, on a bright, bustling market day.

Hugh had planned everything to perfection. Even so, John felt doubtful. He hadn't set foot in Renfrew since that fateful night when he'd been lucky to escape with his life. Now he was riding through the main street in the company of the King's men.

It was a dramatic transformation in fortune, and it didn't go unnoticed. By the time they reined in their horses at the mercat cross, they'd attracted quite a following.

Bute Pursuivant lifted his horn and blew three sharp blasts upon it. Unrolling the parchment, he called out, "Men of Renfrew! Hear you the words of His Grace King James the Fourth of Scots—"

John studied his horse's mane intently as the decree of forfeiture was announced. It was hard not to look elated; the herald's proclamation warmed his heart. From the delighted looks on the faces before him, he wasn't the only one who savoured the prospect of revenge.

"—Furthermore," said the herald, "let it be known that after forty days elapse, then the aforementioned John Stewart, Earl of Lennox, Matthew Stewart, Master of Lennox and Robert, Lord Lyle, will be considered fugitives from the King's justice, and any man who harbours them will be hanged as a traitor—"

Hugh had been perfectly serious. There were to be no half-measures.

"Finally," Bute Pursuivant said. "As a token of their gratitude, the men of Renfrew will present themselves in full array at the butts in Renfrew town. There, the Sheriff and his officers will make the selection for the host." He rolled up the parchment, his work done.

"You heard the words of His Grace King James," John called. "You know what happened through the winter; the hardships, the burnings, the abuse of justice. His Grace has agreed to act against the Stewarts on our behalf. He's been most generous; we must support him."

"Hurrah for His Grace the King!" some courageous soul shouted out from the crowd, and widespread applause soon followed.

John breathed out in quiet relief. So far, so good.

Chapter 64

Just two days after her husband's departure, a cart came to Ellestoun. It had journeyed from Renfrew, carrying bales of ivory velvet and some skeins of crimson and black sewing silk. Alan unloaded everything, and carried it upstairs.

Margaret thanked Holy Mary for William's diligence. Despite the difficulties, he'd slipped away and carried out her errand.

Now she had sufficient cloth, Margaret immersed herself in the task of making a jupon. It was new to her, but the old groom Henry was very helpful. He introduced her to a battered old man-at-arms named Rab, who showed her round the armoury.

It was the first time she'd visited such a place and it unsettled her; all those implements of war, lying ready to maim and kill.

Rab opened the kist that held her husband's plate-mail. The suit was dismantled, but it looked impressive nonetheless. Rab said it would cost five hundred pounds to replace. Small wonder that every piece was polished morning and night to keep the rust at bay.

After that, she saw the linen surcoats worn by the men-at-arms, and the banner carried when her husband's family rode to war.

Margaret spirited a surcoat away to her room. Using an old slate and a piece of charcoal, she practised drawing the arms again and again; the chequered chevron, the three hunting horns arranged above and below.

Henry and Robert helped her measure the garment. Then, when the fabric was cut, she took the pieces away and set to work.

* * *

Every afternoon, she sat by the window, stitching busily in the sunlight. As she worked, she wondered how her husband was faring. He'd been gone four days, and she felt there was something missing. Ellestoun lacked its heart, its soul.

Margaret sighed, and studied her stitching with a critical eye. Every time she heard a noise in the yard, she'd look out for him. She wanted to know he was safe.

Perhaps, when he returned, she'd invite him to her chamber. They'd talk, then one thing would lead to another, and he'd find himself in her bed. They'd lie together, flesh against flesh, he'd put his arms about her and tell her that he loved her more than life itself. . .

She smiled at the thought, then yelped as she stabbed herself with the needle. She sucked upon her finger; last thing she wanted was to ruin all her hard work with a misplaced bloodstain on the fabric.

* * *

John rode to Cunninghame's place at Craigends as he'd ridden elsewhere, with only William in attendance.

318

The gate in the barmkin wall was closed. Leaning on the parapet was Craigends himself, grey-faced and weary. His son Andrew, Master of Craigends, stood alongside.

"So the rumours are right," Craigends said. "Are you lost, Master Sempill?"

"No, sir, I'm not lost." John reined his horse in. He kept a brave face for William's sake, but inside the doubts were growing.

"You must be touched with madness to show your face here." Craigends laughed, chill, mocking. "Do you think I'll open my gates to the dog who fawns at Montgomerie's feet?"

"I'm sorry you hold me in such low esteem. You might have found this meeting profitable."

Craigends drew back and conferred with his son. "I'm forgetting my manners," he said, slouching against the parapet with a broad, unconvincing smile. "You'd best come in."

The gates creaked open a sliver.

William jogged his horse alongside. "Master John—"

"Go back to Ellestoun."

William's eyes widened. "And leave you here alone? My God, I'm not doing that!"

"Then you're a fool!" John retorted. "Let's hope we can plead our case before he slays us."

* * *

Craigends waited in the yard alongside a brace of his men-at-arms. As John halted his horse, he stepped forward and seized the beast's bridle.

"Pray dismount, sir." His face was a mask of insincerity.

The gate slammed shut.

John cast William one last uneasy glance, then swung down from the saddle.

He'd just turned to face Craigends, when he caught movement at the edge of his vision. Before he could respond, his arms were seized, and hauled behind his back.

William, too, had been restrained; he was struggling to free himself.

"William!" John warned.

William caught his eye and gave up the fight. Too late; the Cunninghame retainer raised his fist and thumped William's head so hard he sagged and groaned.

"For God's sake stop that!" John snapped. "What manner of men are you?"

Oblivious, Craigends pulled John's sword from its scabbard and threw it aside. His dagger soon followed, even as the Master of Craigends disarmed William.

Craigends stepped close. "Three good men died at Glengarnock." He grabbed John's hair, hauling his head back so hard that John winced and stiffened. "I should cut you into pieces for the part you played there." His breath was hot and fierce against John's neck.

"Is this the way you always treat your guests, Sir William?"

"You're not that devil Montgomerie, but you'll do in his stead. You'll have a slow death for your treachery." Craigends drew his dagger, and settled the point against John's throat.

John felt the blade pressing upon the blood that pulsed there. Just one brief jab, enough to pierce the skin, but he felt no pain. Yet. . . "What will killing me achieve?"

"I'll be a happy man for doing it."

Blood trickled warm down his neck. "If you slay me, you slay the Sheriff."

"Sheriff?" Craigends' grip eased a little.

"There's letters in my saddle-bags. From the King, and the Justiciar. They acknowledge my right to hold the Sheriff's office, and give me authority to travel through this land unimpeded."

"Find them!"

The Master of Craigends sprang to obey. He extricated the letters, and turned to his father, eyes wide. "Holy Mary!" he gasped. "This carries Montgomerie's seal!"

Craigends spat upon the ground. "Damn him!" But he loosed his hold. And withdrew the knife, too. "Release them both."

"Thank you." John glowered as he straightened his clothes. His bloody neck annoyed him, but he didn't touch it. It was a stark reminder to his host about his lack of manners.

"So. . ." Craigends was suitably sheepish. "What does the Sheriff of Renfrew want with the Cunninghames?"

"A wappenschaw's been called—"

"Another one?" Craigends countered.

"I hope that as my Coroner, you'll be willing to attend."

"Coroner?" Craigends' eyes narrowed. "Does *he* know?"

"Lord Hugh is content with my choice."

"Christ Almighty. . . What's the world coming to?"

"He's not incapable of reason."

Craigends snorted. "Aye, right." Then he added, "What about Glengarnock?"

"He sought shelter for the night. Was I supposed to turn him away? Perhaps I should have afforded him the same hospitality you just gave me. . ."

"Alright!" Craigends glanced away. "You'll dine with us this afternoon?"

"A place at the board would be appreciated," John said. "If you could return our arms, so much the better."

"Of course." Craigends picked up John's weapons himself, and handed them back. "Will you remain with us tonight?"

"Thanks for the offer, sir." John placed his sword carefully back in its scabbard. "But I'm afraid I must decline. My wife lacks experience in running the household. I'd best return, and see what damage she's done in my absence."

Craigends managed a smile. "Come inside," he said. "You'll be well fed before we send you on your way."

* * *

It was an awkward meal. Conversation was strained; they discussed inoffensive things, like family, horses, dogs, and little else.

John was relieved to be gone. But his joy was shortlived. When he turned back to Pennald, the sinking sense of gloom came back.

He was going home. To *her*. And on the way, he had to pass Mary's place.

When he reached the track that led to Nether Bar, he stopped. It was coming to the end of a long and trying day. He'd have given anything to be safe and warm in Mary's arms.

"I'll ride to Ellestoun, if you like," William said. "I'll tell Mistress Margaret you'll be back tomorrow."

Please don't see her again. . . Margaret's voice spoke plaintive in his thoughts.

Frowning, John spurred his horse forwards. "She's been alone more than a week," he said. "I'd best get back to her."

Chapter 65
The Place of Ellestoun

Margaret retired to bed early and was only half-awake when she heard hooves outside. She came to her senses and lay still, listening. A hound barked loud, men's voices called in the yard.

Downstairs, a door creaked open, then closed again. Men were talking in the room below.

Margaret opened her eyes and smiled. He'd come home to her. *John.* . . She whispered his name in the darkness, caressed it with her tongue. She thought it suited him now. A gift from God. A man blessed with the moral courage of the Baptist, and the high-minded wisdom of the Evangelist.

Tomorrow, she'd seek him out. He'd come and sit with her and tell her everything. And finally, her life would be complete.

* * *

The sun was already high by the time John stirred from his bed. He'd missed mass, so he hurried out for a late breakfast, still yawning, and nearly collided with Margaret on the stair.

She bobbed before him like a cheerful sparrow, lit by the shaft of sunlight that drifted through his open door. "Hello!" she said. "I thought I heard you last night."

It seemed so long since their last meeting. Looking on her now, he felt the same way he had when he'd first set eyes on her, foolish, hopeless, painfully embarrassed.

To make matters worse, she was smiling. She looked so lovely when she smiled. . .

"Did everything go well?" she asked, clasping her hands before her.

"It seemed to." He leaned back against the newel-post of the stair. She was uncomfortably close, her skirts swamping his legs. "Hard to say, really. I'll soon find out."

"I thought you'd drop by my chamber and tell me your news."

John averted his eyes. "I've only just risen. And there's much to occupy my thoughts."

"So much you don't have time to think of me?" She peered close. "Oh, Holy Mary! What happened?"

He scratched uncomfortably at the scab on his neck. "A slight disagreement with the neighbours."

"Looks like they tried to kill you."

"Not exactly. And it's all settled now, so you mustn't worry."

Her perfume was all around him, the scent of roses. He desired her more than ever, it was only a matter of time before his body betrayed him. He sidled past. "I'm sorry. There's much to do."

"Why are you avoiding me?" Her forlorn cry echoed after him.

He paused at the curve in the stair. "I'm not avoiding you."

"You're lying, John. I know you're lying because you won't look at me."

"I have to go."

"Wait, please!" she called, but he quickened his pace.

Too much to do, he told himself. And he felt a sudden burst of relief, because he'd put the awkward task of reconciliation off for another day.

The Place of Eglintoun

Robert Montgomerie, the youngest of the Montgomerie brothers, had travelled all the way from Polnoon to speak with Hugh. He wasn't alone; his brother James rode with him, and so did their kinsman John from Hessilhead.

Having so many of the household's senior members present at one time boded ill, Helen Campbell thought, as she trod the stairs to the laird's chamber. Last time it happened, Kerrielaw burned. . .

She knocked upon the door.

"Enter!" Hugh sounded strained.

Helen bustled inside and filled up each goblet in turn. Then she settled down by the window to watch her husband's business unfold.

Hugh was in his big carved chair, while John Montgomerie of Hessilhead sat in the other chair, head slumped against his hand. Robert and James, the younger ones, had to perch side by side on the kist that stood at the foot of the bed.

"You were civil, I hope," Hugh said.

"Of course I was. But—" Robert broke off.

"What?" Hugh sat up. His expression hadn't changed, but he sounded cross.

Robert hung his head. "I don't think you served our interests properly by re-instating a Sempill as Sheriff."

"It should've been Robert," Hessilhead muttered.

"You're talking nonsense," Hugh snapped. "We've enough to do in Cunninghame, without extending the feud to Renfrew."

"True enough," Robert agreed. "But I have my doubts about the wappenschaw."

"Sempill will ask the Cunninghames to attend," Hessilhead grumbled. "He's bound to. And with the forces of Craigends and Finlaystone combined, Robert will find himself heavily outnumbered."

"Unless I know I have enough men with me to equal Cunninghame's," Robert said, "I won't be attending."

Hugh stretched back in his chair with a sigh.

"I can take forty men," Hessilhead said.

"That'll make you very popular with the Sheriff," James Montgomerie replied.

Hessilhead shrugged. "It's about time he learned who's in charge."

Hugh tapped his fingers idly against his chair arm. For a long while, he said nothing. Then he drew himself tall and cracked his knuckles. "I suppose you think I should be present."

"You're not a man to turn aside from trouble," Hessilhead said.

Hugh just smiled.

"So you'll be there then?"

Hugh shrugged. "If that's what you all want, then how can I refuse?"

The Burgh of Renfrew

On the morning of the wappenschaw, Renfrew had the atmosphere of a fair day. Booths selling food and drink had been set up in the town and near the butts, serving people who'd walked miles to witness the spectacle at first-hand.

John rode down the field, taking one last opportunity to assess the numbers. William followed, holding the Sempill banner high.

People cheered, and a band of children raced alongside, screaming with delight. John's horse, anxious to be off, snorted and flicked its ears and fought to canter.

"Ho there, Sir Knight!" A shapely maid sauntered close. "You may prick me with your sword whenever you like!"

William guffawed, but John took no notice. He was counting the Montgomeries.

He'd expected twenty-five, but lost count at fifty. "What the Devil's he playing at?"

"What d'you mean?"

"Look at them! There's a small host here."

"Maybe he's just showing willing." William tried hard to sound optimistic.

"Let's hope so." John steered his horse away.

Near his own tents, he saw the banners of his kinsmen, the Mures and the Crawfurds. Beyond them lay more tents; belonging to Knoxes, Boyles, Flemings and Erskines. Then, last of all, he saw the quartered shake-fork of the Cunninghames.

He sighed with relief. "It's a success."

William was smiling. "There's no doubting that."

* * *

Sempill of Fulwood came to meet him. "We've had over eighty men turn up."

John reined in his horse. "Dear God!"

"I've told some to leave, but they won't. Seems they want to fight."

"If they're so determined, then let the King's officers make the final decisions." He ran his gaze over the assembled men, nodding to some he recognised.

His eyes settled on a thin, flaxen-haired boy: John Alexson of Bar.

"Damn!" He dismounted, pressing his reins into William's hand. "Wait here!"

"But they'll be along any moment!"

"Call me when I'm needed!"

* * *

The Alexson boy smiled uneasily as John approached. He was armed with no more than a pitchfork and wore a stout leather jerkin over his sark.

John hauled him aside. "What are you doing here?"

"Ma sent me." The boy looked up, hopeful. "She said to tell you that she'd have come herself, if she could."

"Your place is with your mother," John told him. "Go home. Before they find you."

"Master John!" William hailed him. "They're coming."

"You heard me." He pushed the lad roughly away.

As he grabbed his horse, he could hear the sound of massed drums drifting ever louder from the town. He cursed under his breath as he scrambled up into the saddle.

He looked round one last time, but the boy had vanished.

* * *

At the head of the procession rode Bute Pursuivant in his herald's tabard. Three knights followed, riding stirrup-to-stirrup. To John's right, mounted on a gold-caprisoned warhorse, was Sir John Ross of Hawkhead, a venerable knight and one of John's more distant kinsmen. Next to Ross was a man he didn't recognise, horse swathed in blood-red velvet. And alongside him was Hugh's familiar figure, grey horse bedecked from head to hoof in azure.

"Damn him!" John snapped to William. "He knew how hard it'd be to coax Craigends out. I thought he'd be a little more circumspect."

William's glance was unconvinced.

John crossed the last few yards and halted before the approaching knights. He felt suddenly insignificant; Hugh and his companions were resplendent in shining plate armour, their velvet surcoats finished off with bright silk threads.

Why, even their horses walk with a swagger, John thought sourly. His own armour was the same set he'd worn in battle last year; scratched and dented, woefully out-of-date. His poor old horse seemed no better than a sumpter nag, ivory caprison stained and patched. And he wasn't even sporting a surcoat.

As for William. . . He had no more than a padded jack over his clothes, and a battered old sallet on his head.

The knights halted, forming an elegant line of polished steel and solid horseflesh. Behind them rode half-a-dozen burgesses, arrayed in the finest arms and mounted on well-bred steeds. They were followed by two ranks of drummers, and about four-score men-at-arms; townsmen mainly, with a respectable number of Rosses and a few Montgomeries thrown in for good measure.

A final flourish of the drums, then silence.

"On behalf of His Grace King James;" Bute Pursuivant called, "His Grace Patrick Hepburn, Earl of Bothwell and Master of the King's Household; His Lordship Hugh, Lord of Montgomerie, and Justiciar of Arran and the West; our noble cousin Sir John Ross of Hawkhead, Keeper of the Castles of Blackness and the King's Inch in the town of Renfrew."

John nodded, curtly.

"On behalf of the burgh of Renfrew; John Sempill of Ellestoun, Sheriff of Renfrew."

325

"My lords." John drew his sword, lifted the blade to his face then swept it aside in extravagant salute. "The men of Renfrew have mustered. They await your inspection."

Hugh gave a distant nod. The courtier's mask was back in place, the warmth and friendship of a few weeks back apparently forgotten. "Good work, Master Sempill." He flicked a sideways look at Hepburn. "This is John Sempill, whom I've spoken of."

Hepburn's expression was inscrutable. "Good day, Master Sempill. Let's waste no more time—" He broke off, scowling, as a horseman approached at a ragged trot.

It was Craigends, red-faced beneath his helmet. "I wasn't told that *he'd* be here!" He jabbed a finger towards Hugh. "You lied, Master Sempill. You drew me here under false pretences!"

"Lord Hugh's the Justiciar," said Hepburn. "He's entitled to attend."

"Well this damned Justiciar won't have any co-operation from me." Craigends jerked his horse's head around. "If Lord Hugh gets on his knees and begs me to stay, I might just change my mind. But I don't see that happening, do you?" He kicked his steed fiercely in the ribs, urging it forward.

Hugh said nothing. He was studying Craigends with the same level of respect he'd grant a turd.

Hepburn's expression didn't waver. "Lord Hugh, you're responsible for the men of Polnoon. Get them ready for the roll."

"My lord." Hugh cast one last contemptuous look at Craigends, then turned his horse away.

"I should've guessed this would happen," Hepburn said to Ross.

"I'll speak to Craigends," Ross offered.

"If he won't listen to you, what hope is there for the rest of us?"

John manoeuvred his horse alongside Hepburn's. Together, they watched as Ross hailed Craigends, who ignored him at first. Eventually, Craigends held his horse back so the sturdy old knight could join him. They argued fiercely for a while, then Craigends turned and rode back towards them.

Hepburn raised his brows. "Wonders never cease!"

"Your Grace." Craigends nodded towards Hepburn. "Sir John Ross assures me that the Lord Montgomerie will play no part in mustering the host, and that the Cunninghames won't be answerable to him. If this is so, we'd be pleased to remain."

"It can be arranged." Hepburn's voice was chill. "Now return to your men." He said nothing while Craigends retreated, then muttered, "Thank God that's over." He glanced at John. "Now, Master Sempill. Come with me. We'll get those damned Montgomeries out of the way first, shall we?"

* * *

Earl Patrick wasn't prone to idle conversation. He carried out his duties in silence, giving just a curt nod to signal his satisfaction.

It was hard to gauge his thoughts. All approval, all displeasure was hidden beneath a polished, courtly façade. John found it intimidating at first. But as the afternoon wore on, he grew more accustomed to Patrick Hepburn's manner. He let the cold indifference wash over him, and got on with his job, counting the men, counting the weapons, and making sure the Notary Public had written everything down correctly.

Eventually, they were finished.

Earl Patrick turned to John with what might have been a smile. "The turnout's a credit to you," he said. "Now let's rescue Lord Hugh, shall we? Before he dies of boredom."

"Do you know his plans for tonight?"

"In what respect?"

"Will he be staying here?"

Earl Patrick gave that little smile again. "If you're *that* anxious to be rid of him, why not ask him to leave?"

"It's a serious matter, my lord. Having Montgomeries and Cunninghames camped in such close proximity is asking for trouble. It'll be a miracle if they can last the night without tearing the town apart."

"Miracles are what you're here for, Master Sempill." Spurring his horse forward, Earl Patrick waved to Hugh, who was conferring with Sir John Ross. "Ho there! Do you plan to stand there gossiping all day?"

Hugh raised his hand. He trotted over, Ross close behind. "You're finished, then?" Hugh's horse fell into step alongside John's. "I was just telling Sir John what a relief it'd be to get back to the King's Inch. It must be time to dine—"

John fought the urge to scowl; Hugh talked over his head as if he hadn't even been there.

"The boards'll be ready and waiting, my lord," Ross said.

"Then let's be off," said Earl Patrick. "No need to inconvenience the cooks."

"Thank you, Master Sempill." Hugh's gaze bored right through him. "That'll be all. Good day to you."

Halting his horse, John watched them make their way across the field. The knights talked and laughed together, warhorses striding out beneath them.

"Well," John remarked to William. "A man soon learns who his friends are. If I'm not fit to grace Lord Hugh's board, I'd best find my company elsewhere."

Chapter 66

They dined in John's town house, then in the evening they relaxed. Adam Mure and Malcolm Crawfurd spun tales of valour and adventure to young Hector, while John and Robert settled down by the fireplace.

Robert gazed into his goblet. "I fear she may be pregnant again."

John clapped his shoulder. "But that's wonderful news! We must drink to her. And to the child, too."

"I don't think I can live with the worry," Robert confided. "Not after what happened before. Now I've been called up for the host, and. . . I don't want to go."

"All you can do is trust in God. Pray He keeps Marion and the child safe."

"You don't understand how hard it is to leave her."

"No, I don't," John agreed, cheerfully. "I'm glad to be away." He looked up, concerned. "Sounds like trouble outside."

"Must be curfew," Robert said. "The poor old bailies. Having to get dozens of drunken men-at-arms back to camp without provoking a riot. . ."

"My lord?" William peered round the door. "The bailies are here."

"Damn!" John sat up. "No rest for the wicked," he said. "What's the betting that war's broken out between the Montgomeries and the Cunninghames?"

* * *

"Are you sure you won't round up your men-at-arms?" Malcolm asked.

"I'm trying to prevent a battle," John said. "Not provoke one." He looked around, wincing. "God, I'll be busy tonight."

Already, the town was in chaos, with running battles being fought in the vennels and closes. And they hadn't even ventured into the market square...

A woman stumbled from a nearby house, hair dishevelled, face red. One eye was bruised, half-closed, and howling children clung to her skirts. "For pity's sake help us!" she wailed. "My husband. . . He tried to get them out. But they threw him down and knocked him senseless!"

"It's alright. We'll get redress—" He broke off as a burly man staggered through the broken door, blood streaming down his face.

Another charged out in hot pursuit, followed by a third, a young lad who staggered beneath an armful of pots and pans and brass candlesticks.

"Put those down!" John roared.

A look of blank surprise crossed the lad's face. He dropped his booty without a word as the bailies closed in.

John stood back and let them knock some fight out of the boy before he grasped the lad's shoulder and hurled him against the wall. "Who's your master, knave?"

The lad gulped a few times to regain his breath. "The Lord Hugh, sir."

"Pray he thinks well of you. Because he'll have to pay a tidy sum to get you out with your ears intact." He hauled the youth over to the bailies. "Get him locked up! His friends can join him."

"What about the Cunninghames?" one of the bailies asked. "We can't put them in together. They'd kill each other."

"That's no great loss to the world," John retorted. "Get the Montgomeries rounded up, at least. And make sure the Cunninghames don't burn down the gaol."

He released the youth into the bailies' custody.

"Ah, God," John said. "I was having such a pleasant evening."

"It'll take more than rhetoric to stop this," Malcolm said.

"We're outnumbered. In case you hadn't noticed. I don't want any swords drawn. Hear that, Adam?"

Adam growled in reluctant assent.

"One night to keep the peace," John muttered to William. "That was all we wanted."

"The Montgomeries started it," one of the bailies said. "They hung their banner on the mercat cross."

"And you didn't make them take it down." John studied the reluctant faces. "I suppose you want me to do it for you. You're damned cowards, the lot of you."

* * *

The Montgomerie banner was still draped over the mercat cross, smothering the crucified Christ beneath its folds.

He'd known what to expect, but the blasphemy of it still made John's breath catch in his throat.

Removing it wouldn't be straightforward. The banner had its guardians; four Montgomerie men-at-arms, sporting studded brigandines, with swords and daggers at their belts. They lounged around the cross, swigging ale from flagons and hurling abuse at any who came near.

"I'll cut that rag down and piss on it!" Someone called across the market square.

"I'll piss on your corpse if you try!"

"That—" John said to Malcolm, "—has got to go."

"Take no part in this," Malcolm said. "They're some of Lord Hugh's beasts from Cunninghame."

"If they're from Cunninghame, then what on earth are they doing here?"

Malcolm grabbed John's arm. "Let them be, John! The Cunninghames'll soon knock them down to size."

John shook him loose. "What's to stop them burning the burgh by morning? I've got property here. I'm not going to lose it." He pushed past a knot of drunken Cunninghames and confronted the Montgomeries. "Take that down!"

All four were staring right at him. "Go and fuck yourself!" retorted one. A battered old soldier, with a battle-scarred face. He was missing an ear; he was either a thief, or someone who'd suffered the Cunninghames' justice at first hand.

John took a deep breath. "Take down the banner." Not that talking would do much good. It was like confronting a pack of wolves; they were biding their time, waiting. . .

The drunken man-at-arms lurched closer. He leered at John and jabbed a finger in his chest. "And I won't tell you again, boy. Go and fuck yourself!" He spat at John's feet. "Who d'you think you are, anyway?"

John pushed him away. "I'm the Sheriff," he said. "And you do what I say. Take that down. Now."

"You can take your fucking Sheriff's office and shove it right up yer arse, *sir*. There's only one man tells me what to do, and you're not him."

"Get out of my way." John shouldered past. As they stood there gaping, he climbed up onto the plinth. He hooked his arm about the stone shaft of the cross and reached out to grasp the banner. He heard growls of displeasure behind him, but didn't look round. Adam was swearing and cursing at his back; John just had to hope and pray that Adam, who had the shoulders of an ox and a bellow to match, would make the Montgomeries think twice before attacking.

His fingers closed about the silken banner. He tugged it gently, but its folds snagged upon the arm of the cross beneath. He was trying to coax it loose when something struck him between the shoulder blades. He couldn't breathe. He thought, for a brief frightening instant, that he'd been knifed.

Then his foot slipped. He hung there in the air, still clinging to the banner, until with a terrible tearing sound, the silk ripped.

He crashed to the ground, landing square on his thigh, right on the edge of the step. The impact made him gasp; white-hot pain ripped through the length of his leg, his head spinning as his face skidded along the stone plinth.

Adam could no longer protect him; John barely had time to curl up before the furious Montgomeries leapt on him, roaring so loud they'd have sent a hell-hound fleeing.

He clamped his arms about his head, groaned as a foot drove into his stomach. He couldn't move; he was buried beneath a torrent of them, kicking, stamping, tearing. *I'm going to die*, he realised, numbly, as he lay there with his leg twisted at a cruel angle beneath him, and the Montgomerie banner crushed against his chest.

He weathered the blows with weary detachment. Eventually something struck his leg, a blunt weapon that hit hard enough to make him yelp. Another blow, then someone had a hold of his ankle and was hauling so hard he thought his hip would give way.

"Got him!" Robert's voice, triumphant. The pulling ceased, hands grasped his belt and he could breathe and move free again.

John sat up with a groan.

Adam towered over him, sword half-drawn. "Get back!" Adam snarled, as the bailies laid into the Montgomeries with the full force of their cudgels. "Stinking thieves! You're no better than animals!"

Malcolm and William grasped John's arms and hauled him to his feet. John shook his head, dazed. He blew blood from his nose and swore as the pain surged fresh through his leg.

Adam's face swam into focus before him. He patted John's cheek, roughly. "You'll live," he said, "but your nose may never be the same again."

Head clearing, John spat out a mouthful of blood, then turned around and surveyed the devastation behind him. The bailies had beaten the offending Montgomeries into submission; they knelt in the square with their hands upon their heads as the townsmen quickly disarmed them. But half-a dozen more prowled beyond.

"Get them to the tolbooth!" John called. "Quickly!" He shrugged Malcolm and William loose. "I'm alright." He soon regretted his words. His leg shook. Wincing, he reached for William's arm, just in time to stop himself falling.

William gripped him tight. "What is there about Renfrew? Whenever you come here, someone tries to kill you."

"It's the company he keeps," Malcolm said.

John moved his jaw, cautiously, pressing his fingers along it. All his teeth were there, at any rate. Glancing down, he groaned disgustedly. His doublet and sark were ripped and bloodied, he'd torn his hose on the rough stone step.

"We should get you back to the house," William said.

"No. I must keep order. Now help me, please." The pain was setting in now; the bile rose in his throat when he put weight on his right foot. He gritted his teeth regardless, and strode off as manfully as he could, one arm wrapped round William's steady shoulders.

* * *

John threw the last of the miscreants into the tolbooth-gaol himself. "You'll stay there until Lord Hugh pays up for your release!" he shouted, as they battered their fists against the hefty wooden door and loudly voiced their protests.

Leaning back against the rough stone wall, he closed his eyes. All that pain and effort, just to win a minor victory in a much larger war. "Get Craigends," he told Malcolm. "I'll find Hugh. It's obvious they won't listen to me. Surely to God they'll do what he tells them?"

"It'll take more than this to coax Hugh Montgomerie out into the night," Malcolm said.

* * *

Inside the Castle of the King's Inch, it felt like a different world. Stewards bowed and scurried before John as he passed. They asked if he might wait, they asked if he wanted to tidy himself up before he entered the hall. *There are ladies present*, one said. *You'll upset them.*

John brushed them aside. He was shaking with rage and delayed reaction. He wasn't sure how long he could go on before his strength finally gave out. He certainly wasn't in any mood to let the erring Lord Hugh finish his dinner in peace.

"Wait here," he told William, once they reached the hall. "I won't hang onto your arm."

Within the hall, a group of musicians played a gracious air, as the diners forged their way through the last few courses. There amongst them at the top table was Hugh, calm, composed and elegant.

The sight of him brought John's blood closer to the boil. He limped resolutely onwards, fuelled by hatred and disgust. Servants tugged his arm, asking him to wait until they'd spoken to Sir John Ross on his behalf.

He paid no heed.

Hugh spotted him first. A look of startled surprise flickered on his face, then the courtier's restraint was back. "Good God, Master Sempill. You look like you've been wrestling a wolf-pack."

Earl Patrick looked up, his meal forgotten. So did Ross, pausing in mid-mouthful.

John scowled. "They bore your name."

"Ah." Hugh squirmed slightly.

He hadn't thought Hugh capable of embarrassment. But there it was, and that one crack of vulnerability was all John needed. "You asked me to keep the peace!" John snapped. "I tried, and what thanks am I given? Not much, just a pack of your men trying to tear me limb from limb. There's decent folk out there, cowering in their homes, while your people run riot. They can do what they like in Cunninghame, my lord, but this is Renfrew."

Hugh sat back, arms folded. "You're the Sheriff. You deal with it."

"There's only eight of us, and at least seventy Montgomeries." He slammed his fists upon the board. The platters jumped, making the ladies gasp further down the table. "You brought those knaves from Cunninghame. You brought them here expecting trouble and you didn't have the decency to warn me. If this is what I'm to put up with as Sheriff, then you can take the Sheriff's office and choke on it, *my lord*."

Hugh cast a mutinous glance towards Earl Patrick and Sir John Ross. They said nothing, feigning disinterest.

Hugh studied his platter, then glowered at John. "I'll be with you shortly, Master Sempill," he said, and drained the remains of his wine with a martyred sigh.

* * *

Sir William Cunninghame of Craigends sat on his horse by the mercat cross, a brace of men-at-arms in attendance. He was watching the running battles with interest, but doing precious little to intervene.

"Ah, Sir William!" John hobbled over to join him. "I need your help, sir."

Craigends looked him up and down, unmoved. "I heard about your woes, Master Sempill," he said. "I'm hoping it'll teach you a salutary lesson about choosing your friends more carefully."

"It's neither the time nor the place for recriminations. Can you gather together your men?"

"My men are defending themselves, Master Sempill." Craigends stretched comfortably in his stirrups. "I hope you understand now," he said. "This is what *he* intended all along."

Stalemate. John cursed beneath his breath as his leg weakened once more.

"Sit down, for God's sake!" said William.

This time, John gave in. He sank down on the steps of the mercat cross. "I'm a damned fool," he whispered to William. "We'll be waiting here all night."

The Montgomerie banner still lay nearby. John picked it up; the evening's antics had wreaked havoc on the fine silk and carefully wrought embroidery. He folded it with a sigh, then watched resignedly as further down the street a man fell and didn't get back up again.

"Put a knife in him!" Craigends called, even as the bailies rushed to reach the stricken Montgomerie first.

"For all your self-righteous talk, you're no better than Lord Hugh," John said. Craigends didn't reply.

Hooves thundered across the timber drawbridge of the King's Inch.

They all looked round. There was Hugh, mounted on his great grey horse and fully armoured, six men-at-arms at his back.

"Christ All Mighty," Craigends muttered. "It's a damned papingo on a donkey."

By now, John couldn't find much consolation from Hugh's arrival. "If you can't say anything civilised," he told Craigends, "then don't say anything at all."

Zephyr bounced along at a sprightly trot, snorting fitfully and fighting a tight rein. "Now then!" Hugh called from the stallion's back. "How can I help?"

John lifted his head. "Get them out of here!" he snapped. "They can tear each other to pieces at the butts for all I care. But not within the bounds of the burgh."

"Certainly!" Hugh smiled, pleasantly accommodating. He set off down the street at a canter. Drawing his sword and waving it high, he called, "*Garde bien,* Montgomeries! To me!"

John glowered at Craigends. "Will you let him restore the peace single-handed, Sir William?"

Craigends growled in reluctant response and sent his horse ambling after Hugh's.

John moaned and let his head fall against his knees. "What a night," he said.

* * *

Once he'd escorted his men back to camp, Hugh returned to see how John was faring.

He soon wished he hadn't. John looked as if he'd rather suffer the bloody flux than pass the time of day.

John pushed himself stiffly to his feet. "At the last count, eight of your men were locked in the tolbooth. Including the ones who assaulted me."

"Ah," Hugh said, cautiously.

"I'll release them into your custody. Provided I have no further trouble from them."

Hugh had expected an outburst. He'd have preferred it to this abominable air of self-righteousness. He smiled uncomfortably as he dismounted. "That's gracious of you, sir."

"And there's this." John thrust a banner into his hands.

In the fading light, Hugh saw the red and blue colours and frowned. It was the standard that was supposed to fly in the midst of his camp. A venerable piece, fifty years old.

"I'm afraid it didn't survive the night unscathed." John sounded unsympathetic.

Hugh shook out the cloth, and saw a gaping hole in its midst. He drew a sharp hissing breath.

"It was my fault." The martyred tone was back. "But if one of your people hadn't struck me with a stone, it would never have been damaged."

"My grandmother wrought that," Hugh said. "She was a Cunninghame. The only worthwhile thing to come from their line—"

"William!" John grasped Master Haislet's shoulder and hobbled towards the tolbooth.

Hugh trailed after him. "It's the first time I've seen you lose your temper," he admitted. "A man'd be hard-pressed to know. Until it was too late and there was a knife in his ribs."

"Let me warn you, *Lord* Hugh. You're coming damned close."

"You shouldn't have tried to intervene," Hugh continued. "You should have spoken to me first." It wasn't much of an apology, he supposed, but at least he'd made the effort.

"You wouldn't have stirred from that board unless the castle was burning down." John waved to the bailie who stood outside the tolbooth. "Open up! Lord Hugh's come to fetch his people."

"Here!" Hugh fumbled at his belt. He had a small bag of coins there; he pressed it firmly into John's hand. "For your pains," he said. "Assaulting a Sheriff doesn't come cheap, I know. My thanks for being prepared to overlook this—"

John's frosty expression hadn't thawed. But at least he had the courtesy to accept the peace offering, even if he didn't voice his thanks.

The door swung open and Hugh's retainers traipsed out, heads hanging.

"Come on, knaves!" Hugh whacked a straggler's head with his mailed hand. "That's for your folly. Don't go battering my friends."

Chapter 67

Archery tournaments were in progress, and further down the field there was jousting. Every so often they heard a loud thump and a cheer as lance met shield or steel plate and another man was unhorsed. The whole town had turned out to watch, but for John and Sir John Ross, the day would be spent drilling two hundred reluctant farmers and townsmen in the skills of war.

Normally, John would have been frustrated at not being able to try his hand at the jousting. Today, he didn't care. It was a hot day, and he was baking in his armour. He felt dizzy; he wasn't sure if it was from the heat or from a surfeit of the *aqua vita*. The gash on his leg had re-opened; he could feel the wet warmth of fresh blood.

"If they spent their Sabbaths training for war instead of kicking a damned ball about the churchyard, we might actually win our battles." Sir John Ross glowered at the disorganised ranks of men. "Left, I said! God, you're like a bunch of old women." He frowned at John. "You all right, lad?"

"I'm surviving," John replied. His thoughts were pleasantly fogged. He'd taken a few measures of the *aqua vita* to help him sleep the previous night, and a few more before venturing out that morning.

"Take yourself home and put your mind on getting better. I won't tell a soul."

It was a tempting offer. John's limbs had stiffened up overnight; now he could barely move. His face was swollen, so wearing his close-helmet brought constant discomfort, while his knee throbbed incessantly.

"Are we ready now?" Ross called. "Let's try again. Form up!" Glancing anxiously at John, he added, "I meant what I said."

John shrugged. "I'll be doing this myself some day. Best I learn my trade from the master."

"That's very kind of you." Ross watched carefully as the schiltron settled. "One thing's for sure; you'll be the talk of the town for weeks. Did you get redress?"

"Ten pounds, in all."

Ross uttered a wheezing laugh. "That's a miracle in itself! Hugh's tighter than an abbess's arse when it comes to reparation." He shook his head. "When I saw you last night, I thought your poor father's ghost had come seeking revenge. You fair took the wind out of Hugh's sails, too. Not before time, either. . ." Taking a deep breath, Ross called out, "Are we ready now? Alright, let's try again. Forward! And left. Hold. Better. Much better."

The schiltron of spearmen wheeled in new-found confidence before them. "That's good!" Ross called. "Very good! You'll have King Henry quaking in his boots."

John closed his eyes, briefly. *Don't swoon, for God's sake. You'll be the laughing-stock of the town. It can't be long now. . .*

The church bells tolled one o'clock.

He could've wept with despair. A fly buzzed round his face and the heat was getting worse by the minute.

What I'd give, for a mug of ale. His mouth watered at the thought.

But it'd be another three hours before he was free to sate his thirst. He gritted his teeth and willed the afternoon to pass.

He wanted, more than anything, to go home to Ellestoun. Then, at least, he could rest his aching bones in peace.

The Place of Ellestoun

Margaret flopped down by the window. Pulling her handkerchief from her sleeve, she wiped her forehead.

It was the hottest day of the year so far. Beneath her gown, her kirtle clung to her.

Hoping for a breeze, she stood by the window. But there was no relief there; it was like standing by an oven. *Mustn't complain,* she told herself. *Crops are turning already, and that's all that matters. . .*

Then she noticed two of the men-at-arms, stationed on the wall-walk. They were staring down the hill intently.

Curious, Margaret followed their gaze.

Half-a-dozen horsemen approached. It was hard to see much when the sun shone so bright, but she could've sworn they were arrayed for battle.

She shivered despite the heat. Managing the household in peacetime was one thing; managing it in war was a different matter entirely.

One of the horsemen broke formation and entered the gates at a canter.

It was William.

Margaret put a hand to her breast, shaky with relief.

But something about his manner unsettled her. She kept watching; she saw him dismount and talk with Henry and Alan. They huddled near the stables; William kept looking back and gesturing down the hill. He was wearing his brigandine; it hung open to reveal his pale sark beneath.

Margaret anxiously peered at the approaching horsemen, seeking John amongst them. She didn't spot him at first, but noticed his red-brown horse.

Then she realised why she hadn't recognised him. He was clad in his plate armour.

Something's wrong. Why would he travel in full array on a day like this? She closed her fingers around her rosary. *He's not sitting right. . .*

The horse ambled through the gates then wandered over to where William and Henry waited.

John didn't even try to dismount.

Henry grasped the reins, while William and Alan hurried to John's side. She couldn't make out what they were saying, but their hushed words sounded tense, anxious.

"What's wrong?" Katherine peered over her shoulder.

"I don't know. I think he's ill." *Or wounded*. . . She couldn't bring herself to say it.

"Maybe he tried the jousting. That makes a man feel out-of-sorts for days."

Margaret said nothing. She gripped the window-ledge tight as she watched John half-slide and half-fall from his horse.

"I'd best see what's wrong," she said.

"Do you honestly think he'll want to see you?" Katherine asked.

"I don't care. I need to know what's happened."

* * *

John perched on the edge of the bed while William removed his armour. Once helmet and *cuirass* had been set aside, John sighed with relief; now, at least, he could breathe freely.

"Should've done this earlier," William said. "It wouldn't have taken long."

"And I'd still be on the road. Believe me, I'd rather be here." He gasped as William unbuckled the *cuisse* that encased his right leg. "Ah! Be careful!"

"I'm sorry!"

John gripped his shoulder. "Steady," he said. "Won't do any good if you rush things."

"Jesus!" William gasped. "When did the bleeding start?"

The leather lining of the *cuisse* was stained black with blood. The cloth of John's hose was saturated, too. "I don't think it actually stopped."

"Should've been sutured," William muttered, as he worked on freeing John's other leg. "I offered last night, but no. You wouldn't let me near it."

"I was tired. You were fussing."

"And with good reason." William sat back on his heels. "There. You're done."

John laid himself down with a sigh. His left leg moved of its own accord, but he had to use his hands to haul the right one up alongside. He couldn't bend the knee without causing excruciating pain.

He closed his eyes. Now he was lying still, his aches were subsiding a little. He wasn't comfortable though. His clothes were sodden with sweat, his head swimming.

"Are you alright?" William asked. "You're very pale."

"Just hot, I think. I need a drink."

"I brought some warm water," Margaret spoke outside. "Can I come in?"

"Oh Saints preserve us! Send her away, William. She can't see me like this. She'll have nightmares."

William shrugged, and went to the door. "Thank you for your help, Mistress Margaret," he said. "He'd rather not speak with you just now. I'll tell you how he fares, soon as I can."

"But—"

"I'm sorry, but he doesn't want to see you." He took the water, and nudged the door closed behind him. "She should be told what's happening."

"Go and speak to her," John said. "But be quick, please. I want this over with. And bring some *aqua vita*. I'll need some if you're going to start sticking needles into me."

William set the flagon down. "Won't be long."

* * *

With William gone, John struggled to sit up. The world turned black, briefly, and bile rose in his throat. He weathered the nausea as best he could; he'd been sick several times on the journey home and he still stank of it.

Clenching his teeth against the pain, he unlaced his hose and eased them off. His knee was swollen, discoloured; it was no wonder he could hardly move his limb.

He'd bound a strip of cloth around the ragged gash on his thigh the previous night. It was dull red and soaking wet now. Reluctantly, he pulled it aside.

The wound still oozed blood.

John sighed and settled down again. When he lay on his back, his head felt worse, and breathing made his chest hurt. He perched on his side, but that felt little better.

His throat burned with thirst. The pain was growing unbearable. He hoped he'd swoon, for then at least there'd be an end to it.

* * *

"What happened?" Margaret asked.

"There was an incident in Renfrew," William said. "His leg's hurt bad." He kept casting guilty glances at the door.

"Is it broken?"

He shrugged. "It's his knee, I think. Battered his head, too. And his ribs. . ."

"Should we summon a leech?" Margaret persisted.

"No!" William visibly recoiled.

"Why ever not?"

"A leech'd take his leg off."

"That's nonsense." She paused. "You're worried about him, aren't you?"

"Yes."

"I want you to go to Paisley, and fetch us a leech."

"He needs me here," he said, faintly.

"Must I ride out myself?"

His shoulders slumped. "He's vile company when he's poorly," he said. "Send word to his mother. I'm sure she'd help."

"I'll manage, thank you," she said. "Now please go."

* * *

Margaret's knees wobbled with fear as she trudged up the stair. *He'll never forgive you for this,* she told herself, as she pushed open the door.

Discarded pieces of armour lay strewn about the floor. She picked a careful course through them, trying not to make a noise. She hoped he wouldn't hear her approach, in case he snarled or shouted.

John lay on his bed, oblivious. He'd shed his hose, and his sark and arming doublet were crushed up around his waist. He faced away from her; she couldn't take her eyes from his long white legs and the firm flesh of his buttocks.

Then she saw the yawning tear in his thigh, and the evil-coloured swelling around his knee.

Fear turned to indignation. *God granted you such perfect limbs*, she thought, *and you've wrecked them*. She marched over. "You were brawling, weren't you?" Grasping him under the oxters, she rolled him onto his back.

He choked back a howl; he'd jammed his foot beneath his injured knee.

"Oh, I'm sorry." She freed his limb and set it straight. His skin was cold and clammy; she winced as she touched it.

He struggled onto his elbows. One eye widened momentarily, the other remained stubbornly half-closed. "Where's William?" His hair was dank with sweat, his face so badly swollen down one side that she hardly even recognised him. He stank to high heaven; of rank sweat and vomit and spilt urine.

"I sent him to Paisley. To fetch a leech."

"I need him here!" He looked close to tears. "We don't even need a leech. We just needed a stout bodkin, and some thread, and some *aqua vita*. . ." He gulped, and whispered, "What am I going to do?"

She sat beside him and gripped his arms. "Calm yourself." His linen arming-doublet was saturated with sweat, the muscles beneath tight and hard. She was relieved he looked and smelled so awful, for it meant she felt no desire for him. "I'll look after you. Is there anything you need?"

He met her gaze just briefly, then looked away. His breathing was rapid, shallow. "I'm thirsty."

"Then I'll fetch you a drink. Just lie still, and I'll see to everything."

Chapter 68

He'd thought things couldn't get any worse, but now he was stuck with Margaret, who didn't know what she was doing. And probably didn't care, either.

John stifled a sob. *She'll find something else to do. She'll leave me here all night.*

The door creaked. "John?" Margaret called.

He tried to sit, but couldn't find the strength.

"Wait!" Setting the ale aside, she helped him, then handed him the mug and held him steady as he drank.

"I'm alright now," he told her, once he'd drained two mugfuls. "I just need rest. You can leave me."

She cast him a sideways look. "Can you manage to the privy?"

"Piss-pot's there, isn't it?"

"And how will you reach it? It's tucked under the bed."

He'd been trying to ignore the growing pressure in his bladder, but now she'd mentioned it, the battle was lost. With a martyred groan, he swung his legs around and staggered to his feet.

She seized him. "Careful!"

He gritted his teeth, trying not to show how much it hurt, while she gripped him with surprising strength for one so small. It took an eternity to cross that tiny stretch of floor. His strength was failing, he hoped it'd last long enough to get him safely back to his bed.

She held back the curtain that closed off the privy. "Will you be alright?"

"Of course."

"If you need me, just call."

* * *

"Thank you," he told her, once he was back in his bed. He hadn't meant to sound so ungracious, but it was hard to be courteous when he felt so crushed with exhaustion.

"Your clothes are wringing," she said. "Let me help you undress." She seized his shoulders and heaved him forward.

"I can do this myself, for God's sake! Leave me be!" He sat there glowering as she unlaced his arming doublet and slid it from his back. He'd never loathed himself so much; he hated being helpless, he hated being so dirty and foul-smelling.

Just his luck that she was there to witness it.

Margaret was, however, handling all this unpleasantness remarkably well. She sat on the bed beside him, his soggy sark rolled up in her lap. "Oh, John." She laid her hand on his. "You look like you've been trampled by a herd of kye."

"I feel that way, too."

"Lie down. I'll cover you up as best I can. I'll leave your legs, though, while you're bleeding like that."

He settled down without a word.

"Something should be done with the wound, shouldn't it?" She arranged the bedclothes carefully over his body.

"Should be washed out," he muttered. "With wine. Or *aqua vita*. The cooks'll make a plaster."

"I'll go and talk to them." She wrung out a soft cloth, and laid it gently against his head. The water had been infused with herbs; its warmth and sweet scent helped soothe his aching head a little.

He sighed and closed his eyes.

Margaret squeezed his hand. "I'll be as quick as I can."

* * *

"The cooks were very helpful," Margaret said, cheerfully. "They boiled up some herbs, and told me what to do." She set down the cloths and the mortar, which held within it a foul green paste. She'd been given a pot of honey, too, and a large flask of *aqua vita*.

Margaret pulled back the coverlet, slightly. She tried not to grimace at the smell of him, but didn't quite succeed.

John sighed, and shifted uncomfortably.

She fetched a cushion from the window seat so she could raise his leg while she cleaned the wound. She grasped his foot. "Yuk!" she said. "Your skin's so damp and cold!"

He cringed. "I'm sorry. I'd bathe, if I could. . ." He struggled to sit.

"Stop it," she told him. "You'll only make things worse."

He grunted and lay still.

After what William had said, she'd never thought he'd be so compliant. She didn't feel quite so anxious as she slipped a cloth beneath his thigh, and perched beside him.

Taking another cloth, she swabbed the wound with *aqua vita*. It looked clean to her unpractised eye; she supposed the bleeding had helped wash it out. But she gave it a good rub regardless.

He clenched his fingers into the sheet and his leg kept twitching. But he didn't utter a sound.

"Was it a sword?" she asked.

"A sword would have taken my leg off," he replied. "If you must know, it was a stone step."

"So you tripped up?"

"No! Not at all. It's a long tale, and my head hurts—"

"In other words, you don't want to tell me. It must've been some step, to do this to you." She emptied the stinking green paste onto a linen pad, dripped some honey around the wound and bandaged it into place. "There. It's done." She patted his thigh.

He didn't answer. He had that faraway look about him again.

"There's a pot of water by the bed," she said. "It should still be warm. I'll bathe your feet if you like, to try and heat them up."

"No, really. There's no need."

341

"You're always so eager to act the martyr. It's no trouble. I'm sure you'll feel a lot better afterwards."

She settled down with the bowl of water, and picked up his feet. One after the other, she wiped them clean and dried them, taking great care not to jar his injured limb. He watched her all the time, wary, faintly hostile.

"There now," she said. His feet still rested against her knees; when she closed her hands around them, he gasped. "I won't hurt you," she told him. She kneaded the soles, gently. The skin was soft, yielding. "I'll be very careful."

His toes were curled tight, through fear or displeasure. But gradually his tension eased. His limbs loosened, his eyes closed.

"Margaret," he murmured.

"What?" She kept running her hands gently over his feet. They fascinated her; they were long and slender, sparsely fleshed.

"I'm sorry. About what happened that first night."

"Hush now."

"No, I mean it. I hurt you, and—"

"It's a long time ago." She slid off the bed. "If you want, I'll wash your face."

"I'd appreciate that."

He sat there quite still as she cleaned out the cuts and grazes with yet more *aqua vita*. She wiped his face and his neck with the scented water, and when he voiced no objection she took a cloth to his chest and his oxters, too.

She'd have washed his loins if she'd had the courage to suggest it. As it was, he was infinitely more pleasant to the nose.

"Poor John," she said, as she pulled the covers over him. "You look so unhappy."

He smiled, grimly. "You can be honest. I'm a pathetic creature."

She sat down on the edge of the bed. "I would hate to be a soldier."

"I'd hate to be a woman."

"Have you fought in a battle?" The thought thrilled and appalled her.

"Yes."

"Wasn't it horrible? To have to kill your fellow men?"

"I don't want to talk about it."

"Alright." She stood. "Don't say anything more. I can see you're exhausted."

"Margaret?" He opened his eyes.

"Yes?"

"Thank you. You were very kind."

She leaned close and lightly kissed his forehead. "I'm your wife, John. That's what I'm here for."

* * *

Katherine was an island amongst a sea of argent velvet. She looked up from her stitching as Margaret approached.

Margaret sat opposite. "I won't be with you tonight."

Katherine set down her sewing, but said nothing.

"Alison?" Margaret called. "Can you go to the kitchens? Fetch me some bread and milk for my supper."

There'd been no time to sit back and think. She'd been too busy. But it was hitting home now. She thought of him lying there; with his pale, fragile flesh, and his manhood all shrivelled and small in his lap.

She shivered.

"How's he faring?" Katherine asked.

Margaret shrugged. "He's not himself."

"Like the Good Samaritan, you tended him," Katherine said. She glanced at Margaret, half-smiling. "Did he squeal when you scrubbed too hard?"

"Of course he didn't!"

Katherine edged closer. "Did you glimpse his flesh?"

"Yes, I did."

"Then what's it like?"

Margaret inched forward. She beckoned Katherine towards her, then, when their faces were nearly touching, she whispered, "Imagine a figure of Saint Sebastian, carved from ivory. Perfect in every respect, but with that fair flesh broken by the blows of a vicious enemy. That's what it's like."

Katherine smirked. "Strange this should happen, after all those things we said."

Margaret sat back with a sigh. She'd tried to put those thoughts from her mind. Those times she'd lain awake at night, imagining what it would be like to inflict endless cruelty upon him.

She'd wanted him passive. She'd wanted him defenceless. He was both now, but knowing it brought no pleasure.

She just wished he was better.

Chapter 69

Margaret sagged in her chair, exhausted. The sun had set hours ago, the sky outside that strange pale blue of midsummer.

John had been dozing, off and on. But he kept waking, troubled by his wounds. William had been a little unfair. John wasn't exactly vile company, but he *was* difficult. He reminded Margaret of the lion with the thorn in his paw; he'd snap and snarl, but every time he'd have good reason to be grouchy.

He'd never volunteer any information himself. Instead, she had to tease through the possibilities. *Are you thirsty?* she'd ask. *Are you too hot?* Eventually, with some coaxing, he'd tell her.

He gave a little moan, and she sat up with a yawn. She'd pulled the coverlet off him earlier, leaving just a sheet in place. At first, she'd found it difficult to settle knowing he was lying there so close. She'd so desperately wanted to find some excuse to peek at him.

Now though, she was too tired to care. She reached out and fondled his hair. "Are you alright?"

Silence. A bad sign.

"Do you need a drink?"

"No." He sounded terse.

"Are you cold?"

He hesitated. "I need to pass water."

"I'll fetch the pot now."

* * *

Judging from the endless stream that poured out, Margaret suspected that he'd been holding it in for quite a while. She wasn't surprised; it was a struggle to help him sit up so he could use the piss-pot. In the end, she had to hold the pot with one hand and his member with the other, while he leaned his hands on her shoulders and braced himself.

"Are you finished?" she asked.

He buried his face against her neck, too spent to move. His breath blew warm against her skin, his flesh was pale in the night's half-light. "Don't pour it away," he said. "The leech will want to see it."

She set the pot down. "Rest a moment," she said. "There's no hurry." She touched his shoulders, cautiously; he didn't react, so she ran her hands over his back.

Closing her eyes, she breathed him in. She wished she could live the moment for eternity. *Ah, God, I don't want to lust after you. It's the last thing you need just now. But when you're so close, with your smooth, soft skin. . .*

He lifted his head. "I'm better now," he said. "I might sleep."

* * *

"John." Margaret shook him, gently. "He's here." She tossed the covers aside.

The door opened and there was William. The leech followed, a stern-looking fellow of fifty years or more who carried his casket of instruments before him.

The leech frowned. "Must the lady be present?"

"I'm his wife."

"Very well." The leech took a long hard look at John's thigh. "We'll mend the wound first," he said. "Then see what needs to be done for the rest of you." He turned to William. "If he struggles, he'll damage that knee."

"We can dose him full of the *aqua vita*," William suggested.

"Two stout men might be more helpful. Or some rope to tie him down."

"You'll do no such thing!" Margaret snapped. "Give him something to deaden his senses."

"Too risky," William said. "It's not as if his leg's coming off."

"He mustn't suffer needlessly. Give him a draught."

John sighed. It made it worse, hearing them talk like that.

"Please, Mistress Margaret," William persisted. "You don't understand the consequences."

"No!" Margaret confronted him, hands on hips. "I won't have him put through that." She looked at John, eyes wide. "John, please!"

"I'll take the draught," John spoke out.

"John, for God's Sake!" William argued.

"I don't care!" John snapped. "Stop chattering and let the man get on with it."

The leech looked askance at John, then retreated to his box of medicines. He brought out a small vial. "Drink this."

The potion tasted bitter. John gagged, fighting to keep it down.

William gave a frustrated moan.

"It'll be a few minutes," the leech said. "You've cracked your head, Master Sempill. Best make sure your crown's not broken."

"You should go now," William told Margaret.

"He needs me here. John, tell them—"

"If it's what she wants. . ." He was almost looking forward to the moment when his senses failed him.

The leech bent close, and John obediently held his ears and nose and kept his mouth tight shut and did his best to breathe out.

"Excellent." The leech nodded in satisfaction. "All's well. That's one less thing to worry about. Now lie down. We'll get you mended as soon as we can."

"Don't you worry, John." Margaret knelt on the bed behind him. "Just rest your head in my lap."

He settled down. As his eyesight dimmed, he swallowed, suddenly frightened. Once sleep took him, there'd be no guarantee he'd return. Hemlock, henbane, hellebore. He'd taken these poisons willingly, because she'd asked him to.

"It's alright." Her voice was receding. "I'll be here, and it'll soon be over."

You're a fool, he thought, *and you'll die for it. Perhaps the innocence is just a front. Perhaps she knows. . .*

He was falling, down an immeasurable chasm. The speed of his descent left him dizzy, nauseous.

He found himself in a grey, blasted world and he wasn't alone. There were shapes everywhere; bent, scuttling creatures with burning eyes that stared from the shadows.

He wasn't bound, but he couldn't move an inch as they came closer. Their claws dug deep into his leg; he screamed and howled, until his voice was hoarse and he couldn't scream anymore. He tried to struggle, but it felt as if his limbs were weighed down with stones.

Cloudy darkness overwhelmed him, and the fearsome pain in his thigh subsided. The murk cleared; he found himself lying in Margaret's lap, naked, exhausted. She was all he could see in the gloom, her face lit pale. *It's alright now.* She stroked his hair. *I'm here. I'll look after you.* There was something about her features, a harsh unreal quality that frightened him.

Faces loomed out of the fog alongside. He saw them clear as day; Katherine, Mariota, Alison. As he lay there helpless, they caressed him. He writhed to escape but they held him fast, laughing loud, mocking him as he begged for mercy. Then Katherine parted her lips and smiled, and her teeth were sharp as a cat's. He wailed in terror as they all leaned over him. Their lips and tongues nuzzled his skin, then they sank their fearful teeth into his flesh.

When they lifted their heads, their mouths dripped with blood. And all the while they scrabbled deep into his belly, his manhood, with nails like claws so he screamed and whimpered some more.

"—What kind of a cure's this?" Margaret's cry pierced the mists. "He's a thousand times worse now! Are you trying to kill him?"

* * *

At first, Margaret didn't know what the fuss was about. The leech threaded the bodkin, and stitched the wound. John twitched and murmured, but nothing more than that, and when she stroked his hair and talked to him, he'd grow quiet.

Once the wound was closed and bound with a fresh poultice, the leech looked carefully at John's swollen knee. *Too much blood there,* he'd said. *That's why it's so hot and distended.* So he set half-a-dozen strip-like leeches in place around the joint.

The creatures gorged on the blood, growing visibly before their eyes.

Margaret wondered why there was such urgency. *Is he so anxious to get back to Paisley,* she thought, as she watched the leech pluck the plump leeches away and plop them back in their jar. Even when they'd gone, the blood kept coming, marking John's pale skin with bright red trails.

"Fetch some cloth!" the leech instructed. "Put it under him. Quickly!"

What's happening? she wanted to ask William. But she couldn't bother him; he looked pale and frightened as he lifted John's hips and slid a thick folded blanket beneath.

"Hold his legs firm," said the leech. "He mustn't wrench that knee."

"Keep his shoulders steady, Mistress Margaret," William said. "Try and keep him still—"

She tightened her grip just in time. A spasm shook through John. And another, more violent this time. As he fought to breathe, he opened his eyes, and his gaze was glassy, staring.

Oh God help me, Margaret thought. *And God help him, too. He's dying. I just know he is.*

She was living through a nightmare. She had to sit and watch while he screamed and writhed like a tortured soul. She held him down as long as she could, until the vile waste started to come out of him and the leech asked her to clean it all up while he kept holding onto him.

Her stomach turned, but somehow she kept going. She trembled and wept, not because of what she had to do, but because John was so obviously suffering. He howled and thrashed so violently that the bedposts shook.

Eventually he was so spent he couldn't struggle anymore.

He lay there whimpering like a child. Margaret touched his hair and called his name but he didn't respond. It was as if his soul was locked in some horrible place where no-one could reach him.

The leech set a handful of herbs in a bowl, lit a taper in a nearby candle's flame and set the herbs alight. The smell drifted through the room, driving the stench of corruption away. "If he's to recover swiftly, then body and mind must be kept clean and pure," he told Margaret. "Wash him every morning, and pray in his presence as often as you can. He can eat when he's able, but only plain, simple food. Some broth, when he can take it. Or a bowl of brose. Until then, he'd best have water. But it must be blessed."

Margaret nodded, too numb to speak.

Chapter 70

He was lying on his back, stretched out like a corpse, with his hands folded across his chest. His guts burned, as if they were packed with red-hot coals.

He could smell herbs roasting nearby. The coarse warm weight of a cloth pressed against his thighs.

A sudden wave of panic tumbled through him. He didn't want to be placed in the ground with just the cold earth and the worms for company. But when he tried to call out, no sound escaped his lips.

He heard their voices, as the shroud of silence fell away. "There," Margaret said briskly as she patted him dry. "That's much better."

"Cover him, for God's sake," said William. "He'll catch cold."

"But what if he soils himself again? We'll be out of clean sheets by morning." She gave a heartfelt sigh. "I don't know what I'll do if anything happens to him. . ."

She talked as if he were dying. John felt relieved somehow, for it meant that if he waited long enough, the pain would be gone.

Her fingers closed tight about his. "I'm too young to be a widow."

"Don't give up yet," William said.

"You don't understand. . ." Her voice shook. "It's all my fault! I wanted him to die. I prayed to God, and begged Him—"

"Don't talk that way!" William retorted. "He might hear."

"How can he? He'll be dead by morning." She drew a great gulping breath. "I didn't think the brew would kill him!"

He opened his eyes, but could see nothing. He moved parched lips and tried to speak *please, I'm thirsty,* but no sound came.

"Oh, God! He stirred. Did you see? John, can you hear me? John!"

Someone shook him, so hard the fire rekindled in his belly. A tiny moan escaped his lips.

"Be gentle," William said. "He's very weak."

"Give me some water. Quickly."

His head was lifted and a little water poured into his mouth. It soothed at first, but as the cool liquid went down his throat, it made him gag. The pain in his guts flared brighter. His whole frame locked in a fearful spasm, and he whimpered.

Her hand clutched his. "Listen to me, John!" she called. "You have to be strong. D'you hear? It'll pass. And you'll get better."

He squeezed her fingers, but even as he heard her gasp and exclaim that he was back amongst the living, the fog was pulling him back under.

"Come on, John!" Her voice called from afar. "You have to get well. Please. . . You mustn't die."

* * *

Let him rest now, the leech said. *He needs to recover his strength.* He'd used the lull to draw more blood, while William rode out to the chapel to fetch a priest.

Margaret sat hunched in John's big wooden chair, tightly gripping the arms. The priest was chanting away, and still John lay there in that dreadful swoon.

She remembered how she'd endured all this before, throughout the week when her father died. She'd sat there, helpless, praying endlessly to the Virgin and the Saints for help, but it hadn't worked. Her father just faded away before her eyes.

Margaret pulled her knees close and rocked back and forth, too frightened even to weep. *There must be something I can do*, she thought. Then she remembered; there was a holy well beside the chapel. And the leech had said he should drink holy water.

* * *

Margaret walked alone to the well, clutching a heavy flagon and the sark that John had been wearing the day he was wounded. It was a long journey on foot, and she was very tired; she hadn't slept the previous night and her limbs felt like lead. She had to cross the river; she took off her shoes and picked up her skirts and waded through the ford.

She could have had a wagon made ready. She could have had Katherine come with her so she didn't have to carry her burden alone. But it felt better this way. As an extra sign of her penitence, she finished her journey barefoot, hoping Saint Bryde would be inspired by her devotion.

The well was thronged with women, dressed in rough, home-spun clothes. Some were swollen with child, others clutched howling, snot-nosed infants to their breasts. There were young maids, praying to be fruitful in marriage, and old women, bent double and groaning from the pain of aching limbs.

Not so long ago, Margaret would have barged everyone aside and demanded that her needs were more important. Today she just weathered the wait in silence.

An old lady asked what had brought her there.

"My husband's very sick," Margaret said. "I hope Saint Bryde will help him."

They shook their heads and murmured their distress. "I know the laird," one said. "He's a fine man, and we don't want to lose him." One after another, they promised that they'd pray for him.

When her turn came, she stepped up to the well. She filled the flagon, then she dropped to her knees and prayed. *Please, Saint Bryde. Grant him strength. And please let him forgive me for what happened. I said such horrible things, but that was when I didn't know what it would mean to lose him.*

Tearing a strip from his bloodied sark, she tied it on the bough of the gnarled old tree that overhung the spring. Then she heaved the flagon up into her arms and started the long journey back up the hill, to Ellestoun.

* * *

The fog receded. John heard chanting, in the Romish tongue. And smelled sweet herbs, burning nearby.

A hand lifted his head. "Come on now," she said. "Let me help you."

He opened his eyes, and saw her leaning close. She had such a lovely face, filled with light and radiating goodness. She seemed familiar somehow, but he couldn't think where he'd seen her before.

She raised a bowl to his lips and trickled cool water into his mouth. He swallowed, overwhelmed by emotion. "Sancta Maria," he whispered.

"No, John," she said. "It's Margaret. I went away, but now I'm back, and I'll stay by you till you're better, I promise."

"Sancta Margereta," he said, and he smiled. He wasn't frightened anymore. She'd look after him, and keep him safe from harm.

* * *

Margaret washed him again that night. She started with his face, taking great care not to aggravate his wounds, then moved onto his body. She whispered reassuring words to him, but he didn't respond.

Tending him this closely brought a new intimacy that touched her deeply. She saw the way the hairs stood taut upon his arms, and how the muscles moved beneath his skin. She saw all this, and marvelled at it. She thanked God for making him so beautiful, and for allowing her to witness his beauty at such close quarters.

Once she'd washed him, she combed his hair, so it was free of knots and hanging loose about his pillow. She pulled the covers up over him, then retreated to his chair, where she settled with a sigh.

William sat close by, keeping silent vigil. He'd hardly strayed from John's bedside all through the day.

Margaret regarded him wearily. "He knew this would happen, didn't he?"

William hesitated. "Yes."

"Then whatever possessed him to do it?"

He dropped his head in his hands. "I don't know."

Margaret mulled it over in her mind, but could make no sense of it. *Did he want to die?* she wondered, and the thought hurt so much that she had to push it aside. "I've been in this gown two days," she complained. "I stink."

"You've done enough," William said. "Get to your bed."

"I told him I'd sit with him." She shifted uncomfortably. "But my arms ache so. And my back, too. I don't think I'll be able to sleep here."

"Then slip in beside him," he said. "He'd understand."

She wasn't sure he would. "I couldn't."

"Might do him the world of good, to know there's someone there with him."

* * *

Margaret lifted a handful of her kirtle and sniffed in disapproval; it was damp and smelly from the heat. She wondered what was worse; to taint John's clean flesh with her dirty clothes or to taint his unconscious thoughts by lying too close.

She wriggled out of her kirtle, then slid into the bed.

The mattress felt comfortable, so she snuggled deep. She tried not to think of him lying there, within reach of her hand, but his scent was all around her, not stale and foul now, but fresh, bittersweet.

She settled close. *It won't hurt, just to touch him. . .* She laid her head against his back, marvelled at the slow thump of his heartbeat, the heat of his skin against her cheek. She breathed deep, intoxicated with joy because he lay so still and calm alongside.

God, give me strength. Deliver me from temptation. . .

She slid her arm about his waist. His flank heaved in steady rhythm as he breathed. As she held him loosely in her embrace, Margaret trembled, filled with such longing that she could scarcely think. She pressed her flesh against his own; he was warm, vital.

I think I love you, she thought. *But it's too late now, isn't it? You don't love me. . .*

Chapter 71

John opened his eyes, to see daylight flooding the room.

She was there at his bedside. Curled up in his chair, with her legs drawn close and a grubby-soled foot showing pale beneath the heavy mass of her skirts. With her hair hanging soft and unbound about her shoulders, she looked young, vulnerable.

His eyes filled with tears; there was so much he wanted to tell her, but he was too frightened to speak, in case it all went wrong and his memories of this moment were spoilt forever.

She shifted with a moan, head sagging. And there was no longer anything beautiful or sacred about the scene; she was just a careworn young woman, racked with exhaustion.

"Margaret. . ."

She started, then scrambled to her feet, eyes wide. "Oh, John!" She leaned over him, cradling his head in her arm. She brushed some hairs back from his brow, smiling. "You're awake. Thank God." Her lips pressed light against his forehead.

When he tried to sit up, she laid a firm hand against his chest. "No!" she scolded. "You're still very frail. We thought we'd lose you, but you're through the worst. There's colour back in your face."

He let her finish, saying nothing.

"Are you in pain?" she asked at last.

"My leg's throbbing. And my head. . ."

"That's all?"

"I feel sick, and so very weak. Like a husk of myself." He swallowed. His throat was dry, his tongue felt furred and thick. "What happened?"

"You don't remember?"

Memories lurked at the edge of his thoughts. Scattered fragments of a time that was dark, and horrible. "I dreamed, I think."

She gripped his hand. "The leech said it would be this way, that you wouldn't remember."

"Remember what?"

"It was as if you were possessed. You screamed and struggled so hard that we could hardly hold you. We tried to calm you, but you couldn't see us, and you couldn't hear us, and when you were too exhausted to fight anymore, you just lay there and cried and it was the most horrible thing—"

"You shouldn't have stayed."

"I thought you'd die. The priest came and absolved your sins. But William said I shouldn't give up hope. So I prayed for you. I asked God and the Saints to spare you, and they listened!"

"My throat. It's so dry—"

A huge smile lit her face. "I'm sorry! You're thirsty, and all I can do is prattle on about how hideous it was, and how pleased I am to see you."

She patted his shoulder, then she was gone.

He closed his eyes, while she fumbled around nearby. She was humming to herself as she poured liquid from a flagon.

"Here. Try and lift your head, and I'll steady you." She slipped a hand behind his shoulders, and lifted the bowl with the other. "It's water," she explained. "It's from Saint Bryde's Well. I asked her for help, John, and she's looking after you, so you mustn't be afraid."

* * *

Katherine hung a fresh gown over the back of the chair. "I don't know how you survived here," she said.

Margaret dried her breasts and shoulders one last time, saying nothing.

"He's poor company at the best of times," Katherine continued. "You'd get better conversation from a corpse."

"He's sleeping," Margaret said. "He won't hear you. And I'm not interested."

"I said you'd soften." Katherine helped her into her gown. "Is he that wondrous to look upon?" She drew the laces tight.

Margaret didn't deign to reply.

"Shall I bind your hair?"

"If you like."

"There," Katherine said, once the hood was in place. "You look better now."

"You can go."

"How is he?" Katherine paused by the bed.

Obscured beneath the coverlet, he was barely visible. Even so, Margaret felt the hairs on the back of her neck prickle. "He's still very weak," she said. "But he'll get better."

Katherine clutched her sleeve. "Please let me see him," she whispered. "Just a little look."

"Absolutely not."

"But it won't hurt! He'll never even know. . ." Before Margaret could stop her, Katherine twitched the coverlet aside; it slid down, exposing his shoulders, his back, where fading bruises still marred his flesh.

Burning with outrage, Margaret snatched Katherine's hand and hauled her away. "How dare you!"

Katherine's eyes welled with tears. "I meant no harm! I thought—"

"Not a word about those times. Not a single word!" She tugged the bedclothes back into place.

He stirred, mumbling incoherently, so she sat beside him, stroking his hair. "Hush," she sighed. "Be calm, my sweet love. I'm here with you."

Katherine giggled. "Oh, Margaret! How your cold, stern heart has thawed. . ."

William's knock sounded. "Mistress Margaret, are you decent?"

"Come in, William."

"There's visitors," he said. "Can you attend?"

Margaret glowered at Katherine. "Upstairs," she said. "William, stay with him, please."

* * *

"Mistress Colville." The burgess bowed.

She remembered him. He was one of the ones who'd visited before. "How can I be of help, Master, em—"

"—Mossman, my lady. Mossman." He looked hopefully at her. "I wondered if I might speak with your husband?"

"He's resting in his chamber. I believe he was involved in some kind of altercation at the wappenschaw." She hoped that was a good enough explanation.

"Oh, dear." He wrung his bonnet. "That's what he told you? That there was an altercation?"

"Yes, why?"

Mossman's broad face beamed bright. "Such a noble gentleman!" he gasped. "I've never known such modesty."

She frowned. "Whatever do you mean?"

"Mistress Colville, he saved the town. The Montgomeries and the Cunninghames. . . They waged war in the streets, and he wouldn't stand for it. He charged into the melee and hauled them back, heedless of the dangers."

"I had no idea."

"We brought tokens of our gratitude. We wanted to present them to him ourselves, but if he's not available, then I hope you'll accept them in his stead."

He gestured to his companions, who stepped forward, and like the Wise Men from the Orient, presented her with packages. And once that was done, Mossman explained that there were more gifts waiting in the carts below.

They went to the yard and Margaret watched in disbelief as the servants unloaded everything. The burgesses had brought coal, beeswax and salt. Some pots of spices, and a big round cheese from Italy. There was a fine hawking glove for John, a smaller one for herself, and a bright-eyed tersal in a cage, which sported a speckled breast and vicious-looking talons and bill. There were three bundles of linen and another three of silk, and a splendid bridle for a horse. And, last of all, there were some elegant lace handkerchiefs from Flanders.

It was all very exciting. But she was getting quite adept at masking her true thoughts. She just folded her hands before her, and gave a benevolent smile. "Thank you, Master Mossman," she said. "You've been most generous."

* * *

That night, Margaret stared out through near-darkness while John slept alongside, his limbs touching hers. She felt the heat of his flesh, and could hardly sleep for the dark thoughts that filled her head. She fancied that she was an Amazonian princess, and that he was a captive Greek warrior who'd been brought to her, wounded, for her to take to her bed before they gave him to their heathen gods as sacrifice.

Margaret shivered. The strength of her desire frightened her. So too did the prospect of losing him, either through death, or, as seemed more likely, through his indifference.

Overcome with fear and loneliness, she hugged him tightly. She wished the night would stretch on forever, that he would remain like this, calm and peaceful.

She dreaded the time when his health was restored. She'd always found him so difficult to comprehend. At best he was distant and unfeeling; at worst, terrifying.

She propped herself up with a sigh. When she moved, he stirred and mumbled something, settling close; she hoped he'd wake so she could tell him how much she loved and desired him, but he didn't.

She brushed his hair back from his face and kissed his cheek. Then she leaned right over and kissed him once on the lips.

He still didn't respond. Half-disappointed, half-relieved, she lay back down again and drifted off to sleep.

* * *

When she tended him the following morning, his limbs weren't a dead weight in her hands. "Are you awake?" she asked.

"Almost," he murmured.

Her heart fluttered. "How long—"

"Since you started pouring water all over me."

Margaret smiled at that. Once she'd dried him, she removed the dressing from his thigh. There was still a fear that the flesh would turn bad. William said she'd know if the worst happened, that the smell would be so putrid that she'd want to be sick. If that happened, John's leg might be lost, and possibly the rest of him, too. William said that some wounds wept and oozed for years, never healing.

But when she lifted the dressing to her nose and sniffed it, all she could smell was crushed herbs and honey. She swabbed the wound with more *aqua vita*, then inspected it closely.

"How is it?" he asked.

"Healing nicely."

"Thank God," he said.

"The burgesses came."

"Oh?" He didn't sound too interested.

"They wanted to thank you. They painted a glorious picture of your heroic deeds."

"They're exaggerating."

* * *

He took a little ale, and then some broth with bread torn up in it. But he couldn't eat much, and soon asked to be laid back down again.

"I still feel sick," he complained, when she scolded him.

"I suppose it's understandable." She paused. "John, why did you take the draught?"

"It's what you wanted."

She didn't know what to say. The implications frightened her; that he'd known he faced death, but he hadn't cared.

She supposed he was jesting. "You look so much better," she said. "You're more like yourself now the swelling's going down."

"Where are my hounds?"

"They're staying with Henry. I didn't want them here. They smell so. It's not good, when a man's in his sickbed."

He didn't answer.

"Shall I read to you?" she asked.

"If you like."

She plucked his bible from the bedside. She chose the Gospel of Saint John, because it was the words of his own saint.

He lay there with his eyes closed throughout. She wasn't sure if he was listening or if he'd fallen asleep, but she kept plodding on regardless, until she'd finished the last line.

"Did you like that?" she asked.

He opened his eyes. "Your pronunciation's awful," he said. "Did you learn your Latin from the altar boy?"

"That's not very fair—" But she had no chance to defend herself, because William was knocking on the door.

"The Laird of Hessilhead is waiting in the hall," William said. "He wants to speak to the master."

"I don't want to speak to him," John murmured. "Margaret, deal with him, please."

* * *

"He asked me to see you," Margaret said, firmly.

Hessilhead paced back and forth before the fireplace. "I want to talk to him."

She halted before the door, so he couldn't charge up the stairs without hurling her aside first. "He's not well."

He stopped, eyes gleaming bright with feral fury. "What've you done to him, witch?"

"What do you want with him?" Somehow, she kept her voice calm.

"There's been rumours." Hessilhead's voice was cold, hostile. "Rumours that Ellestoun's been close to death for three damned days." He stalked close, halting face-to-face with her. "It's your fault, isn't it? You poisoned him!" He pushed her, roughly.

Margaret swallowed. "No, it wasn't. I didn't know."

"When I tell my kinsman of this, there'll be trouble."

She glared up at him. "You've no right to talk to me this way!" she snapped. "It's all your fault this happened in the first place. And it's *his* fault, too. That arrogant kinsman of yours! I don't care if he's a Lord, and a favourite of the King. I hate him. And John hates him, too. We don't need you."

He gripped her shoulders tightly. "If anything ill befalls Ellestoun," he said, thrusting his bearded face into her own, "then we'll have you strangled and burned like the foul witch you are."

"Get out!" she snapped. "William? Fetch the men-at-arms!"

"I'm leaving," Hessilhead said. "Pray your husband makes a quick recovery. Or I'll be back to drag you off in chains."

* * *

John struggled to sit. "What happened?" he asked. "I heard shouting."

She sank down in the chair. Her limbs were trembling; she didn't know whether it was from fear or relief. "He said horrible things. He blamed me for what happened. He called me a witch. . ." Remembering Hessilhead's evil threats, she burst into tears. "Oh, John. I didn't want any of this." Her strength had gone, she felt too weak even to hold up her head. Sinking into her chair, she folded her arms upon the bed, buried her face in her sleeves, and howled, overwhelmed by anguish and exhaustion.

"Hush now." He gently stroked her head.

"I tried so hard to be a good wife," she sobbed. "To look after the place. To look after you. . ."

"You did a splendid job. I'm proud of you."

"Are you?" She looked up, wide-eyed and hopeful.

"Yes." He was smiling faintly. "I am."

* * *

John dreamed that night. He dreamed he lay warm in another's arms, while hands caressed him softly.

He didn't welcome such intimacy, but when he tried to struggle, his limbs were too weak to move. He could only lie there as she pushed her body close, her breasts pressing firm against his chest, her lips moving hungrily at his throat.

John thought he was dead, that he'd paid for his adultery with Damnation, condemned to lie helpless as a nighthag toyed with his flesh for all eternity.

Then he opened his eyes to darkness, and drew a sharp breath.

She lay alongside, clutching him close. Her flesh was hot beneath her linen kirtle, her scent all around him, musky warmth mingling with the smell of roses. Murmuring quiet words, she pulled him closer still.

The crippling confusion was gone. He knew where he was, and who was lying with him. He was still fearful, uncertain, but his prick had a will of its own. He felt a brief glow of warmth in his loins, but the bliss it brought was quickly gone. His seed spilled out, he choked back a sob.

She jerked away. "John?"

The elegance of her strategy stole his breath away. For three long days she'd been kind; she'd worked hard to win his trust so when she struck the hurt would be a thousand times worse. He wished he'd been wise enough to foresee the consequences, but like a fool he'd trusted her. He was too tired, too weak, to care anymore; he wept, overwhelmed with loneliness.

"John, please!" She gripped his shoulders, but when he gasped and froze, she let him go again. "It was a bad dream. Just be patient and I'll clean you up."

He was still too ashamed to reply.

She pulled back the coverlet and wiped his loins, then sat beside him with knees clasped close, rocking back and forth. "God forgive me!" She thumped the mattress with her fist, so hard he flinched. "I never wanted to upset you. I just-" She slipped her arms around him, a shudder shook her slight frame. "I should go. . ."

He wasn't sure if her embrace brought consolation or yet more misery. But the thought of lying there alone brought more terror than having her by his side. "Please don't leave me." he whispered.

"I won't." She took him in her arms again, and this time, he nestled close. He breathed in her scent, as her heart pulsed strong alongside, and his desolation stung deeper then ever. He twisted his fingers into the cloth of her kirtle and silent sobs tore through him.

"Oh, John," she whispered, clutching his head against her breast. "Be brave, you silly old goose. You'll get better."

He trembled as her breath caressed his hair. "It's not that—" Closing his eyes, he steeled himself to say the words, before the moment was gone forever. "I *love* you, Margaret."

She lightly kissed his head. "Are you still feverish?"

"No, I just had to say—"

"You're talking nonsense. Now will you sleep? Or shall I fetch a draught?"

"I'll sleep. I just want to know you're here with me."

"I'll be here. Now just lay down properly." Her fingers teased through his hair.

As he settled beside her, he tried to convince himself that he'd misunderstood everything; that despite all the cruel things she'd said since the wedding, she genuinely cared for him. She kept stroking his hair, his shoulders, whispering kind words all the while, and gradually the panic and fear faded.

He drifted off.

When he next awoke, she'd gone. It was still dark, and he lay there in his bed, unsettled, wondering whether he'd imagined everything.

But if he breathed in deep, he could still smell the scent of roses on his pillow.

* * *

Margaret sat hunched in the bower, knees drawn close, arms folded tight before her. She'd hoped to find solace here, with the scent of the roses hanging heavy all around her, but as the morning crept on she just felt worse.

When she'd tended him that morning, he'd changed. He complied without question when she washed him, but he wouldn't look her in the eye, he wouldn't talk, and every time she laid a hand upon him, his muscles would lock tight with apprehension.

She didn't know what to say. She was too embarrassed to speak about what had happened the previous night. She was too embarrassed to say anything at all.

She'd asked William to spend some time with him, since she couldn't face him. The leech had come back, too, so she supposed John had other things to concern him.

He said he loved you. . . Her spirits lifted a little, then promptly foundered. She kept recalling all the times she'd taunted him, and then she'd cringe, her misery would swell and she'd weep some more.

She supposed that justice had been served. For so long, she'd hoped and prayed that he would fall in love with her. She'd wanted him to burn with desire for her, to know that she haunted his thoughts endlessly. She'd wanted him to endure the torment of having his love spurned, to know he wasn't worthy of winning her heart.

Now she was suffering the fate she'd wished upon him, and she hated it more than anything on earth.

All I want is to hold him in my arms. To hear him say that he loves me, one more time.

"Mistress Margaret?"

She looked up to see William standing over her. She forced a smile. "How can I help you?"

He clutched his bonnet tight in his hands. "The leech is finished now. Master John had an awful time of it; the leech opened a vein in his back to try and get some of the bad blood away. I thought you might want to come in and cheer him."

Margaret closed her eyes, biting back tears. "I'm sorry, William. I can't."

He didn't reply at first. She could sense his bewilderment. "He was in much better spirits when you were there yesterday," he said, eventually.

She studied the ground. "I can't talk to him. Please, William. Go back inside. Be there for him."

* * *

John lay back against his pillow, eyes closed. Today, efforts had been made to tackle the melancholy. A pint of blood had been drawn off him; he'd been given some spiced wine afterwards, to heat the blood, and William was given strict instructions to ensure that he received plenty of red meat to fire his temperament.

His head was spinning, he felt weak as a child. It was disappointing, because yesterday he'd thought his strength was returning.

It's God's way of telling you to rest, the leech had said.

John didn't argue. He'd obediently taken a bowl of broth, just to reassure the leech. He hadn't really been that hungry, and he'd felt a little sick afterwards.

* * *

Throughout the day, he drowsed. Then later in the evening, he revived a little. He hadn't given much thought to Margaret's absence before, but he thought about it now. As his strength returned, he remembered the past few days more clearly, and his recollections disturbed him.

Though Margaret had treated him kindly and with tenderness, John knew her well enough. If there was anything she despised in a man, it was weakness. He'd been weak, and she'd been there to witness every sordid detail.

She wouldn't forget. She'd be mocking him now. Sitting in her room, with Katherine, and the others. Laughing as she told them how she'd won his trust when he lay there helpless in her arms.

He'd tried so many times to convince himself that some day he'd win her heart through valour and acclaim. He'd hoped that once he'd won himself a good reputation at court and gained favour with the King, she'd think he merited her love.

But it had all gone wrong. Now every time she set eyes on him, all she'd see was the hopeless, broken creature she'd nursed through his illness.

Chapter 72

It was still early. The shutters were open, the sky bright, but the air was cool and the sun wasn't yet slanting through the windows.

"How long have I been lying here?" John asked.

"This is the fourth day," William said.

John counted the days off in his head. Something niggled. "What day is it?"

William paused. "St. Barnabas. Day," he said, at last.

St. Barnabas' Day. The eleventh of June.

"Oh, God. . ." John tried to sit.

"What're you doing?" William leapt to his feet. Too late; John had already pushed the covers aside and stumbled out of bed.

"I missed the obit. I can't miss his Mass—" John felt suddenly cold. "The piss-pot. . . Quickly!" He held himself together just long enough; no sooner had William passed him the pot before he'd heaved up the contents of his stomach.

"This is foolhardy," William said.

John wiped a hand against his lips. His limbs were trembling; he grasped the bed-post with both hands to stay upright. "It's my duty." He straightened, slowly. "Now get me washed and dressed."

* * *

William gripped his arm to help him stand, until a priest took pity on him and brought a stool.

John sank gratefully down. He stared at the altar as the singing started. Its weaving beauty struck a painful resonance within; he bowed his head and wept.

He wasn't sure if his tears were for his father, or for himself. He didn't miss his father as a friend. He'd scarcely known him; Sir Thomas had been so distant, disinterested in anything beyond his duties to King and household.

Back then, John had always been overlooked and under-valued. He'd resented it no end. But life had been simpler, more innocent. A year later, he thought he might buckle beneath the weight of his responsibilities.

Dusty sunlight filtered through the glass windows and settled all around. Herbs and flowers were strewn upon the tiled floor, their scent soothed him as he cast his gaze towards the carved tombstone near the altar. *I hope the trials of Purgatory aren't proving too much, Father. Don't despair; we'll try and smooth your path.*

Perhaps his father was the lucky one, for sometimes it felt as if life here on earth *was* Purgatory; an endless rocky path which brought nothing but pain, trial and humiliation. Just when he'd scrambled out of one black pit, he'd slide into another.

Hands were laid upon his shoulder; someone gently kissed his head. He looked up, and there was his mother, smiling through tears. He laid a hand on hers, grateful for her comfort.

Reconciled by their loss, they watched in silence as the priest drew them deep into the magic of the soul mass.

* * *

"You should have a stick," Elizabeth Ross said, as they wandered through the churchyard together.

"Don't be ridiculous!" he retorted. But when she offered her arm, he was glad to accept it.

"It'll mend sooner," she persisted. "In fact. . ." She halted. "You shouldn't be here. He'd have understood."

"I had to come."

Lady Elizabeth patted his hand. "You're a good boy, John." She studied him intently. "You look terrible," she said. "I'm so sorry I didn't come to your bedside. I didn't know. William came when he could, bless him, but by then the worst was over." Lips pursed, she shook her head. "That wicked girl—"

"It was my choice. Not hers"

"—She should've listened to William. She thinks she knows everything, the vixen."

John stared ahead. "Is the dower-house comfortable?"

"Oh, yes. It's quiet, though. I miss the bustle sometimes. And I miss my son. I know you're busy, but I'd like it very much if you'd visit." She looked hopeful. "Would you do that?"

He smiled. "Of course."

"There's one thing. . ." She paused, then, "It's perhaps not the right time, but I hardly see you these days, and I have to know. Is she with child?"

"Not yet."

"Saints preserve us!" His mother crossed herself. "If she's good for nothing else, she should at least be bearing you children." She tightened her grip. "Are you putting it in the right place?"

His face coloured. "Of course!"

"Then why isn't she with child? It's not necessarily her fault. Do you please her? Do you wash before you take her—"

"Stop that!" John snapped.

"You're far too lenient," his mother continued. "You feed her, you clothe her and you give her a roof over her head. Least she could in return is provide you with children."

* * *

"You should rest now," William said.

"I'll sit in the garden. Fetch me in an hour or two."

William shrugged. He helped John down from the cart and steadied him as he limped along the cinder path. It was a slow journey, but at last John settled on a bench in the shadow of the rose trees.

"Don't do anything foolish," William warned.

"I'll sit quietly," John told him. "Send the hounds. I could do with some company."

* * *

John spotted the hounds at last, trotting out from the gates of the barmkin. "Caesar!" he called. "Pompey! Come on now."

Hearing his voice, they tore through the garden at a gallop. They skidded to a standstill before him, tails thrashing; they whined in pathetic delight as he fondled their ears and clapped them so hard he nearly bowled them over. Eventually they settled, slouching at his feet, their long heads stretched out along sleek forelimbs.

John breathed deep, savouring the scent of the flowers. Bees buzzed industrious paths around his ears, birds twittered in the nearby fruit trees. Stretching his leg before him, John sighed as the sun's warmth eased the throb in his knee.

His eyes closed, he drowsed with the heat. And little by little, the melancholy lifted, like the mist burning off on an autumn morning.

Peals of girlish laughter rang out nearby and John sat up, heart lurching. Opening his eyes, he saw her. Striding along the path towards him, her skirts pushing aside the heavy blooms of poppies and paeonies.

The hounds stood erect, stiff with suspicion. Pompey bayed, throaty displeasure.

"Quiet!" John bellowed, and they cowered back down.

Margaret cast them a cautious glance, then settled beside him. She smoothed out her skirts with a sigh.

John reached down and rubbed Caesar's ear. He didn't know what to say. The scent of her perfume brought it all back; disjointed images, snatches of conversation, her teasing presence in the darkness. He wondered what had moved her that night she'd slipped in beside him. Whether it was lust, or just plain cruelty.

He blushed and looked away. Clasping his hands before him, he frowned at the ground.

She laid a gentle hand upon his arm. "You should be in your bed."

"I needed some fresh air."

"Don't you know how sick you were? I thought I'd lose you."

"I'm sorry I disappointed you," he retorted. "Some more henbane in the draught would've solved everything."

"John!"

He had to escape, before he broke down and wept. Eyes blurring, he lurched to his feet, and blundered blindly off up the path, a wounded stag making one last attempt to flee the hounds. He needed William's assistance; he had the awful feeling that at any moment his leg would seize completely and he'd be left in an undignified heap on the ground.

"Wait!" Margaret trotted up behind him. "What're you doing? Sit down, and I'll fetch William."

"I'm alright."

"No, you're not." Her voice was tight with reproach. "You're white as a sheet and the sweat's pouring off you. Let me help you."

He stopped and shrugged, exhaustedly.

"Why are you so proud?" she complained, settling under his shoulder and slipping her arm about his waist. "You'll achieve nothing by pretending that all's well. You'll kill yourself."

John sighed, and focussed his gaze upon Ellestoun. It might've been a dozen miles away.

Margaret walked patiently alongside. "Let me find William."

"I'm alright!" he snapped again. Then he gasped as he misplaced his footing and his knee buckled.

"Oh, be careful!" Her fingers tightened against his side.

He twitched and jerked himself taller. "Did the leech say anything?" he asked. "About how well I'd recover? I'll not make much of a knight if I'm left lame."

"He said you needed rest, and peaceful contemplation. You're not getting either, are you? If you end up a cripple, it'll be your own fault for being so stubborn."

He gave up trying to talk to her after that.

* * *

"I have to rest." John slumped at the threshold of the tower-house, laying his head against folded arms.

Margaret crouched alongside. "Shall I fetch William?"

"I'll manage." Breathing deep, he took her hand, and hauled himself to his feet.

The stairs loomed beyond.

Gripping her shoulder, he staggered up them. Every so often he stumbled, and stifled a moan. Whenever he did, Margaret clutched him closer; by the time they'd reached his chamber, he was hanging heavy round her neck.

At last she had him lying safe on his bed.

He flung an arm over his eyes, chest heaving.

"You must rest now." Margaret picked up his feet and pulled off his shoes. Once that was done, she loosened his belt. "Shall I stay with you?" She sat down on the bed beside him. "I could read to you."

He didn't reply.

"I'll go then." She walked to the door. She hoped he'd call her back, but he didn't. He just stayed silent.

He'd rebuffed her yet again. She should have guessed he would. Angry disappointment engulfed her; she fought back tears. "How can you be so cold?" she demanded. "I sat by your bedside for three days. I changed that stinking poultice and I kept you clean. I even held the piss-pot straight for you."

"Stop worrying me! You're like a dog with a rabbit."

Her face glowed hot. "I can't do anything right!"

"Nor can I." He fought back a sob. "Why do you treat me so unkindly? I try, so very hard, to make things better. But it's not enough. It's never enough. . ."

She'd expected anger. Not this sudden outpouring of despair. It unnerved her; she didn't know how to respond. "John, please!"

He sat up, eyes bright, desperate. "What more can I give you?" His voice shook. "Shall I cut open a vein, and offer you some blood?"

"Don't talk this way."

"—I could slice off my manhood. You could feed it to the dogs. Here—" He pulled his dagger from his belt and hurled it. It clattered to the floor at her feet, making her shriek and shrink back. "If abusing me would bring you pleasure, then do so. With my blessing. I don't care anymore."

"You mustn't say such things!" Margaret picked up the dagger with shaking hands. "You're frightening me."

"I wish to God I'd never set eyes on you." He sounded fierce, but there were tears running down his face. "I wish I was dead. . ."

Margaret swallowed. "Don't be like this. Please. . ." Dropping the dagger, she rushed to his side, and threw her arms around him.

He hurled her aside. "Leave me!" He rolled over, shoulders shaking as he wept.

She approached cautiously, and laid a hand upon his shoulder.

He didn't respond.

"I'm sorry," she whispered. "I never thought I'd cause such hurt." Unsure what else to say, she retreated from his side and left the room as quietly as she could.

* * *

For three days John lay in his bed. He'd wept for the best part of a day, then after that, nothing. He no longer had the strength to love, or hate, or feel anything more than a chill ashen emptiness inside.

He'd let them down. All those ancestors who'd fought so hard to bring success to the family. His coffers were almost empty. His tenants hated him because he'd been unable to protect them through the winter. He'd shown appalling judgement by pledging his friendship to the man who'd slain his father. Though he supposed he'd received his just reward for *that* mistake over the last few weeks...

And Margaret. . .

He'd heard her talking with William as he lay in his sickbed. She'd said she'd prayed to God that he might die.

Marion had talked that way. About their father. To think Margaret harboured such ill-feeling towards him hurt more deeply than he'd ever thought possible.

She'd knocked upon his door countless times over the past few days, begging to see him. But John hadn't responded. He'd felt too weary, too overwhelmed with his worries.

Claws scrabbled outside his room, the door opened. In bounded Caesar and Pompey; they crossed the floor in three long strides and leapt onto his bed, tails wagging. John tried to push them away, for they were treading hard paws all over him. There was no shifting them; they thrust eager muzzles into his face and licked him, whining all the while.

William slouched at the doorway. "It's a fine day," he said. "Let's hunt."

Chapter 73
Edinburgh Castle, 18ᵗʰ June, 1489

Hugh had little patience when it came to Chancery business. When Robert Colville hunted for witnesses to the never-ending stream of charters that passed before the King's eyes, Hugh made sure he was elsewhere.

But there were exceptions to every rule.

"His Grace the King decrees," Robert Colville announced, "that Hugh, the Lord Montgomerie, be granted for life, the lands and lordship of Bute, with all commodities and profits, and the power to assign tenancies as he sees fit. For this privilege, he will pay the King the sum of one hundred and forty-one pounds, yearly—"

Hugh settled more comfortably into his chair. Once hundred and forty-one pounds was a substantial amount, but it was a worthy investment. The island of Bute yielded rich harvests, when the Islesmen didn't pillage its fields and byres. And more lands meant more men, a bigger force with which to keep the Cunninghames in check.

He flexed his fingers before him as Colville continued, "The King further decrees that Hugh, the Lord Montgomerie, be granted for life, the Custody of the Royal Castle of Rothesay, in the Lordship of Bute. For which office he will receive forty merks yearly—" Colville cleared his throat and discreetly sipped some wine. "And lastly, His Grace the King decrees that Hugh, the Lord Montgomerie, be granted the offices of Justiciar and Overlord of Arran and Bute, with the right to impose the King's justice throughout the bounds of these lands, and the power to approve the curates of all parish churches therein—"

* * *

"You're satisfied, I hope?" Patrick Hepburn fell into step beside him.

Hugh bowed his head. "I'm most grateful for the King's generosity. I remain his humble and obedient servant."

Earl Patrick's glance was scathing.

"What about the bombards?" Hugh asked.

"They'll sail to Stirling, then travel by road to Glasgow. We'll take Cruikston and Duchal first; Dumbarton will take somewhat longer. We'll starve them out if necessary."

"A good suggestion."

"I hope your man lives up to expectation," Hepburn grumbled. "He won't know one end of a bombard from the other."

"There's nothing to know," Hugh countered. "He can just point the damned thing in the right direction and wait for the bang. Besides—" he added, "—he'll do what he's told."

"He's his father's son," Hepburn said. "Bear in mind I want Duchal captured. Not reduced to rubble."

"Don't fret," Hugh told him. "I'll keep Master Sempill on a very tight rein."

* * *

All this good fortune left Hugh feeling unusually well-disposed towards the world; normally he thought that charity should begin at home, but tonight he felt much more generous and accommodating

He took to the town after dinner, and gave three silver pennies to a lame old man he met by the mercat cross. *Lost a leg the day King James died at Roxburgh,* the old man said.

After making some appropriately sympathetic noises, Hugh continued on his way. He gave another two pennies to a blind child begging for alms near the fleshmarket, then on a whim, he had Zephyr saddled.

He set off for Leith with a brace of men-at-arms for company. A few well-placed bribes and he found the place he sought; a vaulted strong room close to the harbour.

He knocked on the door of the adjoining house.

A plump merchant answered. "My lord?" he bowed low. "How can I assist?"

"You're holding an item in your stores. A suit of mail. It was shipped from the Low Countries eighteen months ago."

"There's not many of those about." The merchant's gaze flicked warily beyond Hugh, to the men-at-arms who loitered in the wynd.

"Sir Thomas Sempill made the purchase."

"Ah, yes."

"I want to uplift it."

"Begging your pardon, my lord—"

Hugh caught his retainers' glances briefly; they stood tall, hands on sword hilts, as Hugh seized the merchant's gown and hauled him close. "Do you know who I am?"

"Er, yes, my lord. I—"

"I assured Sir Thomas Sempill's heir that I would have his arms transported to the Westland with my own baggage before the month was out. I gave him my word."

"I'm sorry—"

"My men will return tomorrow. See it's ready." He released the sweating merchant, then, as a parting gesture, pressed a gold coin into the man's damp palm.

"Delighted to be of service, Lord Hugh," the merchant called.

Hugh smiled as he climbed onto Zephyr's back. *What a noble thing it is,* he thought, *to help a friend in need.*

* * *

It took a team of sixteen oxen to drag Mons Meg from her quarters at Edinburgh Castle, and a further sixteen to haul her sister. For two hours the oxen toiled through rutted, cobbled streets thronged by eager spectators. More carts followed on behind, laden high with barrels of powder and heavy stone cannon balls.

Eventually, the cavalcade halted at the dockside, where a line of barges waited.

Meg was prepared first, her iron barrel wrapped in a cradle of ropes and straps. Once that was done, Patrick Hepburn checked the lashings.

366

Young James peered over his shoulder. "She seems secure."

"Indeed, Your Grace," said Earl Patrick.

"Alright!" James stepped back. He waved to the waiting labourers. "Let's begin."

The cradle groaned as Meg's vast barrel slowly lifted from the carriage. The jib of the crane creaked and swayed.

Earl Patrick drew a sharp breath, and Hugh lowered his head in silent prayer. The bombard climbed its perilous way upwards; one snapped rope, one broken timber, and the pride of the King's artillery would plummet to rest on the dockside, or at the bottom of the Forth.

Or even, Heaven forbid, on top of *them*.

The jib swung out. High above, Mons Megs' bulk eclipsed the sun. Hugh raised a hand to shield his eyes, unable to look away as Meg rocked gently over their heads.

"That's it!" Adam Hepburn, Patrick's eldest, called out from the barge. "She's in place."

The ropes were wound back, and Meg jolted her tortuous way down. With a hefty thud, she settled against the deck, the barge sagging beneath her weight.

Meg was safe; they could all breathe again.

Walls Hill, Near Ellestoun

A hare burst out from the clump of coarse grass, eyes bulging, ears laid flat against its back. It had the edge at first, but the hounds were on it. Their lithe bodies rippled along at a gallop, their tongues lolling loose as they flung all their strength into the chase. Sensing its peril, the hare jerked and twisted, but the hounds matched it move for move.

John strode after them. His pace quickened to a trot, then, when his knee suffered no ill-effects, he chanced a run. Ahead, the hounds darted, pale, wraith-like, as they pressed the frantic hare back onto its line.

"Go on!" John urged. He pushed himself onwards, revelling in every heartbeat, every fresh lungful of air.

Pompey put in a last burst of speed. The young dog reached the prey first, closing its jaws about the hare's shoulders and lifting it clean from the ground. The hare kicked out, squealing, as it was shaken roughly then tossed high into the air.

Caesar stood back, tail wagging. Pompey, however, forgot his work was done, moving in for the kill as the hare thudded limp to the ground.

"Pompey, no!" John yelled, and when his command had no effect, he put in one last sprint. He slapped the hound aside. "Away with you!"

Pompey sank in submission, whining. John ignored the dog; he picked up the shuddering wreck of the hare and dispatched it quickly with a practised wrench of the neck.

"You've lost the limp!" William called after him.

Letting the hare fall, John braced hands on knees while he recovered his breath. He straightened, grasped the hare's corpse by the hind paws and slung it over his shoulder. He signalled to Pompey, who stopped cringing and crowded close against him.

John ruffled the dog's ears. "Need to curb those teeth a little. . ." He wandered over to the high earthen rampart that bounded the old camp and settled down in the grass to rest in the sunlight. The hounds wandered off, sniffing through the herbs that grew deep in the ditch.

"All this walking," John said. "It makes a man hungry. I don't suppose you brought. . ."

William smiled. "Of course." He delved into his pack. Pulling out a cloth-wrapped package, he handed it to John. Inside was a fresh loaf, and some thick slices of meat.

"God bless you, William!" John tore the loaf in two, and handed a portion back.

"We should head back soon," William said between mouthfuls.

"Not yet." John whistled to the hounds. They came trotting back, burr-covered and muddy-pawed, and slouched at his feet. "For a week I've cared for nothing but my troubles," John said. "In all that time, the world may have transformed itself. I wonder what's been happening?"

"All seems quiet, at any rate."

"For how long?" John leaned forward and scratched Caesar's ear.

"Long enough." William paused. "She asks after you," he added. "Every day."

"Perhaps some day she'll speak with me directly."

"You're not the most approachable of men."

"That's ridiculous." John scrambled to his feet. "Come on, dogs," he said. "Time to go home."

* * *

Margaret stitched deftly away, putting the final touches to the caprison. It had been ten days since John had left his sickbed, and in all that time, she'd scarcely seen him. Every day, he'd rise at dawn and leave Ellestoun. He always went with William, taking his hounds, and travelling on foot.

Weeks had passed since he'd last eaten with the household. Now, when they gathered in the hall, there was an empty void in their midst.

Margaret expected that some evening he wouldn't come home, that eventually his path would lead him where that woman lived. So far, though, her fears had proved unfounded. Sometimes, she'd watch from the window as he strode up the hill towards home. It saddened her to see him so rough and unkempt, but she thought he looked a little better. He seemed stronger, fitter, more like his old self. She questioned William daily, and his words brought more comfort, because, slowly but surely, John was regaining his health. All that walking was giving him an appetite, and he was sleeping better, too.

Keep your thoughts pure, wholesome, she told herself. *Be a shining beacon of virtue. Maybe that way he'll come to you, like the unicorn comes to a maid who's pure of heart.*

* * *

The horseman shimmered in the hazy afternoon sun. His big brown horse shone like polished oak, and gold glinted on his tabard.

It was only when he drew closer that Margaret saw the rearing red lion emblazoned on his chest.

He's a herald, Margaret told herself. *He must be...* She hopped excitedly from foot to foot, willing him closer.

The herald halted and doffed his bonnet. "Am I addressing the lady of the house?"

She curtsied. "At your service, sir."

"Mistress Colville, I bring a message from His Grace the King. For your husband, the Sheriff of Renfrew."

"He's out hunting. But he'll be home soon." *Please God, don't let this be the day he seeks her out. . .* "Would you care to wait? We dine in two hours, if you wish to sit at the board."

The herald bowed his head. "That would be most welcome."

Margaret swallowed, nervously. "Sir," she asked, sweetly. "Might I ask what the King wants with my husband?"

"His Grace the King seeks an audience with the Sheriff of Renfrew. He asks that Master Sempill report to the Abbot of Paisley tomorrow, when the bell tolls noon."

"He'd be delighted to attend His Grace. And he'll be honoured, too, that the King's seen fit to summon him. Pray dismount, sir. The grooms will attend your horse, while I take you to your quarters."

* * *

Margaret came running down the hill to meet him. One hand gripped her skirts, the other clutched her hood. She wasn't very elegant to look upon, but there was something endearing about the way she bobbed along.

Concerned, he quickened his pace. "Margaret!"

She let go of her hood and waved. She was gasping for breath already; heedless, she pushed herself on yet faster.

She tried, too late, to halt her scramble down the uneven ground; he stuck out his arm, ready to catch her. "Be careful!" he called. "You'll hurt yourself!" He gritted his teeth for the impact, but she was so small and slight that she might have been a shred of thistledown. She gasped as he seized her; her body, firm in his grip, came to an abrupt halt, and her legs would have kept on going if he hadn't lifted her up and set her gently back down again.

He clutched her arms. "Are you alright? Is everything alright?"

She buried her head against him while she recovered her breath. "Don't fret." She looked up, face glowing with joy and excitement. "A herald's come."

He relaxed his hold. "Oh, for Heaven's sake... I thought something terrible had happened."

"No. You don't understand." Her smile spread wider. "It's wonderful news. The King's come to Paisley. He wants to see you!"

He could scarcely breathe. "Oh," he said at last.

She still clung to him, and he didn't feel inclined to prise her loose. "I offered him a place at the table," she continued. "And a chamber for the night. But it's not the same coming from me. You should talk to him." She wriggled free. "Come on." Seizing his hand, she tugged him forward. "You should change your clothes. You look like a peasant. You smell like one, too."

"I'll take a bath. . ." He broke off, scowling. "What's that look for?"

"I didn't think men knew what a bath was."

"Well I do, thank you." He strode up the hill with renewed purpose. "William!" he called. "You'd best ride to Paisley and find me some lodgings. But don't go yet! I'll need to organise my wardrobe. I must shave, too."

"And your hair should be trimmed," Margaret added. "It's too long and straggly. You should look after it better, for it's turning a lovely colour now the summer's here. Like the sun on the cornfields in August—"

He shook his head, wondering if he'd misheard her.

She blushed and shrugged. "It's your crowning glory," she told him. "If you don't take care of it, you'll get nits."

* * *

There was an air of excitement in the hall. Margaret sensed it from where she sat at the top table, and she revelled in it. Her flesh tingled with expectation, from her toes right up to her face, because for the first time in a month, *he* was coming to sit with them.

A hush fell about the place, and everyone rose respectfully.

There he was. Dressed in his fine clothes, with his gold chain about his shoulders. Face smooth-shaven once more, and his hair immaculate. He was a little leaner and burned brown with the sun, but it was recognisably John.

Margaret wanted to jump up and down for joy. *He's my husband, and he's the finest man I've ever set eyes on. You should be proud of him, because he's your lord, and he's in the King's favour.*

"May God bless this house, and all those gathered here to dine with us today," John said. "And let us give thanks for this bounty that He lays here before us."

"Amen," Margaret said, with heartfelt enthusiasm.

And then they all sat down, and dinner was begun.

Chapter 74

John Stewart stood by his window, high in the fortress of Dumbarton. It was late afternoon, and the sun was glinting on the waters of the Clyde. Across the river in the lands of Renfrew, the corn was ripening. Harvest was fast approaching, and he was still waiting for word from Ramsay and Ross in London.

Stewart wandered to a nearby table and poured some wine, then settled in his chair with a sigh. Forbes and Gordon were getting restive. *We can do this for ourselves,* Forbes had said, last time they spoke.

Stewart wasn't so sure. Encouraged by the response to Forbes' banner in the north, he'd sent Matthew out to raise the Bloody Sark in the Lennox. But there'd been no rioting in Dumbarton, no loud calls for retribution. Men were more cautious in the Westland, less fired with Northern passion. They looked to Renfrew, to see how the rebellion was being greeted there.

Meanwhile, the King's men had struggled to secure Renfrew's loyalty. Stewart thought that the men of Renfrew would respond with apathy. Instead, they'd switched allegiance and rallied to the King's cause.

An unexpected turn of events, and one which scarcely boosted his confidence.

"I can show myself in!" Matthew called. He stormed inside, hurling the door back so hard the latch nicked the timber panelling. He had his customary scowl upon his face. But behind it, there was something else. A hunted look, a faint pallor of fear behind his strong features.

"Did I give you permission to leave Duchal?" Stewart demanded. "Did Lord Robert?"

His son's scowl grew more entrenched. "I haven't seen Lord Robert for two whole weeks!" He paced back and forth. "I've been told nothing."

"You were given instructions," Stewart retorted. "That should've been enough."

Matthew's anger spluttered out, like a spark in a keg of damp powder. He cast his father a near-desperate look. "They're moving the bombards."

"Yes." Stewart spoke calmly. "I know."

"What are we to do? I can't hold Duchal or Cruikston against siege guns."

"You don't have to."

"I surrender them?" Matthew blinked a few times, then the scowl came creeping back. "I've never backed down. Not in my life."

"Cruikston and Duchal have their uses. They'll hold back Patrick and his people while we wait for word from England. Once they're lost, we'll seek safety here. Not even the damned bombards will dint these defences."

"You've pinned all your hopes on getting aid from Ramsay and Montgrennan. . ."

"Wine?" Stewart asked. "You might as well have some, now you're here."

"My God," Matthew said. "How could you be so trusting?"

"We share a common grievance. We have much to gain."

"It's folly."

"Don't question me!" Stewart thumped his fist upon the table. "I want you back in Duchal. I want it held until you know Cruikston's lost. Then you'll get the women out and you'll bring them here with all due speed."

"Where's Lord Robert?"

Stewart frowned. "It's no concern of yours."

"I'd like to know."

"He's in Kilmaurs."

"So you've betrayed Hugh. . ." Matthew shook his head. "If he finds out. . ."

"We can't pander to him. If Cunninghame joins us, the Boyds'll come with him. So will the Kennedys."

"The Westland will fall."

"And the war will be won," Stewart agreed. "With or without help from Ross and Ramsay."

"He's our kinsman."

"He betrayed us in the first place," Stewart retorted. "My spies tell me that he's just been made Lord of Bute, and Justiciar of Arran and the West." He smiled, thinly. "He's picking our bones clean already."

Matthew sank down by the window. "Then it's my fault," he said. "I spoke with him in February, when you were away." He swallowed. "I tried not to give anything away."

"It's done now," Stewart said. "You did the right thing, giving him a chance to join us. He's snatching scraps from Patrick's hand; he can damn well live with the consequences."

* * *

"It was a pleasure to have your company at the board," Margaret said, as they walked across the yard together. "We've missed you." She crooked her elbow in invitation; he hesitated, then slipped his arm in hers. "*I* missed you," she added.

John didn't reply.

"You scarcely ate."

He shrugged. "I'm not very hungry."

"You must eat!" She looked up, imploring. "I thought this news would lift your spirits. It's a great honour."

"I owe him twenty pounds."

"There must be more to it than that."

John halted. He stared ahead, frowning. "Nothing's certain," he said. "I could say or do something that displeases him. He mightn't even like the look of me—"

"Of course he will! How could he not. . ."

He sighed and scuffed his foot against the cobbles.

Margaret swallowed. She wanted to comfort him, but the words choked in her throat. *What happened between us was different. I just said those things to spite you. I never meant it once. . .*

"I've endured one disappointment after another just recently," John said. "I don't think I can stomach much more." Extricating his arm, he headed into the tower-house.

She followed him up the stair. *William's gone,* she thought. *He'll be alone tonight. He won't sleep, and neither will I, knowing he's sitting here, suffering such anguish over what tomorrow will bring...*

Ahead, he was opening his door.

"John?"

He faced her. One hand was on the latch, poised to close it. "Yes?"

"We mustn't part this way."

He was looking at her, patient, expectant, but she didn't know how to begin. There was so much to say, so many moments that she bitterly regretted...

John gestured inside. "Sit with me a while," he said. "There's wine."

"I'm so sorry!" Throwing her arms about his neck, she buried her face against his chest. "All those things I said, and did. I didn't mean to cause such hurt. I didn't know..."

Everything was going wrong. The words weren't there, and her tongue kept tripping up. She started to sob, angry and frustrated.

"Margaret..." He put his arms around her.

"I think about you all the time. I want to be your friend, and I want you to confide in me, and..." Her voice dropped to a whisper. "I want to lie with you."

He didn't answer, just gave her a comforting pat on the back.

"That night," she continued. "I wanted you more than anything else in the world. It wasn't right, but I just couldn't help myself. And you took it the wrong way." She raised her tear-streaked face. "Can you forgive me?"

He was frowning again. "Yes, of course."

"You hesitated."

"Are you surprised?" John smiled slightly. "You're so forthright. It catches a man off-guard."

Margaret glowered. "I'm sorry."

"I wouldn't have it any other way."

Reassured, she snuggled deeper into his embrace, savouring it. He felt warm, strong. And the way he slowly stroked her back brought comfort, a little tingle of longing. "John," she whispered.

"Yes?"

"I want to see you again." She blushed. "The way you were that night..."

He tightened his grip and sighed, breath blowing soft against the fabric of her hood. "Sweet Margaret," he said. "I'm yours. Do what you will."

* * *

The sheets and coverlets lay heaped at their feet, but with the night air still warm, John didn't feel inclined to retrieve them. He drowsed with his head in Margaret's lap, a willing captive, like the unicorn locked tight in a maid's embrace.

"I remember that day so well," she said. "When I saw you standing there at the kirk door, my heart leapt. But I couldn't love you. They said you were a traitor."

He no longer cared. All that mattered was she'd given herself willingly. She'd been shy at first, and a little frightened, but he'd been careful not to hurt her and she'd assured him all was well each time he'd asked. She must have been telling the truth, for now it was over, she was content to sit with him, naked and unashamed like Eve before the fall.

Her fingers teased through his hair. "I wanted you to hate me, so I could hate you in return."

"I'm sorry," he murmured.

"I never thought you'd take my words to heart." She rubbed his shoulder. "Will you forgive me? So we can put those evil times behind us."

He nestled closer, pressing his cheek against the soft flesh of her thigh. "Forgiveness is a saintly thing. I can't pretend to be a saint, but I can at least aspire to saintly conduct. I shall forgive, and forget."

"It must be late," she said. "The girls will wonder where I am."

"Let them wonder. . ." He yawned and stretched, settling more comfortably.

"Will you sleep better if I stay here with you?"

"Undoubtedly."

"Then I'll stay." She ran a finger over the contours of his face. "John. . ." she said. "Can I touch you?"

He smiled. "In God's eyes, we're of one flesh. You can do what you like with me."

"I'll be very careful." She caressed his shoulders, and his chest, humming a soft little tune to herself all the while. Her fingers drifted lover, straying over his belly, his hips. Her touch was careful, hesitant; she wasn't like Mary, who knew how to rouse, or tease, or bring comfort to a man. He didn't resist as she tugged him gently on to his back; he knew now, that even during that strange, frightening night, there'd been no malice in her actions.

"Oh, John," she whispered. "You look absurd, all sprawled out this way."

"Margaret." He reached for her hand and gripped it tight.

"What is it, my love?"

"My heart is yours. If you want it. . ." He rolled over and looked her in the eye. "But it's a fragile thing. Please treat it gently."

She closed her hands about his face. She smiled, but her eyes were moist with tears. "I shall treasure it," she said. "I promise."

* * *

Birds sang loud outside his window, and he was insufferably hot. John turned over with a groan, and collided with Margaret. He lay still, marvelling that she was here, sharing his bed.

She murmured in her sleep, shifting slightly.

John sat up, studying her. The sheet had slipped down, exposing the curves of her shoulder. Her lustrous brown hair flowed across the pillow; he reached out, and pushed it lightly back from her ears, her shoulders.

She shivered as his fingertips brushed her skin. A smile touched her lips; as she stretched, she yawned, then opened her eyes.

"Good morning," he said. "Did you sleep well?"

"I did, but. . . What hour is it?"

"I have no idea—" He broke off as knuckles rapped urgently upon his door.

"Master John?" Katherine's voice was fraught. "There's no sign of Mistress Margaret."

"It's alright!" Margaret called. "I'm here. I'm sorry. I should've warned you." She leaned forward, clasping her knees. "I should be washed and dressed by now."

John lay back, eyes closed. "No need to panic."

"But I have to dress you, with William away. Katherine, are you still there?"

"Yes."

"Bring my clothes, and fetch some water. I'll dress here." She turned to face him. "Do you mind?"

"I daresay you'll protect me." Reaching out, he tugged her close.

"John. . ." She tried to pull away. But when his lips touched hers and lingered there, she shrugged and relaxed.

"You're so very, very beautiful," he said. "I could lie with you forever."

"You're talking nonsense." She settled upon him, resting her chin against his chest. "You'll be like a pressed hare when you realise there's no time to get to Paisley. . ."

The door creaked open. "Mistress Margaret?"

Margaret jerked free and sprang from the bed like a cat on hot coals. Even as her maids filed in, she was pulling the covers up over him, while he shook with silent laughter. "Stop it!" She smacked his shoulder. "It's not amusing."

She crossed the room. He pretended to be asleep, but all the time he watched her. She knew it, too, putting a little swing in her stride. Glancing briefly over her shoulder towards him, she smiled.

Her maids blushed and mumbled greetings as she joined them.

"You were gone all night," Katherine said.

"Yes, I know." Margaret lifted her arms high as they washed her.

Katherine's reply was barely audible.

"What do you think I was doing?" Margaret retorted. "What else does a woman do at night? With her husband? Anyway, it's my business. Not yours."

The girls continued their duties in silence. They dried Margaret down; soon her ivory limbs were concealed beneath her kirtle, and her gown laced tight.

"Thank you," Margaret said. "That'll be all. We'll talk later."

* * *

With the girls gone, she came back to the bed. "Get up now."

He feigned indifference, so she tossed back the covers. "Come on!" She seized his arm and tugged with all her strength. "Stir yourself!" She couldn't budge him, so she tried again. This time he pulled back, rolling over so when she lost her footing, she fell into his arms. "I am stirring," he breathed in her ear. "But not in the way you intended..."

"John—" She tried in vain to extricate herself. "There's no time."

"I've a fast horse. He'll gallop to Paisley."

"But I've just washed," she complained. "Don't be silly." She made another half-hearted attempt to loosen his grip, then shrugged and laughed as he nibbled at her neck.

"I'm overcome with desire, my love. Would you have me suffer this indignity all day? When I'm supposed to be seeing the King?"

"An hour in the saddle and I'm sure you'll be cured."

"A few minutes now, and I know I'd be cured."

Margaret sighed. "You could charm the fish from the sea. And make them leap straight into a sizzling pan for good measure." She patted his arm. "Alright. But be quick about it."

* * *

There was a price to be paid. Once he'd had his way with her, he had the good grace to relinquish himself into her care. A mistake, for being a woman, Margaret's notion of cleanliness bore little resemblance to his. She was unimpressed by his attempts at washing; she grabbed the cloth and attacked him herself, scrubbing so hard he squirmed and yelped.

"I took a bath yesterday!" he protested, as she pushed his arm up and vigorously wiped his oxter.

"Yes," she replied. "But you were rolling around with me half the night. By the time you meet the King, you'll be stinking. So keep still, and be quiet. Now sit down, so I can do your neck."

When she'd finished, every inch of him was spotless. He was pleasing to the nose, too, for Margaret had liberally tossed perfume all over him. He sat on the edge of the bed, drumming his heels idly against the base and whistling a merry tune, while Margaret burrowed through the kists of clothing.

She sat on her heels amidst a mound of garments. "You sent the best clothes away with William, didn't you?"

"Yes, I did."

"Oh, John!" She hurled a bonnet at him; it bounced off his head and landed on the floor at his feet. "Didn't you think of keeping something back for today?"

"Ah. . ."

"We should've checked your wardrobe. Everything here's worn, or faded, or the moths have been at it."

"There must be something."

"I've found some hose, anyway." She tossed them over.

By the time he wandered over to join her, still lacing his hose, she'd found a shirt that wasn't too frayed about the hems and had moved onto the next kist. "Of course!" she cried, looking up with a beaming smile. "You can wear what you were married in. You looked good in that."

* * *

When he was dressed in all his finery, with his gold chain draped over his shoulders, Margaret stood back to admire him. "There now." She smoothed back the broad fur collar of his gown. "You're a far cry from the filthy creature who treads mud into my hall."

He leaned forward so she could place his bonnet on his head. "Thank you," he said. "You've been most helpful."

"Are you nervous?" she asked.

"A little."

"I've heard things about him. He's wiser than most men twice his age. Don't take him for granted." She paused. "And John. . ."

"Yes, my love?"

She tweaked the shoulders of his gown a final time. "Would you grant me one thing?"

"Of course I would."

"His Grace the King treats life as a tourney. He jousts with his wit as other men joust with their lances. It would mean a lot to me, if I knew you were carrying my favour." She drew a pale silk handkerchief from her bodice and pressed it into his hand. "Would you do that for me? Please?"

He lifted it to his nostrils and breathed in deep. It held the scent of roses on a summer evening, the unmistakable perfume of her. "I'd be honoured." He rolled it up, and knotted it around the cross-guard of his sword. "Margaret. . ." he said. "There's a favour I'd ask of you, too. I don't know if you'll be willing or able to grant it, but. . ."

"What is it?" She eyed him, furtively.

He bowed his head. "I had a mistress. You suspected it, quite rightly. I don't really wish to speak of it, because I know it hurts you." Looking at her, he felt a pang of guilt inside, for a weary, crestfallen air had come over her. "I want to make sure that all's well. But I'd rather have your blessing than go behind your back."

She seized his hands. "It's nothing more? You'd give me your word on that?"

"I swear it on my soul."

"Then go to her, and do your duty. But spare me the details, and. . ." She squeezed her fingers. "Let's not speak of her again."

"Thank you." He kissed her forehead.

"Why is Fate so cruel?" she cried, flinging her arms around him. "I don't want you to go to war."

He held her close. "I must help the King."

"Please be careful. You mustn't die. I couldn't bear it."

"It's just a siege. I probably won't get involved in anything more dangerous than a game of chess with Lord Hugh."

"But you were nearly killed at a simple wappenschaw."

"Come on now." He took her face in his hands. "You must be brave. I'll send word when I can. And when you hear the guns, you mustn't worry, for they'll be ours. Hear me?" He buried his face in her hair and breathed in deep relishing her scent one last time.

Margaret sniffed back tears. "I'll miss you so very much." She clung to him tightly. "Keep safe," she whispered. "And hurry home. Please."

Chapter 75
The Place of Nether Bar

"Ma!" Her eldest called, as he came bounding into the yard.

Mary set down her bucket and straightened. "What's the matter?"

The boy was smiling, for the first time since he'd been sent home from the wappenschaw. "Master John's coming here!" he gasped. "I met him on the road. And he gave me this." He held out the bundle he'd been clutching; it was a longsword, snug in its scabbard. "He says I mustn't steal your pitchfork next time there's a wappenschaw."

* * *

John rode alone on his red-brown horse, but Mary guessed his men-at-arms weren't far away. Seeing him now, as he sat in dazzling splendour astride his destrier, Mary felt the same way she had on that cold winter's night which seemed so long before; uncomfortable, embarrassed by her poverty.

She forced a smile. "Hello, John."

John swung down from the saddle. "Can we walk awhile?" he said. "I want to speak with you." He passed the reins to her boy. "Look after him," he said. "He may want some water."

* * *

They strode side by side across the hill towards the Lochar Water, enjoying the warmth of the summer sun, the songs of the larks and the linnets from the fields and copses.

"I'm going to Paisley," he said. "The King has summoned me."

"Not before time." She eyed him, keenly. "You've made your peace with her, haven't you?"

"You were right. I do love her."

Mary smiled. "Then what in God's name are you doing, wasting your time with an old woman like me?"

"I wanted to thank you. You were there when I needed you."

She rubbed her hands against her skirts. "You were unhappy. I couldn't let you suffer alone."

"You were very kind. I won't forget that." He leaned over, plucked a gowan from the grass and presented it to her.

She took the flower with a gracious smile, and when he offered his arm, she accepted. "Thank you."

"I hope you won't take this the wrong way." He hesitated, before taking a hefty gold ring from his finger and placing it in her hand. "I'd like you to have this. As a gift." He closed her fingers gently over it.

He looked so worried. She supposed he was concerned that she'd slap him and scold him for treating her like a whore. "Johnny. . ."

"I know how difficult it is with your husband gone. This is just a trinket to me, but it would mean so much to you. You could sell it in the town and buy more stock for the farm. Or you could hire some cottars and learn a trade."

"It's alright," she said. "I'll take the gift. I won't resent it, or you."

He grinned. "Thank you!" He looked youthful, exuberant, the way a young man should look, unbowed by fears and worries. "I was wondering, about young John."

"What about him?"

"He'll be twelve soon. The right age to enter my service."

"You'd have him as a man-at-arms?"

"He loves the horses, and he was always eager to lend a hand in the armoury. It'd be cruel to condemn him to a life walking behind an ox-team."

"He'll be overjoyed," she said. "We'll manage without him somehow. And this—" She squeezed the ring in her hand, "—will make life much easier."

"Good." He turned and caught her eye. "You're a mystery to me," he said. "You always have been. I never quite know what you're thinking."

Mary laughed, quietly. "You're a man, John."

"I know I meant nothing to you. I know you only took to my bed so you could keep your family safe. But. . ." He paused, frowning, "you were never a beggar to me. And you were never a whore. I could never be your husband, but I still consider myself responsible for you all. I don't know if we'll meet again, but. . . I'll make sure you're looked after."

"Oh, Johnny." She threw her arms about him, heedless of his magnificent clothes. He didn't mind, either, for he embraced her back. "You were never nothing to me," she told him. "And I know it's over, but it doesn't matter. I'll look at you from afar, as you sit up there on that fine horse, and I'll remember what we had and cherish it."

* * *

The abbey bells were ringing loud as John fought his way through the crowds to the mercat cross.

It was noon. He was late.

He was too heady with joy to be worried. It was all going so well. For once he felt Fate was on his side.

He spotted William at last, loitering next to the cross and looking decidedly glum. William waved, then disappeared into the throng.

He soon appeared alongside.

"It's not good news, is it?" John asked.

William seized the reins. "With the court in town, there's scarcely a room to be found." He rubbed the horse's nose. "Managed to find accommodation of sorts, in a fleapit of a hostel past the fleshmarket. It'll be cosy, mind."

"What about the horses?"

"They'll take four, at a pinch. That'll be cosy, too."

"Just as well I don't have a large entourage," John said. "It'll have to do. Now cheer up, for God's sake. It's not your fault. It doesn't matter if I'm scratching myself to pieces by the morning. Just so long as all goes well today." He urged his horse forward. "Let's head for the abbey. Before the King gives me up as lost."

* * *

Halting at the gatehouse, John glanced towards the Abbot's tower. Hanging limp from the flagpole was the red lion rampant, a sure sign that the King was in residence.

John swallowed. His heart ran faster, he was breaking into a sweat already; he hoped to God the powerful scent of musk and rosewater would hold out a little longer.

The chamberlain approached. "Your name and business, sir."

"John Sempill of Ellestoun, Sheriff of Renfrew. I've been summoned by His Grace the King."

"Come this way, please. How many men and horses are in your retinue?"

"I'm staying in the town."

"You've been allotted lodgings here. His Grace the Lord Montgomerie made arrangements with the Abbot. Shall I tell him you don't want them?"

John blinked. The ground was shifting beneath him, they were playing by rules he couldn't begin to understand. "I'll take them, thank you," he said. "I have a retinue of three men and four horses. I'll send my manservant out to fetch them."

"One of the laybrothers will take you to your chamber now. Just bring the horse inside and dismount, sir; I'll make sure the beast is well-tended."

* * *

It was a small room, in a guest range near the abbot's tower. It would provide cramped accommodation for four men, but it was comfortable enough.

With William still gone, the place was painfully quiet. Settling down cross-legged upon the embroidered coverlet of the bed, John steepled his fingers and tapped them thoughtfully against his chin, wondering when the summons would come.

A quick rap on the door made his heart thud even faster. "Yes?" He winced, for his voice sounded strained.

"It's me," Hugh said. "Can I come in?"

"If you like." He tried not to sound too hostile.

Hugh peered round the door, unusually diffident. "I heard you were unwell," he said. "I'm told we nearly lost you."

John shrugged, wordlessly.

Hugh came a few steps closer, then paused. He glanced here and there, agitated, unwilling to look John in the eye. Opening his mouth to speak, he thought better of it, and snapped his jaws shut. Then he moved, prowling the tiny room with all the demented vigour of a caged lion.

He halted. "You're better now?"

John scowled. "Yes." He wished he had the courage to tell Hugh to leave him be and bestow his gracious gifts on some other poor unsuspecting fool. "No thanks to you," he muttered, half under his breath,

Hugh glared at John. "No thanks to me?" He paused for breath, then roared, "You're a damned idiot! What in God's name made you take a draught for a silly thing like that?"

"I wasn't myself. Margaret thought—"

"Christ." Hugh resumed his pacing. "It's true then. She meant to kill you."

"No, she didn't!" John retorted. With Hugh on the move once more, he felt even less at ease. "For God's sake!" he snapped. "Would you stop that?" Then he added, quietly, "Please. Sit down. You're making me nervous."

Hugh slumped into the nearest chair. "You worry me sometimes," he said. "You're too naïve."

"You're right there. I called you 'friend.'"

"That's enough!" Hugh closed his hands tight about the chair arms.

"Still, a man learns from his mistakes. . ."

"Have you quite finished?"

John sighed, and said nothing.

"When we were in Paisley," Hugh said, "you told me that a package awaited you in Leith. I took the liberty of shipping it back to the Westland, along with my own baggage."

John looked up. Hugh still sat taut and petulant in his chair, glowering at the floor.

"Thank you," John said. "You didn't have to do that. I'll reimburse you, of course."

"I expect no reimbursement," came Hugh's stiff reply. "I thought we might put all this behind us, and remain friends." He paused, then added, "You forget, John, that I've gone out of my way to help you over the past few months."

"Yes, I know that. And I'm grateful, too."

"Then we'll speak no more of the incident in Renfrew."

"No," John said, wearily. "Let's not." He offered Hugh a smile. "Was Helen displeased?"

"She asks that next time you bleed upon those parts already coloured red."

"I don't intend to shed any more blood of mine over that damned banner of yours."

"Glad to hear it," Hugh said. He lifted his head, curious. "You're anxious, aren't you?"

"Yes. I'm incredibly anxious."

"Just keep calm, and keep your wits about you. I'm sure you'll acquit yourself well." Hugh tapped his palms in jaunty rhythm against the arms of the chair. "I'd best go," he said. "I'm wanted for a Privy Council meeting." He stood, and studied John, carefully. "You must learn to trust me," he said. "I wouldn't offer my patronage if I didn't think you were worthy."

* * *

An offer of patronage. . . John had heard it, clear as day, and he didn't quite know how to respond. Of course he was flattered, but at the same time, he could see the disadvantages.

Every fledging courtier needed a patron. For years, John had assumed his uncle Montgrennan would be his. But Montgrennan was gone now, which was perhaps just as well, for he'd collected numerous enemies through the years.

Taking up with Hugh's just as bad, John reminded himself. *He's hardly gone out of his way to avoid controversy. . .*

Beggars can't be choosers. Take what help you can get, and be grateful.

Even if it means placing your trust in him. . .

Another knock on the door made John's heart lurch afresh, but it wasn't the summons from the King.

Instead, two Montgomerie men-at-arms stood beyond the door, carrying a sturdy wooden kist between them. They were typical Montgomerie retainers; big, rough men with impeccable liveries and dog-eared faces. He thought he recognised them from that night in Renfrew, but didn't want to stare too closely, just in case.

As it was, they were on their best behaviour. They bowed and smiled a little sheepishly, then when he gave them both a penny for their pains, they bowed again and thanked him most profusely.

He was just showing them out when William arrived with the others.

"What's this?" William asked.

"My arms," John said. "Hugh brought them from Leith."

"That's uncommonly kind of him." William, for once, looked impressed.

"I thought the merchant would have pawned them by now." John crouched down by the kist and slotted the key into the lock.

"You'll look the part now, Master John," said William. He and the men-at-arms crowded close to get a better view.

"Just as well. I have the impression that here looks are everything." John opened the lid to find a swathe of plush red velvet beneath. Pushing it aside, he glimpsed a flash of shining steel, but before he could inspect it more closely, there was yet another knock upon the door.

"Master Sempill," a boy's reedy voice called. "The King desires to speak with you."

Chapter 76

The page, a fresh-faced boy of eight or nine years, took one look at John and wrinkled his nose in faint dismissal. There was something unsettling about him, an aura of quiet detachment that seemed out-of-place in one so young.

John followed his diminutive guide through the narrow corridors of the range. They crossed the yard, heading into the Abbot's tower. They climbed the stairs but to John's surprise, passed the great hall and reception rooms, moving on to the upper floors, where the private apartments were located.

John's apprehension was back. He'd expected Hugh to briefly introduce him, and nothing more. He'd have a few seconds to bow before the King, before he was ushered away leaving just a name, and—he hoped—a good impression.

The page halted before a heavy wooden door. Beyond, voices were engaged in heated discussion.

Rapping on the door, the boy called, "Your Grace? Sempill of Ellestoun is here, if it please you."

"Bid him enter!"

John took one last fortifying breath as the page opened the door, then stepped inside.

It was the King's bedchamber, no less. He'd walked in on a meeting of the Privy Council.

He knew Hugh and Robert Colville. Bishop Elphinstone was there, too, and he also recognised the Earl of Argyll. Young James sat in the centre, with Hugh at his sinister side and Elphinstone to his right. The rest were unfamiliar.

John dropped to one knee and bowed his head. It wouldn't do to stare, so he studied the brocaded boardcloth carefully. Wine was being poured nearby; he could hear the rhythmic *glug* as it was decanted from a flagon.

His mind went blank; all he could think of was that he must have looked damned silly, kneeling there like a lovelorn squire with a lady's silk handkerchief tied about his sword-hilt.

"Pray rise, my liege," James said, cheerfully.

John straightened, and braved a glance towards his King.

Young James caught his eye, and smiled. The lad's gaze was bright, fierce, searching deep for any trace of deceit or infidelity.

"You come highly recommended, Master Sempill." James lifted his goblet and took a leisurely draft, then slumped back in his throne. There was a faint clink of steel as he moved; John saw then that James wore a heavy chain of iron about his waist. It was the mark of a man who'd sinned so gravely that he would never be free from the threat of Damnation. "I'm told you fought alongside my father last year?"

"Yes, sire. I did." *For my sins.* He fought the urge to scowl.

"Have you had word from your uncle?" James continued, pleasantly.

Montgrennan. It was always Montgrennan. John clenched and unclenched his fists, trying not to let his agitation show. "No, sire," he said. "I have not. I believe his plans were to flee to England."

"You heard that right," James retorted. "Where he's been causing trouble ever since." He looked around his counsellors with a half-smile on his face; they shook their heads and muttered barely audible condolences.

"I'm sorry, Your Grace. If I could make amends for my uncle's conduct, I would, but—"

"A man can't be held responsible for his kinsman's misdeeds," James said. "If he could, we'd have strung you up long ago." He paused. "You'll understand why I'm loath to trust you. Your reputation isn't good. I'm told you were a page in Montgrennan's service?"

"For a year, when I was a boy of ten. My father soon took me away. He thought I'd learn more if I attended university."

"Ah!" James sat up. "An educated man. You have that in your favour, if nothing else!" The smile crept back across his face. "Master Sempill, I apologise. You don't like to be reminded of Montgrennan, do you? If it's any consolation, that makes two of us." He sipped his wine. "Don't worry. I won't let his name slur your own. As I said—" he slid a sideways glance towards Hugh, "you come highly recommended." Another sip, and a long, luxurious silence. "This isn't what you expected."

"No, Your Grace."

"These are difficult times. They require unusual measures. You're here because I would ask a favour of you."

"I'd be pleased to help, sire, if I—"

"Don't be foolhardy! Hold your tongue until you know what's required."

He hung his head. "I'm sorry, Your Grace."

"My request is this, Master Sempill; would you take my artillery to Lord Lyle's place at Duchal, and take the castle in my name?"

The breath caught in John's throat. It took a while for the words to sink in. Panic was quick to follow. *Why me? I know nothing about sieges. I know nothing about artillery. . .* But there was a cold, cynical part of him that understood all too well what was happening. Not one of them wanted to take up arms against their old friend Lord Lyle. Not Hugh, not Argyll, not even Patrick Hepburn.

The fear was gone. He was suddenly serene, secure in the knowledge that he'd reached the defining moment of his life. "I am your humble servant," he said, voice clear and steady. "If this is what's required of me, then it will be done."

He felt the tension lift. It was flattering and terrifying, to realise that as far as all these worthy and eminent men were concerned, he'd said and done the right thing. Even if he didn't quite know what the whole daunting prospect would entail.

"Thank you, Master Sempill," said the King. "You're young and unproven, I know. But I don't judge a man by his years; I judge him by his faculties."

"I'm grateful, Your Grace, for being granted this opportunity to prove myself."

"And we're grateful to you, sir, for showing such restraint through the winter. It's done much to demonstrate your loyalty. Though there are issues which need to be resolved. . ."

A veiled reference to the twenty pounds that weighed heavy in the purse at his belt. John lowered his gaze. "Yes, sire."

"We mustn't let that sour our relations. You'll dine with me today?"

"I'd be honoured, Your Grace."

"Good. Then we'll speak later. Now, if you'll forgive me, I must consult with my counsellors. We have much to discuss before dinner. And the good Abbot will be insulted if we arrive late at his table."

"Your Grace." John bowed low, then straightened. With head lowered, he performed the customary ritual of backing from the King's presence.

An unnecessary nicety, for he'd been forgotten already.

"So that's settled then?" James said. "Duchal will soon be ours. We can turn our attention to Dumbarton, which will, I hope, prove a more worthy challenge to us all—"

The page was waiting at the threshold, studying John with that same insolent look.

John retreated out onto the stair. The door was closed, and he was back in the realms of lesser men.

* * *

There was time to kill before dinner, so Hugh headed back to the guest lodgings. Stopping outside John's door, he knocked smartly upon it.

"Come in, Hugh!" This time, John's voice was buoyant.

Hugh flung open the door, and swept inside. He halted abruptly, his route blocked by a trio of men-at-arms, who sat hunched on the floor playing cards.

John stood by the bed, while William laced him into a fresh doublet. He looked at Hugh and grinned, relieved, exuberant and exhausted all at once.

Hugh sidled round the men-at-arms. "Well done!" he said, engulfing John in a brotherly embrace. "I'm proud of you."

"I did what was required?"

"And more besides. Ah-" He broke off, spotting the dismantled suit of armour that lay upon the bed. "That's a worthy suit of mail. Might I take a look?"

"Please."

"It'll be heavier than your old one. You'll have to work hard if you want to do it justice." Hugh grasped the helmet, tapping it with his knuckles then moving the visor back and forth. "First thing each morning you'll be out there in full array to put some practice in. Or I'll haul you out of bed myself."

"I'd appreciate some guidance with the bastard sword," John admitted. "You're said to be a master. . ."

"That can be arranged." Setting down the helmet, Hugh picked up one of the gauntlets. He held it to his eye, admiring the fluted shape of the sheet metal. "There's an armourer attached to the Royal household. We can get this fitted properly before the host leaves for Duchal."

"Thank you," John said. "Hugh?"

"What?" Hugh murmured, still absorbed with studying the gauntlet.

"About Duchal. . ." John paused. "I don't like to say this so late in the day. But I don't know how to handle a siege. Or a bombard, for that matter."

Hugh thrust the gauntlet into John's hands. "That's why I'm here." He frowned at William.

"The lads are getting bored," William said.

The men-at-arms looked up, hopeful.

"All right," John said. "You can go. Drink and whore as much as you like. But for God's sake don't pick a fight with another man's retainers."

There were delighted chuckles from the men-at-arms, who threw down their cards and scrambled to their feet.

"You don't have to go with them, Master Haislet," Hugh said.

"I appreciate that," John replied. "But I'd rather he did. Someone has to keep them in order."

* * *

John frowned as he sipped his wine. "If my reckoning's correct, we need seventy-five oxen. At least."

"That's right."

"Ten days to hire seventy-five oxen. In a county where half the beasts were roasted in their byres over the winter. . ."

Hugh shrugged. "There'll be carters seeking work in Irvine. And there'll be plenty more in Ayr and Kyle. I'll send word to Campbell of Loudon. And Wallace of Craigie. Together, we'll make up the numbers."

"Just one more thing," John said. "Why me? His Grace said my reputation was doubtful. Yet he's granted me the bombards and put the host at my disposal."

"It's important you're seen to do this."

"At the risk of upsetting you?"

"You think he offered me the opportunity and I turned it down."

John glanced aside. "I didn't mean it that way."

"I wasn't his first choice. Firstly, there's the small matter of gaining the approval of the Cunninghames, and secondly. . ." Hugh grimaced. "He doesn't trust me."

"He doesn't trust *you?*"

"My aunt's married to John Stewart. I'm tainted by association."

"That makes two of us, then."

"Indeed." Hugh lifted his goblet, and dashed it against John's. "A toast," he said. "To those cursed with traitorous kinsmen."

Chapter 77

During dinner, John found himself at the top table. There were just two individuals between himself and the King; Abbot Schaw, and Hugh.

It was a place many men would have killed for.

Hugh was in ebullient mood, giving John no chance to dazzle the King with wit or clever words. Not that John had intended to do anything more than sit quietly and savour the experience, but as the meal wore on, he grew increasingly disappointed. The talk at his board was largely concerned with the unmarried daughters of the lords and barons who peopled the lower tables, and most of the time it wasn't complimentary.

John didn't know the maids in question, and he was glad of it. *You're only a humble laird*, he told himself. *It's not your place to pronounce judgement.* He toyed with his food, wondering if he'd been hauled on as some kind of performing animal for their entertainment. Once he'd been hurled back into the masses, he, too, would become a subject of derision.

He concentrated on eating most carefully, so at least they couldn't fault his manners. It was a fish day, but since the King was present, only the most extravagant of fish would do. The main dish was a porpoise, freshly caught off Ardrossan and brought to Paisley at Hugh's expense.

"There's a deer park here, isn't there?" James changed the subject at last.

"Indeed, Your Grace," Abbot Schaw replied.

"It's enclosed by walls," James grumbled. "I daresay the deer eat out of your hand."

Hugh gulped down his food and took a hasty sip of wine. "There's a Royal forest nearby," he mentioned. "At the Fereneze. Just a few hours' ride would take us there. Master Sempill—" He delivered John an almighty slap on the back. "—has the herd in his care."

All eyes were fixed on John.

"Is that so?" James asked.

John didn't dare look up. "Yes, Your Grace."

"The herd is well?"

"Thriving. They haven't been hunted since your grandsire's time."

"Then it's high time they were! We'll ride there tomorrow. Your hounds, Master Sempill. They're lodged at Ellestoun?"

"I could go tonight and ready them," John offered. It was a welcome thought. He'd escape the trials of court life, if only briefly, and Margaret would be waiting. . .

"That won't be necessary," James said. "We have plans for you this evening." He tapped his fingers against the board. "We'll take the Abbey pack," he decided. "I'll send men out to inform the forester." He slammed his goblet down, smiling broadly. "That's decided, gentlemen. We hunt tomorrow. After that, we'll concentrate on crushing that damned rebellion."

* * *

John was grateful to return to his room.

He was weary, for it had taken considerable effort to maintain a façade of cultured elegance all afternoon. He hadn't eaten much, either, so the wine had gone straight to his head.

He groaned, and stretched along his bed, grateful to relax.

He must have drifted off, for it seemed as if no time passed before William woke him. "A page is waiting," he said. "The King wants to see you."

John sat up, yawning. "What time is it?"

"Past ten."

"What does he want at this hour?"

William shrugged. "He's the King."

"He's probably remembered his twenty pounds. I hope he has, for I'm sick to death of carrying it around with me."

"There's a fresh doublet here." William rummaged inside an open kist. "And a clean sark."

"Third change of clothes in a day," John muttered. "I'll run out before a week's out."

"Let's just hope the novelty of your company wears off by then."

* * *

This time, the atmosphere in the Royal apartments could not have been more different. The room was bathed in the soft light of a dozen candles, while a solitary harpist sat in the corner, playing a melancholy air.

James sat at a small table, flanked by Hugh and Robert Colville. A flagon of wine and some goblets lay before him; he faced an empty chair.

John delivered his knife into the care of the page.

"Ah, Master Sempill!" James called. "You'll join us for a few games of cards before the night's out?"

"It would be a pleasure, Your Grace." John was suddenly grateful for the money in his purse. He could scarcely afford to fritter away funds like this, but currying favour with a King never came cheap. If necessary, he could pawn his gold chain on the morrow.

Better that than his armour. Or his horse…

"Be seated," James said.

John sat down in the empty chair. He glanced towards Hugh, but Hugh was studiously ignoring him, concentrating instead upon shuffling the cards.

"Lord Hugh, would you care to name your stake?" James invited.

"A modest stake, I think," Hugh said. "Three unicorns?"

"Three unicorns it is."

Hugh handed the cards to James, who set them face down. They placed their coins in the centre of the table.

While James dealt the cards, Hugh and Robert Colville said nothing. Their quiet deference unsettled John, but then he'd suspected all along that James had ulterior motives.

"You didn't say much at dinner." James glanced in John's direction.

"I don't like to voice opinions of men I've never met."

"You'll meet them soon enough." James glanced about the table as they pretended to study their cards. "I'm told you have a knowledge of civil law?"

"Yes, Your Grace."

"An understanding of our laws is a valuable gift. And the arts?"

"I found them of interest, Your Grace." John squirmed uneasily.

James looked briefly at his cards, selected one and placed it on the pile at the centre of the table. "You'll know the work of the ancients? Aristotle? Plato?"

"I've little experience of Plato, but Aristotle is familiar."

"And what do you think of his writings?" James leaned closer. "Can we really call him wise, when he had no knowledge of the one true God?"

"I think we should accept that he saw God's truth in his own fashion. He just didn't have the means of seeing it clearly. . ."

"Exactly!" A beaming smile lit the young King's face. "Ah, you don't know how refreshing it is, to find a laird who's even heard of Aristotle."

"You're most kind, Your Grace." John knew now that the game was immaterial. What mattered more was to answer James as confidently and expertly as he could.

The young King's interests were certainly wide-ranging; he established John's views on the latest song styles one minute then asked him to clarify his thoughts on the code of chivalry the next. And all the while, the wine flowed, and the twenty pounds John had kept aside as payment steadily trickled away. Hugh gained a little, so too did Robert Colville. But the man who gained most was James.

Which was, John supposed, the way it should be.

It felt as if hours passed. John was tiring, losing the edge to his wits. He tasted sweat on his lip; every so often he'd get his words wrong and then he'd blush with shame and embarrassment.

It was almost a relief when his twenty pounds was gone. He stared at the table, too tired to be angry, but wondering all the same if they'd deliberately set out to humiliate him. "If it please Your Grace," he said. "I must ask to withdraw. I have no more funds."

James raised his brows. "I'm sorry to hear that," he said. "You've given us great sport." He shared secretive glances with his courtiers, an unsettling half-smile on his face. Then he added, voice deceptively gentle. "It could be said, though, that your downfall was richly deserved. I seem to remember that you owe me some money."

"Your Grace."

"Don't look so glum, Master Sempill." James stretched across to refill John's goblet. "Do you think I'll have you quartered and set at the gates for everyone to sneer at?" He sat back. "It's a dangerous thing, to judge a man by how he conducts himself in victory. There's more wisdom in seeing how he copes with defeat. And you, Master Sempill, are a most gracious loser." James raised his goblet. "Your debts are repaid, your previous transgressions forgotten. Your days in the wilderness are over."

Chapter 78

John rose early the following morning and hurried down to the yard for the hunt. He was the first to arrive. It was a misjudgement, for as more and more courtiers mustered, he remained isolated. Everyone else seemed to know each other, but they all avoided him.

Judging by the derisive glances sent in his direction, John ranked amongst the lowest of the low. *I suppose a man's worth is measured by the company he keeps,* he told himself, sourly. Grasping a goblet from a passing servant, he took a sip of wine.

"Cousin John," a voice said pleasantly in his ear.

He nearly choked, for there at his side was Robert Colville. "Master Colville," he acknowledged.

Colville smiled. "Why the formality? We're kinsmen now. How's cousin Margaret? Is she keeping well?"

"She's very well, sir."

"I'm glad to hear it."

If having Robert Colville's company wasn't flattering enough, Hugh soon appeared. He breezed his way through the crowd, bestowing gracious smiles on all he passed.

He soon joined them. And, once he was safely in their company, he leaned close and muttered scathing comments about the men he'd greeted so cordially just moments before.

Colville smirked into his goblet, saying nothing.

John only half-listened. He was too absorbed by the realisation that the looks in men's faces had changed. Contempt had been replaced by respect, perhaps even a little fear.

The King appeared then, with Archie Campbell at his side. John mentioned Archie's presence to Hugh, who nodded. *Yes, Archie's well favoured just now,* he said. He'd sounded weary, perhaps even disappointed.

James circulated amongst them, briefly speaking to each man in turn, before moving quickly onwards. All the while, Hugh watched intently.

At last James stood before them. "Good morning, gentlemen! You're rested after your late night?"

They murmured their assent.

"You're looking forward to the chase?" James asked.

Hugh swilled the wine around in his goblet. "I've confessed my sins in readiness."

James laughed at that. "We'll speak later," he said, then moved on.

Before long, the musicians struck up a lively air, and the horses were led out. A great long line of them; their coats had been curried until they shone and their manes and tails combed so they flowed in shimmering waves over strong necks and quarters.

There was applause and murmurs of admiration.

John saw Hugh's grey horse Zephyr, but couldn't spot his own lacklustre nag. He was growing increasingly agitated when a groom presented him with a sturdy black destrier.

"This isn't my horse!" he protested.

Hugh glared from Zephyr's back. "Don't argue."

Once John sprang into the saddle, his doubts were forgotten, for he felt like a knight already. He found his stirrups, then touched the beast's sides with his spurs. It arched its neck and shook its head, eager to move off.

The horn sounded, hounds and huntsmen stirred, and John's fine black horse took its place alongside Hugh and Zephyr. John laughed in delight as his steed strode forward, carrying itself with such grace and dignity.

"Oh, for God's sake, John." Hugh sounded bored. "Wipe that daft look off your face. It's a horse. It eats, it shits, same as the rest of them." He urged Zephyr into a trot. "Hurry up," he said. "His Grace doesn't like to dally."

* * *

"I hope you like the horse." James came trotting alongside. King or no, he looked absurdly slight on the back of a huge Spanish grey. "Lord Hugh said you were in dire need of one."

"Your Grace, he is spectacular."

"Have Duchal Castle in my hands by the end of this month, and you can consider him yours."

"That's a most gracious offer."

"And a great incentive to win me that castle," James retorted. "I can see you're besotted already. Much as Lord Hugh is with the noble Zephyr." Then he added, suddenly serious, "Ride with me please, Master Sempill." A whole gaggle of courtiers moved to follow, but James waved them aside. "I don't want company. We'll inspect the traps, and study the line, and then we'll rejoin you."

* * *

James was eager to learn about the forest. He asked endless questions about its management, about how many licenses to clear trees and farm the land had been granted, and whether it was much troubled by poachers.

John answered as best he could, while they picked a careful course through the oblivious deer. There were hinds and young calves amongst them, but James wasn't concerned with safeguarding the herd. He marvelled at a stag that watched suspiciously nearby, its antlers still half-grown and swathed in velvet. "That's quarry fit for a King," he told John. "I'll have him, by God."

* * *

Once they'd viewed the deer trap, they turned away from its high earthen banks.

"There's a straight run for about half a mile," John explained. "The ground's less treacherous there. The forester burns the growth every few years, so the grass is short. We can gallop if that's required."

James nodded vigorously. He cast a practised eye over the undulating ground. "You've known Lord Hugh long?"

"My father helped him once."

391

"Would you call him 'friend'?"

John hesitated too long; James looked at him with those bright, all-seeing eyes. "Is it so hard a question?"

"I called him friend once. I think I was rash to rate him so highly."

Reining in his horse, James settled comfortably into the saddle. "The disagreement wounded you?"

"No."

"Then whatever do you mean?" James looked profoundly interested.

"I can't be angry with Lord Hugh, for he was never at fault." John's face flushed, he was frustrated with himself for saying too much, but the words spilled out regardless. "I'm angry with myself, for not understanding him sooner. The truth is that he cares for very little in this world, except himself."

"You shouldn't judge him too harshly," James replied. "He has many faults, I know, but there's few men whose loyalty I'd rate higher."

"Forgive me, Your Grace. I don't see what this has to do with me."

"Men like him are worth their weight in gold in times of war, but they find it very hard to keep the peace. It takes the influence of a man with steady temperament to curb their excesses."

"I don't think it's possible to change him. He's not a man; he's a force of nature."

"The incident at the wappenschaw coloured your thoughts," James agreed. "That's understandable. But that night, when you asked for his help, he gave it. Freely, and unconditionally. He finds it hard to take commands from any man, but he'll listen to sound advice, providing he respects its source. And he respects you."

"I'm flattered."

"You have the gift of being able to reason with the unreasonable. It would serve me well if you used that gift to keep the peace between the Montgomeries and the Cunninghames. It would serve Lord Hugh, too; if he continues on this present course unchecked, then sooner or later he'll stretch the law so far that not even I'll be able to protect him."

John nodded.

"You deny it, but I think you consider him a friend. You'd help him if you could, just as he's moved heaven and earth to help you."

"I'll do what I can."

"It would help me greatly."

They'd halted on a stretch of high ground that commanded a magnificent view across the valleys of the Cart and the Clyde. Faint plumes of smoke marked Paisley, and further to the east, Glasgow and Ru'glen. Further north lay the hills of the Lennox.

"It's the first time I've seen so much of the Westland," James said. "When I last passed this way, it was autumn. The mists were heavy, and it rained as if there'd never be an end to it. Earl Patrick says it always rains in the Westland and that's why men are so quick to anger here." He sat silent, studying the land. "You and I have much in common," he said at last. "We've been robbed of our fathers, and forced to rely on those who stole them away. It's made us both mature beyond our years. It must sometimes be hard for you to stomach your situation. I know it's hard for me to endure mine."

There was a look of profound sadness on his face. "Your Grace," John said. "It's not right. You didn't take your father's life. Why must you bear the burden for his death?"

"To kill a King's a grievous sin. It's a sin that's tainted the whole land. Scotland's fate lies in my hands now; I must atone for the evils that brought me to the throne." James grasped a firmer hold of his reins. "Talking with you has been a comfort, for I like you. The Stewarts are my kin, and Matthew's a dear friend. It was hard to sign the warrant for their forfeiture, and all for the sake of a man who meant nothing." He spurred his horse forwards, gesturing for John to follow. "We should return," he said. "They'll be anxious, of course. They think I'm reckless and foolhardy. But I won't be coddled. What manner of a King would I be, if I wasn't prepared to risk life and limb for my kingdom?"

* * *

They lined up stirrup-to-stirrup, as if preparing to charge an enemy line.

John tightened his reins one last time, heart beating loud. He'd been issued with a lightweight hunting spear; he gripped the shaft tightly, his palm damp. All around him, horses snorted and stamped. On his left, Hugh cursed as his grey sat up on its hocks and thrashed the air.

Far ahead the hounds fanned out, their deep throaty calls drifting through the still morning air. Deer flushed from cover floated at a leisurely trot beyond the pack.

Still no word from James.

"Forward!" The order came, crisp, loud.

John's black horse sprang away at a canter. Hugh was pressed close to one side, while Sir John Ross hemmed him in on the other. The level strip of grass stretched smooth before them.

The pace soon picked up; before long John was fighting to breathe as the wind slammed into his face, his body. The horse's snorts were loud in his ears, drowning out all else.

A burn split the ground ahead. He saw it just in time and gasped a warning before his horse took a long leap to clear it. Once he'd landed, he chanced a glance to either side, noting with relief that Hugh and Sir John Ross had made it safely.

The line broke. A few men fell back, intimidated by the gruelling pace. They were right, John supposed, for it was madness to run prize horses across ground like this for the sake of a few fat deer.

But James was oblivious to the perils. While the rest of them fought their misgivings, he spurred his grey horse on faster. Danger was like a potent draught to him, fuelling his strength, his vigour. He was alive, and he was glorious, full of light and fire and raw courage.

If James had no time for Death, then why should they? As John fixed his gaze on the young King, his fears faded. Elation gripped him and he urged his horse forwards.

They reached the deer. There must have been two score or more, stags and hinds and a few calves which had survived the onslaught of the hounds.

The pace slowed, and they all looked to James.

He sat tight on his horse, spear held high as he coursed a stag. He threw his spear into the beast's ribs. It staggered to its knees, then collapsed.

The slaughter began.

"There!" Hugh called. "To the left."

Two deer ran there. A hind, and a young buck.

John spurred his horse alongside Hugh's.

"Mark the doe," said Hugh. "Take her when you're ready." He steadied his horse, sent it darting one way then the other. When a gap appeared, he urged Zepyhr forward and split the pair, turning the buck aside.

The doe was alone, wide-eyed and terrified, its path blocked by Zephyr's quarters. It sprang forwards, groaning.

John steered his horse alongside. He threw down the spear with all his strength; it passed straight through and pinned the doe to the ground. When he saw the deer twitching in its death throes, he felt a brief pang of guilt. He never liked to kill a hind, and liked it even less when it wasn't a clean kill.

"Head them off!" Hugh yelled.

The herd scattered as the banks of the deer trap reared high to the left. A stag hurtled towards him from the right; John spun his horse around on its hocks and cantered close, pressing the black stallion's shoulder against the deer's side so it veered back to the mouth of the trap.

It was a hard task, to outwit the terrified deer and force them on into the depths of the deer trap. They worked together; horsemen, huntsmen, hounds. One or two animals escaped, and they let them go unmolested.

Eventually, they reached the point where the banks converged. Thirty deer were huddled in the corner. A line of mounted men enclosed them, while the huntsmen kept a tight hold of the snarling hounds. On top of the banks, more huntsmen waited. There, too, was the Abbot of Paisley, along with some of the older, more sedate members of the court.

"Would the Earl of Argyll care to join me?" James asked. "The Master of Argyll, too? And Master Colville."

The select few. And they didn't include Hugh. John looked at Hugh, but his face showed nothing.

An eerie quiet fell. The deer milled around, snorting.

James and his companions climbed up the bank, joining the men who waited there. Cross-bows were issued; soon the bolts ripped through the air, stirring the deer into a frenzy. The captive deer lashed out and scrambled high on the corpses of the fallen in a vain attempt to escape.

"Mort!" James punched the air as the last deer fell.

The huntsmen moved in to gut the corpses. James scrambled back down the bank to join them, dagger drawn. His face still glowed with excitement.

Hugh dismounted, so John did likewise. Soon they were working together with Ross and Archie Campbell and some half-a-dozen others. It was a gruesome job; they clambered up the pile of carcasses and two of them wrested one to the ground, slitting the beast's throat if it still showed any signs of life. Then they sliced into its belly and hauled out the guts, and the hounds came running up to gorge themselves on the entrails.

When all the deer were slaughtered and gralloched, they were laid out neatly for removal to the abbey pantry. Hounds still patrolled the place, bellies swollen, legs, chests and muzzles caked with blood.

The rest of them looked like they'd walked straight off a battlefield.

Hugh grinned at John from a bloody mask of a face. "A good day," he said. "His Grace is happy, and we've all lived to fight another day."

"Gentlemen!" James called. "We've earned our refreshment. There's tents over yonder."

* * *

Once they'd washed their hands and faces, they sat down together in the shadow of the trees. All were sweaty, dishevelled and filthy, even the King. They were brothers in blood; they stretched out tired legs, shared food and drink and talked eagerly about the hunt.

Then, in the midst of the good humour, they were silenced as a rumbling boom rolled and echoed through the valley below.

James glanced up. "Did you hear that, gentlemen?" he asked. "The Lady Meg serenades us. She sings a song of castles cracked and lofty ambitions thwarted."

John hugged his knees with a sigh. Just over a year ago, he'd been part of a different brotherhood who'd thought themselves incapable of defeat. For had they too not been fighting to defend their rightful King? Against a gaggle of hopeless, misguided rebels. . .

Hugh elbowed him. "More wine?"

"What? Oh, yes. Thank you." He grasped the goblet with both hands.

"You're looking pensive. What the Devil's wrong with you?"

"It's a sobering thought," John admitted. "To know that we're at war."

Hugh smiled. His nostrils flared, briefly; he had that same light in his eyes that he'd had the day he'd raided the fermtoun of Glengarnock. "You can be damned dull at times." He folded a leg in close and plucked some coarse white horse-hairs from his hose. "I suppose your idea of excitement involves fretting over the corn yield."

"It's a satisfying thing, to watch your lands prosper."

"It's another man's job to make them prosper on your behalf."

"I don't begrudge my forty days' service," John said, "but I'd grow tired of constantly riding to war."

"I'm tired of not going to war," Hugh retorted. "I'm tired of Justice Ayres, and of having to be civil to greasy burgesses. I hate pronouncing judgment on petty squabbles about lost chickens and trampled fences." He stretched out along the ground, arms folded behind his head. "I can hardly wait to take up arms again," he said. "It's the only time I feel alive."

Chapter 79
The Place of Ellestoun

"Jamie!" Margaret ran to meet her half-brother. He'd scarcely had a chance to dismount before she threw her arms about his neck.

He gripped her tight, laughing. He was just the way he'd always been; rough, shaggy, pungent. "Hello, my little princess! How are you?"

"It's been too long. . ."

Jamie set her down and stepped back so he could study her. "You look fine," he said. "Are you well?"

"I'm very well." She grasped his hands. "And yourself?"

"Same as ever," he said. "William's coming. With the men-at-arms and the baggage horses. We've been summoned to Paisley for the host. We thought we might stay here tonight."

"But of course! I'll prepare the range."

"Is your husband here?"

Her face fell. "I haven't seen him for days now. I hoped he'd come home to muster our men-at-arms, but he never did. The men left yesterday."

"What's this?" Smiling, he grasped her chin and lifted her head. "Could my stone-hearted sister be in love?"

Margaret jerked away, blushing. "Stop it, Jamie!"

"What did the poor man do to win your heart? Did you make him crawl on hands and knees round the bounds of his estate, dragging a big wooden cross upon his back. . ."

"No! It wasn't like that."

"Told you he was alright." His tone was smug.

"I'm so proud of him." She slipped her arm in his. "He's been restored as Sheriff, and that's not all. He sent word yesterday, and you'll never guess what's happened! The King's made him responsible for the artillery, and he's been ordered to oversee a siege."

"Did he tell you this?"

"That's what I was told. Why?"

"He's prone to exaggeration, then," Jamie retorted. "Being made responsible for the guns probably means he's been told to fire them. If that's the case," he added, "we'd best find you a new husband."

"That's not very amusing."

He patted her cheek. "Why the glum face, little sister? If he survived the troubles last winter, he can survive anything. I'm sure he'll be fine."

* * *

William, Jamie and the rest of her brothers sat down at her table for dinner.

It was the first time she'd set eyes on William since the day she'd left Ochiltree. He'd never been much of a man for conversation, but today he scarcely said a word. He didn't even look her in the eye.

Oh, William, can't you see that I'm happy? she thought. *Fate was working in my favour, though it didn't seem that way at first.*

"So if he's the Sheriff," Jamie said, through a mouthful of roast fowl, "then he'll know what's happening. I don't suppose he told you."

"Of course he did."

"You'll tell us all about it, then." Jamie glanced at William.

"If you like," she said.

So she recounted what she'd heard. She told them about the Stewarts and Lord Lyle, and the way they'd treated her husband through the winter. About how her husband had asked the King for aid, and how the King, to everyone's surprise, had agreed to help. She told them that Lord Hugh was now their Justiciar, and that she thought he might have been the one who'd helped her husband regain favour with King James. They were impressed that she was so well-informed, and amazed that the whole business had unfolded with her husband at the heart of it.

"Do you think you'll see him tomorrow?" she asked Jamie.

"From what you've been saying," Jamie replied, "we won't have any choice. He'll be making us kneel before the bombards and lick them clean."

The Town of Paisley

"Will we see the King?" wee Hughie asked.

Mary hoisted Meg higher. "That's why we're here."

Three hours they'd walked, but neither child complained. They weren't the only ones to abandon their chores; the Paisley road was often busy with pilgrims, but today the men and women who choked it had come to pay their respects to a more earthly figure.

"Will we see John?" Hughie asked again.

"He's Master John to you now," his older brother told him.

"But—"

"Listen to your brother," Mary said. "Forget you ever knew him."

"Why?"

"You'll see why."

Outside the gates, the common grazing was alive with tents. There were lines of horses and cattle, and gaudy banners flying high.

"Can we look around later?" her eldest asked.

"If we do," she said, "you mightn't ever get away again. You've grown an inch since the wappenschaw; that might be enough to make them take you as a soldier."

* * *

Inside the town, the narrow streets and wynds were pressed tight with people. There was such excitement about the place. The news was spreading; *Cruikston's fallen. The bombards are on their way.*

"Bombards!" young John gasped. "We'll get to see a bombard."

"What's a bombard?" Hughie asked.

"It's like a culverin, but bigger," his brother replied. "Big enough to swallow you whole."

"What's a culverin?"

"Keep close now," Mary ordered. "Hughie, hang onto my skirts. Johnny, if I lose you, then meet me at the mercat cross when the crowds wane."

* * *

They headed for the east port, because that seemed to be the focus for all the excitement. As they approached, they found men-at-arms and mounted men mingling amongst the crowd.

"Mistress White," said an armoured horseman. He was clad in a scarlet jupon, with a scarlet caprison draped over his bay horse.

Her heart skipped a beat, until she recognised the face beneath the up-tilted visor. "Master Crawfurd!"

He nodded, brisk acknowledgement. "You chose a bad day to visit Paisley."

"We heard the King was here. We wanted to see him."

"Then you're in exactly the right place," Master Crawfurd replied. "He'll be riding forth to meet the bombards, soon as the bells strike noon."

* * *

Meeting Master Crawfurd was a Godsend. He used his big horse to clear a path right to the front of the crowd. "Stand close," he said. "Castor'll keep you safe from the worst of the crush."

"Have you seen Master John?" Mary asked, lifting little Meg up onto her shoulders.

"Not a glimpse," Master Crawfurd said. "I visited his tent last night, but they said he was in the King's company."

"The King's coming!" someone called.

Master Crawfurd sighed and tightened up his reins. To either side, the eager folk of Paisley pressed forward. But they didn't dare come too close to the horse, or to the Crawfurd men-at-arms who were stationed at regular intervals amongst them.

The bells pealed loud in the abbey tower.

He's on his way. . . The whisper rippled through the waiting crowd, and Mary clutched Hughie tight.

They heard drums, beating loud from the depths of the town. The sound made her heart thud faster with excitement, she craned her head round Castor's shoulder, hoping she'd catch a glimpse...

She smiled. *Stop that, Mary. You're too old for this.*

Cheers erupted, far away. The sound grew closer, and closer, until the clamour was all around her, and she was cheering too.

Then she saw him. He was just a slight lad, sitting up there upon his great grey horse, but he had such a regal air about him. He looked so elegant in the saddle, his face glowed with youthful vigour and he had a gold circlet set upon his thick brown hair. His long gown was embroidered with gold thread, and his horse bore a long yellow caprison, with red lion rampants embroidered on its shoulders and quarters.

"That's him," she told Hughie. "That's our King!"

Hughie jumped up and down and yelled all the louder.

The King turned his head. For a moment, he looked down upon them. Then he'd gone, but the procession wasn't over. Following close behind came the Abbot of Paisley. He was mounted on a jennet, and clad in his finest robes. He blessed the crowd as he passed, flanked to left and right by clergymen who held colourful silk banners aloft, and men-at-arms who marched by on foot.

Hot on the abbot's heels were the barons, and woe betide anyone who loitered in their way, for they rode a wall of high-stepping horseflesh that would crush anything in their path.

"Look!" Her eldest tugged her sleeve. "It's Master John!"

When she looked more closely, she recognised the arms; the ivory-white jupon and caprison that set him apart from the quartered blue-and-red and the gold colours worn by the armoured knights on either side. But she would never have known *him*. His armour shone in the sunlight, white and red plumes stood tall on his helmet.

Tears misted her eyes. She felt so proud and happy.

"That's a new horse," young John said.

"So it is," Master Crawfurd agreed. "Now keep as close as you can."

Master Crawfurd's presence was even more of a comfort as the barons came past, for it was a narrow street, and scarcely big enough to hold them. She pulled Hughie tight against her and pressed against Master Crawfurd's horse as a huge grey destrier passed perilously near. She could see the red depths of its nostril, glimpse the veins standing proud on its legs beneath the blue folds of its caprison. The stallion tossed its head and spattered them with flecks of foam from its frothy jaws, making Hughie gasp in awe.

Its rider was close enough to touch, if she'd dared. For a fleeting second, she saw her distorted reflection in the polished armour. She glimpsed the long shank and cruel jagged rowel of his spur and shivered, frightened and delighted all at once.

She felt like a child again. "Who are they?" she asked.

"The Lord Montgomerie wears *gules*-and-*azure*," said Master Crawfurd. "It's as well you stood back, for he'd have trampled you without a thought. On the far side is Sir John Ross of Hawkhead."

"And there's William!" young John gasped, pointing at the men-at-arms who followed on behind. "He's carrying the banner!"

* * *

The sun glinted on a gun barrel, an excited gasp rippled through the crowds that pressed close on either side.

Pinned between Hugh and Sir John Ross, John couldn't have asked for a better vantage point. Abbot Schaw and James sat side by side just ahead; Schaw was calm, serene amongst the clamour, while James was smiling broadly.

The dust clouds settled, and John glimpsed a knight, riding along at the bombard's side. Jupon and caprison were vivid scarlet, marked with white.

It's Earl Patrick, John realised, as knight and bombard drew nearer. *So that's where he's been this past fortnight. . .*

Patrick Hepburn's plate armour was dull with dirt, his jupon stained and filthy. He'd shed his helmet in the heat, but still wore his mail coif. Even his horse looked weary, picking its way along the newly-built road with its head drooping low.

But as the trumpeters played a rousing fanfare, horse and rider strode forward with renewed vigour. James abandoned his horse and headed for the gate, where he waited between the lines of trumpeters for Earl Patrick to join him.

Earl Patrick approached at a trot. He halted just a few steps away from James, and dismounted. Dropping to one knee at the young King's feet, he presented him with a massive wrought-iron key.

James held the key high above his head. "The Place of Cruikston has been restored to the King," he called, and the cheers grew even louder.

As the roar faded, James stretched out his hand and helped Earl Patrick to his feet. He spread his arms wide and hugged his liege close, oblivious to the dust and the unyielding steel armour.

John settled deeper into his saddle with a sigh.

Patrick Hepburn's task was over; his had only just begun.

Chapter 80
Dumbarton Castle

John Stewart stood at the gateway, counting the arrivals one by one. The last of the ladies came through, followed by the men-at-arms. Once everyone was inside, the portcullis rattled down.

Matthew steered his horse around and halted nearby. He looked anxious, weary.

"Where's Lady Lyle?" Stewart asked him.

"She wouldn't leave," Matthew said.

"What do you mean, she wouldn't leave?"

Matthew dismounted. "I pleaded with her," he said. "I shouted at her. I even tried to reason with her. *I've lived in that place thirty years,* she said. *I'm not leaving it now.*"

"Oh, Christ," said Stewart.

"Cruikston fell two days ago. The bombards might have left Paisley already. They've put Sempill of Ellestoun in charge. . ."

"Sempill! And you left her there?"

Matthew scowled at the ground. "She left herself there, Father."

"You should've picked her up and carried her!"

"I did what I could," Matthew retorted. "She wouldn't listen."

Stewart shook his head. "God help the woman. If he's anything like his father, he'll level the place with her inside."

* * *

The air was hot and muggy as they rode across the common grazing to greet the host. It was hard to ride past friends and kinsmen without offering a nod or a friendly word, but John was at the King's bidding, and it wouldn't do to talk out of turn.

While they baked and sweated in their armour, James remained cool and unflustered. The faces that greeted him were often stern and grim, for these were men who remembered how badly they'd fared through the past year. But as James commended them on their turnout, and asked how their crops were faring, their hostility would thaw. Soon they'd smile, and nod, responding eagerly to their King's questions.

Witnessing this, it was almost possible to believe that James could work miracles, bringing unity where his father had brought division and dissent.

* * *

Hours passed before James finally led them to the bombards.

The two guns had their own cluster of tents, set up close to John's own. Occupying this canvas village was a small army of carters, wheelwrights, carpenters and gunners. Tethered nearby were four ranks of sturdy black cattle, coats cropped short to help them weather the heat. And there were at least a dozen carts laden high with fodder and supplies.

James reined in his horse. "A rest for us all, I think," he said. "Let's discuss the guns, Master Sempill."

Once they'd both dismounted, James took John's arm and steered him over to the bombards. "Well?" he asked. "What do you think?"

"Holy Mary!" It was only now that John could appreciate their vast size. Mounted on wooden carriages, they reached the height of his shoulder, their barrels much longer than a man. John ventured close to one, and peered inside its yawning mouth. Reeking of fire and sulphur, the chasm within could easily have accommodated a child of ten.

"Get away from there!" James hauled him back.

"I'm sorry, Your Grace."

"Remember what happened to my grandsire, and don't step too close. We won't risk the blood of good honest Scots in the firing of her."

"Then how will she be fired?"

"Amongst her entourage you'll find some Danish captives." James slipped a conspiratorial arm round John's shoulders. "They were caught at sea plundering Scots ships. We hanged their companions, but spared them because they knew the ways of artillery. They'll be handling the bombards. Once Dumbarton is mine, they'll be freed—" James leaned closer still, and whispered, "If they survive, that is..." He punched John lightly in the back. "You'll keep them supplied with meat and drink?"

"I will, Your Grace."

"Very good." James caressed the bombard's barrel. "This is Mons Meg. The other. . . She has no name as yet. Treat both these ladies with care, Master Sempill. Give them the tenderness you would lavish on your good wife. Or better still—" he added, with a glint in his eye, "—your mistress. There's two carts of stone for the firing, and another two carts loaded with powder." He paused. "You know a little about the powder?"

"I know better than to roast my meat alongside."

"It mustn't get wet, either."

"I'll place it under cover. And mount a guard over it."

"An excellent plan. There's no better way for a man to sabotage a siege gun than to piss on the powder. "You've spoken to the Laird of Hillhouse?"

"Yes, Your Grace."

"He'll be just ahead, preparing the road. It's customary for the guns to travel with the baggage, but it's such a short road to Duchal that I thought it best if the host remained in Paisley another day. You'll travel on ahead and command the van. You can protect Hillhouse and his men and ensure the safety of the bombards."

"How many men will I be granted?"

"Lord Hugh!" James called. "Remain with Master Sempill. Discuss his requirements and make the necessary arrangements."

"Thank you." James was back on his horse in an instant. "Goodbye, Master Sempill!" he said. "Next time we talk, you'll have good news to report." He waved to Archie Campbell, Patrick Hepburn and the others. "Come on!" he told them. "Let's be on our way."

Hugh stared after them.

"I'm sorry," John said. "It must be disappointing, to be lumbered with a dolt like me when you could be mingling amongst the great and glorious."

"Nonsense." Hugh dismounted and slouched back against the barrel of the bombard, while Zephyr cropped the grass at his feet. "I thought I'd grant you the men from six households. The choice is yours. The only favour I ask is that you allow Sir John Ross and his liveries to travel with me."

John leaned alongside. "I'll have my own men, of course. And it'd be poor form not to invite the Colvilles. Other than that, I'd be grateful for the Mures, the Crawfurds and the Dunlops. And..." He hesitated. "The Cunninghames."

"Christ!" Hugh snarled, so loud that Zephyr flinched. "Why must you burden yourself with *them*?"

"If Craigends comes with me in the van, neither of you'll be granted any opportunity to start scrapping. . ."

"Do you think I'd quarrel with Cunninghame at a time like this?"

"He might quarrel with you."

Hugh scowled. "Alright. If you insist."

"Thank you."

"You'll talk to the lairds?"

"Of course. You may abandon me. Spare a thought for me tonight; while you're basking in the King's company, I'll be discussing Aristotle with the oxen."

"If you mingle with the Cunninghames, then you can forget Aristotle. All Craigends'll want to do is discredit me, the liar."

"You think I'd mock you to win favour with Craigends?"

Hugh didn't reply. He still leaned against the bombard, frowning.

"You should know me better than that." John pushed Hugh away. "Well go on," he said. "The King'll be wondering where you are."

* * *

"If it isn't Master Sempill!" Robert Crawfurd strode towards him. "I scarcely recognised you. A new horse, new arms and bright new trappings, too. It's good to see that some men are prospering in these harsh times."

"That's no way to greet your friend."

"Have they granted you your knighthood? Or do they dangle it before you like a fat carrot before a mule?"

John leaned on his pommel, straight-faced. "How's Marion?"

Robert's face fell. "She's with child again, for sure."

"Is she faring better this time?"

"She's sick every morning, and it breaks my heart," Robert admitted. "But the midwife says it's quite normal for a woman to be that way."

"I'll pray for her, and make arrangements for masses to be sung. I'll visit her, too, once all this is behind us."

"She'd appreciate that. She's been anxious. We heard you weren't keeping well."

"It's all behind me now."

403

"Rumour has it that it was all Montgomerie's doing. That he poisoned you because you berated him in front of Patrick Hepburn."

"Don't men have better things to do than conjure up lies?"

"How can we help you?" Robert asked, voice guarded.

"The bombards leave tomorrow, in my charge. I need men to ride with me."

Robert smiled. "We'd be honoured." He clapped the neck of John's horse. "He's a fine beast. A steed to be proud of."

"He's not mine yet. It all depends on how the situation unfolds."

"Father's inside. I'll fetch him if you like."

"That's not necessary. Perhaps you'd take supper with me this evening?"

"We'd be delighted."

"There's just one more thing. I need a favour. I want Craigends to join me in the van. I want advice on how best to approach him."

"We'll talk to him," Robert said.

"Ask him to dine with me tonight. That might help things a little."

* * *

"Mistress Mary." William touched his bonnet as she approached. He was leaning against his spear, the bombards looming large behind him.

She was glad it was William who'd spotted her first. "Hello," she said, a little shyly. "The boys. . . They came to see the guns. . ."

"Go and speak to Mungo," he told her eldest. "He'll let you take a close look."

Wee Hughie leapt away with a cry of delight, while Johnny followed at a more leisurely pace.

She was left alone with William. "What's in there?" She gestured towards the tent at his shoulder.

"A cart filled with black powder," William explained. "Master John wanted it under cover."

"A sound move." She glanced at the sky. A vast mass of cloud towered over the horizon. "The weather'll break tonight."

"Not before time."

Gripping Meg tight with one hand, she smoothed out her skirts with the other. "We came to see the King."

"Have you a place to stay?"

"No."

"I'll find you a space somewhere." He grasped hold of Meg. "Here. Let me hold her for a while."

"Is he here?"

William glanced back towards the nearby tents. "Entertaining his gude-brothers."

"I didn't expect to see him." She cast a careful eye over the children; Hughie clambered over the bombard, while Johnny talked to Mungo, trying to look manly and responsible.

"Have you eaten?" William asked.

She shrugged. "A few chunks of bread."

He smiled. "Then why don't we go to the town, and find something more wholesome. For you and the children."

"Won't you be missed?"

"Not for an hour or two. Someone else can keep watch while I'm away."

"Alright then," she agreed.

"You're a handsome woman, Mistress Mary," he said. "It's a pleasure to be graced with your company."

* * *

Lightning lit the darkness and thunder crashed nearby. Rain had battered against the tent for an hour or more; lying flat on his back below, John thanked God he'd had the foresight to cover the powder.

He soon gave up all attempts at sleeping; scrambling from his bed, he pulled on a sark and a pair of hose.

He peered outside. A vivid blaze of light showed William standing guard by the powder, so John braved the rain and darted across the open ground to join him.

"I couldn't sleep," John explained.

"Neither could I." William shifted and stifled a yawn.

"I'll relieve you for a while," John offered.

William shook his head. "No need."

Lightning flashed across the western sky, and William crossed himself. "It's an omen."

"Who should heed it? Lord Lyle, or the King?"

William didn't answer.

The world went stark white; in the nearby animal lines, horses and oxen jostled and stamped. Just one creature showed no fear; John's black destrier. It stood like an ebony statue, head held high, gaze fixed on the western horizon.

"I'll call him Storm," said John. "Together, we'll bring Lord Lyle the greatest storm he's ever known."

"There's the makings of a good ballad there," William said. "The Tale of John Sempill and the Siege of Duchal."

"I'm not exactly the Wallace."

"Well, I'm not exactly Blind Harry." William fell silent a moment, then added, "Mistress Mary brought her boys to see the King. I spent the evening in her company."

John laughed, softly. "So there's life in you yet?"

"I was wondering if I might visit her again once this is over."

"Of course," John said. "And if you want to ask for her hand, then by all means do so. I'd like to know she's provided for."

William bowed his head. "God bless you."

* * *

The rain cleared by the following morning, when they gathered for mass one last time. Abbot Schaw conducted the ceremony himself; as well as blessing the gathered members of the host, he blessed the bombards and the beasts of burden for good measure, while King and courtiers looked on approvingly.

Eventually, the Laird of Hillhouse was summoned. He'd remained in Paisley the previous day while the rest of his crew started work on the road. The reason for the delay soon became clear; Hillhouse was presented to the King and knighted.

A good sign, John thought. He watched the proceedings from the back of his horse, flanked by Jamie Colville and Sir William Cunninghame of Craigends.

With mass behind them, they mingled briefly with James and his counsellors before their departure.

But Hugh didn't even glance in his direction.

* * *

"Thank you," John told Craigends later, once they'd started on their way. The road stretched ahead, quarry pits and broken trees scarring the ground on either side. "I wasn't convinced you'd support us."

"I was summoned by my King and my Sheriff. How else could I respond?" Craigends glanced towards the cloud-chequered sky. "It's cooler than of late."

"The storm cleared the air."

"The skies were still blue when you put a tent over the powder," Craigends said. "Men laughed at that. *Master Sempill jumps at shadows*, they said."

"They can laugh all they like."

"No arguing with that." Craigends grimaced. "I must talk with you, Master Sempill."

"What is it, Sir William?"

"My brother the Lord Kilmaurs agreed that we should support the King. But Lord Lyle has already approached him." He paused, then added in a low voice, "My brother is considering Lyle's offer. His Grace the King has done nothing to preserve us from Montgomerie's so-called justice."

"Thank you for telling me this."

"That's not all," Craigends added. "Rob spoke with the Boyds and the Kennedys. If we join Lennox and Lyle, they'll come with us." He looked John in the eye. "You understand the implications?"

"Yes, of course," John retorted. "What I can't understand is why you came here in the first place."

"We think that both you and the King should be allowed to prove your good intentions. But our presence here isn't guaranteed."

"What do you want?" John asked, coldly.

"Nothing much," Craigends replied, with a shrug and a smile. "Just keep Montgomerie off my back. That's all."

Chapter 81

It was the second day they'd been on the road. They'd barely passed the lands of Ranfurly before one of the gun carriages lurched to a halt for a second time that morning.

"Broken wheel," said a carter.

John sighed and sat deeper in the saddle. It must have been around noon; there was scarcely a breeze and he could hardly breathe for the weight of his armour. A fly buzzed about his eyes; he swatted it away.

"How long d'you think it'd take to move these brutes from Edinburgh to Berwick?" Adam asked.

"Six weeks, I'd guess," Craigends said.

"Six weeks!" Adam snarled. "I'd die of boredom!" The fly that had been tormenting John moved in on him; he scowled and slapped it when it settled on his cheek. "I hope to God we make such a damned awful job that we're never asked again."

"Speak for yourself," John said. "If you want to be useful, fetch the wheelwright."

Adam rode off without another word.

John retrieved a flagon from a nearby cart. He returned to the front of the line and halted alongside Craigends. "Some ale?"

Craigends took the vessel and gulped down a few mouthfuls, then handed it back with a gruff word of thanks.

John was taking a drink himself when someone hailed them from further down the line. "Ho there!"

John stood in his stirrups. When he glanced beyond the bombards he saw armoured horsemen approaching; Robert Crawfurd, cantering up from the rear with Hugh Montgomerie alongside.

"Earl Patrick's on his way!" Hugh reined in next to John. "He wants to find a site for the bombards. You'll come with us, Master Sempill."

"Malcolm? The guns are in your care." John handed Hugh the flagon. "Here. There's a little left."

"Jesus Christ!" Craigends muttered. "If I'd known you'd give *him* succour, I'd have spat in it."

"Oh, for God's sake. . ." John began, for Hugh had choked on his ale and was scowling ominously back. "Can't you be courteous, for once?"

"He's a common thief and a murderer. He should hang like one."

Hugh barged his horse against John's. "I won't take this slander from you."

"Hugh—" John warned.

"Your whole damned brood was sired by the Devil," Craigends cut in. "When your mother took Lucifer to her bed, she spread her legs wide and welcomed him—"

Hugh roared and flung the flagon down.

Behind John a dozen Cunninghame liveries readied their weapons. Oblivious, Hugh hauled out his sword with a snarl, his gaze locked on Craigends. He raised his arm to strike, but John moved first.

Reaching out his hand, John closed his fingers tight about the blade.

He'd stopped the fight, but Hugh was glaring at *him* now. John's heart pounded fearfully, but he didn't release his grip. He braved a smile, and a nod. "Gentlemen, please! Lord Lyle would laugh, if he witnessed this." He pressed Hugh's sword gently aside.

Everyone drew a sharp breath. They thought Hugh would strike him, and for a moment, so did he.

Instead, Hugh wheeled his horse around without a word and spurred it down the road at a gallop.

"Come back and fight like a man, Montgomerie!" Craigends called. He smiled wryly at his men. "Damned coward."

"Thirteen against one hardly constitutes a fair fight," John retorted.

Craigends raised his brows. "He's well-used to odds like that."

"If you're spoiling for a fight, then I'm sure Lord Hugh will oblige. It's only fair, though, that the odds are evenly balanced. Then we'll see who's the coward." John coaxed his horse forward. "Malcolm? The bombards are in your care. Tell Earl Patrick that I've ridden ahead with Lord Hugh."

"John, wait-" Malcolm called after him. "Don't be a fool!"

* * *

"Hugh!" John slapped his reins against his horse's neck, urging it onwards. "Wait a moment!"

Hugh pulled his mount to a standstill. He still gripped his drawn sword, face pale, ashen. "I have nothing to say to you."

"I saved your life."

"You interfered!" Hugh spat. "I should have your head for that."

"You were outnumbered ten times over. They'd have hacked you apart."

"That's nonsense." Hugh set off at a trot.

Undeterred, John followed. "You'd be dead!"

There was no reaction at first. Then suddenly Hugh wheeled his horse around. "If I had my way, I'd carve out his guts and stuff them down his throat."

"I heard what he said," John agreed. "I think you acted with restraint."

"I'll kill him." Hugh's voice shook. "I swear to God I'll kill him. And his useless brother Kilmaurs."

"Keep your voice down!" John looked warily back down the track. A flash of scarlet in the distance showed that Hepburn and his entourage were approaching. "If he wants to discredit you in front of Earl Patrick, he's succeeding."

Hugh sighed and sheathed his sword.

* * *

Earl Patrick was accompanied by half-a-dozen of his retainers. In their midst rode two of the Danish captives, clad in torn, soot-blackened clothes. Their pale hair hung loose down their backs, their sullen faces were unshaven. Their wrists were secured to the harness of their horses, which were being towed along by the accompanying men-at-arms.

"I was told you'd be in the Lennox by now," Earl Patrick said to Hugh.

"Your Grace," John said. "Lord Hugh was sorely provoked. No man would've acted differently."

"Quiet, John!" Hugh snapped. "It's not your concern."

"You've taught him well," Earl Patrick remarked. He turned to John. "Master Sempill, come with me." He sent his bay horse striding forwards, so they rode a few yards from the rest of the party. "Is it true, what you said?"

"Yes, it is."

"Ah." Earl Patrick smiled, faintly.

"What did they say?"

"No one said anything. Except Craigends. Who claimed the attack was unprovoked."

The scowl was back, and John didn't try and subdue it. Outrage suddenly overwhelmed him; men he'd once thought fair, and reasonable, like Malcolm and Robert Crawfurd, had shied from the truth because it would mean defending Hugh Montgomerie over Craigends. "Craigends should apologise."

"I'll speak with him," said Earl Patrick.

* * *

When they rode through the fermtoun of the Green, everything seemed normal. The damage done during the Sempills' winter raid had been mended long ago; now the cottages looked quiet and prosperous. The crops were ripening, children played in the sun.

As soon as Earl Patrick and his party appeared, every villager stopped what they were doing and stared. Children gasped and pointed, too young to understand the implications.

Earl Patrick led the way to the little stone-built chapel that squatted in the midst of the village. "Take my horse and wait here." Dismounting, he thrust his reins into John's hand, then strode up the path that led through the burial ground towards the chapel.

The priest was waiting at the door.

"There's still parley to get through." Hugh slipped down from Zephyr's back. "That'll give them plenty of opportunity to abandon the place." He loosed a gauntlet with his teeth. "Hold this, would you?"

"Do you think they know what'll happen here?"

"They're peasants. They don't know anything." Hugh faced the wall of the burial ground. He fumbled with his armour and his hose, then groaned as he emptied his bladder. "God, that's better."

"That's unfair."

Hugh glanced across the village. "No it's not."

John frowned. Judging from the way the villagers were gathering outside their houses, they already suspected that something was amiss.

"The garrison will have abandoned the place, surely," John persisted.

"You'd have thought so."

"So why haven't his tenants left already?"

"The crops are coming along. Their animals are fattening nicely." Hugh retrieved his gauntlet. "In those circumstances, wouldn't you be reluctant to leave?"

"I suppose so."

"There you are then," Hugh replied. "My arse is killing me," he said. "I've been living on the back of this damned horse for the last two days. Any more of it, and I'll turn into a horse myself." Grasping John's mount by the bridle, he added, "I'd make the most of this. Might be hours before you get another chance to stop."

The Place of Duchal

The bombards were set in place on a low ridge overlooking the castle. Lord Lyle's grip hadn't been loosed just yet; the drawbridge was closed, and figures watched them from the wall-walk.

There'd be no escape for the garrison now. The host were camped beyond the main gates, while half-a-dozen Mures and another dozen Montgomeries had been dispatched to watch over the sally port.

Further down the hill, earthen banks were being thrown up to protect the gunners. The fermtoun of the Green lay right in the line of fire, but its inhabitants still seemed loath to leave. They preferred to put their lives in God's hands than risk losing their property.

They were guaranteed to lose at least some of it, though. John had sent the Crawfurds out with his kinsman Fulwood to draw an inventory of all the goods and livestock held on the surrounding farms. He'd seize what was required to make up for what had been lost over the winter.

And take a little extra to cover damages. . .

It was a harsh line to take, but it was astute. He was well within his rights to get whatever he could out of the situation.

He supposed his father would have been proud of him.

He'd followed Hugh's advice and pitched his tents a respectable distance from the bombards, and upwind, too. Hugh had dined with him that evening; now they were whiling away the hours before nightfall with a game of chess.

"How long d'you think they'll hold out?" John asked.

"They'll crack just as soon as the first shot's fired." Hugh deftly removed one of John's pawns and set a Bishop in its place.

"And when's that?"

"That's up to you, isn't it?" Hugh looked up. "D'you think, if they moved the mouths a little higher, the shot'd carry over the hills? It's said the damned things can reach five miles or more."

"Meaning what?"

"It's three miles to Glengarnock, as the crow flies. One to Finlaystone."

"I hope you're jesting."

"How much would it take to bribe a gunner?"

"If you mean the rogues that we've been granted, not much." John batted the offending Bishop aside with his Queen. "Check."

"It'd be a good way of seeing what these ladies can do."

"I'm not listening."

"Why, talk of the Devil!" Hugh sat up, straight, guarded.

The Devil in question was Sir William Cunninghame of Craigends. He stamped up the hill towards them, scowling.

"Ah, Sir William!" John called, raising his goblet. "Would you care to take some wine with us?"

"Thank you, but no."

"Then what can I do for you?"

Craigends cast a sour look at Hugh. "I've come to apologise. I shouldn't have insulted a fellow knight. And what I said about the Lady Katherine Kennedy was unpardonable."

"Lord Hugh?"

Hugh shrugged. "It's forgotten already."

"Eh?" Craigends frowned.

"Master Sempill has convinced me that only great men have the strength of will to walk away from a fight. You are forgiven, Sir William."

"Blessed are the peacemeakers," said John.

"Amen to that," Hugh agreed.

"Take some wine with us," John invited again. "There's more than enough to go round."

But Craigends was already heading back towards his tents.

"There's something to be said for being magnanimous," Hugh said. "It warms the soul—"

"Maybe there's hope for you yet."

Hugh still stared intently at Craigends' retreating back. "—But I draw the line at sharing wine with him."

Chapter 82

Early the following morning, they trod the well-worn track that led to Duchal's gates. Riding alongside Hugh, John seemed calm, serene. But he hadn't spoken a word, and Hugh understood the younger man's silence well enough. John was anxious, and rightly so; there'd been ill feeling between the Sempills and the Lyles for years, ever since Sir Thomas Sempill burned Duchal's outbuildings and orchards in a dispute with Robert, Lord Lyle.

The Place of Duchal loomed ahead. It comprised a tall tower, defended by a high curtain wall and surrounded by a moat of slime-green water. The drawbridge was resolutely closed, the garrison peering anxiously down from the wall-walk.

Margaret Houston, Lady Lyle was amongst them, a grim, indomitable matriarch. She leaned on the parapet, disdain carved sharp on her face as she watched their party approach.

All in all, Hugh thought, it made for an interesting confrontation.

"There you are." Hugh gestured down the track towards the castle gates.

John rode away with the herald. He certainly looked the part now. With a good well-bred horse and a fine set of plate armour, he gave the impression that he'd be a match for any man in battle.

John's skills and prowess had been forged by others; by Sir Thomas Sempill, of course, and by Matthew Stewart, too. But Hugh felt a certain sense of pride because he'd glimpsed qualities that these other worthy men had missed. He'd honed and polished the rough edges, and now he'd been granted a perfect opportunity to see the results of his craftsmanship. Running a hand down Zephyr's neck, he settled comfortably into the saddle.

Bute Pursuivant raised his horn and blew loudly upon it. "Lord Lyle has failed to respond to the charges of treason made against him in Parliament. As a consequence, his lands and goods are considered forfeit. If the said Lord Lyle fails to yield the aforementioned lands and goods into the King's hands, then they will be seized by force of arms."

"Who represents the King in this matter?" Lady Lyle demanded.

"I do," said John.

"And who gives you that right?"

"As Sheriff of Renfrew, it's my—"

"You're not the Sheriff, Master Sempill."

"—duty to enforce the King's will throughout the lands of Renfrew—"

"You're not the Sheriff."

"—throughout the lands of Renfrew." John raised his voice a fraction. "You'll surrender the castle to me, in timely fashion—"

"I will not—"

"—or you'll face the consequences."

She raised her head and looked towards Hugh and Sir John Ross. "I won't negotiate with *him*."

"If you won't hear my terms," said John, in that same steady tone, "then perhaps you'll listen to the bombards."

"You wouldn't dare use them."

"You have two days." He turned his horse.

"Lord Hugh!" Lady Lyle called. "How can you stand for this?"

"Madam, your husband's a rebel," Hugh retorted. "Don't expect any grace from me."

"I'll talk with you," Lady Lyle persisted. "Or with Sir John Ross of Hawkhead. But not with that whelp!"

"You'll parley with the Sheriff. The King and the Justiciar have placed him in charge."

"It's disgraceful. He should never—"

Hugh shrugged. "I appointed him myself."

"Damn you, Montgomerie!" She slapped her fists against the parapet. "Is this world choked with traitors?"

"I take issue with that, Lady Margaret," Hugh retorted. "The King's flag's flying over yonder. That puts us firmly on the side of righteousness."

John returned with the herald. He didn't stop; he just rode straight past. His face showed nothing, but Hugh knew him well enough. *He's livid*, he thought. *Heaven help the woman, if she keeps baiting him like that. . .*

Hugh steered Zephyr around and trotted up alongside. John remained silent, eyes fixed before him. It wasn't until they'd left the castle far behind that he sighed and shook his head. "I almost pity Lord Lyle," he said. "It must be Purgatory, being wed to that harpy."

"And now you're saddled with her," Hugh replied. "Isn't that a comforting thought?"

* * *

John retreated to his tent and flopped down in his chair. The timber creaked ominously beneath him, but John felt too tired to care. The confrontation with Lady Lyle had drained him, a headache prowled in his skull.

William poured him some wine.

John accepted it without a word and downed half the goblet in one draught. It had taken all his strength of will to keep from unleashing the bombards then and there.

She's only a woman, he reminded himself. *Her thoughts are flawed.*

* * *

He thought he'd be granted a rest now that parley was behind him. But he was mistaken. An hour or so later Hugh summoned him, with the instruction that he was to come in full array.

Once he was armed and ready, John reluctantly headed over to find Hugh. He wasn't yet familiar with his new armour; it weighed far more than the old set he'd been used to. Off the horse, he felt he was wading through treacle.

Hugh waited outside his own tent. He leaned idly against his bastard sword, which he'd thrust into the ground beside him. Hessilhead stood at his shoulder; like Hugh, he was arrayed for battle.

John's enthusiasm was wilting already. *Madness,* Malcolm had said. *When Montgomerie takes up the challenge, man against man, a fury comes over him. He'll slaughter you and not even know he's done it.*

Looking at Hugh, it was hard to believe such tales, for he looked bored beyond belief. Unlike Hessilhead, who grinned gleefully, like a Devil welcoming yet another lost soul into his keeping.

John glanced reluctantly around him. Word had spread, and a sizeable crowd was gathering. "You've quite a reputation," he told Hugh.

Hugh smiled, faintly. "Indeed."

"Rest assured, I'm no match for you. It's not my favoured weapon."

"Don't make excuses," Hugh said, then added, *"A pleasance."*

I sincerely hope so, John thought.

* * *

Margaret paused upon the stair. "So how's he faring?"

"He was very well," Alan Semple replied. "Until yesterday."

Her heart lurched. "What happened?"

"He took a hiding from Lord Hugh."

Alan didn't sound too concerned. But Margaret's pulse quickened nonetheless. "But why? I thought they were friends."

"His Lordship meant no harm. He was putting Master John through his paces with the bastard sword, that's all."

"He's not injured?" Margaret couldn't mask her agitation.

"Just a bit bruised," Alan replied. "Lord Hugh knocked him over, again and again. But Master John wouldn't give up." He paused, then added, "We're all very proud of him."

Men, Margaret thought, and didn't deign to comment any further. "Now what exactly are you looking for?"

"There's a list somewhere," said Alan. "Master John set it out back in January. It's an inventory of everything stolen from his tenants."

"I'll find it for you now."

She led the way into the laird's chamber, and opened up the kist where the charter chest was held. Alan helped her lift it out and set it down upon the bed. After unlocking it, she searched through the parchments inside.

She found an inventory amongst the rental rolls. It wasn't a very tidy hand, so she guessed it must be John's writing, rather than that of a notary. The entries listed farms and tenants, and a whole range of items, from pregnant kye to pots and pans.

She handed it to Alan. "Is that it?"

He looked shame-faced. "I don't know."

"If it's the wrong one, then I'm sorry." She rose to her feet. "Maybe next time he'd best send a man who can read." She smiled at Alan's crestfallen expression. "It's not your fault," she told him. "He should've realised that this might happen."

414

"I don't suppose it matters too much," Alan replied. "I've not got far to travel. I can always bring it back."

"I hope that won't be necessary."

"Anyway, he's in no real hurry," Alan added. "Soon as he starts handing out recompense, his army'll melt away faster than the winter snows. They only came to get what's due."

"Doesn't that worry him?"

Alan grinned. "He's got the bombards. He could take the castle with half-a-dozen men now that they're in place."

"That's comforting," she said. "Now, is there anything else?"

"As much bread as you can spare. Some salted mutton, and some salted herrings, too. And beer. Lots of it. Oh, and he wants a barrel of his best claret, so he can entertain his gude-brothers properly."

"I thought the whole purpose of war was that you could live off other men's goods."

"They're our neighbours, Mistress Margaret. Ill feelings can last for generations round here."

"I suppose you're right," she agreed. "Well then, let's go down to the cellars, and see what we can find."

* * *

She watched from the wall-walk as Alan's horse disappeared down the road at a trot. "It's hard to believe we're at war," she told Katherine. "There's Alan, riding out alone like he hasn't a care in the world."

"Your husband's well?"

"As well as can be expected," Margaret replied, bitterly. "Considering he spends his time sparring with Lord Hugh." She shivered. "He could at least try and keep safe."

Katherine studied the parapet. "There's still no sign of your monthly course?"

"It might yet come."

"It's been over a week."

"I know!" Margaret retorted. She didn't know whether to be excited or terrified. She remembered how badly her gude-sister Elisabeth had fared, and shuddered.

"You should be pleased," Katherine said. "He'll be delighted when he hears the news. And so proud of you."

"When I remember that night, I remember being so happy in his company. But the truth is. . . I still hardly know him. The more time passes, and he's not here, the more I look back and wonder if that night was just a dream." She fumbled for her handkerchief and dabbed it irritably against her nose. "If I'm with child, I won't be able to share his bed for nine months or more." She swallowed. "What am I to do? I don't think I can bear it."

* * *

A third day dawned at Duchal, and it was time for the second round of parley.

John left the rest of his entourage and rode down towards the castle with the herald.

Nothing had changed. The drawbridge remained tightly closed, while the garrison still slouched along the wall-walk, faces defiant.

As for Lady Lyle. . . She leaned upon the wall-walk, scowling.

John sat deeper in the saddle with a martyred sigh. The moat stank in the summer heat; a swarm of flies drifted from it and buzzed about his horse, making it switch its tail and stamp.

"You've had one full day to consider our demands," John called. "What response would you have me give the King?"

"I won't negotiate with you."

Was it madness on her part, John wondered, or something more profound? He gestured up the hill. "Then you'll negotiate with the bombards."

"You wouldn't dare use them." She sounded almost gleeful.

He was considering his reply when something stirred on the wall-walk above.

"John!" Hugh's voice rang out.

A projectile hissed; John gasped as he felt his saddle jolt. His horse tensed beneath him, throwing up its head and snorting. He thought at first it had been struck. But when the beast didn't crumple or leap away, he knew it was unharmed.

He reached down to stroke its neck. It was then he saw the crossbow bolt, lodged deep in the pommel of his saddle. It had pierced the wood; the tip had gone right through and was just touching the chainmail skirt that covered his groin.

A wave of rage coursed through him, he glared up at the waiting garrison.

Lady Lyle's face was white with fear. "I didn't authorise this!"

He took one deep breath after another, channelling the fury. Making sure that whatever retribution he took, it wasn't undertaken in haste.

Lady Lyle misread his silence; she sighed with loud relief.

John nodded to her, determined to remain courteous, even now. But when he looked at her, he felt nothing inside; no compassion, no regret.

He spun his horse around on its hocks and cantered back to the brace of men-at-arms that waited by Hugh's shoulder. Barging close, he seized a spear from the nearest soldier. He turned his horse smartly around, and trotted back down the hill.

Almost at the edge of the moat, he hauled his horse to a halt. Then he flung the spear down with all his might. The metal tip lodged deep in the ground, the shaft shuddering along its length.

"Parley's over," he said.

Chapter 83

Hugh hadn't expected hostilities to commence this quickly. But then he hadn't expected one of the idiots trapped in the castle to try his luck at bringing down the Sheriff. Small wonder John had lost his temper, when he'd nearly had his manhood pinned to his saddle by a crossbow bolt.

They watched in uncomfortable silence as John hurled the spearhead down to signal the start of the seige. And when John came trotting past with that pale tight-lipped look about him, not even Hugh felt inclined to question him.

Hugh looked at Ross, who raised his brows and sighed.

They followed John up the hill. At a respectful distance, until they could be sure that his rage had cooled.

Not much sign of that just yet. Hugh hung back a little further. Just in case…

They reached the bombards.

"How soon?" John called to the Master Gunner.

"An hour at most," came the reply.

"Fetch those Danish knaves and get on with it!"

The gunner ducked away.

Hugh reined in his horse alongside. "You've forgotten something."

John scowled. "What?"

"I've a dozen men at the sally port. Sir Adam Mure's out there, too."

"Damn it!"

"Don't delay the firing," Hugh told him. "I'll fetch them now." He smiled. "Everything's intact?"

"Yes," John said.

"Glad to hear it." Hugh pressed his horse away at a canter.

* * *

Hugh assured him that his horse would tolerate the firing, but John felt the beast had suffered enough distress for one day. He dismounted, and handed the reins to William. "Saddle needs mending."

William winced, picking splinters of wood away. "That was too close for comfort."

"It was a perfectly good saddle."

"At least your bollocks are unscathed," said William. "If it'd happened to me, I'd have pissed myself."

"That's comforting to know."

"Master Sempill!" The Master Gunner hailed him. "The guns are ready now, if it please you."

* * *

As they headed over to the bombards, the Master Gunner handed John a lump of beeswax. "To plug your ears," he explained.

Down in the valley, Duchal's tower stood white-harled and defiant. For the last couple of days, John had felt nothing but dislike for Lady Lyle. Now, though, he pitied her. She was only doing her husband's bidding. He wondered if she really knew what awaited her.

The wheels had been removed from the gun carriages, the guns themselves tethered to the ground with ropes attached to stout wooden pegs.

John shed gauntlets and helmet, then took some of the wax and shaped it in his fingers until he could slip it in his ear. Around him, the preparations continued. Casks of black powder were rolled up to the guns; handfuls of powder scooped into the gun barrels then rammed into place. Meanwhile, half-a-dozen Danish captives approached. Two carried a carved stone cannonball between them, the size of a man's head.

John swallowed. His throat felt dry, his heart was thumping. He wanted as much as the next man to see what the bombards could do, but at the same time, he feared for the souls in the castle below.

Whatever happened, he would be responsible. It had been his decision. His alone. . .

The thought sickened him.

There was Hugh, and Adam was with him. They cantered across the slanting ground, their men-at-arms following close behind.

The braziers were already lit, the irons heating in the piles of glowing coals. The line of fire was clear; all that lay before the guns was the castle, which looked suddenly fragile in the still morning air.

"Everything's ready, Master Sempill."

He barely heard the words of the Master Gunner. He took a deep breath, fighting the reluctance. "Fire the guns." His words echoed loud in his ears.

The Danes moved in with the firing-irons and set the tips against the touch-holes. The air trembled with the sound of the explosion and the ground shuddered. Clouds of fire and smoke vomited out from the maws of the bombards, which lurched against their bonds like living things.

John blinked and shook his head. He'd unleashed Hell and he was standing in its midst; clouds of acrid, sulphurous smoke drifted everywhere. He coughed and gagged at the stench, his ears ringing.

Slowly, the smoke cleared. John half-expected to see Duchal in ruins, but the tower was still there. And the curtain wall, too.

Then he saw the fermtoun. One of the houses lay ruined, the timbers of its roof jutting up like broken twigs amidst a cloud of dust.

"It takes a while to perfect the aim." The Master Gunner spoke loud to make himself heard. "We'll realign them before we take the next shot."

John wasn't sure if he was relieved or disappointed. "How soon will that be?"

"It'll be an hour before the barrels cool enough to touch them. If the powder was inserted just now, it'd ignite immediately."

"How much shot do we have?"

"We brought five balls from the Cruikston siege, and we've made another five since then."

"Best conserve the shot then," John suggested. "Cease firing at nightfall. Hopefully, they'll reflect on their situation tonight and surrender on the morrow."

The Place of Ellestoun

They were sitting in the garden with their sewing in their laps when they heard a low, echoing rumble, something like thunder.

Mariota looked up, frowning. "What's that?" she asked. "There's not a cloud to be seen."

"It's the bombards," Margaret said. "He's using the bombards." The thought made her feel warm inside. All that destruction, let loose at his command. She shivered, and wriggled her toes. "I wonder if he misses my company."

Katherine smiled. "There's no-one to satisfy his manly urges."

"There's always his horse," Alison suggested.

The girls giggled, but Margaret remained straight-faced. "So when he sees his horse, he thinks of me. Thank you, Alison!"

Alison blushed. "No! That's not what I meant."

"It must be Hell for him," Katherine sighed. "To be cooped up in his tent, when he knows his wife's waiting just a few miles distant."

Margaret turned back to her sewing. "I'm sure he'll live," she said. "And when at last he returns, he'll appreciate me all the more."

The Place of Duchal

The second time the guns were fired, John was more comfortably situated in the shadow of his tent, in the company of Hugh and Sir John Ross. They were sharing a jug of claret, and finishing their dinner.

They shielded their eyes from the sun and studied the scene before them.

"That's better," Hugh said.

The aim *was* improving. Gaps had appeared amongst the shrubby trees that grew in the valley of the Green Water.

"Here's to the next one." Ross raised his goblet.

* * *

When the next round came, they were so engrossed in a game of cards that they'd clean forgotten the guns were there. John nearly choked on his wine, while Hugh lurched forward in his chair, hitting the table with his knees and sending cards flying in all directions.

Sir John Ross looked up, unperturbed. "You pups should've been at Roxburgh," he said. "Now that was a real siege."

"Don't brag, man," Hugh said. "You lost a King there."

Ross shrugged. He was staring intently at the castle.

A cloud of dust was drifting up from it; when it cleared they saw a gaping hole in the gatehouse.

"That's the aim sorted, anyway," Ross said.

"We'll call a halt now," John decided. "We can start again tomorrow."

* * *

419

John lay awake, savouring the silence.

The stink of burnt black powder tainted the air. To try and banish it, he'd unwrapped Margaret's handkerchief from his sword hilt and placed it beside him on his pillow. It helped a little, though the scent of rosewater had largely faded, with just a ghost of her fragrance remaining.

He could push her from his thoughts during the day. But as soon as he retired to his bed, he found himself thinking of her. He'd have given anything, to see her face again.

He tossed on his pallet with a sigh. He was proud to serve his King, and eager to prove himself. But when the night was dark and silent, he couldn't deny the truth. What he wanted, more than anything else, was to go home.

The Place of Ellestoun

Katherine snuggled up close that night. "Do you think the siege is over yet?"

"If I was defending my place against my husband's enemies, I wouldn't surrender so easily." Margaret lay back, frowning. "I wonder what she's thinking."

"Who?"

"Lady Lyle. Knowing that there's an army camped outside her gates. That they've got big fierce cannon that will blow her walls apart." She shuddered. "She must be so frightened."

"Perhaps the prospect of surrendering to your husband frightens her more than the prospect of being buried alive."

Margaret didn't reply. She couldn't really see how that could be. John was always so pleasant, so restrained. *Don't be foolish*, she reminded herself. *You know what he's like when his temper's roused. It's hard to believe, when he lies docile in your arms and says he'll do anything for you, but. . .* She pulled the covers to her chin, suddenly frightened.

"He wouldn't hurt her, would he?" Katherine asked. "Or dishonour her?"

Margaret didn't say a word. She hoped he wouldn't. But deep inside, she wasn't really sure.

She felt sorry for Lady Lyle. She'd say a prayer for her tomorrow, when she went to the kirk for mass. She'd ask the Virgin to help keep the beleaguered lady safe, and she'd pray, too, that John would be merciful.

The Place of Duchal

John stirred from his tent early, in case Hugh summoned him. Yawning, he looked towards the castle. There was still no indication of a surrender. It was as he'd thought; Lady Lyle wasn't going to give in too easily.

He wouldn't waste shot. He'd make them wait a while, then let the gunners do their work all afternoon and into the evening. That would surely be sufficient.

He supposed he should make a start on distributing the spoils. There wasn't anything to stop him now; Alan had brought the inventory from Ellestoun, and over the last few days several hundred head of cattle and sheep had been rounded up and penned nearby. They were under heavy guard in case some light-fingered laird tried to smuggle one or two beasts away in the dead of night.

This afternoon, John decided. *It'll drive you mad with boredom, but it has to be done sometime.*

That still left him with a few hours to kill.

I'll find Hugh, he thought, *and put in some more training with the bastard sword.*

* * *

A dour-faced man-at-arms confronted him outside Hugh's tent. "What do you want?"

John didn't like being addressed in that manner, but he knew better than to press the point with one of Hugh's men. "Where's your master?"

The Montgomerie retainer scowled back. "He has business elsewhere."

John sighed. He'd thought that by now Hugh would at least have the decency to be forthright.

But Hugh was Hugh. Unpredictable as the weather in springtime. And just as inclement, when the mood took him.

"I'll speak with him when he returns," John said.

The Montgomerie soldier gave a non-committal grunt.

John left then. But as he passed the Montgomerie horse lines, he spotted Zephyr. The grey stallion was tethered with the rest of the horses, hay piled high before it.

John frowned. Wherever Hugh's path had led him that morning, he didn't want to be recognised.

It wasn't a comforting thought.

Chapter 84
The Lands of Glengarnock

Once he'd crossed the line of marchstones that marked the boundary with Lord Lyle's estate, Hugh pressed his horse into a canter. He was in Cunninghame now, in his own jurisdiction.

On such a fine morning, it was a relief to be away from the cramped confines of the encampment. Hugh enjoyed the fierce rush of battle, but he didn't find the boredom of a siege much to his liking. He was tired of dining on pickled herring and salted mutton; he wanted fresh meat once more. It wasn't even as if there was none to be found; there were captured cows and sheep aplenty, just waiting to be slaughtered.

But the effort involved in procuring just one animal dissuaded many men from even trying. And all because John wanted everything to be legal. Why, at that very moment, John would be poring over his ledgers and his inventories, deciding with a lawyer's precision what beast should go where and why.

Hugh smiled. John was probably so absorbed in the intricacies of administration that he wouldn't even have noticed Hugh's absence. Which was all well and good, because for the time being at least, the less John knew of this little excursion, the better.

Hugh frowned. *You're developing a conscience. God forbid. . .*

A thin plume of smoke drifted skywards, about a mile or so to the south-west. He changed course towards it, indicating to the half-dozen men who rode with him that they should follow.

At last he'd found what he'd been looking for.

He spurred his horse onwards. The occasional pang of guilt he could live with. Just as long as it didn't soften his resolve.

* * *

"There's just myself," the woman cried. "I've four bairns to feed."

John looked her up and down. She seemed well-fed enough. "The priest says you're married."

"I'm a widow," she persisted.

"Madam, I won't tolerate lying. You'll take two kye with calves at foot, a half-dozen sheep and two oxen. And you'll be grateful for that."

"But how can I live—"

John sighed. He hated to experience their distress at such close quarters. But every time he saw the tear-streaked, bewildered faces, he'd remember the suffering he'd witnessed over the winter, and then his heart would harden. "There's enough to start again," he said. "Your lord didn't extend such luxury to my tenants. Now be off with you."

William showed her out.

John took a sip of wine, and studied his lists. Mistress Hamiltoun, her name was. She'd been the owner of thirty sheep and twelve kye, eight of which had calved last spring. She'd had three oxen, too, and a pony.

A wealthy woman. Or she would have been, if she'd had the chance to take this year's beasts to market.

He checked his inventory of stolen livestock, allocating the remainder of Mistress Hamiltoun's beasts to his own tenants. Once all the losses were accounted for, he'd give a reasonable number to his friends and kinsmen. The rest would be distributed amongst the host. He was wary of giving everything away; instead, he'd keep a few beasts aside and return them to their original owners at a later date. It was as much a measured gesture of generosity as an act of charity; it wouldn't pay to appear too cruel and unreasonable to the tenants of an estate that bordered his own.

"The Laird of Hessilhead," William announced.

John glanced up. "Send him in."

"No need." Hessilhead swatted William aside.

John fought the urge to frown. "How can I help you?"

"Hugh sent me. He heard you were asking for him."

"He's returned, then?"

"He apologises for his absence. And asks that you dine with him tonight."

John leaned over the rolls, eyes half-closed. The misgivings were back; he rubbed his forehead with finger and thumb, and sighed, deeply. "I'll be there."

* * *

A table had been set up outside Hugh's tent for the evening. By the time John arrived, it was already crammed with men.

He could smell meat. Fresh meat. Roasting on a spit nearby.

John knew the difficulties of procuring meat so far from home. It certainly didn't come from here; Hugh could have taken what he needed from Lord Lyle's herds, but he hadn't even asked.

"Sit down!" Hugh slid aside to make room.

John sat without a word.

Hugh was exuberant. Which was suspicious enough in itself, even before their meal arrived. But once the platter was set down before them, with the newly-cooked flesh piled high upon it, John felt his appetite wane.

"What's this?" he asked.

"Ask no questions," Hessilhead said, as he sliced the meat, "And you'll be told no lies." He served some up on the bread trencher that John shared with Hugh.

"Thanks be to God for the food that He has granted us this night," Hugh said. He gestured to the trencher. "Go on," he invited. "Eat up."

John stared at it. "Wait a moment—"

"It's not polite, to refuse a man's hospitality."

"Is it beef, or venison?"

"Try it and see," Hessilhead suggested.

James Montgomerie stifled a guffaw nearby.

"Where did you get it?"

"It's from Cunninghame," said Hugh.

John studied it, frowning.

"D'you think I'd steal on Renfrew's lands?" Hugh added.

"D'you think he'd steal at all?" Hessilhead challenged.

"Whose lands did it come from?" John persisted.

Hugh smirked. "Glengarnock."

"You seized it from there?"

"Perhaps Craigends'll think twice next time he insults my mother."

"Hugh—"

"You didn't think I'd take that slander from *him*?"

He'd hoped so, but. . . Even a saint would have been sorely pressed by Craigends' words, and Hugh was no saint. "No, but—"

"But what?" Hessilhead asked, ominously.

John said nothing.

"It was perfectly justified." Hessilhead thumped his hand upon the board.

The meat looked delicious. And smelled delicious, too. But John couldn't bring himself to touch it. Once news of Hugh's raid reached Glengarnock, word would go to Craigends and Kilmaurs. They'd take their men and join Lennox. And the last chance they'd had of finding peace in the Westland would be gone.

"That'll teach you, Hugh," Hessilhead snorted. "If you must take a foundling under your wing, then for God's sake choose a real man. Not a lily-livered notary with pretensions of knighthood." He shredded some meat with his fingers, gobbled it down, then belched, loudly.

John closed his eyes and breathed deep, slow.

"Get on with you." Hessilhead drove an elbow into his ribs.

It caught a bruise. John swore, and turned on him.

"What's the matter?" Hessilhead mocked through a mouthful of food. "Can't stomach your meat? You eat like a girl, Sempill."

Anger blazed in him. "You're an ignorant fool!"

Hessilhead roared and drew his knife. At that moment, Hugh reached past John and grabbed his cousin's wrist. "I want no quarrels at the board."

* * *

It should have been a pleasant evening. Instead, the mood was growing frostier by the minute.

"More wine?" Hugh asked.

"No, thank you," John said. He'd dined on bread and salted mutton all night. Each time a fresh piece of meat was dropped onto his trencher, he'd push it politely aside.

But the more rigidly John obeyed his principles, the more determined his fellow diners were to bait him.

"That hair shirt must be chafing," said James Montgomerie.

"Hair hose, more like," Hessilhead retorted. "God knows why you suffer him, Hugh."

Hugh swallowed his wine without a word.

Hessilhead wrapped his arm around John's shoulders. "We'll cut some thorns and nettles for your bed tonight if that's what you want. If it's good enough for Saint Jerome, then it's surely good enough for—"

There was a loud crack as John's fist met Hessilhead's face. The assault took them all by surprise, Hessilhead more than anyone. He blinked a few times, dazed. His cheek was bleeding, his nose too.

John stood without a word, and placed his napkin down upon the table. "Excuse me," he said, as he left them.

Wiping his face, Hessilhead saw blood on his fingers. "Knave!" He lurched to his feet.

"Oh, that's not on my account," John called back. "It's for Margaret. And those cruel threats you made."

"*Outrance!*" Hessilhead slammed his fists against the board. "You heard what he—"

Hugh grasped his cousin's arm. "Sit down."

Hessilhead gaped at him. "You'd let him get away with—"

"Maybe next time you'll think twice before you call a man a coward." Hugh wiped his lips with the napkin.

Further down the table, James Montgomerie snorted into his goblet. "That's you told."

Hugh slapped Hessilhead across the head. "Isn't it about time you learned to be generous in defeat?" He stood. "Goodnight. I must make peace with my guest."

* * *

John hadn't quite reached his tent by the time Hugh caught up with him. "You must forgive them," Hugh said. "They're not used to eating in company."

"I've seen better manners in a pigsty."

"Don't complain. You paid him in full. He's howling for your blood."

"He was baiting me all night. What did he expect?"

"He brings out the worst in men," Hugh replied. "Now," he added, "what's the matter?" He caught John's reproachful look and scowled. "Christ, you're worse than the damned priest at Confession. . ." He paused. "Alright, I took three stirks from Humphry Cuninghame. And, since you seem determined to judge me, I'll concede that I burned four byres for good measure. And I trampled their corn. But that's nothing for you to lose sleep over, is it?"

John hesitated.

"Well?" Hugh's voice rose a fraction.

"The Cunninghames are negotiating with Lord Lyle," John told him. "They say that if you trouble them in any way, they'll abandon the King and ride with the rebels. I'd hoped you might put the feud aside, at least until this business with Lennox was behind us." He sighed. "It was too much to expect. I can see that now."

"You were right to tell me," Hugh said. "This is treason."

John shrugged.

"It's the King's fate that's at stake here. Not yours. Or mine."

"I told you this in good faith," John said, wearily. "I hope you won't use my words as an excuse to punish the Cunninghames."

* * *

Hugh wasn't inclined to go back to his tent just yet. He was in no mood to soothe his kinsman's wounded pride. He sat down by the bombards, perching on the earthen rampart that had been set up to protect the gunners. Wrapping his arms about his knees, he stared into the black depths of the valley.

Lights burned within the tower-house. The garrison were seizing what respite they could before hostilities resumed the following day.

He drew his knife, stabbed it into the ground alongside and rocked it back and forth. The silence cleared his head; he saw the implications of John's words in stark clarity.

John Stewart and Robert Lyle hadn't just turned their back on James, they'd turned their back on him, too. And Cunninghame would make damned sure that a condition of his involvement was Hugh's removal from politics, one way or another.

It wasn't hard to guess what the preferred option would be. His severed head on a spike, outside the main port at Irvine.

Hugh gave a grim smile, and twisted his knife deeper into the earth.

Over my dead body. . .

Chapter 85

"Master John!" William shook him, roughly. "They've surrendered."

John threw back the blankets and sprang from his bed. Propriety got the better of him; he paused to pull on his shirt before he stumbled out into the sunlight, blinking.

His men-at-arms stood huddled by the entrance to his tent. They cheered when he joined them, slapping his shoulders and back and offering their congratulations.

At the castle, a white bedsheet hung over the curtain wall.

John laughed. "Thank God for that! The woman's seen sense."

William thrust a goblet into his hand. "Here's to victory," he said.

John took a token mouthful of wine and wiped his hand against his lips. "Amen to that," he said, then glanced wryly at himself. "I'd best get dressed. Can't take a castle looking like this."

* * *

He ate a quick breakfast then William helped him into his armour.

John flexed his fingers. "In a day or so, we'll be home," he said. "Good food and wholesome company. I can hardly—"

The bombards boomed from their entrenchment.

His heart jumped. But fear soon gave way to concern, and anger. "What the Devil's happening out there?" He clenched his fists, waiting anxiously while William fastened the last few straps.

"There." William patted his shoulder. "All done."

John hurried out without a word.

As he climbed the hill towards the bombards, Robert and Malcolm came running to meet him.

"For God's Sake!" Robert seized his arm. "Put an end to the assault."

John scowled. "What do you think I'm trying to do?"

"What do you mean?"

"I didn't give the order to fire."

"Then who did?"

"I have my suspicions." John quickened his pace.

* * *

Hugh glared at him. "I'm busy." He turned back to his breakfast, ripping the bread into manageable portions.

"Not too busy to explain yourself."

"I don't need to." Hugh bit deep into his bread.

On the face of it, Hugh looked his usual self. A little tired, perhaps. And mildly grumpy.

"Didn't you see the sheet?" John persisted.

Hugh glanced disinterestedly towards the castle. "So they've hung out their laundry?"

"Don't play games with me, Hugh!"

Hugh's expression didn't change. "This isn't a game."

"But the guns were placed under my command."

"You're just a Sheriff," Hugh retorted. "You have as much or as little authority as I decide. Now let me eat my breakfast."

"The Devil take your breakfast!" John swept the platters and flagons aside. "There's women stranded in that castle. I won't have their deaths on my conscience."

"What a shining flower of virtue." Hugh's tone was thick with contempt. "Put the dreams of slaying dragons and rescuing fair maids behind you. If you want chivalry, seek it at the joust. This is war."

"You're dragging my name and my reputation through the mire. I won't let you do it."

"And how, exactly, will you stop me?" Hugh lazed back in his chair, hands behind his head. "Do you want that knighthood, or not?"

"It's not your place to decide."

Hugh smiled. "How do you know?"

John blinked. For once, he didn't know what to say, or do. Lights flashed in his vision, a dull pulsing ache awoke in his forehead. It would have been the easiest thing in the world, to turn his back and let Hugh have his way. But looking at Robert, John saw his friend staring back, anxious, hopeful.

"They're my neighbours," John said, firmly. "I'll have to live with these people, long after you've gone. Raze this place if you like, but at least let me escort the ladies to safety before the firing resumes." He beckoned to Robert. "Come on. We're going to parley."

"You have an hour," Hugh called after him. "Once the barrels cool, the guns will be fired. Whether or not you've returned. D'you hear?"

John didn't look back.

* * *

The ground was treacherous around the north wall of the castle, close to the sally port. Negotiating it would have been difficult at the best of times, but today they were in full armour, with their bastard swords strapped to their backs. They had to protect themselves; Robert was carrying a shirt tied to a spear as a flag of truce, but John wasn't convinced it would carry much weight. The rules of war had been broken already, by both sides.

"This is madness," Robert grumbled.

John smiled, grimly. "He won't kill us."

"He's the Devil Incarnate."

"Hugh's not evil. He's just difficult. When he gets into one of these black moods, working against him's impossible. We just have to work around him, that's all—" John cursed as the turf slipped under his feet. "God Almighty! We'll be lucky we don't break our necks." Half-sliding, half-scrambling down the river bank, John splashed his way across the thin trickle of stinking water that ran past the curtain wall and halted by the sally-port. "Hello?"

There was silence.

Robert crowded close, looking warily about him. His breathing was rapid, frightened, his face gleamed with sweat.

"Hello," John called again. "We want to parley!"

There was a rustle above. John looked up, to see a man-at-arms poised over him, crossbow held ready.

"Summon Lady Margaret," John told him. "Tell her John Sempill wants to discuss the terms for her surrender."

The man-at-arms disappeared.

"One hour, he said," Robert whispered. "Christ, half-an-hour must've passed already. . ."

"Hush, Robert. For God's sake." John wasn't nervous anymore. If anything, he was buoyed up with excitement.

Timbers creaked and the drawbridge that linked the sally port with the adjoining walkway was lowered. "Master Sempill!" A woman's voice hailed him at last.

He waved. "Lady Lyle."

She stood behind the iron yet that closed off the sally port. She was pale, ghost-like, her dark blue gown and hood dusted with crumbling mortar and powdered stone. She'd seemed indomitable when she looked down on him from the distant safety of the wall-walk. Now she just looked bent and tired. "Is this how you conduct yourself?" she asked.

"Do you think I'd be here now if this had my approval?" John retorted. "I want to talk to you." He cast a rueful glance at the slimy pools around his feet. "In more wholesome surroundings, if that's possible. If we come onto the walkway, will you slay us?"

She glanced over her shoulder, to where her men-at-arms lurked unseen. "No," she said.

"Thank you." John motioned for Robert to lead the way up to the walkway.

He hoped he could trust her. For Robert's sake, as much as his own.

* * *

"I'm sorry about what happened. In parley." She didn't look him in the eye. "His brother died when the mill burned; he wanted revenge." She paused. "I won't hand him over."

"The incident at parley had nothing to do with it." Venturing cautiously along the narrow drawbridge, he halted at the yett. Beyond Lady Lyle, he glimpsed the courtyard. Shattered timbers and charred thatch lay strewn there, all that remained of a fallen outbuilding.

Margaret Houston caught his gaze and shuddered. "This is Patrick Hepburn's doing, isn't it? He wants to bury me."

John didn't reply.

She clasped her arms about her. "He's a cruel man. A cruel, cruel man. You should take nothing to do with him."

She was weeping silently.

"Lady Margaret," John said. "You've put up a spirited defence. Your husband will be proud of you. Surely it's time to leave the place to its fate? Come out with your maids and your men. I'll ensure your safety. You have my word."

She shook her head.

"I won't harm you, or anyone in your service."

She gripped the bars of the yett tight and stifled a sob, face grey and worn with despair. "Where would I go?"

"We'll take you to your kin. To their place at Houston. Or to Dumbarton, if that's what you'd prefer."

She let her head sink against the yett. "No." She gulped, again and again, struggling to breathe. "I can't leave."

It made no sense. That she'd rather cower here, enduring the bombardment and the constant fear of death, than abandon her place. *It's only stones and mortar,* he wanted to say. But he knew from the look of her that her fear wouldn't be explained away with reasonable words and assurances. "What about your maids? Your men?"

"They won't betray me."

"I'll do what I can to help," John told her. "In the meantime, take refuge in your strongest cellar, and pray for deliverance."

* * *

The anger was building in him. He'd tried to get the ladies out, he'd failed, and now he couldn't think how best to proceed. He clambered up the river bank, so deep in thought that he stumbled twice and scarcely even noticed.

He'd thought himself capable of dealing with anything Fate could throw at him, but the truth was that he'd been thwarted. He'd been thwarted by Hugh and he'd been thwarted by Lady Lyle.

God, they deserve one another. They're both so damned obstinate. . .

He glanced over his shoulder. They were still in the lee of the valley, beyond the sight of the King's men.

It was the last place of privacy he'd find for a while.

There were some posts rotting in the ground nearby, the remains of an old pen or bothy. John hauled out his sword, and ran at them with a roar. He slammed the blade against the timbers again and again, shredding the wood, cursing and shouting all the while. Once he'd hacked the posts into tiny pieces, he threw his sword aside, and kicked and stamped upon the fragments until he'd pressed them down in the mud.

"John?" Robert ventured.

John flopped down upon the grass with a groan. He looked up at Robert, grinning. "I'm alright. Honestly."

"You tried."

"It's not good enough, is it?" John sat up, and rattled his knuckles against his thigh. "There has to be a way."

"I'd rather you tried to find an answer back at the camp."

"He won't give the order!" Grasping Robert's arm, John lurched to his feet. "But we'd best head back, I suppose. We mustn't let him get too angry."

* * *

430

Hugh was waiting by the bombards. Robert muttered his misgivings, but John was determined to dawdle. And, to cause maximum annoyance, he made sure their course carried them right before the maws of the guns.

Hugh paced back and forth, *panache* twitching in agitation.

He shouted for them to hurry, and when that had no effect, he came to meet them. Ignoring Robert, he channelled all his rage on John. He snarled and ranted, face red with fury, emphasising every second word with a push to John's chest.

John stood there, half-listening. It was something about him being a damned useless idiot and about Hugh wondering why he'd even bothered to wait, because it wouldn't be any great loss to the world if the Sheriff of Renfrew was blown to the Heavens.

John was quite pleased to have provoked such a reaction. It was the kind of response he'd expect from Hessilhead, not from Hugh, and if that meant he'd really pushed Hugh close to the limits of his patience, then so much the better.

He waited for the tirade to splutter out, then offered Hugh a smile. "It's done," he said. "I'm content. Do what you will."

Chapter 86

"You should've let Craigends slay him," Robert muttered. He heaved himself into a chair, scowling blackly. "He's a fiend."

"Don't be so uncharitable."

"We'd all be better off without him."

"Better the Devil you know. . ."

"But something must be done!"

"He's like a mad horse. Once he seizes the bit, there's no stopping him. You've just got to sit it out until the anger passes."

"There's only one thing to do with a mad horse. Knock the legs out from under it so it falls flat on its face."

"And snap your own neck in the process?" John asked.

Robert didn't respond.

John rubbed his forehead, suddenly weary. "There might be a way."

Robert looked up. "What do you mean?"

"I can't stop him. You can't stop him. There's only two men alive who can. Patrick Hepburn, and the King." He sat tall, smiling. "We could ask the King if he wants the honour of capturing Duchal himself. He'll surely agree; what better way is there of proving his prowess in the Westland than to accept Duchal's surrender in person?"

"He's probably in Linlithgow."

"Let's just pray that he isn't." He stood. "I need a favour. I know it's late, but I want you to find Jamie Colville, and ride with him to Paisley. Find out the King's whereabouts, and if he's anywhere in the Westland, seek him out. Jamie can speak to his kinsman."

"But the castle's already surrendered. Taking it now will be like setting the hawks on a dead duck."

"I'll speak to Lady Lyle. See if something can be arranged."

Robert nodded. "Alright. I'll find Jamie, and then I'll go."

"Not a word of the truth, mind. Far as the King's concerned, you, me and Lord Hugh are united behind a common purpose, and that's serving him. It's not that we can't handle Hugh Montgomerie; we've just had to resort to extreme measures to do so."

* * *

John half-expected the bombardment to continue well into the night, but he thought he'd try and talk Hugh into ceasing hostilities. This time, he didn't try and appeal to Hugh's better nature.

"I'd like to get some sleep," he said.

Hugh shrugged. "As you wish," he replied. "Speak to the gunners."

432

Looking at Hugh, who seemed affable enough as he slouched in the relative comfort of his tent, John wondered if the madness had passed. If by the following morning, Hugh might be more amenable to reason.

Somehow John doubted it. The incident with Craigends showed how Hugh could nurture a grudge unseen for days, smiling sweetly at everyone while he plotted revenge. John knew full well that every time a cannonball struck home, there was a part of Hugh that revelled in every smashed stone and shattered wall. It wasn't that Hugh wished any harm on Margaret Houston or anyone else trapped there with her. He just genuinely didn't care what happened to them.

"Robert thought you'd lose patience this morning," John said. "He thought you'd fire the bombards regardless."

Hugh glanced up from his wine. "I should have."

"So why didn't you?"

"Waste of a good Sheriff," said Hugh.

* * *

"Fortune's smiling on you, cousin." Jamie Colville snatched the mug of ale and gulped it down. "His Grace the King was already heading this way. He stayed at Ranfurly last night, and plans to arrive here after noon."

"We took our leave as soon as we could," Robert Crawfurd added. "But word of his coming should be imminent."

"I'd hoped to discuss the situation with Lady Lyle before the King's men arrived." John grasped his arming doublet. "Jamie, can you speak with Lord Hugh? Ask him to delay the first firing by an hour or so."

Jamie shook his head. "God help me."

* * *

"A keg of ale." John set the provisions down beyond the yett. "And five loaves."

Lady Lyle's face brightened. "Oh, thank you, sir."

"How fares the place?"

She shrugged. "The tower's in a sorry state."

"The King is coming here. He'll expect a speedy resolution."

"Thank God!"

"There's just one problem. The bedsheet. . ."

"It will be removed," she replied.

"That's most kind." He turned to go.

"Master Sempill?"

John halted. "Yes?"

"I didn't think you'd be so gracious. My lord was very cruel, over the winter. If this had been your father's time. . ."

"I'm not my father."

"We know that. And we're thankful for it."

"Times are changing, Lady Margaret. We can change with them, or cling to the past." He nodded. "Good day to you. I hope that when we next speak, your situation will be better."

* * *

"The Master of Bothwell's here," the man-at-arms announced.

Hugh cast a sour look towards Lady Lyle's bedsheet. He'd hoped the cannon would take out the offending section of wall, but so far it remained in place.

Adam Hepburn would notice it. Adam noticed everything.

There he was. Striding up the hill in full plate armour, *gules*-and-*argent* colours blazing bright. A younger, more thickset version of his father, with the same imperious nose, the sardonic lift of the lips.

Adam nodded. "Good day, Lord Hugh."

"Morning, Adam. You're faring well?"

"Well enough." He glanced at the castle.

"And Earl Patrick?" Hugh continued.

"He's in good health. He'll be coming to Duchal this afternoon. With His Grace the King. And the men of the court." Adam Hepburn hesitated, then added, "It was most thoughtful, to ask His Grace to attend the closing stages of the siege."

"Oh," said Hugh.

"He's delighted by the prospect. But my father hoped His Grace might witness the guns in action. . ."

John's doing, Hugh thought, and frowned slightly. John had outflanked him, perhaps, but Hugh knew an opportunity to impress James when he saw one. Just one thing remained which might jeopardise everything.

That damned bedsheet. He flashed it a look of utter loathing.

"Has Master Sempill's conduct been acceptable?" Adam asked.

"Impeccable," Hugh said. "Couldn't have asked for better."

"One wonders why there's a tattered piece of linen hanging over the battlements. One might almost think that the garrison has already tried to surrender."

"It's only just appeared," Hugh countered swiftly.

"Good," Adam said. "Father was concerned that young Master Sempill would be a little too eager to exact revenge."

"Not at all," said Hugh. "He's been most restrained."

"I'm pleased to hear it." Adam studied the castle, carefully. "A word of advice, Lord Hugh. Get that rag removed before His Grace gets here."

"It'll be done," Hugh replied. *Somehow. . .* He glanced heavenwards. Some divine intervention would have been most welcome, but he supposed it was a little too late to ask.

Besides, he hadn't heard mass or said prayers for a week. If the Almighty was inclined to grant anyone a miracle, it certainly wasn't going to be him.

* * *

One of the Colvilles came to meet him, once Adam Hepburn had gone. It was the bastard, James; not the most presentable of men, but today his manners were impeccable. He bowed his head and said, "Lord Hugh, I bring word from the Sheriff. He asks that you delay the firing for an hour or so. He's attending parley with Lady Lyle."

Hugh settled back in his chair. "Tell the Sheriff that I want to see him immediately on his return. Tell him I'm whetting my sword in readiness."

He wasn't as angry as he thought he would be. Annoyed, yes, that John had dared to use deceit, but at the same time. . . Given similar circumstances, he'd have done exactly the same thing himself.

* * *

John came trailing up the hill. Looking mildly cowed, nothing more.

"Sit." Hugh gestured to the chair alongside.

John obeyed without a word. His armour creaked as it settled; he shifted to make himself more comfortable.

"Why the full array?" Hugh asked. "Is it Lady Lyle who's put the fear of God into you? Or myself?"

John cleared his throat and fidgeted again, but said nothing.

"I think some explanations are in order," Hugh said. "I've just been told that the King's heading out this way. Seems someone invited him to take command of the siege."

John didn't look at him. "He intended to come here anyway."

"You might at least have discussed the matter with me."

"I didn't think I'd convince you that my actions were justified." John caught his gaze at last, unapologetic, even slightly defiant.

"And why do you think they were justified?"

"Waste of a good castle."

"You're a liar and a rogue," Hugh said, and passed him the goblet.

John accepted it. "Thank you."

"The King is delighted. Earl Patrick thinks it's my doing, and naturally I wasn't going to contradict him. There's just one problem remaining; Lady Lyle's laundry."

"It's being attended to."

"How? Have you summoned the Heavenly Host to pluck it away—" Hugh broke off, for even as he spoke, two figures appeared on the wall-walk. They pulled the sheet back; it was gone from view in moments.

"Sometimes it pays to be civilised." John returned the goblet. "Here. I don't want anymore."

Hugh snatched it away. "You've been whispering loving words too often to Lady Lyle over the last couple of days. What did you say? About her circumstances?"

"She thinks Earl Patrick's responsible," John replied. "I didn't contradict her. It would just have caused more grief in the long run."

"A sound decision." Hugh cast a disapproving look in John's direction. "Polish your arms," he said. "You can't greet James in that state."

Chapter 87

It wasn't just the King who came to Duchal. It was the entire court.

Huge silken pavilions were being set up on the high ground to the west of the bombards as the first of the sumpter-horses and ox-carts arrived. The baggage train trailed as far as the eye could see along the thin strip of the Paisley road. There were courtiers and their retinues, huntsmen, hounds and falconers, cooks, and more carts laden high with provisions. There were trumpeters, too; they lined up near the bombards and blew a fanfare as James came bounding up the hill with Earl Patrick and Robert Colville in attendance. Abbot Schaw and Earl Colin of Argyll followed, at a more leisurely pace.

James waved. "It's fine weather to be out in the field!" He hugged Hugh tight. "Greetings, noble cousin. You've been sorely missed." Then he turned to John. "You're looking well, Master Sempill. You find a soldier's life agreeable?" Before John could answer, he continued, "You've wrecked havoc on the place."

John sighed, wondering how best to respond.

"The guns are effective then," said James. "Has my Lady Meg behaved herself?"

"Lady Meg's a law unto herself," Hugh said. "Half the time, her aim is quite contrary."

"Typical woman," said James. "And the other one?"

"Can't be faulted."

"Then we'll name her *Duchal*, in honour of this day." James peered down into the valley. "They remain defiant?"

"We believe their surrender's imminent," Hugh said.

"Then let's fire the guns, and see if we can press them into capitulating." The King's face was eager. "Show me what's required," he told the Master Gunner. "And if I could light the touch-hole, so much the better."

"Your Grace," Earl Patrick interceded. "Remember the fate of your grandsire. . ."

James wrinkled his nose. "Nonsense. No harm'll come of it."

* * *

James had his way. He wielded the firing-iron with a flourish, whooping with joy as the powder cracked loud and the bombard named *Duchal* heaved itself deep into the earth at his feet. He stood there afterwards, covered in soot but beaming with delight, while everyone applauded and commended him on his excellent aim. Even Mons Meg was on her best behaviour; once the smoke cleared, they saw that one of the corner turrets near the gatehouse had been smashed, and the curtain wall had developed an alarming crack close to the tower-house.

Moments later, out came the bedsheet. The applause started afresh; James was presented with wine in a jewelled goblet, which he soon passed round the rest of them.

436

"Our mission is complete, gentlemen," James said. "Duchal Castle is ours. Let's claim it as our own, and offer our mercy to a bold and noble foe."

* * *

John shivered, and drew his gown closer. The nights were closing in already; braziers and candles had been lit so he could see to write.

It was the first night he'd spent indoors since leaving Paisley, but in its current condition, the hall at Duchal left much to be desired. There was a hole in the timbers above and the splintered remains of a cannon ball were strewn across the flagstone floor.

Keep the fabric of the place intact, King James had said. *The panelling, the slates and the worked stone. Anything else you can keep for yourself. As recompense.*

Everything of value had been removed before the siege. The gold and silver plate, the jewels, and the rental rolls. The only gems that remained were on Margaret Houston's person, and he wasn't quite so churlish as to demand those.

John rubbed his eyes, yawning. He'd worked his way methodically through the castle, taking note of everything, from the bed linen and gowns in the ladies' chamber to the jars of salt and spices in the kitchen. All Lord Lyle's goods would be removed to Ellestoun, even those items John didn't particularly need or want; if Lord Robert wanted any of his furnishings returned, he could pay handsomely for the privilege.

Back in the camp, King James was entertaining the defeated lady in flamboyant style. He'd asked Hugh to join him, and Sir John Ross, too. They were favoured guests at James's table, along with Earl Patrick and Earl Colin of Argyll.

John had almost felt relieved when no invitation was forthcoming. He wanted to go home, and there was still much to do here. Though the items left had little value, there was much that would be useful. He wasn't exactly leaving empty-handed, and every little morsel helped with winter approaching.

Feet crunched on fallen masonry beyond, he heard hushed voices. He presumed it was William, but made sure his sword was close to hand, just in case.

King James peered around the door. "Ah, there you are!" He slipped into the hall with Robert Colville following close behind. "You're quite an elusive man, Master Sempill."

"I'm sorry, Your Grace. I didn't think I was required."

"Time to set your labours aside for the night." James perched upon the edge of the table. His doublet, densely embroidered with gold thread and pearls, shimmered in the candlelight.

"Yes, of course." John set the quill pen down.

James exchanged secretive glances with Colville. "I wanted to speak with you alone, Master Sempill. There's a favour I'd ask you. It concerns your uncle, Sir John Ross of Montgrennan. . ."

John shrugged. "He scarcely knows who I am."

"You're his closest kinsman, if I remember right." Leaning across the table towards him, James said, softly, "We suspect that your uncle has been in contact with Lennox."

"He may even have helped finance the revolt," Colville added.

"I want him back in the fold," James said. "And Ramsay, too. They'll do less mischief here. And if we can entice them away from Lennox, then so much the better…"

"All we want from you is a letter," Colville explained. "You'll tell him that the King is prepared to negotiate his safe return. The charges of treason have been revoked; we want him to know that in return for his goodwill and support, we'll discuss the restoration of his lands and titles."

John studied the table, unwilling to reply.

"By God's Truth, cousin." James reached out and gripped his shoulder. "Your kinsman is safe. I won't trick you into signing his death warrant."

"What am I to write?"

"It's already done." Colville handed him a parchment. "We need your signature, and your seal."

John read the letter carefully. Twice, to make sure he'd missed nothing. It seemed innocent enough; it expressed the King's good wishes and made an earnest plea for a safe and speedy return.

Before he could think better of it, John grasped the pen and dipped it in the ink. He scratched his signature on it and blotted it. Then he folded the parchment, took the wax that Colville offered, and splashed a molten drop onto the document.

He pressed his seal into the wax, and it was done.

"Thank you." James seized the letter. He was smiling, eyes bright with triumph.

John felt sick. *There was nothing you could do. Montgrennan will know that. He'll fear a trap.*

"I've been speaking with Lord Hugh," James mentioned.

"Your Grace. . ."

"He tells me you're the embodiment of knightly virtue and restraint," James continued. "He says you work well together. Which comforts me, I must confess, for I never thought Lord Hugh would work willingly with any man." He grasped John's inventory and leafed idly through its pages. "Archie Campbell will take possession of Duchal and its lands," he said. "But his place is at court, or with his father in the north. If you could arrange for masons to repair the damage, and keep an eye on it in his absence."

"I'll do that."

"You'll be reimbursed, of course." James slid to his feet. "There's one last task I want you to complete, before I release you from my service. It's a knightly quest, one which may appeal."

"Whatever Your Grace requires."

"You'll ride out with Lord Hugh tomorrow morning. Together, you'll escort Lady Lyle to the ferry at Renfrew. There you'll hand her into the custody of her kin. Flags of truce will be carried; I'll tolerate no acts of treachery from either side."

John nodded.

"Good." James set the parchment back down upon the table. "I've sent you on a knight's errand, Master Sempill. It's only right that you ride out as a knight." He beckoned to John. "Come before me, please."

John pushed his chair back and threaded his way round the table. He frowned, hoping he'd heard James right.

"You thought you'd been forgotten, didn't you?" James grasped his shoulders, gentle admonishment. "You shouldn't doubt me. I don't neglect loyal service." He gestured to the floor. "Pray kneel, my liege."

John dropped to one knee, and James drew his sword. He tapped John lightly across the nape of his neck with the blade. "Rise now, Sir John," he said. "You've earned your spurs."

Chapter 88
The Place of Ellestoun

Alan Semple returned first, along with some of the men-at-arms. They came laden with booty; five carts stretched in a line down the hill, and more were coming.

Margaret went to meet him. "Do you bring news?"

Alan grinned, wearily. "He'll be back tomorrow," he said. "And he'll have company. We'll need enough provisions to feed the five thousand."

Tomorrow. She'd see him then. Her heart tripped at the thought. Then curiosity got the better of her. "What's all this?"

"He's picked Duchal clean," Alan explained. "We need to get everything packed away before his return."

"Then let's see to it now." Margaret took his arm, and steered him to the first of the carts.

Her heart sank when she saw its contents. Piles of armour; breastplates, helmets, sallets and brigandines. A sheaf of heavy spears, swords and crossbows. And two bronze, six-sided tubes, the length and thickness of her arm.

"Culverins," Alan explained. "And a small keg of black powder. Just what we need if we're ever under siege."

She tried to look impressed and interested, but didn't succeed.

The next cart was little better. Harness, leather hides and offcuts, buckets filled with old horseshoes and blankets. *He's a man,* she told herself, disappointed. *Of course he thinks of practicalities.*

After that, things improved. John hadn't just raided the stables and the armoury; he'd plundered the kitchens and stores and the living quarters besides.

Margaret sat with the girls and sifted through the contents of each cart in turn. They unearthed pots and cooking utensils, jars of perfume and enough salt and spices to keep them through the winter.

That wasn't all. There were around half a dozen big wooden kists which, according to John's instructions, were to be emptied and placed in storage. They were filled with rich clothes of silk, satin and velvet, some embellished with gold thread or pearls or even tiny gems. John had said nothing about keeping the clothing aside, so Margaret presumed she could now call them her own. There were rolls of cloth, too, and boxes filled with skeins of wool and thread.

And there were some other unexpected treasures.

Margaret gasped as she leafed through a book. It was filled with brightly-illuminated pictures of salamanders, firedrakes and a hundred other creatures besides. "A bestiary! How lovely."

"Poor Lord Lyle," Katherine sighed. "He's lost so many marvellous things."

"It's just reward for trying to ruin my husband." Margaret looked up. "Did you hear that?"

Katherine stared anxiously at the pile of blankets in the corner. "Something moved there."

Plucking up her courage, Margaret pulled them aside.

Cowering beneath was a hound. An emaciated, grizzled old bitch, heavy with pups and too weak to stand.

It wasn't the first beast she'd seen; there'd been a dozen chickens and a half-dozen geese, trussed up and dumped in the back of one of the carts. There'd been a dazed-looking sumpter horse, too. Its dun coat was encrusted with matted dust and blood and it flinched at every sound, but Henry thought he could coax it back to good health.

She found it rather touching, that John had taken pity on the horse and this poor unhappy dog. She reached out her hand. "Come on," she soothed. "It's alright."

The hound thumped its tail, but managed no more than that.

"Henry!" Margaret called. "There's something else here for you." She turned to the girls, smiling. "Well now," she said. "Whatever next!"

* * *

Lady Lyle sat slumped upon her palfrey. She didn't look back as they passed through the shattered remnants of the fermtoun.

Concerned, John rode alongside. "Are you well, Lady Margaret?"

"Well enough, Sir John." She didn't look at him.

John sighed, and steered his horse away. *I paid a heavy price last year,* he reminded himself. *I deserve some recompense. . .*

He didn't need to convince himself of that. But his conscience nagged him all the same.

The lady's life was ruined. She hadn't mentioned the books, but he guessed she'd miss them more than anything else. He'd thought about offering them back, but when he'd lain awake in his tent, glancing through them and admiring their craftsmanship, he'd decided against it. He'd returned her Bible, at least, and her prayer book, and even that was enough to make Hugh roll his eyes and look askance.

Hugh had laughed and called him weak. But somehow John preferred to be weak, than to let all this misery unfold and remain untouched by it.

* * *

Four horsemen awaited them at the jetty in Renfrew town. They carried a white flag, but they were in full array. Three were men-at-arms, armed with spears and swords.

And the fourth. . .

Hugh's face glowed with joy. "Mattie!"

Matthew Stewart raised a hand, then approached at a leisurely trot. "Greetings, cousin." He nodded briefly to John. "Master Sempill."

"Sir John now," said Hugh.

Stewart raised his brows. "Congratulations, Sir John. And next time you toast your own success, spare a thought for my father and myself. If it hadn't been for our tender care, you'd still be wallowing amongst lesser men."

Stewart's tone was jaunty, mocking. But there was a change in him. The last time they'd met, Matthew Stewart hadn't looked like this, near-crushed with weariness and worry.

"I hope you've offered Lady Lyle all due courtesy," Stewart continued. "You're well, Lady Margaret?"

Lady Lyle bowed her head. "I'm well, Mattie."

"Good." Matthew caught Hugh's eye. "We'll be on our way soon enough," he said. "But before we leave, I must speak with my cousin." He scowled at John. "In private."

* * *

They walked together, away from the others.

"Father sends his regards," Matthew said.

"Convey my good wishes." Hugh glanced back towards where John waited with Zephyr. To a man who could read him right, John's disapproval was tangible.

Hugh sighed, and shook his head. *You'll realise soon enough. Some injuries should be forgotten. And some foes forgiven. . .*

"I've brought a message," Matthew told him. "It would be best if you could deliver it to James, but if needs must then give it to Robert Colville." He handed a rolled parchment to Hugh.

"You're determined to go through with this?"

Matthew glanced aside. "There's no retreat now."

"Are those your thoughts, or your father's?"

"There's no discord between us," Matthew said. "My kindest wishes to Helen. When's the child due?"

"Imminently." Hugh broke off. He didn't know what else to say.

"She's strong, Hugh. And healthy. God will keep her safe."

Hugh clutched his kinsman close. "Tread carefully, Mattie."

Matthew returned the embrace. "And you, cousin."

* * *

John made no secret of his impatience. He barely gave Hugh enough time to settle into the saddle before he tightened his reins, ready to move off.

Hugh raised his hand. "Wait!" He couldn't leave just yet. Perhaps he hoped, deep in his heart, that Matthew might yet change his mind.

The last horse stepped aboard and the boat drew away, oars slapping against the glassy calm of the water.

"He'll survive," Hugh said. "I can feel it in my bones."

John frowned, and didn't comment.

Hugh laughed. "What good would it do to hang him? It'd offer you sweet revenge, perhaps, but it wouldn't serve James. Best he has half-a-dozen Stewart kinsmen sniffing round him, all vying for favour. By removing one, you'd make the others stronger."

"Perhaps."

"Besides, you've no reason to complain now, *Sir* John. He's no threat to you." Hugh turned Zephyr around. "Let's go home," he said. "And enjoy the peace while we can."

442

Chapter 89

Margaret sat upon the parapet of the wall-walk, waiting. She'd hoped he'd return before dinner, but there'd been no sign. She'd hardly eaten a mouthful, and now the meal was over, she was so eager to see him that she couldn't bear to remain indoors.

She wondered if he'd be just as pleased to see her. If he'd leap from his horse, swing her up in his arms and kiss her. She trembled at the thought, shifting her hips on the warm stone wall and smoothing her skirts.

At last she spotted a cloud of dust beyond Kenmure, a mile or so away.

Margaret sprang to her feet. The more she willed time onwards, the slower it passed. To make matters worse, the approaching horsemen were travelling at a leisurely speed.

She could wait no longer. She trotted down the steps and out through the gate. If he wouldn't hurry and come to her, then she would go to him.

* * *

There must have been a hundred men-at-arms gathered. Hooves rumbled like distant thunder, sunlight shone on spears and armour. There were brilliant banners flying high; the red-and-blue of the Montgomeries, the ivory-and-scarlet of her husband's household and the silver-and-sable of her own house.

She'd imagined the moment of joyful reunion so many times in her thoughts. But now she began to doubt herself, and to doubt him, too. Perhaps he'd be embarrassed by her devotion. Perhaps he'd be annoyed because she'd got her fine gown wet when she waded through the ford near Kenmure.

It was too late to hide, and far too late to return.

She spotted Lord Hugh's grey horse first, but couldn't see her husband's. She peered into the dusty haze; eventually, she recognised the men. There was Lord Hugh, and her brother William, and her half-brother Jamie, too. Though their men were armed, they'd all put aside their harness for the journey.

Then at last she saw her husband. He had a beautiful new horse. Black as jet, without a single white mark on it. It tossed its head so proudly, and picked its feet up high.

He came to meet her, approaching at an elegant trot.

"Hello," she said, blushing. "Welcome home."

He leaned on his pommel and studied her, in that steady, inscrutable manner of his. "You're wet."

"I wanted to see you."

Hooves battered up close. "Lady Margaret!" Lord Hugh hauled his horse to a halt, just feet away.

She looked into the horse's big white face and swallowed. But Lord Hugh wasn't alone. To her relief, she noticed that Jamie was there, too.

"Well," John sighed. "What're we to do with you, Margaret? You can't crawl through the river again. You'd best take my horse."

"Hold still, John!" Jamie called. "We'll deal with her."

He sprang from his horse, and so did Lord Hugh. They were laughing together, she had no idea what they intended until they seized her, a leg and an arm each. They hoisted her high, heedless of her protests, and thrust her onto the black horse's back.

"Be careful with her!" John instructed, tersely. "Grab hold of me, Margaret."

She wasn't sure if he was anxious, or even cross with her. She wasn't even sure that she cared; she just wrapped her arms tight about his waist and wriggled close.

"Are you secure, Lady Margaret?" Lord Hugh asked.

"Yes, thank you."

"Then let's be on our way. Come on, John. Stop dallying."

She leaned her cheek against John's back as the horse strode forward. Each stride threw her closer; the rough fabric of his gown rubbed against her face. She breathed in deep; he was rank with dirt and sweat, but it didn't matter because he was solid and warm and alive. She wanted to run her hands all over him, just to prove to herself that he was really there, but somehow she restrained herself.

Lord Hugh brought his horse right alongside, so close its shoulder jostled against John's stirrup.

Jamie came barging up on the other side. "It's a fine steed you're riding, Lady Margaret," he called.

"A very fine steed," Lord Hugh agreed. "What a pleasure, to have his tight strong arse pressed close to your own—"

"And when you take that mighty prick inside you—"

"Jamie!"

The two of them erupted into laughter.

"Leave her be," John said.

"Lady Margaret, I'm so very hungry," Lord Hugh said. "If a weary knight could beg a few scraps from your kitchen. . ."

"Stop teasing me," she retorted, "and I might just see what I can do."

* * *

Once he'd settled his guests for the night, John steeped himself in a tub that was normally reserved for the laundry. He scrubbed and scrubbed at his skin, trying to slough away the dirt and grime that had built up over the last few weeks.

There'd been much to do. Guests to be quartered, and so many chores to attend to. Henry had to be introduced to the latest addition to his stable, and then there were more routine matters. Like eating, and attending Mass.

In all the activity, John had neglected poor Margaret. His young wife had been loitering by his shoulder all evening, but he'd never found the opportunity to take her aside and tell her how pleased he was to see her. He hoped she'd know, but he wasn't entirely sure. There'd been so many times when he'd turned around to find her underfoot, looking up at him with an uncertain smile on her face.

She seemed shy. Which surprised him. And unsettled him, too, for it was quite unlike her to act that way.

He emerged at last, dripping and shivering. William flung an old sheet at him, and he dried himself down.

"Are you going to see her?" William asked.

"I'm hoping she'll come to me."

"I'll sleep in the hall, if you like."

"No need for that. But you could leave me for a couple of hours. Things need to be said..."

William grinned. "If you like."

When he'd dried himself properly, John splashed himself with perfume and combed his hair then took great care to clean his teeth. The last time she'd shared his bed, he hadn't had much opportunity to make himself presentable. He hoped she wouldn't hold it against him.

He chewed on a lavender confit, pulled on a clean shirt, and slumped in his chair. He was nervous. His heart was pounding.

"I'll be off then," William said. He patted John's shoulder. "Best of luck," he added. "I'll take the hounds, if you like."

* * *

Fingers tapped light on his door; John sprang to answer it.

She stood there in the darkness, clad in her kirtle. Her long hair hung loose, her eyes were wide with accusation. "Where were you?"

He put his arm about her shoulders and ushered her inside. "Come in."

"You're supposed to call on me—"

"Why?"

"Because you *are*—"

He pressed his lips against hers to silence her. When he put his arms about her, she went limp for a moment, but then she stirred. She pressed close, clutching handfuls of his sark and hauling it up so she could bury her face against his chest and kiss his flesh.

He was roused already.

So much to say, so many things to tell her, but it'll wait. We have our whole lives before us...

"I missed you," she whispered. "I missed you desperately."

He scooped her up in his arms, so fast she gasped and gripped him tight. "Well I'm back now," he said. "We've wasted too much time already. Let's not waste any more."

* * *

The curtains were drawn around the bed, keeping out the world. It was too dark to see, but he was there, stretched out beside her. He hadn't stirred for a long while, she thought he might be asleep.

But Margaret couldn't sleep. *When you tell him, things will change. He won't want to share your bed, for fear of hurting the child...*

She shivered and sidled close. Her limbs pressed warm against his, she reached blindly into the darkness, desperate to touch him. Her fingers traced the curve of his shoulder blade and then she rubbed his back, firmly.

He groaned, a soft contented sound.

She smiled to herself. There was so much to learn about him. And now he was home, they'd have all the time in the world together. "John, there's something I must tell you." She ran her hand down his side, following the outline of his hip, his thigh. The scar from the wound he'd suffered at the wappenschaw broke the smooth flow of his skin; she shuddered at the memories it rekindled. It reminded her that despite their confidence in one another, life was fleeting, uncertain. "I don't know how to say this. . ." She faltered. "My bleeding's late."

He rolled onto his back, but said nothing.

"I'm not sure, mind."

"Have you spoken to a midwife?"

"Not yet."

The covers rustled as he sat up. His hands closed gently about her face. "Oh, Margaret. Sweet Margaret. You should've said. . ."

"No. I wanted you. I don't. . ." Her voice trembled. "I don't think I can live eight months or more without sharing your bed." She swallowed. "I'll pray for a boy. And do whatever I can to make sure you're granted a son."

"Let God have His Will. I'll love the child just as much whether it's boy or girl." His fingers smoothed back her hair. "I've brought you news, too."

"What?"

"I'm a knight." He wrapped his arms about her. "King James dubbed me once the siege was done."

"Sir John Sempill of Ellestoun." She nestled in his embrace, and gently stroked his arm. "That sounds very fine."

"It's what you wanted."

"No," she whispered. "Don't you see? It doesn't matter anymore. It's you I care for. That's all there is to it."

* * *

"He has such plans for the place," Margaret told Jamie. "He wants to create something great and beautiful for his children—*our* children—to enjoy after we're gone."

They were walking arm-in-arm through the orchard, enjoying each other's company while they could. Jamie would be leaving the following day, riding south with the others.

"So that modest façade conceals great ambitions," Jamie said. "Somehow, I'm not surprised."

Margaret glanced back towards the herb garden. John was seated there, basking in the sun like a stately lion. Lord Hugh sat nearby; he wrestled with the hounds as if he hadn't a care in the world, but she could tell from the sober look on John's face that they were discussing something important.

She suppressed a shiver. "He thinks it's about time the men of this land put their feuds aside and worked together. He thinks that's the only way the Scots will prosper in this world."

Jamie laughed. "Good luck to him."

"I think it's a very noble attitude."

"And quite misguided. But if it makes your life pleasurable, then I applaud him."

"He wants to build a new place, down by the loch. He wants it to be big and grand, with acres of garden and trees, and a deer park. He says that if you build a better world, then maybe men will take more delight in preserving it."

"No, they'll just take more delight in burning it down." Jamie squeezed her arm. "You're besotted, dear sister. And I'm delighted for you."

* * *

Pompey grovelled low and growled, trying in vain to haul the stick from Hugh's grasp. Eventually, the hound's grip softened; Hugh hurled the stick across the gardens, Caesar and Pompey bounding off in pursuit.

"Not amongst the flowers!" John glowered at the trail of crushed leaves and blossoms.

"Sorry." Hugh settled back down.

"You seem subdued."

"I shouldn't have lingered. Helen may already have endured the birth."

"She'll forgive you, I'm sure."

Hugh glanced aside. "I'd rather not be present."

"Christ, Hugh," said John. "You've slaughtered countless men in your time. Don't try and tell me you can't abide the sight of blood."

"It's different when it's your wife."

Tail wagging, Caesar ran up and dropped the stick at Hugh's feet. Hugh sighed and tossed it down the path, more carefully this time.

"Last night, when you met with the King," John said. "You discussed the letter from Lennox, didn't you?"

Hugh was silent.

"I just want to know what the future holds."

Hugh shrugged. "There's nothing to hide. You'd probably be quite sympathetic to his demands, considering. . ."

"Why?"

"They want the 'vile and evil persons' who murdered the King to be brought to justice, and insist that King James dismiss those men who've offered him false counsel in the past year."

"They've named names, haven't they?"

"They have."

"And you're amongst them?"

Hugh hesitated. "No, I'm not."

"So they're protecting you still?" John smiled. "There you are, Hugh. You caused all that grief at Duchal because you wanted vengeance, and for what?"

Hugh said nothing.

"I'd hoped there'd be an end to it," John said.

"Not yet."

"Do you think there ever will be?"

Hugh smiled, faintly. "Perhaps."

John frowned, considering Hugh's words. So much doubt and uncertainty remained. And yet, when he remembered how bleak his fortunes had seemed, a year, six months ago. . .

His gaze alighted on Margaret. She was walking through the apple trees with her brothers. She carried herself with grace and purpose, head held high; a young woman secure in herself and confident for the future.

She turned and caught his eye. And she smiled, radiant, vital.

John picked up his goblet and sipped his wine. When she looked at him like that, so full of joy and self-assurance, then all doubts, all fears were gone.

He would have faith in God and King and faith in his fellow man. He'd look forward to the future, for it seemed at last to be something worth believing in.

Notes

1) The Background

The story described here is based on real events, and many of the characters featured (those of noble birth, at least) are recreations of real people.

Some authors claim that historical fiction should represent an accurate reflection of the past, but that's not a philosophy I tend to support. All history is, to some extent, fiction, and every time we re-interpret the past we automatically impose something of ourselves upon it. What I wanted to convey in this novel was not a recreation of the past, but an impression of a possible past. This was made easier by the fact that so little information pertaining to this period of Scotland's history remains extant. I've been faithful to the facts as they are known as much as possible, but where historical or genealogical opinions differ, I've had no qualms about choosing the version of events which better serves the story.

For those of you who are concerned with divining the real truth behind this tale, I've included this list of actual events. For the general feel of the piece, my primary sources of inspiration were two works; Dr Norman MacDougall's book *James IV* (Tuckwell Press, 1997) and Dr Jenny Wormald's account of late medieval Scotland *Court, Kirk and Community* (Edinburgh University Press, 1981). I've also benefited from advice given freely by a number of professional colleagues, whose reactions to this project have ranged from enthusiasm and scepticism to incredulity. No doubt they'll disagree heartily with almost everything I've said, but that's only to be expected. Thanks are extended (in alphabetical order) to Tom Addyman, Derek Alexander, Dr Piers Dixon, Dr Iain Fraser, Duncan MacKintosh, Hugh McBrien, and Geoffrey Stell. Extra special thanks are offered to Dr Norman MacDougall, for his fascinating insights into James IV, Hugh Montgomerie and the Siege of Duchal, and to Dr Steve Boardman, who took the time to give me his views on Hugh Montgomerie and the Montgomerie-Cunninghame feud, and who very kindly sent me excerpts from his unpublished PhD Thesis.

2) The Events…

And now, for historical purists, here are the facts:

?, ?, 1425 The Office of Bailie of Cunninghame passes from the Montgomeries to Sir Richard Cunninghame for liferent, as part of a marriage contract between the two families.

?, ?, 1470 Alexander, Lord Montgomerie dies. His great-grandson Hugh inherits the title as a minor, aged 12 years.

21st April, 1478 Hugh, Lord Montgomerie marries Helen Campbell, third daughter of Earl Colin of Argyll, in Dollar Church.

?. ?, 1481 John Ross of Montgrennan holds the office of Bailie of Cunninghame.

28th September, 1482 Hugh, Lord Montgomerie attempts to recover the title of Bailie of Cunninghame. His case is presented at St. Giles.

Cathedral in Edinburgh. Amongst the witnesses who support Lord Hugh in his claim is Sir Thomas Sempill of Ellestoun.

29th September, 1482 King James III is 'released' from where he's being held by his half-uncles, James, Earl of Buchan, and John, Earl of Atholl.

October, 1483 Sir Thomas Sempill, Sheriff of Renfrew, is ordered to restore goods and property removed from Lord Lyle's Place of Old Duchal, and to restore damage done by himself to the buildings and gardens while exercising his duties as Sheriff.

?, ?, 1487 James, Lord Boyd and Robert Crawfurd of Auchencairn slain by Hugh Montgomerie.

18th May, 1488 Sir Alexander Cunninghame, Lord Kilmaurs, is created Earl of Glencairn by King James III.

June, 1488 John Ross of Montgrennan is appointed Lord Advocate by James III. He is the man responsible for arraying the King's army prior to the Battle of Sauchieburn.

11th June, 1488 The Battle of Sauchieburn. Known supporters of King James III include the Cunninghames and the Sempills, and for Prince James, the Hepburns and the Montgomeries. Casualties included King James III, who was supposedly murdered by an unknown assassin as he fled the field. Also listed amongst the dead were Sir Thomas Sempill of Ellestoun, and Alexander Cunninghame, Earl of Glencairn. John Ross of Montgrennan and John Ramsay of Bothwell fled to England.

17th June, 1488 Robert Colville is made Director of Chancery.

6th August, 1488 Carrick Puirsuivant is sent with summons of treason against John Ross of Montgrennan and John Ramsay of Bothwell.

17th June, 1488 Colin Campbell, Earl of Argyll is amongst a group of magnates sent to Edinburgh to examine the Royal Treasury.

24th June, 1488 Prince James, Duke of Rothesay is crowned King James IV of Scots. On this day, Robert, Lord Lyle is also created Justiciar of Arran and Bute.

July, 1488 The taxes are paid, as normal, by Renfrew burgh.

August, 1488 Abbot George Schaw of Paisley Abbey petitions the Pope to have Paisley created a burgh.

10th September, 1488 Patrick Hepburn, the Lord Hailes, is created Earl of Bothwell.

6th October, 1488 The Scots Parliament meets in Edinburgh for the first time in the new King's reign. One act passed orders the removal of office for a period of at least three years of all those who'd held heritable offices in the reign of James III (Sheriffs, Bailies, etc.). Another demands that all those who inherited lands and titles from men slain defending King James III pay a brieve of service if they are to continue occupying these lands. At the same meeting of Parliament, Hugh, Lord Montgomerie gives an oath that he will seek out and punish 'trespassers' (e.g. thieves and reivers) throughout the lands of Cunninghame.

14th October, 1488 Hugh, Lord Montgomerie is granted a remission by King James IV for the destruction of Turnlaw* and all other offences commited by him prior to August 29th, 1488, in consideration of the 'good and grateful service done . . . in the field near Stirling'.

(Nineteenth century sources state that this refers to the burning of Kerelaw/Kerrielaw, a Cunninghame stronghold near Ardrossan. Modern historians now think it refers to Turnlaw, a Hamilton stronghold near the Montgomerie lands in Renfrewshire. For the sake of the story, I've stuck to the nineteenth century version.)

January, 1489 An extra tax is levied by the Treasury. There is no evidence that Renfrew paid its dues.

15th January, 1489 King Henry VII of England petitions the Pope to have John Ross of Montgrennan restored to office.

24th January, 1489 Sir Robert Colville of Ochiltree dies, leaving the estate to his son William.

?, 1489 Hugh, Lord Montgomerie is appointed to the Privy Council.

6th April, 1489 Letters are sent to the 'Lords of the Westlande' inviting them to join the King for Easter.

8th April, 1489 Bute Puirsuivant is sent to Lord Lyle's Place at Duchal carrying letters (unspecified).

17th April, 1489 Good Friday. The 'Bloody Serk' is raised in Aberdeen by Lord Forbes. A riot ensues.

23rd April, 1489 Letters are sent to the 'Lords of the Westlande', summoning them to join the host at Dumbarton.

18th June, 1489 Hugh, Lord Montgomerie is appointed Justiciar of Arran and Bute.

27th June, 1489 A decree of forfeiture is passed by Parliament against the John Stewart, Earl of Lennox, Matthew Stewart, Master of Lennox and Robert, Lord Lyle.

19th July, 1489 King James IV arrives in Renfrewshire to oversee the sieges of Cruikston and Duchal.

25th July, 1489 King James IV arrives at Duchal.

13th September, 1489 Letters of fire and sword are issued to Sir John Sempill of Ellestoun, Sheriff of Renfrew. They defend his destruction of Duchal at a 'time bygone' and refer to great hardships, burnings, slaughters and injuries committed by the Earl of Lennox, Master of Lennox and Lord Lyle against John Sempill, his familiars and tenants.

3) The Places...

Many of the buildings described are still upstanding, and some are open to the public. Edinburgh Castle (where Mons Meg is now housed), Linlithgow Palace, Dumbarton Castle, Crookston Castle and Stirling Castle are all Guardianship Monuments in the care of Historic Scotland, though I'd argue that of these sites Linlithgow Palace best embodies the spirit and times of James IV. The King's presence chamber, the carved unicorn bosses in the King's Bedchamber, and sculptures adorning the fireplace in the great hall are, I find, particularly evocative.

In Renfrewshire itself, the abbey church at Paisley still survives. It was rebuilt after the Reformation, and remains to this day a working place of worship. It is open to the public.

John Sempill's lasting legacy was the Collegiate Church of Castle Semple, which is also in the care of Historic Scotland. The church, which celebrated its quincentenary in 2004, holds within it John's tomb, though it's uncertain whether his remains are housed there. It can be accessed via the cycle track which runs close to the Castle Semple Visitor Centre near Lochwinnoch, Renfrewshire. The ruinous remains of Ellestoun (or Elliston) Castle also survive. They now lie within a private garden, but can be glimpsed from a public road near Howwood, Renfrewshire.

Monumental remains associated with Hugh Montgomerie are less easy to find. He was probably buried in Kilwinning Abbey, where the medieval abbey church has fallen into decay since the Reformation. Hugh's tomb was probably destroyed; a mob that wrecked the abbey's associated artworks and sculpture during the Reformation was led by the Cunninghames. The Place of Eglintoun has fared little better through the centuries; the seat of the Montgomeries was rebuilt several times, both in Hugh's lifetime and afterwards. The stately home of eighteenth century date that finally occupied the site was eventually used as target practice in WWII and finally demolished in the 1950s. But two tower-houses and one castle linked with the Montgomeries still survive, and Hugh would certainly have been familiar with all of them. Of the tower-houses, Lochranza Castle on the Isle of Arran is in the care of Historic Scotland, while Seagate Castle still survives as a largely intact, though very much ruinous structure in the town of Irvine. It should be noted, however, that much of the surviving fabric at Seagate is believed to date to the sixteenth century, i.e. after the scope of this novel. The ruins of Ardrossan Castle also survive in a public park near Ardrossan town centre. The castle itself was largely destroyed by Oliver Cromwell, and what ruinous fragments do survive have suffered terribly in recent years due to a combination of neglect, erosion, and the predations of local vandals.

Of the other sites, Glengarnock Castle (Ayrshire) and Duchal Castle (Renfrewshire) still remain in varying stages of decay. Though they are Scheduled Ancient Monuments afforded Statutory Protection by Historic Scotland on behalf of the First Minister, they lie on private land, and hence are not accessible to the general public.

About the Author

Photo credit: James Dunlop

Born in Glasgow, Louise Turner spent her early years in the west of Scotland where she attended the University of Glasgow. After graduating with an MA in Archaeology, she went on to complete a PhD on the Bronze Age metalwork hoards of Essex and Kent. She has since enjoyed a varied career in archaeology and cultural resource management. Writing has always been a major aspect of her life and at a young age, she won the *Glasgow Herald/Albacon New Writing in SF* competition with her short story 'Busman's Holiday'. Louise lives with her husband in west Renfrewshire.

Lightning Source UK Ltd.
Milton Keynes UK
UKOW02f1950130317
296541UK00001B/2/P